MATING
LIONS

Graham Duncanson

ISBN: 978-1-326-41744-4

PublishNation, London
www.publishnation.co.uk

Acknowledgements

I would like to acknowledge the help of my many '*Swahili*' speaking friends who have helped me with the '*Swahili*' words and phrases which I have included in the text.

I would like to thank Debbie Withero for her careful proof reading.

Lastly I would like to thank my daughter Amelia for her encouragement in completing this novel.

Dedication

I would like to dedicate this book to the large number of friends which I have made, as a result of being a veterinary surgeon in Kenya and in the UK. However, I would like to stress I was not Jim Scott, at least only occasionally in my dreams.

Prologue

Mines on the road

Monday 9th January 1967

Jim was hot, in fact extremely hot, but that was not the only reason he was sweating. He was afraid. Unlike his previous experience of danger, like picking up the hind leg of an unbroken horse, this danger was continuous. He was walking slowly along a sandy road in the Northern Frontier District of Kenya which, even now in 1967, was still called the NFD by the Europeans living in this independent country. He had been taking a convoy of vehicles along the road inland from Lamu towards Ijara when they had been stopped by two Somalis who said they thought the road had been mined by the '*shifta*'. The '*shifta*' was the name given by the Kenya Government to these bandits, who were trying to cause the succession of the eastern side of the NFD to Somalia. The majority of the populous in the region were actually Somalis but a line drawn at the end of the Second World War had confirmed the area as belonging to Kenya and not Somalia.

Jim aged 22, was a newly qualified veterinary surgeon seconded, to the Kenyan Government from Great Britain. He had been tasked by his boss in Mombasa to go to Ijara and examine, vaccinate and treat two thousand head of cattle recently purchased by the Kenya Government from local Somalis. He was not quite sure if such a task was worth dying for, but he had some pride. The head veterinary scout, an old man called Kassim, had suggested with a smile that they had come to find cattle, not mines, and sitting here was not really an option. So Jim walked. Kassim volunteered to walk with him and held his hand. Jim was not quite sure about the hand-holding but this seemed to be quite normal for two men who were friends in other situations. It did not mean they were gay but they both welcomed each other's support. After several hundred yards their

1

pace got quicker as they saw no evidence of mines in the soft sand and they heard the sound of the vehicles starting up. Suddenly there was an enormous explosion. They both dropped flat on the ground. All the engine noise ceased. Jim thought- now what? He was sure he should show leadership but, as he slowly got up, his legs felt like jelly. They both continued walking slowly, gradually speeding up as their confidence returned. After over a mile they were completely alone, having left the convoy still stationary behind. They rounded a bend. It looked as if they had entered a bush slaughterhouse. There was blood, guts, bones and pieces of skin everywhere in the road and hanging from the road-side Acacia trees. There had been carnage. Kassim found the distinctive head of a 'Topi', a large antelope, as Jim looked at what was left of its body. It had obviously jumped into the road and triggered the mine meant for one of their vehicles. Whether walking slowly they would have seen the mine or indeed triggered it off, Jim did not know. He felt very sick. He knew it was not the sight of the carnage but the fact that he might have been blown to smithereens. They slowly searched the area. Kassim soon found foot-prints in the bush near to the six foot crater in the road. It was obvious the 'shifta' were long gone.

On their return to the convoy they were greeted with some jubilation as everyone assumed they were dead. Obviously Suleiman Mahamid, the Livestock Officer (LO) and Jim's second in command had not known what to do. He had done nothing. Jim had recovered some confidence and now really took charge. As they were expecting parts of the road to be very difficult on account of the black cotton soil, which could turn to a bottom-less morass after heavy rain, there was a tractor in the convoy. Jim moved this to the front. Then with Kassim and himself standing next to the driver they started the whole convey moving at a sedate pace. They did not stop at the carcass of the 'Topi' but continued on, with Kassim, Jim and the driver, keeping a very keen eye out for any disturbance to the sand of the road or any foot prints off to the side. Eventually they arrived at an army road block outside of Ijara. The tropical night came quickly, as the Kenya army soldiers ushered the convoy to a selected area between the army and the village.

Unloading began. The tents went up quickly in good order. The cooking fires were lit. Jim did not feel like any food, which was very unusual. He collapsed into a chair with a large cup of tea and thought about the mine and how lucky he had been. Was it delayed shock that had taken away his appetite? He was sure it was not the sight of the *'Topi'*. He was so familiar with animal death and cutting up animals for postmortem, he was sure the mangled corpse had not worried him. Suleiman came over, bringing a chair and offering him a plate of curry. Jim declined but was glad of the company. Even post independence there was a rigid protocol. Vets socialised with vets. LO's socialised with LO's. Veterinary scouts socialised with veterinary scouts etc. Jim was gregarious by nature and mixed easily with his staff. He was very popular, which is why Kassim had helped him. Certainly the mine had raised his standing. He could hear the other staff chatting away in Swahili about the incident. He was so glad he had learnt the language. It had helped him in so many ways. Watching Suleiman eat made Jim feel distinctly queasy. Then it hit him. He was desperate for a crap. He grabbed a *'panga'* (machete) and some loo-roll and set off into the bush, heedless of Suleiman's warning not to go too far. He hardly had time to scrape a hole. What a relief on two counts. He had emptied his bowels and also found the reason for his anorexia. He had a dose of the trots. It was not the fear from the mine. He instantly felt a lot better. His troubles were not over. Walking back without a torch he alarmed a very jumpy young Kenyan soldier. The soldier fired his 303 rifle as Jim threw himself down. Then two more sentries opened up. It was a full half hour before order was restored, mainly by Suleiman bellowing at the army. Later Major Kapisi came round to Jim's tent, he was full of apologies not only for that fracas but for the incident with the mine. He volunteered an escort for the veterinary convoy in future. He said that the best men for the job were the General Service Unit (GSU). They were actually police, not army but were armed and wore khaki. The major explained that the *'shifta'* were a civil problem and so should be dealt with by the police. He just happened to be up here with his soldiers on an exercise! Kenya was not at war. Jim hoped this was true, not only for the safety of him and his men but also, if there was another incident, there was no way he could carry out the treatment of the cattle in the morning. Suleiman had already sent out messages for the cattle to come to the cattle crush and holding pens in Ijara. Suleiman was a good livestock officer. Jim did not blame him for not taking charge in Jim's absence, earlier in the day. Being in a war zone, although denied by the army, was far outside his training. Was it outside Jim's training? Maybe it was? Certainly Jim knew what to do with the cattle in the morning.

The cattle, all big white '*Boran*' cattle with humps and pendulous dewlaps, came through the big pens and then in to the long races in mobs of two hundred. Each animal was given a mob letter and an individual number with red spray paint. They were vaccinated against Rinderpest and hot branded with a Z on their humps to prove that it had been done. Historically Rinderpest was called Cattle Plaque in England. It is a very virulent virus which nearly always causes 100% mortality. It has been eradicated in Europe and also in Kenya but was rife in Somalia, so the Kenya Government was keen to keep the disease out of the country. The other very serious and dangerous disease of cattle was Contagious Bovine Pleural Pneumonia (CBPP). There was a vaccine against this disease but it was not very effective, therefore Jim had to test every animal to see if it was infected. His veterinary scouts made small cuts on the tail-heads, sucked up a small quantity of blood which was then tested on site. Only animals free of the disease would be allowed on from Ijara. Infected animals would have to be quarantined. What happened after that was decided by vets more senior than Jim, at the veterinary headquarters at Kabete near to Nairobi. These were not the only contagious diseases of concern. Foot and Mouth Disease (FMD) was also a problem. There were some good vaccines but they were expensive. Also it was not good veterinary practice to vaccinate cattle which might be incubating the disease, so Jim's veterinary scouts had to examine the mouths of each animal to check for FMD lesions. Lastly each animal had to be given an injection of '*Berenil*' into its dewlap, to prevent it getting Trypanosomiasis called '*Fly*'. This small blood born parasite was spread by Tsetse flies which were found in the bush near to the coast and near to the Tana River which runs fifty miles south of Ijara. The parasite will cause deaths in cattle and they can only survive in a tsetse area if they receive '*Berenil*' or some other trypanocidal drug. All in all it was hard work. Jim was glad his diarrhoea was so much better in such a short time. He was also glad he had the mobile CBPP testing unit, called the Blood Testing Team (BTT) as this had a generator and several big refrigerators so there were plenty of cold 'cokes' for the day time and cold beers for the evening.

Jim kept them all at work until noon but then called a halt as it was getting seriously hot. They had done four mobs i.e. roughly eight hundred cattle. It was good going and meant that they would finish the job in two more days. The Somalis could then be paid for the cattle. A government buyer, who worked for the Livestock Marketing Division (LMD) had already agreed a price per head for each mob. The money was not handed over until all the veterinary work had been done. The cattle could then start moving down the stock route and were less likely to be stolen back again.

In fact the arrangement suited the Somalis very well. They needed to reduce numbers of cattle as their grazing was limited and they needed to buy maize to feed themselves and their families. There was no other outlet for their cattle. There was an abattoir in their own country, built on the coast at Kismayo by the Russians. However it was not working. The Americans had built a harbour and a water supply for the town and the surrounding area but they would not allow the Russians access to the water! So the Somalis were happy to sell their cattle and live a nomadic existence either side of the border, in either Somalia or Kenya. In fact more in Kenya, as the Kenyan government had not been slow at building small bush hospitals, schools and dams for water. There was nothing of this type of infrastructure on the Somali side of the border. The main problem and the cause of the 'shifta', was oil. There was a rumour that oil had been found in the Somali populated area in Northern Kenya. If there was oil, it was Kenyan oil, as it was in their country but the Somalian government wanted the oil and they would stop at nothing to get it. The British government had close ties with Kenya. If oil was found in Kenya, it would be British oil companies which not only brought it to the surface but also refined it and would then make large profits. On the other hand if oil was found in Somalia, the Somali Government would get the revenue and Italian companies, that brought it to the surface and refined it, would make large profits. Jim did not know if there was oil. He did not know which companies were prospecting. Did he care or were the cattle his only concern?

Jim was particularly interested in pandemic diseases which were often spread by large scale cattle movement. In many ways the

5

Veterinary Department in Kenya had been very far thinking in establishing a stock route from Garissa, down through Ijara to a big holding ground at Bodhei and on to a smaller holding ground at Burgoni. Slaughter cattle could then proceed, in mobs of three hundred on a cattle boat to the slaughter house in Mombasa. The overland route, south from Burgoni, ran down the coast and was not without its difficulties. Physically there were the difficulties of crossing the Tana River which Jim was soon to experience. The whole coast stock route ran in a Tsetse fly belt, so the stock required constant monitoring and treatment. There was a large holding ground called Kurawa which normally had plentiful grazing but was extremely difficult to get to in a vehicle, if there had been any rain.

At 4.00pm Jim thought it had cooled down a little and they could make another start. The BTT had nearly caught up. Jim found Suleiman and together they walked to the nearest herds. They were greeted by a deputation of several senior herdsmen. They complained that they had not been paid for two months. They thought Jim had brought their pay with him. Now they found he had not, so they were not going to do any work. Jim thought, *'bloody hell they did not teach me what to do now, at veterinary college.'*

The conversation with Suleiman began to get heated. Spears were held up. Jim thought, *'there is going to be a riot in a minute and someone is going to get hurt.'* Jim saw out of the corner of his eye a very tall headman away from the arguing group. He recognised him from an escapade with a lorry in Mombasa.

Jim cleared his throat and in a very loud voice said,

"Enough." There was immediate quiet. He beckoned to the very tall headman. "Suleiman I recognise this man from Mombasa. Ask him if he and his men have been paid?" The answer was that they had. Jim told Suleiman to tell the men who had not been paid that he had arranged the pay for these men from Mombasa and that he, Jim did not realise the others had not been paid. So he would arrange for these men to be paid by the LMD buyer when he flew in to pay for the cattle. This *'Bwana mkubwa'* (Important person) would only come once all the cattle had been tested, so the sooner they got the cattle tested the sooner they got their pay. Jim turned smartly round and walked away back to the veterinary staff and got them going.

He did not get a spear in his back. From what Suleiman told him later, the herdsmen all got to work, bringing the cattle up to the race.

Once the work was going well Jim walked over to the army camp to ask Major Kapisi a favour. Could the army get a message to their headquarters in Nairobi, to relay to the LMD headquarters, that money should be brought to pay not only for the cattle but also for the herdsmen's pay for the last two months? Captain Kapisi said that was no problem. Jim prayed that he was right.

They finished the cattle in two more days, as planned. There were no positives found by the BTT to CBPP. At 10.00 am Jim heard the drone of an aircraft. He walked with Suleiman to the air strip. They noticed Major Kapisi had deployed his men in a defensive perimeter. Suleiman smiled at Jim.

"You look a bit pale Jim. How is the diarrhoea?"

"I am fine but if there is no money it may well return!"

Jim's fears were unfounded. Derek Coleman, the LMD buyer had got the message. He greeted Jim warmly and said how well they had all done. Suleiman and Major Kapisi had set up a pay table under a tree in the shade. Jim asked Derek if he would pay the Somali traders but, if Jim could pay the herdsmen as he had promised them that he would get their pay.

"Good idea," said Derek. "It is always good to endorse the fact that you have kept your word. These chaps will not forget."

So it was that Jim made his way back to Mombasa very thankful that a good job had been done and his reputation was still intact, even though he had the diarrhoea at a very inconvenient time.

Chapter 1

Jim's Passion to be a vet

Tuesday 5th July 1966

Jim had always wanted to be a vet for as long as he could remember. As a small boy, on the farm at home in Kent, he loved tending the sheep. In fact he was given a large amount of freedom by his father at a very early age, under the watchful eye of the old shepherd. He was taught compassion at lambing time and common sense. He was taught rough pathology as when a sheep died, the old shepherd did a postmortem. If the cause of death was obvious and was not likely to cause disease, the meat was fed to the shepherd's dogs. If there were any deaths that the shepherd did not understand the vet was called.

His other passion was for wild animals and large open spaces. He longed to go to Africa. It was a natural progression, as he came towards his veterinary finals in 1966, for him to apply to the Overseas Development Administration (ODA) in Stags Place, London to be seconded to Tanzania as a Veterinary Officer (VO).

Jim had to fill in masses of forms and then did not hear anything. On his way through London, after graduation day, he was going by Victoria so he called in at Stags Place, just to see how his application was getting on. He was greeted by two ladies at reception who said they would ring up to the relevant department, if he would kindly take a seat. He was appalled when one of them came over and said, would he go up to the fourth floor, as both Mr. Kent and Mr. Masters were in the office and they would give him an interview now. Jim was dressed in an old, out of shape, black roll neck sweater and a pair of old jeans. He was going to make a very bad impression at the interview. Jim was so passionate about wanting to go to Africa, it would be so sad if he fell at the first hurdle. He rode up in the lift and knocked on the door marked 402, as instructed. A woman's voice told him to come in. He was greeted by yet another very kindly looking lady who said, would he go in, as Mr. Kent and Mr. Masters were expecting him. He tried to apologise about his appearance, but the kindly lady said "Don't worry they are looking for real vets not men wearing suits. You will be fine. Good Luck."

Jim went in. Mr. Kent immediately introduced himself as Grant Kent and held out his hand. He was obviously the most senior as he then introduced his colleague Reg Masters. They both sat down and indicated that Jim should do the same.

Grant immediately kicked off with,

"Congratulations, we understand you graduated yesterday. Well done in coming to see us so promptly. That shows keenness and that's what we want, eh, Reg?"

"Too right," agreed Reg. Grant continued, "You requested a post in Tanganyika, why was that?" As Jim was slightly slow replying Reg added, "That's Tanzania now."

Jim explained how one of his close friends at college was a Tanzanian and he had enthused about his country.

"Indeed he may," said Grant, "but he is still happy to spend another three years in the UK doing a PhD." Jim thought to himself, *'these guys may be office 'Wallahs' but they are well informed.'* Grant continued,

"At the present time we do not have any posts in err Tanzania. Do you fancy doing some lab work?" Jim said that he really was more interested in field work. Grant explained that the job he had in mind actually was in Northern Uganda and was very much field based, doing research into CBPP in a very remote area. Reg chipped in, "Are you married?"

"No," said Jim.

"Do you have a girl friend?"

"No," said Jim, thinking *'damn they will think I am a homosexual'.*

"Good," said Reg, "No place for a woman." He continued talking to Grant,

"I am not sure Karamoja is the right place for a single chap, since all the European administration has left. He might turn bush. Do you remember Old Minns? He had some wonderful stories about his time as Provincial Commissioner (PC) up there. I particularly like the one about him reading the riot act on the front porch to several hundred armed Karamojong, who were about to riot because there was no maize in the shops. All he had were two *'Askaris'* (Armed guards). His wife around the back of the house quelled the riot, by giving them all a cup of tea and all the cake and biscuits she had. Both Grant and Reg roared with laughter. Jim thought *'these two are a real comedy turn but if I want to get to Africa I have got to humour them'.*

"Of course you are right Reg," said Grant.

"He will either go bush or kill himself on the 600 mile road to Kampala to play rugby each weekend." Turning to Jim he asked,

"How good is your rugby?" Jim thought, *'however do I reply? I don't want to sound arrogant and yet I don't want to sound a drip.'*

"I am not as good as I should be. I had to drop out of better class rugby when I moved into final year at Bristol. I could not get much time off, so I only played for a village side at Blagdon near to the field station at Langford."

"I like that approach, young man," said Grant.

"You seem to have got your priorities right. How would you like a job in the field in Kenya?"

"I would jump at it Sir," replied Jim.

"Surely Grant we haven't got any posts in Kenya at the moment," chipped in Reg.

"Of course you are right," replied Grant, "We will have in December. Can you fill in your time until then? We will need you to spend some time at The School of Tropical Veterinary Medicine in Edinburgh. They will bring you up to speed on the current situation in East Africa."

"I am sure I could get a locum job," said Jim.

"Good," said Grant, "that's settled then. Reg can you and Mrs. Isaacs sort out the paper work and the training at Edinburgh. I will just give Jim some fatherly advice on how to behave on his first posting."

After Reg had left, Grant lent forward and, in a quieter voice said,

"I think you are rather a patriotic young man. I read your CV with interest. I noticed you had a Great, Great, Uncle Frank Joslen who was a vet in the Indian army." Jim had not mentioned that it was likely that Frank Joslen, was an alcoholic as he had died falling out of the back of a dog cart, inebriated, according to the 'Bombay

11

Times'. Also he was listed as a colonel but actually he had taught at Bombay Vet School. Grant continued, "I also noted your maternal Grandfather, plus two of your father's brothers and one of your father's sisters were all killed in action in the First World War. Your Grandfather's brother was noted for his bravery in dispatches from Gallipoli. Is he still alive?"

"Yes he is," answered Jim. "I am quite close to him. He is not only a farmer but also a lay castrator. He has given me some useful veterinary tips."

Grant looked Jim straight in the eye and asked,

"Apart from serving the Kenya Government through this Administration, would you be interested in serving the British Government in a more direct way?"

"Certainly," answered Jim, "especially if I could work in Africa."

"Excellent," said, Grant,

"You will be contacted at some stage by a man called John David. Good luck Jim. I hope you enjoy Kenya as much as I did. Let's go and see how Reg is getting on with the paperwork?"

Jim was so delighted that he had got a job in Africa, he soon forgot about this rather strange conversation with Grant Kent. When Jim got home, he looked Grant up in the veterinary register and found that he had been the Director of Veterinary Services in Kenya before independence two years ago but, since then, had worked for ODA. Reg Masters had been Provincial Veterinary Officer (PVO) Rift Valley Province at the same time and he also was listed as working for ODA.

Jim also looked in the advertisement section of some of the recent 'Veterinary Records' (This is the main journal of the veterinary profession) for locum jobs. He found a two and a half month locum job advertised in Rochester in Kent. It was a two man mixed practice. Jim would be the replacement so that each partner could have some holiday. It seemed ideal, so Jim rang the number. A pleasant sounding lady answered. She said her husband, John Mason was out on calls now but would Jim like to come in the evening at about seven 'o'clock for an interview. Jim said he would be delighted.

12

The practice was at Mr. Mason's house in a mainly residential street with houses in their own gardens. The practice premises were actually a converted double garage with a flat above.

John Mason was a genial dark-haired man with a slight Welsh accent. He was accompanied by a giant of a man called Jimmy McLeod who had a very broad Scottish accent. Jimmy was obviously the other partner. Jimmy told Jim that he vaguely knew Jim's father from working at the cattle market. It seems that Jim getting the job was a done-deal. Jimmy was going back to his home area in Scotland the next day for a three week holiday, fishing. Jim would be expected to take over from him. There was the practice Landrover which Jim would drive so he would not need his own car. Jim would live in the small flat above the surgery. He would be responsible for his breakfast but Mrs. Mason would cook lunch and supper for him. He would come down and eat with them after evening surgery. Mrs. Mason would do his washing.

Jimmy McLeod left to go home and get ready for his holiday. He said he had put all his equipment in the back of the Landrover. John showed Jim the practice, which was pretty basic. A waiting room; which doubled up as an office, where Mrs. Mason, who's Christian name was Marjorie, sat during surgery times, a small animal consulting room which doubled up as a treatment/surgery room and a store lined with shelves made up the whole practice.

Jim was very pleased when he left to go home to get his things. The Mason's seemed a kind and friendly couple. Jim had a night at home with his parents and arrived back at the practice, with his clothes and books, at 8.00 am the next morning. Putting it mildly, the back of the short-wheel based Landrover was a real jumble so Jim had everything out on the ground. He got some large cardboard boxes out of the surgery and filled them in some kind of order. Luckily Jim had always been keen on farm animal work at college so he was fairly familiar with all the equipment. He made a note of any omissions, one of which was a Seton needle for stitching a cow's vulva after replacing a prolapsed vagina. When Jim asked John, he laughed and said he used meat skewers but he knew there was one and some uterine tape on a shelf in the store. John suggested Jim looked in the store for any other equipment he needed. It all seemed very relaxed. Jim in fact was delighted with the array of equipment in the store and felt he had kitted out the Landrover really well for most eventualities. One piece of equipment which puzzled him was a hard rubber ball, the size of boxing glove, on the end of a stainless steel rod about three feet long, with a handle on the opposite end from the ball. It looked very new. Once again John was very amused. Apparently Jimmy had bought it at a meeting some years ago and never used it. It was for making sure a cow's uterus was totally back in the correct position after it had been replaced after a prolapse. John said he always used a bottle but he told Jim to take the rod and see how he got on.

John gave Jim a map. He suggested that although Jim was a local farmer's son he would be unfamiliar with some of the area around Rochester. Jim agreed but did admit that the family farm included over 600 acres of marsh land near Cliffe which was not far north of Rochester.

"That's handy," said John,

"There is a call which Marjorie has just taken, to Doubleday's farm near Cliffe. It is to a blown calf. I will show you where the farm is on the map. You will have to go through the farm yard on to a concrete road which will lead you on to the marshes. At the end of the concrete there is a very rough track which leads you to a pound where two men will be waiting with the calf."

Jim was delighted to be off. He found the place without any difficulty. That was lucky because the calf was now down and blown up like a football. Jim knew it was about to die so he did not bother with surgical niceties or local anaesthetic but immediately stuck a trocar and cannular into its left flank behind its ribs and well below its back bone. He took out the trocar and there was a rush of foul smelling gas out of the rumen. The calf seemed to decrease in size before their eyes.

"That was a near thing. I am Jim Scott. I am standing in for Jimmy while he is on holiday."

"You don't waste any time, young man. I am Tom Crane the marsh man and this is Reggie, my helper. I reckon you just saved that calf's life. Mr. Doubleday will be pleased."

Jim then stitched in the cannular, as he said it should stay in for at least forty eight hours. He asked Tom to put a cork in the hole. Jim said, if the cork stayed in and the calf did not get bloat again, the cannular could be taken out. He would come and do that, if Tom could give the practice a call.

Chapter 2

Fun with Dawn Doubleday

Thursday 8th July 1966

Tom did ring after three days and so Jim drove up to Cliffe. Tom and Reggie had got the calf in the pound and they soon put a halter on it. Jim was just looking for his scissors in the back of the Landrover when he felt a nudge in his back. He turned to find a grey pony, which obviously hoped Jim had some food in the Landrover. A girl's voice said. "Blue, get your nose out of there. I am sure the vet does not want your slobber all over his instruments."

"Don't worry," said Jim. "I am glad Blue is so friendly. Lots of ponies can smell a vet a mile away and don't come near us. I am Jim Scott."

"I am Dawn Doubleday. Tom told my Dad that you had saved the calf's life. Dad was very pleased. Are you going to take that silver tube out now?"

"Yes. Do you want to give me a hand?"

"Can I? I like working with animals but Dad is always worried I will get hurt. I will tie Blue up to the pound."

Jim liked the look of Dawn who he guessed was about sixteen. She had an intelligent face, bright blue eyes and blond hair tied in a pony tail. He waited for her to secure Blue and then climbed with her into the pound. Jim smiled at the protocol. Dawn said "Good morning to Tom calling him Mr. Crane and enquired the health of Mrs. Crane. Then she greeted Reggie by his Christian name as he took off his cap to her. Tom said,

"Do be careful, Miss Dawn. The governor does not like you in with the cattle."

"I know Tom. I don't want you to lie to him but can you omit to tell him? What he doesn't know, he won't worry about."

Tom and Reggie just chuckled. Jim got Dawn to hold the Gentian Violet spray. When he had cut the two stitches and removed the cannular, he asked her to spray into the hole formed by the cannular. The spray must have stung the calf as it danced away from the fence and wacked Dawn with its shitty tail, across her chest.

"Are you OK, Miss Dawn?" said a worried Tom.

"I am fine Mr. Crane but I am in for trouble now. How am I going to explain to Dad how I got all this cow shit over my blouse?"

"I will come to see your Dad and explain that I asked you to help me as the spray needed to go in as soon as the cannular came out." Jim chipped in. Tom looked relieved. He obviously was frightened of the governor's displeasure.

Dawn climbed out of the pen and untied Blue.

"I will just put him on this other marsh. Do you mind waiting and then I could come in your Landy? It is really kind of you as I don't want Tom to get into trouble." She led the pony away.

Tom said. "I am really grateful Jim. The girl's mother died when she was born and the governor is a little over protective. He has his own ideas as to what is proper, so to speak. The girl is allowed to do things with her pony, as that is proper for a young lady but doing anything with the cattle is forbidden, as that is men's work. I hope you are ready for a dressing down because I think you are going to get one."

"Don't worry Tom I will survive. I am off to Africa in a few weeks and a lot worse things will happen to me over there. However I may see you again, as I understand from Mrs. Mason that you have a large number of cattle. Let me know if you are not happy with the calf. Goodbye for now."

Jim drove off to the gate of the marsh, which Dawn was just opening, to release Blue. Dawn got into the Landrover and they set off.

"Oh dear you are going to get a real ticking off. I am sorry. You are very brave to volunteer."

Jim laughed. "At least I have not tried to wash your front down with water. That would be fun but then your Dad would be furious."

Dawn giggled. "My front is definitely out of bounds."

"I suppose you could throw yourself into a ditch and say you need to change and then your father will never know you had cow shit on your blouse. You would look awfully sexy with a wet blouse."

"Stop the Landy," commanded Dawn. She got out

'*Oh dear,*' thought Jim. '*I have really over done it now.*'

He got out his side. There was a splash and then he was helping Dawn out of the ditch. She stood laughing and facing him.

"Satisfied with the wet look? You are not allowed to touch but you can have a good look. Your face is a real study!" They both laughed.

"Come on, I have got a towel in the back of the Landy, as you call it. You can dry yourself off. You will get cold. They were still laughing as Dawn was drying her hair with the towel, when a very stern voice said.

"What the devil is going on here?" They both turned around. Jim guessed it was Dawn's father.

"What are you doing with my daughter? Tell me the truth now. I can always tell when someone is lying."

"It was my fault, Sir. Dawn had helped me with the blown calf and got calf dung on her blouse. She said you might be cross, so I told her to jump in the ditch and then you would never find out." Mr. Doubleday swung round to Dawn.

"Is that true?"

"Yes Father, but Jim was only trying to help."

"I know Jim's father and his older brother. From what they say I can certainly believe you. I think I will have to keep you under lock and key until he has gone to Africa." Dawn looked appalled. "Father you can't send him to Africa. I jumped in myself he didn't throw me in. Please don't send him to Africa."

Mr. Doubleday's face lightened and he was almost smiling.

"I know more about this young man than you do. If he wanted to throw you in the ditch he would do. To try to cheer me up at your mother's funeral, Jim's mother told me that her youngest son, Jim was such a stubborn little boy. She had asked him what he wanted for Christmas. He had said he wanted a lion cub. When she said that he couldn't possibly have a lion cub, he said if he couldn't have a lion cub he did not want anything else. His mother was a very wise woman and did not give him anything else. She said he never cried

17

or sulked but said he would go to Africa when he was older and get one. I saw his father at Ashford market on Tuesday. He told me Jim was going to work in Africa."

Dawn went to her father and hugged him.

"I can be stubborn as well Dad. If you had tried to lock me up, I would have gone to Africa as well."

"I can quite believe that," said her Dad.

"Now Jim if you can drive us back to the farm, we can have a cup of coffee and a piece of cake, while this young lady makes herself presentable."

Dawn got in the middle seat of the Landrover. Jim noticed that she sat close to him and put her right leg to the right of the gear stick. He did not mind her wet body next to his.

When they reached the house Dawn went in first, while Jim and Mr. Doubleday were taking off their boots. Jim heard a woman's voice.

"Glory be, Miss Dawn, look at the state of you."

"Sorry to put you to extra work Nanny. I went in the ditch."

"I think you did. You are soaked, child. I have a good mind to put you over my knee and give you the slipper."

"I think I am a bit old for that now, Nanny. Anyway, Father has already given me my punishment. He is going to lock me up until Jim has gone away," said Dawn in devilment.

"Rightfully so," said Nanny. "I suppose Jim is one of the farm boys and he pushed you in."

"No Nanny, Jim is the new vet and he told me to jump in, so father did not see I had been working with the cattle."

"What a carry on! I expect your father will give this new vet a good dressing down. It is a pity, as Mr. Crane told me he is a good vet and saved a calf a couple of days ago. You go upstairs and have a shower, wash your hair and make sure it is dry before you put a dress on. I will have you clean and tidy if you are going to be locked up. What is the world coming to?"

Mr. Doubleday turned to Jim with a twinkle in his eye. "You see, I am not the only frightening disciplinarian in the house!"

As he came in Mr. Doubleday called to a girl, of little more than fourteen, dressed in blue. "Martha, I would be grateful if you could you bring some coffee and cake through to the study, for the vet and I?"

"Yes Sir. I will bring it directly."

"Thank you, Martha."

While they were waiting Mr. Doubleday asked Jim all about his training. He seemed interested that Jim liked horses. He said Jimmy cannot be bothered with riding horses, so he got a neighbouring practice from Ashford to look after his hunter and Dawn's pony. They both needed vaccination so he wondered if Jim would do that next time he came to the farm.

Jim said he would be happy to. Jim then asked if he could take Dawn on his rounds as she seemed interested in animals.

"Did she put you up to this?" asked a shrewd Mr. Doubleday.

"No," replied Jim. "I like her. She certainly has some spirit and I think I could teach her a lot about cattle and horses, for that matter. She may say she can't be bothered. Being in the car all day can be a bit lonely. It's a bit of a change for me, I am used to having all my fellow students around all the time."

"We will have to ask her! If she wants to I would have no objection. I think she is also a little lonely back home. She is at boarding school, so she doesn't really have any friends up here in Cliffe. They all live miles away. However I will hold you entirely responsible for her. I don't want her hurt in any way." He chuckled.

"I think she will do what you tell her. I can't think any of her upper crust school friends would jump in the ditch, if a young man told them to! I think you may have inherited some good sense from your father and mother. I met your mother in the bank yesterday. I said to her that she would be sorry you were not settling down but were going far away to Africa. She said she would be, particularly as he was the baby of the family. Then she said a strange thing to me. She said. "Children are only lent you know." I have taken that to heart. I would like Dawn to take over the farm one day but, if she wants to do something else, I will encourage her. However I would be grateful if you do not encourage her to go to Africa. Going to train in London or going to University are very acceptable but her going off to Africa is not what I would like. It was bad enough for me in the Western Desert."

19

"That is fantastic! Were you in the eighth army when the Africa Corps was beaten?"

Mr. Doubleday laughed. "Yes, I beat Rommel single handed."

At that moment Dawn came in. "What is the laughing about?" she enquired.

"I was just asking your Dad about the war."

"I didn't know the war was something to be laughed about?"

"No, normally war is a horrible thing but I always maintain that nothing is too sacred to be laughed at," said her Dad.

Jim looked at Dawn and said. "You scrub up well."

"I am not one of Father's prize cows," she retorted. By the way she said it, Jim could tell she was not angry and was actually quite pleased with the compliment.

"Jim, I have got a favor to ask you. Could I come with you on your rounds to learn something about animals? I promise I won't get in the way."

"I would love to take you," replied Jim with a smile. "My guess is that you should get your father's permission."

"Please Dad. Do say I can."

So it was agreed that Mr. Doubleday would drop her off at practice in the morning, on his way to get some machinery parts. Jim would then bring her home. Jim suggested she wore trousers and brought an overall and some wellington boots.

"Oh dear I haven't got any overalls," said Dawn.

"Don't worry, just bring an old coat and you can wear my sheep leggings."

"I will buy you some overalls at the machinery store tomorrow. I know they sell them," said her Dad.

Jim said. "I will ask Mrs. Mason to give you some lunch with us. I am sure she won't mind. I had better fly. She will think I have fallen in the ditch!"

Mr. Mason was delighted when he heard that Mr. Doubleday wanted Jim to vaccinate the horses. He said it always annoyed him that the Ashford practice did the horse work. He did admit that, although Jimmy was an excellent farm vet, he did not chat enough to horse owners and so they were not really satisfied. He said he personally would follow up the horse work at Doubleday's when Jim left. He was more guarded when he heard that Dawn Doubleday was coming to see practice. He said he had heard that she was rather prim and proper and therefore would not fit in with the farm work. Mrs. Mason, on the other hand, said she would be delighted to have the young girl for lunch. She said it would be good to talk about something different, rather than the veterinary work all the time. They both roared with laughter when Jim told them about Dawn jumping into the ditch.

"I will have to revise my opinion of the young lady," said Mr. Mason.

"I am certainly amazed that Mr. Doubleday has allowed her to come, after that," said Mrs. Mason.

"I would have thought he would have been scared to death of letting you anywhere near her. You are a very naughty boy. I expect you to be very kind to her and look after her properly. She will not be like your rough and tumble girl veterinary students. Joyce Green, her nanny, is a friend of mine. She will be very worried. I am so amazed that Mr. Doubleday has sanctioned the arrangement. He is quite a big shot in the NFU and in the hunt."

"I think he has been talking separately to my Father and Mother," said Jim. "Apparently, when he was commiserating with my Mum about me going to Africa, she had said, "children are only lent, Mr. Doubleday." He has taken that to heart and is letting Dawn off the leash a little."

"Well Jim, you must behave yourself. Joyce Green will ring your ears if you misbehave." Jim smiled. He wondered whether Mrs. Mason meant that she would ring his neck or box his ears!

In the morning Dawn was indeed very prim and proper in the practice but as soon as she was in the Landrover, alone with Jim, she was totally deferent and relaxed. She was really enthusiastic when she heard they were going to a calving, at Matt Skinner's farm. Apparently Matt Skinner was a tenant of her Father's.

"I think Matt Skinner thinks girls should be confined to the house. I will show him." Dawn said with feeling.

"Very well," said Jim as he stopped in a lay-by, a mile before the farm.

"You had better look the part. You put on my sheep leggings and my parlor top, so you will look as if you mean business."

"What will you wear?" asked Dawn

"I have some waterproof trousers and I will take my shirt off. On second thoughts, as I am the vet, I had better wear the parlor top and you had better take your shirt off."

"Dream on, Jim Scott. I have jumped into a ditch to save you from my father's wrath but I am not stripping off in front of Matt Skinner for all the tea in China!"

They arrived at the farm. Dawn actually looked very sexy in Jim's leggings, as they showed off her pert bottom. He knew better than to say anything. Matt Skinner was a belligerent forty year old. He ordered a farm boy, called Ned, to go in doors and get hot water, soap and a towel from Mrs. Skinner. Jim introduced himself and just said Dawn was a student who was learning the tricks of the trade.

"I hope I don't have to pay double as there are two of you?"

Jim replied. "Oh no. How long has she been calving?"

"Only an hour or so. I can see the feet but she won't get on with it. I think she just needs a pull." Jim guessed he had already given her a pull. Jim had explained to Dawn, in the Landrover, how to put the calving ropes on the legs, like a noose above each fetlock. Jim handed her three ropes, three short lengths of pole and a bottle of lubricant. The water arrived. Jim took his shirt off, winked at Dawn and said.

"Would you like to lead us to the cow, Mr. Skinner?"

The cow was a quiet, old shorthorn cow, secured in her stall by a chain around her neck. Jim asked Ned politely if he could bring him a piece of baler twin. Jim undid the hook of the chain and tied the chain with the string. He gave his pen knife to Dawn. "If she goes down, can you cut the string, so she won't throttle herself?"

"She won't go down," said Mr. Skinner. "She has only been at it two ticks." Jim said nothing but just soaped his arm and felt into the cow. As he thought the calf's head was back. He was sure Mr. Skinner had been pulling.

"The head is back," said Jim. "I will try to put a rope on its head."

He selected the thin rope of the trio and made a loop over the middle fingers of his right hand. Then he asked Dawn for some lubricant. He expected her to put some into his left hand so he could smear it down his right arm. Instead she put a whole lot in her own hand and gently applied it to his arm. It was rather a nice sensation and when Mr. Skinner was not looking he smiled at her. He was not sure but he thought she winked. It was not easy but eventually Jim managed to get a loop of rope behind the calf's ears and in its mouth, like a bit in a bridle. He tied the rope to one of the poles with a bowline knot, so it was easily released and then pulled the head up into the correct position in the pelvis of the cow. He then told Dawn to put the stronger ropes on the calf's legs. Mr. Skinner objected.

"You can't get a weak girl to do something like that!" Jim felt Dawn stiffen beside him. Dawn turned and looked Mr. Skinner straight in the eye. Then she said in a very quiet firm voice.

"A strong woman is much better than a weak man, Mr. Skinner." Then she put on the two leg ropes in the correct position. She tied one with a bowline like Jim had and handed it to Ned. She tied the other and handed it to Mr. Skinner. Then she said, as if she had been calving cows all her life,

"I want you, Jim, to keep the head in the correct position. You two strong men can pull on the legs as the cow strains. I will open the penknife and be ready to cut the string when she goes down. Right-pull."

The head came out and sure enough the cow went down. Dawn stepped forward quickly and cut the string. They soon had the calf out. Before Jim could stop her, Dawn took the rope off the calves head and blew into its nostrils. The calf started breathing.

Mr. Skinner gave them both a grudging "thank you," as they went to go, after they had cleaned up and Jim had put his shirt back on. Jim stopped in the lay by. "You are a real star. I was so proud of you. I could have kissed you but you have such a dirty face, from blowing down the calf's nostrils, I don't think I will. He then produced a clean handkerchief spat on a corner and cleaned the muck off her laughing face.

"I won't forget you refused to kiss me, you cheeky boy. Who said I wanted to be kissed anyway? I certainly did not want my face cleaned up with your spit! Come on, let's go to our next call. This is good fun."

At lunch, initially Dawn was quiet, as she had been first thing in the morning but after Jim had said how proud he was of her and how she had put Matt Skinner in his place, she soon opened up and told Mrs. Mason how exciting it was and how she was really enjoying herself. Jim could see that her enthusiasm had even reached Mr. Mason.

Dawn obviously liked dogs and cats, as she handled them well for Jim during his afternoon surgery. Dawn was quiet when they got near her home. Jim was worried about what had upset her. Then she came out with it. "Was I OK? Can I come again?"

"Of course you can! I would love it. When we get to your home, we will make arrangements for tomorrow." Dawn's face lit up and she squeezed his leg. "Thank you so much. I was worried you had got sick of my girlie chatter."

"Not at all, I love your enthusiasm."

When they got back to the farm, Joyce Green and Mr. Doubleday were both in the kitchen, discussing the order for the butcher. Mr. Doubleday turned to Dawn and said. "Well, how did you get on then?"

With a completely straight face, Dawn said,

"It was a disaster. Our first call was to a calving. Jim was not pleased. He told me to take my shirt off. I refused. I hope I did the right thing Dad?"

"And right you were, my girl," said Joyce. "I have never heard of such a thing."

Her Dad stroked his chin.

"I think you are teasing us. Yesterday you jumped into a ditch when Jim suggested it. I suspect you would have taken your shirt off today, if he had given you a good reason. What's your side of the story Jim?"

"Dawn was a real star. I was so proud of her." Dawn was laughing so much that tears were running down her cheeks when Jim recounted all the details of the calving and the altercation with Matt Skinner.

"How did you know how to do all that?" enquired Mr. Doubleday.

"Well, Jim had told me some of it in the Landrover on the way and, you don't know Dad, but I have often watched Mr. Crane and Reggie calve cows, by hiding in the straw above the calving box."

"I have obviously been too soft with you all these years. Spare the rod and spoil the child. What do you say Nanny?"

"Well it is not my place, Mr. Doubleday but I don't think it is right to laugh at young boys telling Miss Dawn to take her shirt off, in any circumstances and that's a fact." Then she softened and said.

"My friend Mrs. Mason said Master Jim is a good vet and has a wicked sense of humour so I will forgive him this time. I am glad you have bought those overalls Mr. Doubleday. I reckon you must wear those all the time, Miss Dawn." She bustled out of the kitchen so, that she could find Martha to take the tea through.

Dawn continued to come with Jim most days unless she had, in her words, "boring things to do like going to the dentist and visiting elderly relatives." A couple of evenings Mr. Doubleday asked Jim to supper, once when Dawn had gone out with two girl friends to the cinema. The two of them had a pleasant evening talking about the war, particularly the North Africa Campaign. Jim vaccinated the horses that evening. Mr. Doubleday stressed that he must be sent a bill. Jim mentioned that Mr. Mason would be honored to do the horse work. Mr. Doubleday said he did not realise vets were so sensitive. He got the impression from Jimmy that neither of them cared about horses only, farm animals.

One evening Jim took Dawn to supper at his parents. On the way, Dawn asked, "Have I scrubbed up OK?"

Jim laughed. "You look so pretty, you will make my father's deaf aid whistle." Dawn said rather pensively.

"I am sure I will get on well with your father, if he is anything like you and my Dad. It is getting on with your mother that I am worried about."

In fact she got on very well with Jim's mother. So much so that when Jim next went home, his mother said,

"I don't know why you want to go to Africa, when Kent has lovely girls like that. In some ways I wish I had got you a lion cub, it might have got Africa out of your system."

"Or it might have eaten him," said his Dad with a laugh.

On the last night before Dawn was due to go back to school, Jim was asked to supper. Nanny ate with them and she dominated the conversation. "I am not having you three talking all night about vetting. Most of the topics are not fit for the kitchen, let alone the dining room." Dawn laughed at her.

"At least, as you are here, I am allowed to take my overalls off." Nanny was not upset. "You little vixen, I have often seen you without them. In fact, I was appalled by how short your shorts were. You'll get a bad name and give boys the wrong idea!"

"I must say the blue pair did make my heart race when you wore them with wellies," said Jim."You have good legs." Dawn laughed and said,

"I wore the wellies so you would not see my spavins." Mr. Doubleday chuckled at that.

When Jim went to go and was thanking them for supper, Mr. Doubleday said. "Do come and see us for supper. I will be lonely with Dawn away at school. I enjoy your company. Now, you show him off the premises Dawn. I don't want him to pinch anything." Everyone laughed. At the door, Dawn came out with Jim and then shut the door behind her.

"Thank you for making this a wonderful summer holiday and teaching me so much. I am afraid you are not done with me yet, as I have two favours to ask you. You know you said your sister went to my school. Could you come and pick me up at the first exeat? The other girls are so bloody sophisticated. I am proud of being my Dad's daughter and living on a farm. If you arrived in the Landy it would be one in the eye for them."

"I would be happy to, provided the school won't make a fuss. They never did when my brother and I picked my sister up, but then we were siblings."

"I had not thought of that," said Dawn. "I will get Dad to say something tomorrow. I know he hates the job, so he will fix something."

"What's the other favour?" asked Jim.

Dawn said. "Oh yes," as if it had slipped her mind.

"Can I borrow your handkerchief?"

Jim produced one and, in a rather wary tone, asked.

"You are not planning a tearful farewell?"

"Oh no," said Dawn, then spat on the handkerchief and wiped Jim's very surprised face. "I just wanted to make sure your face was clean before you kissed me! Goodbye."

In fact, Jim saw quite a lot of Mr. Doubleday. Mr. Doubleday would often leave word at the practice, asking Jim to supper. They

26

talked about horses, the war and Mr. Doubleday's plans for the future. He said he was particularly pleased at how Dawn had stood up to Matt Skinner. If she was going to take over the farm, she would not only have to run all the farms which Mr. Doubleday actually farmed himself, but also she would have to supervise the six tenant farms, like Matt Skinner's. It was certainly a big job. Jim discussed his own situation. His older brother had always wanted to be a farmer and so his Dad had been pleased and had wrongly assumed that Jim would follow his older brother's example. Jim had always said he wanted to be a vet. Jim told Mr. Doubleday how his father had tried to persuade him to be a farmer. Jim's father had two farms and thought he could give one to each son and make a financial settlement on their sister. Jim's father said that there was much more money to be made farming than vetting. However Jim had been stubborn and so, when Jim was twelve and his brother had finished his National Service, he had given the whole farm to Jim's brother to avoid inheritance tax. Jim did add that his father had made a provision in his will for Jim to receive some money, to help him buy a practice. Jim then said,

"I am telling you this because Dawn may not want to inherit the farm. She is a very willful girl and I am sure, like me, she won't be pushed into a career she does not want to pursue. I feel guilty for encouraging her to be interested in vetting. I would not have done it if I had known your plans."

"Don't worry Jim, I would not have let her come with you if I had not liked the idea. She is the apple of my eye, as you well know. However, I won't push her into farming if she does not want that. I am quite a bit younger than your father. I love farming and particularly livestock farming. I would like to see Dawn go away to university and get a degree. If she studies to be a vet that knowledge will never be wasted. All I beg of you, is not to encourage her to go to Africa. The wind of change has already started blowing there. Farming for colonials will not last for a decade in Africa. I fought together with lots of Aussis and Kiwis in North Africa. They were good men. If Dawn wants to go abroad, I will happily help her to buy a farm or whatever. When her mother tragically died, I very nearly upped sticks and went to Australia myself."

They both sat in silence, dwelling on their thoughts. Mr. Doubleday broke the silence and changed the subject.

"I am thinking of buying a new young hunter. I went down to Lewes, in Sussex, to have a look at him earlier in the week. He is only young but he is a big horse and could carry me easily. I rode him and he seemed honest enough. I wonder if you would come down with me and vet him for me. Obviously you must ask Mr. Mason but I can't think he will have any objections?"

"I think he might," said Jim. "You see Mr. Doubleday, young, newly qualified vets like me are not normally asked to vet big potentially expensive horses. I don't want to know what you are likely to have to pay for him, as that is not my role, but Mr. Mason may not think I am up to the job. I personally would jump at the chance. Obviously, I am going to take longer than a more experienced vet but the fee would be the same."

"Well, I will give him a ring in the morning. I have faith in you, Jim. By the way I saw your Father, in Ashford, on Tuesday. I told him I thought you were doing a good job. Apparently Dawn made a good impression on him. I gather your Mother thought Dawn was very mature for her age, which pleased me. I also gather your Mother wished Dawn was a little older, so that she would tempt you to stay in England. I told your Father you had set your heart on Africa. He said he was resigned about that now and was going to give you all his support."

In fact, Mr. Mason did agree to Jim doing the vetting. He spent over half an hour talking Jim through the procedure. That night, Jim went over his college notes. Mr. Doubleday picked him up at 2.00 pm, after his morning round and a rather hurried lunch. Jim enjoyed the drive down to Lewes, in Mr. Doubleday's Jaguar. They talked about horses all the way there. Jim, particularly, quizzed Mr. Doubleday as to whether there were any faults that he had seen on the horse they were going to. Mr. Doubleday said there was nothing he was particularly concerned about. He did stress that he wanted Jim to really check his age.

They arrived at the yard. Mr. Doubleday introduced Jim to the seller who was a kindly, large, red-faced man, called Peter Curl. He said his son, Len, who was a point to point jockey, would ride the horse for them. Jim talked through the vetting with Mr. Doubleday,

28

as he was his client. He had to concentrate on that, as the seller was waxing eloquent on the virtues of the hunter, which was called 'Prince'. Prince was a big, strong, chestnut gelding standing seventeen hands. Jim asked Peter to put his head collar on and take off his rug in the stable. Jim had brought his stethoscope. He listened to the heart from both the left and right sides. It was beating at 32 beats per minute. Jim breathed a sigh of relief as he could not hear a heart murmur or any arrhythmias. Both these abnormalities are difficult for inexperienced vets to interpret. He listened over the area of both lungs. He also listened at the bottom of the wind pipe and at the larynx. There were no abnormal noises. Jim felt the larynx carefully to compare the muscles on each side. If one had been larger than the other, Jim would have been worried that the horse was a 'roarer'. Jim talked to the horse and started looking and palpating him from head to toe. He peeled back his lips on both sides of his mouth. He was relieved to see he had four canine teeth, which meant he was at least five years old. Jim managed to grab the long slippery tongue so that he could see the grinding surface of the twelve incisors. All the incisors were in wear but Jim thought that the corner incisors were only just in wear. This meant that Prince was six years old. He turned to Mr. Doubleday and said, "I think he is a six year old." Peter chipped in. "That's right, young man, he was six in March this year."

Jim then had a look in his mouth with a small pen torch, while still holding his tongue. He said. "I see he has lost his wolf teeth or did you have them taken out?"

Peter replied. "Yes, we had them taken out when we backed him two and a half years ago."

Jim let go of the tongue and felt all over the head. He was pleased that the horse did not seem to worry about his ears being touched. He felt down his neck and along his back. The horse showed no resentment, even when Jim squeezed his withers. Jim drew his finger hard down each side of his back and the horse bent his back left and right in the normal way. Jim felt around his girth area from both sides and into both his axillae. He looked into his groin from both sides remembering to examine the prepuce, from both sides as well. Jim grasped the tail and raised it so he could examine the anus. He palpated the tail and then, pulling the tail towards him, he pushed on

29

the hip bone. Prince did not object. Jim repeated the test from the other side.

Jim turned to Mr. Doubleday and said. "The examination has gone well so far. Now we will have a good feel of his legs and check his hooves."

Peter Curl chipped it. "You won't find anything wrong with his legs and my farrier says he has the best feet of any he puts shoes on." Jim said nothing but felt carefully down each leg.

Then he said. "I will just go back to the car and get my hoof testers." These are like a giant pair of pliers. A vet can tell if there is pain in the foot by pushing with hoof testers. Jim came back with the hoof testers and asked Peter Curl if he could borrow a hoof pick. While Mr. Doubleday held the horse Peter disappeared to find a hoof pick. Mr. Doubleday asked.

"Do you think his tendons are OK, Jim?"

"I think so," replied Jim. "I just hope he trots up sound." When Peter returned, Jim picked each foot out in turn and then applied the hoof testers. All seemed to be well.

Jim then asked Peter if he would trot Prince up for him.

"I will just get my lad to do that. I am getting too old to run about with horses."

To Jim's relief, 'Prince' trotted up sound when Len got him going on the concrete, in front of the stables. Jim then asked Len to tack him up so that they could give him some fast exercise in one of the fields. Len cantered him around Jim on both reins and then set off for a gallop before returning to let Jim listen to the heart. Jim was satisfied that his heart and wind were OK. Jim explained to Mr. Doubleday that a horse, particularly a big hunter, could have a weakness in its larynx. Then, unlike normal horses which made a noise when they breathed out, a horse affected would make a noise when it breathed in, as well. This was said to be roaring and would have meant that the horse would fail the vetting.

"What does the noise sound like?" asked Mr. Doubleday. Jim laughed.

"It is meant to sound like a leopard roaring. I haven't heard one yet, but I will let you know when I come home from Africa!"

Jim gave instructions that 'Prince' was to be left completely alone in his box, to calm down. He explained that this was to highlight any lameness problems which would then be apparent when they gave him his second trot up. Jim apologized to both Mr. Doubleday and Peter Curl. "I am sorry to have to make you wait but I will sit down quietly and complete the paperwork."

Jim had two forms to start completing. The first was permission, from Peter Curl, to allow Jim to take a bloody sample. This sample would be labelled carefully and then sent to a special laboratory, where it would be stored for six months. It would only be tested if there was a problem with the horse, when it went to its new home. A likely problem would be if, after a couple of days, the horse became lame for no explainable reason. The inference was that the seller had given the horse a pain killer, to mask this lameness at the time of vetting. The blood sample would then be tested and, if a trace of pain killer was found in the blood, the seller would have to give the buyer his money back and refund him any expenses he had incurred.

The second form was the vetting certificate. This was a legal document, which gave all the details of the horse. Any problems found by the vet and whether the vet felt it was fit for the purpose intended. In this case, was it fit as a hunter for a large man? Obviously, eventually Jim would have to sign the form.

When Jim had completed as much of the form as he could, he came back to the horse and, after Peter Curl had signed the form, Jim took a blood sample. Jim had a good look in the horse's eyes with an ophthalmoscope. Then Jim asked Len to do some more trot ups. Not only was Prince trotted up normally but he had to be trotted up, after each leg in turn had been held up in the flexed position for half a minute. Mercifully Prince remained sound throughout.

Then Jim got Len to turn Prince in a tight circle, both left and right, to see that he could cross his legs. Then Len had to push Prince backwards, to see that he did not 'Shiver', a condition of the back which causes hind leg problems. Finally Len had to snatch Prince forward to see that he did not have 'String-halt', a condition where a horse cannot control its back legs all the time and snatches them up in the air for no good reason.

Jim wanted to shout for joy when he had, at last, finished and not found anything amiss, but instead he said. "Good news, Mr. Doubleday. I can't find a thing wrong with him!"

Mr. Doubleday said. "That is excellent. I will give you a cheque Peter, right away, while Jim is completing the forms. I will make arrangements for him to be picked up at the weekend. I will give you a ring with the details."

Once they were in the car, Mr. Doubleday said.

"I was most impressed. You were very thorough. This calls for a celebration. I will treat you to dinner on the way home." They stopped at a smart restaurant, The Tudor House. They both had steaks and Mr. Doubleday bought a bottle of red wine, which cost, as much as Jim would earn in a week. It had been a most enjoyable day.

Jim came home really tired one evening. As he was getting more experienced he was doing more and more farm calls. Mr. Mason was happy to do the small animal work. Mrs. Mason had supper all ready for the three of them. She said. "I feel guilty, Jim. A post card came for you. Here it is. I couldn't stop myself from reading it. Whatever does she mean?"

The post card read; *'Hope all is well with you. Do give my regards to Mr. and Mrs. Mason. They were so kind to me in the summer holidays. I can't wait till exeat. Make sure you wash your face well before you pick me up!'*

Jim went a bit pink. "It is a private joke but it is against me, so I am sure Dawn won't mind me telling you. You remember I have asked for the afternoon off, to go and pick her up from school next week?"

"Oh yes. That will be fine," said Mr. Mason.

"Well the joke started, when Dawn helped me with that calving at Skinners. She got meconium all over her face. When we left the farm, I stopped and told her how well she had done standing up to Mr. Skinner. I told her I was so pleased I could have kissed her, but I wouldn't as she had such a dirty face. Then I got out my handkerchief, spat on it and cleaned her face. She thought it was hugely funny and said she would never forget I had refused to kiss her. She got her own back as, when we said goodbye, when she was going back to school, she asked me if she could borrow my handkerchief. I was worried that she was going to cry. She took my handkerchief, spat on it, and wiped my surprised face and then, roaring with laughter, said, "I just wanted to make sure your face was clean before I let you kiss me goodbye.""

Mr. and Mrs. Mason thought this was extremely funny.

"Good for Dawn," said Mrs. Mason. "I am not sure Joyce Green would find it very funny as she is very protective of Dawn, in many ways more so than Mr. Doubleday. It was kind of Dawn to send her regards. I hope she will have a meal with us during the exeat."

Jim was slightly apprehensive when he arrived at 'Windsby House School'. He could see what Dawn had meant. There were a lot of very smart cars. There were several parents chatting to severe looking ladies, who were obviously teachers. Very demure girls came down the steps, out of the open door, to greet their parents with pecks on their mother's cheeks. Dawn came out, holding a small bag and wearing, a skirt at least four inches shorter than the other girls. She saw Jim. Her face lit up and she started to run towards him. She was stopped in her tracks by a voice, which should have belonged to a drill sergeant.

"Dawn Doubleday. Go back inside and do something with that skirt. What will your Father say? When you have found him, I would be grateful if he and I can have a brief chat." Dawn turned on her heals and went back inside. Jim shivered in his shoes but he had not run away from freshly calved cows that could be very dangerous. He was not going to run away from this one. He walked up to the commanding lady and put on his best smile.

"I am so sorry to bother you but I have been sent by Mr. Doubleday to collect his daughter. May I go in and find her and carry her bag?"

"You certainly cannot. Only parents are allowed into the school."

"I am so sorry, the rules must have changed. My brother and I always came in and picked up my sister Una's trunk."

"That, young man, is allowed at the beginning and end of term with trunks, but not at exeats, when the girls are meant to take the minimum amount of luggage. Una is an unusual name. We had a Una Scott here, who was head girl, but I doubt if you were her brother."

"Actually I am her brother and I am very fond and proud of her. I am sure she would have sent her regards, if she had known I would be meeting you. She has done extremely well at St Thomas' Hospital and is now teaching there."

33

"I am pleased to hear that. Please convey my best wishes. Arrh - there you are Dawn, I gather your chauffeur is the brother of one of our most promising pupils. You could do well to emulate her. I was saying, that girls are meant to take the minimum of luggage home at exeat. I expect you have an enormous bag. Where is it?"

"I only have this, Miss Jewel." Dawn produced a very small polythene bag.

"That is hardly sufficient. What is in it?"

"Only a flannel, Miss Jewel," Dawn produced a bright pink damp flannel and, before Jim could stop her, she wiped his face with it.

In her most haughty voice, putting the flannel back in the bag, she said,

"I do insist that anyone driving me, must have a clean face. Please carry it to the vehicle." She handed it to Jim, turned and walked towards the Landrover. Miss Jewel was speechless. Jim held the door open for Dawn to get in. She hitched up her skirt, showing an unnecessary amount of leg and climbed in. Jim went to the driver's door, got in and they drove off. They only just managed to hold back their laughter until they were out of the school gates.

"Thank God you did not say, I had to have a clean face to kiss you! You were magnificent. I do hope you are not going to get into trouble."

"Oh, I expect I will, but I can't worry about it. You did well to face up to the old bat and not hide in the Landrover. Even if you have got a dirty face, I would like you to kiss me but you will probably kill us both with all the traffic. I hitched up my skirt on purpose, as you said I had got good legs. So you will have to make do with a quick glance at them. Jim looked down, to see her skirt at least half way up her thighs.

"I think your school skirt, when it is like that, is almost as sexy as your blue shorts. I hope this mild weather holds out so you can wear them when we go vetting."

She leant across and kissed him on the cheek.

They had good fun over the exeat. Jim was quite busy working but that did not worry Dawn, as she loved coming on calls. It was not that warm but somehow, much to Nanny's annoyance, she wore her shorts, only hiding them under her overalls in the late afternoon and evening, when it got chilly.

34

On the last afternoon, as there were no calls, Mr. Mason said he would hold the fort. They went for a walk along the top of the sea wall, separating Doubleday land from the Thames estuary. It had been built higher, after the flooding in 1953.

Dawn said. "I know I sound like an over dramatic silly girl, like so many girls at school, but you have really changed me. I have decided to become a vet. Luckily I have just started my 'A' levels and I have picked the right three; Chemistry, Physics and Biology. I will work as a vet for a time and then, when father says the time is right, I will come home and take over the farm." Jim turned her to face him.

"I know you will do it and I wish you all the luck in the world." He kissed her impulsively. It left her rather breathless.

"I am not sure if your face was clean but you must have forgotten to shave this morning in your rush to pick me up as your chin is terribly rough." She reached up and felt his chin.

"I don't mind really, so please kiss me again." Jim did as requested.

"I feel really weak at the knees. Can you give me a piggy back?"

They were both out of breath and laughing when they arrived back at the farm. Nanny was at the stove and Mr. Doubleday was reading the paper at the kitchen table. Dawn burst out.

"I have decided to become a vet and then come back and run the farm, when you want me to Dad."

Mr. Doubleday looked up.

"I think that is a very good idea, but isn't it a little chilly for those shorts?"

"I should think it is, Miss Dawn. You will catch pneumonia. Now be away upstairs, right quick and put a dress and stockings on. I have made your favorite going-back-to-school supper of roast chicken.

Chapter 3

Further training

Sunday 13th November 1966

Towards the end of his locum, Jim received a vast amount of paperwork from ODA. It contained his contract, for two years as a Kenyan Government Veterinary Officer. He was due to fly out on the night of the 9th December 1966. His annual salary of £1025 would start from that date. It also contained a cheque for £40, which was his tropical clothes allowance. There was a list of suggested items, which he would need to take with him and it gave details of the baggage he was allowed to send out by sea. It gave him, not only his ticket but also an extra airfreight allowance of 60lbs, on top of the normal baggage allowance of 40lbs. Jim actually owned very little, so it was very easy to keep within the allowance which he was given as sea freight. The main heavy items were his text books and college notes. He was loath to send them, as he was constantly referring to them during the locum job, but he knew sea freight took a seriously long time, so the sooner they went the better.

Jim was sent all the details of his course up in Edinburgh at the Veterinary Topical Medical School. Jim had only been to Edinburgh as a child, on family holidays. He was looking forward to the course. His mother and father were amused that his accommodation had been arranged at the same hotel which they had used, as a family, fifteen years before. It was on the southern outskirts of the city so that it would be easy to get to Easter Bush, where the School of Tropical Veterinary Medicine was situated, in the mornings, as Jim would be driving in the opposite direction to the rush hour traffic. Equally it would be easy to get back to the hotel in the evenings. In reality it did not matter, as the course did not start until 9.30am, when most people had already arrived at work, and did not finish until 5.30pm, when the vast majority of commuters had already got home. The hotel had been booked for the Sunday night with the introduction to the course scheduled for the following morning.

Jim remembered his childhood, when they had taken two days to drive up from Kent to Scotland. Now, with improvements on the A1, his father said he could easily do it in a day but that it would be worthwhile starting early on the Sunday morning, so that Jim could get through London easily.

Jim's father was right and Jim sailed through London. Some of the A1 was dual carriageway, so Jim was able to pass the coaches most of the time. By mid-morning, he had reached Scotch Corner. Jim was amazed how fast and economical his old Mini was, being nearly empty with just him and a duffel bag of clothes. Normally, in the past, on a long run to Bristol he would be carrying all manner of stuff, including garden produce and food, which his parents gave him to make his meager grant go further. He continued up the A1, although it looked on the map as if it might be quicker to go through Jedburgh. He felt relaxed staying on one road and not having to map read all the time. It was quite chilly but the sun was shining and the views over the North Sea were magnificent. Still, he was jolly tired when he got to the outskirts of Edinburgh and had to find the 'Braid's Hill Hotel'. It was actually visible from the A702 going South out of the city but, finding the entrance was a little tricky, as you had to get on a small street, -Braid Hills Road- and turn left, drive around the back before climbing up the hill of Braids Road to the car park. Jim felt very important parking right near the grand entrance, with its swing door.

Jim was impressed that he was expected by the old man, at the reception, who gave him his room key and offered to carry Jim's duffel bag up to the room. Jim said he would be fine and found his way to an enormous room with its own bathroom. He had a long bath and went down to dinner. He felt slightly lonely, eating alone, in the large dining room which was mainly occupied by elderly couples. He was halfway through his soup when a man, who had obviously had a few drinks, came into the room and weaved his way across to his table.

"Hullo old man. You must be Jim Scott? I am Archie Ledbetter. We are on the same course. Can I join you?" Jim jumped up and shook Archie's proffered hand.

"Of course, that would be great! I was feeling a little lonely," said Jim. Archie slumped down. The waiter came over and brought Archie some soup, which Jim had thought was rather good but Archie complained that it was not hot enough. The waiter went to take the bowl away but Archie said,

"No man, it does not need physically heating up. It only needs some '*Pili Pili hoho*'. Can you get my bottle from behind the bar?"

"You mean your 'Worcestershire sauce' bottle Sir?" asked the waiter.

"Of course man, I am surprised it is not on my table already." replied Archie. The waiter, who had greeted Jim earlier with a welcoming smile, went off in high dudgeon. Jim thought '*I hope the waiter does not think Archie is a friend of mine. It must certainly look like that.*' He said.

"What is '*Pili Pili hoho*'?"

"Don't you know old boy? You obviously aren't an old African hand." Jim thought '*it was pretty obvious he was not an old anything*' but he kept his tongue.

"It's a mixture of small very hot chillies left for many years to flavour in any sort of alcohol. I usually use '*Waragi*'. Of course you won't know what that is either," said Archie very condescendingly.

Archie was fat, in his mid fifties and had BO. He was getting right up Jim's nose in more ways than one. Archie continued to rabbit on.

"'*Waragi*' is a type of gin made, in Uganda, out of bananas. '*Pili pili*' means hot, in Swahili of course, I mean chilli hot not physically hot and '*hoho*' is the noise you make when you taste some." Archie then laughed at his own joke, so loud that other diners turned round. Archie had one eye that turned away from you and one eye that sort of looked past you, so it was very difficult to see where he was actually looking. Jim thought, '*bloody hell this is going to be a long dreadfully embarrassing meal.*' He was right. Jim could not wait to say to Archie that he had driven up from Kent that day and needed an early night. Archie indicated that he thought Jim was a bit of a drip and headed back to the bar.

Jim was down in the morning in good time and was relieved to find Archie had not surfaced. He ate an excellent fried breakfast and commiserated with the waiter, for having to work two shifts back to back. He apologised for Archie's rudeness the night before, having explained that, although they were on the same course, Archie was definitely not a friend of his. The waiter said he was used to rude old buffers from the colonies. He also said he would make sure Jim could sit on his own, by moving the place settings from the table after Jim had sat down, for his evening meal. Jim thanked him and smiled to show how grateful he was.

Jim set off without delay to Easter Bush where the School of Veterinary Tropical Medicine was sited. It was less than five miles and he arrived early. However, a very keen and very pretty receptionist was already at her desk. She had a whole folder of notes for Jim together with a time table. Jim, for some reason, acted differently to normal and asked the young lady her name.

"Fiona, Mr. Scott. Can I call you Jim? Obviously I know that from your notes. Most people call me Fi."

Jim replied, "Fiona is a very Scottish name and yet you don't sound very Scottish."

"Ti-sh! But I am," replied Fi with a very Scottish accent and winked at him. She said that the staff were encouraged to speak in a posh English manner but she was not fussed either way. Fi said she had a variety of accents and Jim could hear them all, if he asked her out for a drink.

"I can do better than that," said Jim.

"Can I take you out for supper? I have been given an outfit allowance for the tropics. I would rather spend it on a night out with you, than on a pith-helmet and a spine protector to keep me safe from the dangerous rays of the sun!"

"I would like that a lot," replied Fi. "You will be in lectures until 5.30 pm. Why not meet me here then and we can make a plan. I must get some notes together for the other chap on the course, a Mr. A. Ledbetter."

"I am avoiding him like the plague," said Jim. "He insisted on sitting at my table last night at supper. He is the biggest, opinionated, old bore you can imagine."

Fi smiled, "So taking me out to dinner is really just to avoid Mr. Ledbetter?"

"No, not at all," stammered Jim, blushing.

"Only teasing you," said Fi.

"You must go to your first lecture, on the first floor, with Jamie Campbell. He is a lovely old boy. You will enjoy your time with him. He has got some wonderful stories about Kenya. He is so enthusiastic; you will want to get out there tomorrow. I will see you here at 5.30pm. Have fun."

Jim climbed the stairs with a spring in his step. He was sure he was going to enjoy this three week course, even if he was sharing it with Archie Ledbetter. Fi had been right. Old Jamie Campbell was a great guy. He was short, round-faced but with a twinkle in his eye. He asked Jim which country he had been posted to. When he heard it was Kenya his face lit up. He told Jim he had been born there, on a farm near Nairobi, in 1905 when the railway line from Mombasa had only just arrived. His parents had come home, with him and his two younger sisters, at the start of the First World War. Jamie had decided, somehow or other that he was going to get back to Africa and, if possible, back to Kenya. Money was tight but somehow he managed to do well at school and got a scholarship to Stellenbosch University in South Africa to read Zoology. On graduation he managed to get a job in Kenya doing research in Trypanosomiasis. He ended up as the 'Chief Zoologist' in the Veterinary Department in Kenya, before he came home, at independence, to take up this teaching and research job. Jamie said he would really enjoy having Jim, for two days, to brief him on all the problems which were being experienced in Kenya with all the types of Trypanosomiasis. He would include information on the Tsetse flies which spread the disease.

Jamie asked Jim where the other candidate who was booked on this course was. Jim said he had met him at dinner last night but did not know why he had not come to the school.

"What's his name?" asked Jamie.

"Archie Ledbetter," replied Jim.

"Oh dear," said Jamie.

"He used to be a field veterinary officer in Kenya until about ten years ago. He developed a severe drink problem. He was given the sack. I wonder why they have re-employed him. Well, if he turns up, no doubt he will tell us. Now let's get down to work. There is a lot to get through. I assume being straight out of college that you do not know much about Trypanosomiasis?"

"I am afraid that I don't," replied Jim.

"All I know is that it is caused by a protozoan parasite and is spread by Tsetse flies."

"Good," said Jamie. "That is ideal you will have no preconceived ideas."

With Jim sitting in a chair by Jamie's desk, Jamie started walking around his room talking about Trypanosomiasis. He kept Jim enthralled for two hours before he suggested they have a break for a cup of coffee. In the canteen Jamie introduced Jim to several other academics who all said they looked forward to teaching Jim in the coming three weeks. Several made grimaces when Archie Ledbetter's name was mentioned. Fi came in and Jamie introduced her as Miss King to Jim. They both smiled and said they had already met at the reception desk. Fi laughed and said she had yet to meet Mr. Ledbetter.

"Aarrh, my dear, you have that treat in store for you," said Jamie. At that moment Archie flung open the door to the canteen and demanded to know where the blasted receptionist was. Without batting an eyelid Fi very politely asked,

"Can I get you a cup of coffee?" Her smile rather knocked the wind out of Archie's sails.

"Err um that would be very nice, thank you," Archie replied. As Fi turned to get the coffee, Jamie held out his hand to Archie and said,

"Hello Archie it has been a wee while since we met at Kabete. I gather you are up here for a three week refresher course. Where would you be heading?"

"Not back to bloody Kenya that's for sure." Archie blustered. "I am going to do some work on Artificial Insemination (AI) in Water Buffaloes in Saba."

"Now that will be interesting," said Jamie. "I understand that they only come on oestrus at night and like to mate in swamps. I hope you've got a wet suit?" Archie obviously did not know anything about Water Buffalo. He looked very uncomfortable and mumbled,

"I won't need any lectures from you, Jamie Campbell." He took the coffee held out by Fi and rudely turned away. Jamie did not seem to be the least put out and he turned to talk to a very distinguished looking man with well groomed, silver, hair.

41

Fi leant forward and whispered in Jim's ear, "What a rude man. However he did me a good turn by making you ask me out to dinner. I think you should buy me a bottle of champagne tonight for saving you from him!"

Jim laughed, "Too right I can't think of a better way to spend my tropical clothing allowance."

"Is that right," said the silver haired man. "We would never have thought of frittering away our clothing allowance like that now, would we, Jamie?" He held out his hand to Jim.

"I am John David. I guess you are Jim Scott. When you have spent all your money on attractive Scottish lassies, perhaps you will dine with me one night. Fi, I wonder if you would you be so kind as to arrange that?"

"Of course I will Sir," said Fi demurely, as John David left the room.

"I had better get back to my desk," said Fi,

"See you later." Jim went with Jamie back to his office and spent the rest of the morning gaining more knowledge about Trypanosomes. The time flew by but Jim was really hungry when Jamie suggested some lunch at 1.30.

The canteen was full but Jim could see no sign of John David, or Archie Ledbetter for that matter. A kindly man with sandy hair sat next to him and asked him where he was going. When Jim replied Kenya, the man, who introduced himself as Richard Hazeltine, told him all the varieties of potatoes he would find in Kenya. Actually Jim learnt quite a bit of geography of the country as well, as the man knew exactly where most varieties were grown. When he left, he said,

"Good luck, I hope you like cabbage, as all the other green vegetables are rather expensive but potatoes and rice are cheap enough."

After lunch Jamie suggested they walk around the buildings, as he thought both of them might go to sleep if they went back to Jamie's rather claustrophobic office. Jim found all Jamie's information about Trypanosomiasis and Tsetse flies fascinating. He felt he was just like a sheet of blotting paper absorbing knowledge. He was sure the knowledge would be useful. He was absolutely correct, as he was going to be working in a Tsetse fly area, with all the problems that would entail. They went back to the canteen at 4.00pm for a very quick cup of tea and continued until 5.30pm in Jamie's office. Jim thought it had been a great day and was glad it was going to be repeated on the morrow. He went off in a great mood in search of Fi. He found her by her desk. She was bubbling with excitement.

"I have got a mass of gossip about your pal, Archie Ledbetter."

"He certainly isn't my pal. What has he done?"

"I will tell you all over supper. Now what's the plan? I can get my usual bus home and you could pick me up from there. I live with my parents in town, in easy walking distance of the Grass Market, where there are lots of good eating places and bars."

"I have got a car. Why don't I give you a lift into town? If you don't mind waiting for a few minutes at the hotel on the way, I can have a quick shower. Then perhaps your Mum will make me a cup of tea, while you scrub up."

"Oh, am I not smart enough like this then?" laughed Fi.

"Of course you are. I think you are the prettiest receptionist in Edinburgh."

"Oh, its flattery now is it? I expect you plan to take me up to your hotel room and have your wicked way with me."

"That is a really excellent idea! Come on, let's get going?" They were both laughing as they went out. They did not see John David watching them. John thought, *'so he is one for the ladies is he? That may be an advantage or disadvantage for the line of work we had in mind for him. I will have to keep an eye on him.'*

Jim opened the car door for Fi.

"Quite the young gent, aren't you?" said Fi.

"Don't worry it is all part of my wicked plan," replied Jim with a smile. Fi laughed.

"I think you are all talk and no trousers but at least you have a car and an outfit allowance! A girl must keep an open mind on these things." Fi giggled. Actually, she rather fancied him and liked him already. So many of the vets thought rather a lot of themselves and Fi found them rather stuck up. Jim seemed very natural and she had no worries, he was going to 'come on' too strong. In fact, she thought *'I think he is a little shy with girls.*

When they got to the hotel, Jim said with a straight face,

"I think we had both better go in, hiding under my coat, in case we see Archie Ledbetter."

"Are you a man or a mouse, Jim Scott?" retorted Fi.

"As we go by the receptionist and you pick up your key, I had better tell him, if I am not back down in five minutes, to send for the police." They went into the hotel laughing. Jim squeezed her bottom as they went through the swing door. Fi turned and whispered,

"You are bloody fast. I had better tell the receptionist to ring the police in only three minutes." Sniggering Jim went to collect his key. The receptionist said,

"Arrh, Mr. Scott, your mother rang. She left a message to hope you were OK. She said she and your father were going out tonight but she would love to hear your news tomorrow." Jim thanked the receptionist and turned to Fi and said,

"So much for my grown-up image, with my mother phoning."

"Don't worry, mine is just the same," replied Fi,

"Heavens knows what she would do, if she knew I was coming up to your room. What she doesn't know about, she can't worry about. Come on lets walk, that old lift looks as its seen better days."

In fact they were both quite natural in the room. Jim took some clothes into the bathroom and had a quick shower. He came out without his socks on, drying his hair. Fi was looking at the hotel bumph on the desk.

"It is quite posh, isn't it, and very expensive. I think it is a good thing your mother did ring. It would cost a fortune to do your laundry here. I hope she will do it when you get home, or I will take it home to my mum's."

"That's why I didn't put any socks on, as I thought it would be too expensive to wash them. Will I be OK in my bare feet, on the grass in the market?"

"Come on you old tease, I am getting hungry and I have got to scrub up, remember. That will take hours."

They drove into town. Fi's home was a town house in Blackfriars Street. She said that many of the neighbouring houses had been made into flats. She said that they had the whole house but her grandparents lived with them and she had three elder brothers, who all still lived at home. Jim took an instant liking to Fi's family but it was very obvious that Fi had surprised them, by bringing Jim home.

Fi's mum wanted him to stay for tea. She said there was plenty. Jim would have accepted but Fi immediately said they were going out for a special meal and Jim was going to buy a bottle of champagne. This raised some eye brows.

"That will set you back young man," said Granddad.

"I have saved Jim from a fate worse than death. He will tell you about it, while I bath and change. I will be sometime so Mum, you can get started with the tea. I will also need plenty of time, as Jim said I was not much of a looker and he hoped I would 'scrub up' better."

"I did not say any such thing." However Jim was speaking to a closing door. You could have heard a pin drop. Mrs. King remedied the situation by saying to the three boys,

"Don't just stand there. Go and wash your hands. Gran, can you give me a hand with the food?"

"Don't worry Gran, I will help," said Jim. Granddad chipped in',

"Well, this is an evening and a half. Fi brings a man home that is prepared to help in the kitchen." Jim laughed and that seemed to ease the tension.

The family was soon sitting down having their high tea. Jim sat, where Fi would have sat sipping a cup of tea while the others ate.

"Well," said Fi's Dad. "Can you tell us what fate worse than death my daughter has saved you from?"

"There is a really unpleasant, loud, drunkard who is staying at my hotel. He is the other person on my course. This morning, Fi met me at the reception desk and I told her about him. He had planted himself at my table last night and had bored me rigid with his bombastic opinions. I teased Fi about her posh English accent and she said that, if I took her out to dinner, I would avoid this dreadful chap tonight and she would talk with a Scottish accent."

"Well," said Fi's Mother."The brazen little hussy and why should you buy her champagne?" Jim laughed,

"I told her I was getting £40 from the Overseas Development Agency as a tropical outfit allowance, so I said we could afford a bottle of champagne." At that moment the door opened and Fi came in. Jim leapt up and said,

"You look like a million dollars and you can kindly tell your family, I never said you were not much of a looker."

45

"Well maybe you didn't." replied Fi.

She added. "The smell of food has made me starving. Let's go." Jim managed a goodbye as she hustled him out the door. She grabbed his arm and they walked down Blackfriars Street towards the Grass Market. When they found a suitable little restaurant, Jim led the way in. They were greeted by a smiling waiter. Jim smiled back and said, could they have a table for two and a bottle of champagne as they were having a celebration. The waiter led them to a booth at the back and took their coats. Fi leant forward and whispered to Jim,

"I am ever so nervous; this is my first proper date. I left school this summer and have only been working a few weeks."

"Don't worry about it. I am only 22 and only had a short locum job before coming up here. Think how nervous I am, going to deepest, darkest Africa in a few weeks. I will be seven thousand miles from friends and family." Fi squeezed his hand.

"Well, I think you are very brave. I could not do it. When I think of the look on my mother's face when I said I was going out for supper. What would have happened if I said I was going seven thousand miles?"

The waiter arrived with a flourish. He poured a little champagne into Jim's glass for Jim to taste. Jim laughed and said,

"Don't worry with that, I have never bought champagne before, I am sure it will be lovely."

The waiter said, "I really hope you both enjoy it. We get so many pretentious folk in here, who make a fuss about the wine and they haven't got a clue what they are talking about." From then on the waiter was really kind to them, helping choose their food. They both relaxed. Obviously the champagne helped. Fi whispered into Jim's ear,

"I feel quite tipsy. It is lucky we are going back home and not to your hotel room, or you could have your wicked way with me and I would not be any the wiser."

"That's a great idea. Let's scrub the food?" laughed Jim.

"No way," said Fi with wide eyes, I am bloody starving!"

They had a great meal, laughing and chattering. They ended with a cup of coffee, which Jim said he needed, to sober him up for the drive back to the hotel. Jim gave the waiter a good tip, as he hoped to bring Fi back to this restaurant again. They walked home hand in hand. At Fi's door Jim said, "That was great fun. I hope we can do that again. See you tomorrow then."

Fi with a very thoughtful look on her face, said, "Aren't you going to kiss me?"

Jim wrapped his arms around her waist and kissed her tenderly. Fi put her arms round his neck and kissed him hard. Her mouth opened and their tongues met. They kept kissing. Fi could feel him hard against her. She was quite breathless when they split apart.

"Take care on the way home," she said. "See you tomorrow and thank you." She turned, opened the unlocked door and went in. Her mother and father were still up.

"I hope you had a good time," said her mum.

"I think he looks a nice chap," said her father.

"Yes, it was fun night," said Fi, as she turned and walked up the stairs.

Chapter 4

Courting Fiona King

Tuesday 15ᵗʰ November 1966

Although Jim was early, Fi was already at work. Jim told her she looked radiant.

"I took time to scrub up." She joked and then whispered,

"Did you avoid Ledbetter?"

"Yes, no sign of him. But can we go out tonight?"

"Sadly not, as I have my Spanish class on a Tuesday night. However, shall I fix you up to have a meal with Mr. David and then perhaps we could go to the cinema tomorrow night?"

"That's a deal," replied Jim. He then leant forward and whispered.

"Can I have my wicked way with you in the back row?" Fi just giggled.

"Now be off with you. You have your second day with Jamie."

Jim had a great day. He was sorry not to see Fi at lunch but he was glad he didn't see Archie either. It was probably because Jamie was so interesting, that they were really late getting into the canteen and the staff were actually starting to clear up. Obviously Jamie was well liked and so they happily gave him and Jim good platefuls of stew, followed by apple pie and custard.

It was well after 5.30 pm when they finished. Jim thanked Jamie profusely and Jamie wished him luck. Fi had gone by the time Jim reached her desk. She had left a note, in an envelope with his name on it. He tore it open as soon as he got to his car. John David was going to come to his hotel at 7.00 pm. Fi also said she was looking forward to her Spanish class. She was going to learn phrases like,

"No we would like to sit at the front, not at the back," and

"Take your hand off my knee or I will walk out." She ended with a row of kisses.

John David arrived promptly at 7.00 pm. Jim had made sure he was showered in good time and was waiting for him, in one of the easy chairs, beside the fire in reception. Jim was surprised when John indicated that they were going to eat in the hotel. John said,

"I am sure we won't be disturbed. Let's have a drink in the bar before dinner as we have plenty of time." When they both had a pint of beer, John said, "We had to send Archie home. Sadly we can't employ him at ODA. He claimed he had beaten his alcohol addiction but either he had not or the stress of meeting up with old colleagues was too much for him. Alcohol addiction is a strange problem. I like a drink like the next man but alcohol does not rule me. Some men just have to have a regular consumption every day and others, like Archie, are binge drinkers and just get plastered on occasions. You will meet both types, rather commonly, in the colonies. It is something to guard against. I gather it is even becoming common in ladies. Anyhow cheers. Here's to your career!"

After they had chatted generally about the course, they moved through into the dining room. Once they had been served their soup they were alone. John said,

"I imagine you are a little confused at what is required of you. Well, first and foremost, you are a veterinary surgeon and employed by the Kenyan Government to go and do whatever they require. The Kenyan Veterinary Department is one of the best and I am sure you will enjoy it. Initially most of your seniors will be British but, as the years go by, more and more Kenyans will qualify. When the first graduates come out of Nairobi Veterinary School in 1968, you may have Kenyans as your superiors. If you work hard and show promise you will be two years ahead of them and may well get accelerated promotion. The ultimate boss in the Department is a Kenyan, who graduated a few years ago up here in Edinburgh.

The other side of your work is for the British Government helping us keep tabs on what is actually happening locally, in Kenya and the surrounding countries. I am your ultimate boss but your local controller is a person who will be known to you as Colin Shaw. After you have settled in, your controller will make contact with you and set up lines of communication. At the present time we do not know where the Kenyan Government will send you. However, as you are young and a bachelor, we suspect you will be given a post requiring a large amount of travelling. You have already said that will suit you well and it will suit us as well. As part of your course up here, you will spend a couple of days with Jim Anderson. He, ostensibly, is going to give you tips on living in the tropics and in Kenya, in particular. In reality, he is going to brief you on what the British Government want to know and how you can obtain that information. He will get you to sign the Official Secrets Act.

John had to continually break off his narrative, as the waiter removed their soup plates, brought their main course and then more drinks. Jim obviously showed some alarm when he was told about the Official Secrets Act. John quelled his fears, saying it was only a formality. It was clear to Jim that John was a very suave operator. He wondered what Colin Shaw would be like. He asked John. John was rather vague and said they probably would not meet. Colin Shaw was not a real name. He said that they liked to keep everything as impersonal as possible. Anyhow said John, Jim Anderson will brief you further. I am just in the background.

From then on, they chatted widely about veterinary work in the tropics and in Kenya and how it was a little different, having so much wonderful farming land up at altitude. John explained how the Laboratory at Kabete was one of the best in the world and how it was so well supported by the other Laboratories nearby, such as East African Viral Research Organisation (EAVRO), East African Trypanosomiasis Research Organisation (EATRO) and the Animal Health and Industrial Training Institute (AHITI).

Jim was still fired up to go to Kenya but he was fairly confused about his spying role and rather wished he was just being posted as a vet. However, he thought he would learn more when he met Jim Anderson. John David was good company but Jim, thought wistfully as he went to bed, that he would rather have spent the evening with Fi.

In the morning he was rather relieved not to have to worry about Archie. Now, in some way, he felt slightly sorry for him. He made a mental note to be careful with alcohol. His father, who had a beer at every meal, had suggested it was never a good policy to drink alcohol on your own.

He was in a sober frame of mind when he arrived at the School of Tropical Veterinary Medicine. Seeing Fi lightened his mood. He told

50

her about Archie. She said she already knew and that was the gossip she was going to tell him but she had spent too long 'scrubbing up'. Then she stuck out her tongue at him and said she would meet him here at 5.30 pm.

Jim was due to spend the day with Brian Thompson who was an expert on ticks and tick-borne disease. In fact Jim was due to spend the next three days with him, so Jim hoped he was as interesting as Jamie. He was not disappointed. Brian was a hunched short figure, who looked a little like a tick. He was extremely knowledgeable and Jim found the day fascinating. Jim felt honored to be taught by men like Brian and Jamie who, even though nearing retirement, still enthused about their subject. As Brian had two more days with Jim, they stopped promptly at 5.30 pm.

Jim found a very cheerful Fi just tidying up her desk before finishing work for the day. "Let me give you a lift into town. Jim said.

"I could have a quick shower, then we could have an early supper at my hotel. Apparently I get my evening meal paid for, like breakfast, by ODA. The waiter is a really nice guy and he said, as I didn't have supper on Monday night, yours could be free tonight."

"That's great let's go?" replied Fi. When they got to Braid's, Jim noticed that Fi had a rather large hold-all as well as her hand bag. However he did not comment. When they got to the room, Jim said,

"I will have a quick shower like on Monday." He took some clean clothes into the bathroom and he was soon out. Fi looked straight at him and said,

"Can I trust you?" Jim looked straight back at her and said,

"I am very fond of you although we have only known each other for a few days. I promise you, I have only been joking about having my wicked way with you. You can trust me one hundred percent."

"I believe you," she replied.

"Can I have a shower and change?"

"Of course you can. I will go down stairs to reception where they have today's papers in giant, strange, wooden clothes peg type things and see what is on at the cinemas in town. I actually am a bit of a softy, so I don't mind if we go to a girlie film. By the way, you look pretty good as you are so there will be no rude remarks about scrubbing up!"

"I should hope not, Jim Scott, or I will tell the whole of the School of Tropical Medicine that you like girlie films!" retorted Fi with a twinkle in her eye.

When he came back to the room, Jim noticed that Fi had not bothered to lock the door. She was sitting on a stool in front of the dressing table putting on some make up. Jim said.

"I didn't think you bothered with make-up, you have a lovely complexion."

"Well I do, for special people." She turned and faced him. "I think a lot of men would have taken liberties, with a girl having a shower in their room. Thank you. Have you picked a good sloppy film?"

"No, I will leave that up to you. I will give you the choices in the car. I shouldn't think we need to book mid-week?" In fact they went to a rerun of 'HELP' a Beatles film which they both enjoyed. They left the car and walked back to Fi's home hand in hand. Jim asked, "How are you going to explain about changing?"

"I don't think, for one minute, any one will ask. They will just assume I changed at work. They would never think I would be so brazen, as to change in your room." Jim laughed.

"Girls at college would not even worry about it, although there were barmy rules about boys not being allowed in girl's rooms, after 10 pm. There were no problems about girls being in boy's rooms."

When they were still a street away from her home, Fi pulled Jim into a door way and kissed him quite hard, with her arms tightly round his neck. She pushed her body up against him and enjoyed the sensation of feeling him hard against her. She also enjoyed the way he put his hands inside her coat and stroked her back, through the thin fabric of her dress. When they eventually, rather reluctantly, pulled away from each other, Fi giggled,

"We'd have got a shock if they had come to the door!"

"Come on, you brazen hussy, let me walk you home. Trusting me is one thing but I don't want us to be caught necking by your family." He squeezed her hand and kissed her again. Jim realized that Fi had been very clever, by putting the onus on Jim to be in control. She obviously found him attractive and would be happy for their relationship to develop but, equally, she was a little frightened of the rise in her desire.

"Do you think I am really a brazen hussy?" Fi asked.

"Of course not," replied Jim. "It is just I have a deep down desire to rip all your clothes off and ravish you. It is very hard to stop myself, when you pull me into a dark door way."

"Am I very strange, as I too want to make love to you but I am a virgin? I don't know what to do. I am petrified of getting pregnant and yet I am dying to see what making love is like. I know I should not be talking like this. My parents would be horrified." Jim kissed her softly again. "I am also a virgin. My body is urging me to make love to you but my mind tells me I will hurt you, not physically but mentally. I know we are going to part in two weeks and then I will be thousands of miles away. There is no way we can build a relationship, so I feel it would be cruel of me to take your virginity, even if you let me. I think, probably, I am just a bit wet and very old fashioned."

"Well I think you are very kind and not wet at all. I trusted you, in the shower, in your room. I knew you would not come bursting in. I did not even lock the door." She kissed him.

"In fact part of me wanted you to come in! I think my mother would think, if she knew what was going through my mind, that I am a nymphomaniac. You are right, we must be sensible." They kissed really passionately and then, almost in unison, they moved apart and continued walking down the street, both of them locked in their own thoughts. When they reached her door, the outside light was on. Jim took both her hands in his and looked into her eyes.

"Can we do something together, tomorrow night?"

"That sounds awfully suggestive but I know you did not mean it like that. My answer is, yes please." She opened the door quickly and went in. Fi was pleased that her parents had trusted her and had not waited up for her. She locked the door and went quietly to bed. She might have dreamt of Jim but it was not for long, as she was very soon asleep.

The next evening, when they met at 5.30 pm at Fi's desk, they both started to speak at the same time. Jim immediately said. "You go first."

Fi replied. "I normally go to the gym on a Thursday night, so I have brought my kit, but why don't we go for a run. I know it will be dark but, if we go out the back from your hotel, we can easily stick to the little roads."

"That's a great idea. Let's go," said Jim.

"Now what were you going to say?" asked Fi.

"I was just going to say I hoped I had not upset you, with our conversation on the way home, last night."

"Of course you didn't, you old goose." She impulsively grabbed his hand as they went to the car.

As they went up stairs at the hotel, Jim said,

"I will look a bit of a clot. I have only got my rugby gear and a pair of gym shoes. I haven't even got a tracksuit, so I am going to be bloody cold."

"Don't worry, I haven't got a tracksuit either as the gym is normally quite warm. We will have to run quickly, or we will both freeze." Fi changed in the bathroom, while Jim changed into his rather grubby kit. She came out of the bathroom looking stunning, in short shorts and a running vest. The old fashioned bedroom was quite large, so she immediately did some stretching exercises. Jim thought *'Christ, she looks lovely and fit. I am going to have a real job keeping up.'*

As they were running down stairs Jim said,

"I feel like 'Beauty and the Beast',"

"You do look pretty scruffy. I don't think they would let you into the University Gym," laughed Fi in reply.

"At least we will be in the dark, so no one will see us." They set off at a very sensible pace and Jim was relieved. They were going slow enough to chat, so it was good fun. After a couple of miles, they came to a school playing field which was totally dark but they had fairly good night vision by then.

"Let's do some rugby type training on the grass? It will be less tiring than running on the road. Also if we do trip over, we won't hurt ourselves. You have got great legs, I don't want you to get scars on your knees."

"How can a girl refuse some rugby training, after a compliment like that? You can be the instructor." They went up and down the pitch, with Jim calling out,

"Sprint, run, walk, five star jumps, and five press-ups." at intervals. Then Jim said,

"You take over Fi." Fi carried on and then suddenly called out, "Three cart-wheels." Jim could just see her in the dark and just ran after her laughing.

"I can no more cart-wheel than fly around the moon."

"OK then, how about you doing a head stand?"

"No way," said Jim but I will hold you. Fi ran towards him and placed her hands on the ground and gracefully jumped. Jim grabbed her thighs and, then with reluctance, let her go. She stood in front of him.

"You great numpty, you were meant to grab my ankles, not wrap your arms around my thighs. It was rather nice though." She kissed him, bringing her body up against him. As they broke apart Fi said,

"Lucky it is dark, or you would have been looking straight up my shorts."

"If we do this again, replied Jim, "I will bring a head torch."

"You wicked, bad boy," murmured Fi, as she kissed him again. Jim felt her manoeuver her thighs so that they were either side of one of his legs.

"Mm, that feels good." Jim's hands held her bottom through her thin shorts. He said, "I can't remember rugby training like this. Come on, we will run home. Someone may turn the flood lights on." Fi took some time to disengage herself. She was very reluctant to release his leg from between hers. They chatted about rugby on the run home. She said, she had never been to a big match at Murryfield. Jim said he had been to Twickenham and the matches were great fun. Jim was going stay with relatives the coming weekend, so they decided to see if they could go the following Saturday.

As they came into the hotel, panting, they met the kind waiter, who said he thought they had deserved extra portions for supper that night. They still had energy to run up the stairs. They were just debating who would shower first, when they both stopped and gazed at each other. Fi broke the spell and croaked.

"You go first." Jim had a quick shower and came out wrapped in a towel. Fi went into the bathroom with her bag but came out of the shower fully clothed; Jim was also ready but was sitting on the bed talking on the telephone. As he put it down, he said. "That's great, there is a game a week on Saturday."

Fi sat down on his knees,

"I am sorry, will you forgive me for wet hair. I had some mud in it so I had to wash it." She put her arm around his neck and he put his hand round her waist his other hand on her thigh just below the hem of her shirt. They both looked at it. Jim squeezed her thigh gently, kissed her neck and said,

"I am very hungry and I need some food." It broke the spell. They both laughed and Fi got on her feet.

The meal was good fun, as not only was there masses of food but also the waiter teased them about going running in the dark and looking so idiotic. There was no doubt that he fancied Fi and liked Jim.

In the car, when they were alone, Fi put her hand on Jim's thigh and squeezed it just like he had done on the bed. She said,

"Bloody hell I was near the edge in your room. If you had rolled me off your knee on to my back, on the bed, and moved your hand above the top of my stockings, there would have been no stopping me."

"When you looked at me when we were about to shower, that's when I nearly lost it. I could tell for two pins you would have been in the shower with me. I suppose it is like in the marriage service when the vicar talks about carnal lust," replied Jim. "It is good that we can talk about it. I can see why the Victorians were covered from head to toe. One look at your lovely legs in those shorts and Wow, I get very excited."

They parked the car right outside Fi's home. As they were getting out Jim said, "I wish we had been cave dwellers, it would have been so much easier! I would have come to your cave with a great big club and dragged you off by your hair to my cave and that would have been that. Job done."

"You would not have to have hit me with your club, I would have come willingly!"

"I think the club was for your family, who would try and stop me."

"I suppose they might have, unless there was television in the cave, then all the men would have been too busy watching football. They were both laughing, as they came into the hall and then into the kitchen, where Fi's mum and Gran were busy washing up. Fi's mum said.

"Well, what's amusing you two?"

"We said all the men would be watching football and we were right," laughed Fi as she and Jim picked up tea-towels and started helping Gran dry up.

Gran said, "Fi your hair is wet, is it raining? I thought we were meant to have a dry night?"

"No it is dry outside," replied Fi, "I washed my hair in the shower after our run and Jim doesn't have a hair drier."

"You will catch your death of cold," said Gran.

"What - did you go up to Jim's room in the hotel? What will the staff think?" said Fi's mum.

With a dead pan face Jim said, "I expect they thought I had my wicked way with her." Fi's mum's jaw dropped open.

Gran could not stop herself from laughing. "If it had been Grandad and me when we were young, he certainly would have," said Gran.

Jim put his arm round Fi's mum's shoulders. "I was only joking. Don't worry, we were the laughing stock of the hotel, going out running in the dark."

Fi's mum was only slightly mollified. "Well, for Goodness sake, don't tell your father. He will have a fit."

Fi leant forward and kissed her mum on the cheek. "To be honest mum while he is watching football, I don't think he would notice if I came in naked. He certainly won't notice my wet hair. Shall I make everyone a milky drink?"

Fi was correct none of the men noticed her wet hair. After Jim had finished his drink, he stood up and said good night to everyone. He waved to Fi and said he would see her in the morning. Gran piped up and said, "I will tell Fi in the morning, if Grandad has his wicked way with me tonight." She laughed with Jim and Fi but none of the men heard. They were too busy looking at the football.

In the morning Fi could hardly wait to tell Jim, as he came to reception, that her mum had come into her room and given her a lecture on how Jim was a really nice boy but that she must not get herself into a compromising situation. She had ended by saying, how she thought he had a naughty sense of humour and, although she was totally shocked, it had secretly made her laugh. She had told Fi to ask Jim to supper on Sunday night, when he got back from his relations.

Fi said, "She obviously likes you. None of my brother's girl friends have been asked to Sunday supper. Oh yes, Gran said to tell you that Grandad did not have his wicked way with her but he did tell her the score in the football match!"

Jim's weekend with his elderly aunt and uncle went much better than he thought it would. Luckily they did not get up early, so Jim had a lie in both on Saturday and Sunday mornings. His aunt was a good cook, so he ate well. He also went running on both days. He missed Fi but he ran faster thinking about her. He also actually enjoyed hearing about his Scottish history. This couple where he was staying, was the only remaining relatives who lived in Scotland, all the rest had moved down to England.

Jim arrived at Fi's house just as everyone was coming through to eat. Obviously, Fi's mum had said nothing about his invitation to Fi's brothers. The youngest not knowing Jim was in the hall, said, "Who is the extra place set for? Not Auntie Pat I hope? She is so prim and proper and we are not allowed a drink." Jim came in with a carrier bag full of beers. He knew they drank and said, "Auntie Pat won't like me if I bring the beers, had we better hide them?"

"No lad," said Grandad, "let's open them." Gran whispered in Jim's ear, "That's done it! He won't be any good tonight." They both laughed. In fact they all seemed pleased to see him. The meal went well and Jim kept them entertained with amusing veterinary stories and stories about his Scottish ancestors, who were so fat they had to be winched on to their horses and were always late for the battles. When he left, Fi came with him to the door. She kissed him and whispered, "Well done, I was very proud of you. Can we go out tomorrow night?"

"Of course, I have missed you," said Jim. "See you in the morning and we will sort something out.

He did not get a chance to say anything to Fi in the morning as, although he was early, Jim Anderson was waiting at reception to take him off for the day. The day's session was billed on his program as a tropical orientation day. Jim had expected Jim Anderson to be a typical civil servant. He wasn't but was really quite humorous. He had lots of anecdotes about notable characters which Jim would meet. He suggested that Jim was just to behave quite naturally and only needed to pass on any information he thought was relevant.

There were various PO Box numbers to write to using Colin Shaw's name. The British Government did not actually know where he was going to be stationed. He said he would get more information when he was settled 'in-country'. He gave Jim two telephone numbers in the UK, his and John David's but these were only to be used in a dire emergency. He stressed that Jim was not to tell anyone about his clandestine activities. He made Jim sign the Official Secrets Act. The rest of the day was spent with Jim Anderson telling him about the political problems in other states in the region, so that Jim could have the bigger picture. They finished early, so Jim sat quietly in reception waiting for Fi to finish. As soon as it was 5.30 pm Fi came over to him.

"Let's go. I have an idea for tonight, if you are feeling energetic. Let's climb Arthur's seat? There is a full moon tonight, so it will be beautiful but very cold. We will have to wrap up well. Do you think the hotel would give you some sandwiches and a thermos of soup?"

"I think so," replied Jim, "Particularly if you ask the waiter as I am sure he fancies you."

It was an exhausting climb as the going was quite steep and, as it was so dark, placing one's feet took more effort. They had a torch but it was not much good at guiding them. It did help pouring the soup when they reached the top though. Jim sat down on a low rock. To his amusement Fi sat on his lap facing him and wrapped her arms around him. They kissed. Jim felt himself getting aroused. Fi obviously felt him as well, as she wriggled her bottom provocatively. She whispered in his ear.

"It is lucky it is so cold because I feel some carnal lust coming on from both of us. What makes you excited? Is it me sitting on your 'willy'?"

"Yes and even more so when you wriggle your bottom," replied Jim. "Come on we had better start down before I start trying to get your clothes off."

"What are we like," said Fi. "Even in this cold I want you to open my shirt and fondle my breasts." Jim kissed her neck and blew hot breath down her shirt. She said. "That's nice. I bet your hand is cold." Before he could reply she lifted his hand and pushed it down her shirt. Jim could not stop himself. He fondled her warm firm breast and felt her nipple harden with his cold hand. She kissed him harder.

"That feels lovely! I have never let a boy feel my breasts. If I undo my bra will you kiss them? Jim did not reply but nuzzled his face in her chest, as she reached in and undid her bra. He kissed her nipples and then started to suck them.

"God that's good," gasped Fi. She started rhythmically moving her bottom in and out. The moon, which had been covered by clouds, now broke free and Fi's breasts glowed white in the moonlight.

"You are so beautiful, Fi," said Jim as he caressed her breasts. To make it easier for him Fi moved so she was sitting normally on his knee. Jim continued to fondle her, moving his hand down her flat tummy. He reached between her legs and rubbed her trousers. She parted her legs and kissed him energetically. Jim was not sure how it happened but her trousers came undone and Jim slipped his hand in her knickers. She gasped but just opened her legs wider. Jim felt her springy pubic hair and then her moist delicate lips. He rubbed them gently. Fi groaned with pleasure. She kissed his neck and then moaned.

"That is so lovely." She started to pant and then suddenly let all her breath out.

"I think I have just had an orgasm. Can you rub me some more? That was bloody lovely." In no time she had a stronger orgasm and slumped into his arms. She was like a rag doll and Jim thought he would have to carry her. However she quickly recovered.

"Oh Jim, I have had all the pleasure and you have not had your wicked way with me."

"My darling," said Jim, "It was just so lovely to feel you, now I am going to be like your Gran. You must get dressed, dear, or you will catch your death of cold." They both laughed as Fi stood up and sorted her clothes out.

"I feel a bit weak at the knees. I am glad the path is downhill and the moon is up."

They had to go down in single file, as the path was narrow. It soon widened out and they walked hand in hand.

"I know I am still a virgin but every time I see Arthur's seat, I will think of you. You are so gentle and kind. I am sure most men would really have had their wicked way with me. I would feel sore and bruised and be worried stiff I might get pregnant." She squeezed his hand. "You were so gentle, it was lovely."

"You felt so soft," said Jim, "I loved kissing and sucking your breasts." He then squeezed her hand.

Chapter 5

Falling in love

Monday 25th November 1966

The rest of Jim's time in Edinburgh flew by. The course was still interesting, now he was back learning about tropical clinical problems. He spent as much time with Fi as he could. On the night of Fi's Spanish Class, he went and bought a small hair dryer. The next night, as they were getting changed to go for a run, he gave it to her. Fi was delighted.

"That is marvellous. I hate not washing my hair after a run. Equally, I hate looking like a drowned rat. I will scrub up well for you tonight." They had a really strenuous run, which included several laps around the school playing fields, but did not involve any cart wheels. No one was about as they raced up the stairs to Jim's room. As Jim had always showered first, he grabbed his towel and said, "I'll be quick," and went into the bathroom. He was standing naked in front of the mirror shaving, when he saw the door open. Fi did not realise that he could see her in the mirror. She also was naked and crept up behind him. He finished shaving and he felt her arms around his waist and her body pressed against him.

"I did not dare to frighten you when you had the razor in your hand, in case you cut yourself." She hugged him, "Can we have a shower together?"

"Only if I can wash your hair, it is so lovely."

So they had a sexy shower together. After drying themselves, Fi sat naked on the bed combing her hair, while Jim dried it with the new hair-dryer. Jim was mesmerized watching her dress. Fi said,

"I have never let anyone watch me dress. It is strange, I don't feel any embarrassment." She kissed him briefly.

"Come on, I feel hungry. Let's go down to eat."

They only got tickets to the match at Murryfield on the day, so they had to stand, as there were no seats available. There were very few girls at the match and even fewer standing. Fi stood very close to Jim. She whispered in his ear,

"It is rather sexy surrounded by all these men. Can we go back to the hotel after the game to warm up?" They ate a bag of chips in the car on the way home to the hotel. As they came to the large imposing swing door, Fi said in a quiet voice,

"I hope there is no one about. I feel ever so guilty. It is going to be obvious what we are going to do." They were in luck, the hotel was the type that was busy in the week but was quiet at weekends. They crept up the stairs. As soon as they were in the room, they were in each other's arms and pulling off their clothes. The room was not cold but it seemed logical to get into bed. After they had been kissing passionately for some minutes, Fi guided Jim's hand down between her legs. He started to rub her gently, whispering,

"You are so soft, can I kiss you?"

Fi murmured, "Of course you can." She thought, *'what a silly question,'* until she realised what Jim meant. He had moved down the bed. She suddenly felt very vulnerable and closed her legs. Jim just kept kissing the tops of her thighs. Slowly she opened her legs and Fi felt his tongue. It was magic. She opened her legs wider and held his hair. This was really something. She felt him sucking her and probing with his tongue. She arched her groin towards him and felt his strong hands gripping her bottom, holding her to his mouth. Then he started to rub her with his nose and chin. She lost control and arched her body rhythmically. She did not even feel his hands fondling her breasts.

"Oh, that is so lovely you must stop." Jim stopped.

"No, don't stop please, more." She pushed up at him again. Jim sucked harder and pushed his tongue as deep into her as he could. Her smell excited him. Goodness he wanted her but he knew he must hold back or she would get pregnant. She was really thrusting wildly and he had to hold her bottom really hard, to keep kissing her. She sort of sighed and groaned and Jim knew she had climaxed. He moved up the bed and kissed her gently. They both lay still, wrapped in their own thoughts.

Fi then snuggled into his arms.

"It is not really fair. You are a wonderful lover and bring me to a climax but I don't bring you to have an orgasm. I really want to feel you inside me and feel you climax."

"It is just too risky," replied Jim. "I would never forgive myself, if I got you pregnant by mistake. It would ruin your life. I feel bad enough, thinking of making love to you, knowing I am going to leave you so soon and disappear to Africa. I don't know what the future will bring but I must not leave you in the lurch."

"Jim, I know you are right but 'Boyo' this has been bloody good fun!" Reluctantly they had to get up and get dressed. When they reached Fi's home, she invited him in for a coffee. All the family seemed pleased to see them. Fi's Mum immediately asked if he would like supper the next night. Jim said he would love that. He said he was hoping to take Fi on a walk on the beach, up at North Berwick, during the day. It would be cold, so they would have big appetites when they got home.

After Jim had left and Fi was washing up the mugs with Gran, alone in the kitchen, Gran whispered with a chuckle,

"Has he had his wicked way with you?" Fi blushed and said. "Yes, very nearly."

"Was it fun?" asked Gran.

"It was wonderful," replied Fi.

"I am glad for you both. I know he is going away but somehow I think there is going to be a future for you both. I am sure you are going to have fun with other men. Good luck. Remember I will always love you."

Fi hugged her.

"Thanks Gran, I know you will. I will be very miserable when he leaves but I know you will make me laugh myself out of my sadness." They both went up to bed, leaving the others watching TV.

Jim had been right. The next day it was very cold on the beach but the walk was spectacular. With all the open sand they could walk close together, arm in arm. Jim was also right that, when they got home they were starving hungry having only had a bowl of soup for lunch. The family supper was very relaxed. Fi loved it that Jim fitted in so well.

The week flew by. As if by agreement, they avoided being intimate, although they kissed passionately on the door step when

Jim dropped Fi off after going to the cinema, or out for a meal. Fi knew Jim would have to drive home on Sunday. Fi's Mum also knew, so she asked Fi to ask Jim for supper on Saturday night.

Fi and Jim discussed it in a very matter of fact manner. They both knew they would be wretched when they parted, so perhaps it was better if Jim said goodbye to the whole family and just drove off. They were sitting in the car outside Fi's house. They both looked at each other and realised they were crying. They both went to speak. "You go first," said Jim.

"I know you don't want to hurt me, but can we spend the whole of Saturday in bed? I know that is very brazen of me," said Fi.

"You lovely girl, I would love that. It will be a day I can cherish for the rest of my life."

During the week, Jim managed to get some time to go shopping in Edinburgh. On the Friday night at the end of the course, Jim picked Fi up and they drove out of town, to a small restaurant that one of Jim's lecturers had recommended. It was a great night out. As they kissed on the door step of Fi's home, she said.

"I can't wait until tomorrow. I have told the family that you are picking me up after breakfast and we are having a day out and then coming back for supper. Sleep well. I suspect you are going to need to keep your strength up for tomorrow."

She hugged him and ground herself against him. "Sweet dreams." She closed the door.

Fi awoke earlier than normal. It was a combination of being excited and a commotion. Her father and her three brothers had decided, the previous night, that they were going fishing. There was a bit of a queue for the bathrooms but Fi managed to get in, with some moaning that she would be hours.

The men-folk had agreed to go out south of the city and so it was easy for them to drop Fi off on the A702. It was a squash in the car with five of them and the fishing stuff. Fi was made to sit in the middle, in the back of the small car. They teased her about her smelling of perfume. Fi soon shut them up, with a retort about them all smelling of rotten eggs and stale beer. The dawn was just breaking as they dropped her off. There was a nip in the air as Fi made her way to the Hotel. There was no one in reception, so she crept up the stairs. She wondered how she could wake Jim up, without waking the rest of the hotel. She had no need to have worried as Jim had not locked the bedroom door. She crept in without waking him and locked the door behind her. She felt very naughty stripping off. She shivered and quietly got into the lovely warm bed.

Jim was naked lying on his side with his back towards her. Very gently, she pressed herself against him. Still he did not stir. She reached over and touched his penis, it was very small and soft. Fi thought, that is not going to hurt when it goes inside me. In fact, she thought, it is so floppy, I am not sure how I am going to get it inside me. Then she remembered in the shower and she was not quite so sure. She gave Jim's penis a squeeze. Instantly he was awake and turned to face her and then rolled on top of her.

"You little monkey, how did you get here?" Before she could answer he was kissing her. When they broke apart, she breathlessly told him about the fishing trip.

"Well, it's great to see you. I must go for a pee, I am bursting. Can you keep the bed warm?" Jim leapt out of bed and rushed into the bathroom. He soon returned and they were kissing again. Fi loved the feel of his hands, as he caressed her. Slowly he got nearer her pubis. Fi thought, please rub me like before. Jim must have read her mind as he started to tease her pubic hair and then, with one finger, he gently rubbed her clitoris. Soon Fi was breathing hard. She had her legs wide apart and was thrusting upwards. It was getting too much for her.

"Don't stop my darling, please don't stop." Then she had an orgasm and they kissed deeply.

Once she had got her breath back, Fi took control. She rolled Jim on to his back and sat astride him. She could feel his penis hard under her. Now she said,

"I am going to try to give you an orgasm but not inside me."

Jim said, "We must be careful."

"We will," she replied. "I ache just to feel you inside me but only for a second." With that Fi leant forward on her knees and reached behind her for his, now hard penis. Slowly she pushed it up inside her. In fact she was so moist that it slipped in really quite easily. She sat down on him and felt herself stretch. It did not hurt. It felt good. She felt Jim's hands on her hips. Jim thrust upwards.

Fi whispered. "That's good but we must stop." She raised her bottom up off his penis, which flopped forward onto his tummy. She rested her bottom down and felt his penis between her labiae. Fi looked down and could see the end of his penis sticking out. With her hands on his chest she rhythmically moved her bottom up and down his body, pressing her weight down on him. She saw Jim had his eyes shut.

"Fi, that is wonderful," Seeing the tip of his penis excited her. She kept moving and started to rub herself with one hand. She suddenly realised she was going to climax. She hardly heard Jim groan, "Is it safe, I can't stop," Fi looked down, to see white semen squirting up his tummy. She groaned herself and flopped on top of him. She did not know how long she lay there but then she felt him sucking her breasts.

"Oh Jim, that it is lovely." Fi suddenly returned to reality. "We must be careful or we will make a mess on the sheets." She threw back the bed clothes.

"You just lie back very still and I will get a flannel." Totally unembarrassed, she ran naked into the bath room and came back with Jim's flannel, which she had moistened with warm water.

"Now, let me wipe you down." She rubbed his tummy and very gently lifted his shrunken penis. Smiling down at him she said.

"I think it is amazing, how big and strong he is one minute and the next he is all soft and floppy. I will just get the flannel warm again and a towel." Jim just lay back, stunned by her beauty and how down-to-earth she was and yet how extremely sexy was her behavior. When Fi came back, she dried him with the towel which was warm from being on a heated towel rail. Jim felt his penis stirring again and was somehow embarrassed. Fi noticed and said.

"He doesn't take long. I wonder what he will think of this?" Fi shamelessly washed between her widely spread legs and then dried herself in a very sexy manner. She got back into bed.

"Let's have a cuddle for a few minutes and then we will have to try and sneak out." She lay in his arms and lovingly fondled his now erect penis.

"Does that feel good?"

"Too right," replied Jim. "You are not only beautiful, with your long blond hair with its reddish tinge, but you are bloody sexy. I want to bury my face in your ginger bush."

"Go on then. I would love that. I should smell OK as I have just washed," laughed Fi. That's what happened. Soon Fi was mewing with pleasure and thrusting her pubis up into Jim's face. When they calmed down at last, Jim looked at his alarm clock.

"Christ, we have almost missed breakfast and the young lady will be along to do the room any minute." They hurriedly dressed and Fi checked the sheets.

"Not a mark, thank goodness," said Fi. "It is going to look mighty guilty, me coming for breakfast."

"Too right," replied Jim, "Let's hope we can slip out and then get breakfast in town."

They were not that lucky. The waiter was behind the reception desk.

"You have no need to worry. We won't charge you extra. I saw you come in earlier, Miss, was he difficult to wake up?" Fi blushed and stammered, "Yes."

"Come on in, I have kept some breakfast for you both. I expect you both need it." They both followed him into the empty dining room blushing, like beetroots. The waiter brought them a bowl of porridge each and a pot of tea and then left them, to prepare the toast and the 'full Scottish' breakfast. Fi whispered, "He knows just what we have been up to."

"Well we are both no longer virgins," laughed Jim.

"When Gran asks me, I can truthfully tell her you have had your wicked way with me."

Jim looked appalled. "Will she ask?"

"I expect so," replied Fi. "She won't tell a soul and will probably ask if it was fun."

"What will you say?" asked Jim. Fi giggled and whispered, "I will say you had a very small 'willy' and I had to work really hard, to get it big enough to make it worthwhile putting inside me." She half rose and kissed him on the lips, just as the waiter came back. He just smiled and said, "I have given you both a slice of white and slice of black pudding. I hope you really enjoy your day off."

"We will." They both stammered in unison.

67

They did not talk, as they ate their breakfast, but just kept smiling at each other. It was only when they were walking down the hill from the hotel, hand in hand, they both had a fit of the giggles.

"That, was the bed and breakfast to end all bed and breakfasts," laughed Jim.

"This afternoon is going to be the laziest, romantic afternoon of all time," replied Fi. "In fact, let's include late morning in that. I am sure they will have done your room soon."

So, in not much over an hour, they were sneaking up the stairs again, tearing off their clothes and jumping into bed. In the middle of the afternoon they awoke, after sleeping for an hour or so. Jim reached into the bed side locker draw and brought out a small parcel.

"I have a present for you, my darling," Fi sat up in bed, totally unashamed of her naked breasts.

"Can I open it now?"

"Of course," replied Jim. "I bought it, as it reminded me of the colour of your breasts on that night, in the cold, on Arthur's seat. It is a Moonstone. I hope you like it?"

"It is beautiful," said Fi. She took out the pendant, on a long silver chain, from its little box. She kissed him and then said,

"You must put it on." She then turned her back to him. With a lot of fiddling about, Jim managed to do it up. The chain was long and the pendant rested between her breasts.

"We are not allowed to wear jewelery at work, but no one will be able to see this, unless they are a really dirty old man, trying to look down my front. I will wear it all the time." Then she burst into tears and buried her face in Jim's chest. Jim just stroked her hair and cried as well.

"I will always remember you Fi, because you were my first love but also because we had so much fun. Christ, I am going to miss you but I know, if I did not go to Africa now I, would regret it and then, in an unkind way, I will blame you."

"I know you are right," came her muffled reply. "You will have other girls, who will be fun. I will have other boys." Then Fi laughed through her tears and said,

"May be they will have bigger willies? Come on, let's have a shower and you can wash my hair. That will make him really big, if you stand behind me and rub up close against my bottom." So it was they had a shower together, with Jim washing Fi's hair. Then he dried it for her as she sat on his knee. They both got dressed, rather subdued, and went down to Jim's car and off to Fi's house for supper. Luckily the fishing trip had been very successful, so the boys were on top form. Fi and Jim managed to stay cheerful and occasionally her hand would stroke his thigh. No one saw the pendant, which Fi was relieved about, as she thought she would cry for sure, if it was mentioned. They all had hot cups of tea at the table. When they had finished, Fi got up first and said,

"Now Jim, you must go. You have got to pack and you have a very long drive tomorrow. I don't want you going to sleep at the wheel." Jim said his goodbyes. Fi came with him into the hall. They hugged each other for some minutes. They then kissed quite gently and whispered.

"Good luck." Then Jim went out the door. He turned to wave to her, waving on the door step. He blew her a kiss and she closed the door, with one hand on the pendant. Fi never knew how she managed not to cry in front of the family but she bravely helped with the washing up. The men folk went to watch television. Fi said good night to them all and went to bed, where she cried her eyes out. In the morning she was in no rush to get up, as it was Sunday, so she tried to read but found it impossible. She got up and tidied her room, which she had been meaning to do for weeks. She heard noises downstairs and went down to breakfast. She thought, I have no need to try and forget him. I will just have to get on and live my life. In many ways, she was glad they had agreed not to write. She would only have been waiting every day for a letter. She told her Mum and Gran, as they were doing the washing up after breakfast, that they had agreed not to write. Fi thought that was better than letting them think Jim had just walked off and forgotten her. Gran gave her arm a squeeze. She smiled at Gran and said. "That was a really lovely three weeks. I wonder what life has in store for me from now on."

"Who knows?" replied Gran, "Now we had better start thinking of Christmas."

Chapter 6

Time to leave the UK

Sunday 4th December 1966

Jim arrived home from Edinburgh with a heavy heart. He was deeply sad to be leaving Fi. He could not believe how he had got so fond of her, so quickly. Was it just lust? They certainly could not leave each other alone but Jim was sure it was more. They seemed to really enjoy doing things together. When they were together, they never stopped talking. He liked her family and he was sure they liked and respected him. They had agreed not to write to each other which, in some way, was strange as he was sure they both wanted to keep in touch. Jim thought they both felt they would be less sad, with a complete break.

It was a long, tiring, journey down to Kent. Jim was irritable when he arrived home. He tried to be cheerful for his mother and father. He knew his mother was worrying about him leaving, to go to Africa for two whole years, in ten days time. He chatted away to his mother, as he helped her get the cold Sunday supper ready and then he chatted about the course, with both of them over supper. He could tell that they were vaguely interested but there was some other agenda which was worrying them. The house was cold, which was always a bone of contention between them. His mother liked it warm and his father begrudged spending the money on the heating. He did not mention Fi, as he did not want any comments on his behaviour which, to them, would not have been honorable.

After supper he helped with the washing up. He was dying to go to his room and sort out the three weeks of post. At last it came out. It was about Christmas. His mother was sad because he was going to leave on the 12th December and, therefore, would not play any part in Christmas. His brother, wife and daughter were going to spending Christmas day at his brother's wife's home. His sister, her husband

and their son were going to spend Christmas day at his sister's in-laws. Mother and father both worried that they were going to be alone. This was not, in fact, the case. His mother's mother, was going to be coming for Christmas lunch. Although she lived in an old people's home, she was still very 'with it'. His mother had no brothers or sisters but his father had one brother and three sisters, who would all be coming but Jim knew that somehow, in his mother's eyes, they were a bit of a chore. Jim tried to cheer them up - particularly his mother. In a strange way, having to make that effort helped him, so that he did not weep when he eventually went to bed. In fact, he was very tired and he slept well.

Jim was glad to get up early in the morning, to help his father castrate and disbud some calves. Jim could see his father was proud of him. Jim was good at the job. He knew his father who was 65, found the task hard work. They were both hungry, when they came in for breakfast. Mother seemed much more cheerful, and was delighted when Jim tucked into a really big breakfast. Jim was dying to go and visit some of his friends from university, who were dotted about the country but he knew that would make his mother sad and cross, so he set to and helped both his father and mother with various tasks they wanted help with. He went to see his Aunts and Uncles. This was rather boring, as his father was one of the youngest in his family. Also, his father had married his mother in his early thirties. The relatives were really almost two generations away from him. Jim suddenly had a great idea. When he was at Bristol Vet School, he had spent some time with his mother's relatives who lived in Gloucestershire and Worcestershire. He suggested to his Mother, that he drove her down to the West Country, to see some of them. His mother jumped at the idea. They had a fun trip. The relatives were delighted to see Jim again and were also pleased to see his Mother, who they had not seen for many years.

There was no doubt that Jim's parents were very unhappy, when it was time to drive to Heathrow and for Jim to fly out. Jim's brother volunteered to drive so, in fact, the journey went very well. Jim tried to hide his excitement, so it did not look so bad. He knew that in his heart, he was sadder at leaving Fi than his family. This worried him, as he thought of all his parents had done for him but then, he thought, they were also proud of him. He had to make his way in the world. At last he was off to Africa.

Jim did not sleep very well on the overnight flight, in the VC 10, from Heathrow to Nairobi. There were three stops and all the passengers had to get out at all of them. Jim bought himself a beer in Rome which was a big mistake, as it cost him an arm and a leg. Things were even worse at Benghazi, as a BOAC Comet had developed engine problems and, as many passengers as possible were herded onto Jim's plane. The couple in the two seats next to Jim, had a very young baby and a toddler. Jim felt very sorry for them. In fact, the children slept very well. Jim was interested to walk around, at the final stop, at Entebbe in Uganda. He felt he had, at last, arrived in East Africa. He noticed some RAF planes on the tarmac but there did not seem to be any British personnel about. They eventually touched down at Nairobi Embakasi at 8.00 am. Jim collected his 40 lbs of hold luggage, without any problem. He tried to pick up his unaccompanied air luggage but, apparently, that would take at least two days. There was no delay at immigration or customs and a delighted Jim walked out into the morning sunshine. The sky was a beautiful blue. There was not a cloud to be seen.

He had been told that there would be a Kenyan Government car, waiting to pick him up. No car arrived, but a dusty diesel-belching bus arrived, which claimed to be the 'Airport Shuttle'. No-one else wanted the bus. Jim asked the driver, a wizened old Kikuyu, where the bus went. There was then a general discussion with the driver, the conductor and two porters. Jim did not understand any of the Kikuyu being spoken but he managed to hear the magic words 'New Stanley Hotel'. Jim had heard of this hotel, which had been nicknamed the 'Thorn Tree', as a large Thorn Tree grew in the middle of the outside restaurant. Jim knew it was right in the middle of Nairobi. He looked on a little map he had been given, at his briefing in Edinburgh. He quickly found the 'New Stanley Hotel' and saw that it was extremely near the Ministry of Agriculture so he clambered, with his big case on, to the bus. There had been rain over night and Jim was intoxicated by the smell 'of Africa'. He did not notice the smell of the bus. He was invigorated by the bustle of activity everywhere. The journey, although Jim knew it was about eight miles, seemed to be over in a flash. He was delighted that it only cost two Kenya

Shillings, which seemed a pittance compared with English prices, particularly as the driver dropped him off exactly opposite the Ministry of Agriculture. It was to the right, on the South side of Delamere Avenue just, before the 'New Stanley Hotel', which was on the corner of Hardinge Street which ran parallel to Government Road. Two street boys offered to carry his case but Jim did not want to let it out of his grasp. He was worried they would run off with it.

He laboriously climbed the steps, through the big doors, into the Ministry of Agriculture. He approached the desk, manned by two men in a heated discussion speaking Swahili, too quickly for Jim to fully understand but he gathered there was a blockage in the toilet and neither thought it was up to them to fix it. When Jim asked for the Veterinary Department they both looked very confused. There was no Veterinary Department in this building. All the veterinary offices were out at Kabete. These, they explained to Jim, were eight miles away. As Jim was pondering what to do, as there was no way he could carry his case eight miles, an old bald man in khaki uniform came into the building. The two men called to him to come over to sort this '*Muzungu*' (European) out. All was well. This was Moses, a Kabete driver, who had been sent to pick Jim up at the airport. They had missed one another, or he had been asleep. When he realised the young vet had gone into Nairobi, to the Ministry of Agriculture he had followed. He readily took Jim's case and they both left, leaving the continuing discussion on the broken toilet.

Jim had read that Nairobi meant 'cool waters' in Masai. It had been a swampy area, when the Europeans had arrived with the railway, at the turn of the century. Kabete was an easy drive eight miles to the west, climbing a few hundred feet. The striking thing of the landscape was the rich looking red soil. It was not as dark red as the soil in South Devon but it certainly looked fertile. Moses took Jim, first of all, through a coffee farm to his hotel. This was a friendly, European run, small hotel all on one storey. He was given an excellent cup of coffee and a piece of cake. Moses said there was no hurry so Jim did some unpacking, as he knew he was staying for ten days, and had a shave and a shower. He felt so much better in clean clothes.

Moses was rather taciturn, or he thought Jim's Swahili was rather bad, but he did say that he would deliver Jim to the main administration block, to meet the Deputy Director of Veterinary Services. He would pick him up at 5.00pm to take him back to his hotel. Jim thanked him and said he would look forward to that. The Deputy Director was rather distracted when Jim came into his office. Jim was not sure whether he was actually very busy, or was pretending to be very busy. He sent him to a building which housed the diagnostic laboratory and said Jim should base himself there but he would see all the departments in the next ten days. He said he did not know where Jim would be posted but that a decision would be made soon.

Jim really enjoyed his ten days at Kabete. He learnt a large amount of local Kenyan knowledge and met, not only several vets, but also scientists working in specialist labs and zoologists working on ticks and tsetse flies. They were all useful contacts. In many ways, it was like a small School of Veterinary Tropical Medicine. Jim missed Fi. He was so tempted to write but he managed to resist the impulse. After three days he learnt that he had been posted to Mombasa. Jim was delighted. He was sure there had been some string-pulling by Grant Kent or John David.

Jim was excited as he got off the overnight Nairobi train, at 8.00 am, on to Mombasa station. It had been a great journey leaving, at 6.30 pm on the previous night. Moses had given him a lift to Nairobi station from Kabete. He was sharing a compartment with another government officer, as he was travelling on a government warrant. There was no sign of his companion so he read a book for a while until he was summoned by a steward, clad very smartly in white, to the dining car. The steward showed him to a table for two, which was occupied by a middle-aged man, who introduced himself as John Perkins. John was drinking a 'Tusker beer'. Jim joined him with a beer. John was very pale and said he had just recovered from a very serious dose of malaria, while he was up in Nairobi on business. He was glad to be coming home to the coast. This was the first beer he had been allowed since he had been in hospital. Jim inquired where John had picked up malaria, as he thought there was no malaria in Nairobi. John thought he had picked it up in Mombasa before he left. Jim was glad he had been issued with some 'Paludrine', an anti-malarial prophylactic by the British Government, before he left. He resolved to keep taking it, all the time he was at the coast. John

Perkins certainly did look ill and the last thing Jim wanted was to get Malaria.

John chatted over the meal, which was excellent but, after a cup of coffee, said that he was going to turn in as he was worn out. Jim was happy to do the same, as he had had a long day. When they got back to their compartment the steward had folded down a top bunk and made up two beds. After cleaning his teeth in the tiny basin in the compartment, Jim clambered up on to the top bunk and slept like a log.

Jim did not even wake up until John, who was fully dressed, shook him and said he would see him in the restaurant car for breakfast. Jim got up, washed his face and put on a shirt and tie and tweed sports jacket, the dress of a country vet. It was totally unsuitable for the tropics. However he had nothing suitable, for his arrival at his posting. Breakfast was great and John looked a bit healthier. The scenery out of the window of Tsavo Game Park was awesome. In no time, it seemed, they arrived at Mombasa station. Jim thought the Provincial Veterinary Officer, an old colonial with a fabled irascible temper, would meet him. He was wrong. He humped his single 44-pound suitcase on to the platform and stood looking around. Everyone else seemed to have someone meeting them. John Perkins offered him a lift to the Veterinary Office. His kindly wife, Rita, said that they were going right past it, on the way to their home at Mariakani.

"We can't miss it," she said "the stink of the public tip next door will remind us!" Jim took them up on their offer. He was grateful to take off his jacket and tie. John enlightened him that it was not only the public tip, but also the town dairies and the Kenya Meat Corporation (KMC) abattoir, which helped to make the smell.

"I am sure you will get use to the smell. I expect often the Veterinary Office itself will smell just as bad." They dropped Jim off at the bottom of the track to the Veterinary Office.

So far, Africa had been better than Jim's wildest dreams. He had always wanted to come to Africa; as far back as he could remember. Jim was twelve when he had announced that his older brother could have the farm. He wanted to be a vet and go and work in Africa.

Here he was, 22 years old, a qualified vet going to, what sounded like, the smelliest work place in the world. He was hot and happy as he got out of the car and walked up the '*murram*' (red earth) track to the series of single storied huts, which were signed as 'The Provincial Veterinary Office'. The first person he met was Jacob, the messenger, on a pushbike. Jim remembered his Swahili, "*Jambo*" (Hello) to which the obligate reply is "*Mzuri*" (Good), even if an elephant is standing on your foot! Jacob had a very broad smile and continued in English. He took the suitcase, put it in a parked Landrover and said he was sorry that Omari, the driver, had not met Dr Scott but his wife was ill and he had taken her to the doctors. He led Jim down to an imposing office door. Personal Assistant (PA) to the Provincial Veterinary Officer (PVO). '*So the violent tempered PVO had a PA, he must be a big cheese*' thought Jim. The PA was a delightful coastal man called Silas. He welcomed Jim to Mombasa. He said he had booked Jim into the 'Hotel Splendid' for 10 days while longer-term accommodation could be arranged. He explained that might take some time, as it was the Christmas Holiday. In fact it was the 24th December 1966. Jim had forgotten in his delight at being in Africa that it was Christmas Eve.

Jim was enjoying talking to Silas, as his office was air-conditioned. The only other office which was air-conditioned, was the PVO's office. This led off from Silas' office. The door crashed open.

"Where the bloody hell is Omari?" roared a short, rotund red, faced man, James Roberton, the PVO. Then he saw Jim.

"I suppose he took you round the tourist's sights in Mombasa! Silas, I want Omari to drive me immediately to the Provincial Commissioners (PC) office". Jim was not about to drop poor Omari, whoever he was, in the shit with this rude bugger, so he volunteered to drive the PVO.

"What! You are a veterinary officer not a bloody driver. You don't look old enough to drive anyway". Silas sort him out. I will wait in my office. Tell Omari to report bloody yesterday". He slammed the inner door. Silas looked at Jim apologetically.

Jim explained the problem of Omari's wife. Silas paled, if an African can pale.

"Oh dear, Doctor Scott, we do have a problem. Chaiko, the only other driver, is due to collect fifty Turkana herdsmen and take them to the KMC jetty."

76

"No problem" said Jim. "I will take the fifty herdsmen in the bus to the jetty and Chaiko can take the PVO to the PC. Please call me Jim. I will never get used to being called Doctor Scott".

"Thank you Jim, I will send Kitchopo, the office *'shamba'* (garden) boy, with you to show you the way. It won't be a bus" he laughed "but a Bedford 4x4 lorry. You collect the herdsmen from the farm, where they are camping at Mariakani. Good luck."

Jim had never driven a lorry before, certainly not a four-wheel drive model. He felt very nervous but was damned if he was going to show it. Silas gave him the keys and quickly found Chaiko and Kitchopo. They both had broad smiles. Jim thought *'I am going to like these folk. Life is a laugh to them.'* He could forget cold, rainy and demanding England, with its hidden agenda. He hoped to God James Roberton was not his real controller only his veterinary boss. Roberton was a bully. Jim was not afraid of bullies. He had been well trained at a public school. The bigger they are, the harder they fall. Roberton would get what was due to him one day. Jim would wait. *'He remembered his father. He never backed up, nor would Jim.'* Jim was going to regret that little thought, in a few minutes.

With his poor Swahili and some good sign language, Jim gathered there was enough fuel in the lorry, which looked enormous. Chaiko went off to report to the PVO. Jim clambered up in to the lorry with Kitchopo, who rarely stopped smiling. With a roar, the engine fired into life. Jim thought he might have been in Australia, as he kangarooed down the *"murram"* road. Kitchopo, still smiling, pointed away from Mombasa as they joined the main road, which was a dual carriageway. Jim remembered John Perkins saying the dual carriage way only lasted a couple of miles up the hill, but there was tarmac all the way past their house at Mariakani for fifty miles, to a place called Mackinnon Road. From there it was *"murram"* for one hundred and fifty miles, through Tsavo Game Park. Jim wished he were going that far.

There were many small farms on the roadside; these were said to be *'shambas'* according to Kitchopo. Jim realised why he was called a *'shamba'* boy. Really he was a gardener. There were small plots of maize and fenced fields, with withered grass, containing thin humped-backed white cattle. The lorry did a steady thirty five miles an hour uphill, so it was not long before the village of Mariakani came into sight. Kitchopo indicated that they should turn left. In a couple of hundred yards, there was a bungalow on the left with a watered garden. Jim recognised John and Rita's car in the driveway. He skidded to a halt in a cloud of red dust. Leaving the engine running, Jim indicated to Kitchopo to stay in the lorry and he ran up to the house. On the veranda were John and Rita laughing.

"You did not waste any time coming to see us. Do have a '*samosa,* (Indian snack of meat in filo pastry) and a cup of coffee". Jim did not have a clue what a samosa was but he readily accepted, saying he must not be long as he had left the engine running. The spicy envelope called a '*samosa*' was excellent. He downed the lukewarm coffee and sprinted back to the lorry. A big mistake! He was hot and the cab, with the lorry not moving, was unbearably hot. It was not yet 10.00am. Jim had some acclimatization to do. Another half mile and Kitchopo pointed to some large corrugated iron barns, with no walls, the cowsheds. Jim swung the lorry in a wide circle and remembered to kill the engine. A short, slight, Indian man approached, from a similar type of low building as the veterinary office. He had a sad face and a weak handshake. He looked kind and he was obviously stressed.

"Who are you, sir?"

"Hello, I am Jim Scott, the new Veterinary Officer".

"Welcome Doctor Scott, I heard you were coming to take over from Miss Whitehead but I did not expect you to be driving a lorry. I am Mr. Patel. How can I help you?"

"I have come for the Turkana herdsmen, as Omari's wife is ill. I am helping out with the driving."

"You are most welcome. I was at my wits' end. The 'Turks' are frightening the farm staff. The sooner they go the better. Please follow me." With thoughts *'of Gallipoli and Lawrence being buggered by a Turk,'* Jim followed Mr. Patel around the corner of the office and neighbouring feed store, with some trepidation. He could see Mr. Patel's problem. There was an area the size of a football pitch, in total squalor. It was one hundred times worse than any gypsy encampment on the farm, at home, in fruit picking time. There were small fires, with filthy cooking pots, small bivouac-type tents, and rows of spears, stuck with their butts in the ground. Fifty, very tall, very black men, wearing dirty grey blankets over their shoulders and nothing else, sat in groups. No wonder a lorry had been sent, rather than a bus, thought Jim. Mr. Patel took Jim to the Headman, who stood four to six inches above Jim, who himself was a good six feet. Jim grinned as he said, *"Jambo Habari"* (Hello how are you). The headman remained impassive, just bobbing his head slightly. Jim wondered if he did not want to speak to him, or if he did not understand Swahili. Then he made a guttural sound, spat and, in a very deep, voice said *"Muzuri. Habari Mzee"*. Jim was at a loss *'was he a 'Mzee'* (An old man)?' He turned to Mr. Patel and asked him if he could explain that he needed all the Turkana and their belongings in the back of the lorry as soon as possible. The headman nodded his head and in a deep voice, which probably could be heard in Mombasa' said two sentences. Jim thought *'Oh hell, how do I get this job done.'* He had no need to have worried. Instantly, all the Turkana were moving purposely, with the minimum of fuss and talk. Four men had the tailgate of the lorry down in a second and clambered up into it. Others started packing up the tents and throwing them up to the men in the lorry. The cooking pots were stowed in hessian sacks and thrown into the lorry. The fires were stamped out, with feet protected by sandals made of car tyres. Up onto the lorry, went the men with their spears. The headman and two Turks stayed on the ground. With a nod to Jim and a guttural sound to the men, the headman walked purposely round to the front of the lorry. For one dreadful minute Jim thought, *'he was going to drive.'* However, with a bold leap, he was on the bonnet and then sat on the cab. Meanwhile the two men swung up the tailgate and clabbered up in to the lorry, like Nelson's seamen of old.

Jim thanked the now effusively grateful Mr. Patel and got into the cab with the now very nervous Kitchopo. Jim pushed the starter. The engine groaned, fired and roared into life. *'Hell'* thought Jim *'I am sure it is illegal to ride sitting on the cab,'* but there was no way he was going to ask the headman to get down. Even if he concurred there would be a loss of face, which was to be avoided at all costs. Jim was not sure whether he was more worried about the police or being laughed at by John and Rita Perkins. In spite of the fact that the lorry was badly overloaded and complained on every corner like a bad tempered elephant, the journey went quicker on the way back to Mombasa. It was downhill. Mariakani was some 800 feet above sea level. John and Rita were lucky; their home was slightly cooler than homes in Mombasa, certainly cooler than houses in the town, away from the sea and the on-shore breeze.

Jim was beginning to relax as he started down the dual carriageway into Mombasa. Kitchopo had been inattentive. He cried out, that they had over shot the left hand turning to the KMC. With great presence of mind Jim gradually slowed the lorry, mindful of the headman perched precariously on the cab, his long lean legs and his penis hanging over the windscreen. Jim drove the lorry, very slowly, a further 500 yards until he came to a gap in the curb in the middle of the road. Luckily nothing was coming, so he swung through the gap. Bloody hell the lorry seemed to have a turning circle like a battleship. He was right across the other carriageway. He would have to back up. Where was reverse? Jim was sure Chaiko had probably told him but his Swahili did not run to such complicated instructions. Jim knew "*toa*" meant pull out and "*tia*" meant put in. He tried "toaing" and "tiaing" with the sweat pouring down his face. His shirt was dripping and then he heard the first sound of a horn. He was blocking the whole carriage way on the main road out of Mombasa, Kenya's second biggest town, ultimately arriving 310 miles later in Kenya's capital Nairobi. The horns got louder. Jim's efforts became more frantic. Kitchopo wanted to smile but thought he might get blamed for the debacle. He had not a clue how to drive a lorry. He was only the '*shamba*' boy. Bugger it. Jim was in a real mess. He was, after all, a veterinary surgeon not a lorry driver. Then with a smile Jim remembered his father. Never back up. This time he would have to. He jumped down from the cab, waved to the headman and pretended to push the lorry backwards. The headman was not just a headman because he was tall, but also because he was quick witted. He scrambled down to the ground and croaked to his laughing men. The horns had reached a crescendo. The '*Turks*' were out of the lorry in seconds all carrying their spears. One or two '*Turks*', looking very warlike, wandered over to the now 300-yard queue of cars. The noise of horns certainly abated somewhat. Jim was back in the cab with the hand brake off. The lorry inched slowly backwards as he swung the steering wheel hard left hand down. Out of the corner of his eye, he saw three '*Turks*' standing abreast across the other carriageway. Jim had no need to worry about the traffic coming down from Nairobi.

The lorry inched backwards; although it was heavy there were forty strong fit men, under good leadership, pushing. A second shunt and the lorry was ready to proceed back up the road towards Nairobi. Jim blew the horn. The headman leapt back on to the top of the cab. The *'Turks'* scrabbled back into the lorry, up the sides as well as over the tailgate like drowning men climbing up the nets into a rescue ship. A second blast of the horn, a crunch of gears, a broad smile from Kitchopo and Jim was on his way back up the hill, to the roundabout at Changamwee.

On the return journey Jim made no mistake and the lorry roared into the car park at the KMC. Slaughtering, which started at 4.00am, was over. The car park was filled with Africans in bloodstained white clothes, preparing to go home. Jim noticed that on the back of each bicycle was an Ox tail. Kitchopo explained that this was *'buckshish'*. Every slaughter man got an Ox tail, as well as his wages, for each day's work.

As the now sweaty, grimy Jim got out of the cab he was greeted by a very black man even taller than the headman and considerably wider.

"Welcome. I am Daniel Oket, in charge of this abattoir. How can I help you and your men?" Jim said, "Hello" and said that he had brought the fifty herdsmen, to go on the cattle boat from the KMC jetty to Lamu, a remote island on Kenya's northern coast. Daniel seemed relieved that his role was so easy and suggested that Jim lead the *'Turks'* down the cattle race to the cattle boat, called Bonanza. The cattle on the boat had all been unloaded. Daniel explained that they had killed half of the 300, which the boat had brought early that morning. The other half would be kept and fed in the lairage, until the day after Boxing Day. However Bonanza was returning to Lamu, in a couple of hours, as the captain wished to spend the holiday on Lamu.

It was a weird spectacle as Daniel led Jim and the fifty Turks in Indian file, down the long cattle race down to the small jetty, alongside which was the 200-foot long boat with cattle pens on its decks, covered with awnings. Daniel shouted to one of the Arab crew to get the Captain. Obviously, Daniel had no intention of getting on to the smelly, dung covered vessel.

Olaf, the captain, was a very red faced Dane. Jim guessed he was an alcoholic. He greeted Jim enthusiastically and invited him on board for a drink. Although Jim could have murdered a beer, in fact several, he declined knowing, somehow, he had to return with the lorry. The captain said the '*Turks*' could camp on the deck. They seemed oblivious of the dung and smell. Jim said, "*Kwaheri*" to the headman, who studied him carefully and then to Jim's surprise offered his hand. Jim really was pleased to shake hands, although slightly taken aback, by the headman bringing his left hand round to clasp Jim's hand in both his hands. Jim felt somehow that he had gained the headman's respect. He certainly hoped he had.

All was quiet at the veterinary office when Jim and Kitchopo returned. Jim learnt from Kitchopo that everyone had a two hour lunch break, because it was so hot. Both of them drank long drafts of water from the tap. Jim had been warned at his familarisation briefing, that he should never drink the water unboiled. Somehow the briefing had not indicated he would be driving a ten ton lorry on his first day. Thank goodness every one drove on the left side of the road. It was not long before Jim was to learn that the English drive on the left, the French on the right and the Kenyans on the best side of the road!

As Jim was rummaging in his suitcase, in the back of the Landrover, for a clean shirt, he was surprised by a tap on his shoulder. A thickset, bald, man shook his hand saying, "*Jambo bwana mimi Omari* (Hello master I am Omari)".

"*Habari Omari*". Jim's mind went blank. May be it was the dehydration. He could not remember the Swahili for wife so he continued,

"*Habari a wifey?*" Omari replied "*Mzuri sana, mtoto ingini na kuja* (Very well, another child has come)". Jim shook Omari's hand again. At least his absence had been justified in Jim's mind, even if James Roberton would not see it that way. Omari suggested he took Jim to the Hotel Splendid. Jim readily agreed.

The hotel did not quite live up to its name. It was, at best, very seedy. The reception was dark and full of flies. The Asian man was friendly as he led Jim to his room which, he claimed, was the best. It was up three flights of stairs. Jim was sweating again from carrying his suitcase. The room had a slow ponderous fan, which at least kept the flies flying. The view from the tiny balcony was actually rather good, showing much of Mombasa. There was little movement of cars. The mosques shimmered in the heat. Jim felt it could have been the same as when his Grandmother had visited, on her way to India, at the turn of the century. She had declared to him. "A dreadful place! I had to wear my mosquito net the whole time!"

When left to himself, Jim found what passed as a bathroom. It had a tiled floor with a hole for the lavatory, which did have a flushing mechanism. There was a water pipe coming out of the wall at head height, the shower. No hot water but Jim was not worried-he had a long shower. What was strange for him was that he did not feel hungry. He dressed in clean clothes and went down to find Omari, waiting patiently for him. It was about 3 'o'clock when they reached the office. The effect of the cool shower was quickly lost.

"You have had a bloody long lunch break. Don't make a habit of that" fumed James Roberton.

"I want you to go to the town dairies across the road. They report they have a cow with something hanging out of its back end. Michael, the veterinary scout will come with you. He will make sure you don't make a cock up on your first job."

The cow did indeed have something hanging out of its back end, a very rotten uterus. Jim was used to dealing with uterine prolapses within a few hours, not one that looked as if it had been out for two weeks. The Asian dairy workers said that the owner was away, so they had not done anything, hoping he would come back. He had not returned and they knew the veterinary office closed at 4.00pm until after Christmas. Jim gave the cow an epidural anaesthetic and with his shirt off, assisted by Michael, tried to replace the uterus as he had done in previous cases. After half an hour he realised replacement was not going to happen. He remembered a long winded lecture from the Professor of Surgery at Vet school, on how a uterus could be removed. He decided to have a go. After ligating the two large uterine arteries he just cut off the organ. This was removed by the dairymen. Jim had a nasty thought that they were going to eat it later. He pushed in the stump and put a large stitch in the vulva. Then he gave the cow an injection of penicillin and an injection of calcium. To his amazement she got up and started to eat the cut maize stalks, which were in front of her.

Back at the office, he was met by the PVO and a lady, who he assumed was his wife. "Well have you killed it?" asked the PVO belligerently.

"No, she is up and eating" said Jim holding out a rather bloody hand to the smiling lady.

"Well done, I am Anne Whitehead. Thank you for doing that job. I will show you around. Have a good Christmas, Dr. Roberton."

"Happy Christmas, Sir" said Jim. The PVO just grunted and walked away.

Anne turned to Jim with a smile. "Don't worry about him, his bark is worse than his bite"

'He certainly does not seem very festive,' thought Jim. *'I wonder why?'*

Anne answered the unspoken question. "He is rather a lonely bachelor and I expect the thought of being away from the office two days on his own, is not very appealing. I am sorry, you are going to be a bit lonely tomorrow. I would like to invite you to my house but I have been invited to a beach Christmas with some old friends. However I hope you will come to mine on Boxing Day evening, when I have some younger friends coming".

"That will be great, thanks; I will find something to do tomorrow. A long walk on the beach will be fun. I have never been on a tropical beach". At that moment a large, friendly, German shepherd cross dog came round the corner of the building. It greeted them both.

"Is this your dog?" asked Jim. "What is her name?"

"I call her Karli, which means 'fierce' in Swahili. In fact she is very friendly but she looks fierce, so she has the desired effect."

"Can I be really cheeky and borrow her tomorrow? It would be much more fun walking her on the beach, rather than on my own."

"Of course you can. Come around to my flat anytime tomorrow. It will only take you ten minutes from your hotel. I will give you a lift into Mombasa and show you where to come, before I drop you off."

Chapter 7

Christmas Day

Sunday 25th December 1966

Jim awoke on Christmas Day an hour after dawn. It was seriously hot in the 'Hotel Splendid'. He had a shower and went down for breakfast. Jim was fascinated by the marvelous tropical fruit provided. He really enjoyed the pawpaw, with a squirt of lime, and the mangoes, which he learnt were from Lamu, were excellent. He made a pig of himself by having about a pint of fruit juice, as well as a bowl of cereal, closely followed by a fry up. Taking his rucksack and a book, wearing a settler type hat which he had bought in Nairobi, he set out to walk the ten minutes to Anne Whitehead's flat. He was dripping with sweat when he arrived. This convinced Jim, that he should buy a Landrover as soon as possible after the holiday.

He was slightly concerned that he was rather early for Christmas morning but it was obvious Anne had been up for sometime, so he need not have worried. She, in a very old fashioned manner, shook him by the hand and said,

"Happy Christmas."

Jim hoped that all the girls in Kenya would not be quite so reticent. His thoughts rushed back to Fi. *'He was glad he had left her safe and sound with her family. He felt sure they would cheer her up. He remembered her Gran as being particularly good value.'*

Anne said. "I won't ask you in, as I am rushing around doing jobs. However I will hope to see you later but here is a key. You can open the door and let Karli in, if I am not here, as I don't think they will like her at the hotel. I will look forward to entertaining you tomorrow night. If you could come around 6.00pm that would be great, then we will have time to have some drinks before supper."

"That all seems good. Before I go, could I borrow a water bottle as I guess I am going to get thirsty," replied Jim.

"Of course, let me give you two big ones and this plastic bowl for Karli and here is her lead."

Jim was off. He headed up Kilindini Road and then turned right southwards towards the Likoni Ferry. There was a big queue of cars, all containing people off to the South Coast for the day. They looked very hot in their cars. For once Jim did not envy them, as there was no queue for foot passengers and, even better, the ferry was free of charge. As he was walking down to the ferry he bought a 'madafu' (a green coconut cut open to make a bowl from which to drink the cool coconut milk) from a young boy, who expertly opened the top of it with a 'panga' (an African *machete*) and gave him a straw. It was lovely and cool and refreshing. He had put Karli on her lead and she walked very happily on to the ferry beside him. However he noticed the Africans gave her a wide berth. Her looks gave her a reputation to go with her name.

On the other side, the cars streamed off onto the main tarmac road heading south. Jim took a small 'murram' (red earth) road heading out to sea. The main Kilindini channel, for the large boats to enter the docks, ran to his left. There was no beach-only a coral shore. Soon the road turned to the right in a more southerly direction and Jim could see coconut palms to his left. He guessed the sea was in that direction, so he vowed to take the next left and hope he came to a beach. Local dogs had been a pain, coming up to Karli and threatening a fight. Jim wished he had a stick, as his voice was not much use in frightening them off. They followed along behind until he and Karli had walked out of their territory and then another group would arrive. Luckily he soon came to a turning, down on his left, which he guessed was down to the beach. There was a stall on the corner selling Africa carvings. Jim bought a stout long stick with a notch at the top for his thumb. The local dogs, often called 'pie dogs', had better beware.

The track did, indeed, lead to the beach: soon he could see the sea. There were several tracks, to houses and bungalows, to his right and left. It was great to get on to the beach. He let Karli off the lead. She was delighted and rushed to the sea to chase the sea birds. Jim took off his boots and socks. He also took off his shorts, as he had worn his swimming trunks underneath them. He stuffed them all in his rucksack and had a good long drink of water.

He was off. It was better than his wildest hopes. *'Here he was, in Africa, in the most beautiful country. He had an excellent posting to the coast and he was being paid for living in a tourist paradise. Coupled with that, there did not seem to be a tourist in sight. There were no Africans on the beach, so he had it to himself. He could just see a few fishing 'dhows' out to sea.'* He had a spring in his step, as he felt the warm sand under his feet. He moved his track, so that he just had his feet in the shallow surf. He walked for about an hour and he reckoned the tide was coming in, as he was walking higher and higher up the beach. He saw lots of beach houses, with people sitting on verandas. He was surprised that there were no children on the beach but he guessed they were still opening, or playing, with their presents. Karli was having a great time rushing up and down the surf. He was so glad he had brought her, as otherwise he would have been lonely. He did not miss his home, as he could picture all the elderly relatives and the endless clearing away and washing up. He did miss Fi. He could imagine her father, grandfather and three brothers, going down to the pub for a drink, while the women got the lunch ready. He had a pang of remorse that he had not sent them a Christmas card but he knew it was for the best. He and Fi, had said they would not write and he was going to stick to that. However, he really missed her. In his heart, he knew she was the girl for him but they had met at the wrong time. He imagined her out here, really enjoying the beach and the game parks, but then he thought of him being away most of the time, for his work, and her being left at home without a job. She would soon get bored with sunbathing in the garden. No, he decided they had taken a sensible course of action. He was sure they would both find someone else.

He was so deep in his thoughts that he did not notice that Karli was no longer in the surf.

Then he heard a call from the coconut trees. Karli was with a girl, in a bikini, wearing a large floppy hat. The girl was waving at him. He walked up the beach towards her. As he got near, he could see that the girl was waving a glass. She called.

"I am drinking the good health to a wandering man and his dog. What's her name?"

"It is Karli but, as you can see, she isn't. My name is Jim. What is your name?"

"I am Annie. Would you like a glass of white wine? It is still lovely and cold. My friends have gone for a walk on the beach. They are really lucky, they get wonderful tans. I just get red in the face, so I sit in the shade."

"I would love a glass of wine. I was just thinking how lucky I was, to be on this beautiful beach and then I became sad, as I thought of the girl I left behind in the UK."

"There you are." Annie gave him a big wine glass, full of chilled white wine.

"Is she very pretty? I bet she would take a tan."

"Yes, she is pretty. I only knew her for three weeks, in November, in Scotland. There is not much sun there, for a tan."

"Well, I will do my best to cheer you up. Take off your shirt and come and sit with me. You are whiter than me. We will let those bronzed beauties bugger off. I bet they have chatted up some men at 'Twiga Lodge' and left me to prepare lunch. I am a bit pissed, so you had better help me finish this wine before it gets warm. In fact, would you like some lunch? You can help me prepare it."

"I would absolutely love some lunch, with a gorgeous red headed girl. Surely you can take you hat off as we are in the shade."

"For compliments like that, I will do anything," replied Annie with a naughty smile. "Now tell me about yourself. What is your surname? I am Annie Sanderman and I live and work in Nairobi. I am just down here, with two girl friends, for Christmas and New Year."

So Jim gave her a brief life history and ended by saying. "I want to make this my home already and I have not been here two weeks yet."

"I think you are going to have a ball," replied Annie. "Come on, let's go and make the lunch? If you have to help me to the house, I will be delighted. Let's give a real white man a hug." With that she put her arm round his neck and they walked up the beach, under the palm trees, to the little house. Jim realised that she was indeed a bit pissed but he thought, '*What the hell. She is a little Rubenesque but she seems good fun.*' When they got into the house Annie went straight to the kitchen and looked into the fridge. "As I thought, there will not be enough beers."

"Why don't I go and get a crate? There must be a '*duka*' (shop) or bar nearby. It can be my contribution to Christmas. I can see you have all been preparing masses of food. It will make me feel less guilty."

"That would be great. You can leave Karli with me. In fact, she has made it her home already. She is already guarding the veranda. Take my car. Here are the keys. It is an old Austin Westminster, with dreadful pre-ignition, but I am sure you will manage."

Jim did manage and was back before the other two girls returned. Annie made him put several beers in the deep freeze with strict instructions not to forget them.

"They will blow up if you do and we will have a devil of a job clearing out the glass. Can you get us one out of the fridge? I suggest we share and then we won't have hot beer."

Jim got a beer out of the fridge and replaced it with one out of the crate. He found some pint glasses in the fridge and thought. '*How very civilised that was.*' He half filled one glass and took it over to Annie. She was bending over the table with her legs slightly apart. He could not resist it. He raised the cold bottle between her thighs.

"Wow," exclaimed Annie. "You are a cheeky monkey. I did a double take for a moment and thought it was your prick. I think you are really wicked." She kissed him on the lips.

"Well, well," said a girl's voice behind them. "I see Father Christmas has come after all. Stop talking to the dog, Ronnie. Come and see what Annie has found in her stocking."

The girls were back. They were very brown and had lovely figures. They had on small bikinis, which left little to Jim's imagination. "I am Charlie, I want a kiss like Annie. You can wait your turn Ronnie." With that she kissed him on the lips, having put her arms around his neck. Ronnie, who Jim realised was short for Veronica, did the same. Ronnie rubbed the front of his swimming shorts. "Oo, that feels nice. You are right Annie I think Father Christmas is really wicked. What's your name, Santa?"

"I am Jim. I think you need to take me everywhere with you, as my whiteness will show off your tans. I bet you have great strap marks."

"What are we going to do with you, Jim?" asked Ronnie. "We have only just been introduced. You have an erection like a tent pole and now you want me to show you my tan marks. Where did you find him Annie? We had no luck at 'Twiga Lodge'. It is a very long, hot, walk and was even worse on the way back, after a couple of beers."

"Can I get you both a beer?" said Jim. "Annie and I are sharing one so that we don't have hot beer."

"Wow," said Charlie. "This must be serious. Annie is really possessive of her beer."

Soon they were all sitting on the veranda, in the shade, having a lovely cold meal. There was cold chicken, ham and masses of prawns, together with salad, potato salad and cold baked beans. Jim remarked.

"I've never had them cold."

Charlie said. "I think it was a Kenyan thing because I have never had them cold in the UK." It transpired that she was out here on holiday, staying with Annie and Ronnie, who both had jobs in Nairobi. Charlie was a lawyer in London.

Pudding was fruit salad and ice cream. When they had finished, Jim stacked the plates and asked if anyone would like coffee.

"Yes please," was the chorus. "It's a pity you have a job as a vet, Jim. You would make a marvelous houseboy. I would love a man at my beck and call," said Ronnie. When they had their coffee, they all did the washing up. Jim enjoyed it, as it reminded him of the UK but now he was slightly pissed, he was mellow and not sad any more. He also enjoyed it, as he would not have been comfortable leaving a houseboy to do it all on Christmas day.

Ronnie and Charlie took their towels and went back to sun worshipping on the beach. Annie, Jim and Karli stayed on the veranda, in the shade. Annie read a magazine, in a rather desultory way, and Jim read his book. In fact all of them were either dosing or asleep. Jim woke to a hand over his mouth. It was Charlie, indicating that he was to be quiet. She went and got her camera. Annie was fast asleep, with her mouth open. She took a picture and then, moving very close to Jim, whispered,

"She says she doesn't snore, but listen to her." Her breast brushed incitingly, on his shoulder.

"How about a swim?" she mouthed. Jim nodded and they walked down to the sea. The water was almost too warm.

Jim said. "Let's swim out a bit, the deeper water maybe cooler, now that the tide has come in." Indeed it was. Jim could only just touch the bottom on tip toes.

"I am out of my depth," spluttered Charlie. "Can you give me a rest?" With that she wrapped her legs around Jim's body and put her arms around his neck. Jim found it delightfully difficult to breathe, with her bikini top in his face. Charlie laughed at his difficulties.

"You rat," she shrieked, as Jim undid the back of her bikini. Instead of letting go of his neck she pulled his head into her breasts.

"Now, no pervert will get a look at my tits. Ronnie and I have seen a man, with binoculars, in the next door house but one. He is pretending to be a bird watcher. Now, you naughty boy, you must tie my bikini back up before I drown you."

They did a bit more swimming before going back to the beach. They had to walk along a little, as the tide had washed them along the beach.

"There he is, on his veranda. The dirty old sod. I saw the lens flash." Charlie moved to the seaward side of Jim. Jim moved his arm up around her shoulders. Charlie grasped the front of his swimming trunks when Jim moved his hand to the back of her bikini.

"Don't you bloody dare, Jim?"

"I thought I might solve your problem. He might have a heart attack, or at least it would fog up his lens."

Charlie said. "You are a naughty, bad, boy." She then pushed him hard so he fell backwards on to the sand.

"Race you back, for tea."

The others had made tea and were eating some cake when Charlie arrived, hotly pursued by Jim.

"Girls, you will have to watch this young man. He undid my bikini top in the water." Jim could tell she wasn't really upset as, she ruffled his wet hair and said.

"At least he protected me from the peeping Tom, two houses down."

"I have a suggestion," said Jim.

"Let me take you all out to 'Twiga Lodge' for supper. I only have my shorts but they are clean, as I took them off as soon as I got to the beach. I have got a clean shirt in my rucksack. If you can lend me some shampoo, I can have a shower in the one to the side of the house, which I assume has fresh water and is meant to wash off the sand."

"No, we could not possibly let you pay for the three of us and we have plenty of food here stocked up for the holiday," replied Annie.

"I have an idea," said Ronnie. "Let's ponce ourselves up and go down for a drink, before supper. We can then see if any talent has come out of the wood-work. If we go in the car we won't all be sweaty, when we arrive."

So that was agreed. Jim was banished to the garden, to shower.

"That will be a disappointment to the peeping Tom," said Charlie.

"I think you had better take Karli with you," said Ronnie with a laugh. "He might be queer!"

The girls all scrubbed up really well. There was a lot of laughter as Annie insisted on taking a photo of them all, with a timer, so they could all be in the picture. In her haste, she slipped and would have gone a real purler, if Jim hadn't grabbed her.

"That will be a great picture, Annie. You throwing yourself at Jim," said Charlie. Charlie did the running for the next photo and that was more successful.

"Come on, let's hit 'Twiga Lodge', said Ronnie.

"It's your car so you had better drive, Annie. I bag the back seat with Jim," said Ronnie.

"Then we can have a snog."

"I am terrified," replied Jim.

"You are a bloody liar," said Charlie.

"Watch out Ronnie, he will have your bra undone before we get onto the coast road!"

They arrived at 'Twiga Lodge' in high spirits.

"Jim is not much of a snogger," said Ronnie. "However it was lucky I had big pants on. I had a job stopping his hand going up under my skirt."

"Really, Jim we are surprised at you. Is that how you treat respectable young ladies?" chorused Annie and Charlie.

"Only in my dreams," laughed Jim.

Jim bought a bottle of chilled white wine and came back to the girls, who had taken a table. He brought four glasses. The place was nearly deserted.

"We can have another bottle of white wine with our supper" said Ronnie. "I bought one in Nairobi."

"Sadly we can't," said Annie. "Jim and I drunk it before lunch, when you were down here."

"You piss-heads," said Ronnie. "No wonder we caught you snogging."

It was a good drinking session and it was after 9.00pm, when they headed home. "Pity there wasn't any talent," said Ronnie.

"We have got our own," said Charlie as she snuggled up to Jim on the back seat.

"Be careful of that hand up your knickers, Charlie. I saw them when you were dressing. There is no way they will deter a rampant vet." giggled Ronnie.

"Look out Annie, you nearly hit that bicycle. I think it is getting pretty steamy in here," added Ronnie.

Karli gave them a lively greeting, when they opened the door.

"Wow," said Annie. "Your cold nose, Karli, was worse that Jim's beer bottle."

"So, what have you been doing to my friend, with a beer bottle," said Ronnie slightly aghast.

"Don't worry, just cooling her thighs," said Jim. "You have no need to worry, now I know you have big pants on." Ronnie stuck out her tongue at him.

While the girls were laying out the cold supper, Jim opened the second bottle of wine he had bought. They all thanked him and raised their glasses. "The toast is our surprise Santa Claus."

It was a pretty raucous meal. The wine was soon finished and then they all went onto beer. After the washing up, they moved inside as the '*dudus*' (insects), attracted by the light, were driving them bonkers. They shut the veranda doors and only had candles as lights. They had two big movable fans which they had to position carefully, or they blew out the candles.

"I brought a bottle of Tequila, down from Nairobi," said Ronnie. "Let's have some slammers?"

"What are slammers," asked Jim

"What a naïve young boy you are. Now I will educate you," said Ronnie as she went off into the kitchen.

Charlie lent forward and whispered into Jim's ear. "I haven't a clue what they are. Please help me."

Ronnie came back with the Tequila, a lime and the salt cellar.

"I can't find any lemon but I am sure lime will do. You go first, Annie. You know the form. In Mexico they call them muppets, which is what I think you are, Jim, for being so ignorant."

Ronnie put a little salt on to the back of Annie's hand. Annie then licked the salt, swigged back a shot of Tequila and crammed a slice of lime in her mouth. She made a face which would have curdled milk and said, "Ronnie, that was yuk! You can have the next one."

Ronnie had one and then Jim and Charlie were made to have them. "Now I know what you are talking about but they made my brother have something slightly different, at his stag do," said Jim.

"OK smart-arse, you show us," said Ronnie who was getting slightly aggressively pissed. Jim thought Charlie was a sweet girl, very feminine and very attractive but Ronnie was rather over the top.

"I need a tumbler and some fizzy drink. Have you any soda or tonic?"

"I will get some tonic but I don't think it is cold," slurred Annie. She staggered into the kitchen and came back with the tonic.

"What you do, is put the shot of Tequila in the tumbler. Add some tonic. Put your hand over the top of the tumbler. Give it a shake. Put your mouth up to your hand."

Jim brought his hand up to his mouth and then expertly let the gassed up liquid squirt into his mouth.

"Bravo," shouted Charlie. "You try Ronnie?"

Ronnie had a go and did not get her mouth over the glass quick enough. All the drink went down her top.

"Who is the muppet now?" laughed Charlie

"Right, Jim Scott, my wet top is your entire fault. I have a dare for you. I want you to suck it clean."

"OK, raunchy Ronnie," replied Jim. "Before I do it, I have a dare for you."

"So I am raunchy Ronnie, am I?" said Ronnie. "What's your dare?"

"It is that you take your bra off first," demanded Jim.

"He has called your bluff now, Ronnie. Go on, take your bra off," called Annie.

"Let's all have another straight shot first," said Charlie. She poured four shots. They all raised their glasses and necked the Tequila.

Then Ronnie came over to Jim. She had on quite a short skirt. She sat very provocatively, facing him, with her legs astride his. She did not take off her top but managed to wriggle out of her bra. She gripped his hair and pulled his face to her breasts. "Now you young ram. Get sucking, until my nipples are so hard that they ache."

After a couple of minutes, Ronnie sighed. "That is bloody good. You two ought to try a slammer and have your breasts sucked. Thank you Jim. I wasn't sure you were up to that."

"I have a better idea," said Annie. "Let's play strip poker? You can put your bra back on to make it fair Ronnie. We girls will then have shoes, a skirt, a top, a bra and a pair of knickers."

Ronnie was still sitting on Jim's lap. She leant forward and kissed him.

"Poor Jim." Ronnie was all soft and loving now.

"You are certainly going to lose this game. You are bare foot. You don't have a bra." The girls all laughed.

"And," said Ronnie, conspiratorially,

"You don't have any pants on, as you were wearing your swimming trunks under your shorts and I can feel a little gentleman trying to get himself into my knickers."

Jim blushed crimson and all the girls roared with laughter.

Ronnie got up and turned her back on Jim and with a flourish took her top off and then put her bra on. "You have felt my tits with your tongue, Jim, but you have to win the poker game to see them."

Annie found some cards and they all sat around the table. She said. "We will make it simple as we are all pissed. I will deal five cards to each of us then, starting to my right, you can ask to change any number of cards you like. There will be no straights, only a flush of the same suit, which beats two pairs but loses to three of a kind. A full house loses to four of a kind. There are two jokers so, in theory, you can have five of a kind. The game ends when someone is naked. Does everyone understand?" Charlie looked doubtful. Jim wondered, *'how he could help her.'*

Jim knew, *'he would have to be careful. He was sure he was not as pissed as the girls and he had always been good at maths and odds. He just hoped he would be lucky.'* He thought he had been with the first hand, as he ended with three nines but he was beaten by Ronnie, who shrieked with laughter with three jacks. She came over and sat on him again and insisted on taking off his shirt. She wriggled her bottom. "Oo, that little gentleman is getting very hard."

From then on, Jim was both lucky and careful. The girls all lost their shoes. Charlie looked gorgeous in her lacy bra, having lost her top. Ronnie lost her top and said. "Lucky I put my bra back on."

Then disaster struck. Jim had two pairs and he was sure Annie was bluffing but she had three fives. The girls, who were really pissed now, insisted he face them and drop his shorts. There were howls of laughter, as he still had an erection from looking at Charlie.

"So," said Ronnie admiringly. "I have got to hand it to you Jim, you have got guts and you might be blushing but you are a bloody good loser." With that she let him pull up his shorts and gave him a hug.

"Christopher Columbus," said Jim. "Look at the time. Its past midnight and I must get Karli back to her mistress. It will be a long swim if the ferry stops."

"Don't worry," said Annie. "It stays going all night. I will give you a lift back to the ferry, then you can cross on foot."

"No way," said Jim. "I would never forgive myself if something happened to you, all alone on your way back."

"We will all go," said Ronnie and Charlie. "I know you are a bit pissed, Annie, but I will be spotter for you. Charlie you can snog Jim in the back, to thank him from us all for being a bloody good sport. So they all staggered out to the car. It was a hatch-back, so Karli was made to jump in the back. All the girls were fully clothed and Jim collected all his stuff, as well as his stick.

The journey back was good fun, as Charlie took her role seriously. After a little reluctance she parted her legs and Jim gave her a gentle rub, through her knickers. Sadly they arrived at the ferry all too soon. They all gave him big hugs and Jim begged them to be careful on the way home.

"Do come and see us one evening, if you get a chance," said Annie. This was endorsed by Ronnie and Charlie.

There were not many people on the ferry, nor were there many cars. Jim was soon across. He just prayed that the girls would get back safely. He reckoned all three of them were quite accustomed to alcohol, as they had got pretty pickled with the shots but had soon recovered. The night was cool now, as Jim and Karli walked back to Anne's flat. Jim thanked goodness that he had a key, as it was just on 1.00am as he let Karli in. He heard her run through and start eating her food, which Anne must have put out for her. He filled up the bowl, which Anne had given, her with water from his rucksack and quietly closed the door.

It was even moderately cool in the 'Hotel Splendid'. He had a cold shower, drank two pints of water and crashed on to his bed. What a Christmas Day. It was a hundred percent better than waiting on several elderly relatives.

Chapter 8

Boxing Day

Monday 26th December 1966

Jim woke at dawn feeling a little worse for wear but went down and had a big breakfast. He was just finishing his third cup of tea when the hotel owner came in, to say he was wanted on the telephone. It was Anne Whitehead. "I hope you had a good Christmas and that you weren't lonely? Also I hope you can come to my place tonight."

"Yes, that would be great. What time would you like me? Can I bring anything, like some beers?"

"Yes, beers would be good. Sadly, there is a job I wonder if you can help me with. It is a farmer, Fred DeArth. He is a funny old bachelor but he loves his cows. He lives on the south coast. He has got a cow with a roofing nail stuck in its front hoof. I wonder if you could go and get it out for him. I have organized for Omari to come and pick you up from your hotel. He will bring passes for the Likoni ferry. I said you would ring him, when you are ready. There is some veterinary stuff in the Government Landrover, ready for such an emergency. I know it is a Bank Holiday but I thought you would not mind."

"I am really happy to go. I will ring the office now, as I have finished my breakfast. I look forward to seeing you tonight."

Jim was really pleased, as it gave him something to do and, more importantly, he now had an idea of going to join the girls for lunch. He rang Omari and asked him to pick him up as soon as possible. He also asked him to bring the Veterinary Office bicycle, which he had seen Jacob riding. Omari thought he was totally mad! When he arrived, Jim asked him about his wife and he said, both she and the baby were doing well. Once again, there was a queue at the ferry. Having a Landrover, rather than being on foot like Jim had been on Christmas Day, they had to wait. It was a very hot half hour. Omari knew the way to Fred DeArth's farm. Jim noted it was past the *'duka'* (shop), where he had got the beers yesterday.

Fred was really quite elderly but was very grateful to Jim for coming out on Boxing Day. The cow was a big *'Sahiwal'*, a breed which Fred said did well at the coast. They were a big breed of Indian red cattle, which had originally been bred in Pakistan. They had got it into the crush, where it was chewing maize stalks contentedly. It was holding up its right, front foot. Jim got one of the herdsmen to put on a halter and another to make a noose of rope around the right cannon bone, so that he could hold the leg, up by putting the rope over the top bar of the crush. Jim could then see the nail, which was embedded in the outside claw. Jim thought that it had penetrated the soft tissue in the claw but hopefully had not damaged anything vital, like the pedal bone. Jim grabbed the nail with a pair of pliers, which Omari supplied from the Landrover's tool kit and gave a yank. It came out with a little bleeding. The cow only struggled momentarily. Jim then put on a cold poultice, of Epsom salts and cotton wool. He bound it all up with Gutter Tape. He gave the cow an injection of penicillin and left two more days worth of penicillin, for Fred to give and advised that Fred took off the poultice on the third day. Fred was very happy and insisted that he had a cup of coffee and some biscuits.

On the way home, Jim got Omari to drop him off at the *'duka'* (shop). He told Omari he would bicycle down the track, to some friends in a house on the beach. He said the bicycle would be useful for him to bike into the office in the morning. Omari was quite relaxed and said he would go home and leave the Landrover at the office.

Jim could not take a crate of beer on his bicycle, so he just filled up his rucksack. He found the house easily. There was nobody about, so he put on his swimming trunks and went onto the beach. The tide was half way in. He could see the girls swimming, about eighty yards out. They were standing with their heads out of the water, splashing about in a circle, laughing and giggling. They did not see him, as he kept low in the water. When he was about ten yards away he swam under water. The water was lovely and clear and he could see the girl's bodies. He was not sure which was Charlie or Ronnie but he swam up to one girl. He grabbed her bikini bottom and pulled it

99

down. It was Charlie. She leapt in the air, so that Jim easily swam away with the bikini bottom. He stood up waving his trophy. "You bastard, Jim," cried Charlie and came through the water towards him. "Help me girls," she cried. "That pervert will see me with his binoculars." Annie and Ronnie were laughing. "Don't worry Charlie. The pervert can't see under water, but Jim can! You grab him and we will have his trunks off in a second."

This is what happened. Charlie hugged him and the other two pulled his trunks off. Jim noticed that Charlie kept hugging him longer than she need have done. While the other two made their way to the sand, Jim held on to Charlie and pulled the bow on the back of her bikini top. Instead of getting cross, Charlie kept hugging him and then kissed him. Annie and Ronnie had now got to the beach and were waving Jim's shorts in triumph. Charlie said at last. "However are we going to get you back to the house? You can't walk up the beach naked. I am sure that pervert will be watching with his binoculars."

"I have an idea," said Jim. "Let's get your bikini back on." This was achieved with lots of giggles. "Now," said Jim, "I will carry you up the beach and when we get into shallow water your body will hide my modesty."

It was hard work for Jim carrying Charlie in his arms so, after thirty yards, she put her arms around his neck and her legs around his hips. "I think my bottom will cover your 'willy'. You bad boy, I can feel him getting excited."

"There is not much I can do about that. It is very sexy holding on to your bottom. He will calm down in the cold, fresh water shower at the house."

They both had a fresh water shower. Charlie grabbed a towel for Jim and they both came to receive a large amount of good humoured teasing. Jim produced the beers, which were gratefully accepted and then they had a good cold lunch. The afternoon went all too quickly and Jim was soon on the Veterinary Office bike, heading back to the Likoni ferry, after promising he would come and see them again. The ferry crossing was quick, as having a bike meant that he was considered a foot passenger and therefore did not have to queue. He had time to get back to the Hotel Splendid for a shower and a change, before bicycling to Anne Whitehead's flat via another '*duka*' to buy some beers.

It was a good sized and airy with big ceiling fans. It was a small, very informal party. Jim was the last to arrive but that did not seem a problem. Anne said she was so sorry to get him working on Boxing Day. She wanted to know how he had got on. Jim reassured her that he had got the nail out without much difficulty and Fred had been very happy with the outcome. One of the other guests was a vet from Uganda. He was an academic and had been teaching vets in Uganda for some years. He had decided to return to the UK and go into practice. He, his wife and their teenage children were leaving, by boat, the next day. When he heard that Jim had only just arrived in the country, he immediately made Jim an offer of his Landrover. Jim was delighted, as he knew he could not afford a new one and, obviously, this Landrover was up and running, as the family had driven down from Uganda three days before Christmas. While the others were having pre-supper drinks, Jim went out to have a look at it. The owner was an enthusiast and was delighted to show the vehicle off to Jim. Jim guessed that he was rather desperate to sell it, as he was leaving and therefore not trading the vehicle in for a new one.

After a good supper, they reached a deal and Jim became the proud owner of a Landrover. It was agreed that Jim would buy it with a UK cheque. Jim would pick the family up after lunch and drive them to the port. It was a really fortunate arrangement. They were both delighted, as Jim had a really cheap good vehicle and the retiring vet had money in the UK. Jim was thankful that he had done the locum job, so that he had enough money to pay for the vehicle outright and not go through the paper work of getting a Government Loan.

That was not the only bit of luck Jim had that night. One of the other guests was a rather grey man who, initially, Jim thought was Anne's boyfriend. However, he was only a friend who Anne had felt rather sorry for, as he was all alone over Christmas. He lived down near the port, in a large building called 'The Smith Mackenzie Mess'. This building used to provide accommodation for the young, unmarried men who worked for this large company. Now this chap lived all alone. There were fourteen other small flats which were empty. He was interested in Jim taking one of these flats, rent free, provided Jim would share the cost of the servant. This was ideal, as it meant Jim could move out of the 'Hotel Splendid' immediately and stay, without paying rent, until a subsidized Government house became available.

Jim was very busy the next day. After checking out of the 'Hotel Splendid', he moved into the 'Mess'. Then he had to arrange insurance for the Landrover. Anne held the fort at the Veterinary Office but she needed sometime with Jim to complete her handover, as she was off on leave. Then Jim had to run the family to the port.

At last he was free to unpack at the 'Mess'. Actually, this was not a big job, as Jim only had his airfreight luggage. His sea freight stuff had not arrived. He was just boiling a kettle for a cup of tea, when there was a shout of, "*Jambo*', Jim." It was the girls. They had tracked him down, via the 'Hotel Splendid'. There were hugs all around. "That hotel is a real dump. You are well off out of there," said Annie. Jim made them all a cup of tea and then suggested that they go down to the Mombasa Sports Club, in the Landrover. It was a bit of a squeeze, getting all three girls and Jim in the front of the Landrover. It was very enjoyable for Jim, as Charlie's bare leg was rubbing up against his. Also, she managed to get both her legs between the gear stick and Jim's legs. Jim was not a member of Mombasa Sports Club but he hoped to join, as they had a rugby team and there was a squash court. They managed to get in, as Annie and Ronnie were members of a club in Nairobi, called Parklands. Parklands had a reciprocating arrangement with Mombasa Sports Club. Annie bought the first round. Jim was embarrassed, as he was not allowed to buy a drink but Annie said he was not to worry as he had been so generous, buying them food and drink over Christmas. It was not long before two men came in, Richard and Justin. They both knew Annie and Ronnie and were delighted to see them. When they found out that Jim was a keen rugby player, they immediately got a proposal form from the office. Jim just had to put down his details. They proposed and seconded him and then handed the form in. Apparently, there would be no problem and Jim would be voted in, at the next committee meeting. Jim was delighted. He was really looking forward to the start of rugby training, in March. It was a good evening. After several beers they all went for a curry, in a fairly filthy looking curry house, on Kilindini Road. It was that dirty, that most people had their table moved out into the car park! However the curry was hot and excellent. Justin assured Jim, that the hot curry would kill any enteric bacteria. Jim doubted this but did not argue.

After the meal, they all wanted to go to a night club on the seafront, called the 'Florida'. Jim was very tempted but he knew he had to work in the morning. The others were still on their Christmas break. They teased him for being so wet but Jim was adamant. Jim said his goodbyes and was just getting into the Landrover, when Charlie came running over. She said she had left a thin cardigan in Jim's Landrover. Jim was certain she had done it on purpose as, when she was out of sight of the others, she gave him a big kiss and said, please would he come to their house the following night. Jim said he would do his best. She gave him another kiss and ran to get into the car with the others, as Justin was blowing the horn.

Chapter 9

Blood testing camels

Tuesday 27th December 1966

Jim was summoned to the PVO's office, in the morning, which was ominous. He was glad he had not gone clubbing the previous night. Silas, in the outer office, greeted him cheerfully so Jim thought things can't be too serious. He went in, after knocking, even though he had not heard a response. The old air conditioning was making such a racket, he thought he would not have heard an acknowledgment anyway. Jim, now that he had got acclimatised, did not like air conditioning. He thought it probably was OK if you worked in it all day but, if you had to go in and out like he did, it just made you break out into a sweat each time. The PVO did not look up, from reading a file on his desk. Jim wondered if he had not heard him but thought it was more likely to be a ploy to put Jim in his place and show how important the PVO was. Jim remembered advice an old drill sergeant had given him. Don't apologise, in fact don't say anything, just fix your gaze on a spot six inches above the officer's head. Eventually the PVO looked up.

"You took your time." Jim said nothing. You could have cut the silence with a knife but eventually the PVO backed down and said, "I have a friend in the Sudan, who is doing some research into Trypanosomiasis in camels." Jim thought, 'so this is an unofficial task and he feels guilty.'

"He needs serum from four hundred camels, from Northern Kenya. I want you to go up to Wajir and take the bloods. Can you manage that without making any cock ups?" Jim just said, "Yes sir." The PVO looked slightly deflated, like a punctured inner bladder from a rugby ball. Jim then turned on his heel, saying. "I will see to it directly," as if it was a very simple task, like checking on a sick cow in the lairage at KMC. The PVO started to speak but found he was talking to thin air-conditioned air. Silas said to Jim, as he came out, "let me know if there is any help you require but I must warn you, we are very short on Landrovers, so you may have to use your own." "Many thanks," replied Jim, "I will do my home-work and then let you know."

Jim went back to his office and got out his map of Kenya. He could see that he would have to go up the coast, through Malindi, to Garsen on the Tana River then, staying south of the river, travel up to Garissa. That way he would stay out of the dangerous area for 'shifta' (bandits) and cross the Tana in Garissa. That was a journey of 320 miles. He would then have another 300 miles, going north to Wajir. He thought to himself, it sounds like I won't get a GK (Government of Kenya) Landrover but if I take my own, I will get a good mileage allowance. I won't get a driver if I take my own but so much the better, as I won't have all the rigmarole of Government Local Purchase Orders (LPOs), having to go to the garage which has won the government tender, putting the vehicle in the government pound at night, staying in the government rest house etc. I will get up and back much quicker but I will estimate it is going to take at least two weeks, so I will have some time on my own to look around.

He went back to Silas. "Silas, as you are short of vehicles, I will take my own up to Wajir. Could you get a letter, signed by the PVO, copied to the PC authorizing me to go up to Wajir via Garsen and Garissa in my own Landrover? I will leave tomorrow morning, after the radio round up, when I can alert the Livestock Officer (LO) at Wajir to get the camels mustered. I will be away for two weeks." "That is fine, Dr Scott. Thank you for being so helpful about the Landrover," replied Silas.

Jim went into town and got enough provisions for two weeks. He was conscious that he had no fridge and so everything was going to be out of a tin, except for anything he might shoot. Obviously, he could take potatoes and carrots, together with dry food like cornflakes, coffee, tea, sugar etc. He would take plenty of Ultra Heat Treated (UHT) milk. He would not bother with a tent but just a mosquito net, which he would tie in a tree over his camp bed. He would take a small gas stove, in case it was difficult to make a fire; a gas light and a torch. He had made a camp shower out of a canvass bucket, which he was keen to try out. He would take a chair and a table, but try to keep everything to a minimum. He would need a thousand or so blood bottles to suck off the serum and then, somehow, get it frozen. The standard method was to take a 'Jablo box'. This was an enormous tin trunk, which filled with hay and dry ice. In the middle of the trunk was a smaller metal box which would take the bottles of serum, in metal racks. It was very tempting to put bottles of 'Tusker' (locally brewed beer) into the 'Jablo box', to give him a supply of cold beer but Jim resisted the temptation. He knew that if he kept opening the box, the dry ice would go in three days. Also, there was a real danger of freezing the beer and breaking the bottles. He was pleased he was going to be travelling light. Obviously, the water and petrol would be rather heavy but there was no way he could avoid that.

After he had got everything organised, he drove across the Likoni Ferry to the girl's beach house. It was dark by the time he got there. There was a note on the door from Charlie, saying they had all gone to Twiga Lodge for a drink, so Jim followed them down. They were a little subdued, as they had got very drunk at the 'Florida' and had not got home until after 5.00 am. Jim thanked his lucky stars that he had not gone with them. They had slept most of the day. After a couple of drinks, they cheered up but then Charlie seemed genuinely sad that Jim had to go off on 'safari', early in the morning. Jim only stayed for a third round of drinks, as he knew he had an early start and a really big day driving, next day. Annie was appalled that he was going the whole way to Wajir on his own. Charlie said she wished she was coming with him but Annie said Jim was going through a very dangerous area and there was no way that it would be safe for her. Also, she would be too late to return with Annie and Ronnie to Nairobi, as Jim was going to be away for a fortnight. After Jim had said goodbye to Annie and Ronnie, Charlie came out with him to the Landrover. Jim was amazed at her passionate kiss. It was as if he was going off to war! Annie had laid it on a bit thick. Jim knew there was some danger but he doubted it was that bad. Charlie made him promise to be careful. She hugged him until they were both very sweaty. Jim gave her a final kiss and drove off. He actually was sad to leave her, as she was a sweet loving girl but he was excited to be going off on a real 'safari'.

He was very happy, when he set out at dawn. He drove the whole 75 miles to Malindi with only a brief stop at Kilifi ferry. He filled up at Malindi and carried on the 85 miles to Garsen, with just a cold coke for sustenance. In Garsen, he filled up again, as he knew fuel would get more expensive, the further he was from Mombasa. Jim was delighted as he got to Garissa, a further 160 miles, around 5.00pm. He filled up, yet again and drove out on the Wajir road, where he had to stop at the police barrier. The PVO's letter worked magic and he was allowed through, but was made to promise that he would stop before dusk. Jim was happy to stop within a few miles, as he was bone tired and he wanted to set up camp before it got dark. The bush was very sparse north of Garissa so, to get some solitude, Jim turned off the road twenty miles north of Garissa and went *'Bundu bashing'* (a term for off-road driving through the bush) for at least half a mile. He only managed to find a suitable tree, twelve foot high, but he thought that would be OK for the mosquito net. Ideally, he wanted a second tree to pull up the camp shower but, he thought, he would just have to manage to wash himself in a big plastic bowl. At least the ground was nice and flat and sandy.

There was plenty of really dry wood, so Jim immediately made a small fire. Near it he put a metal bucket of water to heat for washing and washing up. He had a small piece of strong wire mesh, set on four metal legs, which he put over the fire, with a kettle of water for making tea. While the kettle was heating, he made up his old-fashioned 'senior officer's' camp-bed under the tree and strung up his mosquito net. He set up the table and chair and had started peeling the potatoes and carrots, when the water boiled. The large mug of tea tasted like nectar, even with the UHT milk. Soon he had the vegetables on to boil. The temperature was still quite warm, so having a hair and body wash and a shave was still very pleasant.

He made corn beef, potato and carrot hash, which he washed down with another cup of tea, as the light was beginning to fade. It was magical, sitting all alone in the bush. There was no light pollution and the stars shone brilliantly above him. He thought how lucky he was to be here and being paid for it. He could never afford to come on '*safari*', in such a remote area of Africa, if he had to pay for it. By light of a torch, he did the washing up and made another brew of tea. He must have been more dehydrated than he realised.

There did not seem to be any mosquitoes. He just sat back in the dark with the dying embers of the fire.

He thought of all the improvements he was going to make to his safari kit. He was going to get a roof rack for the Landrover, so that he could have a tent up there permanently. He could have a mattress, in an A frame 'Quick-pitch' type tent. This would lie collapsed, on a large piece of ply-wood on the roof rack. He could easily pack light stuff on top of it, for travelling, when he was short of space in the Landrover. He would have to get some method of cooling beer and milk. On the whole, he thought he was fairly comfortable. He then thought about obtaining information for London. This would not be so easy but at least this trip to Wajir was a very good start. He would find out as much as he could, about any oil exploration up there. He would spend a little time in Garissa on the way home but he thought it was unlikely he would find out anything new, as Garissa was much nearer to Nairobi. Soon he went to bed. He actually, hardly needed his sleeping bag, as it was still warm. He did not really need his mosquito net but, like the fire, it made him feel somehow more secure. He was soon asleep.

He awoke before dawn, with the sound of trucks on the road. Obviously, they opened the police barrier fairly early, to allow the trucks to get going in the cool of the morning. The fire was still alight, so Jim threw some small pieces of wood on to the embers and it was soon crackling. He put the kettle on for a brew and had some cornflakes with most of the remaining UHT milk. He made a mug of tea and also a thermos of tea, for the journey. He packed up the camp and covered the fire with soil with the '*panga*' (an African machete). It was already light as he moved off, following the tracks which he had made the evening before. He thought it was strange, as the noise of the trucks seemed to be coming from his left as well as from straight ahead. When he reached the dirt road he turned left. After half a mile, he realised why the trucks had sounded to his left. The road to Mado Gashi and on to Wajir, branched off to the left. The other road led on to Dadaab and the Somali border. He took the barren road to Mado Gashi. There was very little bush, as the road ran through virtual desert. He had been lucky he had stopped where he had, as there were no trees and the ground was very open. There was nowhere nice and secluded to camp. The road was rutted and it was a hard slog, the hundred miles to Mado Gashi. There were no villages. Jim stopped by the side of the road to have his thermos. He seemed to be totally alone. He was obviously not catching up the trucks and there seemed to be none behind him. He was glad he had plenty of fuel and water. He hoped the Landrover would not break down or he would be in a muddle. No wonder the PVO made a big deal of the trip.

He reached Mado Gashi before noon. It was a real dump. Jim guessed it was only there as his road from Garissa met the bigger road from Isiolo. He bought a coke in the '*duka*' which only seemed to sell cokes and maize. Jim was actually glad to be going again, having turned right to Habaswein and on to Wajir. He reached Habaswein in an hour. He was really glad he had plenty of fuel, as the petrol pump at the small shop was empty. The Somalis in the shop were not very welcoming but he did buy another coke. This seemed to be the only drink available. Nearer to civilization there were 'Fanta Orange' for sale, but Jim did not like their rather synthetic taste.

There was a bore hole supplying Habaswein with water. The bore hole was the reason for the village, which was in the middle of the Lorien Swamp. The area did not look like a swamp and, in fact, was very dry for nine years out of ten. However to the west, a large river called the *Uasin Nyro* (Literally 'Black Water' in Masai) disappeared under ground and ran beneath the Lorien Swamp. In very wet years, the area became a complete morass for two or three weeks. A myth was that the river flowed all the way underground, to the island of Lamu, where the bore holes never failed and always had sweet water.

Jim filled up his water cans and carried on to Wajir.

It was a hard, tiring, drive through very hot dry country. There were areas of real desert with either soft sand or harder shale but mostly it was sparse low bush. There was little traffic on the road, mainly trucks, or trucks being used as buses. Jim was very glad to arrive in Wajir. He had completed the 620 miles, all except 35 of which were '*murram*', in two days. At the start of the main street was a garage and Jim immediately filled up the Landrover and his entire number of petrol jerry cans and bought, yet another, coke. The Arab, who owned the garage, was friendly and directed Jim to the

Veterinary Compound. This was quite a large walled area, with various offices and stores. They were all locked but, as Jim was trying the door of the third, a young Somali man wearing veterinary uniform, ran up and greeted him. "Welcome Dr Scott, we were expecting you. Mr. Matua, the Livestock officer has gone home but he told me to look out for you. He suggested you should camp here in the compound, under that big acacia tree. He said that four hundred camels had been ordered by the PVO and would be arriving in the main street, soon after dawn." Jim thought *'surely not four hundred on the first day. There must be some mistake'* but he only said "Great, I will certainly camp over there. It looks a beautiful tree." Indeed it did, with its yellow bark and high canopy of branches, covered with small green leaves and vicious thorns.

Jim asked the Veterinary Scout his name. "It's Zebedee *'Bwana'*. I have the keys for the *'Choo'* (Lavatory) and the water tap. Can I help you set up camp?"

"That is really kind and would be great help," replied Jim. While they were setting up camp, Zebedee told Jim about Wajir and his family. It sounded as if he came from quite a big, influential family. Many of the camels, to be blood tested tomorrow, belonged to them. Zebedee also told Jim about the Italian oil exploration camp, in the desert to the east of Wajir. Jim listened carefully to the details, as he would include them all in his report for his controller, Colin Shaw in Nairobi. He hoped he could find a reason to visit the camp.

When the camp was set up, Zebedee left to go and have some food with his family. The veterinary *'askari'* (guard or soldier), called Joseph, had arrived for his night of guarding duty. He also was a Somali and seemed an easy-going chap. Jim made himself some pasta, with tomato sauce and onions, and more bully beef. When he had finished, he was sitting back having a large mug of coffee, when Zebedee came running back into the compound. Apparently, one of his father's female camels was having difficulty giving birth. Zebedee had felt inside but the head was back and he could not see how the calf was going to come out. Jim's heart sank as, although he had attended many calving cows, the only mare he had attended was a disaster, with a dead foal and a very torn mare. She had lived but it was a nightmare experience. Jim imagined camels were similar to mares. He did know that they had the same type of placenta. He

110

would just have to do his best. With Zebedee's help, he left the Landrover in the compound, and carried his veterinary gear.

Zebedee's home was very similar to the veterinary compound. Jim's patient was standing under an acacia tree looking miserable. However, Jim thought, most camels looked miserable, so that was not necessarily a bad sign. Zebedee introduced Jim to his father, who spoke good English and thanked Jim for coming, particularly as he must be very tired after such a long drive.

Jim asked for some soap and water, which soon arrived in a large metal *'karai'* (a very large bowl). He took off his shirt and washed his arm thoroughly with soap and water, into which he had poured some iodine. Zebedee's father told two of the younger boys to move a heavy cut log behind the camel, so that Jim could stand on it to make his job easier. Zebedee had been correct, the head was right back. There was no way Jim was going to be able to reach it. Luckily, only Zebedee had put his hand inside the camel, so it was still slimy and fresh. Jim thought a caesarean section might be an option. He told Zebedee's father the problem and how he had two options: either to slaughter the camel to prevent further suffering, or carry out a caesarean section. Zebedee's father immediately requested a caesarean.

Jim clipped up an area below the animal's ribs, on the left hand-side, and got Zebedee to clean it well with cotton wool and dilute iodine. At the same time, he got Zebedee's mother to boil up his stitching up instruments, including a scalpel blade, in a *'sufaria'* (cooking pot). With Zebedee's father holding the camel firmly by the head and Zebedee holding up its left front foot, Jim injected local anaesthetic under the skin, in a line about fifteen inches long on the camel's belly, below its ribs. Jim then injected more anaesthetic into the muscle layers underneath the skin. All the time the camel did not actually move very violently but it kept growling and spitting. Then Zebedee released the leg and, luckily the camel stayed standing and did not go down into the *'kush'* position. Then Jim scrubbed his hands and arms. He asked Zebedee to do the same, then to make sure he did not touch anything other than what Jim indicated he should touch.

Opening the abdomen went well. The anaesthetic seemed to have worked OK, as the camel did not seem to feel anything. Jim plunged his right hand and arm into the abdomen and grasped one of the unborn calf's back legs, through the uterine wall. He had the scalpel in his left hand and made a foot long incision in the uterus. He told Zebedee to hold that leg, while he found the other hind leg. Then they drew out the calf which was, mercifully, still alive. Jim and Zebedee had to concentrate on stitching up the camel, so they left looking after the calf to Zebedee's mother and two children, who were watching with looks of awe on their faces. Stitching up was not easy, particularly as the camel had become weary and kept trying to go down in the *'kush'* position (The position when a camel lies down sitting up on its brisket). Zebedee's father kept shouting at it, in Somali. The light was failing when they had finished and Jim gave her two injections, one of penicillin and one of a hormone, oxytocin, which would make the womb contract. Hurricane lamps had been lit. The calf, which was now standing, was held under its mother so that it could suck the colostrum: which is the first milk and contains vital antibodies to protect the calf from disease.

A table and chairs had been set up and Zebedee's mother insisted that Jim had some food, after he had washed himself and put his shirt back on. Jim could converse with Zebedee's mother in Swahili. He was surprised that the younger children spoke some English, which they had learnt at school. Certainly this family was very pro-Kenya. Jim would have to keep his ears open and see whether this feeling was general. It was the sort of thing London needed to know. He was the only way they could get this sort of intelligence, in such a remote area.

Luckily Jim had a good appetite, as he had already had a plate of pasta but was given a large plateful of stew which he guessed was goat. It was half way between a curry and chilli con carne and was a bit chewy but very tasty. Jim washed it down with a bottle of coke. After the food, they all went back to see the camel, which was now in the *'kush'* position and was chewing the cud. The calf was lying beside her and seemed to be contented. Jim told Zebedee that it was very important that the camel had an injection of penicillin, every day for four more days. Zebedee came back with Jim to the veterinary compound, to help carry the gear and also to show Jim the way, as it was now pitch black.

Jim slept very well but he was woken before dawn with the noise of shouting and of grumbling camels. He had a good wash and shave. He made some tea and had some cereals and a tin of pineapple. He was ready to face the day. As it got light, he could see the camels. Zebedee had been correct, there could easily be four hundred. Mr. Matua, the Kikuyu LO arrived, with several other members of staff. Jim explained how he required the blood bottles, after he had filled them, to be returned to their trays and left to settle. When a good clot had been formed, he explained how the serum had to be sucked of with the pipettes very carefully so there were no blood cells in the serum. Then this was to be squirted into fresh bijou bottles which were in other racks. When five racks of twenty had been obtained, the Jablo box was to be opened quickly, they were to be put in, then the box had to be closed really quickly to prevent the dry ice evaporating. In fact, the staff understood all about the dry ice, as they all had taken part in Rinderpest vaccination campaigns.

The bleeding began. Each camel was made to 'kush' (lie down sitting on its brisket) by its owner, who then held it by its halter. One of the veterinary scouts, wrapped a leather thong tightly around the camel's neck. This raised the jugular vein, which was as big as a child's fore-arm. Jim then stuck in the four inch bleeding needle. Another veterinary scout held a blood bottle under the flow, to collect the blood. When the bottle was full, the first veterinary scout released the leather thong and Jim pulled out the needle. The second veterinary scout then put on the top of the blood bottle and took it to the racks, in the shade. All the staff set about the task with a will and formed a chain, so that Jim never had to wait for a camel to be ready and a blood bottle to be held. They were soon bleeding a hundred camels an hour. The owners were pleased, as they could take their camels away as soon as they were bled. Mr. Matua recorded their names and the number of camels they had presented. After they had bled three hundred, Jim called for a break. He gave some money to Mr. Matua, to buy some cold cokes for all the staff. Jim checked up how the serum harvesting was getting on. Obviously, they were somewhat behind but Jim was absolutely delighted that they already had one hundred bijou bottles, in the dry ice.

It was getting really hot now and Jim was glad of his bush hat, to keep the sun off his head and face. As Wajir was such a dry place,

113

there were very few flies-which was one mercy, however, the last hundred camels seemed to take forever. Jim was very relieved to flop down in a chair, in the shade of the veterinary office veranda. He send out for some more cokes. Zebedee's mother then arrived with a plate of food, hidden under an upturned plate. It was a kind of risotto dish with meat, peppers and *'brinjals'* (Egg plant or Aubergine). It was delicious. Jim knew that the official office hours meant, that the staff, who were separating the serum, were working in their two hour Government lunch break. He asked Mr. Matua to sort out some sort of roster, so that no one had to work more than their statutory hours, but the serum separation still carried on. Jim helped with the separation. Everyone was delighted when the last rack was put in the Jablo box, which was then packed carefully so there would be no breakages. Although Zebedee's family and the veterinary staff urged him to stay, there was nearly three hours of daylight left, so Jim, after much hand shaking, left for the journey home. As he had explained to them all, if the serum got hot all their hard work would have been in vain.

Two hours of driving got Jim into the Sabena Dessert, just past the left hand turning to Dadaab. He thought he would not make Habaswein in real daylight, so he drove five hundred yards off the road, over a shingle ridge, so that he was not visible to passing traffic and stopped for the night. There was no wood and Jim did not really want to draw attention to his camp by lighting a fire, so he used his small gas stove to brew tea and make some supper. The water in the jerry cans was tepid, so he had a good wash. He laughed at himself, as he wrapped a towel around his waist. It did not matter if he walked around naked; there was no one to see him.

During the night, he did not hear any traffic so he slept really well. He actually slept in, as the sun was properly up by the time he awoke. He had a cold cereal breakfast but did make himself a mug of hot tea and, made a thermos of tea. He packed up quickly and was soon going on the road south. He resisted the urge to check the serum samples, as he knew he would only waste the dry ice. He did not bother to stop at Habaswein and he reached the big left hand turn off to Garissa, in Mado Gashi, soon after 8.00am. He rolled into Garissa, before the staff at the veterinary office went for their lunch. He knew they had a deep freeze, so he transferred the serum samples into the safety of their freezer. There was precious little of the dry ice left but he did wrap a few cokes in towels and put them in the *'Jablo box'*. The LO explained that he was used to storing vaccine and that he could easily have the frozen samples taken to Kabete, by Landrover, in the next few days.

Jim was nervous about leaving the samples, having made such an effort to take them but he knew he had to trust the LO. There was no way he would get them, still frozen to Mombasa. He filled up with petrol and water and set off, as the staff went for their lunch break. He kept going all through the afternoon, at a steady pace. He drank his thermos of tea and all the cokes. He filled up just before 5.00pm in Garsen. He bought more cokes and some bananas and got going. Even if he had to drive in the dark, he was determined to reach civilization for the night. He knew he was mad but he was sick of camping on his own and being dusty and dirty all the time.

The light was failing as he passed the left hand turn to Kurawa, but he pressed on. There were no other vehicles on the road. He frightened himself, when a Warthog came charging out of the bush and hit the side of the Landrover. Jim stopped to see whether he had killed the poor beast, only to see it charge off, into the bush on the other side of the road. There was a bit of a dent in the Landrover, just in front of the back wheel arch. Jim set off again but made a mental note to keep his speed down. If he hit some larger game animal, on this sandy dirt road, he could easily lose control and roll the vehicle over. He was thankful he was in his own Landrover, as he could cheaply get the dent knocked out. Being aluminum, the metal would not rust, even at the coast where the air was so salty and seemed to corrode everything. If he had been in a Government vehicle, there would have been all manner of forms and reports to fill in. There would even be a record on his personal file. Jim crossed the bridge over the Sabaki River, just North of Malindi at about 9.00pm. Although he could have stayed in a tourist hotel in Malindi, he decided to carry on for another fourteen miles to Watamu. He had been told, it was a really beautiful spot on the beach, with only two hotels, the smaller of which was owned by a retired LO from the Veterinary Department. It was just after 10.00pm, when he drove down the beach road past the sign, on an old piece of drift wood, announcing 'Ocean Sports'.

Jim knew he looked an absolute mess, dirty and filthy with dust and sweat. He hoped they would give him a bed, after all this effort. He did not fancy driving three more hours to Mombasa. He found his bag, with his clothes in, and walked into the wooden porch which acted as a reception. There was no-one about, so he dumped his bag and walked through to the bar, where he could hear muted voices in the semi darkness. Behind the bar was a large, jovial man who immediately gave him a 'Tusker', saying Jim looked as if he needed one. Jim gratefully accepted it. The beer was ice cold. The first draught went down without touching the sides. There seemed to be no problem with Jim having a room. A young African was summoned to take Jim's bag from reception. Apparently there were only four '*bandas*' (Individual rooms, usually with their own bathroom) and Jim's was the furthest away. They had finished serving dinner but a big plate of ham sandwiches arrived, which Jim tucked into with gusto. When Jim explained he had driven all the way from North of Habaswein that day, having been working in Wajir, he was given another beer and the proprietor said it was on the house. The proprietor said he was bloody glad he did not have to go up there anymore. What with tiredness and heat, Jim felt fairly woozy after this second beer, so he made his excuses and staggered to his '*banda*'. He had been told that his bed was prepared with a mosquito net but the lights were not on, to save the electricity and to cut down the number of '*dudus*' (Any type of insect), which would fly in through the wide open windows. In the torch light, his '*banda*' looked delightful. Jim did not turn on the light but just looked around the room with his torch.

The roof was quite high and was thatched with '*makuti*' (Palm leaves made into tiles). The walls were wattle and daub and painted white. There was a small verandah, with two wooden chairs and a wooden table. Jim left the door open to let the breeze in. He could see the line of the surf, breaking on the sand fifty yards away. The room had two beds, one of which had a mosquito net hanging down over it. There was a wooden bedside table between the beds, with a candle on a saucer and some matches. There was a thermos flask, which Jim found contained ice cold water. He immediately drank a large glassful. Through a curtain to the side was a shower, a basin and a *'choo'*. It was pretty basic but was just what Jim wanted. The windows were wide open and the breeze blew the curtain about.

The water was warm in the shower and Jim stood under it for a long time. He washed his hair twice and hoped he had cleaned himself but he imagined the sheets would look pretty dirty in the morning. He could not worry about it, as he was so tired and could not see much in the torch light.

Chapter 10

Susie Cameron

Monday 2nd January 1967

He slept 'the sleep of the just' with the gentle sound of the surf. He woke up at dawn. The view of the ocean was spectacular. Jim could not wait. He put on his swimming trunks and ran down to the sea. He rushed into the water and dived through a big wave and swam, as if his life depended on it, towards India. He must have swum nearly a quarter of a mile before he turned back towards the idyllic beach. He came in with the waves and just lay, face down, in the surf. With each wave, he was washed in a little further. He was just thinking, *'what a wonderful life he had',* when his head bumped into a pair of small, pretty feet.

"Hullo," said a beautiful dark haired girl, wrapped in an orange and black *'kikoi'* (A cotton loose-weaved cloth, long enough to be wrapped around the body and secured by tucking into itself).

"I thought you were exhausted from your long swim and were lying here half drowned, but I see you are just playing the fool. You are lucky. I am not allowed to swim on my own, in case I get cramp and drown."

"Well," said Jim getting up, covered in sand, "you are with me, so now you will be fine."

"Great, I will risk it. Let me just put my *'kikoi'* above the water line, as the tide is coming in. She ran athletically up the beach. She was wearing a one piece orange swim suit on her return, which showed her young lithe body off to perfection.

"I am Jim. What is your name?"

"Susie." She held out her hand and Jim shook it.

"Come on, let's get back in the water and I can wash all this sand off."

They ran out together into the water, splashing along, until Susie made a graceful dive through a wave and came up laughing.

"I am going to get into trouble, as now my hair is all wet and it will have been obvious I have been swimming. Come on, let's swim out? I might as well be hung for a sheep, as a lamb."

Jim could see she was a good swimmer. She swam breast stroke beside him and then started a fast crawl. Jim had difficulty keeping up with her. He was relieved when she rolled on her back and pushed herself slowly along, with her legs.

"I wish I was a boy. My elder brother can swim whenever he likes. Surely, he is just as likely to get cramp as me. I heard you talking in the bar last night. My father was totally gob smacked that you had driven and camped, on your own, all the way up to Wajir and back. I know you must be older than me but I don't think by very much. You have total freedom. I long to leave school. I long to become more independent. My parents have other ideas and want me to stay on and take 'A' Levels. I want to be a nurse, so I don't need 'A' levels, but they think I should do a diploma in nursing and then I would get more rapid promotion in my nursing career"

"Yes, when my head bumped into your feet, I was just thinking how lucky I was. I did not get time to think how doubly lucky I was, to bump into a beautiful girl who was likely to become Matron of a hospital in five years!"

Susie splashed him playfully.

"You are a bad tease. Race you to the beach." She beat Jim by several yards. Jim laughed as he stood up and walked up to her, in the shallows.

"Would it do any good if I spoke to your parents and said what a marvellous swimmer you are?"

"Sadly, the answer is definitely, NO. They already think you are a lunatic, driving up into the NFD alone. I should think I will be in trouble even talking to you, let alone going swimming with you. Come on, I must rinse my hair under the shower before breakfast. I suspect it is going to be a stormy one."

They walked up the beach, to an outside shower set over a slab of concrete. Susie turned on the shower and rinsed herself off. Jim thought she would get into more trouble if she was seen showering in front of him but he thought it would look ridiculous if he turned away. Then he had an idea.

"I will just run and get your *'kikoi'*." He raced back down the beach.

When he got back, Susie said.

"That was really kind of you. Whatever my parents say, I think you are a real gent, not a cowboy at all! I hope we meet later on." She turned and walked away to her *'banda'*.

Jim thought, *'I have really arrived. A beautiful girl thinks I am a gentleman and her parents think I am a Kenyan Cowboy.'*

Jim showered in the same shower and walked to his *'banda'*. It was already hot on the soles of his feet and he was dry by the time he reached his veranda. He quickly put on a clean pair of shorts and shirt, found his sandals, grimaced at the red dust on his sheets and went for breakfast. He was greeted by the happiest waiter, who asked him, in Swahili, what he would like. Jim had forgotten the Swahili for a mango. He tried,

"Iko mangoi?" (Jim meant is there a mango?).The waiter replied.

"Ndio Bwana mwenbe tayare." (Yes Sir, Mangos are ready) Jim laughed.

"He *pali la gari moshi indani Mombasa."* (That is the name of the railway station in Mombasa).The waiter thought this was hilarious and turned away, dying to tell his friend in the kitchen, that there was a chap in the dining room, who did not know a mango from a train station. He soon brought back a mango, a slice of pawpaw and a cut lime. The fruit was excellent and obviously totally fresh. Jim loved it. The waiter soon brought a mug of tea, some toast and a large plate of fried breakfast. Jim was seriously hungry. He ate the lot, together with more toast and honey.

There was still no sign of Susie or her family. He hoped she had not got into too much trouble. Jim walked back to his *'banda'*. He sat on his veranda with his binoculars, looking at the spectacular bird life and then started to read his book. He heard Susie and her parents going to breakfast but they did not look his way. Then Susie came running back. She gave him a discrete wave and went into her *'banda'*. She emerged carrying what looked like two guide books. She waved again and hurried after her parents. Jim carried on reading. It was such a magnificent setting. He could really relax, after several days of hard work. Soon a young man came to tidy the room. All in Swahili, he asked if Jim minded if he cleaned the room. Jim apologized for all the dirt on the sheets. The young man had heard all about Jim's epic journey and said it did not matter, as he had brought clean sheets. He said it was a pity that the young 'memsahib' (European Lady but actually an Indian word) had not been allowed to stay with Jim. She had been made to go to the ancient ruins of Gedi, for a day trip out. Jim felt sorry for Susie. Obviously she had got into trouble. Oh dear, he felt guilty, as he had encouraged her. Equally, she had not needed much encouragement. Jim asked if it was possible to go water skiing. He was told that the hotel had a good boat, round in Mida creek. Jim thought that would be good fun, later in the day.

Having read for maybe two hours, Jim went for a walk-North from the hotel. Although it was hot on the sand, the views were spectacular. He climbed over a rocky spur and found another bay, which was totally deserted. Jim thought, sadly, that it was only a matter of time before it was developed.

He came back and went to the bar for a beer. The proprietor was very friendly and they had a good chat. Jim was offered lunch but declined, saying he had enjoyed his breakfast so much that he would skip lunch and wait for supper. When he asked about water skiing, the proprietor's face lit up. He said he would be delighted to take Jim. He said the boat was around in Mida creek, as it had just been serviced but he wanted to bring it back round, so that it could be moored, as usual, opposite the hotel. He suggested that if Jim was feeling strong, he could have a tow all the way from Mida creek to the hotel. He would only charge the cost of the petrol. Jim thought that was a great idea. He said Jim could ride with him to Mida creek at 3.00pm. Jim said he needed exercise, so he would walk round to Mida creek. The proprietor laughed and said Jim must be a glutton for punishment, as he guaranteed Jim would be totally knackered if he walked there then skied back. Anyway Jim could always drop into the water, if he was too tired and get a lift in the boat. Jim went back to his verandah to read for a bit, then he set off on his walk. Although he put on his swimming trunks he also wore a shirt, a hat and his sandals. He also drank a pint of water out of the thermos. He had been wise. It was a very long walk in the hot sun. He was very glad of his sandals, as he had 400 yards of coral to walkover on the point. However, he had done well because he had plenty of time at the boat yard to dose off in the shade.

He was woken by a hand on his thigh. He looked up to see Susie laughing at him. Actually, he must have been in a deep sleep, as he could not think immediately where he was.

"Hello, how did you get here? Anyway, it's good to see you. I hope you did not get into a lot of trouble."

"No, only a little bit. It was mainly the sin of swimming with strange men."

"I must say, I do see your parent's point of veiw. I am rather strange!"

Jim laughed. "Now how about coming water skiing?"

"Will you teach me? That would be awesome."

Soon Jim found himself in Mida creek, holding a very beautiful young girl round the waist and shouting to the proprietor in the boat.

"Get ready to hit it."

He shouted to Susie. "Keep your arms straight and your knees bent." Then, reaching down, he grasped her thighs, making her bend her legs so her knees were on her chest. Then he shouted, "hit it." Susie was good. In fact she was a natural, with excellent balance. Jim rather resented her getting up on her third attempt. It was rather good fun, holding her in the water.

Susie did three small circles around the creek and managed to cross the wake several times. When she released the rope and glided to a stop, near to Jim, she was ecstatic.

"Thank you so much for helping me. You are a marvellous teacher. I have tried twice before and never got up. It made all the difference, you making me bend my legs and holding me up. Now you must have a go. I gather you are going to ski back to the hotel."

Jim said, "I am going to try but it is a long way."

"You will do it. I know you will. I can't wait to tell Mum and Dad that I got up, thanks to you," gushed Susie.

The boat came near them and Jim put his hand under Susie's bottom and posted her up into the boat. Jim had seen a big, long mono-ski in the boat. He asked for that, as he thought it would be his best bet. Ideally, for a really long ski, particularly out at sea, he would have preferred a pair of large long wide jump skis but he knew there were none available. He handed up the normal skis, which Susie had used, and put on the mono on his left foot and tucked his right foot in the strap behind his lead foot. He shouted. "You can start whenever you feel the rope goes tight." Jim took a deep breath and the boat shot forward. With a massive effort, he came up and broke the surface. He was away. He did a couple of steep slalom turns, just to get the feel of the ski, and then he coasted along in the smooth water of the creek, conserving his energy. He was feeling fine, until they met the choppy sea, as they rounded the headland. Although the boat was at full revs, as it climbed each wave crest it slowed. Jim was constantly bending his legs. He knew the advice he had given to Susie was vital. Keep your arms straight and bend your knees. However, occasionally the boat slowed so much, that he had to take up the slack rope with his arms otherwise the force, when it went taut, would have pitched him into the water.

When he was beginning to think he could not take any more, they rounded the headland into calmer water. There was still a swell now, coming in from his right hand side, but the speed of the boat increased and was steadier. He could relax a little but he could see there was still a considerable way to go. He hooked the bar of the rope in his left elbow to give his arms a rest. This was a powerful boat. They were travelling at 35 mph, so they soon covered the distance. When they were nearing the hotel Jim put in a really tight slalom turn. It slowed the boat by about 10 knots, but as soon as the boat speeded up, he put in another tight turn. He put in two more really aggressive turns before throwing the rope away and gliding into the shallow water, where he just walked off the ski. He turned and picked up the ski and carried it above the surf, then came back into the sea to help get the boat in. The proprietor tied the boat up to its mooring buoy and then jumped into the water. It only came up to his mid-thigh. Susie was about to jump in when she saw Jim coming. She waited and then jumped into his arms. With great gallantry, Jim carried her out of the water before he set her down. She whispered in his ear.

"The proprietor has never seen a skier as strong as you. You were fantastic." The proprietor came up behind them.

"That was some great skiing. Come on, let's get you a beer. You deserve it."

When they were in the bar, Susie's parents came in. Before they could say anything, Jim said, "Your daughter is a star, she got up third time and then went round the creek, crossing the wake. You must be very proud of her. Sorry I should have said, I am Jim Scott." Jim held out his hand. Susie's father shook it and said.

"Thank you for looking after Susie. I am Colin Cameron. This is my wife, Freda." Freda grasped his hand and looked him keenly in the eye. "You are a very good skier. We watched you come in. I think you must have been a big help to Susie. Thank you. I gather you are on your own. Would you like to join us for dinner? Shall we meet in the bar at 7.00 pm?"

"That is really kind, I will be delighted," replied Jim.

Jim made sure he was in clean clothes and arrived in the bar exactly at 7.00pm. Colin and Freda Cameron were already at the bar but had obviously only just arrived, as they were buying drinks. Colin Cameron turned as Jim came in and said. "There you are, what can I get you to drink?"

"A Tusker would be marvellous. Where is Susie?"

"Still dressing, you know what these girls are like!" was the reply.

"Well, I will forgive her for being a slow dresser, as she is such a quick learner. I have never met anyone get the hang of it so quickly. I took forever, in England and nearly froze to death."

Susie who had come up behind him said. "I would not have liked to have learnt in the UK. The thought of lying in the water, while the boat got the rope in the right position, gives me goose pumps thinking about it. Can I have a G & T with lots of ice please, Dad? Hopefully that will cool me down. I feel hot already and I have hardly been out of the shower ten minutes?"

The conversation flowed very naturally at the bar and when they sat down to dinner, Colin asked. "Now Jim, tell us why you were up in Wajir and what prompted your rush to get here."

"I was in Wajir to blood test 400 camels, for my irascible boss in Mombasa. I think it was only semi official, as the bloods were required by a pal of his. I was pretty naive and thought the task would take me much longer. I allowed a fortnight but, as I got through the job, I thought I would skive off here at Watamu."

"I think I had better stop you there Jim, before you say anything more and get yourself into trouble. You obviously don't realise that I am Chief Veterinary Research Officer (CVRO) at Kabete, down here on holiday. I think you deserve today off, after your hard work, but I am afraid I must insist that you return to your station, after breakfast tomorrow."

"Of course," replied Jim. "That will teach me to keep my big mouth shut."

Susie piped up. "I feel partly to blame. You could have carried on with some days off, if I had not talked to you this morning. Could you not stay dumb for a couple more days, Dad?"

"No Susie that would not be fair on your Dad. At least I have had a lovely day today. Also I am very superstitious and so, if by misadventure, the blood samples do not get to Kabete, I really would be for the high jump." Colin was glad the subject was closed. He did not seem to notice that Susie had drunk several more G & Ts. The party broke up after coffee. They all said good night and Freda said, "I am sure you have no need to go at dawn Jim, so why not stay and have a good breakfast with us. Shall we meet here at 8.00am?"

"That sounds a good plan. I will easily get to the office before everyone comes back from lunch, at 2.00pm." Jim went off ahead of them to his room. He quickly packed most of his things. At supper there had been talk that, as it was the dry season, there were no mosquitoes about, so Jim slung the mosquito net back up and got naked into bed, after he had turned out the light. He was soon asleep and did not see the slim figure in the moonlight, silently open and close the veranda door. Susie discarded her *'kikoi'* and slipped into his bed. She felt Jim move so she clapped a hand over his mouth and whispered in his ear,

"Don't make a sound or we will get caught."

Jim nodded his head. Susie then took her hand from his mouth and kissed him passionately. Jim immediately realised she was naked. He returned her kisses and then thought. *'This is madness. It might be good fun now. However I am sure it will all end in tears.'* His thoughts went to Fi. He had probably broken one girl's heart. *'He must not do it again. He remembered Fi saying, you were so kind Jim. He must be kind to Susie but it was not going to be easy.'* Susie's hands were caressing his back. She had one of her legs between his and was rubbing her bush on his leg. Jim knew he had to act now, or he would roll her onto her back and enter her. He broke away from her kisses, stroked her hair and whispered,

"Susie, you are too lovely. I will lose control in a second. Please stop. I am sure you can feel my erection. It would be totally disastrous if I got you pregnant. You are such a beautiful girl. I don't want to ruin your life." This had the desired effect. Susie stopped rubbing her bush. Jim longed to rub her himself and feel her having an orgasm, but he willed his hands to stay away from her groin. He just kept one hand on her back and kept stroking her hair. Her breathing came back to normal.

"You are right. I have been a very naughty girl. Can we blame it on the gin? I can't think what my parents would say. I was lying in bed and I remembered the feel of your hands on my body, in the water. I just wanted to feel them again." Then she silently started crying.

"What will you think of me?"

"I will think of you as a very lovely, sexy girl. Don't cry. You have done nothing to be ashamed of. It is perfectly normal to want to make love. I hope you do it a million times again."

"Jim, you are so kind and understanding. In some ways, I want you more now."

He could hear the laughter coming back in her whisper. "Well, I am still a virgin. Can I just feel your 'willy'. I don't think there would be room inside me for it and yet my vagina feels wet. Would it have hurt me?"

"Yes, I think it would have hurt you, unless we had been very slow. Now, what we must not do is fall asleep in each other's arms. That would be too ironic, as we would get into serious trouble and your parents would never have believed we had not actually made love."

So reluctantly they got up. Susie flung her arms around his neck and kissed him. "Thank you for being so kind and wise. I will always remember you as the boy I gave myself to but was too sensible to ravish me and yet, he said, I should try to make love a million times!" They went to the door and stood looking out over the moonlit beach.

Jim hugged her.

"I hope you get back to your room OK," whispered Jim. He watched her get back to her room. As he got back into bed, his erection subsided and he went to sleep.

In the morning Jim had a shower, cleared his room and put his stuff in the Landrover. He was just paying his bill, when the Camerons came to breakfast. They had a great meal, with a lot of laughter. They all came out to wave him off. He shook hands with Freda and Colin. Susie hugged him and said,

"Can I write to you, when I am back at school? It will be boring girlie things, but you can tell me about long night drives in the NFD and how you have managed to skive off work, without my boring father finding out. You are definitely my best and wisest teacher?" She kissed him on the lips and said,

"Take lots of care."

Jim got in the Landrover and shouted,

"I will look for the post." He then drove away. Freda said,

"Susie, I think he is a very nice boy but I don't think you should have kissed him on the lips or even hugged him so close. You will give boys the wrong idea." Colin expected an argument from his impulsive daughter, but he was wrong. Susie just said. "Sorry Mum. I just felt like hugging and kissing him. Don't worry, I won't hug or kiss any old bloke, except maybe Dad." She kissed her father on the cheek.

Colin thought. '*I don't know or want to know what happened last night. Something certainly did, yesterday morning Susie was a girl. This morning she is a woman. I don't think Jim Scott hurt her in any way. I think he is a very bright guy and I think he will go a long way in the department. I will follow his career with interest?*

Chapter 11

A party at the Gurneys

Saturday 7ᵗʰ January 1967

Jim got called, at about 10.00am, by a European Lady on the telephone at the Veterinary Office. Kimuta had taken the call and transferred it to Jim.

"So sorry to bother you on a Saturday morning, but my Jersey house-cow is having difficulty having a calf. My headman is perplexed, as the calf seems to have two heads and three front legs. I would be very grateful if you could come and help. I am having friends around for drinks at lunch time. I do hope you will be able to stay for the party." Jim had read Anne Whitehead's reports. He knew the farm was a large farm, which ranched-milked a herd of a thousand cows on the grass, between the rows of sisal on the North Coast, South of the Kilifi Ferry.

Ranch milking was where the cows were milked in the morning, having been separated from their calves during the night. The calves were allowed to run with their mothers all day. Jim already had his calving stuff ready. He collected a car permit to cross Nyali Bridge and another to cross Mtwapa Bridge, from Silas, and set off. He had to go through Mombasa, which was busy on Saturday morning. He was impatient but then he relaxed, as he imagined the cow had probably been calving all night. He was met at the dairy by the headman, who bowed slightly and introduced himself as Juma. He took Jim to the cow, which was tied up in her own box. Talking to the cow were two European girls, with long blond hair and brown faces. They were obviously identical twins. Jim thought they were about eleven years old.

Jim greeted them with, "Hello you two, what is the cow's name?"

"Rosie," was the chorused reply. Jim asked Juma for a '*karai*' of warm water and some soap. The girls said their names were Emma and Amy.

"To help you, Emma is wearing blue shorts," said Amy.

"My shorts are green."

"Can we help you with Rosie?" said Emma.

"Certainly you can. First of all we must give Rosie an injection of Penicillin. Can you each shake one of these little bottles?" Jim injected Rosie into her rump and then took his shirt off and washed and soaped his right arm. He had been wrong. This was a nice fresh calving. It was twins. However he did not say anything except,

"We must get some ropes on these legs."

"Can we feel inside," chorused the twins.

"Of course you can. Soap up your arm like I did." Both of them took off their shirts. '*Oh dear,*' thought Jim. '*I don't think I should have encouraged young girls to take their shirts off. However it is too late now.*'

They were really excited when they felt inside the cow and could feel the calf's feet. Jim put some calving ropes on to the calf he thought would come first. He got Juma to pull on the ropes as he guided the head into the pelvis. Soon the calf was coming. The girls did not stand back but helped to pull the calf and to stop it falling on to the ground, as the cow was still standing up. They got covered in the yellow amniotic fluid.

"Quick," said Jim. "Rub its chest, get the mucous out of its mouth and poke a piece of straw up its nose to make it breathe." Soon the calf was breathing nicely and moving its head.

"Now, each of you take off a rope and wash it. I have a surprise for you. Put your hand into her vagina and tell me what you feel. There is room, so you both can put your hands in at the same time." Jim did not want a fight as to who went first.

"There is another one," shrieked the excited girls. They soon delivered the second calf. Jim examined the cow carefully, to see that she was not torn and that there was not a third calf. Jim thanked Juma for being so vigilant. He also gave Rosie a bottle of calcium, as Jim was sure she would be likely to go down with milk fever. He gave the calcium with a long tube, called a flutter valve. This was attached to the bottle at one end and a large-bored needle at the other end. The calves were both sitting up and, in fact, one was trying to stand. Juma released the cow and she immediately started to lick the two calves.

"Come on you two, hop in the Landrover and we will drive up to the house."

There were several cars at the front of the large bungalow. The party had obviously already started. Jim drove around to the back of the house. Inside the back door was a large sink. Jim kicked off his filthy safari boots and was about to wash.

"Kick off your boots you two and we will get washed up." The twins could not wait and rushed through. He heard,

"Mummy. Rosie has had twin heifer calves. Jim let us help. It was all slimy but so exciting."

"My goodness, look at the state of you. Your shorts are filthy and where are your shirts?" inquired a woman's voice.

"Jim told us to take them off so we could feel inside Rosie."

"Did he now and where is he now?"

"Washing in the back sink," was the reply.

"Well that's where you had better go and clean up. You can't go through the house without shirts on, with all the guests here." They both came running back to Jim, followed by their mother.

Jim said. "I am sorry about the mess and their shirts. I'm Jim. I can see where they get their good looks from." Jim had filled the enormous sink with warm soapy water. He was wrapped in a towel and had finished cleaning himself off.

"Well, I am Emily and I will forgive you as you are so complimentary, but I am trying to make the twins into young ladies and running around with their shirts off, is not to be encouraged. However, you girls are so filthy I suggest you take all your clothes off and let Jim lift you into the sink. Maria can you get them some clean pants and shorts? I gather their shirts are still clean. I am sorry to be so rude but I ought to be giving my guests drinks. Jim, can I leave you in charge of them? Once you are all cleaned up, you can all come through and I will do some introducing."

Emily did not have to, as when Jim came through holding each twin's hand, he was set upon by three shrieking girls.

"It's Jim." It was Annie, Ronnie and Charlie. They all hugged and kissed him. Charlie said to the twins, "Can you be very grown up and get us each another G & T? I expect Jim would like a beer?" The girls all wanted to know why Jim had neglected them. When they heard he had been up to Wajir, blood testing camels, there were gasps of,

"That's bloody miles away."

"Don't they spit?"

"Can't you get syphilis?" Jim patiently explained that yes, it was a long way away but they rarely spit and they do not carry syphilis. The twins came back with the drinks, in relays. They stayed close to Jim, who was now their hero. Jim noticed that they, like him, were not wearing shoes. Then disaster struck. Jim was waving his arms around, demonstrating how a camel gets up, when he knocked a glass clean out of the hand of a passing guest. It smashed on the concrete floor. Jim commanded. "Emma and Amy, jump into my arms. You don't have any shoes on." Jim lifted the two girls up. "I am sorry but I can't safely move, as I haven't any shoes on either" said Jim. He turned to Charlie. "Can you be an angel and sweep up the broken glass?"

It turned out to be a really good party, although Jim did receive some rather disparaging looks for his lack of foot wear. In fact, his whole attire was not approved of, as he was the only man wearing shorts. However, after a couple of drinks, Charlie seemed to Jim to be very attractive. She did not seem bothered about his lack of long trousers. When she said she was dreading going back to Nairobi with Annie and Ronnie, as they had to return to their jobs, Jim said, "Why don't you stay in Mombasa with me? I know I will be at work but I am sure you can top up your tan during the day in my garden, which is right on Tudor Creek and we can have lots of fun after I get home, which is normally soon after 4.00pm?" Charlie jumped at the invitation. So it was agreed, Annie and Ronnie would drop her off at Jim's house at coffee time on the next day, on their way through from the South Coast, before they started the long drive back to Nairobi. Jim gave Annie directions to his house.

Jim then went with, the twins in tow, to check on Rosie and her calves. When they came back to the house, the last guests were leaving. As they drove away, Jim said to Emily. "I am so sorry about the glass and being so slovenly dressed. Otherwise, I thought the party went really well."

"You are a very kind and generous young man. In fact, the twins and I have enjoyed having you. Isn't that right girls?"

"Oh yes," agreed the twins.

"I am also grateful for your help with Rosie. Why don't you stay and have some lunch with us?"

"That would be great," replied Jim.

Jim enjoyed Emily's company. She was obviously ten or more years older than Jim but had a very young outlook on life, for a mother of two eleven year old girls. Her husband was a professional hunter, who mainly took clients to Tanzania. She stayed at the coast and looked after the farm and the twins. The twins were delighted, as Jim asked them if they would like to come with him, if he had any interesting calls in future. He made them promise that they would not take their shirts off even if he did. Telephoning was not really a problem on the coast. It was just calling Nairobi and upcountry, which was a pain.

It was a fun lunch. Jim left, promising that he would be in touch soon. He was glad to go home and get himself organized, as everything had been a bit chaotic, as he had only received the keys to his government house on the previous day. Anne Whitehead had left to go on leave for four months. Some friends, who lived in Nakuru, had agreed to look after her dog, 'Karli'. Jim had welcomed her idea of him taking on her old cook, called Katana. He was a kindly old man from the Kikuyu tribe. Anne said she would find another cook on her return.

Jim noticed that Katana had done a wonderful job, in his first two days, cleaning the house. It had been lived in by another European family but, like any house when some of the furniture and fittings are removed, it looked a bit shabby. It came with a complement of hard government furniture, so it did not look too bare. Jim only had his air freight but he did have enough bedding and a spare mosquito net, so that he could roughly furnish a second bedroom for Charlie. He did really like her but he had some reservations. He was pretty certain she would want a room of her own. Because Annie and Ronnie were such dominant characters, he had not had much of a chance to talk with Charlie on her own. Most of the time they had been together, they had been either a little drunk or totally pissed. Luckily, the

132

house not only had three bedrooms but also two bathrooms and a third lavatory and hand basin.

The following day, Jim set to and totally unpacked his things. He tried, rather in vain, to make the place look like a home. He put some flowers in two jam jars and some candles in four wine bottles. He put two towels in the spare bathroom.

Although it was Sunday, the food shops were open. He and Katana made a list of food items they required. Jim was just about to take the Landrover into town, when the girls arrived. Charlie seemed on good form but Annie and Ronnie were subdued. Jim guessed they had hangovers and did not relish the long, hot drive to Nairobi. They also were depressed at having to start work in the morning, after their extended Christmas break. They did not even stop for coffee but left for the garage, to pick up a puncture from yesterday. They said they would fill up and then set off and stop for Lunch at 'Titty Andy'.

Jim asked, "Where the devil was 'Titty Andy'?" It turned out to be Mitito Andei which was half way to Nairobi. No wonder they were in a hurry-it was one hundred and fifty miles away. Only the first fifty miles to Mackinnon Road, was tarmac. However, those were not the only reasons that Annie and Ronnie were out of sorts.

As soon as they had left, Katana brought Jim and Charlie coffee on the veranda. Charlie said, "Jim, the girls are cross with me. I admitted to them, last night, that I have a steady boy friend back in the UK. They said, they did not think I have been fair to you. When you and I have been together, we have had a few drinks and things have led on from that. I am sorry, I think I have encouraged you. I like you and find you attractive but, they feel, by accepting your invitation I have gone too far. I really am sorry."

"Don't worry about it," replied Jim. "I am glad you have told me. I find you very attractive as well, but I guessed you had some reservations. I had anticipated them and that's why I have got Katana to make up a bed for you, in a separate bedroom. You will have your own bathroom. We can have good fun. I hope you will enjoy your week here." Charlie squeezed his hand.

"I knew you would be sensible and down to earth. I also thought Annie and Ronnie were dramatising the whole thing. I think, perhaps, they were a little jealous that you paid so much attention to me rather, than them."

So it was. Jim and Charlie had an enjoyable week. Jim was not too busy at work. He managed to get home at lunch time. Charlie seemed happy sunbathing in the garden and reading in the shade, when it got too hot. Jim's sea freight arrived. Charlie set about it with gusto. She really helped to make the house into a proper home. Jim was delighted with the 'woman's touch'.

They discussed which would the best way for Charlie to get back to Nairobi. Charlie was obviously a little short of money and so, flying or the train was not a very good option. Jim was not keen on her getting a so called 'Happy Taxi', which were cheap but had a reputation for, at best, breaking down or, at worst being involved in serious high speed accidents. Charlie was due to fly out on Sunday evening, checking in at 5.30pm. Jim guessed she did not want to be a burden to Annie and Ronnie but equally, she secretly hoped that they would come to the airport to see her off.

Jim tentatively suggested camping in Tsavo Game Park on Saturday night. Charlie jumped at the suggestion.

"Will you be OK sharing a tent?" asked Jim.

"Of course I will be happy. You have been a real gent all week. I would much rather share a tent with you, than be on my own. I would be seriously scared."

The next morning, at work, Jim put through a long distance call to Annie at work. He made it sound official and Jim thought no one would notice. He got through to Annie. "I am bringing Charlie up to Nairobi on Sunday. I gather you were a little cross with her. I have not told her that I am ringing you but I know she would love to see you and Ronnie, to say goodbye."

"That is really kind of you. Have you had fun together?" asked Annie, who was probing for information.

"She told me all about her boyfriend in the UK. She has been really helpful sorting my house out. You and Ronnie must come down and stay. She checks in at 5.30pm. I don't really want to leave her alone at the airport but equally, I really would like to heading back to Mombasa before then."

"Of course you must. It is so sweet of you to bring her up. Why don't we meet at the airport for a late lunch, say 2.00pm and then you can head back and we will entertain her until check in?"

"That sounds great. See you then. Love to you both. *'Kwaheri'* (Goodbye)." Jim rang off.

Jim told Charlie what he had done at lunch. She got up from the table and kissed him. "You are a very naughty boy, but thank you. I am really grateful. Annie and Ronnie were really kind to me and I did not want to go without saying goodbye. I am looking forward to our *'safari'*."

When Jim got home from work, Charlie helped him pack everything up for the *'safari'*. She had to pack her case for going home but Jim lent her a small grip, so she had stuff for one night in a tent. They planned to make an early start, so that they would reach the park at dawn, or soon after. Charlie had been shopping and not only had bought food for a special supper, but also a bottle of white wine. They were hot, having packed up the Landrover, so they had a beer and then showered. Supper was not quite ready, so they had another beer on the veranda in the cool of the evening. They drank the wine with the meal. Katana brought them coffee and then said good night. He said he would make them a light breakfast in the morning, at 5.30 am. Charlie was wearing a long but light skirt, which blew in the wind, when she stood up and leaned over the rail of the veranda, looking at the moonlit creek. Jim got up and joined her and put his arm around her shoulders. She did not resist, when he turned her towards him and kissed her. Then he said,

"We must be good and go to bed. I know it is not yet 10.00 pm but 5.30 am will come rather quickly." Charlie said rather wistfully,

"It is so beautiful. Just hold me close for a few minutes." She cuddled up to his chest. Then she broke away.

"Jim, I am sorry, I am being a real bitch. You have been really kind to me and I am doing just what Annie and Ronnie said I must not do." She reached up kissed him quickly.

"Goodnight and thank you for a lovely evening. See you in the morning." She went to her room and shut the door. Jim was pretty sad.

They were both cheerful and excited in the morning and were on the road before 6.00 am. There was little traffic and they were clear of Mombasa before the sun came up. However, it was well up by the time they had travelled the fifty miles of tarmac road to Mackinnon Road, where Tsavo East Game Park started on their right hand side.

135

Immediately they started to see animals. There was a herd of female Impala, mixed in with a group of Burchell's Zebra. Charlie shrieked with delight, when a family of warthog ran across the road, the mother led and was followed by a line of piglets, all with their tails up. On their left were large ranches but they too had game animals. Charlie saw ostriches and a lone *'kongoni',* the Swahili for Hartebeest. There were Tommy's (Short for Thompson gazelle) and Grant gazelle, all mixed together. She was overjoyed when they came to two large bull elephants, quietly feeding on the bush not far from the road. The bush had been cut back from the road, to give drivers some warning of game animals crossing. They stopped to watch the elephants for a few minutes. The *'murram'* surface of the road was good, so they had quite a smooth ride. Soon they came to Voi, which meant they had driven a hundred miles from Mombasa. They stopped for fuel and a cold coke. It was getting hot. Once they were going again Charlie asked, "I have got my bikini on so can I take my shirt off?"

"Of course, I will enjoy that," said Jim.

"Don't you get any ideas of undoing my bikini top? We are not on the beach now." She said this with a laugh and Jim realized, she was not too bothered about what he saw.

Ten miles after Voi they had to stop, to let a large herd of Buffalo cross the road. There was a car coming the other way and the occupants waved. They shouted. "There are lots of elephants behind us." Sure enough, a few miles on, there were elephants both sides of the road.

"This is marvellous," shouted Charlie.

"This is much better than Nairobi Game Park, where Annie took me." Jim really enjoyed game watching. His pleasure was added to, by Charlie's enthusiasm.

They arrived at Mitito Andei, where they filled up again. Jim knew that, as they got further from Mombasa, the fuel became more expensive. The cokes were very welcome. They journeyed on. By staying on the main road, they were no longer in the game park. There were not so many animals to be seen and, of course, game was harder to find, once the temperature rose. To Jim's delight, Charlie wriggled out of her shorts, so now she only had her bikini on. Somehow, it was much more erotic having an almost, naked pretty

136

girl, in the Landrover than just seeing a bikini clad girl on the beach. Jim had to keep his eyes on the road, as the '*murram*' was not so good. He was also keeping a close look out for a turning, on his right. He knew it was about twenty five miles from Mitito Andei. There was, apparently, only a small wooded sign, pointing to a cheap camping place called 'Bushwhackers'. Charlie, on the other hand, was looking to their left at the Chyulu Hills. She was hoping to see Kilimanjaro, which was sometimes visible behind their southern end. Sadly, she was unlucky.

Jim found the sign and they turned down the single rough track. When Jim had been at Kabete a young vet, who worked at the vet labs, had told him about 'Bushwhackers'. Apparently, you did not necessarily have to use their '*bandas*' but could pay a much reduced fee and camp up the Kibwezi river. The chap had said to Jim, if he really needed an adrenaline rush, he should find the small cataract in the Athi River and swim there. They came to the small wooden hut, which served as the 'Reception'. It was manned by an old man, who was from the 'Kamba' tribe. They populated all of this area, north of the road. Charlie grabbed her shirt. She wanted to get out, as she had seen some wooden carvings for sale. She had wanted to buy some for presents, in Mombasa, but somehow there had never been enough time. Jim paid the five shillings, which was their camping fee. The old man said they were welcome to use their showers and lavatories. Charlie was pleased, as she knew she would be going straight to the airport the next day and this might be her last chance of a shower, before flying home.

Jim laughed. "I have got a camp shower. I was looking forward to helping you to wash your hair."

Charlie replied, "No way am I standing naked, showering in front of you! You can use your camp shower. I will come back here to shower and buy some presents to take home. Some of these carvings are beautiful and they are much cheaper than those I have seen in Mombasa, down the 'Kilindini' Road."

They said goodbye to the old man but said they would come back later, when they had made their camp. They drove along the track which went behind the '*bandas*'. After they had gone a hundred yards, they found a beautiful camping site with a large tree. They stopped the Landrover.

Jim said, "Let's go and have a look at the river. It is meant to be spectacular swimming." They had to walk about three miles before they could hear the river. As they walked, it got louder and louder, until they came to a very rocky place. The river was only twenty five foot wide at this point. It crashed and frothed, muddy brown, through large rock boulders for thirty or forty yards before coming to a large pool.

"Wow, that is terrific," shouted Jim, above the roar of the river.

"I am going to swim down to the pool right now. The chap at Kabete said it was really exciting." Jim started taking off his clothes.

Charlie was horrified. She clutched him to her and said, "Please don't Jim."

Jim misunderstood her and said, "Don't worry there is no one about. You have seen me naked before."

"No, you bloody fool. I don't mind you being naked. It fact I would enjoy it. I just don't want you to get drowned." No pleading would stop Jim. He jumped into the water, stark naked except for his trainers, in a place free of rocks. He was grabbed by the current and driven through the rocks at break-neck speed. It certainly was exhilarating. He was soon at the pool. Charlie sprinted down beside the river, bounding over the dry rocks. She ran straight into the pool in her shirt. She splashed up to him and held him to her. "You are an idiot."

Jim replied. "You are a very sexy girl with your wet look."

"I can do better." Charlie untied her bikini top and took it off. Her shirt clung to her and her hard nipples showed clearly through. She kissed him.

"Now bloody Annie and Ronnie will say I am encouraging you. They are bloody right. You are a sexy animal!" They walked hand in hand, back up the river, to Jim's clothes.

"I bloody well hope no one comes along with a camera. I would be mortified if my boyfriend saw a picture of me with my wet shirt holding hands with a guy with a 'hard-on!"

When they got back to Jim's clothes, Charlie said, "Now cram yourself back into your pants and shorts."

Jim was pleased to see she made no effort to put her bikini top back on. When they got back to the Landrover, Jim got out the camp table and a couple of camp chairs, while Charlie found two cold beers in the cold box. They sat in their semi naked state, looking at the view of the Kitu hills and enjoying their beer.

"This is really beautiful," sighed Charlie.

"I wish I could forget about the UK and reality. Is it possible to want two men? Ronnie said I was a sex manic. She saw your hand up my skirt, when we drove to the Likoni Ferry on Christmas night."

Jim went red and said, "I am sorry I should never have done that."

Charlie giggled. "I should never have let you. Perhaps I am a sex maniac but that criticism, coming from Ronnie is really the pot calling the kettle black. We must forget it and blame it on the drink."

Then she added, rather softly, "I do remember rather enjoying it and regretting the arrival at the ferry." She got up to get another beer and gave Jim a playful slap on the hand.

"My boyfriend in the UK would never get drunk or be so bold." Jim said nothing but he remembered things were a little different in the UK. Then, with a pang of sorrow, he remembered Fi. She was a really fantastic girl. Had he been a fool to leave her? Africa was beautiful and exciting but Fi was a girl for life. He came out of his reverie with Charlie laughing, "I don't feel bad at all now. Be honest you weren't listening, you were thinking about another girl-admit it. I will kill you if it was Ronnie." She got up and sat astride his legs, facing him, and held his head firmly.

"Was it Ronnie? You rat."

"I have to admit it was another girl but I promise, on my life it wasn't Ronnie."

"I believe you. Your face looked so soft and loving. I knew you weren't thinking of Ronnie. However, now I know, I don't feel half as bad." With that she kissed him, rather passionately, and said, "However I don't expect you to take liberties with me. I definitely won't be having too many beers tonight."

In fact, they had lots of laughs cooking supper. Charlie had no qualms about asking Jim to come with her to the showers, as she was nervous about walking on her own in the dark. He volunteered to share the shower with her, in case there were any snakes.

"Definitely NO. I will risk a Black Mamba rather than a certainty of that one-eyed trouser snake!" She let Jim hold her hand, as they walked back to the camp. He was certain she was not that frightened. They had made a small fire, so they sat and had another beer, gazing at the flickering light. They both were nervous, not quite knowing what to do about going to bed. Jim had erected the tent on top of the Landrover, on the roof rack. He wondered if Charlie now regretted saying she would share with him. Would she choose to sleep in the Landrover and be uncomfortable instead?

His question was answered by her saying, "You must look the other way while I put my *'kikoi'* on. I think this fire gives off quite a bit of light. I really ought to find my pyjamas but they are packed in my big bag, ready to go home. I can't be bothered but you must go up the ladder first, or you will have a good view." She giggled, turned her back on him, took off her shirt and shorts, and then wrapped her *'kikoi'* around her body above her breasts. Jim took off his shorts and wrapped his *'kikoi'* around his waist. As he climbed up the ladder, he said, "I don't know why I bother with a *'kikoi'* you have seen it all before."

Charlie laughed. "Only in Africa, or in Scotland, does a girl get a chance to look up a man's skirt!" She came up behind him. Jim turned on a torch, which he had left in the pocket of the tent, so that he could see to zip up the tent flaps, to stop any mosquitoes coming in. The tent had mosquito netting at either end, so it was not too hot. After they had sorted out their pillows and lain down under the spread out sleeping bag, there was an awkward silence.

Then Charlie said, "Do you mind if I cuddle your back, it is a little bit cold?"

"That will be nice," replied Jim.

"I hope you sleep well?" He felt her against him. It was a lovely feeling and, although he was quite excited, he went to sleep. He awoke sometime later as he felt Charlie's arm flopped over his body and a little bit cold, because the sleeping bag had slipped down. He felt her roll over, as he pulled the sleeping bag up over them. He rolled over behind her. He was not sure if she was awake but she moved back close to him. Of course he then got an erection but she made no move to get away from him. Thus encouraged, he put a hand on her hip. After a minute he was further encouraged as she rolled towards him, onto her back, letting his hand fall on to her body as her *'kikoi'* had come undone. He could not resist moving his hand on to her springy bush. He was sure she was just pretending to be asleep, as she moved and just opened her legs a little further apart.

He moved his hand down and felt the soft lips of her vulva. She moved again and he thought he had gone too far and that she was going to roll away from him. However she just moved slightly and parted her legs even further. He gently started to rub her clitoris. Initially there was no reaction, but then Jim felt her pushing up her pubis and he rubbed slightly harder and quicker. Jim was breathing a little harder and he could hear Charlie breathing. Then she started gasping. He went to stop but somehow he knew she wanted him to keep going. She opened her legs further and pushed up her vulva to his hand. He slipped two fingers into her vagina. Her hand grasped his and he thought she was going to pull his hand away but she just pushed his hand harder against her pubis. She thrust up violently and then relaxed. Jim was not sure later if he had dreamt or actually heard Charlie whisper, "Christ, that was bloody good."

They both woke at the same time, with the dawn. They were naked, as their '*kikois*' had come off. Charlie was not shy. She rolled on to him and said, "I thought I felt something in the bed last night. Luckily it was really gentle, not like I can feel now, or I would have to have woken you to protect me. You are a real bugger. It was bloody lovely even if you were dreaming of another girl. Can we have a pact not to tell anyone?"

"Agreed," replied Jim.

"However, if you keep rubbing my cock with your thigh I will roll you on your back and ravish you." He kissed her.

Charlie rolled on to her back, pulling him on top of her and said breathlessly, "For God sake don't ravish me. I want to remain a virgin until my wedding night. Please kiss me as I feel so bloody horny and I can't blame it on drink. That was a night to remember." After a few passionate kisses she cuddled Jim to her and, in fact, they both dosed off to sleep.

When they had woken up properly, dressed, climbed down and made a cup of tea, Charlie said, "Can we go back to the river? I feel much braver today. I want to swim naked down the river like you did. The thought of it makes me feel really sexy and I hope the shock of it will stop me wanting you to make love to me all the time. If I have a grin like a Cheshire cat when we meet Annie and Ronnie, I want them to know it was because I had a real adrenaline rush, not that you gave me the best orgasm I have ever had."

141

Jim replied. "It will help me not to feel so randy. Come on, let's go. I can pack up the camp while you are buying presents to take home."

Charlie kissed him. "You are too bloody nice to be true. Come on." She started sprinting towards the river. She was true to her word. She did not hesitate but stripped off in front of Jim and jumped in to the river, at the spot where Jim had gone in the previous afternoon. Jim followed her and stood up in the pool, as she came up spluttering and laughing. She hugged him. "It has not made any bloody difference. I still feel randy. I love holding this hard body of yours. You were fast asleep last night and I was willing you to wake up and touch me. You and Africa have not seen the last of me."

It was with that last thought, that they made their way back to the camp and ate an enormous breakfast. Although Charlie volunteered to pack up the camp, Jim insisted she went and had a shower at 'Bushwhackers' and then did some shopping. He had finished, when she came back with an armful of paper bags. She proudly showed him her presents. She became rather shy when she came to the last two bags.

"This is for you to, say thank you for having me. You haven't actually had me. Even although I have really wanted you to! I hope it will remind you of me?" It was a beautiful female Impala gracefully standing with her head cocked on her side. Jim said.

"Thank you it is really beautiful. I will treasure it." Then, even more shyly, Charlie opened the final bag. It was a proud male Impala, with magnificent lyre shaped horns. His front legs were straight and held his body, so that his prepuce was in evidence. She laughed but there were tears running down her cheeks.

"This is a present for me to remind me of a man in Africa, who has really made me glad to be a woman." They kissed. When they broke apart, Charlie said.

"Can I be a real pain and get you to get out my bag for the UK. I want to wrap my Impala in my knickers so, not only will he not be damaged, but I will be excited when I unpack him.

They were a little subdued, compared to the previous day, as they drove the one hundred and twenty five miles to the airport. They still saw quite a lot of plains game. A big herd of Giraffe crossed the road in front of them. They also saw a large herd of Eland.

Jim said, "I bet I will see hundreds of female impala on the way home. They will remind me of you and make me sad."

Charlie said. "Rubbish, you will be fine. It is me who will go bright red in the face when the customs man unwraps my knickers. I must remember not to wear tight jeans or I may get a little damp spot thinking of your hand. You gentle old devil!"

They reached the airport a little before 2.00 pm. Jim went to park but Charlie stopped him. She was crying, "Do you mind if you go before Annie and Ronnie arrive? I am a complete wreck. I don't want them to realise that I have totally fallen for you. I will tell them I have got conjunctivitis from swimming in the Athi River."

Jim stopped, as she had requested, in the drop down lane. He got her bag and all her other things out of the Landrover. She did nothing to hide her tears but flung her arms around him.

"That other girl you were thinking of yesterday is bloody lucky. Take care." Jim had begun to cry. He kissed Charlie, got in the Landrover waved out the window and drove off. He was not sure if he was crying from saying goodbye to Charlie or from the loss of Fiona. He did not see Annie and Ronnie, coming the other way into the airport, waving at him. It took them some time to find Charlie, who had composed herself a little but still had red eyes.

"What did I bloody tell you, Charlie? We have just seen Jim driving out of the airport crying. I knew you would hurt him."

Charlie was angry. "Don't talk bloody rubbish. We both have been swimming in the Athi River. My eyes are still stinging from the muddy water. Jim's were as well. It was really exciting swimming down the cataract. I got thrown all over the place. I have ruined my tan I expect, with bruises." Annie and Ronnie believed her and they went away to have a drink and get some lunch.

Chapter 12

Learning to fly

Tuesday 7th February 1967

Jim had learnt to water-ski as a teenager when his brother, Gordon, had bought a speed boat with two other farmer's sons, when they were in their early twenties. Therefore Jim soon found there was a water ski club in Mombasa, in Tudor Creek. He became a member and often used to go down in the evenings, after work and before sunset for a quick ski. It was very refreshing after a hot day working in the sun. That day had been particularly hot and stressful. He had called into the Veterinary Office after everyone had finished, as he needed to drop off all the blood samples to go in the fridge. As he was driving away, Jacob had run after him with his bundle of post. He did not have a private PO Box and all his mail came to the Veterinary Office. He thanked Jacob and threw the bundle on to the passenger seat of the Landrover, with his swimming things. He took them all down the steps to the ski club. There was a friendly family, from the Kenyan Navy, who were just leaving. Jim was sorry they were going as Joanne, the mother was a pretty blond, with a great figure. She really made Jim's heart race when he watched her ski. Jim had a ski and then signed for a beer which he took to one of the tables. There was no one else at the club, so he sipped his beer and opened his post. Most was pretty boring. A letter from Colin Shaw, his controller, was good news saying London were pleased with his reports from the NFD and would he keep sending them. It stressed that even the smallest detail might be of relevance. Then he saw a sealed air-letter. It was quite bulky. He looked on the back. It was from Charlie. It contained a letter and several photographs. Jim looked at the photos. One was a much posed photo of Charlie and a young guy. On the back she had written. I have taken the plunge. This is one of our engagement photos. The second photo was of

Charlie naked sitting on a bed with the carving of the male Impala. On the back was written. This is a self portrait taken with a camera timer. I was a bit pissed and thinking of you. You can never find a male Impala when you need one!

The letter read:

My darling Jim,

I know I should not write like that, now that I am engaged. However, there is rarely a night that goes by without me thinking of your hand. Anthony proposed to me when he met me at the airport. My excuse was, that I was in a weakened state after our night together followed by an overnight flight. I accepted. He is a nice guy but somehow not quite as exciting as you. However he loves me and I am sure will be a good husband.

I was given hell by Annie and Ronnie at the airport, as they had seen you in the Landrover crying. They said I had hurt you. I told them they were talking rubbish and that it was the muddy water in the Athi River. I think they believed me, so please stick to that story when you see them. I know I am being a complete cow but somehow I will be cross if you get in Ronnie's knickers. Actually I don't know what to think. I am sure there is another girl in your life. Perhaps she has dumped you but somehow I don't think she has. She is a bloody fool if she has let you go, as obviously she means a lot to you.

Thank you so much for being so kind to me and giving me such a good time. I am sure we will meet again. I am tempted to ask you to our wedding but that would be very hurtful or perhaps it wouldn't. At the moment, I think if you did come to our wedding, I would grab hold of you and put your hand up my wedding dress. God, what am I saying? Ronnie is right. I am a real bitch and a sex maniac. I know I should not have written this letter. In fact, I should tell you to totally forget me. In my heart, I don't actually want you to forget me.

SO TAKE CARE.

Lots of love from your Impala.

Jim sat slowly sipping his beer. He tried to analyse his feelings. Certainly he was sad. Was he sad because he had lost Fiona forever? Was he sad because Charlie had gone home? Somehow having a great and exciting job, living in a beautiful place and coming down to water ski were no longer enjoyable. Jim watched the vapour trail of a jet flying high over head. Jim knew that the rugby season would start at Easter but he needed something else to focus his energy on. There and then, Jim decided to learn to fly.

There was a very active aero-club at Mombasa Airport. There were two assistant flying instructors, Ken Gibb and Richard Catling. There was also a fully qualified flying instructor, Tom Dove. Tom tried not to be involved with the instructing as he was also a qualified examiner. The authorities did not like it, if he examined his own pupils for their flying test. The club had several planes but the usual plane, used for pupils was a Piper Colt. This was the simplest plane available and therefore was the cheapest. As one of the requirements for obtaining a Private Pilots License (PPL) was the completion of forty hours of flying, the cheaper the hours were, the better.

A Piper Colt is a high wing canvass airplane, with a nose wheel. It is extremely simple to fly and therefore is an ideal airplane to learn on. Jim went up to Mombasa Airport which was large enough to take big jets. Actually, the majority of the big jets were British Overseas Airways Corporation Comets, which brought in charter passengers from Germany on package holidays destined for Malindi. There were two scheduled flights from Nairobi, which were East African Airways DC3s or Turboprop small passenger airplanes. The aero-club had its own hanger on the opposite side of the Airport from the main terminal. It shared the hanger with two small charter firms, which each had two Cherokee six type planes. These could ferry six passengers around the game parks, mainly Tsavo East and West, and take six passengers up to the island of Lamu, up on the Kenya coast, near to Somalia. Although intrepid travellers like Jim, went to Lamu by road, tourists went by air.

Jim had rung ahead and was met by Ken Gibb. Ken was a jovial slightly overweight man in his early forties. He worked as an engineer for the Ministry of Works, mainly in keeping the supply of fresh water going to the whole of the Coast Province. He was using teaching as a way to build up his flying hours, so that he could take his commercial flying license. Jim took an instant liking to him. He obviously loved flying and also, more importantly, loved the country. He showed Jim the Piper Colt and talked him through the pre-flight checks, which every pilot had to perform to the outside of the aircraft. Jim was amazed at how thorough this had to be. Jim was used to checking the oil, at most once a week in a car, but Ken suggested the oil was checked every flight, unless the plane had just been stopped to allow a passenger to alight. Then Ken took Jim up for his free initial flight. Jim had never been in a light aircraft before. He was fascinated. Ken showed him the simple controls. The Colt had a stick like a steering wheel, not a joystick like most of the tail wheel airplanes. If you pushed it forward, the nose went down. The airspeed increased but you lost height. If you pulled it back, the nose came up. The airspeed decreased but you gained height. It was so simple but, as Ken continued to pull the stick back, the plane lost so much airspeed that it suddenly stalled. The nose dropped alarmingly and the plane seemed to be plunging straight towards the ground. Jim nearly panicked but Ken calmly pushed the nose down and brought the plane back to straight and level. He told Jim to look at the altimeter. Jim could see that they had lost over two hundred feet. Ken said that there were important lessons for Jim to learn. First of all, that you lost a large amount of height quickly when the airplane stalled and that you must never do aerobatics at low altitude, for that reason. Ken told Jim a tragic story of a young guy who flew over his girl friend's house. He started going up and then roaring down on the house. The girl friend and her parents came out on to the lawn to watch. The guy then pulled back on the stick too rapidly. He went into a high speed stall. He did not have enough height to pull out and crashed to his death, in front of his girl friend. Jim thought. *'Perhaps flying is not quite as simple as I thought?'*

Apart from going up and down, the stick controlled the ailerons, the flaps on the wings. If you turned the stick to the left the plane turned to the left. However, Ken explained that there were also rudder pedals which made the plane turn left and right. The pilot had to use both together, so that the plane made a smooth turn. He explained that a rate one turn, was a thirty degree turn, which was relatively mild. When he showed Jim a rate two turn, which was sixty degrees, Jim felt sick.

The Colt, unlike most planes, did not have flaps. Flaps were used, to get the plane into a stable rate of climb or descent. Obviously the throttle was also involved, the faster the revs, the quicker the plane climbed. Jim was surprised that there were no gears, like in a car. The pilot in control, sat in the left hand seat, so he worked the hand throttle with his right hand. Ken, who was an assistant instructor, was in the right hand seat. However, he was still the pilot in charge and so logged the hours, which went towards the total number he would require for his Commercial Pilots License.

The free half hour was soon over. Ken talked to the Air Traffic Controller, in Mombasa Control Tower, on the radio and was given immediate permission to land, as there were no other planes in the area. He lined the plane up on the approach to the enormous runway. Then Ken turned to Jim and said. "You have control." Earlier, Jim had been quite happy when they were high up, well away from the airport, playing with all the controls, turning left and right, going up and down. Now his palms were sweating. Ken talked him down. It was quite bumpy as they came over the palm trees. Jim had throttled back, as Ken had instructed, and their air speed was down to sixty knots. They actually were losing height steadily but to Jim, with no experience, they seemed to be bumping all over the place. They came over the end of the runway at about one hundred feet. They were soon down to thirty feet and Ken told Jim to pull back on the stick, to flatten out their trajectory. Jim was too keen and pulled back so the plane went up slightly but Ken quietly corrected him and the plane then settled onto the tarmac. Most planes have foot brakes but the Colt only had a small hand break. Jim went to put on the brakes but Ken suggested that it was not really necessary, as the runway was so long and they were losing speed rapidly. Ken then got Jim to use his feet, which not only controlled the rudder on the tail but, also the nose wheel to guide the Colt to the aero-club. Jim learnt that, when an aircraft is on the ground, it is said to taxi. Ken showed Jim how to shut down the engine. The plane only had one door. Ken got out first and then Jim slid across the second seat and got out. Jim shook Ken's hand.

"Thank you so much for that. I am hooked. When can I start?"

"First of all you need a medical. There is only one Doctor, registered by the Civil Aviation Authority, in Mombasa. His name is Doctor Robertson. He is a lovely old chap. You should be fine unless you are colour-blind. When you have passed that, you apply for your provisional flying license and your provisional radio telephony operator's license. They are jolly quick at sending them but you can actually start as soon as you have passed the medical. If you are really keen to start, why don't we book your first lesson now?" So

Jim booked several lessons, before work in the mornings. This suited Ken and Jim, as they both worked from offices near to the airport.

Jim booked a flying medical that afternoon. When he arrived at Doctor Robertson's surgery he was met by a very pretty receptionist. She was Doctor Robertson's niece and was just helping out her Uncle until she went back to the UK in two days time. She told Jim to get a urine sample, in a bottle which she gave him. She noticed Jim's hesitation. "There is a basin just behind the screen here." Jim went behind the screen but did not need a wee and was too embarrassed to do one. The girl realised his problem and laughed as she came around the screen. "Shall I turn the tap on in the basin, for you?" Then she started to whistle. Jim immediately started to wee. The girl said. "That always seems to work." Jim was blushing as he handed her the bottle. "I hope you pass. You can go through to Uncle now. I will test the sample and come through with the result."

Doctor Robertson was, indeed, a very kind man. He went through the examination thoroughly but chatted away to Jim about working as a vet. His niece popped her head around the door to say Jim's urine was fine. She added, that she hoped Jim had passed the rest of the medical. She teased him by saying. "Most of the pilots who come in are very arrogant but you are a little bit shy. I hope every time you hear a whistle, you won't wet yourself?"

"That's quite enough, Morag. You will terrify the lad out of his wits," said Doctor Robertson. He turned to Jim and said. "She is only here for one more night. I don't know what to do with her?"

"Well, I could take her down to the water ski club and see if I can drown her for you," said Jim helpfully.

"Wow. Could you?" said Morag. "I would love to have a go at water skiing. I can ski on snow."

"That is a help. Perhaps I won't have to drown you after all!" replied Jim.

"Can I go with him now, Uncle?"

"Of course you can. I am grateful for all your help here in the surgery," said her Uncle. Turning to Jim, he said. "You have passed with flying colors. Good luck in your career."

Morag grabbed her bag and followed Jim to his Landrover. "I am sorry about teasing you. Thank you so much for taking me. Aunt and Uncle are rather staid. It will be good to have some fun. I have got my bikini in my bag, as I go to the Sports club at lunch time to sunbathe."

Jim said. "We will go via my house, to pick up my swimming things. I will also find a pair of old shorts, for you to wear over your bikini. I don't want you getting a salt water enema."

Morag was a real laugh. She had a beautiful figure but had quite a job to get into Jim's shorts as they were tight on him normally and she had, what she called, good child-bearing hips. Jim also gave her a shirt as he said, "Much as I would enjoy it, I don't want you falling out of your bikini top." Morag gave him a peck on the cheek and said. "You are most thoughtful. If you are really good, you might be allowed to see my tan marks."

"That's a deal, would you like some supper?"

"That would be lovely, provided I don't swallow too much salt water."

Jim had a word with Katana and then he and Morag went to the water ski club. There was no one else down at the club, only the boat driver who was nicked named 'Sea Lion'. He was happy to drive the boat, so Jim got Morag into a life vest. This had clips at the front. He helped her do them up. She said with a laugh. "I will have to watch you. I don't think you are quite as shy as I thought you were." Jim went red.

Jim got her a pair of skis and helped her get them on, in waist deep water, by adjusting the rubber bindings. He got her facing out, into the deep water of Tudor Creek. "Now," said Jim. "I want you to lean back into my arms, with your legs bent and your arms straight."

"Not so shy, are we now! I will try," replied Morag. "I suppose if you really were trying to grope me, you would not have made me put on these ridiculous old clothes."

Morag managed very well and leant back against Jim, as he stood up to his chest in the water. "OK," shouted Jim. "Let's have the rope Sea Lion. When I shout, "Hit it," give it all you have got." "*Ndio Bwana*," (Yes Sir) was his reply.

To Morag, Jim said, "Now keep those legs bent and your arms straight. Are you comfy?"

"Yes, but I am nervous with you behind me and threatening to give it all you have got." Jim knew she was teasing. Sea Lion slowly took up the slack of the rope and Jim held Morag's thighs.

"Hit it," shouted Jim. Morag was away. She did very well but fell as Sea Lion turned, to avoid going straight across the creek. He came back and picked Jim up. When they got near to Morag, Jim dived in off the boat. "Well done. You went for over two hundred yards." Jim retrieved her skis and, going under water, got them back on her feet. Then he got her steady in the water, as Sea Lion went round in a large circle to bring them the rope. Morag said, "Thanks for the shorts and shirt. I would have been in a right bloody muddle without them. What did I do wrong?"

"You just had your weight wrong on the turn. It is slightly different from snow skiing. Here is the rope-have another go?" The next pull Morag bent her arms and went head first into the water. She came up spluttering. "Without your shirt, I would have lost my bikini top for sure. I am determined to do it this time. I knew, as soon as I bent my arms, I was going to fall." In fact, she did exactly the same thing the next time. However on the fourth attempt she really got it and was soon crossing the wake, as Sea Lion went up and down the creek. Eventually Morag steered into the shore, threw away the rope and glided into the shallow water. Sea Lion went to pick Jim up. When he got near to the shore, Morag splashed up to him, wrapped her arms around him and kissed him. "That was marvellous. Thank you so much. Now you must have a go. Can I sit in the boat and watch you?

"Of course you can. I will help you get in." It was fun giving her bottom a big shove, to get her over the gunwale. As Sea Lion took the boat out again Jim stood on his right leg in the shallow water with a mono-ski on his left foot. He held about three small coils of the rope. As the rope became taut, he threw the coils in the water and shouted. "Hit it."

Sea Lion gave the boat full power and Jim just floated off the beach, onto the water. Morag stood up in the boat and clapped. Jim did not ski for more than five minutes but he really worked hard, doing very tight hard slalom turns. These almost made the boat stop in the water. He was really breathing hard as he threw the rope away and drifted into the beach below the club house. He kicked off his ski and came to help Sea Lion with the boat and give Morag a hand to get into the water. She did not need a hand but jumped into his arms and nearly knocked him over. "That was really something. You are a marvellous skier." They helped Sea Lion bring the boat up the beach as it seemed unlikely that anyone would come down now for a ski, as it was quarter past six and would be dark in half an hour. They both washed off under the fresh water shower. Then, after Jim had signed the chit to put the skiing time on his bill, they said good-bye to Sea Lion and made their way up the steps back to the Landrover.

"Won't we make a mess in the Landrover, with our wet clothes? I can easily change under a towel," said Morag.

"Don't worry, the seats will dry in no time. However I would enjoy watching you change." Morag gave him a playful push. "Come on my shy, boy let's go to your house and have some supper. I have not swallowed much water and I am starving. Katana had anticipated their return just before dark. He said supper would be ready in quarter of an hour. Jim showed Morag one of the showers and he went in the other one. When he came out, he called to her. "I am sorry, I haven't got a hair drier but there are plenty of towels in the cupboard next to the basin. You can put one on your shoulders and let your lovely long red hair, dry in the air." When she came out, she had done what he suggested. She came to him and kissed him. "That is for being so complimentary about my hair. I don't really like it. I would really like to wear pink or red clothes but I look awful and so have to wear green or blue. I lied to you about my tan marks. I am hardly tanned at all, as I have to be so careful in the sun. It is infuriating."

"I bet the white bits are just as exciting," said Jim gallantly. He received another kiss.

Katana had made a cottage pie, which he served with carrots and cabbage. They both set about it with gusto. They shared a beer so that they could have a second cold one, rather than let the beer get warm. They had mangoes and ice cream and then had a third beer on the upstairs veranda, overlooking the moonlit creek. They thanked Katana, when he brought their coffee and said, "Goodnight."

Morag got up and came and sat on Jim's knee. She was wearing the white blouse and thigh length skirt she had worn in the surgery.

She said, "I think my first assessment of you was right. I think you are a bit shy. It is a bloody good thing, as this is a very romantic setting and heaven knows what might happen. I am going to rest my head on your shoulder and get you to put your arm around me but there it must stay. I hardly know you and I am off to the UK tomorrow night. You are a great guy and I don't really trust myself." She sighed and let her head fall. She gave his neck a little kiss and sighed again. They stayed like that for several minutes. Her hair was now dry and Jim stroked it.

"Come on you lovely girl, let me take you back to your Uncle and Aunt. I won't forget this evening." She kissed him on the neck again and got up, offering him her hand. He led her to the balustrade. They kissed. As they broke apart Morag said.

"I won't forget this evening. Thank you for being so kind."

It was only nine 'o'clock when they reached Doctor Robertson's house. They went in and Morag introduced Jim to her Aunt. Her Uncle asked how she had got on water skiing. Morag said it was great fun and she was really happy that she had managed to do it. Her Aunt seemed pleased that she had enjoyed her last evening.

She said, "Thank you Jim, for giving her some fun. We have loved having Morag to stay, as we have not seen her since she was a little girl but we are rather dull company." She turned to Morag. "You look radiant, dear."

Jim chipped in. "I have really enjoyed looking after Morag. She thinks I am just flattering her but I do love her auburn hair." He stroked it. "Mine used to be that color," said her Aunt, wistfully. Morag hugged Jim.

"You know, I said in the surgery to Uncle, that I thought he was shy. I think he is but he is ever so gallant. I think it is rather lucky I am leaving tomorrow as I think I might fall for him. Come on Jim, I will come with you to the door." Jim said goodbye to Doctor and Mrs. Robertson and went with Morag to the door. When they were out of sight, Morag kissed him passionately. Jim undid the buttons of her blouse and kissed her breasts. Morag murmured.

"That's bloody lovely. It is lucky I did not kiss you like that at your home or, my shy Jim, I think there would have been no controlling you. You must be off. Good luck and take lots of care flying. Jim drove home with a heavy heart. He thought how lucky he was to be learning to fly, or he would be day dreaming about Morag and Charlie all the time.

Initially the first three, one hour, flights went well. Jim readily got the hang of keeping the plane straight and level. He mastered climbing and descending using the power or using his height. Ken said his turning was a bit sloppy, as he could not seem to coordinate his rudders i.e. his feet, with his ailerons i.e. his hands but his turns did improve. He did not seem to master side slipping i.e. the method of keeping the plane straight when flying in a cross wind. Ken was not unduly worried, as he said that would come.

In the fourth lesson they did stalls, which Jim did not find difficult. Jim found it was a natural instinct to push the stick forward and feed in more power. The next lesson was correcting a spin. Jim found this quite terrifying. He became totally disorientated, so that when he was meant to apply opposite rudder, he sometimes put on more rudder and the spin got quicker. Ken tried to encourage him. Ken explained that many older high winged planes, like the Colt, would come out of the spin without intervention by the pilot. They climbed to six thousand feet. Ken took control. He brought the nose up into a stall and applied right hand rudder, just as the plane stalled. He then totally let go of the controls. The plane spun twice and then went into a very steep dive. The dive made it naturally increase air speed and so the spin and stall corrected themselves. This certainly gave Jim more confidence. Ken explained that Jim would not be expected to get out of a spin, in his flying test, but Ken would have to certify that he had managed it under supervision. After that, they left stalls and spins and concentrated on the nitty gritty, which was landing and taking off. The latter Jim mastered very quickly. The Colt just needed full power and then there was a natural feel to gently pulling back on the stick and becoming airborne. Ken explained that it was slightly more complicated with a plane that had flaps, but he did not think Jim would have a problem.

Landing was not so easy. Sometimes it went well and Jim managed to land, without Ken doing anything, but often Ken had to intervene. Having had two lessons, of an hour each, devoted to so-called circuit and bumps and with little improvement, Ken very wisely used the next lesson for Jim to get the hang of doing forced landings. Ken would suddenly cut the engine. Jim had to get the plane stable. Then he had to select a safe place to land, like the beach, a large grass field or even a road. Then he had to position himself so that he could land where he had selected. At the last minute Ken would say, "OK climb away" and Jim would open the throttle and climb to safety. Because Jim enjoyed this exercise, he was good at it. If only he could master landing the blasted thing. Ken was quite philosophical about it and just said, don't worry it will come. Jim did worry, as he had now done ten hours. He had spoken to another trainee pilot, who Jim thought of as rather arrogant. He was German. This chap told Jim that, in the German Air Force, if you had not gone solo in six hours, they would never bother to train you as a pilot. He also said that, if you were just a private trainee and you had not gone solo in twelve hours, they suggested that you gave up. He then, rather smugly, told Jim that he had gone solo in four hours. Jim was depressed as in the next lesson, even though he had done quite well at several landings, Ken had not let him go solo.

Jim's next lesson had to be cancelled at the last minute, as it started to rain quite heavily. Ken and Jim went for a coffee in the main terminal. Ken could not wait to tell Jim the gossip. Apparently, this arrogant German worked for a tour operator. He had passed his flying test and only had two hours to go before he would have completed the statutory forty hours flying time. He had been sitting in the right hand seat, in a Cherokee six, with a professional pilot actually flying the plane in the left hand seat. There were four tourists behind. He had suddenly had an epileptic fit. Luckily, they were at a decent altitude and so the pilot had managed to keep the airplane airborne, while two of the passengers held him down until he passed out. No one had been hurt, except for a few bruises but there would have to be an investigation. Ken reckoned that the chap had tried to learn to fly in Germany and had a fit before. He had left it for some years and not had another fit, so he had started to learn to fly again. This would account for how very quickly he had mastered flying. Obviously it was illegal, as pilots had to declare that not only had they never had an epileptic fit but also no one in their immediate family had suffered from the condition.

It was a sad story but it cheered Jim up, because he realised that he was just a slow learner and not absolutely hopeless.

The next lesson, in two days time, was going well with Jim doing four landings totally on his own and Ken not doing or saying anything. After they landed for the fifth time, Ken got Jim to stop the plane in the middle of the enormous runway. Ken got out and shouted above the engine noise,

"Do a couple of circuits and bumps on your own. Then taxi to the aero club. There are no commercial flights due. Good luck." He shut the door and walked away, making sure he was well clear of the propeller. Jim was both nervous and elated. He managed to do two perfectly presentable landings before taxing to the hanger and cutting the engine. He was seriously sweating but felt like punching the air.

After that the flying went well. Ken met Jim at the hanger and he would go off and do a whole hour of circuits. From then on he could fly on his own, provided Ken knew he was going. Ken did not have to be at the airport. Jim loved it. He had to keep within fifty miles of the control tower but, other than that, he could do what he liked provided he kept in radio contact. Jim found the radio work easy, having had so much experience with the veterinary morning call up. Jim used to fly low along the beach and frighten girls sunbathing. Obviously that was strictly illegal but no one reported him. His excuse would have been that he was practising forced landings.

Ken and Jim then managed to combine trips, to do with their work. Jim had to fly to Mackinnon Road, to blood sample a mob of cattle and Ken had to inspect some government buildings at Malindi. They set off together, for what was to be Jim's first cross country. Jim had to have planned all the navigation, before the trip. He had to file a flight plan, under Ken's supervision, carry out all the radio procedure and do the in-flight navigation. They flew first to Mackinnon road which was pretty straight forward, as there was not only the tarmac road but also the railway. To be logged as his cross country, the trip had to be at least triangular. It did not qualify if it was just a straight, there and back, trip. After they had dealt with the cattle, they set off on the second leg, to Malindi. The wind had got up so they were blown off course. It was not a problem, as they soon could see the sea. All Jim had to do was decide that they had been blown slightly south and then follow the coast line up, until they could see Malindi airport. There was a Government vehicle waiting for them. The driver dropped Jim off at the Blue Marlin Hotel so he could sit by the pool, drink a coke and read his book. Ken went off to do his work.

Jim had a very happy two hours. He thought to himself. *'This is the life!'*

The flight back to Mombasa was really simple, as all they needed to do was follow the coast for sixty miles. Apart from completing forty flying hours, Jim had to do a solo cross-country. He decided to at least get some of the money back, by doing a work related trip. He made the first leg, to go to do some work at Voi. He landed on the ranch belonging to Amanda and Luke Cuddington. Luke had several jobs for

Jim to do, but to help, so that Jim was not too long on the ground, Luke managed to get all the mobs of cattle to crushes near to the airstrip. Jim had to forgo a nice lunch and fly the second leg to Aruba dam. The dam helped navigation, as it was clearly visible from the air. Once again, the final flight of the triangle was easy, back to Mombasa. Jim resisted the impulse to fly low to see some game. As it was, there was a massive herd of elephants at Aruba.

Jim had not done much book work, to study for the written part of his PPL, so he did not do anything social on the weekend before the exam on the Tuesday. He spent the whole weekend revising. It was like being back at Vet School. If fact he found the exam a doddle, as it was multiple choice and very straight forward. It cheered Jim up, as he felt his brain had not totally died, having left University. The flying test was quite another thing altogether. Tom Dove had a reputation of being very strict. Jim had never flown with him. Jim had received one lesson with the other assistant flying instructor, Richard Catling. Although Richard had been helpful and a good instructor, Jim had stayed loyal to Ken who, he knew was keen to accrue as many flying hours as he could. However, Ken suggested Jim had one more lesson with Richard, to see if he could correct any faults that Ken might have missed.

Jim's flying exam was scheduled for 4.30 pm on Thursday. He met Tom Dove in the club house. They walked out to the plane together and Tom watched him check the plane over. Jim was very nervous. In fact Tom was very kind. He turned to Jim and said. "Don't be nervous, just fly as you normally do. I am sure you will be fine." Jim relaxed a little and in fact was fine. After a gruelling hour, they taxied back to the club house. Jim checked the magnetos and cut the engine. Tom said. "I thought your forced landing was very good. You were very positive. Your rate two turn was a little sloppy but I suppose you are not training to be a fighter pilot. You are a strange flier, in that when you are flying straight and level you always have your left wing slightly down like an old pheasant that has been shot." Tom got out of the airplane and Jim was sure he had failed. As they were walking across to the club house Tom was asking Jim about worming his dog. Ken greeted them in the club house. "Did he pass?" "Oh yes, he is safe enough. He walks with a shambling gate and he flies like it!"

Jim had got his PPL. He bought drinks all round.

Chapter 13

Rinderpest strikes

Tuesday 11th April 1967

Veterinary surgeons first got together, to form themselves into a profession in the UK over a hundred years ago, as a result of the devastating effects of 'Cattle Plague'. This disease, which was highly contagious and almost 100% lethal, spread through the town dairies, interrupting the supply of milk. It also affected beef herds in the countryside. Nowadays this disease is called by the German name of 'Rinderpest'. It was eventually eradicated from the UK in 1866. Slowly, it has been eradicated from Europe and then, from most of the rest of the world. It is a virus disease which is spread from cow to cow. There is no treatment. Eradication has been helped in Africa by the use of a marvellous vaccine which was developed in Kenya. All cattle in Kenya have to be vaccinated twice, by law, once when they are calves and again when they are between one and two years of age. They then receive a Z brand on their humps or, with European cattle, on their flanks. Jim had taken part in several 'Rinderpest' vaccination campaigns in the Coast and North Eastern Province. All the LMD cattle were vaccinated.

Jim was summons, by Silas, to the PVO one morning. Silas warned Jim that the PVO was in a foul mood. Jim knocked on the inner office door and walked into the air-conditioned office. As always, the PVO just ignored him. Eventually, the PVO looked up and spat out. "I have just had the Director of Veterinary Services (DVS) on the phone. There is a possible outbreak of 'Rinderpest' in your area." The way he spoke, it made it sound as if it was totally Jim's fault. Then he started ranting on about staff letting the vaccine get hot. Jim said nothing but just waited for him to calm down and come to the point. Eventually, Jim realised that the report had come via the Garissa Veterinary Office and the outbreak was centered in

Habaswein. Jim knew the village, as he had been through it on the way to Wajir, to blood test the camels. He remembered it had a bore hole supplying the water to the village. He imagined by now, after the rains, there would be plenty of grass. "Shall I go up there tomorrow and confirm the diagnosis?" asked Jim.

"How will you bloody well do that? You have never seen the disease."

"We spent plenty of time on viruses, at the School of Tropical Medicine in Edinburgh, so I think I am fully briefed. I will report in three days." Jim turned on his heal and walked out. He suddenly felt very sad as he thought about Fi. He felt tears come to his eyes. Silas saw he was upset and thought he was upset with the PVO. Silas said, "Why not take Karissa the driver? It would be much less tiring for you?"

Jim rallied, "That is an excellent idea. Could you sort that out? He will need bridge passes, petrol LPOs and a letter from the PVO, endorsed by the PC, authorizing our journey. Will Karissa mind camping?"

"I don't think he will be very keen but I am sure he will find places to stay. He is a graded driver, so he gets a subsistence allowance. I will sort everything out and get him to pick you up from your house tomorrow, at 6.30 am."

"Thank you so much, Silas. You are a star."

Luckily Jim was playing rugby that Monday night and would, hopefully, be back in time for the Saturday game. Jim always enjoyed the games, which he much preferred to the training sessions. He was careful to have only a couple of beers, after the obligatory two pints of lemonade and lime after the game. He needed to help Katana pack up his safari stuff tonight so he would be ready, having had his breakfast, at 6.30 am the following morning. Jim also packed up his normal post mortem kit, before he left the Vet Office. If it was Rinderpest, he would be able to make a clinical diagnosis but virology samples would be a useful back up, to calm down the PVO and, ultimately, the DVS. If it was not Rinderpest, Jim would need lots of samples, to find out exactly what was killing these cattle.

It was a hard rugby game, against another Royal Navy Frigate team. They had been in port for three weeks and so had managed to get match fit. All the crew was back from trips upcountry, as they were due to sail on Tuesday morning. Jim scored two tries but they still just lost the game. The rainy season had only just begun, and so the ground was hard and the grass was rather sparse. Jim could have done without the bruises but he was ready for Karissa in the morning. Karissa was a good and fast driver. He had good control on the '*murram*', which started just North of Kilifi ferry. They filled up both in Malindi and at Garsen. Jim bought himself and Karissa a coke at both places, as it was a hot, dusty journey. They managed to get to Galole before dusk, which was good news as Karissa was friendly with the DC's driver and the DC, Leonard Baloala, was a particular friend of Jim's. Leonard loved entertaining, so Jim had to be careful to limit the number of beers he drank. Leonard insisted on giving Jim a good breakfast so they were not on the road until 7.30 am. However, they made good time to Mado Gashi. Luckily, they had filled every available jerry-can with petrol in Garissa. As normal, the pump was empty in Mado Gashi. To both Jim's and Karissa's annoyance there were no cold cokes. They set off for Habaswein. After thirty miles, when they thought they were only two miles from Habaswein, the sky was nearly black with circling vultures ahead of them. Jim thought, ' *this looks ominous.* ' They arrived at a large '*boma*' (an area for keeping cattle enclosed), next to the road. Nearby was parked a GK Landrover. They stopped next to it and Karissa sounded the horn. A driver, who had been sitting in the shade of an acacia tree, got up and walked over. He confirmed that Abdul Mohamed, the LO from Garissa was just inside the '*boma*', with the dead cattle. Jim suggested the two drivers stayed in the shade. He walked through to find Abdul. He was holding a small meeting with five Somali traders. He shook hands with Jim and said how pleased he was to see him. The traders looked very angry. Apparently, this mob of 480 steers had come in from Somalia, North of El Wak. They had obtained a movement permit from the LO Mandera, to move them South to El Wak and then on to the northern edge of Garissa District. They had then moved them illegally to Habaswein. Abdul confirmed that he had not issued a 'movement permit'. Jim guessed that Abdul, like him thought they had started to die and the traders had thought it was lack of grazing and so had pushed on to Habaswein. Jim asked to see the original 'movement permit'. This, although badly crumpled, was produced. Jim suspected it was a forgery but he said nothing. There was nothing on the permit indicating vaccination against Rinderpest and Foot and Mouth Disease, which was mandatory. Jim also knew that they had not been tested for CBPP, which was also required before movement. Jim asked how many cattle had died. The traders growled that over 300 were dead and all the rest looked sick. With a heavy heart, Jim asked to be shown animals that had recently died. They all had deep erosions on the lips and around the eyes. They all showed evidence of diarrhea, as did the live animals which were listlessly walking around. Jim went back to the Landrover to get his Postmortem box. This certainly looked like Rinderpest. Very few diseases caused such a high mortality. Foot and Mouth disease, was not a serious disease in African Zebu cattle. Where these animals had come from and where they were now, was hot dry country. There was no tick born disease. Equally there were no Tsetse flies and therefore no Trypanosomiasis. Jim got the traders to keep the vultures away, as he opened up one of the newly dead cattle. Although he looked at all the organs, the most interesting was the rectum. This showed the tell-tale stripped zebra markings of Rinderpest. Jim took some samples, as the disease would have to be reported internationally. He was relieved to see that the animals had not been vaccinated against Rinderpest, as they did not have the statuary Z brand on their humps.

Jim got Abdul to call the owners all to a *'barazza'* (a meeting). He then had to lay down the law. None of the cattle were to be moved. They were all likely to die. He thought it would be kindest if the remaining animals were shot, but that he could not actually enforce this immediately. He would require confirmation from Nairobi.

Jim was surprised that the traders, after a brief discussion, agreed for the slaughter. They obviously were familiar with the disease and knew that he was right. They also knew that they would not be popular with the local people and so, the sooner they went back to Somalia, the better. Jim's job was done. He could return to Mombasa and report to the PVO and, of course, to his controller in Nairobi, but he sort of thought he had only done half a job. Was the 'movement permit' a fake? The only way to find out, was to go to Mandera and see if there was an original. He was reluctant to return home, only to have to drive all the way back up north again. He made a decision. He and Karissa would proceed on to Mandera. He thanked Abdul for all his help and stressed that this outbreak was not of his making and that he would get an excellent report from Jim. Jim walked over to the two drivers sitting under the tree. He apologised to Karissa, but said sadly their '*safari*' had not finished. Did Karissa mind going on to Mandera? Karissa laughed and said he would be delighted, as he would earn more subsistence allowance. They said their goodbyes and started on their journey.

As it was late in the day, Jim decided that they would see if they could reach Wajir. There was little traffic on the road and the surface was good, so they drew into the Veterinary Compound in Wajir well before dark. Zebedee, the Veterinary Scout, was delighted to see them. He said he would help Jim set up his camp but first he would run to his home and make sure there was supper for Jim and Karissa. He soon returned with some of his younger brothers and sisters. They quickly set up camp. Karissa said he would sleep in the back of the LWB Landrover, as he had a bed roll. Jim gave some money to the two youngest children, who he sent out to get enough cokes for all of them. The younger children were delighted. Jim sent them all ahead to Zebedee's home, saying he would stay and write his report and come on as soon as the '*askari*' (guard) arrived.

The meal reminded Jim of coming home for supper, when he got a chance, when he was doing a locum. It was good fun and he really relaxed. He knew he had a big day in the morning, as they would be travelling in new territory for him. He questioned Zebedee's father about the journey and any possible dangers. He was told that everything was pretty quiet, as far as was known, over the Somali border. He would be travelling very near to Ethiopia, just below the escarpment, for the final part of the journey. Security issues were unknown but no news was, hopefully, good news.

They made a good start in the morning. Karissa was not only a good driver but he was well organised. The going was good, as they were travelling on a shale road across the Gora Dudi Plain. After less than an hour, they had covered the 36 miles to a tiny village called Tarbaj. There was no garage or even a shop but it was important because they needed to fork right, to take the most direct route to El Wak. The road, which appeared to be larger, headed due north through Takabba to the Ethiopian border. Jim was tempted to go that way, as it was safer, because it was further away from the Somali border. There was an airstrip at Takabba if there were problems but equally there was an airstrip at El Wak. Jim's two problems were that he did not have authorisation to go further north than Wajir, and the nearer he was to Somalia the more dangerous the journey was, on account of the '*shifta*'. However, Jim had learnt that this area was not as dangerous as the more southern areas, between Garissa and the coast north of the Tana River.

Jim knew that this whole trip was well worthwhile, from a disease control perspective, as it was vital to find out how the infected cattle had got so far into Kenya. It was also important for the British Government to know, whether there was any Italian oil exploration in the area.

The direct road became rougher, which cut down their speed, but was easily passable in the Landrover. Apparently there were two deep bore holes on their route. They never saw them but they were not concerned as they had plenty of water. They had covered fifty or so of the 85 miles to El Wak, when they got problems. The road just ended in a sea of sand, which was the Laga Katulla. Karissa stopped, on the ridge above the lugger, and they surveyed the problem. They were in a LWB Landrover with good tyres and, in theory, if they kept going in the soft sand they would get across OK. Jim asked Karissa to wait with the Landrover and he set off to walk across. The wind had blown the sand across a concrete road which was not visible from a vehicle but Jim could see it as he walked. In the middle, there was a massive hole in the concrete, where there had been a six foot culvert. This had been smashed by a heavy lorry. Karissa could easily have driven into this hole, as he would have been trying to go quickly to avoid getting stuck in the sand. Jim made marks in the sand, so he could guide Karissa. After the hole, the concrete track was straight forward.

Jim came back, after about half an hour, to explain to Karissa the problem. Karissa had not been concerned, as Jim had never disappeared out of sight. It was decided that Jim would run ahead of the Landrover on the concrete road and Karissa would then follow Jim off the concrete into the soft sand, avoiding the hole and giving the Landrover full power, in low range, to keep the speed going. That was the plan. It was time to go. Karissa gave Jim a twenty yard start. Jim could hear the Landrover behind him. He kept running and

Karissa kept a steady distance behind him. Jim came to the hole and turned, ten yards before it, to the left into the deep sand. Running in the deep sand was very hard work. Jim was really labouring; he heard the Landrover roaring behind him, as Karissa fed in more power and went up a gear. He tried to keep going. The concrete road was still seventy yards ahead. He had to keep going until he knew Karissa could see it. He dared not look round. He heard the Landrover laboring. It was sinking. He heard Karissa change down to the lowest possible gear. The noise of the Landrover did not diminish. It was not stuck yet. Jim was really tiring. The noise was getting louder. Karissa must not stop. He was catching Jim. At what seemed the last minute, Jim threw himself to the left and fell face down into the sand. Karissa kept grinding on passed him. Jim got to his knees and stood up, so he could turn and see the Landrover. Karissa had obviously seen the concrete road, as he had veered off to the right. Even thirty yards away, Jim could hear the note of the engine change, as Karissa changed up. The Landrover had made it but Karissa did not stop and wisely kept going up the far edge of the lugger. Jim trudged over the sand but he was elated that they had made it. Karissa came down to meet him. He offered Jim a hand but Jim was recovering quickly and so they walked up the ridge together. They were both smiling. Karissa laughed as Jim brushed off the majority of the sand. "Well done, Dr. Jim. You won the race!"

They drove the remaining miles into El Wak in high spirits. Two miles out, they could see the Arab made fort. This was their target, as that was where the police and the DC were based. There was no Veterinary presence. Obviously, Government visitors were rare and came in by air. The police and the DC were pleased to see them. The lack of a permit or a letter of authority did not seem to be a problem. They were really interested in the state of the road. They did remember the cattle coming through. They had checked the Movement Permit but as it was signed by the LO from Mandera, they did not see a problem. Jim assured them that they had done just the right thing. He would journey on to Mandera and find out what had gone wrong. The police regularly patrolled the road, which ran parallel to the Somali border. They reported it was in good condition for the 95 miles to Rhamu, on the Ethiopia border. It went due North so, although El Wak was only five miles from Somalia, the distance

164

between the road and the Somali border increased on their right hand side. There was no likelihood of Jim veering off and crossing the border by mistake. They said they had no first-hand knowledge of the rest of the road east but the Police from Mandera reported that it was passable, but rough. They thought Jim was in no danger from bandits from Somalia, north of the Dawa River but, if he had been driving a mob of cattle, then he would need a large number of guards as stock theft was a real problem. They gave Jim and Karissa a cup of tea and a very welcome coke. Sadly there was no petrol available but Jim knew he had sufficient. Karissa checked all the cans and all the water cans. They set off soon after noon.

The ninety five miles took them two and a half hours as the road was good. After half the distance they could see the low Somali escarpment, as a grey smudge in the distance. Slowly it got bigger, as they travelled across the Awara plain, with first the Danisa Hills and then the Raiya Hills on their right.

The tiny village of Rhamu was set three miles short of the Somali border, separated by the Dawa River, which was the actual border, by the airstrip. There was no fuel but there was a small shop. They had a rather warm coke each. Jim would rather have brewed a cup of tea but he knew they should push on. They still had nearly fifty miles to go, to get to Mandera. Jim knew they were no villages before Mandera but he also knew that he would have the Dawa River always on his left. Both Jim and Karissa were very relieved when they reached the town of Mandera. There was a 'duka', which was also the petrol station. The fuel was very expensive but Jim was not taking any chances, so he got Karissa to fill up every can. He had to pay cash, as Karissa had not known about this journey and so had not obtained an LPO from Silas. Jim was not concerned, as he knew the Kenyan Government would reimburse him. They then went to the Veterinary Office. The 'askari' said that the office was closed but would be open at 8.00am the next morning. He said Jim was very welcome to camp in the Veterinary compound, under a big tree. He said he thought if Karissa went to the staff lines and knocked on the door of the second house, the driver who lived there would be likely to let Karissa stay.

As it was not quite dark, Jim got Karissa to park the Landrover in the vine covered car-port, next to the Veterinary Office. Before he unpacked, Jim, having got directions from the '*askari*', decided to walk first to the DC's house to report his unannounced visit and then to the LO's house, to say he would look forward to seeing him in the morning. The DC was very welcoming and offered Jim a cup of tea. He told Jim that the border situation was really quiet at the moment. He also said that he had not heard of any oil exploration in the district. When Jim told him about the arrival of Rinderpest from Somalia, the DC became very grave. He said, naturally the LO was under the control of the Veterinary Department but that he had noticed that the whole Veterinary Office was very slack and, in fact, if Jim had not arrived, he was going to bring the problem up when he flew to Nairobi, at the end of the month, for a DC's meeting. He said he would rather not comment any further but let Jim see for himself. Jim thanked the DC for being so hospitable and said he would make a report through the correct veterinary channels. The DC seemed relieved that something was going to be done and that he did not have to get involved. Jim thought he would leave his meeting with the LO until the morning.

As Jim walked back to the Veterinary compound he pondered that he was not going to have an easy morning. He was rather glad he could just have a simple supper and get an early night. In fact he was really tired. He was so grateful to Silas for sending him with a driver. Jim was up soon after dawn. He packed up and had some breakfast. He then walked around to the front of the office and started talking to the clerk and the veterinary scout. They showed him the old movement permit books. The main entries were either, local movements of small numbers of cattle for slaughter, or large numbers of sheep and goats to go by lorry down to Garissa. They all seemed in order and had been duly signed by the LO. It was only when they showed him the current book, that Jim found the copy of the movement permit he had seen at Habaswein. Jim wondered whether the LO had been bribed or was just incompetent. He looked at his watch. It was 8.40pm. The chap was seriously late. Outside, Jim saw there were quite a number of Somalis milling around in front of the office and his Landrover. He was not concerned, as Karissa was there happily chatting to his fellow driver. He went back into the office and was given a cup of tea. He studied the map on the wall. It had obviously been a major cock up but, hopefully, if they

166

could get vaccination teams up here quickly, there was no need for alarm. It was just unfortunate that Kenya could not claim that it was free of Rinderpest with the OIE.

Suddenly there was a crash and the bumper of a Landrover came through the wall of the office. There was quite a bit of dust but it was remarkable that it only knocked out three breeze blocks. There was a large amount of noisy chatter, so Jim when outside to investigate. It appeared that the LO had arrived and, knowing he was rather late, had been going too fast. He had gone to turn into his normal parking slot in the car-port. Jim's Landrover had been hidden from view by all the visitors to the veterinary compound. The visitors had all scattered on the approach of the speeding Landrover. Only at the last minute did the LO see the visiting Landrover. He had tried to brake and then, to avoid hitting the other vehicle, he had driven into the wall of the office. Jim wanted to laugh but he held himself in check and walked to the window of the Landrover. To help stop himself smiling, he said in a very pompous voice, "Good morning, a little late I see." The LO, who still reeked of drink, was too shocked to reply. Jim turned and walked back into the office. You could have heard a pin drop. Jim had a few moments to collect his thoughts and decide how to proceed. He decided that there was nothing to be gained by having a row. When the LO came in Jim just pointed to the movement permit, which had authorized the infected cattle to move and asked. "Did you sign this?" The LO replied. "Yes."

"Did you vaccinate or examine these cattle."

"No, I forgot."

"These animals have brought Rinderpest into Kenya from Somalia. I suggest you write a report, through the DC, to the DVS immediately. The DC will take it with him when he flies to Nairobi at the end of the month. You had better file an accident report about this!" Jim pointed to the bumper of the Landrover. "I will be on my way, as soon as I have said goodbye to the DC. I have roughly five hundred miles to journey, before I reach Garissa and then I will drive to Mombasa and report to the PVO. Goodbye and Good luck. I think you are going to need it."

After briefing the DC, Jim and Karissa set off for the return journey. It was actually further than five hundred miles, as they avoided Laga Katulla by turning right ten miles south of Rhamu.

They then had a journey of seventy miles, below the Ethiopian escarpment, to the airstrip at Banissa, where they turned due south to Takabba. There was no fuel at Banissa but there was some at Takabba, at the '*duka*' near the airstrip. The fuel was horrendously expensive but, although Karissa and Jim thought they would have enough to get to Wajir, they did not want to take any chances. They camped at the bore-hole at Didmutu. There was a Kenyan Army detachment camped there. They were happy to let Jim and Karissa camp with them. There was plenty of water for washing and the army captain gave them each a beer. He told them, they rarely got visitors except Somalis, on foot with their camels and cattle. However, he had good news that the road south was in good condition and that there had been no reports of any '*shifta*' (bandits). Jim and Karissa were soon asleep, as they had decided to try to get going by 5.00am. Although it would be dark, it would be cooler and they now knew that the road was safe.

The captain also told them that he thought it was safer to follow the road they had come up on, south of Wajir. He said there were reports of mines, on the road across the Sabena desert, north of Dadaab. This was confirmed by the '*duka*' owner, when they filled up with fuel in Wajir. Jim called in briefly at Zebedee's home, just to say hello. He and Karissa were keen to get back to Mombasa, so they did not stop for any food. Zebedee's mother insisted they take a '*kikapu*' (basket) of food and drink, both cokes and fantas, for the journey. They were very grateful, as it took them two whole days to get to Mombasa. They arrived at about 9.00pm. Karissa dropped Jim and his baggage, of at his house and then returned to the Veterinary Office. Katana helped Jim unpack and offered to make him some supper. Jim declined and just had a large mug of tea, some bananas and one very cold Tusker, before showering and crashing into bed.

Jim was still asleep, when Katana brought his tea in the morning. He showered and ate breakfast quickly, so that he could get to the Veterinary Office in good time to write his report, not only to the PVO but a separate report to Colin Shaw. While he was on the radio to the veterinary outposts, he got the clerk to type up the report to the PVO, so that it would be on his desk when he arrived. Obviously, the report to Colin Shaw had to be written long hand and sent to the special PO Box in Nairobi. He was sorting out the petrol reimbursement, when he was summoned to the PVO. Silas, in the outer office, said he was glad to see Jim safe and sound after such a long journey. Obviously he had heard about it from Karissa. As usual the PVO kept him waiting, standing in front of his desk. At least, Jim thought, it is cool here in the air conditioning.

"Well you seem very sure of your diagnosis, considering you have never seen the disease. I hope the samples prove you wrong."

The samples did not prove Jim wrong. Rinderpest had entered Kenya and the country had lost its freedom from Rinderpest status. It took six months of hard work, vaccinating, to regain it.

Chapter 14

Extracting 'Somali One'

Tuesday 6th June 1967

It was ten o'clock in the morning and Jim had just got back from Mackinnon Road, after a dawn start, to blood test fifty big steers destined for the KMC. The Head of LMD wanted them tested for 'fly', as he hoped to keep them for another two months to really finish them so that they would get top grades at the abattoir. Kitchopo had brought Jim a strong cup of coffee. The telephone went. Kimuta, the telephonist said, "There is an old man on the phone. He would not give his name but said he needed to speak to you urgently." As soon as Jim heard the husky voice, he knew it was his controller, Colin Shaw, speaking through a handkerchief to disguise his voice.

"We have a herd boy up in Somalia, who is extremely ill. Can you get up to Kismayo and bring him out for hospital treatment in Nairobi? He will wait, unobtrusively, in the departures lounge at the airport. He will know what you look like and approach you. He will limp and say "Hello, I am Somali one and I have hurt my leg. Can you give me a lift?" If that is possible, you will reply, "Fine, come with me." If you are compromised you say, "Sorry, I am not insured." You then just walk away. The husky voice then said, "Good luck, I am relying on you."

Jim knew he could trust Kimuta, but Jim did not want to get him or himself into trouble, so he tapped down on his phone bar to get Kimuta's attention. Kimuta came on the line saying, "Can I help you Sir?"

Jim replied. "Did you hear any of that, Kimuta?"

He replied, "Sorry Sir, I didn't. I was speaking to the PVO, who was saying he would be staying in Nairobi for another night and would get tomorrow night's train. Can Omari meet him the following morning at the station?"

"That will be fine Kimuta. Can you get Silas to organise that? I need to go up North to sort out some possible cattle for KMC. I will be out for the rest of the day," said Jim. That was great, the PVO was away so Jim could try and get up to Kismayo that day. He rang the flying club and booked out the Piper Tripacer. He rang Shell at the airport and ordered five extra cans of aviation fuel, to be left at the flying club. He had a can of water in his Landrover, so he got going immediately. He knew it was going to be a near thing, to go today but he had to try. He went straight to the control tower and filed a flight plan to Bodhei, a veterinary holding ground near to the Somali border. He knew this was an unmanned strip. The veterinary staff all lived ten miles away, at a second holding ground called Burgoni.

The flight to Bodhei took under two hours. Every 30 minutes, Jim had to report 'operations normal' to the East Air Control Centre. The trip was uneventful, except that the bush strip was extremely rough and, obviously, had not been used for years. He was glad when the plane eventually came to rest. As Jim got out, two *'Topi'* (Large russet coloured antelope) crashed away through the bush to the side of the strip. Thank goodness they did not run across when he was landing. A Tripacer is a high wing, nose wheeled, very old fashioned plane. The wings are canvass. In theory, it should be able to take four passengers but in reality three adults is top weight. The top speed is 90 knots, so you do not get any where very fast. A friend of Jim's with a five series BMW thought that, when the road was tarmac from Mombasa to Nairobi, he would be able to get there quicker by road than Jim could in a Tripacer!

With all the fiddling about in Mombasa, it was now past one o'clock. Jim wished he had brought some food, other that a hand of bananas and a packet of biscuits. Luckily, he found an old 44 gallon oil drum at the end of the airstrip. He commandeered this to stand on, as the fuel tanks filled from on top of the wings. It was fairly precarious but Jim managed to fill both tanks. He was airborne in 25 minutes. This time he did not file a flight plan. His flight time to Kismayo was only half an hour. Kenya was not quite at war with Somalia but any flight into Somalia would be totally banned. He was on his own.

He was certain there was unlikely to be any radar but certainly they would see him come in, on final approach. He would have to pretend that he had got lost, on the way to Lamu and had kept flying up the coast. He also saw that there was a military airfield marked on the map. He just hoped they would not bother about him. Jim flew the first part of the journey at four thousand feet, to conserve fuel, but dropped down to one hundred feet when he was twenty miles out and came along the beach. The beach looked beautiful. It was totally deserted, unlike the beaches around Mombasa which Jim often flew over to see if there were any girls sunbathing. Luckily, the radio frequency for Kismayo tower was 118.1, which was the same as the frequency a pilot should use, when landing on an unmanned airstrip. So Jim called on this frequency pretending he was trying to land at Lamu. Initially the controller just gave permission to land. He obviously had not really listened and thought it was a Somali based aircraft. Jim kept coming in on this heading and hoped for the best. He was cleared to land which was marvellous. Then, his troubles started as he taxied towards the rough looking control tower and tin sheds which were, what he assumed to be, the official terminal. A very stern voice commanded the pilot of five Yankee Kilo Juliet Hotel (5YKJH) to report immediately to the control tower.

Jim's heart rate went up as he parked the plane. He just hoped Somali One was ready. Jim walked into the tin sheds, as if he thought that was the way to the control tower. There was a poorly dressed policeman guarding the door. Jim said,

"Hello, I am a pilot. I am looking for the control tower but first I need to go to the lavatory." Jim slipped him a ten dollar note, which Jim imagined was a month's wages. The policeman just nodded, made no acknowledgment, and waved Jim through. The inside was very squalid, with people milling about and others just lying on the floor sleeping. A very important looking older Somali, wearing a dark suit, came towards Jim. He thought, I am in trouble now- this guy will not be easy to fool. Then Jim noticed his limp. Was this Somali one?

The man said. "Hello, I am Somali One I have hurt my leg. Can you give me a lift?" Jim replied. "Fine, please come with me."

He smiled and said. "I am glad you are insured." Jim said rather breathlessly,

"We are in a bit of trouble. They want me to report to the control tower but I am pretty certain, at best they will detain me until it is too late to fly home and at worst, they will lock me up. If you are game, I suggest we get out of here as quickly as possible."

"Too right! Lead on. I know I have a limp but I can move fairly quickly."

"Great, let's walk briskly to the little plane over there." Mercifully the policeman at the door totally ignored them. The fifty yards to the plane seemed like ten miles but nothing happened. Jim directed Somali one to the right hand door and jumped into the left hand seat. He started the plane immediately, as he saw three figures running from the control tower. He did not bother with any checks but gunned the engine and took off down-wind, which was very bad practice but Jim felt haste was of the essence. The figures were catching them up but the plane was soon out-stripping them. It seemed to take forever to get airborne, as Jim had not bothered with the flaps. As soon as he had built up some airspeed, he didn't climb but banked left and headed south. Jim turned to Somali one and suggested he fasten his seat belt. He grinned and said,

"Sadly, I think the lack of a seat belt is the least of our problems. My real name is Mohamed Abdi but most 'wazungu' (Europeans) call me Tom. I used to be Minister of Agriculture but was sacked yesterday, for opposing the president on a proposal to divert the Juba River. I was due to return on a scheduled flight to Mogadishu this afternoon and face the music. I got a message from Nairobi to say 'Animal boy' would come, which I presume is you. I am very grateful. I think my days in Somalia are numbered but, hopefully, I will be able to return to Northern Somalia. My home is actually Hargeshia district. You Brits used to call it 'British Somaliland'. Luckily, my family is safe up there but I think my life is in jeopardy now. I had booked my luggage in for the scheduled flight, which was why they had not bothered to arrest me. It is also why I don't have any luggage. Perhaps that is for the best, as this seems a very small plane. Sadly, I think they will have seen me get into the plane, so I don't know what will happen now."

Jim said, "Hopefully, it will be out of sight, out of mind. We will be out of Somalian airspace in half an hour. There will be an official complaint that this plane arrived in Kismayo without authority but I will just say I was looking for a veterinary holding ground in Northern Kenya and got lost, I saw a town and thought it was Lamu and landed to find out. When I realised I was in Somalia I panicked and took off immediately. I will totally deny I had a passenger. What will you do when you get to Nairobi?"

"I imagine I will fly to London and be totally debriefed and then I will return to my home in Hargeshia. My days of being a politician are over. What is your name? I can't keep calling you 'Animal Boy'," said Tom.

"I'm Jim Scott and a vet, which is why I am called 'Animal Boy'," said Jim. Suddenly there was a 'woosh' as a fighter jet went tearing past them. The radio crackled. "5YKJH you have entered Somali airspace illegally. Return to Kismayo immediately. You have kidnapped a Somali national."

"Oh shit." said Jim. "I think I had better not say anything and pretend we can't hear him."

"Kidnapped my arse," said Tom. "They know bloody well I escaped with you and that there was no force used. I am sorry to have got you into this, Jim." Jim was doing a rough calculation on the map. They were only at two thousand feet and he could see the coast line very clearly. They were only thirty miles from Kiunga, which was in Kenya. Then there was a crackle of cannons and another whoosh.

"Change heading and return to Kismayo or we will shoot you down," said the voice in the radio.

"Can you see if there are two of them, Tom?" shouted Jim. "I am going to dive to increase my speed." They soon were doing One hundred and sixty knots, which was their maximum but Jim knew that was no match for the Jet.

"I can only see one," said Tom.

Jim said, "Tom, hold on to this handle. When I say 'now' just pull it upwards. You will feel three clicks." It was the handle which put the flaps down. Jim kept turning round looking for the jet. There it was dead astern and closing fast. It seemed to fill Jim's vision. He could see the flashes of its cannons.

"Now, Tom," commanded Jim. As Tom pulled on full flap, Jim cut the power and pulled back on the stick. There was a terrible shuddering noise. Jim thought the wings were going to fly off. The

174

airspeed dropped rapidly and they were in a high speed stall. Jim fed in full power, pushed the stick forward and shouted at Tom. "I will take the flaps. Let go of the leaver." The pilot of the jet, which was right on their tail, thought he was going to hit them. He panicked and pulled back on the stick too rapidly. He went into a high speed stall but, unlike the Tripacer, he needed more height to correct it. Jim was struggling to keep the Tripacer airborne. He managed to correct the stall, with only a hundred feet to spare. Jim thought to himself. *'Lucky there is no stall warning in this plane or there would have been one hell of a racket.'* The jet had long since shot by the Tripacer. There was a flash on the beach. The jet had crashed. Jim kept flying south at top speed. He stayed at one hundred feet. The sand and coral raced below him.

"Keep looking for another jet, Tom," shouted Jim. He turned. Tom's normally coal black skin, was grey. He managed to look around and say, "I can't see one." A small coastal village raced by on the right hand side.

"Hopefully that is Kiunga, which is in Kenya," shouted Jim.

"We will keep going along the coast, to make sure. I don't trust them not to send another jet after us. They will know Kenya have no radar up here. The Kenya Air Force (KAF) is based at Eastleigh, which is two hundred and fifty miles away." Jim then saw a thick green forest inland.

"That must be the Dodori forest. I have been shooting forest Guinea-fowl in there. They were jolly good eating."

"Don't talk about food! I feel bloody sick," said Tom. As the large island of Pate appeared on their left, Jim swung the plane due west. He would only relax when he crossed the Tana River, which was an hour away. Jim thought it would be very unlikely for Somali jets to trespass that far into Kenya. They both cheered up when they crossed the Tana and Jim landed at a small red *murram* strip on Galana ranch. They filled up with the remaining cans of fuel, drank some water and had a few biscuits, before getting on board for the last leg to Wilson airport at Nairobi. It was strictly illegal to carry fuel in cans, actually in the aircraft, but many Kenyan pilots did it, as the distances were so great and proper fuel facilities few and far between. The first time Jim had done it, he had nearly jumped out of his skin when the cans had made a clanking noise as they expanded with the increase in the altitude. The two hours seemed to take forever. Jim filed an airborne flight plan as if he was flying from Bodhei to Wilson. It was heard by a British Overseas Airways VC10, thirty thousand feet somewhere above him, who relayed the message to East Air Centre. There was no mention of any reported crash and Jim was relieved. He wondered when the shit would hit the fan. He had not mentioned his passenger when he made the flight plan.

"When we get to Wilson, I think the best thing is for you to just get out, Tom and walk round the back of the aero club, where I will park. As far as the authorities are concerned you never existed. What will you do then? Have you got any money?" asked Jim.

"Don't worry about me, Jim. I have got both Kenya Shillings and Dollars. I will get a taxi and get dropped off in the middle of Nairobi. I can then walk to a 'safe house'. I imagine I will be spirited away to the UK to be totally debriefed and then, hopefully, I can get back to my home."

The Tripacer seemed to take forever to get to within fifty miles of Wilson Airport. Jim was getting extremely anxious about the fading light. He reported, to Nairobi control, that he estimated his time of arrival (ETA) to be 18.40 hours. The controller was fairly relaxed and just said. "Cutting it a bit fine Juliet Hotel? Report the visual marker." Jim said to Tom "at least the visual marker will be easier to spot in the gloom as there is a beacon light. Also the tower won't be able to see you if, when I give you the word, you can put your head down?"

"Certainly," said Tom. "If I don't get a chance later, can I say a big thank you? I won't forget that you risked your life for mine." Jim just smiled. Jim had to put on his landing lights but, as he was so late, there was no other traffic and he landed before seven 'o'clock and taxied to the aero-club. He cut the engine. Tom opened his door, said "goodbye" and disappeared into the tropical night. Jim was totally exhausted but he managed to get the plane refuelled and tied down. There were a few faces he knew in the aero-club but he was relieved there was no-one he would have to chat to. He checked into a room. He bought a toothbrush; tooth paste and a razor at the reception. Often, he camped by the plane but he had no spare clothes and certainly no camping gear. The rooms were little more than cells but the beds were clean and there were towels. There were communal showers and lavatories, which was fine with Jim. He had a shower. He then had some supper which was sausages, chips and baked beans. He had a mug of tea and bought some sandwiches for the morning. He asked for a wake-up call at 5.45 am. He would have to take off at first light, as he had to get back to work as soon as possible or there would be some awkward questions asked.

Chapter 15

Jane Morton

Wednesday 7th June 1967

He suddenly had a great idea. He would fly home via a ranch at Mackinnon Road which was three quarters of the way to Mombasa. The rancher, Bob Ritchie, had asked for a routine visit last week, as he had some trouble with 'fly' and he wanted some heifers tested for pregnancy. This was an ideal opportunity and would be a marvellous excuse for Jim's absence. Jim filed a flight plan to take off at daylight in the morning. He knew it would get down to Bob's ranch in time for one of Mary's legendary breakfasts. He wanted to go to bed but he knew he ought to report in to his controller. It was after 9.30 pm, which he knew was a good time for his controller. He went to the pay phone, in a booth by reception and dialled the agreed number. The phone was picked up almost immediately. Jim said. "This is 'Animal Boy'. I am reporting that I have extracted Somali One. He should be getting in contact with you very soon." The husky voice said, "Very well done, I am very grateful. He has just reported in. I gather you have had some adventures. I will wait for your written report in the normal manner. Once again, thank you for your prompt help."

Jim flew low over Bob Ritchie's house, before landing at Mackinnon Road. Bob came out to fetch him and, when he realised it was Jim, he was really pleased.

"Come back to the house and join Mary and me for a late breakfast. You could not have come at a better time. I will get the lads to get the heifers into the pens. They are not far away."

When they arrived at the house, Jim immediately realised something was wrong as, normally, Mary would have been out to greet him with a big hug. She never made any pretence that she fancied him, although she was old enough to be his grandmother. He found her sitting at the big dining room table, with her foot up on a stool.

"Mary, you poor girl, what has happened to you?"

"I have been bitten by a cobra and I can't seem to bear any weight on my leg." Jim took one look at the leg and could see it was very serious. To Jim, it looked like a horse's leg with severe cellulitis/lymphangitis. He had seen one put to sleep, at college.

"We must get you onto antibiotics immediately. Do you mind if I inject you?"

"Of course not, dear, I am sure you will be very gentle, as I know you treat dogs and cats, as well as cows." Jim went straight to his emergency bag, which he always took with him on safari. He drew up a dose of penicillin for a Great Dane and, with a fine needle, injected it into Mary's arm. "Now Bob, I want you to rig up a stretcher with two brooms and several shirts, so that we can carry Mary down to the airstrip. Mary, I think you will be more comfortable being carried rather than hitched into Bob's truck and then out again. It will be bad enough, I am afraid, getting you into my airplane but at least I have a back door. The cattle will have to wait until another day."

"Oh dear," said Mary. "Is my leg that serious? I did think it might be, as my glands are all swollen in my groin."

"I didn't want to feel your groin. I thought Bob might give me a clout," said Jim trying to lighten the situation. Jim gave Bob a sharp look and saw that he realised how serious the problem was. While Bob was getting the stretcher prepared, Jim, under Mary's instruction, got her nighty and wash things together with a book, in a small bag. "If I wasn't feeling so bad, I would be very excited about coming for a flight with you, Jim," said Mary, trying to make the best of it. Bob was obviously a good organiser as, very quickly, four strong Africans had been recruited and they were carrying Mary carefully down the track to the airstrip. Jim ran ahead to do his flight checks and get the seat organized, so Mary could sit in the back and put her leg on the passenger seat, which he moved forward and he managed to get the back of the seat almost flat. He ran back to the stretcher party and chatted to Bob, as they continued onto the airstrip.

"I will get an ambulance organised, by radio, to take Mary to the Katherine Bibby Hospital and to get Ted Hughes, the chief surgeon, to see her as soon as possible. I know you will have to get things organised here, on the ranch, before you can drive to Mombasa but I wonder if you can ring up your sister, who lives at Nyali, to come down to the hospital. I know you don't have a phone at the ranch but I think you can ring from the railway station."

All the jolting of the journey, down to the strip and getting into the plane, took its toll on Mary. She was deathly white but managed to give Bob a smile and told him not to worry about her. Bob shut the door and stood back from the plane. Jim started the engine and was airborne in minutes. He thought, '*I hope I don't have to do this too often? It's the second time in twenty four hours!*'

He was only thirty five miles from Mombasa Airport and so he made an emergency radio call to the tower.

"Mombasa Tower, Pan, Pan, Pan, this is Five Yankee Kilo Juliet Hotel in bound from Mackinnon Road, with a very sick woman on board who has been bitten by a cobra. I request immediate permission to land and would be grateful if an ambulance could be arranged to take the lady to the Katherine Bibby Hospital."

"Roger, Juliet Hotel I have copied your message and I will expedite your request. Ted Hughes is a friend of mine and I will get him ready to receive her. You are cleared to land on runway 150. Please report field in sight."

"Wilco, Juliet Hotel out," replied Jim.

"What is all this about pots and pans?" asked Mary. Jim thought, '*she is a marvellous woman, I hope she won't lose her leg.*' Jim laughed. "You won't have to do any cooking Mary. It is a code to indicate an emergency. If the aircraft was going to crash, I would have said, "Mayday, Mayday, Mayday," but the Pan business says I want a bit of quick action. I will soon have you on the ground."

Jim quickly did his pre-landing checks, which were minimal as the Tripacer was such a simple plane.

He then called the tower. "Mombasa Tower, Juliet Hotel, Your field is in sight. I estimate arrival at 10.36."

"Copied, Juliet Hotel. You are cleared to land. An ambulance is waiting at the aero club."

Jim came in high, to reduce the turbulence from the palm trees and then, when he was over the enormous runway, put on full flap and came in for a copy-book landing. Mary managed to say. "Thank you my dear" and then she passed out. Jim kept his head and said on the radio, "Tower, Juliet Hotel taxi over. Thank you for your help."

"Clear taxi, wish your passenger good luck. Tower out."

The ambulance had its doors open as Jim taxied up. Jim saw Bob's sister, Judith Morton. She must have moved very quickly to get up to the airport. Jim was relieved.

"Judith, thank you so much for coming. Mary has just passed out. She is in a pretty bad way."

"Don't worry Jim, I will take over now. You have been a star. I will ride in the ambulance. James and Jane will come up and pick the car up later."

Jim was relieved, as he ought to get back to work. Bob Ritchie, unasked, had done him a good turn. He had rung the Veterinary Office and told them what had happened, so there were no problems. The PVO was not due back until the following morning's train from Nairobi. Still, Jim had a lot of work problems which needed sorting out. He managed to get finished by 4.00 pm. He went home for a shower and to touch base with Katana, who had been worried about him. Then he walked down to the Katherine Bibby Hospital. In the lobby, he saw a very pale girl wearing thick rimmed glasses, who had obviously been crying. He took a chance and walked up to her and, putting his arm around her said, "You must be Jane. Can you give me news of your Aunt Mary?" The girl was obviously very upset and did not really register that Jim had put his arm around her shoulders. She burst into floods of tears.

"It is dreadful, the surgeon is examining her now. I was told to leave but my grandmother had told me to stay with her. I could not argue. I feel I have done the wrong thing. I think she may be going to lose her leg, or even die. Grandma told me that if a marvellous vet had not flown her into hospital, she would have died already."

Jim thought, '*Poor Mary. I did think it was bad.*'

He said, "Jane, we will just have to hope for the best." Jim then turned to the receptionist and said. "We will be in the garden near to the creek. Could you call us if there is any news?"

180

He then led Jane out into the fresh air. He made for a seat which looked over the creek. The evening wind had started to blow and the atmosphere was fresher. When they had sat down Jim said, "I should have introduced myself I am Jim Scott. My house is just further down the creek."

"Thank you for being so kind to me. It is the first time I have travelled on my own. I managed to hit a '*hamarli cart*' (A four-wheeled hand pushed cart) this morning, bringing Grandma's car in from the airport. Grandma and Grandad told me not worry about it. They were so kind, which made me feel even guiltier."

"You don't need to worry, if no one was hurt there is absolutely no problem. Where did it happen?"

"It happened on the causeway onto the island. As soon as it occurred, I was surrounded by Africans. A really kind African stopped and saw that the cart was not really damaged and told them all to get on with their lives. He said I should drive on. He said he worked just off the causeway and these small accidents were always happening."

"Was he quite a large man with a smiling light brown face, dressed in an immaculate white shirt and blue tie?"

"Yes. How did you know?"

"His name is Silas and he works with me. He is a really kind man and is always helping me out. I will thank him for you when I see him tomorrow."

Jane, now that she had told someone about her problems, seemed to have calmed down. Jim suggested they go back inside and see if there was any news. Ted Hughes was in the lobby. He greeted Jim. "Good news. I think we are going to save that leg. Since Mary has been on the drip, the circulation seems to have returned. You did well giving her penicillin and getting her in. I guess you chaps see a lot of snakebites, in animals. I always think it is amazing that there are so few humans bitten in Kenya. In fact, you rarely see a snake, not like in Australia, where I worked as a young man. People were always being brought into Perth General. I must be going. See you down at the Yacht Club sometime."

Jim turned to a wide eyed Jane. "Are you the vet?"

"Yes," replied Jim.

"You are marvellous," said Jane. She hugged him so hard she knocked her glasses off. Jim was very embarrassed by this adoration and was pleased with the excuse to bend down and pick the glasses up. "Let's go and see Mary?"

They went along to her room. Mary still looked very pale but not as white as Jim had seen her at the airport. She was all hooked up to a trip but was remarkably bright. Jim said immediately, "I am glad to see you looking better. I thought, at the airport, my flying had killed you."

"I can assure you, it would take a lot more than a bit of turbulence to kill me." She turned to Jane. "You poor girl, you have been told to stay with me all the while. You must get out and have some fun. I know Jim lives near here." She turned back to Jim and said. "I want you to take Jane back to your house. Give her a stiff drink and some supper. Go along now. You both must be starving."

"I certainly am," said Jim. "Katana always makes enough food for an army, so there will be plenty for you, Jane. I will bring her back, high as a kite, to wish you good night, Mary. See you soon." Jim steered Jane out the door. As soon as they were out the door, Jane protested, "You don't want me boring you over supper. Mary is really naughty, telling you what to do. You have probably got a girl friend and you won't want a cry-baby like me."

"Rubbish," said Jim. "I shed a tear when I left the UK." He did not add, it was because he was leaving the most wonderful girl in his life. He could not help comparing the mischievous Fi with this poor frightened girl. He thought. *'We all have our strengths, this girl is probably super bright and plays the cello.'*

Jim was nearly right, Jane told him she was going to Oxford in October to read Maths but that her greatest love was music. She played the violin. Jim was also right that Katana had made plenty of food. Jim tucked into a large portion of cottage pie and cabbage. Jane only took a small portion but Jim noticed she was very polite and ate all she had taken and thanked Katana. Somehow, he thought, she probably would not like beer, so he gave her a lemonade and lime to drink. She looked straight into his eyes through her thick glasses, "I guess 'high as a kite', means drunk. Has this got alcohol in it?"

"No, it hasn't. I thought you wouldn't actually want any and it is a good refreshing drink. I often drink it after rugby."

"You are right. I did not enjoy it, when I got drunk at my older sister's twenty first. I was very sick in the basin and then was too drunk to clean it up. I was so embarrassed. You are very kind. I totally trust you. I am sure you would not get me drunk and try and take advantage of me."

Jim had had enough of this hero worship and, through devilment, said," I don't need you drunk to try and put my hand in your knickers." He expected a shocked silence. Instead he got a cheeky grin and a "so, I might be a lucky girl tonight?" It was Jim's turn to be shocked into silence. Luckily, Katana came in with mango and ice cream. Jane said. "That is my favourite. Thank you so much, Katana."

Jim changed the subject and talked about Oxford. He had been at school near there and so knew quite a lot about the city. So actually did Jane. She told him how lucky she had been to get a scholarship to St John's College, which was so beautiful. There were no awkward silences and the supper was in fact good fun. It was hardly dark when they started to walk back to the hospital. Jim took Jane to the end of his garden, near to the creek, so that they could walk along looking at the water.

Jane asked, "Is the sea deep here?"

"Oh yes," replied Jim. "I often dive off and go spear fishing."

With that, with Jim looking aghast, Jane took off all her clothes, laid her glasses carefully on top of them and dived in. She called to him. "It is beautifully refreshing. Come in, or are you scared of the dark. Don't be shy. I won't be able to see you. I am as blind as a bat without my glasses." Jim took off his clothes and dived in, not half as neatly as Jane.

"Shall we swim to the other side?" asked Jane.

"I should think it is quarter of a mile?" replied Jim hesitantly.

"Oh, that is fine." Jane was off at a fast crawl. There was no way Jim could keep up with her, as he had kept his gym shoes on, knowing they had to climb up the sharp coral to get out. He was pretty knackered when he got to the far side, mainly because he was worried about getting back. Not Jane, she set off with a beautiful back stroke. He was admiring her pert breasts when she stopped and said, "You will have to keep up and guide me or I might swim in the wrong direction. Poor you, wearing shoes. They will slow you down.

I guess that it will be difficult getting out over the sharp coral cliff. I am sure you will help me so I won't cut my feet." After what seemed an age, they reached the home bank. Three times Jane had stopped and just floated on her back, waiting for him to catch up. Jim thought. *'She is a real monkey-she knows I can see her breasts. It just shows, how easy it is to totally read someone the wrong way.'*

They had to negotiate about six feet of vertical coral, with the slight swell going up and down.

"Now, I am not sure how we can do this. I think the safest way to avoid your body being scratched, is for me to climb up, facing the coral, and you to climb up my back. The top of the coral is soft grass, so you will be able to stand on my shoulders and wriggle on to the top without hurting yourself. You are a wonderful swimmer so, if you feel you are going to fall, just push well out and fall back into the deep water."

"I am sure I will be able to get up," replied a confident Jane.

Jim climbed half way up the coral wall. Normally he had gloves on but he just had to hold on to two good hand-holders, on the coral wall, and then grin and bear it. Actually, the distance was not great. His feet were only about six inches out of the water and the top of his head was about the same distance below the top, when he stopped and called to Jane to take care but start to climb. Jane had not got a spare ounce of fat on her, so she had a very good strength to weight ratio. She somehow thrust herself, with a power breaststroke kick, out of the water. She gripped Jim's bent knees and got one foot on top of his. Then her arms went around his waist and her other foot stood on his foot. Then she grabbed his shoulders and stood up, with her body flattened against his. She whispered. "This is cozy?" then, with a giggle, she bent one leg and stood on his thigh which was almost horizontal. Jim was straining, with every ounce of his strength, to hold on. Luckily he had his shoes on, so they took the majority of their combined weight. Still, the coral bit into his hands. Jane did not hang about. She held his shoulders and brought her other leg up. Then she bent her first leg and managed to get it on to his shoulder. Jim gasped. "Hold on to my hair. You won't hurt me. With one hand holding his hair and the other on the top of the cliff, she hauled herself up so that she was lying on the grass. Immediately, without her weight, it was much easier for Jim. Jane quickly turned around and reached her arms down to him and he easily got up the rest of the cliff. They both stood there panting. When Jim had got his breath back enough to speak, he said, "I will never try to shock a girl again."

Jane laughed, "When I come swimming here with you tomorrow night, I will bring my trainers and a sensible one piece swimsuit. At least you now know what is inside it, you rascal. Can I borrow your shirt to dry myself, then I will get dressed and not terrify Katana by being naked. I am sure you have got more dry shorts and shirts."

Jim put on his shorts, which were soon soaking. He handed her his dry shirt. She dried herself all over. She was just drying between her legs, when she realised he was looking at her. She threw the now wet shirt at him and said, "You have seen enough." She turned her back on him while she put on her knickers and bra. She turned back and pulled up her shorts and put on her T shirt. She smiled at him as she did up her shorts and he handed her glasses to her.

"I thank you, kind Sir. You are not quite a gentleman but, I suppose, I am not quite a lady. I will blame it on being the youngest of three girls." They walked back to the house, for Jim to get some dry clothes, before heading back by the direct route to the hospital.

Good news greeted them at the hospital. Mary seemed a little better and, in Bob's words had turned the corner. Bob had driven down to see her but was going back to Mackinnon Road that night. He had brought a driver but, all the same, Mary was worried that he had not left yet. While Jim was talking to Mary, Bob was whispering to Jane in the corner. Jane left the room. When she came back, she was obviously cross and Jim heard her say to Bob,

"They won't let me bring her in."

"Well, I will take Jim outside, while you stay with Mary," said Bob.

"Stuff and nonsense, you all go out. I don't need anyone to stay with me."

So, Jim followed Bob and Jane out to Bob's truck in the car park. Beside Bob's truck, his driver was standing holding a black Labrador bitch. "I have brought you a present, Jim, to thank you for saving Mary's leg and, indeed, probably her life. The dog's name is Lucy. I have trained her to the gun and I think she will be a loyal servant." Jim was delighted and squatted down to talk to Lucy.

"Bob, I am delighted. That is really kind of you. Thank you. Now you ought to get going home, as Mary is getting agitated. I will stay out here with Lucy. You go in and say goodbye. I am sure Jane will look after Lucy while I pop in, when you come out."

Thus Bob had left and Jane was holding Lucy, in the car park, when her grandparents arrived. They were delighted, when they heard that Mary was on the mend. They said they would just go in to say hello but they would not stay long, as they felt Mary should sleep now.

"Also, Jane, you must be starving as you have not had any supper."

"I have had masses Grandma. Jim took me back to his house. I know you said I was to stay with Aunt Mary but she insisted. She said I was in need of fresh air. I have said goodbye to Aunt Mary, so I will stay out here with Lucy. Uncle Bob has given Lucy to Jim, to say thank you. I think Jim is delighted."

"How lovely," said Judith Morton, as she and James went into the hospital. They were soon out again with Jim and were thanking him for feeding Jane, when Judith noticed her wet hair.

"Did you manage to have a shower at the hospital?"

"No, I had a swim in the sea."

"What-on your own?"

"Oh no, Jim came with me."

To try and help Jane, Jim said, "I have never seen such a wonderful swimmer. You must be very proud of her. I am willing to bet twenty Kenyan Shillings, that she swims for Oxford."

"What a kind thing to say, Jim. Perhaps you would like to come out to supper with us tomorrow night?"

"I would love to. I will bring Lucy with me and perhaps Jane and I can take her, with your dogs, for a walk along the beach."

With that, they said good bye and drove off, leaving a delighted Jim to lead Lucy back to his house. When the Mortons got home, to their beautiful house on the sea front at Nyali, Judith said to Jane, "I should hang your wet swimmers out, on the line on the veranda. They get so smelly if you leave them wet." Jane said nothing.

In the morning, as they were having breakfast on the veranda, Judith noticed there was no swimming costume on the line.

"Jane, that is most unlike you not to do as I suggested. Pop and get your swimming costume and hang it up to dry."

"Sorry Grandma. I didn't have one with me."

"Oh well, it was dark and I expect your bra and pants were quite respectable but I would hang them up and then put them in the wash, when they are dry."

"Yes Grandma," replied Jane, who went to her room and found her bra and pants from yesterday. She then dutifully hung them up. She had a very naughty grin on her face, when she did as she was told.

Jim had been really busy at work, so he had not had a chance to go and see Mary. He was hungry for news, when he arrived at the Mortons. He was delighted, when Jane ran out to greet him and to tell him she was much better and was no longer on a drip. "I am sure there is not a vet in England, who would have injected a lady with penicillin. Weren't you worried something might have gone wrong?"

"I suppose I was but I thought speed was of the essence." Jane squeezed his arm. "Well, I am very grateful. I am very fond of Aunt Mary. Where is Lucy?"

"I have left her in the Landrover because I thought it was best for her to meet your dogs on mutual territory, like the beach. We don't want a fight. Anyhow, she seems devoted to the Landover and I have parked it in the shade. By the way, Mr. Silas sends his regards. I said I would bring you in to see him. I hope that is OK."

"Oh yes, does that mean I could come and work with you for a day. I would love that."

"Well, if you don't mind an early start, I could pick you up tomorrow. I have to go to the prison farm and castrate thirty bulls tomorrow. It is only fifteen miles from here but they like to start at 6.30 am, so it would mean picking you up at 6.00."

"I will be ready and waiting. Now, you must come in for a drink. Grandad and Grandma have already started." With a giggle Jane said, "I was going to get 'high as a kite' before our walk but, if I have to be up at 6.00 am I think I had better not."

"Knowing you, during our walk, you might strip off and try to swim to India."

"Please be quiet about that. Grandma thinks I was in my bra and pants."

"Not a word," said Jim.

They went through the house onto the veranda. James Morton asked Jim what he would like to drink. "I would love a tusker," replied Jim. "Could I have a little of yours?" said Jane. "I don't really like beer but I think I should start getting to like it, before I go to Oxford."

"Oh, Jane dear, I don't think it is very lady like to drink beer. Why don't you have a Gin and Tonic like I'm having?"

Jim laughed. "I don't think boys will like buying her Gin and Tonic at University, Mrs. Morton. Certainly you can have some of my beer."

"Do call me Judith, Jim, I feel so old being called Mrs. Morton and I notice you call Mary by her Christian name."

"Of course I will. Cheers," said Jim. He raised his glass and took a big swig and then passed the glass to Jane. She did the same and said. "It is much better than English beer. It is all cold and fizzy. English beer is flat and heavy."

"I agree," said Jim. English beer is great on a cold evening in the pub. 'Tusker' is good out here in the heat."

Judith and James were good hosts and they had a very nice evening. Jim noticed that, between them, he and Jane had drunk four pints. He reckoned she had very nearly drunk half. He wondered if she would be up in the morning. It was not late when they took the dogs out on the beach, having said no to coffee. When they were out of sight of the house, Jane took his hand. "I am not 'high as a kite' but I know I have had a drink. In fact, I feel a bit frisky. I am ready, Mr. 'I will shock this little girl' Scott to feel what it is like having your hand down my knickers." Jim laughed. Jane continued. "I hope I will enjoy it as much as I have enjoyed drinking your beer. I purposely drank beer, as I assume you are going to kiss me first and my breath will smell just like yours."

"Jane Morton, you make me feel I a dirty old man corrupting a young, innocent girl."

"Well, aren't you?" replied Jane. She could feel him chuckling in the darkness.

"I suppose I should have expected this, from a girl who just stripped off in front of me, but what is meant to happen is that I kiss you very delicately, then I touch your breasts and eventually, I let my hand slide down the front of your knickers."

She kissed him and then broke away. "It seems to me," said Jane. "That it would be a lot simpler if I just took all my clothes off, like last night. At least I can take my glasses off and lay them carefully on my clothes and we won't spend half the night trying to find them in the sand, when you have knocked them off."

Jim said, "Come here, you naughty but lovely girl. At least let me have the pleasure of taking your clothes off."

"Yes, that would be nice, but I expect I will have to help you, or you will pull all my buttons off. It is all very fine in the romantic novels, when he rips her bodice open but they had sewing maids to sort it all out afterwards."

She put her arms around his neck and said. "Come on, then." Jim felt her hand in his back pocket as she kissed him. It was a very passionate kiss. She had been sensible to put her glasses in his pocket. In fact, Jim did not take all her clothes off as he could not wait but started to rub her the front of her pants. This was greeted by a very breathless gasp, "That is a lot better than a glass of beer!"

In their passion, they had forgotten about the dogs. They must have seen some Africans on the beach, as they started barking. They broke apart and both started calling. Luckily, all three dogs returned to them but the spell of passion was broken but not the humour. "Next time," said Jane, "I want you to wear pants, so I can feel what it is like when I put my hand down them. I am sure men in England wear pants. Why don't you?"

"Mainly because you tend to get prickly heat, wearing tight pants," answered Jim.

"Should I not wear knickers then, because they are tight?" asked Jane.

"That would be very racy, if you didn't," said Jim with a dirty laugh.

Jane was still laughing when they reached the veranda, as she had told Jim she would have to put pairs of knickers in the wash, or Grandma would want to know why she wasn't wearing any.

"Well Jane," said Grandma, "I thought you were a really serious blue stocking but I am delighted, ever since you have met Jim, you have never stopped laughing. Lots of silly girls giggle when they are embarrassed, but you laugh as if you haven't got a care in the world."

"I like to hear a girl laugh properly," chipped in James Morton. "Look, the dogs agree with me." All three dogs were wagging their tails.

"Well, on that note, I must go," said Jim. "Thank you for a wonderful supper and a great evening. I will see you in the morning Jane, at six."

"I will be ready."

"Where are you going tomorrow?" asked Judith.

"Jim is taking me to the prison farm, to castrate some bulls." Turning to Jim, Jane said," I know we are going to be in the sun so I will be wearing a big floppy hat. If you laugh at me I will certainly not be happy."

"Don't worry Jane, you can always smear your face with cow dung to keep off the sun," said Jim. Before she could hit him, Jim and Lucy were running to the Landrover.

"What a nice boy he is," said Judith. "I wish I was young again. Now you must not get in his way, Jane. You must do exactly as you are told. I will get Salim to bring you a cup of tea before six, to help you get up. I will get him to pour some juice for you and you can eat a couple of bananas, as you will not have time for breakfast. You must not keep Jim waiting. Grandad and I will stay in bed. We are too old to get up at dawn."

Jim was surprised, not only was Jane up when he reached Nyali, but she had walked down to the end of the short lane that led to the house. She had on a large floppy hat but it was a sensible colour of khaki, which matched her shirt which had long sleeves. She was wearing shorts, which were not fashionable as they came almost to her knees.

Lucy was delighted to see her. Jim greeted her and thanked her for walking down the lane. "I did not want the sound of the Landrover to wake Grandad and Grandma. Grandma gave me strict instructions that I was not to be a nuisance or get in your way." Jane laughed and said. "She said I was to do exactly what I was told. I can't imagine there is a seventeen year old girl anywhere in England, who is allowed to go out at dawn with a twenty three year old sex maniac and be told to do exactly what she is told!"

"I think it is a little hard, saying I am a sex maniac. I was gob smacked when you took off all your clothes and dived into Tudor Creek. However, I must admit, I admire your style. I have to laugh, as I think you are going to terrify the eighteen year old school boys, who will be going to Oxford at the same time as you."

"Would you have been terrified, when you first went to Bristol?"

"Too right, I am fairly apprehensive now."

It was her turn to laugh. "I am totally amazed. I am sick to death of all the stories about the brave marvellous Jim Scott, the flying vet who takes oranges out of cow's throats and pretends it doesn't hurt, who slaloms so sharply that he pulls the ski boat backwards and yet he is frightened to death by a naked seventeen year old."

"I am sorry," said Jim. "I read you all wrong. When we first met, you were crying and I assumed you were in a strange country and you felt very vulnerable."

"I am just honest, Jim. I was upset. I was crying. I thought my Aunt was going to die. I had just been involved in that nonsense on the causeway. You, however, took one look at a pale girl with thick glasses and made a snap judgment that I was immature, had a flat chest and I was silly."

"Where did the flat chest business come in? I don't mind telling you that you have great tits."

"You only say that, now you have seen them. If I had been a pretty girl, bursting out of a tight T shirt, you would never have put your arm around me and led me out into the garden. Go on admit I am right!"

Jim hesitated. Jane laughed. "I knew I was right. Anyway, what you don't know is that I enjoyed having your arm around me. It was actually kind of you. Also, I am glad you like my tits. Now I have got that off my not-so flat chest, let's have a fun day. I am sorry I am grouchy but my excuse is that you have got me up too early. I bet you thought I would not be ready?"

"That did cross my mind, but I hoped you would be. Honestly I did."

"Did anything else cross your mind?" probed Jane.

"Well, I was thinking how sexy your body felt when you were climbing up my back, up the coral wall. You are very athletic, you know."

"I will give you a compliment now. You were very brave and strong holding on to the coral, because I think it hurt."

Then Jane really laughed. Jim asked her what was so funny. "I was just imagining when Grandma is listing your achievements at one of her totally boring coffee mornings, whether she will say how you helped her granddaughter get up a coral cliff, when they were both stark naked."

They were still laughing, as they turned into the gate of Shimo La Tewa Prison. The guard told Jim, Jonathan was expecting him. Jim made Jane laugh again, when he told her that Jonathan had been the farm manager but he had been caught stealing milk, so that they had sent him to prison, where he did just the same job.

Jonathan was a relaxed happy person. He seemed genuinely pleased to show Jane his cows. Jane took an instant liking to him. Jonathan and all the other prisoners, were wearing wellington boots. The cows were in long lines, tied to posts, with rope around their necks under 'makuti' (Palm-leafed roofing) roofs. They were standing on smooth flat concrete. The bull calves were all penned up. There was liquid shit everywhere. Jane quietly told Jim, she did not have any wellington boots and she thought Grandma would murder her, if she got her trainers all covered and stained with cow shit. "Don't worry," said Jim cheerfully. "I have got a spare pair. Your feet are so small you will be able to keep your trainers on inside these big old boots."

Jim took his shirt off and hung it on the mirror of the Landrover. He then only had on his shorts and wellies. He walked near to the bull calves had a laugh and a joke with Jonathan and some of the other prisoners and then the rodeo began.

Jane had seen the local Giriama women walking around with their breasts bare, so she took off her shirt and bra. The sun was hardly up and they were under the 'makuti', so she knew she would not get burnt. She then stood behind Jim. The calves were quite small but that did not stop them shitting all down Jim's shorts. Jim did not turn but just handed Jane the large pair of Burdizzos (instrument for carrying out blood-less castration), as he injected local anaesthetic into the first calf's scrotum. He had explained to her, in the Landrover, what was going to happen. He continued to inject more calves. Jane moved up close behind him and said, "Can I have a go injecting them?" Jim still did not turn but said, "Of course, come up beside me and I will show you where to inject. Because they are being held properly you won't get kicked, only you will probably get shit on your shirt. "Will Grandma be cross if your shirt gets shitty?"

Jane laughed. "My shirt won't get shitty, as I hung it with yours on the mirror of the Landrover. Grandma won't be cross as she told me to do just what I was told.

"Fair enough," said Jim. He stepped back and saw that Jane was totally topless. He said nothing but thought, '*what a girl she is? God help some young undergrad at Oxford. He will be terrified. Equally, is it me? Maybe I don't understand modern girls.*'

"Now grab the testicles and inject some local, into the cord you can feel at the top of each testicle."

"Yes, I can feel it," replied Jane

"That is the cord, which we are going to clamp with the Burdizzos." Jim moved forward to make sure she had the correct place and managed to smear shit all over Jane's left breast.

"Sorry about that. I will have to help you wash that off afterwards."

"I bet you will," replied Jane, grinning.

They steadily worked down the line, working very close together, their top halves got covered in shit and also their shorts got pretty filthy. Jim was amazed how quickly he got used to Jane's naked chest, as if it was the most natural thing in the world.

When they had finished that group of calves, they went to another group. Luckily, these were also under '*makuti*' and so Jane did not have to worry about the sun. Jim smiled to himself, as Jane made no effort to cover herself.

Suddenly he had a little worry. All the herdsmen were prisoners. Could they be sex offenders? Jim thought that was extremely unlikely, as most of these chaps would be thieves. Sex offences were extremely rare in Kenya and child crime was unheard of.

When they had done all the calves, they had to take blood from a group of cows. Jim did the first few and then, after she had watched how he had done it, Jane took over. She had a good eye for the jugular vein. So much so, that Jim said, "Well done! The Masai would be proud of you."

193

Jane commented, "I have heard about them but I think they use a bow and arrow with a very sharp V shaped point."

When they had got all the samples they went to the dairy. Jim stood, as he normally did, for one of the dairy guys to hose him down, from head to toe with cold water. He was hosed on both his back and his front. It took his breath away. He thought he really should get a pail of soapy water for Jane and offered. Jane said she would be just fine and would be washed down like he had been. He watched her and saw her nipples become erect. She saw him watching and put her tongue out at him. They went back to the Landrover and Jim found a clean towel for Jane to drape round her shoulders, as she said she would dry before she put her bra back on.

They said good bye to Jonathan and the dairy staff and set off, having waved to the men on the gate.

Before they got to the main road, Jane said. "Shall we have a swim before we go back to Nyali? I am sure I still smell of shit." She leant forward and smelt under Jim's arm. "You certainly do."

"That is a great idea. I have often thought of going for a swim but I have always felt self conscious on my own. Now I have Lucy, I expect I will go more often."

"Well, this time you will have me with you as well," said Jane forcefully.

"Now, you promised not to laugh at me wearing my hat and my shirt. I only need to be in the noon day sun for ten minutes and I will burn."

They went down one of the tracks to the beach. Jane took off her shirt and bra as they were going along and then put her shirt back on. "At least I don't need a bra," she said with a grin. "You have been gazing at my breasts all morning. Now you can see my sexy wet look."

When they stopped, Lucy was very well behaved and only jumped out when Jim called to her to get out, even although she was obviously very excited.

Jane asked. "Have you got any soap? I think I am going to need it." Jim brought a bar of soap and they walked down into the shallows. Jane splashed in the shallow water and then, to Jim's amazement and delight, took all her clothes off. He could not take his eyes off her. "Come on, you said you would wash me when we were at the prison?" So Jim set about washing her really thoroughly and she did the same for him, once he had taken off his shorts. Then he picked up her shorts and washed them well and rinsed them, as best he could, in the sea. Jim laughed. "I see you took me at my word-no knickers today. We had better hurry up or you will get burnt. Jane put on her wet shirt and then ran up to the Landrover and came back wearing her hat. "Well, what is the verdict on my wet look?"

"Ten out of ten but, if you don't cover that bottom up, you will get seriously burnt."

"You are right but it is so tedious."

"You will just have to remain a fair English rose. Your skin will look much better in fifty years from now, than a girl who is always tanning. Anyway, these much tanned girls are fairly boring. All they want to do all the time is lie in the sun. They don't want to castrate calves or blood test cows. I was very proud of you. I bet you any money you like, you will be the only girl to get a first in Mathematics at Oxford, who knows how to castrate bull calves."

Jane was really encouraged. "I am going to work bloody hard to prove you right. You can say the nicest things, when you are not trying to shock me."

"I am not trying to shock you but you have done the buttons up wrong on your shorts. I can see your pubic hair."

"Thanks-helpful comments like that are totally acceptable."

"I have another proposal which you might find acceptable. You must say if you don't like the idea and I will totally understand. I think your Grandparents are likely to volunteer to take Aunt Mary back to the ranch in their comfortable car, rather that Bob's truck. I still have to do the pregnancy diagnosis on Bob's heifers. Normally, as it is all tarmac, I would go up in my Landrover but, if you were coming and would like, we could go up in the plane?"

"Would I like? I would really love you to fly me up."

"Well, that's settled then. There is one other thing."

"I know, let me guess. I might be too heavy, as we will have to take all your veterinary gear, so I would have to fly naked to keep the weight down!"

"Well, it might be a good idea," said Jim smiling and stroking his chin. "What I was going to suggest was, that we flew on from Bob and Mary's to an airstrip just outside the Tsavo Game Park on the

Voi River and camped for the night. We might see some game or we might not. We certainly will be bitten by mosquitoes. You can bring your clothes but weight will be an issue, as we will have to take all our water. One thing for sure, is there will not be anyone else around. The area is very dry and often there is no water in the Voi River."

Jane's face lit up. "I can't think of anything I would like to do more. Of course, there are lots of people I would rather go with but beggars can't be choosers!" She laughed when she saw his rather crestfallen expression. "You old goat, I would love you to take me. I was only joking. You are so delightfully easy to tease."

Jim relaxed. "We will have to be a little circumspect about asking your grandparents. They may not approve of you going off in the wild with me."

"They certainly would not approve knowing what scrapes you get me into. Fancy letting me swim in Tudor Creek without any shoes or gloves, so I had to climb up your body, Grandma would have had a fit!"

Jim just laughed. There was no point in reminding her whose idea it was to dive in.

They arrived back at Nyali at the right time for lunch. James and Judith had just got back from visiting Mary. They were delighted how well she was doing. As Jim had expected they were going to take her up to the ranch in three days, time. It was ideal as, being a Saturday, Jim could work in the morning pregnancy diagnosing Bob's heifers and then, after lunch, fly off and camp. They could then fly back on Sunday, whenever they liked. Jim left Jane to pick the right time to ask if she could go camping. She was sure that the flying would not be a problem, as Jim had proved himself bringing Mary down to Mombasa.

Their fears were totally unfounded. Judith thought going to watch game was fine. Jane suspected that her Grandparents felt slightly guilty that they had not taken Jane on 'safari'. Also, as Jane had said, they had not a clue what the two of them had been up to.

Chapter 16

A flying safari

Saturday 10th June 1967

Jim picked Jane up after breakfast. He had told her he would bring everything they needed and all she had to bring was her sun hat, some sun block and a lot of mosquito repellent. James and Judith were going to pick Mary up at 10.00 am and have lunch at the ranch and then return before dark.

Jim was sad he had to leave Lucy behind with Katana but she would not have been safe just let loose, so near the game park when they camped.

Jim drove Jane out to the airport and parked at the aero club. Then they got out the pitiful amount of kit they were taking with them, for their one night '*safari*'. Jim teased Jane, saying the water they were taking weighed as much as her. They managed to pack it all in. Although it was light, the piece of foam they were going to use as a mattress was very bulky and seemed to fill the back of the plane. Jim took Jane up in the control tower to file their flight plan, as he knew she would be interested.

When they got back to the plane, while Jim did his preflight checks on the outside of the plane, Jane went into the aero club. Jim thought she had gone in to go to the loo. She came out with his aviation map and a piece of paper. On it, she had written the headings they would need to take, if there was no wind, and then the likely headings they would need, allowing for the wind speed at the moment on the ground. She had worked out the distances for each leg together with the times, if there was no wind, and once again the times they would need allowing for the wind speed at the moment on the ground. Jim was most impressed and said so. Jane just smiled and said, "I do enjoy maths, you know!"

They got into the plane and, before Jim started the engine, he showed Jane all the controls and the instruments. Then he helped her strap herself in and he shut and locked her door. After he had started up and done the magneto check, he shouted to Jane above the noise, "You put your hands on the joy stick and your feet on the pedals. It is totally dual control, so you will feel me moving the controls. In this way you will get the hang of it."

Then he got permission to taxi from the control tower and he was cleared to go to runway 180. As they moved along the taxi-way, Jim tested the rudder, the elevator and the ailerons. Jane found it a strange sensation, with the controls moving, this way and that way. When Jim was happy the controls were in order, he shouted, "You have a go." He took his hands off the stick and his feet off the pedals. Jane was concentrating hard but, he could see she was enjoying it. He gave her directions to the end of the holding area, by the runway. He told her to stop there. He cleared take off and said, "OK, you get her lined up." She manoeuvered the plane on to the runway and gasped, as it looked so enormous. Jim said,"I will feed in the power and you can take her off."

"Wow, can I really?"

"Yes, but if I think we are in trouble, I will say 'I have control'. You must let go of everything and take your feet off the pedals."

Jim increased the throttle to full revs and the plane quickly gained speed down the runway. Although he had his hands and feet ready to take action, he let Jane carry on. She did very well. As they reached take off speed, Jim shouted,"OK, just let her fly herself off the tarmac." Jane, very gently, eased the stick backwards. Jim could just feel her pulling back a bit too quickly. "Don't pull back anymore, just let her build up speed. That is great. You are a natural. Well done, keep her like that. She is climbing nicely." As they reached the end of the vast runway, they hit the turbulence created by the coconut trees. The light plane lurched sideways and upwards. Jane did not panic but just pushed down slightly on the stick, to keep the plane at the right angle. Jim was concentrating in case he had to take over. He did not notice the tip of her tongue poking out between her lips, as she was living every moment. There was some more turbulence and then they were flying straight and level.

Jim reported to the tower that they were leaving the circuit and heading for Mackinnon Road. He was told to report to East Air Centre. This he did, as Jane continued to climb. He was also told to report Mackinnon Road in sight.

He turned to Jane. "Very well done, now let's do a climbing turn on to the heading you had worked out?" Jane did not have to look at her piece of paper, as she had memorized the heading. Jim shouted, "I will keep an eye on the road, to see if I can see your grandparent's car but I think we are ahead of them. You keep climbing, as we want to be a little higher so it will be cooler." It was only then, that he noticed the sweat droplets coalescing between the top of her breasts. It was very sexy.

"OK, I think we are high enough, you can level off and I will show you how you use the trim to make it easier for you to fly level. I have control."

Jane said, "I am sorry I am not talking but I have been really concentrating. Thank you so much for letting me fly." She rubbed his thigh with her left hand. "Sorry, my palms are a bit sweaty." Jim was not sure whether she was apologising for having sweaty palms or whether she was just drying her palm on his leg.

Soon they could see Mackinnon Road airstrip, beside the Mombasa Road. Jim called East Air Centre and reported that they were going to land and that he would report again when he was airborne. He changed on to frequency 118.1 which was good practice, as they were coming into an unmanned strip.

"There is no need to buzz the house, as I can see Bob's truck already on the strip. Do you want to try landing the plane?"

"Yes please, but keep watching me. I feel a bit scared."

"You will do fine. We will save money and come straight in. I will throttle back for you. You have control. Just keep pushing the nose down and aim at the red runway." Jim trimmed the flap for her. "See, you are losing height on your altimeter. Keep the speed at 65 knots. Well done." Jim controlled the rate of descent with the throttle but he let Jane fly the plane. They were well positioned and there was no wind. They were thirty feet up, as they came over the end of the strip. Jim cut the power to idyll. They were descending perhaps a little too fast but he calmly said, "OK, start to pull back on the stick. Well done, you are flattening out nicely. Pull back a bit more. Bring the stick right into your tummy and keep it there." There was a little bump but it was a very good landing, considering they had not used the flap. "Well done. You keep the plane straight, I will put on the brakes." The Tripacer only had a hand brake but they came to a stop, at the bigger area at the end of the runway.

"Can you park it? I am totally knackered," said Jane.

"I have control," said Jim. He quickly parked it out of the way. Then he did a magneto check and cut the engine and turned off the fuel. He opened the door and Jane virtually fell out. Bob came towards them, "Are you OK, Jane?"

"I am fine. Jim let me fly and then let me land. It was so exciting I have lost all my energy. Can I hug you Uncle Bob, otherwise I think I will fall over."

"It is good to see you both. The others have not arrived but they know where to go, so we will go and PD the heifers. The herders have got cattle into the crush."

They did not have far to go before they came to the race and holding pens. Jim took off his shirt and handed it to Jane, who went behind Bob's truck. She took off her shirt and bra and put on Jim's shirt. She felt a little aroused as it smelt of him. Jim did the PDs. He came to one heifer and said, "This feels like a freemartin." He turned to Bob and said, "Sadly you will have to send this one to KMC, Bob, as she will never breed. When she was in her mother's womb there was a twin calf, which was a bull. The bull developed before the heifer and so the heifer did not develop her proper reproductive organs. Bob, can you ask your chaps if this was a twin?" After some general conversation among the herdsmen it was agreed that, indeed, this animal was a twin to a bull. Jim turned to Jane and said, "Would you like to feel inside?" Bob did not say anything but his astonished face said it all, as Jane got into the crush. "Don't worry, Uncle Bob. Jim has told me what it feels like."

Jane loved it as Jim got close to her. They had ten cows to blood test and Jane did all of them. Both Jim and Jane were filthy so they rode in the back of the truck. Then they got covered in red dust as well. They arrived back at the house just as James, Judith and Mary arrived. Both Judith and Mary were shocked. "My goodness Jane, however did you get so dirty?" said Judith.

"I was helping Jim PD Uncle Bob's heifers. I have decided I am going to be the only person to get a first at Oxford in Maths, who knows how to feel if a heifer is a freemartin and how to castrate bull calves," said Jane proudly.

"Well, I don't think it is proper for a girl to get so dirty. Mary, can she use your shower?"

Jim said. "I will go to the outside shower. Sorry to delay everyone, I expect you are ready for lunch?"

Bob said, "I think we all need a drink. Mary, you must sit down, you must be tired after your journey. Are you allowed alcohol?"

"I think so but I should only have one." She was obviously delighted to be home. Their cook had prepared an excellent lunch. Jane came out from her shower looking very fresh and clean. They all had a good lunch. Jane noticed that Jim did not have a beer. She was just about to say something, when she realised he was not ill, it was just that he would be flying. He had told her, he never had any alcohol within eight hours of a flight. She thought, I wonder if he will make up for it tonight. She suddenly became apprehensive. She had never slept all night with a man. In fact, she had only ever kissed and cuddled two different boys and, although she had not disliked it, being just near to Jim was very different. She longed to touch him and let him touch her. She thought, '*I am not actually frightened. It is that I hope I can please him. I don't think just doing what he says will necessarily please him. I want to excite him as much as he excites me.*' Jane was delighted that they did not sit drinking after lunch but Jim suggested they get going. They said their goodbyes and Bob drove them to the airstrip. Bob thanked Jim, once again, for his help with Mary. Bob hugged Jane and said he hoped they both would have fun, as there would be no creature comforts out there. He was sure they would make the best of it and he left them to go back for, in his words, 'an afternoon session'.

They checked the aircraft together. Jane could not reach the petrol caps on top of the high wings, so Jim lifted her up. He was once again amazed at how little there was of her and how light she was. Jane, for her part, loved the feel of his arms around the top of her thighs.

Jim got her to do virtually everything. There was no doubt she was an extremely bright girl. She remembered everything. It was a short flight and they were soon landing on a rough airstrip near to the Voi River. There were no trees and so they would have to use the plane's wings to provide some shade. They got all they needed out of the cab, which soon became very hot. Jim had packed a cool box with a little food and a lot of beer. He found his old pewter beer mug and suggested they walk the hundred yards to the nearest tree and have a drink in the shade. He took off his shirt and folded it on a log, as a seat for her.

"You sit down and I will sit on your lap, if you can bare my weight?" said Jane.

"I am horribly sweaty. You still look so clean and fresh, after your shower," remarked Jim.

"You do talk a lot of twaddle. I can feel the sweat running down between my breasts. I will take my bra and shirt off but I must put my shirt back on when we go in the sun." She folded them up and put them on top of his shirt.

"That will be more comfortable for you." She giggled, as he sat down and put her arm around his neck.

"What is so funny?" asked Jim.

"Some girls who are a bit flat-chested or whose boobs droop a little, have bras with metal wires in them, to keep their tits up. If I had a bra like, that you might have got a piece of wire up your arse." They both laughed.

Jim said, "So, I am doubly glad you have got great tits." They swallowed the cold beer contentedly. The cold of the beer made them both sweat more. Jim told her how he often drank tea, as that did not make you sweat like a cold drink. There were beads of sweat on her breasts. Jim lent down and licked her nipples. Even in the heat, Jane shivered with delight. She asked, "Is it nice if I lick your tiny nipples?"

Jim replied, "Not really, it doesn't turn me on at all but I think it does for some men. You are a good statistician, I am sure. So you will have to keep records. You can then tell me if I am normal or abnormal."

"Why don't you ask your friends?" queried Jane.

"I would be much too embarrassed. Men never discuss things like that."

"Oh well, I suppose that is a good thing. I would hate the thought of you saying to your pals, 'Cor, that, Jane she loves having her nipples licked and kissed.' Can you do it again? I suppose a girl should not ask?"

"I think you are right to ask. It is so difficult to know, sometimes, what a girl wants you to do." With that he delicately licked each nipple several times.

"Yes, that is lovely. You are lovely and gentle and I like that, but I have read in books how some girls like men to be rough. I suppose we are all different. I don't think I would like it if you spanked me but certainly I have read that turns some girls on."

"Well, you must tell me Jane, what you do like," said Jim

"Can I be really honest?"

"Of course, go ahead."

"You will laugh at me but it is the little things which I love. It is feeling your hard 'willy' against my thigh. I feel it nudging me like a dog's nose. It is feeling your hand on my thigh. You are going to really laugh now that I am bare chested, but I love it when I have a shirt and a bra on, then you take a little peep down the front. Am I right? Do you enjoy just peeping?"

Jim roared with laughter, "You are right. I think I am totally weird as, in many ways, having your tits bare is not as exciting as catching a glimpse of them." He leant forward and licked them, "That is exciting."

"You have taught me a lot in the last few days," said Jane. "Now that I have felt inside a cow I think I know what is happening to me. When you lick my nipples, I feel a contraction in either my womb or my vagina or somewhere down there. It is a lovely deep feeling of satisfaction. I was really feeling that, when you were rubbing me on the beach, before the dogs started barking and spoilt it. I have read about girls rubbing themselves and having an orgasm but I have never done that. Tonight, will you rub me and give me an orgasm? I think I would love that?"

"That will be great fun. Will you do something for me?"

"Yes," said Jane a little hesitantly. She was wondering what he was going to ask.

"Will you take off your shorts and run back and get us another cold beer? I would love to see the muscles in your bottom rippling and I will enjoy drinking the cold beer!"

Jane got up and, with a grin on her face, stood right in front of him and tantalizing undid and then took off her shorts. She flicked her dark bush and then turned and ran to the plane. She came back breathless, with a bottle and the opener. She picked up her shorts. "I don't think I will burn now, so we can add them to our cushion. Now, you must take your shorts off, so I can see how pleased you are to see me back. As Jim took his shorts off his penis sprung out. Jane kissed him, "I am conceited enough to think it is my body but, sadly, I think it is the beer! There is hardly any room to sit on your lap."

With that, she sat astride and facing him. She offered him the beer, which Jim poured into his tankard and handed it to her. She took a really long swallow. "I am getting to like this stuff. I can imagine me, in the rain sitting outside a pub in Oxford, by the Thames, drinking warm flat beer with masses of clothes on. I will think of you and feel a warm glow."

"You won't," said Jim. "You will be thinking how nice it is to be talking about some stimulating mathematics problem, with a very clever young man who is not always trying to get your clothes off and is not constantly lusting after your body."

Jane laughed. "That's what you thought when you first met me but, hopefully, I have pointed out your mistake. I love being warm and naked and feeling your erection against my pussy. My only sadness is I can't go rushing in to Grandma and say how wonderful it is. Mind you, she did tell me to do what you tell me to do. Let me have a swig of the beer and lick my nipples again."

Two more beers went down and then Jane announced that she did not need to put anymore clothes on, as the sun was not burning now. In fact, her back was now just in the sun as it had sunk down. She was wrong as, in the morning, Jim teased her because there were white hand marks on her bottom, which was slightly pink.

They set up what little they had as a camp. They put the mattress under one wing and tied the mosquito net to an eye on the wing, which was meant to be used to tie the plane down if there was a wind. Jim had brought two pillow cases, which he said they could stuff their clothes in to act as pillows. Jane had always worn pyjamas, as the bedrooms in her grandparent's house were air conditioned. When Jim saw them, he suggested she stuff them in the pillow case as, he said, he thought she would be seriously hot in the night. Jane retorted. "Are you boasting or complaining?"

It was lucky they had this banter as, after they had eaten their supper, which was sausages cooked on thin metal rods, baked beans in the tin and baked potatoes in tin foil all cooked on a small fire, they were somehow shy, even though they were still completely naked, except for their shoes.

The fire was some distance from the plane, as they were worried about the fuel. They had taken the seats out of the plane to sit on but they had no table. They got really mucky, eating a pineapple in their fingers. Jim boiled some water and made a tankard of coffee, which they were going to drink black and share and then Jim remembered the miniature bottle of African Cream Liqueur, which he poured into the coffee.

"A bit tinny but very sweet and tasty," was Jane's comment. They drank it in silence, gazing into the fire. They were both lost for words. At last Jim said, "We should be careful with the water but I think we could have a little warm water in the saucepan and wash a little. We won't see most of the dirt, until the morning."

"I will wash you," said Jane. "I think I will be more economical with the water."

She washed his face, then his hands, under his arms and then his groin. Jim immediately became erect. She washed him very delicately and told him to stand and dry. The warm air dried him immediately. She then bent down and kissed his penis. "Is that nice?"

"Yes, it is lovely."

"Can I suck it, now it is clean? I don't think it would taste very nice all gritty. It would be like unwashed asparagus."

"For a mathematician, you have a marvellous way with words."

She licked the tip and then, gently sucked it into her mouth. "Is that nice?" she said, as she stopped.

"Yes, its lovely, but let me wash you now." He washed her like she had washed him, ending in her groin. She stood with her legs apart, letting the warm air dry her. Then Jim squatted down in front of her and licked her very gently. He stopped. "Was that nice?"

205

Jane giggled. "It was ticklish. However I think it would be awesome if I was lying down. Let's go to bed?"

They got onto the piece of foam and tucked in the mosquito net, although they had not noticed any mosquitoes. Jim had brought a large duvet cover for them to get into, but Jane lay on it on her back with her legs wide apart and said, "I think this is going to be fun. Probably not as exciting as flying but I gather you haven't got a 'night rating'."

"You are a very cheeky monkey." Jim drew her towards him and buried his face in her groin. He licked, sucked and nibbled. Jim felt her have an orgasm. Then he pushed two fingers very slowly into her and started moving them in and out. He kept on but moved up her body and started to kiss her breasts, at the same time as moving his hand really quickly. Suddenly he stopped. "Sorry, would you rather go flying."

"Don't stop, you bastard. Please don't stop. It is heavenly."

Jane was under him gasping and pushing her slim hips up on to his hand and then, suddenly, quick as a cat she had rolled him on his back and was lying on top of him with her legs wide apart. Using both hands, she thrust his erect penis inside her and ground her pelvis on to it. Her knees flexed and she moved her pubis in and out. Jim knew he was going to ejaculate and, just in time he lifted her whole body off him. He only managed it because she was so light and he could grasp her hips so easily. She clamped her thighs and he ejaculated between them. It was only then that he heard a gurgling sound and realised it was her laughter. "I knew I could do it," said the voice in his ear. "That was marvellous, 'I am in control' Jim Scott lost it then." They fought then with Jim rolling on top of her and trying to silence her laughter with his kisses. The laughter stopped when he started moving two fingers inside her again. "Yes, oh please, yes, move them quicker." She thrust up and then, with a groan of deep seated pleasure, Jim felt her relax under him.

When they had both calmed down, were lying on their sides, with her little bottom pushed into his tummy and her hands holding his, which were holding her breasts, Jim said. "I thought I had hurt you and then I realised you were laughing. Did I hurt you?"

"No, you conceited bugger, you aren't well enough endowed for that! It was a wonderful feeling but I was laughing as, in books, the girls are often trying to fight to save their virginity but I was fighting to lose mine. Admit it, you were still in control and would not have entered me?"

"I was too worried you would get pregnant." Jane turned and kissed him. "You are a kind boy and I should not laugh at you. I never would in front of anyone else. It was just great having you in my power." Then she laughed again. "Your semen has stuck my thighs together, so don't worry, you can't come in again!"

Then, after she had peeled her thighs apart, she said, "Put him back, high up near my fanny. I like the feeling of him up there. Hug me tight."

Neither of them really remembered anything, until the rising sun woke them in the morning. Jane whispered in his ear, "Wake up, you lazy boy. Don't make a noise. I want to go down near the Voi River and see some game." Jane pulled back the mosquito net and put on her trainers. Jim said nothing but put on his trainers. He was reaching for his shorts, when Jane whispered, "I want to go in the nude. Come on Tarzan, me Jane."

"Wait," said Jim. "We are much too white. We will terrify all the game." Jim splashed himself with water and lay in the dry red dust, which had blown to the side of the airstrip. Jane followed his example. They followed a track down to the river. They were lucky. In the river, which was just a muddy mess, were a group of elephants. The nearest was only ten yards away. The very slight wind was blowing in their faces, which meant they were down wind. The elephants were eating the bush. Jim guessed there must be some water higher up the river, as there was no way they could drink at this spot. Jane touched him and indicated that he should sit on the ground, so she could sit on top of him. Jim put his filthy hands around her and held her thin body close to him. He kissed her neck and she kissed his cheek.

Slowly, the elephants started to move up stream. They followed at a safe distance. Jim had been right. There was some standing water. The elephants seemed to queue up and each one had a drink, without disturbing too much mud. Jane had got Jim to sit down again and was sitting astride his legs, Jim saw some Zebra coming to the other side of the water. He touched Jane and pointed. They did not seem frightened of the elephants and came to drink. After that two waterbuck arrived, also to drink. They were followed by a fairly big group of female impala. Jim could feel Jane's body tense with excitement, at seeing all this game. He was excited, not only by the game but by her body, as she moved over his groin. He started to get an erection but suddenly felt they were being watched. He turned slowly and there, two yards away, was a big male baboon. Jane said later that the first thing she felt, was his penis shrinking. She slowly turned and saw the baboon. She said, she was sure he winked at her before he slowly ambled away.

It was now bright sunlight and all the animals moved off in various directions. Jim indicated that they ought to return, as she would soon start to burn. He was also worried that the baboons might have trashed their camp but it was just as they had left it. He went to the edge of the camp and started to have a wee. Jane crept up behind him and, when he was in full flow, held his penis and wiggled it about. "I have often wondered what it is like for you men to have a wee. It certainly takes longer than us girls but we have usually got more clothes to sort out." Jim was speechless.

When it came to cleaning themselves up, they actually didn't too bad a job, as Jim had gone over the top with the amount of water he had brought. He thought, what a beautiful little body Jane had, as he watched her wash herself, several times, in the tiny bowl they had brought with them. He thought she had read his mind, as she turned towards him and said, "I am glad you like my body, you voyeur."

"How did you know I was thinking that?"

Jane just giggled and pointed at his erect penis. "Now, come here and let me wash you properly, as I am not letting you anywhere near me in that filthy state." Jim decided being washed was rather nice. They both were dry in no time, in the dry air. Jane quickly went to cover herself, as she was worried about getting burnt.

"Please stay naked. Why don't you sit on the mattress, under the wing in the shade? I will move the mosquito net away and make you a cup of tea."

"That would be lovely. I don't think you men realise, it is nice for us girls to look at a boy's body." Jim laughed. "Actually I am quite shy, in fact, much shyer than you. I wonder why? We were a very open family when I was growing up. At boarding school we got no privacy at all but, of course, we never saw a girl's body only, dreamt about naked girls and had pictures stuck up on our locker doors."

"You must have been so frustrated at school. We three girls, as sisters, at home were always naked but I was at a mixed day school, so boys were no big deal, in fact, they were just annoying most of the time. I never saw my Dad naked that would have been totally taboo. I have read about apes. When the females want a male, like me now, their vulvas would swell but mine doesn't. Do other girls?"

"I don't know," said Jim as he brought her tea and sat beside her. "I think that male baboon fancied you."

"I don't think he did but I am sure he winked at me," replied Jane.

The high wing of the airplane was a good shade provider but it soon started to get very hot. "Now, Miss Top Navigator and Ace Pilot, I have an idea as I don't think we will see anymore game here. How about packing up and flying to Kilaguni Lodge, which is not far away by air? We could have lunch and use their pool?"

"That would be really great, in all respects bar one. I will have to put some clothes on! Come on, don't let's hang about." She sprang up like a gazelle and started to get dressed. "Do I have to wear underwear?"

"That's your answer," said Jim, pointing at his erection.

"I am going to call your 'willy', Jake the Rake. Thank you, Jake. That was the right answer." She leant down and kissed Jake.

Once they had got the plane packed up, Jim got Jane to do all the checks on the outside of the plane. He enjoyed lifting her up, to do the physical check of the fuel. Then, when they had got in, he got her to start the internal checks. She had remembered the magneto check, from the night before. Jim did turn on the radio to check, on the 118.1 frequency, that there was no one trying to use this unmanned strip. He shouted to Jane that he would not bother with East Air Centre, as he knew they would not hear him. He said, he would if he was on his own but he wanted to help her with the controls, as this time he wanted her to use the throttle as well as the other controls. Then she was taxing down the runway, so they could take off into the wind. He made Jane do the take off checks. She giggled when he told her the mnemonic for remembering them. 'Try my prick for instant happiness. This stood for trim, mixture, pitch, flaps, engine, harness and hatches.

"What is prick?"

"We haven't got one." Jane raised her eyebrows.

"It is the pitch. Only bigger engines have a variable pitch, so you can alter the angle of the propeller and cut a bigger slice of the air."

"I will make do with Jake."

"Now, I want you to do everything. First, put on the brake, we only have a hand brake. Then push the throttle forward, as far in as it will go. Now the engine is racing. Look up and aim down the runway, as you release the brake. Off we go."

The little plane gained speed quickly and Jane let it fly itself off the runway. Jim got her to push the nose forward to build up speed and then slowly release the ten degrees of flap. Then, with his hand over hers, he got her to throttle back the revs so that they were on a good climbing speed. Once they were over five hundred feet above the ground, he got her to turn on the heading he had worked out for Kilaguni. He had done the calculation, as he knew she was not experienced enough to do everything.

He shouted. "Let's stay at this height, we might see some game. We will be too far north to see Bob and Mary's house."

Jane was a natural, she kept the plane beautifully straight and level. She mastered the trim quickly, so the plane virtually flew itself.

They passed the Aruba Dam, slightly to their left. Further to their left they could see the Taita Hills. Jim thought he could see Voi to their left. Then they crossed the railway and the main Nairobi Road, which ran together. Jim was impressed as Jane did not wait for him to tell her but climbed five hundred feet, as they had to fly over an unnamed hill. He then showed her how to lean out the mixture, now that they were higher, to preserve fuel and make the engine run sweeter. He also showed her how the carburetor heater worked but, obviously, at this altitude in the tropics, there was no icing.

Jim shouted, "Now we have to look out for a line of dark green trees and that will be the Tsavo River. There is the Chaimu Crater ahead, so we should see it soon. You can lose a little height. I will just check there is no other plane in the area." There was no response to his radio call.

"I can see the river," sung out Jane.

"I can see the strip, dead ahead. If you turn thirty degrees to your right, you will be able to do a gentle turn when we are past the runway and then line yourself up to land. I would do your landing checks now. They are hardly relevant, as the plane has a fixed under carriage but it is a good habit to get into."

With minimal help from Jim, Jane landed the plane. She parked up and did a magneto check before cutting the engine. Jim squeezed her thigh and said. "Well done, that was magic. I can't believe how you have picked up everything so quickly. You are a marvellous girl. You never have to be told how to do anything twice." With a big grin she said. "You are a bit the same, just a little slower." She pushed his hand, which was still on her thigh, up under her skirt. Somehow the concentration of landing had really aroused her. She very soon came to a climax, as Jim's fingers entered her. Jim opened the door to let some air into the plane which as they had stopped, had rapidly heated up. Her whole neck and throat were bright red. He got out and she fell into his arms, almost fainting. "Are you OK?" he asked, in a concerned voice. "Not really," was the reply. "I feel really weak at the knees and dizzy. That orgasm was something else. It seems I am a quick learner about sex, as well as flying. Can you sit on the ground, under the wing and let me sit on your lap. I will soon recover. Either my blood sugar is low, or my blood pressure dropped dramatically." As they sat, she let her head drop on his shoulder. They stayed there for a couple of minutes and then she kissed his neck. "Sorry for being such a goose. I feel much better now."

Jim stroked her hair and said. "Let's just sit for a couple more minutes and then I will find your hat and your bikini and we will go for a swim. The water in the pool is quite cool, not like the pools at the coast."

Jane soon got to her feet and held on to the wing strut, while Jim found her hat and their swimming things. "I think we only brought one towel, so we will have to share." He knew she was feeling better, as she jokingly said, "I know you only brought one towel, so you could see me naked. Look, what's happening to Jake?" It was Jim's turn to blush. She laughed again. "The cold water will do him good! On second thoughts, I feel like doing a take-off check." She dropped on to her haunches, undid his shorts and kissed Jake. Then to Jim's pleasure and amazement, she put her arms round his neck and

211

jumped, with her legs around his waist. Jim, with a reflex action held her naked bottom and took her weight. She reached down and he felt Jake inside her. She was so light, he could easily hold her as she griped him, thrusting her pelvis. He groaned, "I am coming." She reached down and he came into her hand, as he let her legs drop and she took her own weight. He was breathing really hard. "Christ that was a near thing." He looked on in surprise as she casually wiped her hand on her naked thigh. "Time for that swim, I think," said Jane.

They had a great time by the pool, swimming. Jane wore her hat and a shirt over her bikini and they both sat under umbrellas, by a table at the pool. There were a few other people initially but they soon went in to have lunch. A kind waiter brought them a sandwich and a pint of lemonade and lime, out to the pool.

They chatted away all afternoon until, at about 4.00 pm, they both fell silent. Jim said rather glumly, "I feel I have let you down and not planned ahead. I would love for us to have stayed the night here and watch the animals come to drink in the flood-lit waterhole, but your grandparents would be worried stiff if we don't get back tonight. There is no way of contacting them and, as you told me last night, I haven't got a night rating!"

"You are a silly boy. I had more fun on that bit of old foam, than I think some girls have in a life time. I loved all the flying and our game watching at the river. Come on, let's fly home now in plenty of time and go to Nyali, laughing all the time as they say we always do?"

Jane did almost all the flying on the way home. She loved it. When they landed, she again said she felt a bit weak and would he hold her. It worried Jim that she had felt weak several times. In the Landrover he said. "I am worried about you, Jane. I don't think it is normal for you to feel faint, like you did when we landed just now. Will you promise, when you get back to UK, you will go and have a checkup?"

Jane laughed. "I don't think it is anything to worry about. It may be the anti-malarial tablets. Or, of course, it might be the devastatingly good looking Jim Scott?" She put out her tongue at him.

"What is sad," she continued, "Is that I am now hooked on flying but I would never be allowed to because of wearing glasses."

"Rubbish," replied Jim. "Of course you can fly privately, like me. It is only if you wanted to be a commercial pilot, that it would be tricky. You are much too bright to waste your life being a commercial pilot. You must be an Oxford Don or a nuclear scientist."

"Stop the car," commanded Jane. Jim thought. *'What have I done to upset her?'* As the car stopped, she threw her arms round his neck and kissed him. "You are lovely. You are the only man who does not put me down, because I look like the back of a bus with these thick glasses."

"I don't put you down because you have great tits." Jane roared with laughter. She grabbed his penis and said. "I am going to squeeze Jake harder and harder, until you say I am a beautiful girl. Go on say it."

"Actually, Jake is rather enjoying being squeezed but you are a really beautiful girl, with great tits."

"You are a bastard. You always have to have the last word." Jim knew she was not cross when she said, "Drive on my man. You have control."

As they were coming up onto the veranda, they were talking about the game they had seen. Jim said. "I bet that baboon thought you had great tits when he winked at you."

"That is quite enough from you, Jim Scott." They both laughed.

"Still laughing, I see," said Judith. "You look as if you have been pulled through a hedge backwards, Jane." Jim stood up for her. "She has been on a really rough safari and has not uttered one word of complaint."

"Well, I am glad to hear that but I still think her hair is a mess."

"Sorry Grandma. It was the chlorine in the pool at Kilaguni that did it."

James laughed, "It does not sound a very rough safari to me, if you have been at Kilaguni."

Jim could tell that, actually, Judith and James were relieved that they were back safe and sound. They all had a good supper, with Jim and Jane eating massive amounts.

When Jim went to go, Jane asked Judith if Jim could come to lunch the next day, as she was leaving on an afternoon flight to Nairobi and then flying back home to UK, in the evening.

"Of course he can."

Jane walked with Jim to his Landrover. She kissed him and said. "Thank you for everything. I mean everything. I think I might burst into tears at the airport and see if another guy will put his arm around me." Jim hoped she was not crying but he thought she might be, as he drove off.

He arrived early for lunch. Jane came onto the veranda to greet him. "Can you give me a hand to close my case? I have bought too many presents." Did she wink? Jim was not sure. She led him into her room and shut the door behind them. She pushed her case, which Jim could see was shut up, against the door. Then she pulled him to her and lent back against the door. Then she kissed him. Jim knew immediately what she wanted. She had a fairly short skirt on. He reached up under it. She had some knickers on. May be he had read her wrong, yet again. She whispered into his ear. "I had to have knickers on, so you could shock me and reach inside them." Jim felt her. She was moist already. With one hand he rubbed her and he put the other over her mouth. She did not resist. She knew he was trying to stop her making a noise. Her legs were wide apart and she rhythmically pushed herself on to his two fingers. As she came, she bit down on to his hand and fell into his arms.

They both heard Judith calling. "Lunch is ready. Have you managed the suit case?"

Jim answered, "We have nearly got the zip done. We did not want to break it."

As they came into the dining room, Judith said. "You are poor dears that must have been a struggle. It has even stopped you laughing." Both of them just grinned.

After lunch, Jim put Jane's suitcase into the car. Then he put his arms around her and said, "Make sure you ask the stewardess if you can go up into the cockpit. You know flying is the most exciting thing you have ever done. Have fun at Oxford. Thank you for being such a great co-pilot. Good luck."

She kissed him and got into the car. Then she waved, with both arms out of the window, as James drove off.

Chapter 17

High Commission Reception

Saturday 24th June 1967

Sir Richard Rochester had been very successful in the diplomatic service so, at a relatively young age of 57, had achieved the office of Kenya High Commissioner and, with it, his knighthood. His career had stagnated as he reached 50 as he was an unmarried bachelor. There had been talk that he was a homosexual until he had a whirl-wind romance with Claire Foster-Stand, which ended in a high profile wedding. Claire was 32 years his junior. She knew, when she agreed to marry him, she was being foolish but she had left school six months earlier and was totally miserable and bored. She had never known her mother, who had died at her birth. She had been brought up by a series of nannies. Her father, a diplomat, was a close friend of Sir Richard. Her father was kindly and she had had a normal rather distant relationship with him during her formative years. When she was fifteen, he had married a thirty year old. Claire loathed her step mother. She had managed to stick it out while she had been at boarding school but then, when she left school, life became intolerable. Marrying Sir Richard was a way of leaving home.

Their wedding had been a very grand affair, which had been organized by her stepmother. During the wedding preparations Claire had, what might have been called, a brief fling with a 24-year-old, very good looking Irishman who had been employed to look after the families' horses. He was an accomplished lover and had seduced her. Luckily, he was sensible enough not to get her pregnant. She was, therefore, not a virgin on her wedding night. To be fair to Sir Richard, he did try to make love to her but could not get an erection however hard Claire tried to stimulate him. He made an excuse that he had had too much champagne but Claire, although she was only

215

18, guessed there was a problem. They were in a suite at the Savoy, so there was no problem for them to sleep in separate rooms. Claire was a forthright girl and therefore had it out with him in the morning over breakfast in the suite. She was more cross with herself, than with him. He admitted that he had never had a relationship with a woman and swore blind that he had never had a relationship with a man. Claire actually believed him. Even though she was 32 years younger she took control, when he broke down and begged her not to leave him. He said his career, which meant everything to him, would be finished. Claire said she would stick by him. She would be the model diplomat's wife but she might well take a lover. If so, she would be very discrete and the world would not know any different.

Thus Sir Richard and Lady Rochester were standing in the hall greeting their guests, who had been invited to a cocktail party to celebrate the Queen's birthday.

Unknown to anyone except her boss in London, Lady Rochester was not only the high commissioner's wife but also the head spy master for East Africa. Her alias was Colin Shaw. She ran several agents, not only in Kenya, Tanzania and Uganda but also one in Somalia and one in Southern Sudan. She collected information from the agents. She endeavored to cross reference it and therefore verify it, before sending it on to London. No-one suspected all the letters to various 'girl friends', sent in the diplomatic bag, were her reports. Sir Richard was totally unaware of her other existence. It was the ideal cover. The agents knew of the existence of a controller but had no idea it was Claire. Recently she had had a serious problem. Agent 'Somali One', had been detained in Kismayo. She had sent in a very new Kenyan agent 'Animal Boy'. She had never met 'Animal Boy', as he had only been in the country six months. She was very reluctant to use such an inexperienced agent but had no other agent suitable. 'Animal Boy' had shown extreme courage and ingenuity and had rescued 'Somali One' with no damage to the network.

Tonight she knew 'Animal Boy' who was Jim Scott, was coming to the party. She knew him on paper and in black and white photographs, but had no idea what he was really like. She guessed from his dry reports, that he might be arrogant. He certainly was very bright to be a vet at 22. She thought she would dislike him, but knew that she could act the part and he would never know. How wrong she was.

Most of the guests had arrived. Claire said, "You go through Richard. I will meet the tail-enders and join you in twenty minutes or so."

"Very well, my dear, as always that will be an excellent idea. I never said before, as we were so rushed, but you look radiant tonight."

Claire did a small curtsy and replied. "Thank you for your compliment, kind Sir."

As she stood near to the front door, she heard a small commotion at the bottom of the steps. There were two *'askaris'* (Guards) stationed at the bottom of the steps. They were laughing with a European. He was chatting to them in very bad Swahili. He was bringing *'Salaams'* (Greetings) from one of their fathers and asking about their wives and families. He was also asking about their cows. Claire thought. *'Could this be 'Animal Boy? Surely he had only called into the Vet Labs at Kabete for a few days, before going to Mombasa. How could he be so friendly with these guys?'* Claire got on really well with the African staff at the High Commission. In fact, she got on well with Africans everywhere. She seemed to understand their humour. She hated it, when Europeans spoke down to Africans. She thought 'Animal Boy' was going to be arrogant. This chap sounded really friendly and full of fun. She must stop calling him 'Animal Boy'. He was Dr Scott. As she came out of the door, she heard one of the *'askaris'* teasing him about needing an *'ahya'* (Nanny). She could see why. Clambering up the steps, with ruffled hair, was a young man desperately trying to tie his black tie. Claire stepped forward and said "Come in, I won't be your *'ahya'* but I will be your *'malimu'* (teacher)".

"Oh thank you so much. I am a complete mess. Heavens knows what Sir Richard and Lady Rochester will think of me?"

"I am not sure what Sir Richard will think but Lady Rochester will do her best to help" Jim's jaw dropped. "You are Lady Rochester?"

"If you call me that, I definitely won't help you. I am Claire." Claire held out her hand. Jim took it and blurted out "But you are lovely." Still holding her hand Jim asked, "Can I kiss your hand?"

"That's a little formal, even for the High Commission. I meant you to shake my hand. As you have been so complimentary, why don't you kiss me?" Without any hesitation, Jim kissed Claire on the lips.

"What am I going to do with you? You come here late, looking a mess. You bring out all the charm. Then you kiss me on the lips. Next thing you will be trying to get in my knickers." Jim went bright red and dropped her hand as if it had burnt him. He mumbled,

"I am so sorry, somehow I couldn't help myself. You looked so lovely and I expected an old matron, with buck teeth and a massive bosom." Impulsively, Claire grabbed both his hands and looked straight into his eyes.

"So where is all your charm now? Aren't my tits big enough for you?" Jim immediately dropped his eyes and realised he was looking straight down Claire's cleavage. His eyes shot up to hers. He exclaimed,

"I didn't mean they weren't big enough, they are great. Oh Christ, I can't believe what I am saying. I am so very sorry."

"Don't keep saying sorry. I'm glad they pass inspection! Now, turn your back on me so I can tie your tie. I can only do it from behind," giggled Claire. She put her arms round his neck and started to tie his tie. She thought, I can't believe I just said that and giggled again. Talk about love at first sight and she pushed her body a little closer to his back, than she need to, so that she could tie his tie. What the hell, she thought, I really like the look of him and I haven't had a man touch me for years.

When she had tied, his tie she told him to turn and face the 'askaris'. They both had wide grins on their faces and they both brought their feet together and saluted. Jim said, "'*Memsahib muzuri sana*' (The lady is very good)." "'*Ndio*' (Yes)," they both answered.

Claire now led him into the Commission, through the hall and into the vast dining room. She said, "I will introduce you to some of the guests. Most of them you will find very stuffy. There will be some massive bosoms! I will have to circulate and do 'the hostess' bit. However, please don't go until we have had a much longer chat. In fact, would you like to go to Nairobi Game Park early in the morning?"

218

"I would really love that," replied Jim. We will touch base when you have done your entertaining. Don't worry about introducing me around. There is a girl over there, I know, called Annie. I will go and talk to her." Claire felt a pang of jealousy but said, "Great-you have a good time. See you later."

Claire thought, I wonder how he knows her. She is a Nairobi girl. As Claire went around the room chatting animatedly, she passed the three girls who worked at the High Commission. Claire wondered if Jim would go and chat to them. Claire felt another pang of sadness. They were all young, free and single. He was bound to go for them. However Claire was wrong. Very soon he came up to her, as she was talking to The Swedish Ambassador and his wife. Claire introduced them and then said,

"Please stay here Ambassador, I just want to bring over the Minister of Agriculture to meet you. I am sure Jim can entertain you for a moment. He is a vet from Mombasa but has travelled extensively, not only in the Coast Province, but also in the North Eastern Province. He has some veterinary stories to tell, about all manner of animals like camels." With that she was gone. Jim wondered how she knew he had dealt with camels but he dutifully regaled the Ambassador and his wife, with stories of doing a Caesarean section on a camel and blood testing 400 hundred camels in a single morning. Soon she was back with Bruce Mackenzie, The Minister of Agriculture in the Kenyan Cabinet. Claire did the introductions and then admitted to the Swedish Ambassador that she had an ulterior motive in introducing him to Bruce Mackenzie, as she knew the Kenya Artificial Insemination service for cattle were in desperate need of finance and the Kenya Government thought the Swedish Government might be persuaded to enlarge their aid project.

She then grabbed Jim by the arm and said she needed him to entertain some other guests with his stories. Before Jim quite knew what was happening, they were on their own outside on a veranda. Jim turned to Claire and said,

"I am so sorry I was late and behaved so badly when I arrived."

"Don't worry about it. I enjoyed having someone to tease. I don't get much chance here. Everyone is so serious. Now tell me about yourself. How are you getting on? You have been in the country for six months now."

"How did you know about the camels?" replied Jim. '*He doesn't miss much,*' thought Claire. '*I will have to be very careful or he will guess, I am more than the High Commissioner's wife.*'

"We get a lot of stuff, about all the Brits in the country, coming through the information service. We particularly hear about expatriates, who are on Overseas Development Agency (ODA) contracts. That is why you got an invitation tonight." replied Claire calmly. Jim was not totally convinced but thought, '*I will let it ride. At least a bad report has not been sent by the PVO.*'

Jim said, "I am really enjoying life. I love the job as it is so wonderfully varied. It would be great if we could have a look round Nairobi Game Park tomorrow. Obviously, I have driven through Tsavo several times and have been to the small Shimba Hills National Park but otherwise, on my safaris, the sighting of game has been rather fleeting."

"I love going round Nairobi Game Park, as you see so much in a very short time, but I would love to go on a real, dare I say it, rough safari in the NFD," answered Claire.

"I would love to take you," said Jim. "I am improving my kit every time I go, but I still have not solved the problem of keeping things cool. Apart from that it is fairly comfortable. It is a far cry from what the professional hunters take e.g. mess tents, loo tents, bath tents etc, but I rather like it that way."

"I am sure I would be the same," said Claire.

They went on chatting about safaris and Game Parks in a very relaxed way oblivious, of the reception inside, until they were stopped by a discrete cough behind them. Claire turned to see one of the senior high commission servants behind them.

"Eli, I was talking to Dr Scott and I had completely forgotten about the party. People must want to go. Thanks for calling me."

"Yes '*Memsahib*' there are a few people in the hall. Is this the Dr Scott who did the operation on my father's camel? It is the talk of Wajir. My mother thought you were marvellous '*Bwana*', not because of the camel, but how you talked to all the children. My youngest brother wants to be a vet and my youngest sister wants to be a nurse!"

"Well Eli, we will have to see what we can manage," said Jim holding out his hand. Eli lent forward and grasped Jim's hand. *"Asanti sana bwana."*

Claire thought to herself. *'Jim is a really good guy. This has been my lucky day.'* She said to both Jim and Eli.

"I must fly or there will be chaos at the door. See you both soon."

It was pitched dark with no hint of dawn. Jim was slightly early and was grateful that he had not drunk too much, at the party the previous night. He shivered and set off at a brisk walk, left out of the gates of the Norfolk Hotel, down Government road. He had an uneasy feeling that Claire would stand him up. Yet he knew he was being silly. She seemed totally sober, when she shook him by the hand at the door of the High Commission and lent briefly forward and whispered,

"See you at the first junction". He hoped and prayed that she would be alone. She was so lovely, he did not want to share her with anyone. He couldn't believe, she had been so kind to offer to take him out to Nairobi Game Park. She had laughed at him, when she suggested her old Landrover might break down and he had denied any real mechanical knowledge.

"You can always push! I will let you know if I see any lions creeping up on you".

There was Claire, flashing her headlights. She was on time. He ran across the road and swung himself into the Landrover.

"Well done. I was dreading you would not be here. The last thing I wanted to do was go into the Hotel Reception." Claire cheerfully greeted him. "It would be just my luck for some pissed upcountry farmer to be staggering in and recognise me!"

"I am so sorry. Would you have got into trouble?" asked Jim.

"Of course I could. The High Commissioner's wife, is not meant to be picking up strange men in the middle of the night! Don't look so worried. It didn't happen. Now, we are free of all the bloody formal protocol nonsense. We are off to see some game on our own. What would you particularly like to see?" Claire enquired.

"I suppose I must say, lion, except if the Landrover breaks down". Jim replied.

"I was only teasing you. Don't be such a worry guts. I have got a picnic and plenty of water. I even have a tow rope, so someone can tow us home."

With a giggle she said, "You might have to hide under a blanket in the back. I am damn cold. Can you come into the middle seat and put your arm across and keep the window closed. Now the road is rougher, it keeps sliding open."

It was only as Jim slid across, that he realised that she only had a cotton dress on, which only came halfway down her thighs. He was in his shorts and he immediately felt himself becoming aroused. He wished he had not taken an old settlers advice, "Never wear underpants Dear Boy. You will only get prickly heat". At least it was still dark and there was no interior light in the Landrover, so Claire would not see his discomfiture. As if she had read his mind, Claire changed gear and her thigh pushed hard against his. They lurched even closer together.

"Well done, keeping the window closed. It is much cozier without that draft."

They had come off the tarmac road and were on a dirt road, signed to the Game Park.

"I hope the rangers will let us in this early. The park does not officially open until 6 am. However, it is so much better to arrive at dawn. Not only is it cooler but you see so much more exciting game." Jim confessed, that he had been obsessed by African game animals as a little boy. He had wanted to come to Africa, even before he decided to become a vet.

Claire ruffled his hair. "I bet you were a lovely little boy".

"I doubt it, but I suppose my mother thought so. I was the youngest and certainly her favourite." At that moment, they lurched into a big pot-hole and Claire's left hand slipped off the gear stick and on to Jim's thigh. She just left it resting there. Jim could not remember when he felt so embarrassed. He prayed that his erection would subside, before it got light. Equally, he could not imagine that it would. What would Claire say? Would she tease him? Somehow Jim could not imagine her being shocked and getting cross. It was just so humiliating. Then disaster happened, as they hit a bigger than normal pot-hole. His shorts rode up and the tip of his penis came out of the bottom of the leg of his shorts. At the same time, Claire's hand went further up his leg and felt his extremely swollen organ.

"Wow, I never have had anyone like my driving that much. What an honour!" Claire giggled delightfully, giving his penis a little squeeze before grabbing the steering wheel with both hands, as a sharp bend loomed up in the road. Around the corner was the Park entrance. As Claire drew up to the barrier, Jim moved across into the left hand seat as he flicked the right hand window open, which he had been holding closed.

Claire charmed the game scout, with a joke in Swahili about a new foreigner from England mad keen to see some lion. The game scout advised them to head for Leopard's Rock, as he had heard a lion roaring up there in the night. Claire gave him five Kenya shillings, with a plea not to tell anyone else for a couple of hours. Claire let in the clutch and, with a friendly toot, drove off into the dawn. Jim's mind was racing. He knew he was pretty ignorant about girls. Here he was, in the middle of Africa, with a beautiful girl who must have been five years his senior, who was married to someone else. That someone was the High Commissioner and he could have him put on the next plane to England, sent home in disgrace.

Claire drove on and Jim could just make out a rocky hill in the distance, in the dawn. He moved into the middle seat and reached behind Claire, to shut the sliding window which had managed to work open again. Claire turned and kissed him very quickly on the cheek.

"Thanks, I thought I might have frightened you." Jim went crimson with embarrassment, as that is just what she had done. He managed to mumble,

"Sorry, I got a little excited."

"Don't be sorry." Claire was smiling and brought her left hand back on to his thigh.

"I have to be so prim and proper all the time, with so many old farts, it is great just to be ME and tease someone my own age. I am only twenty five, so I expect you are a bit younger than me but we are the same generation."

"Yes, I am only a baby. I am only just twenty three."

"Not that much of a baby," said Claire as she calmly rubbed his penis which to Jim's relief, was still in his shorts but getting big again rapidly. "How did you manage to qualify so early? I bet you are super bright and I was a dunce at school. My parents were delighted to get me married off and therefore off their hands."

Although Jim's commonsense was screaming at him, he could not resist moving his right hand on to her lovely smooth, brown neck and caressing it gently.

"Mmm, that's nice. I love having my neck fondled. Don't stop." Jim had moved to close the window, which had vibrated open again. He obediently started gently massaging her neck again. "Your hand will keep my neck warm. I won't notice the draft. Jim certainly was not noticing any draft. In fact he was radiating heat." Claire dexterously undid Jim's fly buttons and gently held his throbbing penis. "I hope my cold hand does not make him collapse," Claire giggled. "I will have to leave him now, as this bit of the road is steep and the gravel is loose. Sorry, I will have to drive with both hands."

She was right. They had reached the hill, which was very rocky and lived up to its name of Leopards rock. The road went round the rock, which allowed the Landrover to climb. Claire had already rammed the red gear stick forward, so it was in low range and four wheel drive. The engine was groaning. Stones were flying up and hitting the mud guards, but the old Landrover was still climbing. They rounded the corner onto a flat area and there, twenty yards away, were two lions. Claire killed the engine and they quickly stopped, with the lions fifteen yards away, on their left hand side. The male roared once and then flopped down next to his mate. Jim looked down. His flies were wide open but he could barely see his penis.

Claire whispered in his ear, "We must not talk or we will scare them off." Jim moved towards the left hand window to get a better view of the lions. He forgot about his open flies. Claire moved half over into the middle seat and lent up against him. She whispered, so that Jim could feel warmth on his ear, "They have been making love. Look at the saliva on her neck. I have never seen lions copulating. I do hope they have another go. Sadly they look shagged out." She moved her hand into Jim's groin. "A bit like you! Goody, I feel some movement." Jim was not sure if she was talking about his penis, which was definitely swelling again, or about the male lion which was stretching lazily.

Claire snuggled against him, to get more comfortable and Jim saw her dress ride up, revealing a large amount of golden brown thigh. He could not stop his hand caressing it. Claire reached up and kissed him gently on the lips. Her tongue licked around his lips and then moved into his mouth, to meet his eager tongue. Jim was in heaven as he continued to caress her thigh, allowing his hand to go up under her dress. Jim felt her break off the kiss and he thought, for one dreadful moment, that he had gone too far, but she whispered "both you and the lion are getting excited." She was right, Jim's penis was rock hard as her hand encircled it and the lion had got up and was standing over the back of the lioness.

"Christ, this is sexy," Claire whispered, as she managed to move more across the seat. She had not dislodged Jim's hand, which was now under her dress and almost in her groin. She wriggled again, opening her thighs. Jim realised, to his amazement that she had no knickers on. He kissed her softly and she reached for his hand. He thought she was going to push it away but she guided his hand higher, into her pubic hair which felt electric to his touch. She moved his index finger to the top of her vulva and whispered, "Can you rub me just there?" Jim murmured, "You are so soft," as he gently rubbed her.

"Can you rub a little harder?" Jim seemed to realise she wanted him to rub, not only harder, but quicker.

"My darling, that is so wonderful-you are a very quick learner. Christ, I am coming already. Don't stop." There was a grunting noise from the lions. The male was right on top of the female, who was arching her bottom up to him. With a roar he convulsed into her. Instinctively, Jim pushed two fingers into Claire and rapidly moved them in and out. Claire pushed her lips into Jim's neck, to stop her scream and shuddered. Jim felt her tacky liquid on his fingers. Without thinking a conscious thought, he put his fingers in his mouth and felt the wonderful taste of her. She immediately reached out and kissed him very hard and held him to her. The lion roared again and she broke away from his kiss. "That was wonderful. No-one has ever brought me to such ecstasy before. You are gorgeous. I can't wait to get you to bed. In fact, why wait? Mount me from behind, like the lions." Claire rolled onto her knees. Jim was on his knees behind her in a flash. He flipped her dress over her bottom and started to thrust at her thighs. She immediately realised his inexperience, and reached round to guide him into her. "Come, my lion." With just two thrusts he ejaculated into her. "I'm sorry, I'm sorry." Jim sobbed. "I came so quickly, I could not stop"

"Don't worry. I loved to feel you inside me. I hope I won't get pregnant. I loved to feel your semen running down my thighs. Thank goodness my dress was over my back. You will have to hold it up as you withdraw, or I will be in a hell of a mess." She reached for a towel, which was pushed down between the seats, and rubbed her thighs and his now flaccid penis.

The lions had gone. Jim and Claire sorted themselves out and made themselves decent.

"How about having a bit of breakfast? I am starving."

"So am I," said Jim with a smile. Having looked around carefully to make sure the lions had really gone, they got out of the Landrover. Jim got the two collapsible chairs out and put the picnic basket on the tail gate. Everything was dusty but was readily cleaned with a cloth. With big cups of tea each, they set about the ham sandwiches with gusto. Luckily, the lions had frightened away the monkeys and baboons which, in normal circumstances, would have been plaguing them. The sun was now warm and, even in this high spot above the Athi Plains, there was no wind. They felt they were completely alone. "It will only be an hour or so before the bulk of the visitors will be arriving. We had better go soon, or there will be questions asked at the Commission. I am known as an early riser and the cook knew I was going out, because of the picnic, but I will be expected back at mid-morning coffee time. Thank you so much for this morning. I have loved every minute of it. Many of the minutes I will remember for the rest of my life." Claire said with a lascivious grin on her face. Jim astounded himself with his courage. "I certainly loved every minute too but I have one more request, which is very rude and very cheeky." Claire raised her eye brows and gave a doubtful nod. "You are so beautiful. Can I see all of you naked?"

"You are a lovely boy. What a wonderful thing to ask me. Of course you can." She jumped up, put her arms around his neck and kissed him long, hard and deep. Then she stepped back and looked very serious. "Now, I have gone all shy. I hope to goodness you like what you see." Looking steadily at him, she reached behind her to unzip her dress. Her breasts rose and then her dress fell to her feet and she looked down. Jim gasped "You are so beautiful, I want to eat you up." He jumped up and flung his arms around her. He kissed her mouth. He kissed her neck and he kissed her breasts. Then, very tenderly, he cupped each breast and kissed each nipple very, very gently. Claire giggled, "I am not made of china. They won't break. Kiss them harder and then suck them. I love that. In fact, you had better not or I will have another orgasm. Oh shit, that is so good but we must be sensible and go."

Jim released her and picked up her dress and handed it to her. "You are so sexy and naughty not wearing underwear."

"Talk about the pot calling the kettle black! Look at you." She laughed and pointed to his massive erection. Before he could stop her, she wrapped her arms around him, kissed him hard and ground her pelvis into his groin. It hurt a little but Jim loved it. She broke away and said, "Come on, we must go or we will be caught out." She hopped into the Landrover and started up, while Jim got into the passenger seat. They saw masses of game on their way out of the park: Giraffe; Impala; Waterbuck; Warthog and of course Baboons. Jim was in heaven, but really he only had eyes for Claire.

At the park gates, the cheery game scout who had told them about the lions called out, "*Na ona simba*" (Did you see the lions?). "*Ndio. Simba na fanya shibli* (The lions were mating)," replied Claire. "Tu simba?" (Only the lions?), laughed the game scout. "And us" sang out Claire, as she let the clutch in and roared away. "Oh dear, I must have, 'I'm in love' written all over my face," said Claire. "I will have to be bloody careful. I had better drop you on the outskirts of Nairobi. Will that be OK?"

"That's fine. I can easily get back to the Norfolk. I will check out and head back to Mombasa. When can I see you again? I know it will be difficult. I can't safely ring the Commission. You can't ring out either, as I bet there is a telephone operator on duty all the time." Claire bit her lip. She wanted him so badly. She knew she could not see him but she could not bear the thought of not hearing his voice. "Surely, I can hear you somehow?" Claire almost sobbed in desperation. Jim laughed. "You can hear me every morning if you like, on the long wave vet radio. I am on from 7.30 am until 8.00 am." "Marvellous" she cried, as she squeezed his thigh with affection. "I can listen in. We can work out a code. I will write to you at the vet office. I will also get a private P.O.Box which you can write to. I will scheme something up, so that I can come down to Mombasa."

"I will try to find reasons to come up country, even if I can only glimpse you across a crowded room, it will be worth it. Why not turn up the next dirt road on the left. I can easily make my way from here, but I want one last kiss and a hug. I am going to feel so empty when you are gone." Claire swung the Landrover off the main road, drove a quarter of a mile up a dirt road and parked under some trees. They both jumped out and ran around the back of the vehicle, nearly running into each other. They hugged, like the world was trying to tear them apart. One long kiss and Jim led Claire back to the driver's door. "Remember, the frequency is 9738. I will say some idiotic things, just so you know I am longing for you. Now go. I love you." Claire burst into tears and could not speak as she drove away, watching his waving figure diminish in the mirror. What they had forgotten, was that Claire could always ring from a telephone box if she was prepared to wait, sometimes up to half an hour, for a line to Mombasa. Claire had completely forgotten she was his controller.

Chapter 18

The hippo in the water hole

Monday 10th July 1967

Claire was very surprised when the butler at the High Commission brought her a letter addressed to Lady Rochester, as she was having a mid-morning cup of coffee with her husband. She nearly panicked when she recognised Jim's hand-writing. She managed a

"Thank you Eli. I wonder what this is about." Luckily she was so afraid she did not blush. In fact she felt the blood drain from her face. Then instantly she thought, *trust him, he knows the form.* She tore open the letter.

Dear Claire,

I hope you don't mind me calling you Claire, rather than Lady Rochester, but you did say that was OK, when we met in June at the High Commission function. I remember you saying how you longed to go on a real bush-type safari with a real purpose, rather than drinking sundowners in a tent as big as a marquee. Well, I am being very cheeky and asking you on one. A hippo has got stranded in a waterhole at Addi, 60 miles south of the Tana River. The Game Department in Tana River has asked me to help them relocate it back to the river. The safari will take four or five days. I will have all the normal safari gear and can easily take a mossy net, camp-bed and tent for you. However, sadly, there will be no fridge so the menu will be rather limited. I would not have asked you, if there was any danger of shifta. All the attacks have been north of the Tana River. I will take my Landrover. There will be two Bedford 4 X 4 lorries, with a dozen or so Game Department staff. I plan to go next Monday morning and will meet the Game Department at Galole. I could pick you up, either off the train or off the morning Nairobi/Mombasa flight.

There were rather a lot of people at the reception but in case you don't remember me, I was the idiot who arrived late and could not tie my bow tie!

I do hope you can come.

Yours sincerely

Jim Scott

Claire laughed and handed the letter to Sir Richard.

"I would never have believed anyone would have asked me on a proper safari. I know how you hate 'roughing it' Richard. This will get you out of having to go without your creature comforts."

"I hope you will enjoy it, my dear. After four or five days without a shower you will smell like a warthog," said Sir Richard rather pompously.

Claire flipped open her diary and said,

"Dammit, I will go. I don't have anything fixed for next week."

At that moment Christopher Martin-Jenkins came into the room. He was Sir Richard's Personal Assistant (PA). Claire disliked him. She was sure he was gay but that was not why she disliked him. There was something else. She did not trust him. He had done everything to under-mine her at the High Commission. He always treated her as if she was a brainless idiot. Her boss, in London, had warned her to be careful about him. They were sure he was a traitor but they had never been able to nail him. One of Claire's tasks was to catch him. As yet she had been unsuccessful. She was sure that he had something to do with the exposure of Somali one, but she had no proof. One thing was certain, she was going to be extremely careful that he did not expose Jim.

Sir Richard passed Jim's letter to his PA saying, quite casually, that Claire was going on a real safari and would he arrange transport for her to Mombasa and notify Dr. Scott that she would be coming. Sir Richard added, that the expenses could be borne by the High Commission, as it was a good Public Relations (PR) exercise. Claire had a flash of insight. She suddenly realised that her husband did not like his PA. So when Christopher protested that he did not think it was proper for the wife of the High Commissioner to go on such a trip, she said nothing. Christopher went on about how hot and dangerous it was in that area. Sir Richard just smiled and asked when Christopher had last camped in Tana River District. Claire was delighted to see Christopher's discomfiture, as it was obvious to both Claire and Sir Richard that he had never been north of Malindi. Sir Richard might not be very manly, but he was a diplomat and Claire knew that the High Commissioner of Kenya was a post not given to 'yes' men.

To get his own back, Sir Richard's PA did not get Claire a flight to Mombasa but booked her on the train. Claire was actually pleased, as she loved the slow train journey with the chance of seeing some game on the way. Claire spent the rest of the week in a bit of a daze. She could not think what to take or wear. She smiled when she thought about Jim. At least she knew, the less she wore the more pleased he would be. However she knew she needed to be practical. Shorts, short-sleeved shirts and '*tackis*' were easy. She put in a very short summer dress, in case there was time with Jim in Mombasa. She went out and bought a pair of low cut shortie pyjamas. She also bought two white lacy bras and four pairs of white lacy French knickers. She felt confident that Jim really wanted to see her otherwise he would not have invited her. She knew he did not realise that she was his controller. However she was worried that she had never been on a real working safari, nor had she been to the Northern Frontier District (NFD). She thought London would be pleased that she was seeing the NFD for herself but without risking any involvement of Her Majesty's Government. Sir Richard was in meetings all afternoon and early evening. She said "Goodbye" to him after lunch and had a lazy afternoon. She made sure the High Commission car got her to the train station early.

At the station, she saw she was booked to share a carriage with a Mrs. Middleton. She went to the carriage and quietly read a book. Mrs. Middleton bustled into the carriage with only five minutes to spare at 6.25pm. She seemed a friendly, round- faced, woman with a florid complexion.

"Hello, I am Grace Middleton. You won't remember me but you and Sir Richard were so kind to me and my husband, at the reception at the High Commission last year to celebrate the Queen's birthday."

"Of course I remember you. You have a farm at Miritini, North West of Mombasa. Your husband served with distinction in Burma, in the last war," said Claire.

"You have a marvellous memory. May I call you Claire? It is a bit formal if we are sharing a carriage to call you Lady Rochester. Also, may I be really naughty and ask if you would sleep in the top bunk, when the time comes for bed. I will make a real 'Horlicks' of climbing the ladder and I suspect you will leap up it like a *Klipspringer.*" "Of course," said Claire laughing. "I have never seen a *Klipspringer* but I take it as a compliment."

"Claire, my dear, of course it's a compliment," said Grace. "*Klipspringers* are fairly rare in Kenya but they are more common down south. They are a beautiful, very athletic, graceful small antelope."

The whistles blew and the slow old train started out from Nairobi. Claire and Grace were chatting away. They did not see much of the game on the Athi plains, as the African night fell quickly.

"So, what are you travelling to Mombasa for?" asked Grace. Claire was very enthusiastic.

"I am going on a real rough safari, up into to Tana River District. I am going to help transport a Hippo 60 miles back to the Tana River, with the Game Department. Richard hates roughing it, so he is delighted to send me off on a so-called public relations exercise."

"What great fun, my dear. It is rather wild country so I hope you are not going alone," said Grace.

"No, I am going with a vet called Jim Scott who was at this year's Royal Birthday party," replied Claire.

"You are a lucky girl! He is such a charming young man. He often comes to our farm. Guy thinks he is a really good vet. He really makes my heart flutter. He makes me wish I was young again," said Grace with a laugh. Luckily, the train steward arrived as Claire felt a warm feeling in her tummy and felt a blush rising up her neck. It did not go unnoticed by Grace, but she said nothing except, "Come on, my dear let's go now, then we can have a drink before the food arrives."

The old dining car had tables for four on one side and tables for two on the other side. Grace sat down on one of the tables for two and whispered into Claire's ear, "We don't want to sit at a table for four or a man might sit down and try to 'chat me up'. Chance would be a fine thing then." She laughed at her own joke and insisted Claire joined her for a '*Waragi*' and tonic. She explained to Claire, that

'*Waragi*' was a type of gin made in Uganda, that it was very cheap and quite pleasant. Claire had to agree and enjoyed her drink. It was a set menu. They both had soup with added sherry and another '*Waragi*' and tonic. The main course was roast Guinea fowl, which was excellent. Grace explained to Claire how Guinea fowl were really common in Tana River District and in the NFD. She said that Claire should make sure that Jim Scott shot one for their supper, one night.

"If you haven't got a fridge, my dear, it will make a good variation to 'bully beef'.

"What is 'bully beef'?" asked Claire.

"Sorry," said Grace, "I should have explained, it's what, in England, you would call corned beef. These men, if left to their own devices, would go on safari with just a crate of 'Tusker' and a case of 'bully beef', and think they have done a wonderful job catering. You must insist that you stop at a '*duka*', before you go off into the wilds, and get some decent provisions. You need some UHT milk and cornflakes for your breakfast. Eggs are a disaster, as they always break and bacon goes bad in a day in that heat. Do attract the steward's attention and we will have another *Waragi.*" Claire had no difficulty in attracting his attention, as the only other dinners had long since left, after their apple pie and custard desert.

Grace said, "I am getting excited, just thinking about you both setting off together on an adventure. I don't think I could imagine a braver young man. After one veterinary visit, Gerald said. "There would be a place in my platoon for that young fellow."

"What has he done that was so brave?" asked Claire, who felt another warm feeling inside of her.

Grace replied, "One of our best cows had got an orange stuck in its gullet. It had started to get bloat and Guy knew that he ought to stick a knife into its flank to release the gas, but he could not remember exactly where to cut with the knife. Jim arrived just in time. He got the handle of a hammer in the cow's mouth and got our headman to hold it, while Guy held the cow's head down on the ground. Jim put his hand and fore-arm into the cow's mouth. The cow threw its head up. The headman and Guy let go. I could see Jim was in agony but he did not take his arm out, and somehow managed to grab the orange. He then pulled out the orange. The cow gave a great belch and sat up. She has never looked back, but Jim's fore-arm was covered in blood from all the bites. We washed it off with running water and then put on some mercuricum. Jim never made any fuss. He was marvellous. Now, my dear, we must go back to our carriage and get some sleep."

Their beds had been made up with crisp white sheets. Claire climbed up the ladder on to the top bunk and got into her pyjamas. Grace took her flannelette nighty with her and went to the loo. It was then that Claire realised she had a problem. She needed to go to the loo and Grace would see her skimpy pyjamas. If only she had not had several '*Waragis*' she would have put her dress back over the top of her pyjamas but, she thought, '*Oh what the hell.*' She was climbing down when Grace came back into the carriage. Grace smiled and said,

"Jim will be a lucky boy, to see you in those."

Before she thought, Claire said, with a laugh, "He will be even luckier if he sees me without them!"

Grace roared with laughter, "Your secret is safe with me. I hope you have a great safari. Guy knows how to hold his tongue so, if you ever want to come together to stay at the farm, you will be really welcome. I will leave the light on for you until you come back from the loo." Grace was good to her word, so it was easy for Claire to climb back up onto the top bunk. They both said,

"Good night, sleep well," as Grace put out the light.

Claire awoke with the grey light of dawn. They had gone to bed without drawing down the blinds, so she could quietly move to the foot of the bed, without waking Grace, to look out of the window. They were in Tsavo Game Park. In the distance, on a slight rise, Claire could see some elephants feeding. She thought how lucky she was, to be able to wake to such a glorious sight.

The rapidly brightening light woke Grace, who stretched.

Claire said, "I hope you slept well?"

"I had a wonderful night," replied Grace. "I always sleep well on the train. Now I must go to the loo." While she was away Claire quickly climbed down. It was much easier to change when she could stand up, rather than on the top bunk. She didn't bother to close the blind. She thought, '*I don't mind giving the elephants an eye full,*' as she stood stark naked in the warm carriage. She quickly put her dress on over her new racy underwear. She thought, '*she must not make Jim think I am too forward all the time, like in Nairobi Game Park.*' The linen dress was cool and was just the right length. It came to four inches above her knees. It had big buttons down the front.

Grace came back into the carriage having put her dress on in the loo.

"You look ravishing, my dear. Guy and Jim won't be able to keep their eyes off you. Jim may not be there to meet you. Vets get called out all the time. We will look after you, if he is not at the station. You can come home with us. Let's go and get some breakfast?"

However, Jim and Guy were at the station. They both came down the platform to carry the bags. Claire just had a small rucksack, but Grace had a suitcase and some bags from her shopping expedition in Nairobi. Jim immediately introduced Claire to Guy. He could see she had been talking to Grace. While Grace hugged Guy, he longed to kiss and hug Claire, but he thought that would not look correct, so he, rather gravely shook her hand. Claire laughed at him, saying,

"Your '*safari impishi*' (camp cook) is reporting for duty. Would you like to see her references before you take her on?" Grace immediately laughed and said,

"Don't worry, Jim, we shared a carriage so I have checked them out. Now you two must get going as you have a long dusty drive ahead of you. However, Jim, you must stop at the '*duka*' (shop) and get some more provisions. I know what you men are like. I have given Claire some ideas. You both will need to eat well if you are going to get that hippo back to the Tana River."

Guy added, "Good luck and you know you are both welcome at the farm at anytime."

Jim and Claire walked briskly out of the station and, as soon as they were out of earshot of any of the other passengers, Jim blurted out, "I so want to hold your hand. I also wanted to bring you some flowers but I did not want to draw attention to us." "My darling, you did just the right thing. You did so well writing that letter. I can't wait for us to be alone. I was so naughty in Nairobi Game Park. I was worried I would have frightened you and you would never want to have anything more to do with me." They had reached Jim's Landrover. Jim immediately opened the passenger door for Claire. It was quite a high step up. Claire lent towards him, as she put her foot on the floor and whispered.

"Have a look down. I hope you like them?" The bottom of the front of her dress fell open, revealing the small scrap of lace. Jim remarked dryly,

"That's the best view I have had since Leopard's Rock!" Somehow, he managed to rub her thigh before he closed the door.

They were soon over Nyali Bridge and heading towards Mtwapa Bridge, on a good tarmac road. Claire moved across into the middle seat, so she could rest her hand on Jim's thigh.

Jim said, "I don't think we need to stop at a '*duka'*, as I think I have everything we need. Grace is a lovely person so I expect she was worrying about your creature comforts. Why did she laugh so much about your references?"

Claire smiled, "We got on like a house on fire. We had a good supper on the train. Grace introduced me to '*Waragi'* so I was a little pissed when we went to bed. I had bought, especially for you a pair of very revealing pyjamas. I forgot I might be sharing a carriage. When she saw me in my pyjamas she said,

"Jim will be a lucky boy to see you in those my dear."

"Without thinking, I said, he may be even luckier and see me without them." She roared with laughter and, obviously, she guessed we were lovers. However, I trust her. She will tell Guy but it won't go any further. They think the world of you. How is your arm where the cow bit you?"

"That is fine. They were only small bites but it was bloody sore when it happened," answered Jim. "I am so glad you could come on this trip. I racked my brains for a reason to see you again and this job came up out of the blue. By the way, that dress is lovely, but you must take it off after Kilifi creek, as we will then be on '*murram'* roads and it will get filthy."

"Here we go," said Claire, "Only with me for a couple of minutes and you want me to take my dress off. A right '*dume'* (Male animal) you are." Jim blushed. Claire laughed.

"I'm glad you can feel embarrassed. You have seen my knickers already and if you care to look round, you can see my lacey bra too." Claire had undone the top two buttons of her dress.

Jim gulped like a fish and managed a "Wow, this is going to be a fun safari."

"When we stop, I will put on a pair of bikini bottoms and a top," said Claire.

"When we are going to be in a village, I will put a pair of shorts on. For now I will let my dress ride up and I want you to stroke the inside of my thigh." Jim did not take his eyes off the road but he felt her hand guiding his left hand. He duly stroked her warm thigh. They both started to speak together. Claire said,

"I dreamt, all last night of the feel of your hand."

"I dreamt of your lovely brown body," said Jim, "You are totally gorgeous."

As they came to Mtwapa Bridge, Claire did up the dress buttons and pulled down her skirt. Jim greeted the man on the bridge, who took the money, with, *"Habari imbuzi* (How are the goats)*?"*

He replied, *"Mzuri sana* (very well)*."* As they drove on, Jim explained that his three nanny goats had nearly died, the previous week, with a bad dose of 'Barber's Pole worms' which can cause death from severe anaemia. Claire leant over and kissed his neck.

"I am so proud of you," she said and rubbed his thigh. She went on. "But you are a bit boring wearing pants. You have stopped the one-eyed trouser snake from coming out! We both were so naughty in Nairobi. I can't wait to have you again. Look, there is a track up there through the sisal."

Jim swung off the road, went a hundred yards up the track and parked under some trees. They both jumped out and nearly knocked each other over, running around the back of the Landrover. Claire's arms were round Jim's neck in a second and she was kissing him. He drew her tight towards him and felt her lithe body through the dress. She pushed him urgently away and pulled his shirt over his head. Then she was kissing his neck and his body. Her hands undid his belt and his shorts, and she pushed his shorts and pants down his legs. She kept kissing him, as she pushed him against the back door of the Landrover, and then had her arms tightly around his neck again.

Jim reached down and easily undid the big buttons down the front of Claire's dress. He gently pushed his hand in the top of her knickers. She kissed him harder and pushed herself on to his hand. Jim moved his fingers and felt how soft she was. She stopped kissing him and just let her head hang over his shoulder. Claire was panting now. She started to moan,

"Yes, my darling. God that is good. Don't stop! Please don't stop. I'm coming. I'm coming. Enter me." Jim just tore her knickers and reached both hands behind her and lifted her buttocks. She was wide open and he thrust deep inside her. He kept pulling her buttocks towards him, while she was undulating her pelvis. He could stand it no longer and he ejaculated deep inside her. He groaned as she took her weight again. She looked deep into his eyes and said,

"You are a lovely boy." Then she laughed and said, "I am glad I gave you a glimpse of my knickers earlier, they are certainly trashed now!" She took off her dress and bra and, naked, guddled around in her rucksack for her bikini bottoms. She put them on and a faded brown top. Jim noticed that she didn't bother with a bikini top. He kissed the back of her neck and cupped her breasts with his hands. He whispered, "I love you."

She turned and said, "I think I love you too."

Claire asked if they were near the ferry at Kilifi. Jim said they were, so she put a pair of shorts on over her bikini bottoms. Jim had put his shorts back on but put his pants into his rucksack. He found two cold 'cokes' in the cool box. Jim sighed and said, "Sadly, we won't have cold cokes for very long."

"Don't worry," said Claire, "We will manage. We will have to save our mad passionate sex until the dark, when it is cooler. Still, I can't wait. I have never had sex in a tent. Come on night!" She laughed.

They crossed the ferry, holding hands discretely in the Landrover, as there were plenty of people about. Then the 'murram' road started. There was red dust everywhere. The surface was good and it only took them just over two hours to get into Malindi. They stopped at a road-side 'duka' for another cold coke each and they each had a 'samosa'. Jim bought a couple of 'mdafu' for drinking later on. They set off again. The road was quite good as far as Mambrui but then it deteriorated and it was a hard, hot, dusty grind for two hours to Garsen. It seemed more humid and hotter in Garsen because of the wide brown Tana River. They filled up with petrol but did not have to go across the ferry as they were following the road on the south west of the river, up to Galole. They drove for another two hours.

238

Jim thought they were getting near to Galole, so he asked Claire to look for an easy place to come off the road. Most of the road had been graded so there was quite a ditch, but Claire found a place and they headed off into the bush. They went for approximately a quarter of a mile until they came to a sandy clearing, which had been made during the recent flooding but was now bone dry.

It was lovely to stop. They both staggered out of the Landrover.

"Well, we have made it this far and in quite good time. I think there is at least two hours before dark. I have brought lots of mosquito repellent, as they are really bad up here. We are actually only a mile or so from the river." He opened the back door of the Landrover and slid out a wooden camp table and two canvass chairs.

"You flop down in one of these while I make you a cup of tea."

"No way," said Claire, "I am here to help." She squeezed his hand.

"Show me where all the cooking stuff is, or would you like me to collect wood for the fire?" Jim replied that if she could make a fire that would be great. Claire went off to get wood. There was plenty of dried stuff as, although this area had been flooded, the water was long gone and the sun dried it all very quickly.

Jim soon had the very small one-ringed gas stove going on the table, with an old blackened kettle. He had two mugs out with a tea bag in each. He half filled an old black metal bucket with water. He was just reaching into the Landrover to get out the cold box, when he felt Claire's arms around his waist.

"Well-lover boy, I have come for some matches. He left the cold box, reached behind and ran his hands down her thighs.

"They feel hot. Has anyone ever told you that you have the loveliest legs in the world?"

"They maybe hot but they are not hot enough to light the fire," Claire giggled.

"The matches are in the Landrover, on that shelf under the windscreen on the driver's side." Claire went off to find them. She realised that he was very methodical and he must have put them back in their special place, after he had lit the gas stove. The kettle was whistling as she went back and lit the fire. Claire had always been a bit of a tom-boy and so was good at lighting fires. She put the matches back as Jim called, "tea is ready." The tea was heaven. She said, "I didn't think we would have fresh milk."

"Sadly, only for tonight and tomorrow's breakfast, then we are on to UHT stuff, which is OK but not so nice."

"Grace told me to make sure you brought UHT milk but I was so excited to see you, I forgot." Claire admitted.

Jim said, "You have made an excellent fire. Could you put the half bucket of water near to it, to heat up for our shower?"

"Wow, I thought this was a rough safari. I didn't think I would get a shower. I hope you will share it with me?"

"I would love to," said Jim.

"Shall we put up the tent and get the supper ready, then we can have a shower when the water is hot?"

Claire was surprised how easy it was to put the tent up. It was a simple 'A' frame on the roof rack. The front guy-rope tied to the bull-bar on the front of the Landrover. There was a large window covered in mossy-net. The back guy rope tied, with a long thin rope, to any suitable tree. Jim explained that it could be tied to a peg behind the Landrover, but this way it was totally out of the way so it was easy climbing up to get in and out. Also, it was not in the way as one walked behind the vehicle. On the floor of the tent was a mattress, off a normal single bed, covered with a fitted sheet. There were a couple of pillows, another sheet and folded up blanket.

"I don't think we will need the blanket as it is going to be quite hot," said Jim.

"We will have to let the mossy-net down over the door or we will be eaten alive. Up-country, I often leave the door wide open to let the breeze through. Of course you never know your luck. A girl with sexy pyjamas might come into your tent by mistake," said Jim with a laugh.

"I think tonight, Jim Scott, you just might get lucky!" replied Claire with a wide smile.

"I can imagine Gerald getting very red faced and excited when Grace describes them to him. I totally trust them. I am sure our secret is safe with them. However, there will be some gossip in the High Commission, so we must be careful when we are in public."

"Don't worry, I will be very prim and proper all the time," answered Jim,

240

"I have, in fact, brought a spare mossy-net which I can sleep under on my own, if we are worried at anytime. I think we will be fine with the Game Department chaps. They would think we were very odd NOT sleeping together."

Claire was most impressed as they then set up a wood and canvas camp basin, which even had a pocket in the canvas for a piece of soap. She was not very impressed with the grotty soap it contained. They selected a suitable tree, to be used as the shower tree. A rope was thrown over a branch about twelve feet up. This was tied to a large canvas bucket, which had a pipe coming out of the bottom. There was a tap on the pipe, above a shower-head rose. This was then pulled up empty, about seven feet above the ground. An old ground sheet was laid out directly below it. On top was a wooden and canvas camp bath. This also had a canvas pocket, which Claire guessed was for soap or even shampoo but that was empty.

With a raised eyebrow, Claire asked whether there was a lavatory.

"Oh yes," said Jim. He reached into the back of the Landrover and produced a *'panga'*, some lavatory paper, and a box of matches.

"You dig a small hole with the *'panga'*. Once you have wiped your bottom you set light to the paper and then fill in the hole."

"I hope I don't miss," giggled Claire.

Tonight was the last night of fresh food so they were going to have barbecued steaks, big tomatoes and peppers cooked over the embers of the fire, on a rusty old piece of mesh with four legs. Potatoes were wrapped in tin-foil and were going to be cooked in the embers. Claire wanted to put them in then, as she said they would take an hour to cook. Jim said they were not too big and would only take twenty minutes. Claire said nothing. She was glad she hadn't as, in the end, she found Jim had been right. She made a mental note not to question his judgment. He seemed to be a person who was quite authoritive when he was sure about something, but was quite happy to say he didn't know if he was not so sure. Claire was happy because, although she knew she was in love with him, he was also under her control. She did not want to send his reports back to London if they were bull-shit. She was still worried about his safety. She was quite happy they were on this safari together and might be in some danger but she dreaded having to send him into danger on his own, like rescuing Somali One. She sighed to herself and thought, I will just have to face the problems when I come to them, there is no point worrying in advance. She went up behind him, put her arms around his waist and kissed the back of his neck. He turned and kissed her on the lips. Their tongues played together. As they broke apart Jim said,

"Let's have that shower before supper?" Claire was aghast and said,

"What? I have got to get in the shower stark naked, in broad daylight!"

"You lovely shy girl," said Jim,

"You are happy to make love in the middle of a sisal field but you worry about being naked, in the remote bush in the shower. I do love your quirky ways. I remember you were shy when I wanted to see you naked in Nairobi Game Park." Claire blushed. "You are right. I am a bit barmy. I think it is maybe because I never let my father see me naked. I never knew my mother and I didn't have any brothers or sisters. I bet you were from a totally uninhibited family, all having a bath together and running round the house naked."

Jim laughed, "You are right about the bathing but it always seemed to be bloody cold at home, so no running around naked. That's one of the reasons I love it here in Africa, the warmth and wearing few clothes."

Then he became suddenly serious. "Poor you, not knowing your mother. I am sad for you. I love my Mum and Dad. They will come out here sometime I hope you will like them. I am the youngest and my mother's favorite but I somehow think my Mum will like you. She is very perceptive, a bit like Grace. I don't think she will need a clue like your sexy pyjamas. However I will try to behave I am sure she will know I am nuts about you. She will see you are fond of me but will think you are such a nice girl that she won't guess we are lovers. I could see you are fond of your husband. What went wrong? I am sure it is not just an age thing." Jim put his arms around her. Claire looked up at him and knew she could trust him.

"I have never told anyone else but poor old Richard couldn't make love on our wedding night. I had had a sexual experience, God that sounds formal, with our groom, so I knew something was very wrong. I didn't love Richard, but I liked him well enough and I saw him as a way to get away from my dreadful step mother. I had it out with Richard and I agreed that I would stay in all appearances, as a dutiful wife but we would just sleep apart. I said I would be unlikely to stay faithful to him but I would never let the world know I had a lover. So we have lived quite happy lives until bang along you come and I just knew I wanted you. When I heard you laughing with the *'askaris'* and saw you walking up those steps I wanted you. Did you feel me press against you as I tied your tie?"

"Too right," said Jim.

"I can still feel your body now." Claire said, "You know I was jealous when you said you knew 'Annie'."

She looked at him very seriously, "How well do you know 'Annie'? She has the reputation of being a Nairobi Bike?"

Jim laughed, and replied, "I met her down on the south coast on Christmas Day. She and two friends were good fun. I will bear what you said in mind, if I have no transport in Nairobi." Claire grabbed his ears and kissed him.

"Oh no you won't, you young *'dume'* you will bloody well walk! Come on, let's have this shower." Before Jim could catch his breath, Claire had stripped off her shirt, bikini bottoms and shoes and stood in front of him.

"You will have to carry me to the Landrover first, so I can get my washing kit, as there are so many thorns. I need some decent soap as that piece in the basin is worse than hideous."

Jim enjoyed carrying out her instructions. Once she was safely standing in the bath, he fetched the bucket of warm water from the fire. He tested it with his elbow and then, having lowered the canvas bucket, he filled it up. He raised the bucket up again just out of reach of Claire. He then walked over and sat down in a chair and looked at her standing naked, waiting for the water.

"You rat, Jim Scott," moaned Claire and stamped her foot.

"You always look sexy but you look bloody gorgeous now," said Jim as he walked to the ground sheet, took his clothes off and kicked off his shoes. He stepped into the bath and opened the tap and let the warm water pour over them. He turned the tap off to save water. Claire wrapped her arms around him and said,

"You are a naughty, bad tease but I forgive you because of this lovely shower. Also, I will never be worried about being naked with you again. I have learnt my lesson well. Oh my God, there is a couple of Europeans walking towards us!" Jim spun around, nearly falling over the canvas of the bath. He felt two hands around his waist as Claire grabbed his penis.

"You are not the only one who can tease," she whispered in his ear. "I will let go of you, if you shampoo my hair for me."

"It's a deal," said Jim. "If you are like me, it feels as if you have half the soil in the NFD in your hair."

They washed each other's hair and then each other's bodies, before Jim turned the tap on to wash off all the soap and grime.

"Let's just dry in the air?" said Claire. "I don't actually think I am totally clean but it feels so much better and I won't wipe all the remaining dirt of on the towel."

After putting on their shoes they walked over to the table. Jim put the supper on to cook. Claire found they had two cold beers. She poured them into two pewter tankards she found in the wooden camping box. She handed one to Jim and said, "You sit down. I will just get my hair brush."

Jim said, "Sadly, there will be no more cold beer until we get back to civilisation. I will have to sort out some sort of refrigeration in the Landrover. Electric fridges need generators which are so noisy or, if they work off the battery of the Landrover, they flatten it. A pal of mine takes a paraffin fridge with him but it takes hours to set up because it has to be level. It is OK if you are staying in the same place for several days."

Claire came back with her hair brush.

"Are the chairs strong enough for me to sit on your lap?"

"I think so," said Jim. "Can I brush your hair?"

"Would you, I would love that." So, as they drank their beers and cooked their supper, Jim brushed Claire's hair. When they had finished supper Jim said,

"I think it is time I saw these racy pyjamas and we covered up with mossy repellent, or we will be eaten alive. Jim started clearing up, as Claire went off to the Landrover. Jim turned as she returned,

"Wow, I see why Grace guessed something was up. Hell they are sexy."

"I was so stupid," said Claire, "not only because of the train, but also because I won't be able to wear them, with the Game Department chaps in camp."

"Well, I love them," said Jim. "They won't camp right on top of us, so your pyjamas will be fine after dark. Let's face it, they cover more than a bikini. It is just with the low top they are so sexy." Jim found his '*kikoi*', which he wrapped around his waist. They covered themselves in repellent.

When they had cleared up and washed up, they made a cup of coffee. They used up all the fresh milk, as Jim was sure it would be off in the morning. Claire sat in his lap again and wriggled her bottom. Jim felt his arousal. She turned and kissed him and whispered,

"I don't think he is too upset from being grabbed. I was a bit worried, as he seemed quite asleep while you brushed my hair."

"I was concentrating, so that I would get all the knots out without pulling your hair. It is strange getting an erection. Sometimes I just have to think about you and I am instantly aroused, and yet you were sitting in my lap and, as you say, he was asleep. Mind you, you did not wriggle your bottom in that sexy way." Claire half turned to him and put her arm around his neck. Jim laughed. "I can see right down your cleavage and I am getting really excited."

"So you are," said Claire and wriggled her bottom again.

"Can I ask you a very intimate question? I have never had a man to ask. I might ask other women girlie questions, but there is so much I want to know about men, and you in particular. Now we are in the dark and in the wilds, I feel I can ask you. I am blushing but you can't see that. Do you masturbate?"

"Oh yes," replied Jim. "Actually, since I have met you I can hardly leave my cock alone. In bed I just have to think about you and I get excited. I could not go to sleep without masturbating. Before I met you, I did not masturbate very often and then I would ejaculate in my sleep. Boys at school, call it a 'wet dream'. Do you masturbate?"

Claire kissed him and said rather breathlessly,

"I am so embarrassed now. Yes I do, but it is not very satisfying now that I have had you. I have never had a climax like in the Game Park or this morning in the sisal field. I got excited when the groom rubbed me but it was nothing like the same. With you I feel wide open. As soon as I have climaxed I want you inside me. In fact, I really want you now. I know it is early but can we go to bed? I will

245

just have a pee before we climb up. Can I have a pee right near as I am a bit frightened to go away from you and the fire?"

"Of course you can. I think some men get excited seeing a girl having a pee, but it doesn't turn me on," said Jim.

"I want to know ALL THE THINGS that do turn you on, Jim Scott." said Claire, as she climbed the ladder.

"I will just make the fire up and follow you up," said Jim.

When Jim climbed into the tent he found Claire still in her pyjamas sitting cross legged on the mattress, holding a torch. He drew the mosquito net across the entrance and pulled off his *'kikoi'*. Claire handed him a second torch and said,

"Come and look down my cleavage. I want to see if it really does excite you or, actually, you need to be touched and kissed."

"I love this sort of experiment, in the interests of science," said Jim. He took the torch and held it in his mouth. He lent forward on to his hands and looked down her cleavage. Instantly he felt arousal. Claire gasped,

"Wow that is all it needs." She laid down the torch so it was still pointing at Jim and took off her pyjama top. Then she got on to her knees and very provocatively slid the shortie bottoms onto her thighs.

"Now, he looks really big in the torch light. What would turn you on now?" asked Claire. Jim took the torch out of his mouth and said,

"Lie back and lift up your bottom and let me take your pyjamas right off. Claire wriggled her bottom and she was naked. She thought it was so strange that, just playing around with Jim, she also felt so aroused and yet they had not even kissed. Jim carefully lay on top of her and they kissed very slowly. He took some of his weight on his elbows as he kept kissing her. Claire had her legs wide apart and was pushing up towards him. It was so sensual, she wished it could go on forever. They kept kissing and Claire became more breathless. She reached down and guided Jim into her. He immediately thrust and Claire groaned with pleasure. They pushed in unison and managed to climax together. Jim kissed her neck tenderly. Claire felt him about to move.

"Don't move, my love. I love to feel you get smaller inside me. In a silly way, it makes me feel that I have some power over you. Thank you for our scientific experiment. Can we do others?"

"Too right," said Jim.

"However now, I just want you to curl up in my arms and let me cuddle you to sleep." With that they wriggled around but actually did not go immediately to sleep, as they caressed each other and just slowly dropped off.

They were woken with a loud thump, as if a giant was stamping near them. It was just dawn.

"What the hell was that?" said Claire.

"It was the Geo-seismic survey. No cause for alarm but I will just go and check up. You can have another half hour sleep." With that, Jim went down the ladder on the back of the Landrover, grabbed his shorts and shoes, picked up the compass from the shelf in front of the driver in the Landrover and ran off in the direction of the thump. He was helped by a second thump. Claire watched him go. She thought, now 'Animal Boy' is doing his job. She put on her bikini bottoms and a rather low-cut, clean top thinking, Jim will like this and went down the ladder. She easily got the fire going and put some water in the bucket, near to fire, to heat for washing up. She set the kettle on the small stove. She laid breakfast i.e. she put out the UHT milk, the cornflakes and cut up a banana into two bowls. She put tea bags into two mugs. She remembered Jim said he did not take sugar. She found two spoons. She lowered the empty shower bucket and, having collapsed the camp bath, she put them both by the back of the Landrover. She folded up the ground sheet and laid it with them. The kettle boiled and she filled the two mugs and turned off the stove. She was on the top of the Landrover bonnet undoing the front of the tent when she heard voices. Looking up, she could see Jim walking back towards the camp, chatting to a European. She hopped off the front of the Landrover, re-lit the stove and filled up the kettle. She had just found another spoon, when they came into the camp.

"Hello, would you like a cup of tea?" said Claire. The stranger, who was very dark and tanned, replied,

"I would love one."

Jim said, "Claire, I would like to introduce you to Luis Stephano. He is carrying out the survey nearby." Claire gave him a wicked grin as she shook his hand and said,

"I don't think you deserve a cup of tea, as you woke me up with your thumping but you can earn your forgiveness by sitting down and cutting up a banana into this beer tankard, as I am afraid we have not got a third bowl." Luis was all flustered and said, in very passable English,

"No, no, I am so very sorry. Tea alone will be just fine."

"Rubbish", said Jim, "She is only teasing you. Come and sit down in this chair. I will get a couple of seat cushions out of the Landrover." So it was that they had a very friendly breakfast. Jim noticed that Luis could not keep his eyes off Claire's cleavage. Claire chatted away and made it much easier for Jim to gain all the information about the survey, and the oil exploration being carried out by the Italians. Claire could not help smiling to herself, as she knew she would be receiving all the information in Jim's accurate reports. Both of them were amazed that the Italians had been allowed so far south. Were they just trespassing and no-one in the Kenyan Government knew they were there or, more likely, had they paid a large bribe to some senior official? They both thought, independently, that it would be very useful for the British Government to know the personalities involved. They both said they hoped they would meet Luis again. Claire made sure she lent very far forward when she gave him his second cup of tea. She actually asked him how they were allowed to survey so far south. Luis said he did not know but he would ask his boss. He was totally unaware that both Jim and Claire were obtaining information for London.

After Luis had left they hurriedly packed up the camp, doused the fire and got going, as they did not want to keep the Game Department waiting. It was only in the Landrover, when they were back on the road, that Jim reached over and stroked Claire's thigh and, laughing said,

"Young Luis was fascinated with your chest. You know you look particularly sexy. I don't think he was very discrete, giving us all that information. Will you tell them at the High Commission?" Claire replied, honestly, that she probably would not say anything at the Commission, as she might get Luis into trouble. She didn't tell Jim that she did not want to give anything to Christopher Martin-Jenkins, as she did not trust him. However, Claire knew that London would be pleased with the information. She thought she would play down her involvement, and infer that the majority of the information came from Jim. Claire moved into the middle seat and stroked Jim's thigh and loved his instant response.

"You don't mind Luis looking down my cleavage?" asked Claire. Jim replied,

"When there is a beautiful view you don't mind sharing it with others." Claire kissed him on the cheek and put her hand on his crotch.

"You have got on boring old underpants. I was so delighted when your cock popped out in Nairobi Game Park."

"I was mortified," said Jim. "I thought you might stop and throw me out of the Landrover, and make me walk home through the lions."

Claire said, "I still can't believe how forward I was. However, I am bloody glad I was because you were quite shy initially. On the other hand when you saw the green light, it was up with my skirt and thrust away."

Jim replied, "I am so sorry, I am such a useless lover. I get so excited I come too quickly."

Claire kept stroking his thigh and said, "I have never heard such rubbish. I love you as you are but I am sure we will have great fun learning together. You talk as if I have had sex with hundreds of guys, when I only had sex with the groom." She squeezed his thigh.

"I can't wait until tonight. We will have to be really quiet but we will have some fun. Is this Galole? The sign says 'Hello' in Spanish."

It was indeed Galole, which had a second name of Hola. Jim swung off to his right and followed a smaller '*murram*' road, which led straight to a belt of large green trees marking the Tana River. Opposite a T junction, 100 yards before the trees, was a tidy compound of white washed breeze block houses, all in a line, whose roofs were of shining new corrugated iron. The gates of the compound had a barrier, manned by two very smartly dressed '*askaris*' who both saluted Jim and Claire. The '*askari*' nearest to Jim, came to his window, and asked if he could be of any assistance. Jim said, although he was from the Veterinary Department he really wanted to go to the Game Department, but he would like to report to the DC. Jim was told to park his Landrover under a tree, then Claire and Jim followed the '*askari*' to the middle of the houses, which they could now see were offices. A new sign, on the lintel of the open door proclaimed that this was the office of the DC. A very imposing man sat behind a large desk and looked up as they entered.

"Welcome to my District. My name is Leonard Baloala. How can I help you?" The DC was a very tall strong man. He rose from his chair, came around his desk and offered his hand to Claire. Her small hand disappeared in his enormous fist. "Leonard, we have met before at the British High Commission. I am Claire Rochester. You won't remember me, but you and my husband had a long talk about rowing, which you had enjoyed in Cambridge."

"Of course, I remember your husband. How rude of me not to recognize you. You were wearing a very lovely ball gown, but I prefer you in your safari clothes. My real home is much further north, but Tana River district could be said to be the start of the NFD. I am always pleased, when I can greet friends who have taken the trouble to come to northern Kenya. Now tell me, to what do I owe this honour?"

Still holding his hand, Claire replied, "I am here, with Jim, to rescue a Hippo from Addi water hole." Leonard let go of Claire's hand, with reluctance, and turned to Jim. "It is good to see you again Jim. The District Game Warden is getting all his team ready to leave at first light tomorrow, so I insist that you stay in my guest house tonight. We will have some supper at my house and then I will take you both to Galole Club, as we have a darts night tonight. We can all be a team of three. My district staff will be delighted to meet you. The winning team gets a crate of "Tusker". Now, sadly, I have got some work to do so I will get Christmas, the office messenger, to take you first to my guest house for a cup of tea and then on to the Game Department compound, so you can meet Justin Kipech, the District Game Warden, and make your plans for tomorrow. Christmas will then guide you back to my guest house. You can then have a siesta. My cook will bring you a cup of tea about 4.30 pm and we will eat at about 6 pm. Darts start at 7.30 pm so we will have plenty of time." Jim and Claire both said, in unison that would be fine and said they would look forward to seeing him later. Claire added that she was a rubbish darts player and hoped she would not let them down. Leonard laughed and said, either way, he would enjoy the game.

As if by magic, Christmas was at the door. Leonard gave him instructions very carefully. With a smile on his face he saluted them all, and turned on his heel and walked briskly to their Landrover. Claire hopped up into the middle seat and put her legs either side of the gear stick. Christmas sat next to the window and said Jim should turn left out of the DC's compound. Claire knew it was not chance that Jim tried to put her knee into reverse!

Christmas directed them to a large, brick-built bungalow, surrounded by a six foot high wall, recently painted white. There was a barrier at the entrance, manned by a cheerful '*askari*'. He raised the barrier and said,

"Welcome, my lady and welcome '*Bwana*' Scott. Christmas will take you around to the guest house. The guest house was a '*rondavel*' (round house), with two doors off a small veranda, with a table and two chairs. Christmas helped them with their small bags into the two bedrooms, which each had a door to a communal bathroom. Each bedroom had a single bed, already made up, and a chair. There was a basin, a lavatory and fairly large bath in the bathroom. Jim thanked Christmas and asked if he could give him a lift back to the office. However, Christmas said he was happy to wait with the DC's cook, and show them the way to the Game Department Compound. After he had gone Claire came into Jim's room through the bathroom.

"What a great looking bath. Do we have to be very respectable or can we have one together?"

Jim replied, "We certainly can. No one will know or care. I think Leonard just felt we ought to look respectable. I am sure he is a man of the world. It is an ideal guest house, with a big bath, and small beds we can snuggle up together in. It will be quite hot. I see there are mosquito mesh screens on the windows and mosquito nets over the beds. I hope you are taking anti-malarial tablets, as this area near the Tana is bad."

"I am," said Claire, "I am also taking the pill. I was worried I would get pregnant after the Game Park adventure." Jim looked guilty, "I am sorry, it was totally irresponsible of me."

"Don't be such a clot. It takes two to tango. I was such a brazen hussy, on my knees with my dress over my head, but Christ it felt good. I think you would have stabbed me to death with that prick of yours, if I had not helped you inside me." With that she wrapped her arms around his neck and kissed him. There was a shout outside, "*hodi, chai tiari* (Can I come in, the tea is ready)." They sprung apart and then both laughed like school children and called, "*karibu* (come in)". In came a young boy with a really cheeky smile, carrying a tray with tea things laid out on it. Claire was certain he had been looking through the window but, she thought, what the hell.

Jim said, "Shall we have it outside? " Then he turned to the boy and said,

"*Jina ake* (What's your name)?"

"Dubi, *Bwana*," replied the boy. Then Jim said in Swahili, "I think you are a tracker. Do you want to come with us to catch the hippopotamus tomorrow?"

"Oh, yes I would," replied Dubi.

"I will ask the DC if he can spare you. I will tell you what he says, when you bring the tea tomorrow morning. It will still be dark, so I want you to make a hoot like an owl, so that a big chap like you does not frighten the '*Memsahib*'", said Jim with a chuckle.

"*Ndio* Bwana Scott. I didn't mean to frighten the *Memsahib,*" replied a shame faced Dubi.

When Dubi had gone and they were sitting having their tea, Claire said,

"You are a clever chap. I suspect Dubi will be your friend for life. If you had really reprimanded him, it would have got you nowhere. I am sure he had been looking through the window. If he had not said '*hodi*' he might have caught us making love. I was just about to reach into your shorts," Claire giggled.

They sat and had their tea, which Jim noticed was made in the English way with a teapot. He had expected African tea. African tea was made by boiling the hot water and adding tea, sugar, and milk and then, to continue boiling the result. Jim did not dislike it and, in fact, he thought it was probably a good idea, as there was plenty of Brucellosis in the grade cattle, which could be spread though raw milk. Milk, sold in the shops in Mombasa and Nairobi, was all pasteurized and so it was safe. Luckily, there was no bovine tuberculosis in the country, so that was not a worry. When they had finished their tea, they both walked to the back of the DC's bungalow, where Jim was sure he would find Christmas and the cook. He carried the tray. When Dubi saw them coming, he ran forward to retrieve the tray. Jim suggested that Dubi could come with them. Then Jim said he would drop Christmas back at the DC's office and Dubi could show them the way to the Game Department compound. Dubi beamed a smile of pleasure. His father, the cook, spoke in Orma to his son, obviously telling him to be on his best behaviour. Jim asked the cook his name. It was Durey.

Dubi easily guided them to the Game Department Compound. After Christmas got out of the Landrover, he quickly climbed over into the front seat next to Claire. He said he was twelve years old. He had finished primary school, but his family could not afford for him to go to secondary school and so he was actually unemployed, but he helped his father doing odd jobs and the DC paid him sometimes, to do work for him, like cutting the grass in the garden after the rains.

There was an organized chaos in the Game Department compound. One group of game scouts was pushing a big old tank of a petrol tanker, up some planks, on to a Bedford 4 x 4 lorry. Another group was making a giant pallet, to act as a sledge to strap the hippopotamus onto, to get it up into the lorry. Others were making the sides of the lorry higher, so that the hippopotamus could not get out. The game warden, a tall Orma, was standing in the middle of the compound issuing orders. He immediately came over when he saw Jim and Claire. Jim had parked outside the compound and left Dubi guarding the Landrover. Claire had found a new baseball hat in her bag. She had given it to Dubi, who wore it with pride.

Justin Kipech was a tough looking man. He greeted them solemnly but he soon warmed to Jim's enthusiasm for all the preparations. He admitted he was worried that the hippopotamus, which had a fearsome reputation, would attack his men and kill one of them. Jim reassured him, with an optimism he actually did not feel, that his '*dawa*' (medicine) would make the animal go to sleep, so they would have plenty of time to rope it to the sledge and get it on to the lorry. Jim said his main concern was keeping the animal cool. Justin assured Jim that he would have plenty of water. He had one proper water bowser, which he had borrowed from the Water Department, and one make shift bowser, which his men would soon have ready. He said the plan was to move off in the morning, at dawn, and make the 60 mile journey to Addi in one day and camp just outside the village. Jim said he and Claire would be at the compound before first light and travel with the Game Department convoy. Jim said they would go back to the DC's guest house and see Justin at the club for the darts match. Justin had relaxed with them now and said he would look forward to beating them.

They parked the Landrover near to the guest house. Dubi said he had to help his father with the cooking, as the DC wanted a special meal for his guests. Claire and Jim went into their rooms through separate doors but of course they met straight away in the bathroom. "I wonder if there will be hot water?" said Claire, "I am jolly hot but it would be good to have a hot bath to get rid of the dust. Then we can have a cold bath after that. First of all, I think we will close the curtains! I don't want young Dubi disturbing our bath." They were pleased the water was not that hot, but it was far from cold, so got into the large bath together. Claire made Jim wash her hair and rinse it thoroughly. Although he made a fuss he loved it really, as she knelt between his legs and let her long blond hair hang down on to his chest. Having his hair washed was even more fun, as her breasts were right near his face, so that he could kiss them. Eventually Jim lay back in the bath and Claire lay with her back to him and encouraged him to fondle her breasts. They let the dirty water out and let in some almost cold water to cool them down. Then Claire's nipples were rock hard and Jim was really gentle with them.

It was nearly dark, by the time they had dried and dressed. Claire's hair was still wet but she said it would soon dry in the heat. Someone had brought a hurricane lamp, so, after putting some mosquito repellent on any exposed skin, they sat out on the veranda. Claire had obviously paid attention to Justin, as she made Jim promise to be careful with the hippopotamus. Soon Dubi arrived, to lead them to the DCs bungalow for supper. While Dubi was present, Jim asked Leonard if Dubi could come with them tomorrow to help. Leonard was delighted as he told them, after Dubi had left, that he was keen that Dubi got more education, as he was a bright kid and deserved better than herding goats all day. Leonard reminisced that was what he had to do, until his father got a job with the Game Department and the whole family moved to Marsabit, where there was a secondary school. He urged Jim and Claire to go to Marsabit, as he said it was a most beautiful place. It was a mountain in the middle of the desert. Leonard was an excellent host and, obviously Durey was a good cook. The time flew by and Leonard said he would drive them to the club, which was called the Tana River Club. Jim was grateful, as he had had a couple of Tuskers and, although he was fit to drive, he did not want to lose his way in the dark.

It was a ten minute drive to the club. When they arrived, there was a row of Government of Kenya (GK) Landrovers in the car park. Jim was amazed as, in Mombasa, the rules were very strictly upheld and GK vehicles were only allowed to be used on Government business. The party had already begun. Jim could see the club had obviously been built in colonial times. He imagined a group of a dozen or so Europeans, either unmarried or posted without their wives, in this out of the way spot. Now all the GK staff were male Kenyans. Here, they were having a get together without any ladies. He looked at Claire.

"Don't worry my love; remember, I am a diplomat's wife. I will be fine, except I am hopeless at darts!"

Leonard introduced them all to Jim and Claire. They all seemed amazed that Claire was up in Tana River District. Justin said to the group, how honoured he was to take them on safari and that he and his staff would really look after them. Jim said he also would look after Justin and all his staff. Jim bought Claire and Leonard a cold tusker each. Claire whispered that it looked like they were in for a real session. She was delighted as no-one would notice how bad she was at darts. However, she was determined not to let Jim down. She also did not want to let Richard down. She would show bloody Martin-Jenkins.

As planned Leonard, Jim and Claire were a team of three. There were three other teams of three. Claire wasn't as bad at darts as she feared. Jim was quite good but Leonard was excellent and so they kept winning. This meant that the opposition had to buy them more tuskers. Claire asked Jim if he could help her out. He said he would but he said he wasn't a big beer drinker. He enjoyed a few pints but not a real skin-full. Claire, very discreetly, asked Leonard. He said of course he would help a lady and he loved beer so there was absolutely no problem. Actually, the party broke up pretty early but not before Leonard had downed a large number of pints. Yet he seemed to take his beer well. The barman, however, recognized the problem and he sent the second barman off at the run, to summon Leonard's driver. Obviously Leonard was well loved and highly respected so, there was not an issue. Jim hopped up into the back of the Landrover and Claire sat in the middle seat. When they reached the DC's house, Jim came around to help Leonard but he was fine. He thanked his driver and wished them a good safari in the morning and peaceful rest tonight. Jim also thanked the driver. He and Claire made a fairly drunken course to the guest house.

There was a hurricane lamp on the veranda, but Jim suggested they left it there as it would definitely attract '*dudus*' (insects) inside. They, very properly, each went in their respected bedroom doors. It was hot. Jim took off all his clothes as he heard Claire in the bathroom. He heard the door open and felt Claire's arms around him from behind. She whispered,

"Wow, naked already. I am a little pissed but I feel very sexy." Jim turned to face her and, as he kissed her, he reached his hand up under her dress and inside the wide leg of her knickers. He rubbed her and felt her sticky juice. He whispered, "Christ, I want you but I will be bloody useless. I am bound to have brewers droop."

"What is brewers droop?" asked Claire as she rubbed herself against him.

"It's when you are a bit pissed and you can't get an erection," replied Jim.

"Even with a little encouragement," said Claire, gently fondling him.

"In fact I can feel him getting harder. Yes, definitely he is getting harder. Let's do like we did in the game park. I will kneel on your bed. You push my dress over my head. That's it. I can feel him but you will have to take my knickers off, you pissed old ram, otherwise you will never find my pussy." She giggled. "You couldn't when you were sober and I had no knickers on." Jim was kissing the back of her neck. Claire arched her bottom towards him. He reached down and started to rub her through her knickers. The silk felt good. He could feel his erection. Claire moaned softly as he pulled down her knickers. Then he drew them down her legs and off her feet. Claire immediately moved her legs apart and backed onto him. He reached for her and she pushed hard back at him. He reached down and helped his penis into her and then, with his knees between hers, he

256

started to thrust. His arms held his weight. His face was in her dress. He was intoxicated with her smell. Unlike in the game park, he did not have an orgasm but just kept thrusting. He felt Claire undulating her bottom. He felt her muscles tighten. He reached under her, partly resting his weight on her. He rubbed above her bush. He felt her stomach muscles tighten hard but still he did not come. They both were gasping now. He whispered.

"Can you roll on to your back?" Before she could take her dress off, his mouth was on her vulva. She was moaning, "Yes, yes, yes." He was in a complete frenzy now. He still kept sucking and rubbing her. He just ripped her dress and then her bra. He fondled her breasts. Claire too was in ecstasy. She moaned,

"Oh, don't stop," when she felt his mouth leave her. Jim had no thoughts of stopping. He knelt on the bed with his knees slightly apart and pulled Claire's thighs over his. She was so wide open he went straight into her. She groaned again, as he thrust twice more, then she felt his hot semen on her tummy. He collapsed on top of her and deeply kissed her lips.

As she regained her breath, she whispered,

"You must get brewers droop more often."

Chapter 19

Nearly a tragic accident

Wednesday 19th July 1967

They both woke with Jim's alarm.

"How do you feel, my darling?" asked Jim.

"Actually, not too bad considering I was raddled half the night but an old ram. How are you?" asked Claire.

"I am in love with the most beautiful, sexy girl in all of Galole'" replied Jim. After she had kissed him she said, "That wasn't much of a complement. I think I am the only girl in Galole! You, young man, owe me a new bra and a new dress! I will run a quick bath then you can have my water. Sadly, we haven't any time to share. Dubi will be hooting like an owl very soon.

Sure enough, Claire was only just out and Jim got in, when they heard the hoot. Claire wrapped a kikoi around her and was careful to open her door.

"*Jambo Dubi. Bwana safisha indani ya batho. Mimi na tengenaza chi. Habari ake* (Hello Dubi. The Master is washing in the bath. I will pour out the tea. How are you)?" "*Muzuri Memsahib. Meme tiari kwa safari.* (I am well Mistress. I am ready to go on the trip)."

"*Muzuri, Bwana hapana sahow wewe nakuja indani Landrover ya Bwana Jim* (Good, the Master has not forgotten you are coming in his Landrover)."* Claire could not see him in the dark but she was sure he was smiling.

She took a cup of tea into Jim's room. She stuffed her ruined dress and bra into Jim's bag and quickly packed the rest of her stuff into hers. It was just light enough for her to see. Jim came out of the bathroom with his washing things, and hers which she had forgotten. Claire went back into her room for a quick room check and to ruffle the bed to make it look slept in. Then they slurped their tea and they were off to the Landrover. Dubi was already there, with his belongings wrapped in a cloth. He had a stick, but he was not old enough to have spear. He directed them unerringly to the Game Department compound. To their surprise, all was very nearly ready. Justin waved to them. His driver ran over with some bananas. Justin then shouted to the lead lorry driver and they were off.

Claire sat in the middle seat. She was glad she had shorts on and a light shirt top. As soon as the sun got up, it began to get hot. Jim kept to the back of the convoy. He soon stopped and showed Dubi how to remove the whole window section on each of the doors. Obviously, it let more dust in but it was considerably cooler. As the vents under the windscreen were open, Claire and Dubi put their feet up. At 10 o'clock, they stopped for everyone to stretch their legs. Jim kindly whispered to Claire, did she need a pee. She said she didn't. She was so hot she thought she might never pee again. Jim made her drink plenty of water. They had seen little game, only glimpses of Topi, Zebra and Dikdik, as they fled away. The convoy moved off but Jim waited while Claire had one more drink of water. Dubi pointed off to their right. Two '*francolin*' (partridges) were sitting motionless under a tree. Normally, Jim was a sportsman but this was supper. So he took his shotgun out of its sleeve, from behind their seats. He took careful aim. He fired one shot only and hit both birds. With a whoop, Dubi ran to them and rung their necks to make sure they were dead. He proudly brought them back. Jim tied them separately by their necks in the back of the Landrover, making sure they would not bleed over anything vital. It was hardly a problem, as everything was covered in dust. The convoy had gone, but Jim had no trouble following their tracks, although Dubi volunteered to run in front. When they stopped for a lunch break, Dubi told everyone about their luck with the francolin. Jim was slightly worried as they were with the Game Department, but Justin was not concerned when Jim gave him one of the birds.

Although Claire and Jim had not had any breakfast, they felt too hot to be hungry. They ate some bananas and a melon, which Jim had carefully packed in a bed of a towel in a bucket. Jim teased Claire, but she just laughed, as the juice ran down her chin. Justin had got out a gas stove and Dubi brought them a cup of black tea with lots of sugar which, in a strange way, was quite refreshing. Jim

259

looked at the milometer in the Landrover and saw that they had done 48 miles. Even with all the bends in the track, they must be getting near to their objective. Jim knew there was a small rock outcrop near Addi. Jim asked Dubi if he would like to climb one of the biggest Acacia trees. It would be dangerous, but Dubi was not concerned. He had thick soled shoes, made from car tyres. Jim gave him a leg up to the lowest branches. He climbed and soon was shouting that he could see the rocks. Jim was worried that he was so excited that he would fall, but he climbed safely down. Claire squeezed Jim's hand and whispered that she could not wait for night to fall and Jim could wash her in cool water.

They all got into the vehicle for the last push to Addi. Everyone was tired; particularly Jim and Claire after their escapades the previous night but, now that everyone realised they were near to their goal, the mood lightened and some of the game scouts in one of the lorries began to sing. In fact, it was really a chant, and Jim could hear them from his position at the back of the convoy.

The children of the village must have heard them as well, because there was a big group of them waiting by the track. A convoy like theirs was a very rare occurrence. Jim thought it was amazing, that only a few weeks ago, all the land except for rock out crops and some low hills had been under water. He noticed that Dubi had proudly put on the baseball cap which Claire had given him. After they had passed the waving children, they came around a bend and a group of village elders stood in the middle of the road. Jim left all the talking to Justin. Obviously they were very welcome. The children grew bold and crowded around Claire. Many of them just wanted to touch her hair. Jim wished he could take a picture, but he did not want to frighten them or spoil the celebration mood.

The elders showed Justin where they could camp, under some large 'Fever Trees'. It was a good spot, but it was still very hot, so unloading the camp stuff was done at a very leisurely pace. Jim and Claire walked into the village to find the water hole.

It was not difficult as it was the focal point of the village, which was just under the rocky out crop. The water had receded further than Jim had imagined and the water level was at least six feet below the surface. There was a way down to the water, which was obviously used by both the hippopotamus and the villagers. Jim could see the villager's problem. It was narrow and, if they were coming up with water when the hippopotamus was coming back from his night time feed, there would be a dreadful accident. Now that the whole area was drying up, the hippopotamus would have to travel further to reach any fodder. He would be competing with the villager's cattle, which also had to use the waterhole. The sooner the hippopotamus was back in the Tana River the better. There was a snorting noise and the Hippopotamus came to the surface and opened his enormous mouth lazily.

Jim and Claire went to find Justin to make a plan. They found him in the camp making preparations for supper. He volunteered one of his chaps to pluck and dress both '*francolins*'. Jim gratefully accepted. Justin and Jim agreed that this was not going to be a simple operation, and timing would be important. Jim was worried that when he darted the animal, it would have time to lumber back into the water. Justin suggested that he positioned the trucks across the way, in and out of the water hole, after the hippopotamus had gone out to forage at night. He said they should not move the trucks until the animal was well away from the water hole, in case he heard the trucks and immediately ran back to the water. Jim suggested that, if they made a giant net between two trucks, the animal might get tangled up in it particularly if he was half sedated. So, it was agreed that they would have an early supper and get some sleep. Game scouts would act as sentries. When the hippopotamus left the water, the game scouts would follow but one would come and get Jim and Claire, so they could also follow. Dubi would come so, as soon as Jim was in a good position to fire the crossbow with the dart, he would return and tell Justin to be ready to start the trucks and position them and the net. As soon as Jim had fired the dart, Claire would blow a whistle and Justin could start the trucks.

The '*francolin*' wrapped in tin foil, and some potatoes also wrapped in foil, did not take long to cook, so they ate before the sun went down. Jim filled two darts and got the crossbow all prepared but not cocked. Dubi announced he would sleep in the Landrover. Jim winked at Claire and said they would sleep in the tent on top. He then whispered to Claire,

"No hanky panky tonight!"

"Bloody good job," replied Claire, "I am bloody knackered." So, they were a very chaste couple going to bed and were quickly asleep. In fact, it was 4 am when Dubi made an owl hoot which woke them, but it felt as if they had only been asleep for ten minutes. They quickly dressed. Jim grabbed the crossbow and darts. Claire took the big torch without putting it on, and the two of them quietly followed the game scout with Dubi behind them. They had a long frightening walk. Not a word was spoken. Jim reckoned they walked for nearly an hour and covered about two miles. Luckily there was a moon, so they could each see the person in front of them. Jim thought how good the game scout was, to know where he was going in the dark. The scout stopped when he saw the other scout, who was a sort of link man, as there was yet another scout about 100 yards away, nearer to the hippopotamus. They all went very slowly forward. They could hear the animal eating. They stopped at about 10 yards from the Hippopotamus, which had not heard them. Ever so quietly Jim cocked the crossbow. He indicated to Claire to move a couple of paces to his right so that there was no danger of being in her light. They had agreed that he would aim at where he thought the animal was and shoot, as soon as Claire turned on the light. They both felt their hearts were going to leap out of their chests. On went the light. There was the hippopotamus' bottom. Jim fired. Jim immediately reloaded the cross bow, but as he did so, the hippopotamus wheeled and came straight at the light and, of course, Claire. To her eternal credit Claire was made of very strong fibre. She stood stock still, held the lamp up high and kept it aimed at the beast. Jim leapt in front of her to protect her, then knelt and fired the second dart. It hit the animal straight between its nostrils. It swung away and crashed through the bush, heading back to the water hole. Jim shouted.

"Claire, are you OK?"

"I am fine but I have dropped the whistle." In the excitement, Jim had totally forgotten it. They found it quite quickly with the torch. Claire blew one very long blast. They were now totally disorientated and did not know which way to go. They had lost all their night vision. Jim said, we will just stand still and wave the torch in an arc in the night sky. That was how Dubi found them, and led them quickly back to the chaos at the water hole. The hippopotamus had made it back to the waterhole but, luckily, the effect of the drug had slowed him considerably. Jim obviously did not know if it had received two doses or, if one of the darts had misfired. Jim thought *'thank goodness, the second dart into his nose had turned him away from Claire. It made him feel weak, at the thought of Claire being crushed by two tons of very angry hippopotamus.'* This giant was now thrashing about in the makeshift net, making the two anchoring trucks rock like boats in a storm. Jim had no time to load a dart for the crossbow. He quickly drew up yet a third dose into a normal, non-disposable syringe. He locked on a Luer fitting three inch needle. Claire guessed what he was going to do.

She screamed, "Be careful." Jim ran at the hippopotamus' rump. He lunged with the syringe and injected all in one motion, as he had been taught to inject pigs at college. He slipped as the hippopotamus lunged forward even further into the tangle of the net. Jim rolled to the side and quickly got to his feet. He must have been very lucky, and injected into a very vascular area of muscle, or the effects of the first two darts started to kick in, as the animal lay still as he backed away. Then it started to snore and Jim knew he had done a good job. Claire was instantly close beside him, hugging him as if her very life depended on it.

The Game Department team was then galvanized into action. Using the vehicle head lights, the hippopotamus was strapped, with webbing hobbles, to the wooden pallet that they had made two days earlier. Strong metal ramps were laid on to the ground, from a lorry which was backed up to the snoring beast. Using rollers, the pallet and animal were pulled and pushed up onto the lorry. When the tail gate was up, the net was securely anchored round all the sides of the lorry. Some game scouts rode actually on the lorry, while others rode in Justin's Landrover, which led the way back to the Tana River. The dawn had not broken. Jim was delighted. The lorry with the hippopotamus followed Justin's Landrover, while one of the water carrying lorries followed behind. The rest of the game scouts quickly broke up the camp and loaded everything left onto the remaining empty lorry. Jim, Claire and Dubi also broke up their camp and loaded the Landrover. Claire managed to brew some African tea on the remnant of the fire. They had some cornflakes and UHT milk. Dubi looked at the cornflakes with suspicion, until he tasted them after Claire had added some sugar. His face split into a wide grin.

The second convoy, of the Game Department lorry, the makeshift water bowser and Jim's Landrover was soon under way. They could easily follow the tracks of the others. Now that the excitement was over, Claire felt rather deflated and quite cold, as the dawn was only just breaking. She sat as close as she could to Jim, and put her right arm around his shoulders. He immediately asked,

"You must be cold. Shall I put the windows of the Landrover back in?"

"No, don't worry. My guess is it is going to get hot pretty quick." Claire was right. The tropical dawn was very quick in coming. Soon, they could see the dust of the first convoy. Jim was uneasy. He wondered whether those three doses of sedation and anaesthetic would last. He just hoped the hippopotamus would not have a violent recovery. Claire must have read his thoughts. She squeezed his thigh and said,

"I am sure everything will be fine. How soon will Justin stop, to pour water over the hippopotamus? I wonder if he will have a sore nose from that second dart" Claire shuddered, thinking how close the hippopotamus had been to killing her.

"Justin said he would stop at 9.00am. I think his nose will be fine. Thank God it hurt him enough for him to turn, or we both might have been killed," replied Jim.

"I won't ever forget, you saved my life, Jim," said Claire giving his thigh another squeeze.

"I won't ever forget how cool and brave you were, holding the light up high and steady." Dubi, who had been following the conversation with his limited English said, "The game scouts said you were both as good as any hunters."

"That's good to know," said Jim.

They were all hot when they caught up with the others. The hippopotamus was still snoring and they had poured masses of water over him, so the first vehicles got going as Jim arrived. Jim called to Justin that they would not stop, but would all travel in one convoy in case there were problems. Justin, very wisely, did not let the lorry with the hippopotamus actually stop again. Every 15 minutes, he made it slow to walking pace, and four game scouts would run to catch it up and pour a bucket over it. Then it would increase speed again but, obviously, as they were just on a dirt track, the pace was very slow. It was nearly 11.30am when the whole convoy stopped, as the hippopotamus was totally awake and trying to get up. Jim was so relieved they had tied him down. He managed to lunge with another full dose of anaesthetic. They poured a large volume of water over him. Then, even though he was rocking the lorry they, set off. Luckily, the motion of the lorry must have made him sleepy, as Jim could see the rocking motion gradually becoming less. Claire could see how worried he was but she said nothing, just squeezed his thigh.

At 1.30pm they could see the green belt of trees, which was the Tana River, but Jim could see the lorry rocking again. He had told Justin that it would be very dangerous to give the animal another dose of anaesthetic, so the lorry kept going. The driver did not accelerate, as he knew he might have an accident. They came up to the main Garsen to Garissa road. There was Leonard, with some 'askaris', stopping the traffic. They went onto the slip-way down to Tana River. Leonard had stationed more 'askaris' there, to keep it clear. The lorry turned round in a wide circle, rocking very violently. The game scouts kept throwing water over the animal. The lorry backed down the slip-way. Jim, Claire and Dubi were out of the Landrover. Leonard joined them at a fast trot. The game scouts managed, with great difficulty, to get the metal ramps tied to the lorry. Quickly the tail gate was dropped. The sledge was already moving and needed little help to get it down the ramps. Jim could do nothing to help, so he ran to the bank and took some photos. The scouts were cutting the ropes and then the Hippo from Addi was free. He roared and set off at a brisk run to the water's edge and, with a dive of several feet, he splashed into the Tana. Jim got some great pictures, not only of the hippopotamus, but also of the people's faces. There were wonderful expressions of delight. Leonard put his arm around Claire and said how delighted he was that it had all worked out so well. He encouraged them to stay the night but Jim said they ought to get some way home that night, so that could get to Mombasa the following night. Justin thanked them both, as he shook their hands vigorously. Leonard promised to look after Dubi and to make sure, somehow, he got to school. In front of Dubi, he told Jim if he ever needed Dubi to come with him on safari, he could always send word via his office. Claire was delighted, as when they left, a great cheer went up, not only from the Game Department staff but also from the Orma villagers, who lived on the river.

The first part of the journey went well. They managed to get through Garsen and turn south towards Malindi. They turned off the road and did some '*bundu bashing*' (bush driving) so that they would have Africa to themselves as the sun was going down. They set the tent up on the roof of the Landrover. They did not bother with a fire, but just cooked some tinned soup and a cup of tea on the gas stove. When it was totally dark, Claire came up behind Jim and whispered in his ear, "The water in the plastic jerry cans is tepid. Shall we wash each other, standing up in the canvas bath?"

"Great idea," said Jim, "that sounds fun. We will probably be almost as dirty when we have finished!"

It was before 8 pm when they clambered naked up into the tent. Jim closed the mosquito net door but left the canvas doors open both ends, so there was some air flow. They lay naked on top of the sleeping bags. Claire reached down to Jim's groin and whispered,

"You have not got brewers droop tonight and no company. I am really worn out but I still want you to make love to me." She rolled on top of him and kissed him. Trapping his penis on his tummy she rubbed herself on him and, all the while, they kept kissing. Suddenly Jim could bear it no longer. He reached down below her bottom, parted her thighs and thrust upwards. He missed his target but then he felt her gentle hands guiding him.

"Slowly, my great stallion," whispered Claire as she undulated her bottom.

"Now you can thrust. Yes, that is lovely. Now try to think about something else, so you won't come so quickly. Think of the charging Hippo. Oh yes, that is good. Keep going slowly. Christ, that's good. I am almost there. Yes. Yes. Oh yes. Come now my darling." Jim squeezed her bottom hard and climaxed deep inside her.

Chapter 20

Marvellous public relations

Saturday 22nd July 1967

Christopher Martin-Jenkins was very quick to point out to Sir Richard, at his daily morning briefing that Lady Rochester seemed to be taking an extra long time to return to Nairobi. Sir Richard just grunted and said, "I am sure no news is good news." Christopher Martin-Jenkins did not show Sir Richard an article on the third page of the "Daily Nation", with a headline of 'Game enthusiastic wife of the British High Commissioner personally helps the DC of Tana River District, Leonard Baloala, to rescue a stranded hippopotamus'. There was a great picture of Leonard with his arm around Claire, with both of them smiling. Sir Richard found the article himself and called Christopher back to the morning briefing.

"Christopher, what a marvellous PR exercise. I knew Claire would come up trumps. I gather you sent her down on the train, rather than flying her down. No wonder she took longer to come home. Claire came into the room.

"Ah there you are my dear, I was just saying to Christopher how well you had done. You must be really tired having to come back on the train."

Claire replied, "No problems darling, on the way down I shared a carriage with Grace Middleton, who gave me some excellent tips on going on safari and on the return journey, I had a carriage to myself and slept like a log." Claire did not say she was completely knackered after her last night with Jim, which ended up with her putting her racy pyjama bottoms on Jim's head. She had to sleep in a shirt on the train as, somehow, the pyjama tops had been ripped down the front by Jim, in his haste to kiss her breasts. Oh well, she thought, I will know always to be naked at the coast from now on.

Actually, she was surprised by the article. Jim had not said anything about it. In fact, after he had seen her off on the train, he had gone round to see a pal of his, Mark Young, who was the Coast correspondent for the "Daily Nation". Jim had saved the sight of Mark's dog, which had been spat at by a spitting cobra. Mark was delighted with the story and had managed to get the photographs developed that night and sent up to Nairobi, to make the first edition. In fact, it was quite a scoop for Mark. He was happy to leave any reference to Jim out of the article. Jim said it would have got him in trouble with his boss, as he was meant to look after food producing animals and game animals were not in his job description. Jim felt a bit bad, as Mark immediately thanked him again for saving his dog.

Sir Richard seemed genuinely pleased by her return and was interested in her edited version of the safari, particularly when Claire told him about the Italian seismic survey. She did not tell him that the Italian had divulged more information than he should have, while he was looking down the front of her T shirt. Sir Richard said he would forward the information to London. Of course, he was totally unaware that Claire would also be briefing London.

Jim had a beautiful house, whose garden ran down to Tudor Creek. It was in between the Provincial Commissioner's vast residence and the Catherine Bibby Hospital. Next door to the hospital was the Mombasa Club. As the club dropped down towards the water, it was called the 'Chini' (meaning 'below' in Swahili) club. Therefore Jim was actually only a stone's throw from the 'Chini' Club. Jim was not a member of the 'Chini' Club, as he thought it was rather stuffy compared to the Mombasa Sports Club, where he played Rugby, Hockey and Squash. However, he was actually allowed into the 'Chini' Club, because he was a member of an upcountry club, The Nanuyki Sports Club, which reciprocated membership with the 'Chini' Club.

Jim had put Claire on the train three days ago. He had not heard from her, which was hardly surprising. He was a little despondent when he came home for supper after rugby training. The phone was ringing and he hoped it was not a call to a cow calving at the dairies, or a steer down on the "Bonanza" on arrival at the KMC. His heart missed a beat, it was Claire.

"My darling, I am in a call box and haven't got long, but I will be down in Mombasa next Saturday. I have persuaded Richard to let me come with him to an official dinner at the Chini Club on Saturday night. Isn't the 'Chini' Club near to you? Richard and I will be in separate rooms so I can easily slip out when everyone is a sleep. I will make my way to the swimming pool. Can you break in and meet me at 2am? I will wear sensible clothes and shoes so, somehow, you will have to get me out".

"I will be there," said Jim but the line went dead. He called the operator, but that was it, he could not ring back to the call box.

They had not had a chance to work out a code for Jim's morning veterinary radio broadcast. He would have to concoct something. He daren't ring the High Commission and there certainly wasn't time for a letter.

In the morning, he broadcast the following message; "I confirm to the farmer with the white Shorthorn cow that I will examine his cow on Sunday morning down by the water on Tudor creek at the agreed time." Jim prayed that Claire had got the message. He transmitted the message again on Friday morning.

On Friday evening, straight after work, Jim reconnoitered the area. First of all he walked down the path from his house, past the hospital to the 'Chini' Club. Although he could get down near to the swimming pool, there was no way he could climb over the wall, as it was topped with glass. However, he could see that he could climb up the coral wall between the sea and the pool. He knew he would have no bother, as he regularly dived off the similar wall at the bottom of his garden for a swim and then could climb up to his house. In fact, he had managed to get Jane Morton up some months earlier. It would be hard for Claire but, if he brought a rope and tied it to the steps of the pool, they could dive off together and then he would help her up the rope to come home. Could she swim? Somehow Jim was sure she would be a swimmer. What about her clothes? She would have to hide them by the pool and dive in, get dressed in them on her return for the journey back to her room. He walked back home with some doubts but he thought it might work. Before it got dark he put on his swimming trunks and went for a swim off the bottom of his garden. He always wore his gym shoes and a pair of diving gloves to make climbing up the coral easier. He would have to buy a pair of gym shoes and gloves for Claire in the morning. That would be easy enough, but there was no way he could buy a bikini, as he knew the girl in the ladies clothes shop, and she would not only ask questions, but might well say something at the rugby game on Saturday afternoon.

The swim from his house was easy, a little over 50 yards. He knew he could return to his house OK, but he carefully checked out the climb up to the Chini Club Pool. He was sure he could manage it and he hoped with the aid of a rope, Claire would be able to climb on the way back, after their tryst.

There was not much work for Jim to do at the Veterinary office on Saturday morning, so he had no problem buying a pair of ladies size gym-shoes, from one of the African shops down Kilindini Road. There was a bustle in the diving shop so the owner, who knew Jim, just waved to him. Buying a small pair of neoprene diving gloves from the African assistant did not raise any eyebrows.

Jim was always on edge before a rugby game. Today he had the real butterflies and Katana remarked, as he ate so little lunch that he hoped Jim was not getting Malaria. Jim hoped he wasn't and, in reality, he knew it was the prospect of seeing Claire again. Had she heard him? Had she got the clues on the radio message? Would she come to the pool?

He arrived in good time at the sports club and, all the banter with his pals helped to take his mind off the prospects of the night. He played hard and, in fact, had a good game. It was not part of his character to save himself. They always had pints of lime and lemonade straight after the game, so Jim drank a couple of those as normal. After there had been a couple of comments about him continuing to drink lime and lemonade and not 'Tusker', Jim let slip that he wondered if he was getting Malaria, as he had not wanted any lunch.

"Rubbish" said one of his team-mates. "I bet you are love sick for one of the Nairobi 'fillies' you met last weekend". Jim coloured but it was hot in the bar and, luckily, no-one noticed so he didn't get any more ribbing. After a rugby tea, Jim managed to slip away before the serious drinking got started. He didn't think anyone noticed but there might well be questions asked at training on Tuesday.

Back home Jim didn't think he would sleep, so he didn't get into bed but read a book in an armchair on the veranda. The moon was up over the creek. It looked really beautiful. Jim saw it with new eyes. Luckily, Jim set an alarm as he must have dosed off to sleep. He was up in a flash but, in fact, he had plenty of time. He got into his swimming trunks. He put the small pair of gym-shoes in his waist band and he split the small pair of gloves one in each pocket. He walked down the garden in his gym-shoes and dived into the water. It took his breath away as it seemed quite cold, but he soon warmed up as he started to swim. He could see first the hospital and then the Chini club, easily in the moonlight. He breathed a sigh of relief that there were no lights on at the pool. Also, the bar behind the pool was dark. He had thought it was unlikely that there would be drinkers after one 'o'clock, but it would have just been his luck if Claire was trapped in her room and he had to tread water for hours, out in the creek.

He swam into the coral wall under the pool. It was not a vertical climb and so, actually, he climbed it quite easily. Damn, he had forgotten the rope. However, it was so easy, he thought Claire would manage and he would be able the climb up underneath her. He longingly thought of her little naked bottom above him. All was quiet by the pool. He carefully stayed in the shadows. Then he saw a figure sitting on a sun chair. It was too big to be Claire. It was the night-watchman. His regular breathing showed he was asleep. Jim crept up to him and stood by the edge of the pool. It was a risk but he had to let Claire know he was there, and he was sure she would be able to see his silhouette. He stood for what seemed like an eternity until he felt a light touch on his arm. She had come. Without a word he took her hand and they moved like ghosts over to the creek side of the pool. Jim guided Claire to the end of the pool, nearer to the hospital, where he remembered the coral wall was nearly vertical. There was a flood light there, where she could hide her clothes. He whispered in her ear, "You are marvellous, I love you so much". She just squeezed his arm and immediately took off her shirt. Her breasts were like white lights in the moonlight. No bra and then he saw no knickers either. He handed her the small gym-shoes which she quickly put on, leaving her flip-flops with her clothes behind the light. Quickly she put on the gloves and, before he could say a word, she did a beautiful dive into the sea without a splash. When he was sure she was clear he followed her but, he thought, I bet I make a splash. The cold did not make him gasp, but the hard little body with legs that tightly wrapped round his waist certainly did. Her arms were round his neck and she kissed him really hard, as they slid below the surface. However one kick of his legs brought them both up, with Claire still wrapped around him.

"Shit, it's cold. What a way to treat a girl". Then she giggled "My nipples are so hard they hurt. I bet your cock is tiny but, when we get out, I will do something about that!"

"Come on then," whispered Jim. "We have a 50 yard swim before the climb up to my house". She let him go and immediately was swimming breast stroke towards the sea. Jim had a job to keep up with her. To think, he had worried she would not be able to swim.

It took a little longer to get to his house, as the tide was coming in, but soon they were beside the familiar coral wall. Jim swam up to the easiest place for Claire to climb. She let the sea bring her in close before she grabbed the coral and scrabbled up. He got a lovely view of her pretty white bottom, with its cleft, before she was over the edge. He was quick to follow her. At the top she flung her arms round him and kissed him hard. He could feel her rock hard nipples on his chest and the sea water in her kiss.

"Come on, it may be the tropics but we will freeze to death, up here in the wind". They ran, hand in hand, up the grass and across the drive into the unlocked front door of the house. The stairs were straight ahead and led, not only to the bedrooms, but also to an upstairs veranda, where Jim often sat at night and watched the sea. It looked wonderful tonight in the moonlight.

"This is so beautiful," sighed Claire and hugged him again.

"We had better not turn the light on, or we will be on view to all and sundry. Let's have a shower." He led Claire to a large wet room type shower. It had a frosted window and a basin, which drained into a drain in one corner, with the lavatory in the other corner. After shutting the door, he pulled the light switch. As he went to take off his swimming trunks, he turned away from her and felt her arms around him from behind.

"Oh no you don't. Here am I, only dressed in a smile, and you won't let me see a full frontal!" said Claire. She still had her diving gloves on, when she grabbed him.

"Poor little 'willy', I will soon make you big and strong". Letting go of him, she turned him to face her by the shoulders, looking him straight in the eye and smiling. She took off her gloves behind him and sank to her knees in front of him. She took his small penis with her hands and lasciviously started licking the end. Instantly, Jim started to become aroused. Then she started to very gently suck him. Jim groaned and delicately pushed her wet hair off her face. Very soon Jim could not contain himself anymore and pulled her head back before he ejaculated. Claire felt his hot semen on her breasts. She got up slowly and kissed him.

"You silly boy, I wanted to take you in my mouth but your hot semen on my cold, hard nipples felt lovely. Now, I want you to wash me all over. I know you are still shy but make sure you don't miss any bits!"

Claire grinned. "Don't worry. I will make sure you do a proper job. Now let's get the shower to the right temperature."

Jim replied, "this isn't like Nairobi, it is only tepid I am afraid, but I think you will soon warm up". Sure enough, after making Jim take several attempts to wash between her legs, Claire was soon satisfied and started to dry herself, which was why she was the first into the bedroom. She tripped over the rope, Jim had forgotten to take with him to help her up the coral cliff.

"Wow, so you aren't so shy after all. You were going to tie me up?" Claire queried as Jim spluttered, "that it was to help her up the coral cliff." Turning and hugging him Claire laughed. "You liar, one day I am going to tie you to a bed and bounce up and down on you until you beg me for mercy. Tonight I want you to come under this mosquito net and kiss me until I can bare it no longer and then I am going to guide you inside me and you can come as quickly as you like. However, as you have swum all that way and come all over my breasts, I don't think you will come quite as quickly as normal. Come on, my beautiful lover." She was quickly under the mosquito net pulling Jim's head between her legs. Jim did not need any second urging. He kissed her. Claire initially directed him but soon laid back and let that glorious feeling wash over her. "I will forgive you, for

273

calling me a white cow on the radio." She started making small mooing noises which encouraged Jim. He moved his hands up to hold her breasts. He felt her belly muscles harden as she started to gasp. He felt her thighs gripping his head and her fingers lacing themselves in his wet hair. She shuddered and moaned. "Don't stop. Oh please, don't stop. Yes. Yes. I am coming." She almost dragged Jim up her body. "Kiss me hard and enter me." Her legs were wide open and she raised her pelvis to him so that it needed no guidance. They both started to thrust together. Claire had been right, although Jim was in ecstasy he was not quite ready to ejaculate and he found he could hold back for a few seconds. Then it was too much and he thrust as deep into her as he could, with Claire thrusting up to meet him. As his orgasm came and came again he felt Claire keep thrusting towards him. She cried out. Jim slumped on top of her burying his face in her neck and kissing her.

The alarm woke them with Claire still on her back and Jim lying half on top of her. They both groaned as Jim flicked on the bedside light reaching, through the mosquito net. Claire stroked his hair.

"You stay put, my darling. I can easily swim back to the club on my own."

"No way! Of course I am coming with you. Sadly we ought to go, as we must get you back in before day-light. Let's hope the askari is either still sleeping, or on his rounds." After putting on their gym-shoes and gloves they walked, hand in hand, down the garden. The tide had come in so there was not such a big drop.

"It will be much easier to get out at the other end. Make sure you dive well out my darling." Claire dived and, as soon as her head surfaced, Jim followed her.

"Phew that's cold and now I want a pee" Said Clare.

"Be my guest" said Jim. They both started to swim to the Chini club. Luckily, it did not seem as far as the swim down the creek. The sky was just beginning to lighten. Dawn would be coming very quickly, so near the equator. They both scrabbled up the coral wall. There was no sign of the 'askari'. Claire got into her clothes, as quick as she could but it was not easy, being wet, and they stuck to her. Jim had no trunks on, so he just took her gym shoes. She gave him a hug and a kiss and scampered away to her room.

Once inside, she had a quick shower and, combing out her hair, she crawled under the mosquito net. She was now quite awake, so she pulled the spare pillow under her and dreamed it was Jim. In fact, she was dog tired and was soon asleep.

Jim stood by the edge of pool and watched her inside, and then turned and dived into the sea. Arriving opposite his garden, he threw Claire's gym shoes up onto the grass and climbed wearily up to follow them. He was seriously tired and just towelled himself and fell into the still warm bed. He could still smell Claire and their love making. He was asleep in seconds.

Jim slept until noon and woke sweaty and sticky. He was sad, as he showered, thinking that he did not know when he was going to see Claire again. He was sorely tempted to go to the Chini club for lunch but he knew that was ridiculous, as none of his friends would be there. Anyhow Claire might well have left, so what was the point. No, he would stick to his plan, which he had mentioned to Claire, about going sailing from the Mombasa sailing club. He would think of some excuse to go to Nairobi. Poor Claire, he thought, she would have had to have got up for breakfast with her husband, and then had a hot, five hour drive up to Nairobi.

Jim drove the short journey to the yacht club, after having a bowl of cereal for breakfast. He thought to himself *'that he must really be love-sick, as he should be starving hungry.'* He so wanted to see Claire again. It was so tempting to find some pretext to go round to the Chini Club, but he resisted it. He felt better when he went into the yacht club and was greeted cheerily by several friends. He booked a club '505' for the afternoon's racing, and put his name down as wanting a crew. He hoped he would get someone friendly. There were lots of guys who had girls as regular crews but Jim had not sailed that often, while he was learning to fly and playing rugby. So now he had to take pot luck. He sat down at a table and started reading 'The Sunday Nation'. He jumped when Claire put her hand on his shoulder and said. "Hello, we met at the High Commission. I hope you don't mind, but I have put my name down to be your crew. I have sailed a little as a child, but I have never sailed with a trapeze. I am afraid I will be rather hopeless. I will quite understand if you would rather take some more experienced girl." Jim was flustered but he managed to blurt out.

"I would love to take you. I have not done much, so I am sure we will come last but, I am equally sure, we will have some fun. I had a very late breakfast. Do you want some lunch first?" With a mischievous smile Claire said. "For some reason, I slept in. I can't think why, so I also had a late breakfast. Let's go down to the boat and you can give me some instructions."

As soon as they were out of earshot, walking down the sand, Jim said quietly. "You are a real angel. I was so miserable when I thought I would not see you for ages. I nearly came down to the Chini Club on some pretext, just to see you from afar. Then I thought you would have probably set off for Nairobi and I would have made a prat of myself. It is so wonderful to see you."

"I was very naughty. I left a note for Richard saying I felt a bit sick and that I would stay another night at the Chini Club. I suggested he got the Driver to take him back to Nairobi and that I would come up by train. He left a note saying he hoped I would feel better soon and would see me in Nairobi. Can you put up with me for another night? Before you say "yes," remember I am a real novice on the trapeze."

"I don't care if you capsize us a hundred times. Please stay. I am like a dog with two tails. We will have a couple of races, just because it would look odd if we don't. Then we will bunk off home. You look ravishing." Claire felt she looked sexy. She had a new white bikini, which really fitted her breasts. She had a white blouse with all the buttons undone and the ends tied under her breasts. In fact, she was not showing off anything more than she would have, just wearing the bikini top, but it gave a much more risqué look. Over her bikini bottoms she was wrapped in a mainly white 'kikoi', with gold threads through the weave. Jim thought she looked like Aphrodite. Claire pulled off the 'kikoi' as they reached a pile of trapezes. She picked one up and turned to Jim saying,

"I think you will have to help me get into this?" With a smirk Jim agreed. They were standing facing each other and somehow Jim's hand slipped in the top of Claire's bikini bottoms. She moved closer to him and said,

"You are a sexy beast. I can't wait for this evening." They moved apart as Zachariah, the head boatman, walked over.

"I am very sorry, Bwana Scott, but you won't need a trapeze. The boat captain said that, as you don't sail very often and won't get in the team, he has allocated you the Hornet rather than one of the 505s."

"Don't worry Zachariah. The Hornet will be fine. In fact, I am more familiar with a Hornet from sailing in '*Ulaya*' (UK). The Hornet will be great. We will have a more favorable Harbour rating. Can you give us a hand to get it down to the water? We will have a practice before the race starts."

"Of course, thank you for not making a fuss. I will give you a help launching her." They both put on life-jackets and then they got the boat into the water. Jim said,

"You hop in, Claire. Zachariah and I will get the sails up." Claire got into the boat, while Jim and Zachariah held it steady, and then she turned to Zachariah and said. "Thank you for helping, I am rather hopeless as I don't know what I should be doing."

"Don't worry '*Memsahib*' you will soon get the idea. Bwana Scott will teach you. He is a kind man." Claire felt a warm feeling inside. She loved to hear people saying nice things about Jim. She was also totally confused about Jim being one of her agents. She knew she would defend Jim whatever but could she send him into danger, like rescuing Somali One. What was worse was she knew he would risk his life for someone else, if he was sent on a mission, whether she, as his control sent him or whether he knew his control was her. She was brought out of her revelry by Jim's hand brushing against her thigh.

"I just have to tighten the mainsheet," said Jim. Claire thought the mainsheet was tight enough but he just wanted an excuse to touch her thigh. Claire was right.

"OK, all set. Zachariah and I will push us off. I will jump in and, if you could pull on this rope, which is called the jib-sheet, we will be off." The manoeuver went off smoothly. As soon as Jim was in the boat, he pulled in the mainsheet and the boat gathered speed, heading out into Kilindini Harbour.

"Many thanks, Zachariah," Jim called out. Claire turned to wave to Zachariah, as his figure grew small on the beach.

A hornet is not quite as fast as a 505, which has the crew on a trapeze. It has a sliding seat, which the crew has to slide across as the boat "goes about". As they left the shore, they were on a broad reach so that, by spilling some of the wind from the mainsail, Jim could keep the yacht upright, while he explained to Claire what she had to do. When he was going to turn he would warn her by saying "ready about". Claire would then have to come in from the seat and uncleat the jib. When he said "lee ho" he would push the tiller away from him so that the yacht would turn into the wind and go onto the opposite tack. All Jim had to do, was to keep his head down below the boom and move over to the other side of the boat. Claire had to slide the seat over, loose the jib, move over to the other side of the boat and then haul in the jib, cleat it and move her weight out on to the seat. Instinctively Claire ducked down under the boom. Jim could not stop himself from squeezing her bottom as they both moved over. Laughing, Claire said, "I am going to enjoy this 'lee ho' business."

Very soon Claire had got the idea and they were racing across the harbour close-hauled. Spray soon soaked Claire, as she managed to get her feet on the gunnels and her bottom right far out on the seat. She was arching her back out over the water and shouting,

"This is great, it is really exciting. What happens if the wind suddenly dies?"

"Unless you can get your weight in quickly, you will get very wet and we will capsize, like this." shouted Jim as he took some pressure off the tiller. He had purposely dumped Claire in the water. She came up spluttering. Jim quickly turned the yacht and raced back to her. He turned the yacht into the wind and so it was stationary in irons. Claire had only three yards to swim until she was behind the stern.

"You rat, Jim. You did that on purpose. You wait until we are in bed tonight. I will get my own back."

"Come on, give a big breaststroke kick with your legs and wrap your arms round my neck. I will lift you out," said Jim, as he neatly pulled her out of the water, without Claire getting scratched by the rudder.

"Even with your life jacket, you look a hell of a sexy maiden with the wet look."

"I will give you hell of a sexy maiden!" said Claire but Jim noticed that she still had her arms around his neck. He was dying to kiss her but he knew there would be binoculars trained on them from the yacht club. Claire felt his erection as she slithered past him to get to the movable seat. Jim knew it was not chance that she grabbed his swollen cock.

"You just wait, Jim Scott. Thank you for providing a good hand-hold, for a maiden in difficulties. Now let's get sailing and show these fancy 505s how to race." As if on cue, the five minute gun sounded across the choppy blue water. Jim got the yacht under way and headed to the start line.

"Actually, getting you wet was good policy in this breezy weather, as there will be more weight on the end of the seat and we can go faster," said Jim with a grin.

"I remember, when we first met you said my tits were not big enough. Now, you say I am not fat enough. There is no pleasing you, Jim Scott," said Claire.

"Oh yes there is! You promised great things tonight. I can't wait to find out what they are," said Jim. Claire stuck her tongue out at him and said. "There is a clue. The second clue is the number of the boat." It was 69. Jim was non-plussed but thought, *'somehow I think tonight is going to be very memorable.'*

With some careful manoeuvering letting the 505's tear about, Jim managed a really great start but, of course, his lead did not last long. He tried to get the best out of the hornet. He loved watching Claire arching her back, as she leaned out from the very end of the sliding seat. Soon they were far enough behind, so that they could talk without being over heard. Claire shouted, "This is almost as exhilarating as watching lions mate."

"Not quite," shouted Jim. "I will never forget my hand creeping up under your dress and finding you did not have any knickers on. What a wonderfully sexy girl you are."

"I will never forget how wonderful you were asking, to see me totally nude. I still feel shy thinking about it. I love you so much that, if you asked me, I would rip all my clothes off right now. For God sake don't ask me. The old buffers in the club house, watching us with binoculars, will have heart attacks."

"Ready about," shouted Jim.

"Remember where to put your hand when we lee ho" shouted Claire. As they rounded the buoy, Jim managed to reach forward and gently stroke Claire's thigh, just below her bikini bottom.

"Want more lee hos" shouted Claire, waggling her bottom provocatively. On the next tack, as they were racing after the other yachts, they had a bit of luck as the wind veered and they were able to make the next buoy more easiley than the other boats. They had to do two more tacks. None of the 505s were paying attention to them, which was lucky, as when Jim looked at Claire, she had slipped her bikini bottoms down and he could see her bush of pubic hair.

"I am just getting ready for the next lee ho. I bet you can't touch my fanny?" She shouted. They had gained several yards. Then they lost them again as, when they next went about, Claire took an extra couple of seconds crossing over so that Jim could touch her.

They finished the race behind the rest of the fleet and came into the shore in front of the yacht club. Jim shouted. "Let's call it a day. I am starving hungry and could do with some tea."

Claire whispered as they drifted in, "I hope you like what I have for your tea. You will find out what 69 means."

Zachariah had a wide smile on his face, as he helped them draw the hornet out of the water.

"Well done Bwana Scott, you were the winner."

"We can't have been," said Jim. "We were way behind the others. You are just teasing us."

"No, honestly Bwana, they were so busy fighting amongst themselves that they let you get too close so that, with your handicap, you beat them. I am glad they made you have the hornet."

"We are really grateful. Thank you Zachariah."

The club captain congratulated Jim, when he got into the club house. Jim introduced Claire. The club captain, who had an eye for pretty girls, said he was going to propose Claire for membership and said she was welcome anytime. He said Jim had done the correct thing coming in now, as the wind was dropping and the 505s were much stronger, being lighter in a soft blow.

Claire and Jim said their good-byes and walked to the Landrover. They walked well apart back to the Landrover and drove the mile and half back to Jim's house. Lucy, Jim's dog, gave them a lavish greeting but soon walked off into the shade. They both went into the tepid shower in their clothes, and let the water wash the salt out of them. Jim's hands shook, as he untied the knot of Claire's shirt and let it fall to the ground. Her bikini top was tied with a bow at the front. Jim delighted to let it fall and gaze, at her perky white breasts which stood out from her tanned chest. He tugged down her bikini bottoms to reveal a triangle of white containing her pubic hair. He moved his hand down to rub her. Claire stopped him with her hand and kissed him.

"Wait until I show you 69. Now let's have your shirt and swimmers off." She striped him and then, lovingly, put her arms around his neck and kissed him passionately, pushing her naked body against his. They let the water run over them. Then they each washed each other's hair. After all the shampoo was rinsed out they turned off the water, dried each other and walked into the bedroom.

Claire wrapped a dry towel around her long hair like a turban. "Now for 69" she whispered. Jim asked whether the turban had any significance.

"No, I don't think 69 is in Karma sutra" replied Claire. "I hope you like it. Remember, I stuck out my tongue. You lie on your back on the bed." Claire instructed. She then lifted one leg over Jim's body, so that she was facing the bottom of the bed. She knelt with her legs either side of him and with her head over his semi-erect penis, she leant forward on to her elbows and started, very slowly and deliberately, to lick him. Jim did not need to be told what to do. He started to lick her. Claire started to move her bottom in undulations. Jim gripped her waist with his hands and helped move her body backwards and forwards while he still pushed his tongue deep inside her. Claire was panting like a dog. With a final gasp she fell forward groaning.

"I am sorry, my darling, I could not make you come. God that was good." Jim had not finished stimulating her. Claire moaned "Oh yes, don't stop. Please don't stop. Yes. Yes. Yes." Jim could see the muscles of her tummy contracting violently and then she collapsed again burying her face into his crotch.

It was several minutes before she could roll off him. They were both dripping with sweat. Jim had not had an orgasm, so he still had a hard erection. Claire gently stroked him, as she started again to passionately kiss him. She rolled on top of him. She started to rock forward and back with her pelvis. Jim cried "Claire, Claire," as he ejaculated. Claire rolled her spent body off him and Jim cuddled her from behind very gently kissing her neck. He whispered

"Was that a punishment for tipping you into the sea?"

"No, that was a rather energetic way to say I love you. The punishment will have to wait." Jim kissed her neck again,

"I love you too Claire. I love to see your tummy muscles tighten as you have an orgasm. It is more enjoyable than me having an orgasm myself." Claire thought how lucky she was to have found this man. So many of her married friends had stories of slightly pissed husbands just going through the sexual act to their climax and then rolling off their wives and falling asleep. She turned to Jim and kissed him on the lips.

"Come on, you must be starving. I promised you some tea." Jim laughed,

"I have just eaten the best tea I could ever want!"

Chapter 21

Another trip to the Tana River

Monday 24th July 1967

Soon after his return from the trip to Addi, Jim received the following coded message from his control:

There is an indication that there is some seismic surveying occurring in an area, just south of the Tana River, east of Garsen, towards the sea. London would be interested in any information you can obtain. I am very aware that this area is difficult to travel in, so please take care.

Jim was not surprised by this instruction, as he had reported on the seismic surveying he had observed, when travelling with Claire to Addi. He was slightly surprised by the final phrase. London had sent him to rescue Somali One and had not really been too concerned about his safety. That was an extremely dangerous task. Now, although the area was very remote, it was not likely to be a very hazardous assignment.

In fact, he was delighted with the instruction, as it would fit in with his veterinary work. The PVO had tasked him to investigate a possible outbreak of Contagious Bovine Pleural Pneumonia (CBPP), in that area. Also, he had an on-going task to keep abreast with the incidence of trypanosomiasis in the whole of the coast province. There was no doubt in Jim's mind, that the numbers of tsetse flies were not diminishing and so, the disease risk was still very real.

He sent a memo to the PVO, to get his permission to fly over the area to estimate the numbers of cattle involved before he took a foot safari. He was fairly confident that it would be granted, as the PVO was always talking about the advantages of foot safaris and yet, it was the last thing he would actually want to do himself.

Before Jim had received an answer to the memo, Kimuta was on the phone. Would Jim take a call from Josiah Kibariti, the Livestock

Officer in charge of the Sabaki holding ground? The line was not good, but Jim gathered that Josiah had received 500 cattle, belonging to the Livestock Marketing Division (LMD), twenty five days ago from the Kurawa holding ground, which was further north up the Coast Stock route, and sixteen had died. Then the phone went dead and Kimuta could not raise Josiah again. Could this be CBPP? It would be disastrous, as Sabaki was only five miles north of Malindi and CBPP had never been recorded on the coast, so far south. Although it was past noon, Jim set off with Chaiko, in a Government Landrover, to investigate.

Chaiko was a good driver and kept up a steady pace, but the ferry at Kilifi was congested and the road north of Kilifi, which was 'murram', was being graded, so the journey seemed to take forever. Chaiko and Jim did get two packets of locally ground cashew nuts, from the children at the ferry and washed them down with a 'madafu' while they were waiting. They arrived at the Sabaki office, as the sun was setting, to be greeted by a very shamefaced Josiah. He reported, that the herdsmen had buried the carcass of the steer that had died today. Jim was not pleased, but he just suggested to Josiah that he got into the Landrover and they drive to the cattle. The cattle were already in their 'boma' (cattle enclosure) and the herdsmen were sitting around their fires cooking. As there was still some light Jim, asked Josiah to ask the headman to get his herdsmen to dig up the carcass. There was considerable resentment at this request but Jim was insistent. He knew just what the burial was going to reveal, but he needed to have some proof. Sure enough, there was no real carcass but a load of fresh bones. Jim asked where the skin was. He was shown the skin stretched out in the hides and skins store, drying as per government instructions. He asked Josiah, if the number of hides tallied with the number of deaths.

Josiah confirmed that there was a skin drying for every animal that had died. There was a palpable relaxation in the atmosphere. Jim turned to Josiah and said, in Swahili,

"Fine we will return to your office. The vultures here on the coast must be very big to eat so much meat so quickly. I hope the animal did not die of Anthrax, as any human who eats the meat will be dead in the morning. Vultures are immune to Anthrax so they will be fine. When the skin was flayed, did anyone notice anything unusual?"

"Oh yes, replied the head herdsman," now trying to be helpful, "There were lumps under the skin, in front of the fore-legs."

Jim asked, "What were the lungs like? Were they the colour of my face?"

"Oh yes," said the headman, "perhaps not so red." There was some laughter.

"Good," said Jim, "I will be back if another animal looks sick, or dies."

When they got back to the office, Jim explained the blood slides he wanted to be taken, from any new sick animal. He also explained how Josiah should take a sample, from the lumps which had been seen. These lumps Jim knew were, in fact, Lymph Nodes (LNs). The fact that they were noticeable, meant that they were swollen. This was a very strong indication that the cattle had died of East Coast Fever (ECF). This normally fatal disease was caused by a protozoal parasite, spread by the Brown Ear Tick. Josiah should have been dipping these cattle every week. Either they had not been dipped, or the dip was under-strength. Although it was now dark, Jim got a sample from the dip, for testing at the Veterinary Research Laboratory at Kabete. Jim had a look at the dipping book. The records showed that the cattle had been dipped at suitable intervals but there was no record of the dip being topped up with the concentrated solution. Jim obviously did not know whether there had been some theft of the concentrate, or that there was just general incompetence. It was good news that the lungs of the cattle had appeared normal. It meant that it was unlikely that they had died of CBPP.

It was really late by the time they got back to Mombasa. Jim told Chaiko he had done really well and that he should have the day off the next day, to make up for the overtime. Jim knew the PVO would not be pleased but Jim was not going to worry about that. After a cold meat supper Jim was soon in bed. He spent only a few seconds, daydreaming about Claire, and he was asleep. He awoke at his normal time and immediately turned on the Long Wave Radio (LWR). He knew that the LMD had their slot, before the coast stock route came on air, which was when Jim normally tuned in.

Jim quickly established contact with the Head of LMD. He immediately told him what he actually knew, but was careful not to elaborate on any conjectures, and certainly not to accuse anyone of incompetence or theft. Obviously the Head of LMD had a large amount of experience and, although he was not a vet, he had a handle on likely diseases. He immediately authorised Jim to purchase some *'Coopertox'* (Dipping fluid to kill ticks) on LMD's account and get the dip totally cleaned out and then replenished to the correct strength. He said, it would be useful to have a dip sample but did not want to delay awaiting the results. He also suggested that Jim implemented twice weekly dipping, to act as a belt and braces approach. He agreed with Jim that ECF was the most likely diagnosis and that, sadly, the deaths would continue for at least ten days. He then said he would move the cattle to Mackinnon Road as soon as the deaths stopped, as he wanted to auction them there. He hoped to sell them to ranchers, who could then take them by rail nearer to their ranches. He said they were only stores and not ready for KMC. When Jim told him of his worries concerning the possibility of CBPP south of the Tana, he said he would send the BTT down, at LMD's expense to help Jim. He asked Jim whether he needed any other help. Jim said he was hoping the PVO would authorise a flight over the area. The Head of LMD said, Jim could send him the bill if there was any problem, although he said it really should come out of the PVO's budget. He said he would send down a boat with the BTT, to make Jim's foot safari less arduous. As further help, he would send down ten donkeys he had at Burgoni, the holding ground near to Lamu, which appeared to be resistant to Trypanosomiasis, to help Jim make his foot safari into the wet areas of the Tana River.

Jim was really grateful. He had been worried about a bollocking from the PVO, for going to Sabaki without authorisation. Now, he knew he would have some backing from Nairobi. He ate a good breakfast and arrived early at the Veterinary Office. He immediately got Omari to go to Mombasa to buy the *'Coopertox'* and continue to Sabaki, so that the dipping could be carried out that afternoon. He asked Kimuta to telephone Josiah and get him cleaning out the dip. Jim got the dip sample packed up, to go on the evening train to Nairobi. He then set about doing post mortems on some laying hens, which had been brought in from Kwale district, on the slab around the back of the veterinary office. Apparently, quite large numbers were dying.

He heard a great commotion around the front of the building. Kitchopo came around, to warn him the PVO was on the war path. Apparently, his car would not start and he had rung up the office to send a car and a driver. He was not pleased that one was not instantly available, as Chaiko had been given the day off and Omani was on his way to Sabaki. Luckily, the LO from Kwale was still in the office, having brought in the chickens and had been loading the new staff uniforms for his district staff. Silas, the PVO's PA, immediately realised the problem and sent the LO to the PVO's house.

The PVO's temper had erupted when he got to the office. He stormed round to the post mortem slab and demanded why Jim was fiddling about with chickens when there were cattle dying of CBPP just north of Malindi. Jim looked him in the eye and said, if he would just authorise the flight he would be off in an instant, as he now had a diagnosis for the chicken deaths.

"I am not sure if it is justified financially." Spat the PVO. "You are always off gallivanting. I gather you were in the flesh pots of Malindi and were late home last night and had the nerve to take Chaiko and then give him today off."

Jim went very white with rage and just glowered at the PVO, who realised he had gone too far. Without taking his eyes off the PVO Jim washed his hands in the prepared bucket of disinfectant and said, in a normal voice,

"Newcastle Disease. I suggest you gazette the whole district, as I understand from the LO it is widespread. I will report my findings on my return or via the radio, through the Head of LMD." Without another word, Jim turned away, got in his Landrover and drove out of the office complex.

He went up to Port Reitz airfield. Luckily, 5Y KJH, the Tripacer was available at the aero club. He filed a flight plan and did his preflight checks. He was airborne in no time. Navigation was easy. He flew straight up the coast, across the bay South of the Tana River. The sea was all muddy for several miles out from the delta, due to all the erosion. He could see the large Kurawa Holding ground, which was nearer to the sea than he realised. He could make out the large number of LMD cattle held there. He knew there were 3500. The 500 animals which were dying at Sabaki were from that group. From the edge of the holding round, he started flying a grid, so that he could

287

count the number of cattle. They stood out well, as although the bush was quite thick, it was not high. He counted the cattle and also the number of villages. All the villages had tracks leading down to the Tana River, There was no road south of the river but there was a clear road north of the river, which ended at the coast at Kipini. Jim worked out that there were eighteen villages and a total of 2200 cattle. He was working out a plan as to where he would have the testing team camping North of the river, and how he would have to ferry the staff across with the LMD boat, when suddenly the engine of the plane faltered and cut out. He immediately flicked the fuel switch but nothing happened. The gauge showed empty. Surely he had not used up that much fuel. His heart was in his mouth, as he was looking for somewhere to land. Suddenly he realised what he had done. Because he was still so angry with the PVO, he had started the plane on the left hand tank. The plane only had one fuel gauge but that had been on the right tank. When the engine had, cut he had flicked the gauge on to the left tank, which was now empty. He straight away switched the tanks so that fuel was coming from the full right tank. There was a clonking noise and the engine fired into life. In fact, he had over 300 feet to spare, but Jim was bloody glad to have the engine running sweetly. He flipped the gauge switch, showing he had a full tank on the right side. He climbed away and headed for Malindi. His brain was alive and, while all the information was in his head, he marked the villages and cattle numbers roughly on his large scale map. He refuelled at Malindi and was very tempted to spend the night at Watamu, just to put the finger up to the PVO. However he thought that is probably what he would be accused of doing, so he quickly filed another flight plan and flew home. The sun was low in the sky but he had half an hour to spare, as he touched down safely at Mombasa.

Once again, he was up early to catch the Head of LMD on the radio. Obviously, he had to be careful what he said, as anyone could listen in to the radio. However, he reported that he had seen the 3500 head of LMD cattle at Kurawa and that there were 2200 villager's cattle in the area. The head of LMD said,

"Well done young man. You are quick off the mark. We like that approach in the service. Just send the bill for the plane to me. It is in the interest of the LMD to make sure all the cattle are free of CBPP. I have dispatched the testing unit. They will bring the boat I mentioned, down. It is a rubber zodiac with a 35 horsepower engine. The boat can be carried, inflated, on the top of a long wheel base Landrover. I will issue it to you, so you can keep it for your use. I will send an extra fuel tank, as you will be travelling some distance on the river. I have got the donkeys on the move." He broke off and said,

"Break, break, Abdi. How are they getting on?" Another voice came on the radio. "They spent last night at Witu, Sir. They will have left at first light and will reach Garsen before dark. They have full packs, as you instructed and I have doubled up the Turkana to six, as the lions are so bad in the area." The Head of LMD was back on,

"Well done, Abdi. Good thinking. I want you to give full assistance to Dr Scott."

"Jim, I know you will have to report to the PVO but I would be grateful if you could keep me in the picture, not only on the radio but I would also like to meet you. If you do get a chance to come to Nairobi, please let me know. LMD over and out."

Jim was delighted. He had been given a boat, which he could water ski behind, and all his plans were working out.

'Bugger the PVO.' Unbeknown to Jim, Claire was listening in. She had just been getting up and had taken off her pyjamas and danced round the room punching her fists in the air. She was thinking 'Jim has an excuse to come to Nairobi.' Yippee. She immediately got into her very tight jodhpurs. She thought, 'No Visible Panty Line (VPL) for me. Jim loves it when I don't wear knickers.' She felt really naughty, as she rubbed herself on the saddle as she trotted out in the cool of the morning. She thought, 'I had better gallop. Thinking of Jim and trotting will make me come, and without any knickers on, it might be obvious.' She was gasping after a long gallop up beside a long row of coffee bushes, but she did not have an orgasm. 'Bloody hell,' she thought, 'I can't wait for Jim to come to Nairobi.'

Jim arrived, ahead of time, at the veterinary office. He was greeted by Alex the microscopist, who looked crest-fallen. "Three more steers have died at Sabaki, Bwana. Omari brought the lymph node smears back, after he had delivered the 'Coopertox'. They are all positive for ECF."

"Do the blood smears show any Tryps?" Jim asked.

289

"No '*Bwana*', they were all clear and there were no Anaplasma or Babesia," Replied Alex.

"In some ways that is good, Alex, at least we know what we are dealing with and Omari got up there with the dip. Sadly, the deaths will continue for ten days but then they will stop. The BTT is on its way down here. We will get them to stop and test all the remaining animals at Sabaki. If they are clear, as soon as the deaths stop, we can walk them down to Mackinnon Road to the South of Tsavo Park. We will give them a shot of '*Berenil*' on arrival, as they are bound to pick up Tryps. Can you make sure we have plenty in stock?"

"*Ndio bwana* (Yes Sir)," replied Alex.

Jim was pretty busy, during the day, with routine local work. He noticed the PVO kept out of his way, locked in his air conditioned office, protected from visitors by Silas. Silas was very friendly, when they met at coffee time. He stressed to Jim that he must come and visit his home in Wundanyi. He said, it is as high as Nairobi and lovely and cool, just right after a foot safari near Kurawa. Silas, like the PVO, did not envy Jim working in the hot country. However, Jim loved the remoteness and the wild. He was not too worried about the lack of creature comforts. He did think he would take a crate of beer with him, as the blood testing unit had a generator and a fridge.

It was arranged that the unit would camp at the veterinary office that night.

Jim was due to play a game of rugby, against one of the Royal Navy ships which had arrived a couple of days ago, having been on station off Beira for four weeks, on the so called 'Beira' patrol. It was the British attempt to stop Oil getting to Rhodesia. It was successful, in that no oil came through Beira, but everyone knew that plenty was coming up from South Africa.

He planned to leave early in the morning, ahead of the blood testing unit and find a good camping spot for them at Garsen. Then, they would have to go over the river on the ferry, and find camping spots north of the Tana River. They would then move slowly down the road, at intervals, and Jim would help them bring their equipment across the river. Jim knew there were cattle crushes in the villages, as they had been used for the annual Rinderpest vaccination campaign.

Jim enjoyed a great game of rugby. The navy team were not at all fit, having been at sea and so, quite a strong Mombasa team made mincemeat of them. Jim ended up scoring three tries, as the Navy back row became seriously worn out, in the second half, by the heat. After they had showered and drunk two pints of lemonade and fresh lime juice to rehydrate themselves, the others started on the 'Tuskers' and 'White Caps'. Jim disappeared outside of the bar, to the pay phone in the club. He rang his pal, Mark, who worked for the Daily Nation and gave his report for the game. The reporter was a lazy chap and found it much easier to sit on his veranda, with his feet up, rather than watch the game. Naturally, Jim gave a glowing report of his performance. Jim also gave him a report on the disease at the Sabaki holding ground. He told him, obviously, not to mention Jim by name but that quick action by a Kenyan Government Veterinary Officer had prevented a major loss of Government Cattle. Jim thought his boss, the PVO, would probably take all the credit for the job but at least the Head of LMD knew it was Jim.

The veterinary article was read by Sir Richard at breakfast the following morning. He handed it over to Claire.

"I wonder if that is your friend who took you on 'safari'? From what you say, he is a very capable chap. I have met his boss, who seems like a pen pusher to me. I can't believe he would rush up, to post mortem cattle in such a remote area?"

"Certainly could be," said Claire, noncommittally. She knew it was Jim, as she had been listening in on the radio. She realised she would probably get his report later that day. She knew it would be dry and strictly factual, but she loved getting his reports. It somehow made him feel closer to her. After Sir Richard had gone to his office, she idly looked through the rest of the paper. She came across the rugby report. Mark had done Jim proud. *23 year old Jim Scott, a veterinary surgeon based in the Coast Province, helped crush a very unfit Royal Navy side, with three tries in the second half of the game. His superb fitness and his ability to move rapidly into any hole in the defence, secured all three tries.*

'Good for Jim,' thought Claire. 'No wonder he can make love for hours. He certainly finds all the holes in my defence. Why is Mombasa so bloody far away?'

Jim was careful not to drink too much beer after the game, as he knew he had to be up early in the morning. Chaiko arrived before dawn and Katana helped load all the safari stuff in to the long wheelbase Government Landrover. Jim left Katana at home, to look after the house but he took his dog Lucy. Lucy could not contain herself and bounced about, while they were loading up. Jim always took some dog medicines for Lucy, in case she got ill on safari. Jim had sent word, on the radio, to Michael Ngulu, the LO at Galole, to send word to Dubi to meet him at Garsen.

They made good time and were at the front of the queue for the ferry at Kilifi, just as the dawn was coming. However, the sun is so quick to rise in the tropics, that it was fully light before they bumped off the other side. Jim was day dreaming about Claire. He resolved, one day, to take her across the 'Singing ferry' at Mtwapa rather that the pontoon bridge, which obviously was much quicker. The ferry was free but there was a fee to cross the bridge, which was owned in part by the Gurneys, where Jim had made such a fool of himself when he had first arrived. Government vehicles had to have a pass, which was issued by their offices. Silas always issued them to Jim or any of the drivers.

They swept through Malindi, so much for flesh-pots thought Jim but, as they were so near, they called in at the Sabaki Holding Ground. Josiah seemed pleased to see Jim and reported that there had been no deaths the previous day. However, he gave Jim the slides from the previous days, to verify that the cause of death had been ECF. He confirmed that ALL the carcasses had been buried, under his supervision. Jim let the matter drop. He could see Josiah was relieved that he had not been disciplined. Jim thought, '*What the hell, the government actually had not lost anything but he was glad he had stepped in. It would have been easy for the herdsmen to just kill an animal to eat when it was sick, rather than treat it. Not all diseases were like ECF which, at that time, was thought to be invariably fatal. Jim knew that they got good recovery rates from animals infected with other tick-borne diseases like Anaplasmosis and Babesiosis.*' Dogs also got tick-borne diseases but they were caused by different organisms. Luckily, Lucy seemed to have immunity but he always took the '*dawa*' (medicine) with him just in case. Jim always made sure that Lucy was bathed weekly in Benzene Hexachloride to control the ticks. Dog owners had to be careful, as the cattle dip '*Coopertox*' was very toxic to dogs.

North of Sabaki, the road got really bad and so they stopped for a break at the Kurawa holding Ground which was only ten miles off the road, to the right, down towards the coast. Jim had never been so he was keen to meet Matua, who was the Veterinary Scout actually in charge of the holding ground. He was answerable to Josiah at Sabaki but, as they were so far apart, most of the control was by radio. Jim liked the sound of Matua, who seemed a very practical man, well liked by the junior staff. He said they had no deaths in the 3500 head of cattle on Kurawa. However the '*Fly*' problem was very bad and so they had to inject them every two weeks with '*Berenil*'. This was very labour intensive, as there were only two collecting places with cattle races. Jim said he would try to persuade LMD to build more. He was pleased that the cattle did not need to be dipped. Obviously the Sabaki mob had picked up ECF either on the way to Sabaki or actually at Sabaki. Matua said that they would be running out of grazing with such a large number. Jim said the first 500 would be moving off Sabaki soon and then Matua could send more cattle down, in mobs of 500. Matua also said that they were due for '*Berenil*' (An injection to prevent and treat trypanosomiasis) tomorrow. Jim decided to get the Blood Testing Team (BTT) to do them at the same time, to save the labour. Matua said they normally injected 1000 a day but they could half that number, so the BTT could keep up.

Without chatting any more, Chaiko and Jim went back to the road, so they could stop and divert the BTT. Jim was pretty certain they would be in time, as he had left before dawn and the BTT were not due to leave before 8.00am. They parked in a very obvious place, under a biggish tree beside the road. Chaiko was charged with not going to sleep and stopping the team, which consisted of two long wheel-based Landrovers each towing a two wheel trailer. Jim elected to take his shot gun, and a very excited Lucy, to see if he could shoot a guinea fowl for supper. He told Chaiko to keep blowing the horn intermittently when he had stopped the BTT and had directed them down to Kurawa. He took a panga so that he could mark the acacia trees as he went. So that he would not get lost, he also took a compass. It was no use trying to use the sun as a guide, as it was now high in the sky and blazing down on him.

The road ran due north and so Jim set off due west. The unrelenting sun burned down from the clear blue sky. He was glad of his bush hat. Lucy seemed oblivious of the heat and trotted beside him with eager anticipation. He kept marking the trees. He had covered about a mile, in what he thought was a due westerly direction, when he saw a flock of guinea fowl moving away from him. He guessed they had seen him, so he ran after them with the shot gun in his left hand and the '*panga*' in his right. He overhauled them so that he was only 30 feet from them when they took off. He stopped, dropped the '*panga*', brought up the shot gun and fired left and right. Two guinea fowl dropped. One was fluttering about on the ground, the other was up and started to run. Lucy was on it and soon brought it back to Jim. He rung both their necks, to make sure they were dead, then he ejected the two cartridges and started back to the road. Very sensibly, he carefully followed his foot marks which were plain to see as he had been running, and soon he came to the panga marks on the trees. Then he started going from tree to tree. It was rather slow but he was glad to see each mark, as he knew he was not lost. Then he heard a continuous horn blast and knew the BTT had at last arrived. The horn continued but seemed to grow fainter so Jim kept following his marked trees. Soon he could not hear the horn at all but imagined Chaiko did not want flatten the battery and so was sitting waiting for him. He arrived back at the road to find it empty. Where was Chaiko? He was sure he was at the right spot, as he could see the tyre tracks under the tree off the road. Lucy flopped down in the shade. Jim was cross with himself, as he had not thought to bring any water and he could see she was thirsty, as was he. He was undecided what to do. He was certain he had heard the horn but why had Chaiko not waited for him? Surely he could have directed the BTT down the clearly marked track across the road which led to Kurawa. He was tempted to set off to Kurawa, where he knew there would be water but he resisted the temptation. He was sure Chaiko would come back for him. So he joined Lucy in the shade and sat back leaning against the tree. The air was oppressively hot. He must have dropped off to sleep as he woke with a start, when he heard the sound of a vehicle approaching from the north. He stood up and soon he could see a Landrover approaching. It was Chaiko. The Landrover drew to a halt. Behind him was the BTT. Apparently the BTT had not stopped, when they saw Chaiko's Landrover. Why should they, it was just a standard grey government Landrover? Chaiko, who promised he was not asleep, had blown his horn and set off in hot pursuit. With the dust from the trailers, they had not seen him when he had caught up with them, and started flashing his lights and blowing his horn. Luckily, they had stopped for a break ten miles or so up the road. Then Chaiko had led them back to the meeting place. Anyhow, now they all greeted Jim and Chaiko gave Lucy some water. Jim was tempted to have a beer but thought it would go straight to his head, so he had some water instead. With Chaiko leading, they all set off for Kurawa.

They had a pleasant camp at Kurawa. The BTT had a very large tent which was meant as a laboratory, so they could work in the rain. It had mosquito netting at the large windows. Once they had set it up, they used it as a mess tent so all the veterinary staff could eat together. It made all the difference, as the mosquitoes were ferocious. It was a good fun evening. Jim found it interesting that no alcohol was drunk, probably because some of the staff were Moslems, but there was quite a happy party atmosphere. They were not late to bed and so it was easy for Jim and Chaiko to load up the rubber boat onto their Landrover, as soon as it was light in the morning. They left for Garsen, leaving the BTT to test and treat all the LMD cattle.

They made good to time to the Veterinary Office. Michael Ngulu, the LO from Galole was waiting for them. He had brought Dubi, who was delighted to be working with Jim again. Lucy also gave Dubi a greeting. The donkeys had arrived, with their extra herdsmen from Witu.

The whole blood testing campaign had to be organised like an army operation. Initially, Jim would go in south of the river with the donkeys, taking some materials to repair the crushes and to make some new ones. He would decide on sites for the crushes and get the villagers to start on their construction. Michael Ngulu and Chaiko would go north of the river along the Kipini Road and then turn down a track to the Tana River at Kau. They would set up a camp there. The BTT would work from there and Jim would use the boat, to ferry personnel and blood samples across the river.

The donkey safari went well. It was pretty rough, as Jim did not have his usually items of 'safari' equipment like he did in the

Landrover, but the ground was drying up and the mosquitoes were not too bad, except at dusk. He often ate his supper sitting under a mosquito net. The donkeys behaved extremely well and never made any attempt to escape. Jim was glad of the extra men to guard them at night, but he did not hear any lion.

Jim loved this type of organising and his enthusiasm was infectious. He had one problem. He was the only person who could drive the boat. He had two options; he could either walk back to Garsen, after he had got crush repairing under way or he could swim across the river at Kau. He decided to swim, so he told Dubi to go with Chaiko and look after Lucy until he joined them. Dubi was not happy but Jim was firm, as he thought Dubi might drown if he tried to swim.

When Jim reached the opposite side of the Tana River at a small village, the river looked ominously wide, very muddy with a relatively fast current. They arrived at mid morning, which Jim thought was ideal for his swim, as he was not at all tired. The main camp was well set up on the opposite bank. There was a lot of waving, but the river was so wide that it was difficult to hear anything shouted from the opposite bank. Jim put on his swimming trunks and then walked with one of the herdsmen, five hundred yards up river. He was relieved that there did not seem to be any evidence of crocodiles or hippos on this stretch. He was in two minds as to whether he should wear his gym shoes. They would be a big help walking through the shallows but they would certainly make swimming harder. He remembered the night with slim Jane, swimming across Tudor Creek.

There was no point in any delay. He gave his gym shoes to the herdsman to look after and slithered down the bank into three foot of water, and very sticky mud. There were no stones or rocks. He was glad he had not worn his gym shoes as they would have been sucked off in the mud. He clabbered away from the bank until he was in four foot of water. He slipped totally into the water and started swimming. There was very little current. He did not fight it but swam a steady breast stroke towards the opposite shore which, now that he was low in the water, seemed a very long way off. He kept going steadily, but he soon realised that the current was getting stronger, until he was suddenly flying down the river. He knew he had not reached

296

anywhere near the middle. He nearly panicked, and tried to swim upstream, but he calmed himself and just kept swimming towards the opposite bank, letting the current race him along. He was beginning to tire but he doggedly kept going. He thought. '*I bet slim hipped Jane would be over by now. I wonder if she will get a swimming blue.*' Then almost by magic he was out of the main current and, although he was drifting, he was making good progress towards the bank. He kept swimming until he was only in two feet of water. It was difficult but, with the help of the vegetation, he clambered out. He expected to find people, at least Dubi and Lucy, but there was no one and the bush was thick. Actually he was not as exhausted from the swimming as he thought he would be. It was fortunate as it was hard work getting through the bush. Eventually, he came to a track and he started walking up stream. It was then that he wished he had some shoes. He had been taken much further down river than he had imagined. He was blissfully unaware of the panic, which was occurring with all the staff further up river, who thought he had been taken by a crocodile. It was a long walk, the current had been much stronger than Jim realised. What a greeting he received back at the camp. They all thought he was dead. All Jim was thinking about was having a cup of tea and finding some shoes.

However, soon he started to ferry equipment across the river. As he was doing that he started teaching Michael Ngulu how to drive the boat. Each time they stopped on the northern side he taught Chaiko and Kibeer, the driver from Galole, how to look after the 35 horse power out-board motor.

Jim stopped all work at 5.00 pm, as he thought they had all worked hard enough. He left all the staff relaxing in the camp and drove with Lucy down to Kipini, to report in to the DO, who was a tall man from western Kenya called Claude Mzungu. He was a kind man and offered Jim a cup of tea. He seemed to love dogs and so the two of them had a pleasant walk along the beach, with Lucy, to see the Arab ruins at Ungwana and Shaka. Claude was appalled when he heard Jim had swum across the Tana.

Jim was rather reticent but, eventually, he asked Claude how he had got his name. Apparently his father had worked as a cook for a professional hunter. The hunter had a French client called Claude, and so he had been named after this man. His father had been called

Mzungu which meant European in Swahili on account of his pale skin. Claude, in fact, was very dark.

Even with the large number of hungry mosquitoes, the base camp at Kau was a happy place. The next morning, it was full steam ahead to get as many cattle tested as possible. Jim was very relieved that there were no positives in the first whole village they had tested. The next day, Jim was on the radio to LMD and the PVO to report the good progress. Even the PVO was pleased. Martin Riley, the head of the LMD, asked the PVO if Jim could attend a top level meeting at the Ministry of Agriculture in Nairobi. The PVO could hardly refuse, as Martin said LMD would pick up all the expenses. Now that Jim had got everything going, it would be easy for Michael Ngulu and Wenceslas, the LO in charge of the CBPP BTT, to carry on and complete the task. It was decided that Jim and Chaiko would leave at dawn the next day and, hopefully, reach Mombasa by dark. Dubi had been put on the LMD pay roll as a herdsman. He would remain with the donkeys. When the job was over they would go to Kurawa and remain there until Jim organised their next assignment. The rubber boat and engine would also be stored at Kurawa, until it was required again.

Chapter 22

A flying visit to Nairobi

Sunday 30th July 1967

Jim was glad to get home for a night, after being on quite a rough safari. He made some telephone calls, to make sure it was OK for him to hire a Cherokee Arrow first thing in the morning. The Arrow was pretty fast, with its retractable under carriage. He just managed to make the meeting scheduled for 10.00 am, at the Ministry of Agriculture. Martin Riley greeted him warmly and introduced him to the others. There was George Ball, Head of The Water Development Department, a silver-haired, rather frail looking man who was a senior water engineer, called Ian Mather and David Matata, the Permanent Secretary. Martin chaired the meeting and opened by saying,

"You might be surprised that I have invited a vet to this meeting which is about water supplies in Tana River District. However Jim is only just back from the area. I lent him a boat from my division's stores, but he decided not to use it and swam across the Tana River instead, so I think he should be a welcome member of our team. They all laughed and Jim looked embarrassed. Martin then looked to David and said. "I know, Permanent Secretary that you want to push further water development in this area, to help the people and their stock move away from the dependency of the Tana River. I have two goals; the first is to move cattle down from the Eastern NFD to the rail head at Mackinnon Road, avoiding the disease ridden coastal stock route, and the second is to buy cattle from the Orma people in the area. If we can come to an agreement and put together a package, I am sure we can get funding from overseas under an aid programme."

Soon agreement was reached and then there was a discussion on how this project would get off the ground. It was decided that Jim would make a safari, due west from Galole, to the very small village of Mutiboko which was on the sand lugger called the Thua. Then he would journey due south, aiming at a hill called Dakawachu. All the way at regular intervals he would make large letters with white paint, after clearing the bush, so that these could be seen from the air. Then Ian Mather and George Ball would fly over the area and decide where water points for a stock route could be sited. Then the department would prepare to do the work, after preparing an estimate of the likely cost. Martin Riley with David Matata would then try to get foreign aid. Jim told the meeting of the airstrip on the Voi River, which would be very useful to monitor the route south of the Galana River, down to MacKinnon Road. He remembered his night with Jane there. It seemed years ago.

The meeting broke up at lunch time and they all went for a Danish Smorgasbord at the New Stanley Hotel, which was virtually next door to the Ministry.

After lunch, Jim went in a taxi to check in to his hotel which he had booked. He just prayed that Claire had deduced where he was staying. He did not dare to ring the Residence. Then Jim used the same taxi to take him to Veterinary Laboratories at Kabete. He had some tasks to do for the PVO and then he went to Colin Cameron's office. Colin was delighted to see him and took him to his home, for tea with Freda.

Jim and Susie's correspondence had become very lax and so it was good to hear how she was getting on. She seemed to be really enjoying the UK. Colin and Freda ate early and so it was not much after eight when Colin drove Jim to his hotel. Jim had refused any alcohol as he was flying in the morning.

Claire was delighted when she heard Jim's summons to Nairobi. She smiled when Jim went over the times and dates twice with Martin Riley. She was sure he was doing it for her benefit. Contacting him at such short notice was going to be very difficult. If only he had said something about accommodation. *'What a silly bugger,'* she thought. *'I want to spend a night with him, not just meet for half an hour at the aero club. Surely he won't camp. They will pay for his hotel.'* She put on a pretty dress and went down to breakfast. She idly chatted to Sir Richard. He was going to be away, showing a senior UK politician various aid projects in the Rift Valley, which made her life a little easier. She had little organised which could not be wriggled out of.

They had talked, in the past about Jim staying in a small hotel in Muthaiga near to the High Commissioner's Residence. She wondered if he would remember. There was only one way to find out without using the embassy telephone. She would walk to the hotel and make enquires. She often went out riding and walking, and so it was no big deal for her just to tell Eli she was going for a walk.

There was no one in reception at the hotel so she rang the bell on the desk. A silver-haired African arrived and gave her a broad smile. Claire asked him casually if there was a party of vets coming to stay in two days' time for a meeting at Kabete. He said he did not think so, but he would make sure by looking in the book. He produced a big ledger. He peered at it. It was obvious to Claire that reading close to, was difficult for him. She was sure, if there was a lion in the grass a hundred yards away, he would spot it in an instant.

She asked helpfully. "Can I look for you?"

"That is kind '*Memsahib*' my eyes are not so good these days."

Claire had struck lucky. Jim had been booked in for a single night in two night's time. He was booked into room five. He was not such a silly bugger after all.

Claire thanked the old man and said she was sorry to bother him. She felt like singing on the walk home.

Claire could not wait, on the night in question, for the time to pass. She ate alone early, which was not unusual when Sir Richard was away. She then told Eli she was having an early night and went to her room. She changed into sensible trousers and a khaki shirt and crept out of the side door, without anyone seeing her. She locked the door behind her and pocketed the key. She easily got past the '*askari*', who did a regular small circuit around the drive. When she was out of the grounds she became slightly scared, as the night was dark and she felt very alone. She wished she had brought a heavy torch. Then she saw a car's headlights in the distance. She dived into the hedge. It was bound to be someone she knew who would want to give her a lift. A story about not being able to sleep and wanting a night walk would sound very strange. It was only just past eight 'o'clock! She should not want to sleep anyhow. She wanted to make love to Jim. She brushed herself down and continued to the hotel.

Once again, getting past the *'askari'* was a doddle. She had decided that the best way to room five, was just walk boldly in and ask for the key. As it turned out she did not need to. There was no-one in reception. She reached over and grabbed the key. She walked to the room and unlocked the door. Jim had obviously been and changed. Thank goodness he had handed his key in when he left. So she walked back to the reception and hung up the key. Back in the room she was suddenly nervous. What if Jim came back with another girl, someone like Annie or, even worse Cynthia from the High Commission? She thought, *'don't be so bloody silly you know he loves you.'*

Claire remembered a James Bond story, where Bond waited behind the door playing patience for the villain in his hotel room having put pillows down the bed. The villain had fired his silenced gun six times into the pillows. James Bond had said. "Good evening." The villain had whirled around and aimed his gun. Bond had calmly said. "That's a Smith and Wesson and you have had your six." He had then shot the villain with one shot. Claire decided she would surprise Jim, in a similar way. What would make him whirl around? A lascivious smile came on her face. She took off her trousers and her knickers. She put her trousers back on. She had chosen a pair of sexy French lace knickers, when she had dressed earlier. She stuffed pillows down the bed to look like a body and laid the knickers on top of the blue quilt. Jim would have to be very drunk not to see them. She picked up a book, which was obviously Jim's, on the bedside locker, 'Teach Yourself Swahili'. Well, she would spend the time usefully. She pulled an upright, but not uncomfortable, chair behind the door and began to read.

She could not concentrate. She kept imagining all the disasters which could happen. Jim would try to find her at the High Commissioner's residence. He would be drunk and demand that she was woken up. She knew Jim would, firstly not be so stupid and secondly, she had never really seen him drunk. He had been a bit pickled but then he was always very benign. In fact, Claire knew that Eli would do anything for Jim, as would the High Commission *'askaris'*. His popularity made him such a successful agent. 'Somali One' had written such a glowing report about Jim, that Claire was surprised he had not received a knighthood!

Then she heard the unmistakable sound of someone trying to unlock the door, which was already open. The door slowly opened. Jim, who was stone cold sober, was apprehensive, as he was sure he had locked it and had not left the light on. Claire suddenly forgot what Bond had said. She said. "And whose knickers are those on your bed?" Jim did whirl round. He hugged her so hard, she could not breathe.

"If I had been carrying a Smith and Wesson, you gave me such a fright I think I might well have shot you. I can't remember how many girls Bond seduces in that book. I am bloody sure I am going to seduce you. First of all, I want to know how you got here. I somehow thought you would scheme something up. I had, in my mind, to somehow ring the High Commissioner's Residence and have a word with you. I was going to leave it until I thought dinner would be over."

"I got all your information when you were talking to Martin Riley. You sounded a complete pillock when you repeated everything but I knew it was for me. Now, I want you to lock the door and I will race you into bed." Claire won by several lengths but Jim showed a strong finish, by holding on to her and kissing her, as if he had not seen her for a year. She just could not stop him from kissing her. At last, as he was kissing her breasts yet again, she cried,

"Jim, you must stop. I am exhausted. I love you. We have got all night."

It was as if he was a frightened horse and he suddenly found he was galloping away from the rest of the herd. He instantly stopped.

"It was just so wonderful to see you, feel you and kiss you. I will be gentle now."

"You are a wonderful boy. I love you for your eagerness. I remember the first time in Nairobi Game Park. You had my skirt over my head in a second and heavens knows what would have happened if I hadn't guided you into me."

"I remember, I think I came with my second thrust. Not the way to woo a girl."

"Well it worked for me but what really clinched it was when you asked to see me naked." She sat up.

"Am I still worth looking at?"

"All I can say is, if I could not have seen you tonight, I would have waited all night outside the residence just for a glimpse of you."

She kissed him slowly. "I doubt that is true, but it was a lovely thing to say. Now tell me what you have been up to and also, I am very cross with you for swimming across the Tana River. If you ever do something as stupid as that again, I will just keep my thighs tightly together and keep you out."

"Will you now?" Jim kissed her, where he knew she loved to be kissed on her throat, just inside her collar bone. He moved his hand down her body. Claire could not be cross or stop herself. She opened her legs and whispered in his ear,

"Christ I want you. I have missed you so much. After I heard you might be coming to Nairobi, I went riding and caught myself rubbing on the saddle. Come on, you eager beaver."

Jim was a different man from when he had first met her. In fact, he was a different man from ten minutes earlier. He slowly brought her to a climax and, only when she insisted on riding him, did he let himself go and have an orgasm. She hardly let him gather himself before she was on her knees wanting him to mount her, like their first time. Only then did she cuddle him into her arms and then both slept. Jim woke in the night to hear a glass being filled. The light was still on. Claire came back into the room carrying a glass of water. She saw he was awake.

"I was thirsty. You must be as well. You must have this and I will bring you a second glass. As she came in again he said. "The sight of you naked is worth running three hundred miles for. All I did was fly here."

"I know you did not stop for a drink, as you were back here cold sober. I thought I was going to have to wait much longer. I even had visions of you bringing back another girl."

"Well, you silly girl, that is much worse than me swimming the Tana." They then had a mock fight and made love again.

Jim woke in the morning to find Claire crying quietly. He drew her to him and stroked her hair. "I am being a stupid woman. My hormones are in a muddle and I know I should be all sexy, as we have so little time together. If we were a normal couple, I expect I would be a bit grouchy, send you off to work and be better when you came home for your supper. As it is, I don't know when I will next see you. You might do something damn silly, and I might never see you again." More tears flowed. Jim did not know what to say and, wisely, said nothing but continued to stroke her hair.

"If only we could do things together. It is very exciting creeping about in the dark and, I am sure, it makes our love making more satisfying but I long just to be able to go down to a pub together. The only time we can be really ourselves is when we are out in the bush. I do so love those times." Then she pulled herself together.

"Part of my problem is that you are so bloody far away. I feel as if I have to compete unfairly with all those girls, wearing very little, at the coast."

"You must not worry," said Jim. "Most of the time they are so flimsy, I just tear them off."

"You bugger. I bet you bloody do." With that she made love to him. She teased him. She would not let him enter her. Then she ground herself onto him and would not let him move in and out. At last, she let them move together in harmony and they both had orgasms. After they had calmed down, she said,

"That was very loving and memorable. Perhaps I should be hormonal more often." They cuddled together. They had a hot shower and then turned it to cold and clutched their bodies as close as they could, to beat the cold. Claire had no makeup on but Jim thought she looked all the more lovely, and said so.

"You are lovely too Jim. Where are my knickers? They were on the bed when you came in."

"They are in my pocket, as a keep sake, and to remind me not to do anything damn silly." They both laughed.

"Katana will think you are a complete sexual pervert. Now I must try and get out of the hotel without being seen. These damn bars on the windows from Mau Mau days are a pain."

"I noticed there are some French Doors at the end of the passage. You could go out of them and pretend you were going for a walk in the garden. Perhaps you should put your trousers on first?"

"I have a good mind to walk out without them on. You would not forget that in a hurry."

Jim took her in his arms. "Claire, there is no way I am ever going to forget you. You are always in my mind. I have a hell of a job doing any paperwork or even to read a book." He reached his hand down and rubbed her bush.

"Yes, I like that. Can you rub just a little lower?" She kissed him. She thought, *'There is not much wrong with my hormones. That is bloody lovely.'*

Somehow Claire, with wobbly legs managed to get out into the garden unseen. Getting back to the Residence was easy. No-one had really missed her. She could not feel deflated, that she was of no importance and therefore had not been missed. She was strangely elated and started to plan their next meeting.

Jim had a massive breakfast at the hotel and got a taxi to Wilson airport. The flight was uneventful and he was back in the office for the afternoon. He had to start planning for the tasks he had been set by Martin Riley. How could he get a meeting with Claire, all tied into that. He also reported to Colin Shaw for transmission to London, that there was no evidence of any oil exploration in the Tana River Delta.

Chapter 23

Muthaiga Ball

Wednesday 9th August 1967

Jim had started seriously early that morning. He had driven 100 miles up the Mombasa Road to Voi, then turned left up a steep 80 mile *'murram'* road up into the Taita Hills, to attend Wundanyi Agricultural show. The PVO had been commanded to send a representative as the President, Jomo Kenyatta, was opening the show. As there was no way the PVO was going to attend, he sent Jim. Jim wanted to get up there early as he wanted to check out the District Veterinary Office, not only before the show but also before the President's motorcade drove its ponderous way up into the Taita Hills. Maybe the President would be so browned off that he would order a tarmac road to be made, which would make everyone's life easier. It had been a long day and Jim was pleased to get back to the Mombasa Veterinary Office before the office closed at 4.00 pm. He was doubly pleased, as he saw he had a letter written by Claire. It was in an official envelope from the High Commission. He was dying to know what it contained. He was damned if he was going to let anyone look over his shoulder, so he quickly put it into a pocket in his safari jacket. He collected all the gear he needed for the next morning and got in to his Landrover to go home. He would have time for a quick cup of tea before going to play rugby. It was a mid-week game against a Navy side off, one of the visiting frigates. The drive from the office seemed to take forever with Claire's letter burning a hole in his pocket.

"*Jambo* Katana, *Habari*" (Hello Katana, how are you)? "*Jambo Bwana, Habari* (Hello Master, how are you)?" "*Muzuri sana. Tutakula chai haraka tafadhali. Nakwenda na fanya mpira usiku.* (I am fine. I will eat tea quickly, as I am playing football this evening)." He slumped in the chair and tore open the envelope.

There was an official invitation requesting his presence, to accompany Sir Richard and Lady Rochester to the Muthaiga Club Annual Ball. Tucked inside, was a hand-written note from Claire.

My darling I know how you hate these formal occasions but I have to go and it will be a chance to see you. You never know, we might find a chance to be alone together. I have invited one of the High Commission girls to complete the table. I will be madly jealous every time you even talk to her but that is my problem. I am sure you will be your usual friendly, cheerful self. Just to encourage you, I haven't decided on a dress yet but one thing is for certain, I won't be wearing any knickers! The fashion these days is to have a slit up the side of long dresses. Perhaps that will encourage you to come up to Nairobi, as the slit will make it easier for you to check for the lack of knickers! I can't wait to see you. Take care. Lots and lots of love, Claire.

He was totally flushed after he had finished reading the letter and Katana brought the tea. He thought he would be bloody rubbish playing rugby. He was wrong. Somehow, the thought of seeing Claire gave his legs wings. Jim even scored two tries.

"What got under your tail today?" asked Big Mick after the game, as they downed pints of lemonade and fresh lime.

"I just had a bloody long day driving and working up at Wundanyi. I decided to take my frustration out on the Navy." Jim replied.

"You should drive to Nairobi for away games. It might make you play better!"

"I always feel bloody dead when I play at altitude. Regardless as to how I get up there." Jim lied, knowing that it was normally because he had spent the night with Claire that he had no energy, when he played up in Nairobi.

It was very lucky that he had been picked for a Coast Team i.e. players from Mombasa, Dar es Salaam and Tanga in Nairobi, on the Saturday of the Muthaiga Ball. The rest of the team was going to drive up on Friday but Jim had to work on the Friday and some of Saturday morning. He decided to fly up. The Mombasa Aero Club only had an old Tripacer available but still, this would be quicker and easier than driving up in his Landrover. He would have to skive off work at 10 am but, with a bit of luck, that would be OK. The

Tripacer was very old fashioned with canvas high wings, but at least it was cheap. He would need a bit of cash for the ball, so he decided to camp under wings at the Nairobi Aero club. He thought there was no chance of Claire staying with him after the ball, so there was no point in wasting money on a hotel. He could easily change into his Dinner jacket at the Impala Rugby Club.

The game went well but, as usual, they were beaten by the fitter upcountry side. However, the lads were happy after the game and he got a lot of ribbing for going to the ball. As might have been expected, he was slightly late as he had to get a taxi. Luckily, he arrived before the guests had been called for dinner. Claire came straight up to him with a radiant smile.

"Well done, getting here. How did the rugby go?"

"We lost, but only by a couple of tries which is not bad at altitude, but I am so sorry I am late."

"So, you are a rugger bugger are you?" said Sir Richard, rather condescendingly. Before he could say anymore Claire said, "Let's go through to our table. Jim, I will introduce you to everyone when we sit down, but you sit next to me, as you don't know anyone else. Cynthia you sit on Jim's other side so you can help me look after him. I notice you have made a brave effort with your bow tie. I remember having great fun helping you tie it at the reception at the Commission." It was the first time Claire had met Jim and she had admitted later, that she had purposely come behind him to tie the tie and had pressed herself unnecessarily hard against him.

He remembered the feel of her and he began to go red thinking about. To hide his embarrassment he said, "I always have difficulty tying the damn things."

Cynthia said, "How silly." Claire winked at him behind Cynthia's back.

He just wondered then if Claire had been true to her letter and not worn any knickers. She certainly had on a great, figure hugging dress with a slit up one side. He could not think how he was going to keep his hands away from her. He was going to have to be very careful with Sir Richard. He noticed, that somehow, he was sitting next to Claire on the side of the slit and Sir Richard was on the other side. When they got to the table, Claire did all the introductions. They actually all seemed to be a nice crowd. He thought they were mainly in their late thirties or early forties. Cynthia was obviously his age and was quite new to both the country and the diplomatic service. He thought he must make a bit of an effort, so he started chatting as they sat down, although he had held Claire's chair for her, before he had held Cynthia's. He was determined not to let the side down. It was not long before he felt Claire's hand on the inside of his thigh. He carefully gave it a slight squeeze. She then put Jim's hand on her bare thigh. Jim loved stroking it and was reluctant to start eating. Throughout the meal, Claire was a little monkey. She would be chatting away then, at the same time, would be stroking his leg with her foot, rubbing his thigh with hers or even gently rubbing his crotch. It was lucky Cynthia was rather starchy and kept her hands on the table. The conversation went very easily during the meal. Everyone seemed interested in Jim's job and also about the flying. There was a lot of laughter about Jim sleeping under the wing of the plane, in a tent, that night. Claire was slightly concerned that he would be safe and wanted to know where, exactly, he had put the plane. As soon as the dancing started, Jim asked Claire to dance as he thought that was the correct think to do. Also, he just could not bear not to hold her at least once. Both of them knew they were on parade and therefore had to behave so they danced well apart. Jim couldn't resist leaning forward and saying.

"You look stunning. Have you got any knickers on?" She laughed, as if Jim had made a funny joke and whispered, "I am sure you will get a chance to find out."

As well as the dancing, there was also a roulette game in one corner. Jim had done a bit of dancing with Cynthia and several of the other ladies. He noticed Claire by the roulette table, leaning over Sir Richard who was seated and enjoying his gambling. There was quite a crowd around the table. He went over and managed to get in the throng directly behind Claire and slightly to her right, where the slit was in her dress. By masking her with his body, he managed to get his hand on to her thigh and gently stroke it. She tensed but did not actually move. He moved his hand slowly around her thigh. He knew she thought it was him, as she moved her legs slightly apart. Then he slowly moved his hand upwards. She did not have any knickers on. She opened her legs a little wider. He gently rubbed her. She pushed her bottom back into his thighs. Jim kept rubbing until he felt his fingers becoming damp and Claire's thighs tightening on his hand. He removed his hand. He could see Claire's back colouring, as she straightened up and turned towards him.

"Hello Jim. Have you been lucky tonight?" asked Claire with a grin.

"Oh yes," said Jim. "I enjoy a gamble."

"I imagine you are happy to take some risks in life," replied Claire.

"Certainly, but luckily I know when to stop. Can I get you a drink?" asked Jim.

"I would love one but let's have a dance first," said Claire, leading him on to the dance floor. The music was quite loud so Claire did not worry that they would be overheard, even though they were dancing very formally, a little apart. In a very matter of fact voice, as if she was discussing the weather, Claire said, "I am glad that was your hand. I would have caused a real scene if I had turned around, to find it was some dirty old upcountry settler! Now you have really turned me on. Bloody hell I want you, you sexy bastard but I can't have you, so let's get that drink?"

As it was nearly time for the bar to close, they both pushed together into the crush at the bar. Normally, Claire would have stayed back and let the man get the drinks but she wanted to push against Jim. Obviously, she had to be very careful but she kept whispering in his ear and rubbing her breasts against him. Jim had to lean forward to hear her.

She whispered, "I hope you have a good view down my cleavage."

Jim whispered back, "Sadly, I can't see one of those lovely pink nipples I long to suck." Claire raised her arm as if to attract the barman and mouthed, "Is that any better?" Jim got a little peak.

He whispered, "Hell, my cock aches. You get me so bloody excited, you sexy minx." Claire moved her hand quickly across his flies and said, in a matter of fact way.

"Just checking you weren't fibbing." Then, laughing, she said, "Now you are in trouble when we get out of the crowd!" At that moment, Jim had the attention of the barman and he put in his order. Luckily, the barman took his time and Jim had calmed down, before he had to turn from the bar and be greeted by a grinning Claire. They managed to take their drinks outside of the marquee and talk quietly.

They were so busy chatting that they did not notice that the last waltz had finished and the music had stopped. They heard Cynthia calling, "Claire, the Commission taxi is ready."

"Damn," said Claire, "I won't even get a chance to kiss you goodbye. Don't come, I might cry" She changed her voice,

"Coming Cynthia." She squeezed his hand and she was gone.

Jim stayed outside for a few minutes, looking at the magnificent African night sky. He had a tear in his eye but he got a grip on himself and walked back into the marquee. There were some young folk he vaguely knew at the bar, who asked him if he wanted a last drink. Jim declined, as he said he was flying first thing in the morning. Two couples said they were going to Langata and offered him a lift. Jim said that would be great. It was not a large car and so one of the girls, who was quite pretty, was pushed up against him. Jim was very frustrated, as her thigh kept pressing up against his. She let her hand drop idly onto his leg. Jim gritted his teeth and thought, '*I miss Claire already and I have only been away from her for half an hour.*' The girl asked Jim where he was sleeping. He said,

"In a small tent under the plane's wing."

"Oh that sounds exciting and romantic. Can I join you?" Before Jim could reply her boyfriend, who was driving said, "No you bloody well can't."

The girl gave a small shrug but said nothing. As Jim was getting out she said.

"Take care, Nairobi Park is really near and there are masses of lions." She leant forward and kissed him on the cheek. The wheels spun as the car pulled away. Oh dear, Jim thought, '*someone is not pleased.*' However, the incident had cheered him up and he walked quite briskly to the plane. The place was totally deserted, except for the '*askari*' (guard) on the gate. Jim greeted him, "*Jambo Mohamid, Habari.*" (Hello Mohamid, how are you)?

"*Muzuri Bwana Jim,*" (I am well, Master Jim), was his relaxed reply. Jim walked to the tent and the plane. The plane had a lock, so he left all his cloths inside and locked it. He crept into the tent and crawled into his sleeping bag. He rolled his '*kikoi*' (Kenyan cotton sarong) up as a pillow and was soon asleep.

Jim awoke without moving. He was sure he felt that girl's hand caressing his thigh through the thin sleeping bag. He pretended he was still asleep and rolled with a quiet grunt on to his back. He must have been dreaming. Next thing, he would think he was being attacked by lions. Then he felt the hand fondling his penis. As quick as a flash, he grabbed the hand. The hand did not pull back. A very quiet voice whispered,

"It is your little minx. I thought you said this little chap ached. I have come to make him feel better."

"Claire you are an angel. How did you get here?"

"I waited until the house was quiet, left a note that I was going for an early morning walk to clear my head, (actually it is not yet 2 'o'clock) and crept out of the house past the sleeping *'askari'*. I will have to be home in time for a late breakfast. I ran down the road and hailed a taxi, which was on its way back to the Muthaiga Club to pick up late night revellers. I was going to really surprise you, by crawling naked into your sleeping bag, but it is so small and you are sleeping over the zip."

"We can soon sort that out," replied Jim.

As Claire was taking off her trainers she asked,

"Were you dreaming about me? You were mumbling and had a hell of an erection."

Jim teased and said, "No, some other girl. I can't remember her name."

Claire grabbed his cock and his balls.

"I will give him an ache. Who was it?" Claire demanded. Jim told her the story of the car and the irate boyfriend. Claire relaxed her grip.

"I will forgive you this once." Before she could protest, Jim had rolled her on to her back and was kissing her. Before she realised it, Jim had undone the button of her shorts and had his hand down the front of her knickers. He rubbed between the lips of her pussy and she immediately opened her legs wide, to make it easier for him.

As Jim kissed her neck, she whispered,

"That is lovely, I can't believe I had an orgasm at the roulette table surrounded, by all those people. You are a very naughty boy, but don't stop now." Jim protested that she had led him on, by not wearing any knickers. Rather breathlessly she said, "I have got some on now, but somehow you seem to have got inside them." Her breathlessness only encouraged Jim more. He was still kissing her neck and he pushed two fingers inside her. She arched her pelvis in time with his thrusts.

"Please don't stop, that is wonderful, please more, and yes, please more" and then she buried her mouth in his neck to stop herself crying out. Then Jim slowly kissed her lips again, as her heart rate slowly came back to normal.

Jim turned on his small torch. He shone it on Claire. She giggled, "I must look a right mess."

"Maybe, but you look bloody sexy with your knickers half down so I can see your pubes. You were a seriously naughty girl, showing me one of your nipples last night. I can feel my prick aching again."

"I am going to make him ache even more," said Claire. On her knees, with Jim pointing the torch at her, she slowly and very sexily undid the buttons of her shirt. Then, pushing forward her breasts, which were only partly covered by a lacy bra, she let the shirt drop from her shoulders. Jim was mesmerized, as she put her hands on her bra and fondled her own breasts. Then she slipped each of the straps lasciviously off her shoulders. She reached up behind her, not taking her eyes off him and unclipped her bra and let it fall to her thighs. Then, kneeling forward, she wriggled her shorts half way down her thighs. Slowly, she did the same with her knickers. She leant forward and kissed him and then whispered,

"You will have to help now." She rolled onto her back and Jim very slowly, pulled off her shorts and pants as she held her bottom off the ground sheet. Jim was still partly in the sleeping bag, so he unzipped the whole thing so that they could wrap it around them, as she lay on top of him with her thighs outside of his. Claire felt his rock hard prick pushing against her tummy. She whispered,

"Is he still aching?"

"Bloody hell, yes, I think he is going to burst," moaned Jim.

"Just hold on for me a little longer. If I rub him on my pubis, he stimulates my pussy." She slowly undulated her pelvis up and down. She said, "Wow, that's good." Jim was gritting his teeth trying to hold his orgasm. He could not reply. To take his mind off his prick, he grasped Claire's bottom and helped her move up and down. Claire groaned,

"Fuck, that's good. I am coming." Jim just came with one thrust on to her tummy. Claire felt the hot semen on her tummy and up between her breasts. She felt him shudder as he finished his climax. She was wonderfully wet. They kissed several times, very slowly, having to break their lips apart to breath. They slept.

After a couple of hours Claire awoke and, kissing Jim whispered to him with a giggle, "I think your semen has stuck us together. I have cold bottom can you let me roll on my back on the sleeping bag, and then

314

you can roll on top of me and bring the side of the bag over the top of us."

"What a lovely invitation." Somehow, as they were sorting themselves out, Claire let her legs flop open and Jim found he was lying between her legs.

"Does that invitation mean some real warming up measures?"

"I think it does," replied Claire. "Maybe my pussy aches, as it has not actually had a hard prick in it for several weeks." She reached down and felt Jim's flaccid penis.

"Oh dear, I suppose at least it means you weren't dreaming of the girl in the back of the taxi. Was she pretty? Did she rub her thigh up and down yours, like this? Did she happen to let her hand drop into your crotch and rub you gently, like this?" Jim could feel himself harden in response.

"Does that mean 'yes', Dr. Scott?" As Claire moved her legs tightly together she said, "I don't think my pussy aches after all."

"You little tease, Lady Rochester. I see I will have to undertake some corrective measures." Jim grasped Claire's wrists and held them above her head. He put them both in one big hand, reached down with his free hand and pushed her thighs apart, even with Claire trying to keep them together. Claire giggled, as he managed to get his thighs between hers. He ran his fingers over her. "Poor little dry pussy." He brought his fingers up to his lips. Claire could hear him suck them and then she felt him gently rubbing her. She could not stop herself from drawing her knees up to open herself wide for him. He kept rubbing and Claire no longer felt the slightest bit cold. He still held her wrists but she managed to find his lips with hers, and they kissed long and deep. Then he stopped and she felt momentarily bereft, until she felt the tip of a very hard cock nudging its path inside her. She thrust up to meet it and felt the shaft going deep inside her. Jim now let go of her wrist and reached behind and grasped her bottom. He murmured, "I think you were fibbing. It does not feel cold to me. I love you, Claire, with all my heart."

"I love you too, my darling. I am just a jealous old bag. I don't want any other girl near you. Now push that bloody great prick inside me and fill me with that sticky semen." They started to move in that time honored missionary fashion, with Jim taking some of his weight on his hands beside her and Claire holding him as tightly and hard as she could. Claire knew that, in this position, she was not actually stimulated but somehow, the very closeness of him and knowing he loved her, aroused her and she felt herself tighten as Jim climaxed. She loved him so much that she did not care that he went straight to sleep. She rubbed his back and brought the sleeping bag over them. Then she went to sleep.

The sun was well up when they woke. They kissed. Jim said,

"You are a truly wonderful girl. Thank you so much for finding me last night. I hope you won't get into trouble getting back."

"Don't worry, they will think I am out on a long walk. I often go. It is such a beautiful country. I stink of sex, but don't really want to put my clothes on until I am cleaner." "Not a problem," said Jim, "I have water and washing stuff in the plane." He grabbed his 'kikoi' and unzipped the tent. He had great fun hand washing her and towelling her dry. They shared his toothbrush.

"Aren't you going to wash?" asked Claire,

"No," replied Jim, "I want to smell of you for as long as I can." Claire smiled,

"You lovely boy, can I borrow your shirt and then I can smell you?"

The airport was stirring, as they walked into the aero-club to go to the loo. Luckily, they did not see anyone. Jim walked with Claire, down to the Nairobi end of the Langata Road. Claire could not stop herself from crying as they hailed a taxi. They kissed. She hugged him and said.

"Take special care. You know how much I love you." Jim replied, with a frog in his throat,

"I love you too. I hope it is not long until we can see each other. It is not 'Kwaheri' but au revoir. Keep safe." She got in the front of the taxi. As the taxi man drove off, she waved out of the window. Claire got the taxi to drop her over half a mile from the High Commission, so that she could walk and compose herself. In fact, although the staff were up, their house quests and Sir Richard were still asleep. Claire actually did not feel too bad, as she was still on a high, so she started on a hearty breakfast. Soon she was joined by some of the guests. She was back in her other life, but she had wonderful memories of a very memorable night.

Chapter 24

A lucky meeting

Monday 21st August 1967

Although Jim was rarely out of her thoughts, Claire took her other life very seriously. She had not only her clandestine role, as Chief of station, but also her role as the High Commissioner's wife. It was in this latter role that she was entertaining, at dinner, important visitors from the UK. The most important was the Minister of Overseas Development, David May. She was seated next to him and, although he was obviously well on in his sixties, he could not hide the fact that he found her very attractive. She asked him what he had planned for the next day. He said he was flying up to Tana River District to see for himself the results of an aid project which his Ministry had financed. Claire knew all about the new stock route and the water development project. She said how marvellous the project was. She remarked how she had visited the area some time ago. How the people were really in need of water. She said how she would love to visit the area again, as she had made many friends in the area. David May said. "Why don't you come with us tomorrow? Your husband is coming and we have spare seats in the plane."

"That would be wonderful. I would love to come. I will make sure we take a really good picnic. I am sure Richard won't mind. I think he was rather proud of me when I helped rescue a Hippo up there. He said it was excellent PR."

Claire thought, '*I doubt it will happen but I might get a chance to see Jim. It is certainly worth a try.*'

So it was, that Claire was at Wilson Airport with Sir Richard and Sir David, at the very civilized hour of 11.00 am. She had brought an excellent picnic. The High Commission had chartered a Cherokee six, so there was plenty of room. Sir David, who had been a bomber pilot in the war, sat next to the pilot. Claire and Richard sat behind

317

them, with the small fold down seat between them. The picnic was on the two seats behind them. In the luggage compartment, at the very back, was a camp table and four collapsible chairs. The idea was to fly down to Mackinnon Rd and then turn and head north up the stock route, over the Galana River and then turn north east to the hill called Dakawachu. They would land there to see the dam; bore hole; cattle watering facilities; cattle dip and cattle pens. There was going to be no pomp and ceremony, but just a day for the Minister to see firsthand the area and the project. He would get an idea of how remote the area was, without having to travel for days over bad roads.

Sir David obviously loved the flying. The pilot let him have control whenever he felt like it. They flew low over the stock route, so Sir David could see the mobs of cattle and the game in Tsavo East Game Park. Claire kept an eye out for Jim's Landrover but did not see one. All the way Claire listened to the radio, in case she heard Jim's voice. There was nothing.

They landed on the new airstrip at Dakawachu and walked up to the top of the dam wall. The dam had little water as yet but obviously it would fill, if there was rain in the coming months. They returned to the plane and carried the table, chairs and picnic to a shady spot under a tree. It was very hot but, as it was so dry, it was not unpleasant and there were very few flies. The mobs of cattle had taken them with them.

The pilot was a very well informed 'Kenya Cowboy'. Claire did not find him attractive but he kept the men entertained with his stories and so the picnic was very pleasant. Claire was pleased the pilot only drank water but the two men got stuck into the chilled white wine. Claire knew not to have too much, as drinking wine in the heat gave her a head ache. There was plenty of water and masses of food. They even had a cup of coffee after the meal. It was only when they were carrying everything back to the plane that the relaxed atmosphere ended. The pilot noticed that the nose wheel of the airplane was flat. There was no way they could take off. There was no spare, as light airplanes did not carry them. They were stuck in the middle of nowhere.

The pilot tried to be cheerful and said he would see who he could raise on the radio. Claire suggested the rest of them carry their chairs back into the shade. She poured them another cup of coffee. She could tell that her husband was very angry, but his breeding stopped him from showing his annoyance openly. The flies seem to suddenly become worse. Claire saw why. There was a herd of goats coming down to drink. A young boy was with them. His keen eyes focused on Claire. He ran towards her.

"*Memsahib Claire Habari* (Mistress Claire How are you)*?*" Claire recognized him immediately he was a younger version of Dubi. She remembered his name.

"*Habari Tuku* (How are you, Tuku)*?*" He wrapped his thin arms around her and clung to her. Sir David said. "I must apologise to you Claire, I did not believe you last night when you said you had many friends in the area. The first child you meet is obviously a close friend. Let's hope he has a friend who can fix our tyre."

Claire laughed. "I don't know about that but we will have plenty of goat meat." She asked Tuku, who was now standing beside her, holding her hand.

"*'Dubi iko hapa'* (Is Dubi here)?"

"*Ndio Dupi uku ju* (Yes, he is up high).*"* Claire immediately looked up at Dakawachu.

"*'Hapana'* (No),*"* said Tuku. "*'Dubi indani ndege. Bwana Jim nakuja. Sikia'* (Dubi is in the airplane. Listen).*"*

David and Richard did not understand any Swahili but they instantly realised there was good news, as Claire laughed. She had heard the sound of Jim's airplane. Then they heard the plane. Soon it was taxing towards them in a dust cloud. The engine cut, the door opened and Dubi and Lucy were running towards her followed by Jim at a fast walk. Luckily Lucy gave Claire a terrific greeting and Dubi hugged her, otherwise Claire and Jim might well have given themselves away.

"Well, I never did," said Jim. "I don't remember organising this at Muthaiga Club. Thank you, Sir Richard, for such an excellent evening."

Sir Richard, ever the gentleman, introduced Sir David May who shook hands with Jim. Claire gave Jim a peck on the cheek but her hidden squeeze of his hand told him much more.

The pilot told Jim their problem. Claire was amazed how Jim seemed to take command of the situation. "Right, I only have a four-seater so I will fly you three back to Wilson. Claire you can stay here with Dubi, Tuku and Lucy. Chaiko and Michael Ngulu will be here soon with two Landrovers, followed by the vaccination team in a lorry. Claire, there is no way you can leave Tana River District without seeing Leonard. I will fly you up to see him when I get back. Right, we must not hang about or I will be out of day light. It is lucky I have this Cherokee180."

Once again, Claire marvelled at how her husband and Sir David got in the back and the pilot got in the front, with Jim without any further debate. Claire was left with the picnic, the table and chairs. She poured herself another cup of coffee and looked forward to the night to come. Dubi's English was quite good and Tuku certainly understood the gist of the conversation. Dubi entertained her, with the story of Jim swimming the Tana River.

Jim flew a direct course to Wilson. He was interested to listen to the conversation in the back.

"You are a lucky man, Richard, to have married such a remarkable girl. She organised an excellent dinner party last night. Then we had that super picnic. But, what I think is so amazing, is she is happy to be left with two young African boys and a Labrador, in the middle of nowhere. Who is Leonard that Jim was talking about?"

"He is Leonard Baloala, the District Commissioner for Tana River District. Claire got to know him when she helped rescue that Hippo. You are right, I am a lucky man. Equally, Kenya is lucky because Claire loves the country and its entire people. The people seem to recognise that and respect her in exchange. The Residence is a very happy place with her at the helm. It allows me to do my job much more efficiently."

The pilot did not say much on the flight. Jim guessed he was pissed off, by having to be rescued by an amateur. Jim could not worry about that, as he felt that, that was his problem. It was no big deal, the pilot would take another plane in the morning, together with an engineer and a second pilot. They would fix the wheel and both fly home in the two airplanes. There was no need for Jim to help him anymore. Jim just wanted to fly back to Claire, as quickly as possible. Sir Richard was delighted to be getting back to civilization. He had a horror of roughing it out in the bush. He was fond of Claire and respected her. He knew she would be happy and not at all cross at being left alone. He looked at his watch. He was no fool and he soon calculated that it would be touch and go, for Jim even to get back to Dakawachu by dark. There was no way he was going to fly Claire back to Nairobi that night. He knew Leonard had a quest house and he thought they would go there.

Sir David knew he had an official dinner that night and a full day of meetings in the morning, so he was relieved to be getting back. However, he was still very young at heart and he envied Jim with his adventurous life. He knew he would actually hate sleeping out in the bush, but Claire was a very beautiful woman and so he was just a little sad to leave her.

When they reached Wilson, there was a lot of shaking hands and then they went their separate ways. Jim immediately fuelled up and took off again for Dakawachu. He reckoned he just had time.

As Jim had told Claire, Chaiko and Michael Ngulu soon arrived and took her back to where they were going to camp. Obviously Lucy came with her. Claire persuaded Dubi to stay with Tuku and the family goats, which would make their way back to their temporary boma, now that they had drunk for the day. Claire mused that it was a hard life for a goat, only drinking once a day and she guessed, before this dam had been built, it would often have been that they only drank once every two days.

She busied herself helping to make camp. She knew the timing was tight and she worried about Jim getting back before dark. She prayed he would not do anything stupid, just to get back to her. She knew there were plenty of airstrips he could land on nearer Nairobi. She cussed the tropical night for coming so quickly. Eventually, she could bear it no longer and got Chaiko and Michael to both drive to the airstrip, so that they could light either end of it. The dark came down and she became more agitated. Michael and Chaiko understood her worries and consoled her. They said Dr Jim was a very careful flier and he had probably stayed in Nairobi and would bring the engineer, to repair the plane back in the morning.

Claire let them drive her back to the camp with a very heavy heart. She was not worried, as she knew she would be totally safe and well looked after, but she just knew how Jim might try anything to get to her. She prayed he would not try a night landing. She did not really eat any supper as she was so worried. Soon Michael and all the staff started to get ready for sleep. Claire had prepared a bed, on top of the Landrover, for Jim and her. She knew all the veterinary staff knew she was Dr. Jim's woman. She washed her face and hands, after she had gone a little way out of the camp for pee. Lucy had come with her but was now safely in the cab of the Landrover. With a very heavy heart she climbed into the tent, on top of the vehicle. It was really only then that she realised that she only had what she stood up in. She was somehow hesitant to look in Jim's bag, but then thought this stupid and rummaged around to find one of his shirts which she could use as a night dress. She smiled, when she found a pair of her knickers wrapped up in his kikoi. They were the pair she had put provocatively on the bed, when she was playing at being James Bond. She got into a clean shirt, but opening the bag had brought the smell of him into the tent. She was not cold but got under a sheet for comfort. She was tired but there was no way she could sleep. However, eventually she dropped off.

She woke to the sound of a vehicle. She was confused. Had Michael and Chaiko been to the airstrip? Surely she would have woken if a plane had flown over the camp. It was pitch black when she opened the tent flap. Jim would not have been able to see the camp from the air. The sound of the vehicle had stopped. There was a quiet conversation in the dark and then there was total quiet.

Claire got her torch but did not put it on, as she wanted to keep her night vision. She climbed down the ladder and stood at the side of the Landrover, listening. She could hear Lucy moving in the Landrover behind her. Then she saw a figure approaching the vehicle. She whispered,

"Jim, is that you?"

"Claire, my darling, I thought you would be in bed?"

She was in his arms in a second. "I was so worried about you. How did you get here?"

"It was getting dark, so I landed at Galana Ranch and borrowed a pickup and drove here. I didn't mean to worry you. Have you been standing in the dark long?"

"No, but I woke and thought I heard a vehicle. I did not want to wake the whole camp, so I just stood in the dark and hoped it was you. We will go to bed and you can tell me your news."

They cuddled up in the dark, and whispered their news like naughty school children. Then they behaved like very naughty teenagers, but very quietly, although Jim was sure the whole camp was fast asleep. They fell asleep in each other's arms.

After breakfast, Jim and Claire, with Lucy, took the truck back to Galana, while the vaccination team got to work. When they returned by air, you could see the dust clouds of moving cattle from several miles away. Jim helped the vaccination team, while Claire disappeared into the bush to have a good clean up. She washed her clothes and wore one of Jim's shirts and his '*kikoi*'. She put her clothes out to dry and went back to camp and, with Dubi's help, made a giant '*sufaria*' (saucepan) of tea for everyone. It always amazed Claire how Jim, and his team liked, hot drinks in the heat. Then, leaving Lucy with Dubi, they flew up to Galole to see Leonard.

He was delighted to see them and listened to their adventures with interest. They had an enjoyable lunch, before setting off in the plane for Wilson. Claire was weary, and was soon asleep with her head in Jim's lap. He stroked her hair. He made sure he concentrated on keeping the plane on the correct heading, because he was worried he might fall asleep too. He woke her gently, before he had to start transmitting their landing intentions.

"I have a favour to ask you," said Claire. "I think you will like it. I know you were planning with Chaiko that you would drop me in Nairobi and then fly to Mombasa before dark. Could you not stay in that hotel for the night and so a naughty visitor could spend the night with you?"

"I think I would like that a lot! Has that visitor caught up on her sleep and might it be a rather lively night?"

"Maybe she has caught up on her sleep but, how lively she is depends on you?" was the reply.

So, they parked up the plane at the aero club and both went in the same taxi. Jim got out, well away from the Residence, so he could walk with his small bag to the hotel.

Claire asked how he would pass the time.

"Oh, I will probably ring up one of the Nairobi girls." She put out her tongue at him as the taxi drove off. She smiled, because she was certain he would not go out with any of Nairobi girls. She also thought it was likely that he would write a report to Colin Shaw!

The hotel had a small pool, so Jim spent the late afternoon beside it, after he had a swim. He did, indeed, write his report for Colin Shaw and also the various other work reports to the PVO and the Head of LMD. He ordered a taxi for 5.00 am the following morning, as he knew he would have to get an early start to Mombasa or he would be late to work. He was not unduly worried as, Chaiko would have arrived well after office closing hours and so he would not be expected until the following morning. He had an early supper, after a shower, and then he went to bed, as he was tired. He made sure he left his door unlocked. He wondered how late Claire would be. He woke just after midnight and got up for a wee. He had hoped Claire would have got to him by now. He was slightly concerned, but thought she must have been delayed by entertaining at the Residence. Jim knew that Sir David was not due to fly out until the following evening. As he was fully awake, he got dressed and wrote Claire a note which he laid on his bed, in case they missed each other in the dark. Leaving his door unlocked, he went out. He told the old man at reception that he could not sleep and was going for a walk. He said he would keep his key so the '*mzee*' (Old man) could have a sleep. The '*mzee*' chuckled. He told the same story to the '*askari*' at the gate. He also told the '*askari*' not to shoot him with his bow and arrow, when he returned. This provoked more laughter.

The dinner party at the Residence seemed to go on forever, in Claire's mind. She was not tired, having slept on the plane, but she longed to go to Jim. Sir David obviously enjoyed her company and so was in no hurry to go to bed. Claire thought he was no fool, and wondered if he had guessed she was having an affair with Jim. She was pretty certain Richard had no idea. It had been a bit of luck, Jim tipping up at such a remote destination. Then Claire gave it some more thought. Sir David had only invited her the night before, so it would have been totally impossible for her to have arranged the rendezvous in such a short time. She resolved to be doubly careful tonight, leaving the Residence. Because her mind was elsewhere, she did not realise Sir David had been asking her a question. She very politely asked him to repeat it. It was a very probing question about the value of British aid in the NFD. Eli was in the room refreshing, the coffee pot. Claire turned to Eli, who she was sure had been listening to the question but, so as not to embarrass him, Claire asked, "Eli, Sir David is asking how useful is British aid in the NFD."

"Sir David, Eli comes from North Eastern Providence. His home is Wajir."

Eli took his time on answering. "I think targeted aid is of immense value, particularly when well respected personnel are available to oversee its administration."

Sir Richard was obviously annoyed that Claire had asked Eli, but he said nothing. Sir David was fascinated, that a butler would be so well informed. He asked Eli if he could give an example.

"That is very easy, Sir," replied Eli. "I know the vet, who administers the whole of the North Eastern and Coastal Provinces, is part of British aid. He is extremely well known and highly respected."

Sir David added. "I assume such a responsible job is carried out by a very senior vet from Kabete, who has been in the country for many years."

"Oh no, Sir," replied Eli. "He has only been in the country for a few months and is based in Mombasa."

Sir David chuckled. "Thank you Eli. I have been lucky enough to be rescued by the young man. I am glad my Government has recruited so well."

Eli turned to Sir Richard. "Can I bring in some liqueurs?"

"Yes, that would be nice. Thank you Eli."

Claire felt a flush coming up her neck and she knew it was not the prospect of a liqueur. She thought. '*Thank goodness I have a tan, it won't be so noticeable.*' Mercifully, Sir David did not appear to notice. However, he had noticed that Sir Richard was not happy with the turn of events and more, to protect Claire than for any other reason, after Eli had left them with their liqueurs he said,

"I am sorry Richard. You will have to forgive me. I may be a Cabinet minister but I come from a very different background to you. I have to know what the man in the street is thinking, as well as the men in power. Thank you Claire, I have learnt a lot from you in the last couple of days. That knowledge has made this whole trip worthwhile."

He raised his glass. "Cheers, and thank you both for a most enjoyable stay."

Sir Richard seemed to be mollified. Claire just wished they both would go to bed and, more importantly, go to sleep.

The party did break up and they went to their rooms. As Claire and Richard slept on a higher floor than the guests, Sir David did not know that they had totally separate bedrooms. Claire locked her room and then changed into a navy blue, long sleeved shirt and navy blue trousers. She sat in a chair and tried to read a book. She could not concentrate. She knew she must not make her escape too soon. Her only consolation was that she thought Jim would be sleeping peacefully. She worried about him not getting enough sleep and then having an accident in the plane, through tiredness. She would be devastated if, by sleeping with him she brought about his death. How she wanted him. She willed herself to be patient.

Eventually, when she was totally certain the Residence was quiet, she crept down stairs and, with her own key, let herself out of the side door. She locked it behind her. She moved cautiously in the garden but was pleased to see the '*askari*', on the gate, was asleep as she slipped past him. It was a very dark night and she was quite scared as she moved along the road. Any tree she went by could hide a man who, at best, might mug her and, at worst, might rape and kill her. She tried to console herself that there was very little crime and that she was probably much safer on this tree lined street, than in London.

Suddenly a hand was over her mouth and a very strong arm was around her waist. She was so shocked that she froze like a rabbit caught in the headlights of a car. A voice she knew so well whispered in her ear. "Christ I want you." The hand was off her mouth and they were passionately kissing. Initially, she had her arms around Jim but soon she was reaching down and undoing his belt and pushing down his shorts. She undid the buttons of her loose trousers and they fell to the ground. She felt his hand in her knickers. Jim kept kissing her and she was desperate for oxygen. She had an intense orgasm and tried to get him inside her. She only succeeded when Jim ripped her flimsy knickers away. She felt that wonderful sensation, as he seemed to fill her. He stopped kissing her and they both gasped for breath.

Claire giggled, "I am not sure whether that counted as rape as I was very willing so I am sure it wasn't. I don't think I have ever had such an intense orgasm. Come on, we have got a few hours, let's find your room?"

At breakfast, Sir David remarked when Claire and Richard joined him,

"Thank you for last night. I hope I did not keep you up too late? You both look in excellent health, so I don't feel bad." Claire did, in fact, feel well as the little sleep she had was wonderfully peaceful, in Jim's arms.

Claire spent the rest of the day, not really concentrating on her mundane tasks of running the Residence, but daydreaming how she could get down to the coast again to see Jim. The weather was getting better again in Nairobi. They always called August the suicide month, as there were often several weeks of low stratus cloud cover, which made the temperature fall and depressed everyone with the lack of sunshine. The following day, the sun did come out and Claire invited the Danish ambassador's wife around for a light lunch, by the pool at the Residence. Ute was not a close friend, but loved the sun and was always up to date with embassy gossip.

Ute was delighted with the sunshine and told Claire that she and Helga, the Norwegian ambassador's wife, had got so fed up with the weather that they had decided to go down to Mombasa and spend a few days at the Oceanic Hotel. She invited Claire to join them. That was certainly a chance Claire was going to miss.

Chapter 25

Removing Judas' eye

Monday 11th September 1967

When Claire arrived at the Oceanic, which was on the East of Mombasa Island with a fantastic view of the sea she, like the other two ladies went to her room after they had checked in. It had been a long hot drive but Claire could not wait to contact Jim, so she rang the Veterinary Office from her room. Luckily, it was a few minutes before 4 'o'clock and so Jim was still at the office. They both knew that they had to be careful what they said, as anyone could be listening to their conversation. However, Claire could tell how excited Jim was. Jim suggested the three girls should come to his for supper. They could come in the Danish Embassy car, with their driver, but he could then go to his lodgings and Jim would drive them back to the Oceanic.

After Claire had put the phone down to Jim, she rang Ute's room. There was a long delay before Ute picked up the phone.

"Sorry Claire, I was having a shower. I could not wait to get rid of the red dust. I am sure Helga would like a supper out of the hotel. I will organize the driver for 7 'o'clock. I am meeting Helga at the pool in a quarter of an hour. Why don't you join us?"

So it was, that the three of them had a swim and some cocktails by the pool, before going to their rooms to change for supper. Claire was so excited, but she knew she had to be so careful and not let anything slip by saying anything foolish. She wished she had not had the two cocktails, as they had gone to her head. However, she had a shower and dried her hair, which sobered her up. She still had butterflies in her stomach, when she met the other two girls in the lobby. They immediately started to quiz her about Jim. As he did not live in Nairobi, he was not on the embassy circuit and so neither of them had met him. Claire guessed they both were in their mid thirties. Their English was excellent and they both looked very smart. Suddenly, Claire had cold feet and was delighted when the driver arrived. She sat in the front seat, so she could give him directions. However, she need not have bothered as he knew the way to the 'Chini Club' and Jim was only fifty yards passed the Katherine Bibby Hospital from there.

It was totally dark when they arrived but Jim's house looked quite imposing, all lit up. Claire had really only seen it in the daylight or in the pitch dark before. Jim was on the front drive to greet them. Claire longed to kiss him properly but she just gave him a peck on the cheek.

Katana pulled out all the stops for supper. They had a small Caesar Salad for a starter, followed by Red Snapper for main course. The evening went really well. Jim kept them entertained with his animal and veterinary stories. Claire noticed he drank very little but he kept both Ute and Helga's glasses well topped up. She was glad he did not give her much, as she was so worried that she would say something compromising. She was right to be worried. There was a lot of laughter on the journey home as, although Claire volunteered to go in the back of the Landrover, the girls said there was plenty of room for them all in the front. Claire was virtually sitting on Jim's lap, which was fun, but she was very careful where she put her hands. There was no way she could stop her dress riding up her thighs. When they got to the Oceanic Hotel, Ute asked Jim in for a nightcap. Jim thanked her but said he would get home, as he had drunk a bit and another would be dangerous, as he had to get home through some of the town. So the three girls waved him goodbye and went into the hotel. Ute and Helga bullied Claire into coming into the bar for one drink and then started asking Claire all about Jim. They said what a nice man he was, but they wanted to know how Claire knew him. That was easy, as Claire could say she had met him at the High Commission and then at the Muthaiga Ball. She said nothing about the safari to dart the hippo, but she did tell them about Jim rescuing her husband and the Minister. She did not tell them that there had been insufficient room in the plane and so she had been left in Tana River. Claire hoped she had fielded all their queries but she was not totally sure they did not suspect something. She was glad when the party broke up and they went to bed. Then Claire had a

329

problem, as she and Jim had not made a plan. She decided to leave a note for the girls, at reception, to say she had gone for an early morning run and she would meet them beside the pool sometime in the morning. She dressed in her running gear and went down with the note to reception. She asked the night porter to get her a taxi. She prayed neither Ute nor Helga would come down. She thought it was unlikely. The taxi soon arrived and she walked out of the lobby and got in and gave the driver directions to Jim's house. They had only gone a few hundred yards when Claire saw a vehicle behind flashing its lights. It was Jim's Landrover. Her heart missed a beat. She asked the taxi driver to stop, saying it was a friend's car behind. She paid him, including a very generous tip and ran back to the Landrover.

Breathless, she jumped in and said, "You are a star. What luck!"

"Not really," said Jim. "I was waiting just out of sight, outside the gates. I saw the taxi draw up and hoped it might have come for you. Then I rejoiced, as I saw you come out of the hotel. I like the running shorts." He ran his hand up her thigh.

"You are a lovely boy. Thank you for waiting for me. Now, we have all night together." She put her arms around his neck and kissed him. Jim had difficulty in staying on the road.

They had a long peaceful night together, after going to sleep. In the morning they were still sleepy but revived with Katana's tea. Claire had a couple of biscuits and, after getting into her running gear, she set off for the Oceanic Hotel. Mombasa was awake and the populous were going about their normal business. No one paid any attention to her. She retrieved her note from reception and managed to get to her room without anyone seeing her. She had a shower and was eating a hearty breakfast when the other two girls joined her. They all went down to the pool to sun bathe in the relatively cool morning sun. It was a welcome change from the recent grey weather in Nairobi. Although she was holding a book, she actually was almost asleep, when one of the hotel staff said the local Veterinary Office was on the phone for her. She snatched up her 'kikoi' and, tying it around above her bikini top, went swiftly to reception. A rich deep voice said on the phone that he was Kimuta, the telephonist, from the Veterinary Office. He said Dr Scott had asked him to call, as he was going to be doing an operation on a large bullock in an hour's time and he would be delighted if she could help him. Claire gulped. Would she pass out if there was a large amount of blood? Claire said she would get ready and would wait by reception for the transport. She couldn't help herself from asking, "What is the operation?"

Kimuta said. "He had overheard a conversation and he understood 'Judas' had a malignant tumour of his eye and Dr Scott was going to try to remove both the tumour and the eye.

Claire asked, "Who is Judas?"

Kimuta replied, "He is a very tame old *'Boran'* bullock, which led the cattle off the cattle-boat, up the race into the abattoir. I am blind myself. Dr Scott has taken me to Judas and let me feel all over him, so that I could then imagine what a bullock was like. I think Dr Scott is a very kind man."

This made Claire feel less frightened. She thanked Kimuta and hoped they would meet later in the day. Claire went back to the pool to tell the girls where she was going. She quickly changed into jeans and shirt and, putting on some trainers, went down to reception to wait. Now that she had time on her hands, she began to doubt herself. She knew she had done well with the hippo. However, removing an eye made her feel sick. Then she pulled herself together. If she fainted, she fainted. She was sure Jim would pick her up. Kimuta, who she did not even know, had said what a kind guy Jim was. She knew he was. He might tease her later but he would always look after her.

She looked up and, looking through the big glass doors into the car park, saw Jim's Landrover come in. She was coming down the steps as Jim leapt out of the vehicle. She could see, by his body language that he really wanted to kiss her.

"I am so glad you can come. I am really nervous, as I have never done this operation before. The anaesthetic will be really difficult and 'Judas' is a very special bullock."

Claire replied, "I hope I won't embarrass you. I am also really nervous, in case I faint. Removing an eye sounds particularly gruesome."

Jim gave her a broad smile, "I hope you faint into my arms. I so want to hold you and kiss you but I daren't, in case the other girls are about."

"I want you to hug me too but I want to be conscious when you do it," laughed Claire. They were soon moving through the traffic. There was a mixture of donkeys, '*hamali carts*' and motor vehicles. However they were soon speeding out of the town on the causeway to the mainland. Jim explained, that they were going to do the operation on 'Judas' at the KMC as that was where 'Judas' was kept. The KMC staff were very fond of Judas, which was why they had not told Jim about the tumour. They thought Jim would have 'Judas' shot. The staff, and Daniel Oket the manager of the KMC, had begged Jim to try and do anything to save him as they thought 'Judas' would know what was happening if he was made to go into the abattoir. Jim told Claire that he had told them he would try to remove the tumour but it was a risky business. Jim said it had to be done as the tumour had grown so large that 'Judas' could not shut his eye and the flies were driving him mad.

They were still killing the days quota at KMC so, it was with some relief that Jim and Claire could have a quiet look at 'Judas' in his pen and Jim could tell Claire how he was going to do the operation and what she would have to do. Soon, Michael the veterinary scout from the Veterinary Office, arrived. He helped Jim and Claire carry all the equipment down to the pen. 'Boniface', the lairage man, was sent to get two buckets of warm water. Michael put a halter on 'Judas' and Jim gave him an injection of sedative, into the muscles on his rump. After about ten minutes, 'Judas' slumped onto his brisket with a groan. After a further five minutes, they were able to roll him onto his side. Michael and Boniface tied his two front legs together and his two back legs together. Luckily, he had fallen with his bad eye uppermost. Jim asked Claire to trim off all the hair around the eye with a pair of blunt-ended, curved scissors. Claire had felt a little queasy but, once she started doing something, she realised she was fine. Jim was giving 'Judas' an injection of penicillin. Once Claire had cut off the hair, Jim carefully washed off the area with antiseptic. Then, he injected some local anaesthetic along the eye lids and a large quantity with a long needle, at four points deep behind the eye. Claire took three or four very deep breaths. Jim did not look up from what he was doing, but just lent forward near to her and whispered, "Are you OK?" Claire was grateful he had not made a fuss and said she was fine. Jim asked her to scrub up her hands in one of the buckets. After cleaning the eye again, Jim did the same. Michael had laid out the instruments carefully without touching them, from a sealed bag onto a sterile drape on a tray. Then, Jim carefully stitched the eyelids together over the tumour. He explained that the idea was to contain all the bacteria and tumour cells within the eye sack, and then remove the whole eye sack without contaminating the eye socket. He handed Claire a pair of scissors and explained how it would help if she cut the suture material, near to each stitch, after he had tied it. It was not easy, as the tumour involved much of the conjunctiva.

When this was done, Claire thought it looked so much better. It seemed a pity to remove the eye but Jim explained, the tumour would burst out in just a few days. Michael layed out a new set of instruments, as Claire and Jim scrubbed up again. Jim then cut two careful incisions along the eye lids and started to peel them away from the conjunctiva. He got Claire to hold the skin, with a pair of forceps, to keep the tension and make it easy for him. Claire was really interested now, and had totally forgotten her reservations. Jim had to cut the eye muscles with a pair of curved scissors. Obviously, the local anaesthetic had not totally numbed the area, as 'Judas' made the occasional movement of his legs. However, he made no attempt to get up, with Boniface kneeling on his neck.

At last, Claire could see the enclosed eye ball was just hanging from a bloody looking piece of tissue. Jim explained, this was the optic nerve. Jim asked Michael to sit on 'Judas' and Claire to move back a little, as he cut through the optic nerve. His anaesthetic must have worked, as 'Judas' did not move. A large amount of blood welled up into the socket but Claire was totally absorbed in the operation and was not at all fazed. Jim unrolled a cotton bandage and pushed it all into the socket. He then started to stitch up the skin, as he had totally removed the eye sack. Once again Claire helped by cutting the ends of the sutures, after they had been tied. Jim was just putting in the final suture around the end of the bandage, which was going to be pulled out slowly during the days to come when 'Judas' gave a deep sigh and Jim immediately realised he had died. He did not breathe and Jim felt under his jaw and there was no pulse.

One look at his face and Claire realised he was devastated. In a calm voice Jim said "Poor old 'Judas' has given up the ghost. I will have to go and see Daniel Oket and say how sorry we all are." Michael and Boniface both said "Jim was not to worry, as he had done his best and now Judas was at peace. At least he had not had to go into the abattoir."

Claire, without a second thought put her arm around Jim, and realised she was crying. She sniffed and said "I will stay here and help Michael clear up." Claire was not sure if she was crying for Judas or for Jim. Probably she was sad a little for each of them. Daniel Oket was not in the least upset. "Don't worry, Dr. Jim. I have just been going through our records. He was 21 years old, which is an exceptional age for a *'ngombe'* (cattle). We will bury him and everyone will be relieved that he did not go into the slaughter house. Please don't give it another thought. They will soon train up another animal.

Michael was waiting with Claire at the Landrover. Jim said, "Oh dear, what a disaster but apparently he was 21 years old. Daniel Oket told me not to give it another thought, so I will put it down to experience. Michael, I will drop you off at the Veterinary Office and pick up the blood tubes to take to Kwale district to blood test those goats. Pius will have them organised. I will drop off Claire on my way to Likoni Ferry.

On the way into Mombasa, after they had dropped Michael off, Claire asked casually,

"Would I be in the way blood testing goats?"

"Of course you would not be in the way. I would love you to come. You would be a great help. I did not like to ask, as it will be hot and I thought you would rather sunbathe at the pool."

"You are an ass, Jim Scott. However hot it is, I would rather be with you."

"That's wonderful! When we have done these goats, we can go and have a swim at Diani." There was a bit of a queue at the Ferry but they sat in the Landrover, sharing a *'madafu'* .It was amazing, in all the heat the liquid was always cool. The goats were only ten miles down the road to Kwale. Pius saw the Landrover and stepped into the road waving. He greeted Jim and Jim introduced Claire, as a young lady who wants to be a vet. It made Claire smile. When Pius was not looking she gave Jim's thigh a gentle stroke. Half the village seemed to have turned out to see the goats blood tested. They were high milk producing goats from Machakos District. They were part of a smallholder scheme. Jim wanted to test them for Brucellosis, a nasty disease which could infect humans if they drunk unboiled milk. The disease, in man, is called Malta fever and, in fact, Jim's Godfather had died of Malta fever in the Indian Army.

There were forty to blood test. The villagers caught the goats individually; Jim put a large bore needle in the jugular vein in their necks. Pius held the bottle until it was full and then handed it to Claire, who had to put the top on and write the eartag number on the bottle. Jim made a colored spray mark on the goat, to show it had been bled and then Pius let it go. It went like clock-work. Pius lived at the station where the goats were kept. He only went to the road, to make sure Jim did not miss the turning. They said goodbye to everyone and set off, in theory, to Mombasa. In reality they turned right, when they met the road along the coast, and headed south. They then cut down to the beach to reach the Diani Beach Hotel. They had a very leisurely, late lunch with a cold beer, and then decided to go for a walk on the beach. Diani Beach Hotel was frequented by upcountry farmers, not by package tourists so, after 100 yards, they were on their own. They walked, hand in hand, in the surf with the warm water just up to their knees. They kissed and Jim said,

"What about a swim?"

"Great idea," said Claire, "I have got my bikini on under my shorts."

"What a shame," said Jim, "I hoped you would have to swim in the nude. Your tan marks are so sexy."

"Well, hard luck, you dirty old bugger. Actually, if you come up close to me, I will let you look all you like. However, I don't think you have any swimmers on, so you will have to swim in the nude. I am a lucky girl." Claire ran up the beach, whipped off her shirt and shorts, and ran laughing into the sea. Jim felt a little bit self-conscious, as he took his shorts and shirt off and ran after her. By the time he reached the water, she was dancing up and down, singing, "I can see your 'willy'." Jim did not think it was the small exertion of running which made him go bright red. He tried to catch her but she danced away from him.

"Woo hoo, Jim's 'willy' is bouncing up and down," sang Claire. When Jim got near her, she ran straight out to sea and dived under the water. Jim was after her and soon managed to grab her legs. He could still stand easily, so he pulled her back towards him. She tried to kick him off but he was much too strong for her. He ducked her under the water and, as she came up spluttering, he grabbed her with a bear hug. She immediately stopped struggling, and wrapped her arms around his neck and her legs around his waist and kissed him. They broke off the kiss, with both of them laughing. Neither let go of their grip. Then Jim, before Claire could protest, pulled the bow at the back of her bikini. As Claire held her unfastened bikini to her breasts, Jim reached down and tugged at the two bows at the sides of her bikini bottoms. Claire gasped and reached around his neck and held on to him again.

"This is my favorite bikini. I am just going to hang on to you and leave you the responsibility of grabbing the two bits." With that she kissed him again. Jim enjoyed the kiss and the groping to retrieve the bikini. The water was lovely and warm and Jim could feel himself becoming aroused. Claire could also feel him. She suddenly let go with her arms and legs, pushed him away, turned and ran in to shallower water. Then, she ran as fast as she could, splashing in the shallows along the edge of the sea. Jim had to retrieve both bits of the bikini and run after her. She made such a lovely sight; he did not make a big effort to catch her. She suddenly realised what he was doing and so she turned and held out her arms to him. They laughed together.

"I can still feel your willy hard, between my legs. Does it hurt, running with an erection?"

"It would do if you had shorts on, but not when you are naked," replied Jim. "Shall we run back to our clothes on the hard sand? We will soon dry and then we can go home and make love, before I drop you back at the Oceanic Hotel?"

"So, you are not offering tea and sandwiches? What a way to treat a young lady who wants to be a vet. Mount her. Have your wicked way with her. Then drop her back at her hotel." teased Claire, as she started running,

"Come on slow coach, if we are quick, you will have time to kiss my fanny before you mount me. Do catch up." She held out her hand to him. They soon reached their clothes and got them on. Jim kept hold of the special bikini and they ran on down the beach to the hotel. Claire suddenly stopped, "I am sorry. You had an erection and it must have hurt running in your shorts."

"Don't worry, it soon collapsed."

Claire looked concerned, "It might have taken umbrage and not come hard again."

"You have no need to worry about that! One glimpse of your tan marks in the shower and it will spring up like a sapling."

On their way back to the Oceanic Hotel, Claire said she had better eat in the Hotel with the girls, as she had been away all day and they would be upset, but could he pick her up after they had gone to bed.

"Of course I can," replied Jim. "I will park the Landrover outside the gates of the hotel, behind some Frangipani bushes on the left hand-side of the road. I will come at 9.30 pm, but don't worry, I don't mind how long I have to wait. As it happened, Jim did not have long to wait, as both of the girls had over done the sunbathing and were ready for an early night. They were fascinated by Claire's description of the veterinary day. They both said there was no way they could have helped to take a cow's eye out.

Jim and Claire had a lovely night together and Claire ran back to the Oceanic in the morning. She spent the day with the girls, shopping in Mombasa. Luckily, for Claire, Ute suggested inviting Jim for supper with them at the hotel, so Claire rang the Veterinary Office before it closed at 4.00 pm. Jim was not at the office. Kimuta told her that he gone to see a sick horse at Miritini. However Kimuta said he was sure that Dr. Scott was playing rugby, that evening, at the Mombasa Sports Club as the match secretary had rung earlier in the week. He said the kick-off for the game was 5.00 pm. Claire thanked him for his help. Claire was, once again, reminded how all the Kenyan staff knew exactly what was going on. When she had put the phone down, she rang Ute on the hotel phone. She suggested they all went to the club to watch the game. Ute said that she did not know anything about rugby, but she thought seeing 30 young men must be worth a ten minute car journey. Helga thought the same so, by 5.30 pm, the three girls were on the touch line. As soon as Claire saw the game, she regretted coming. The ground seemed to be like concrete and Claire thought Jim was bound to get hurt. He waved to them at half time. Claire chatted to another girl of her age who was watching. Apparently, Mombasa was winning and the Royal Navy side was very unfit. Claire was very relieved, when the final whistle went and Jim was unhurt. He came over and greeted the three of them. He led them into the club and bought them drinks as, not being members, they could not buy their own. He said he would have a quick shower and join them.

Three unknown girls arriving, caused quite a stir in the changing room. However, it was the navy players who surrounded the girls at the bar. Ute and Helga were delighted with all the attention. Going back to the hotel was soon forgotten and some serious drinking began. Claire managed to take a back seat, so to speak. She tried not to drink too much, but it was difficult. She was saved by Jim, who had been tracked down by a man who had a sick dog in his car. This turned out to be a case of tick fever. Jim had the '*dawa*' (medicine) in his car, so Claire came out of the bar, with the excuse that she could hold the dog. Once the man had gone she whispered, "How are we going to get away from the others?"

"We will take them, with some of the Navy lads, down to the 'Florida nightclub'. Then, once they are all happy, we will slip away.

They managed to get Ute and Helga, together with four Navy chaps, into the Landrover and went the short distance to the sea front. The 'Florida' was on the front and, in fact, was not far from the Oceanic. After one drink, Jim and Claire managed to get away with an excuse that Jim had another sick dog. They made sure that the Lieutenant Commander, who was the most senior navy Officer, and seemed to be relatively sober, would look after the girls and get them home to the Oceanic.

"Now we have got a problem," said Jim, as they got into the Landrover. "If we go home, it will be just our luck for the revellers to come back to the Oceanic and knock on your door wanting you to join the party. If you are not there we will be rumbled, as the girls will know you have gone home with me."

"What a sod," said Claire. "I know, why don't we creep into the Oceanic and go to my room. Then you will have to hide in the bathroom and I will pretend to be half asleep and send them packing. Anyhow, they may just go to bed and not think about me." Jim hid the Landrover and they walked nonchalantly through the reception, praying that they would not meet any one. When they got into the lift, Claire breathed a sigh of relief.

"Our worries are not over yet," said Jim.

"Why is that?" asked Claire.

"This is the only lift in Mombasa. Otis employs one engineer to live down here, in Mombasa, in case it breaks down. They have two engineers in Nairobi but they would take too long to get down if it got stuck."

"Is it likely to get stuck?" asked Claire nervously.

"Not really, but he is a bit of a piss-head. I saw him at the Mombasa Sports Club after the game. He would love it if he caught us stuck in the lift!"

They both were out of the lift, when it stopped, like jack-rabbits. They ran to Claire's room and collapsed onto Claire's bed, giggling. They started kissing.

"Did you lock the door?" asked Claire

"Too right," replied Jim. "I am so nervous about being caught. I have got 'Brewers Droop'."

"I will have to do something about that." Claire pushed him on to his back and straddled him. She teased him by, very seductively, taking her clothes off-one article at a time. Then, she moved her bottom on his groin. She leant forward and whispered,

"I definitely can feel him stirring. Will you suck my nipples? Oh yes, he is really awake now. She reached behind her and drew down his zip.

"You have got boring old pants on." As she was trying to get his penis out, Jim lifted her in the air and moved so her groin was just over his mouth. As he begun to suck her, she groaned. "That is heavenly, don't you dare stop." He didn't, until she collapsed on top of him. No one disturbed them during the night. They awoke in a panic at 7.30 am. Jim was not only worried that he would bump into Ute or Helga, but also that he would be late for work. Totally naked, Claire kept distracting him as he tried to find his clothes. He crept out, promising to come back to the hotel at lunch.

When he did, he found Claire at the pool. She said.

"Did you have a good morning at work? You had no need to have worried, the girls have not surfaced yet and it is past noon."

"Great," said Jim. "How do you fancy lunch at the Mnarani Club? They have got guests staying, with a tame cheetah with a bone stuck in its mouth."

"Bloody hell, I will certainly come. However will you get it out?" Claire quickly got into her shorts and shirt. They left a note, at reception, for the girls and drove the thirty five miles to Kilifi as quickly as they could.

The cheetah was certainly tame as it was being stroked by a small boy, aged six, who said his name was Peter. He said his family had brought up the animal since it was a new born cub. He said his father was out deep-sea fishing and so he, Peter was in charge of the animal, which was constantly rubbing its mouth.

Jim asked, "What's her name?"

"Susan," was the reply.

"Can you get her to open her mouth?"

"Normally, if you tickle her under jaw, she will yawn but I am not sure she will, with the chop bone stuck across the roof of her mouth."

"Can you try for me?" asked Jim. Peter tickled Susan under her jaw and her large mouth opened. Quick as a flash Jim pushed his hand into her mouth and pushed the bone further into the mouth. Claire was horrified. Susan did not bite Jim, but angrily shook her head and the bone flew out.

"Oh, thank you," said Peter. "I thought you were going to have to give her an injection. Susan hates injections and so do I."

"Funnily enough, I am not that keen on them myself," said Jim. Peter laughed.

"It looks as if the lady does not like them either." Jim turned to see Claire's ashen face.

She stammered, "I thought Susan was going to eat your hand for lunch. How did you get the bone out so easily?"

"It's a trick really. The natural thing is to try to pull the bone out forwards but, of course, the upper jaw gets narrower towards the front. On the other hand if you push it further down the throat the upper jaw gets wider and it comes out. Come on, I am starving, how about some lunch?"

"I am not sure about food. I need a very stiff G & T," said Claire.

They were joined for lunch by Peter's parents, who were jovial upcountry farmers. Although they introduced each other, they only used Christian names and they did not recognise Claire. They were so grateful for Jim's treatment of Susan, that they paid little attention to Claire. Claire soon recovered herself with a G & T and so it was a most enjoyable lunch.

When they returned to Mombasa, Jim had to go back to the Veterinary Office. He dropped Claire at the Oceanic Hotel and promised to come back for supper. Claire found Ute and Helga at the pool. They both were still feeling dreadful and were much more worried about themselves, than worried about what had happened to Claire the previous night. She was very relieved that there was not an inquest.

They did drink some fruit juice but, when Claire mentioned dinner, they both groaned and said they would just have a snack in their rooms. They were both worried about the long hot drive up to Nairobi in the morning. Inwardly Claire rejoiced, although outwardly she was sympathetic. So Claire was alone when Jim arrived, smartly dressed for dinner.

"I am afraid you will have to put up with just me tonight, the others are still poorly." Jim's face lit up. "Come on, you look like a million dollars. Will you do me the honour of coming out to dine, Lady Rochester?"

"Do keep your voice down, Dr Scott but I would love that. Where can we go that is quiet?" whispered Claire.

"I know just the restaurant. It is a new tourist place called 'The Casuarina Hotel'. There will be no locals there." replied Jim quietly. "You look so gorgeous. You look good enough to eat."

"I might just let you do that," giggled Claire.

Although the hotel was quite full, the guests were obviously tourists, mainly from Switzerland Jim guessed. Claire read his thoughts.

"I have no worries here. This is so lovely just being the two of us, girl and boy. I feel ten years younger, like a young girl on her first real date."

"Will you go all-the-way, that is the question," enquired Jim with a grin.

"Certainly not, I am surprised you can even consider it."

"So I won't order oysters?"

"Well, I might allow some inappropriate touching," said Claire wistfully, as she rubbed Jim's leg, with her foot, under the table. Then she looked him in the eye and said fiercely,

"Don't you ever dare to give me such a fright, as you did before lunch today? Promise me. I know it is your job but please take more care. I worry so much about you, when we are apart." Then she immediately lightened the mood.

"Tell me what other tricks you get up to with big cats." Jim then told her about doing a caesarean section on a lioness at the Great Indian Circus.

"Bloody hell, I didn't mean you to take that request literally. I wish I was a female Bilharzia worm. Don't they keep the male wrapped up inside them for safe keeping?"

"Let's pretend we are Bilharzia worms. We could be a floor show for the tourists," whispered Jim.

Claire giggled. "I am up for it. I would love to see Christopher bloody Martin-Jenkins reading out a cutting from the Daily Nation to Richard at their morning briefing. *'Tourists on the Kenyan coast were given an erotic natural history lesson, after their dinner, by Lady Rochester and Doctor Scott. The couple, stark naked, gave a demonstration of Bilharzia worms to an applauding audience.'* They both had difficulty controlling their laughter.

The meal was good fun, but their love making that night was even better, with Claire wrapping herself around Jim pretending to be a Bilharzia worm. They were both really sad when they parted, early in the morning, a hundred yards away from the gates of the Oceanic Hotel. They both promised to think of ways of getting together again soon.

It was Claire who managed it. She persuaded her husband to let her come down with him to the official State welcoming, to the new three ships which had journeyed out from the UK, to form the Kenyan Navy in Mombasa. The President, Jomo Kenyatta, was entertaining the President of Zambia, Kenneth Kaunda and the Ruler of Ethiopia, Haile Selassie. The High Commissioner was invited to attend. Claire lied to Sir Richard and said she would stay with a couple of girl friends at the coast, after the official ceremony and come home to Nairobi with them. She then spent a blissful two days with Jim. Naturally they could not go out, in case they were seen together but neither of them thought it was any hardship to be living in Jim's lovely house. Claire would sunbathe in the secluded garden while Jim was at work, and then they had a marvellous time all evening and all night.

So that Claire could stay one night longer, Jim managed to swing it so he could start his morning blood testing cattle at Voi. So the plan was for Jim to hire a Cherokee Arrow plane from the Mombasa flying club. Fly Claire to Wilson Airport, Nairobi which would take two hours and then fly back to Voi to blood test the cattle. No one at the Veterinary office in Mombasa would be any the wiser.

Chapter 26

The mile high club

Tuesday 19th September 1967

It was hell for Claire and Jim, getting up at 6 o'clock after a night in each other's arms. They managed to get to the airport, load up all the blood testing stuff and take off by 6.45 am. They had a right turn out from Mombasa and were soon heading for Nairobi. They climbed away steeply, as the Cherokee Arrow had a retractable under carriage and was a powerful plane, particularly as there were only two people on board. As they flew over Mariakani, Jim turned to Claire and asked, "Would you like to join the mile high club?"

"Are you a member?" replied Claire.

"No," said Jim, "but we could both join together."

"What do we have to do to become members?" asked Claire innocently.

"Oh, just make love while flying a plane over a mile high," replied Jim with a laugh.

"You have certainly got a taker here," said Claire starting to take her blouse off.

"Steady on," said Jim. "We are only at 3000 feet we need to get twice as high as that."

"I like to be prepared for these things. Do we have to meet the club secretary?" said Claire, with a grin, as she unclasped her bra. She reached over to Jim and said,

"I will help you with your clothes. This is certainly the way to travel". Claire soon had Jim's shirt off then undid his flies. His penis popped up.

"As always, no pants you naughty boy," said Claire.

"What about you?" said Jim.

"As it so happens, I have on a very pretty, white lacy pair of knickers today," said Claire.

"As you have made such a good suggestion, I will let you see them". With that Claire wriggled out of her shorts. She turned around and managed to kneel on the seat. "What's the verdict?" asked Claire. Jim took his eyes off the altimeter which was reaching 6000ft.

"They are bloody sexy! I can see through the lace holes! We are over 6000ft, so you can take them off now."

"Always the way with you Jim, no time for compliments. It is just, off with your knickers girl, let's have a shag". Jim went very red.

"Now, let's get you out of those shorts," said Claire.

"However, I had better get a towel out of my bag for you to sit on, or we will have your semen all over the seat! I am sure the club secretary of the mile high club needs some evidence, so we can show him the towel. If I have to be a virgin, he is out of luck!" said Claire with a giggle. She then lent over his shoulder to rummage in her bag. Jim could feel her lovely breasts.

Claire managed, with some effort, to get his safari boots and shorts off, and then get her towel under him over the seat. Jim enjoyed the whole shemozzle enormously. He thought she did as well, as she never seemed to stop laughing. She then turned to him, dressed only in her impish grin and said.

"Well pilot, can you tell me how you are going to make love to your stewardess, before we have to select doors to manual?" Jim could not stop laughing, even when he realised they had been flying for one hour and five minutes and needed to report in.

"East Air Centre, this is Five Yankee Alpha India Quebec reporting Operations normal".

"Roger India Quebec, please report in contact Nairobi control".

"So, do you always have a naked girl with you when operations are normal?" asked Claire with a grin.

"Seriously Jim, this is not going to be easy. I want you to keep flying this plane while you Roger me, Roger me over."

"I think the best way, is for you to sit in my lap with your legs slightly apart. I will have my arms around you, holding the joystick, while I push my joystick inside you"

"Aye aye, skipper" was Claire's comment as she wriggled over on to Jim's lap. He felt her gentle hands guide his penis inside her.

"I am sorry it isn't longer," said Jim. Claire somehow managed to turn and kiss him and said,

"I love it just as it is. I am so excited, my vagina is wet already I don't need to rub myself. I will just have to hold you as I bounce up and down or you will slip out. I know you, even though we made love several times last night it will only take a few bounces and you will be coming all over the place." She was right. Feeling her tight around his penis and imagining her tiny clitoris pressing on the under-side of his penis, made Jim ejaculate in five thrusts. He kissed her neck.

"You must come now, my darling. Masturbate for me".

"Shall I?" said Claire "It will feel funny. I don't know whether I will be able to have an orgasm. How long before you report to Nairobi control?"

"Don't worry, we have half an hour. I will help you by kissing your neck and putting my tongue in your ears. I know you love that. I can even rub one breast at a time and fly the plane with my other hand. Jim kept kissing her neck and fondling her breast. He could feel her rubbing.

"Come for me, my darling" he whispered.

Claire started to get extremely excited. She started to make mewing noises. Jim moved his hand down and rubbed her flat tummy.

"Help me, my darling," whispered Claire. Jim's penis after his orgasm had become flaccid and had dropped out of her. He reached two fingers in its place and started to move them rapidly.

"Yes, my darling, that's wonderful-can you do it quicker and harder? Yes, yes, don't stop. Christ that's good. Oh yes," Claire sighed.

"Can you feel my knees trembling?" Jim felt her thighs, which were indeed trembling. "I think I would collapse if I had to get up!"

"India Quebec reporting visual marker. Estimate landing in eight," said Jim

"India Quebec report finals," replied the controller.

Claire turned and kissed Jim, "You sexy beast, how long before we land?"

Jim laughed, "As I said eight minutes."

345

"Bloody hell," said Claire. She managed to get on to her seat, on her knees, and vigorously wiped her groin and thighs with the end of the towel. Then she wiped Jim. "I hope the mile high club secretary does not come to the plane. It stinks of sex!" laughed Claire as she pulled on Jim's shorts. She helped him with his shirt.

"India Quebec Finals," said Jim calmly

"Finals number two, India Quebec," replied the controller.

"You had better put your blouse on, in case the controller has a pair of binoculars. Have I ever told you that you have great tits?"

"You bugger, Jim Scott. I will give you great tits. Now I have buttoned up my blouse wrong. Stuff my bra and knickers in your pockets while I try to get my shorts on. I hope to god, semen does not run down my legs when I stand up.

"India Quebec, you are clear to land," said the controller.

"Wilco, Wilson. Can I be cleared for immediate take off after my passenger has disembarked?" requested Jim.

"Roger, India Quebec. Make sure you instruct your passenger to stay well clear of the runway."

"You are a real gentleman aren't you? You take all my clothes off. Make my legs weak. Kick me out of the plane and expect me to walk to the aero-club," admonished Claire. Seeing Jim's crestfallen expression she added with a wicked grin.

"That was a bloody good shag! Keep safe and hope to see you as soon as possible."

Claire hefted her small bag off the back seat.

"Don't go near the prop," shouted Jim as Claire got out.

"Too right," shouted Claire, "I will be expecting a serious present before I go near your prop again." She flicked him a V sign, laughing at him as she started walking across the grass to the aero-club.

Jim really laughed at himself, on the flight back to Voi. He was bloody hot and got his hankie out to mop his brow and found he was using Claire's knickers.

Jim always enjoyed going to Voi ranch. The owner, Luke Cuddington, was a very friendly, jovial, sixty year-old. His wife, Amanda, was very hospitable. Jim knew he was in for a good breakfast. He had been on the veterinary radio from the airplane, so Luke knew he was coming and had managed to stop his herdsmen from taking the two mobs of cattle for treatment too far away. As Jim was flying down, they were being driven slowly into large holding pens, so they could be filtered into the cattle race. Jim had taken off from Wilson and reached the ranch, which had its own airstrip, in under two hours. The distance was just a little over two hundred miles. Jim often flew to the ranch, as flying was just as cheap as driving the Landrover, so Luke did not think it was unusual. Obviously, Luke did not know Jim had flown from Nairobi. Jim had told Luke he would need some blood slides which, together with some needles, Luke always had available. Taking blood slides and slides from lymph nodes, was a standard practice when faced with a sick cow. A diagnosis of tick-born disease could readily be established which would alert the rancher, not only that there was a problem with his dipping regime, but also how he could treat the animal in question. Ranchers did nearly all their own treatments. Jim's role was more in an advisory capacity. Ranchers also had their own veterinary scouts, who Jim found to be very capable like the Government staff.

The following morning, Jim was tired and slightly depressed when he got to the Veterinary Office. He had a lot of boring paper work to do. Jacob Messenger brought in his post. On the top, was a letter from Jane Morton. It was hilarious and made him laugh. She wrote;

My dearest 'I have control' Jim,

I remember what a softy you are and I am sure you would have written if you had been sad when I left. My guess, is that you have found another girl with great tits and you are shagging her. I bet I am right.

I did as you instructed, well not actually, the University made me go to the doctor as a routine in fresher's week. You were correct, I was slightly anaemic. The young doctor was rather pompous. He asked me if I had ever fainted. I could not resist it and said yes, I had several times, when a boy I met in Kenya had put his hand in my knickers. I thought the doctor was going to faint. He went bright red in the face and mumbled about the nurse giving me a diet, rich in iron. He could not get me out of his room quick enough.

Oxford is really fab. The work is actually fairly easy. I just hope I can remember what a bulls scrotum feels like, so that I can live up to your expectations of getting a first and being able to castrate bulls.

347

I have joined the University Air Squadron and I am learning to fly. My instructor is a kind old man. He said he thought I must have had a good instructor, to have learnt so much in just three short flights. I did not want to shock him but I was dying to say I had learnt a hell of a lot more on a piece of foam under the wing!

There is a guy, reading Chemistry, who is also keen on flying. I think I fancy him. Believe it or not, his name is Jake!!!! He is the complete opposite to Jake the rake. I am sure he is very bright, but he is very slow. It has taken him four dates to just squeeze my breasts, through my bra and sweater. I am dying to say to him, "For God sake, put your hand in my knickers." I really like him, so I don't want to frighten him off.

I can't really believe I was naked climbing your hard body up that coral wall, after just having had supper with you. I will keep you posted. I know I am right about you having another girl. I bet she is as wanton as me. In fact, I bet you have actually shagged her while flying (An RAF guy was showing off and told us about the mile high club).

I hear the odd snippet of news of you, from Judith. I heard you rescued a hippo in the wilds somewhere. So, I will end by saying.- Live well, Laugh often, Love much.

I still can't believe I had an orgasm, with Judith just the other side of the door!

Lots of love

From

'I am in control' Jane (I think I am in control, when I hold Jake's hand!!!)

Chapter 27

Malaria

Tuesday 17th October 1967

Jim sent off his normal report, to his control in Nairobi. He ended by saying, if there was a delay with further reports, it would probably be because he was sick with Malaria, as he had run out of '*Paludrine*' (A malarial preventative) on his last visit to Tana River District, ten days ago, and had only started taking it again on his return. In fact, Jim had been a fool. As soon as he got back to Mombasa, he should have taken a curative dose of '*Nivaquin*' (A malarial curative). '*Paludrine*' was only a preventative and therefore, if he was infected, it would not prevent the disease. Next morning he felt really ill. He hardly managed to get out of bed, to ring Kimuta at the Veterinary Office, to say he would not be at work, as he thought he had Malaria. He was not hungry and just managed tea and fruit juice for breakfast and then went straight back to bed. He did not ring the doctor, as he did not want to make a fuss. Lots of his friends, who had been in Kenya all their lives, did not take any '*dawa*' and regularly seemed to get the disease but it only laid them low for 48 hours. Jim thought he would soon be better. He wasn't. All through the day and the following night, he had violent episodes of fever and massive sweating attacks. Then, even though the air temperature was very hot, he would feel icy cold. Katana just kept encouraging him to drink tea and juice.

Claire received his report and was delighted by all the information and quickly relayed that back to London. She started to worry about him getting Malaria. She had not heard him on the radio that morning. She telephoned his home, which had recently been connected, from a phone box while she was out shopping. It was very frustrating as there was a delay of 30 minutes. She was worried she would be caught by one of her friends, who would think it was very strange she was hanging about in a telephone box. At last the call came through. It rang and rang and there was no reply. Then Claire was cut off. Katana had been out the back of the house and did not hear the telephone. Jim had heard it, in his semi consciousness, but had not had the energy to go down stairs to pick it up.

Claire tried to relax and say to herself that Jim was just out working. She went back to the High Commission Residence but could not stop herself worrying. She was dying to ring Kimuta at the Veterinary Office but she could not think up a suitable excuse. She tried to busy herself about the house but her mind was not on the job of sorting out her under-wear. Somehow, she put her pants in the sock draw. She jumped, when their private line rang in her bedroom. Could it be Jim? No he would not risk ringing the High Commission's private line. Richard could easily pick the telephone up. She grabbed the phone. It was the operator asking if she could take a call from Mombasa. Her heart leapt. The line was bad but she could hear a woman talking. It was Grace Middleton who was saying,

"Are you alone, my dear? Can I talk?"

"Of course Grace go ahead before this phone dies."

"I have bad news dear. I went into the vets this morning and Jim is off sick with malaria. I thought you would want to know. I know it may be difficult for you to get away, but perhaps you could say I am ill and you could come down and visit me. Guy has a driver, bringing a Landrover with some stores down to Mombasa. The driver has been instructed to call at The Norfolk Hotel at noon and check if there is anything extra to bring. If you were there, he could easily bring you down."

"Grace, you are an angel. I have been worrying about him. I will get to the Norfolk as soon as possible. I wish you both lots of love."

"Safe journey, my dear." Grace rang off.

Claire thought, '*I will have to be quick.*' She knew Richard was in a meeting, so she wrote him a hasty note saying she had gone to the Middleton's, as Grace was ill, and Guy had sent a driver up for her. She did not like lying but she thought, at least I am not hurting anyone. She asked one of the drivers at the front of the Commission, if he was free. He said,

"I think so '*Memsahib*', until Sir Richard goes to the club for his lunchtime meeting." Claire then remembered his name.

"That is marvellous Andrea. Could you take me to the Norfolk to pick up a lift to the coast?"

"That would be a pleasure, '*Memsahib*.' My wife, Martha, was so pleased with the clothes you sent for our new baby. The car is totally ready. Please do get in." He held open the back door.

Claire said, "I will ride in the front with you. You can tell me about your family." Andrea's face lit up, as he opened the front door. On the short journey, Andrea told Claire about his family, who lived in Kisumu. He was of the Luo tribe and so came from the area around Lake Victoria.

At the Norfolk Hotel, Claire saw an empty Landrover out at the front of the main entrance. It had its engine running. She had just made it.

"That's my lift. Thank you very much Andrea for helping me. You rush back. You won't keep Sir Richard waiting and you won't get into trouble. Do tell Sir Richard what you have done. He will be proud of you, showing so much initiative." Claire thought '*best to be totally open and no one would be any the wiser.*' She was like a young teenager, as she ran to the Landrover. She thought, '*not very lady like, Lady Rochester.*' She blushed, as she remembered picking up Jim early in the morning and seducing him. God I hope he is OK. Just as she reached the Landrover, a smiling, short, rather rotund African came out of the reception. She ran up to him and blurted out,

"Thank goodness, I caught you. Can you give me a lift to Mombasa?" The driver did not hesitate,

"Of course, '*Memsahib*'. My name is Daniel. I am sure Bwana Middleton would want me to help you. Do get in." Daniel opened the door for Claire. It was only then that Claire thought '*how totally unprepared she was, for a 300 mile journey. She had only the rather flimsy short fawn cotton dress, which she was wearing. She had no water, no food. What if they broke down while they were still at altitude, she would freeze to death.*' As if reading her thoughts Daniel said,

"I have plenty of water. We will stop at Hunter's Lodge for some food and more petrol. I know '*Memsahib*' Middleton would like me to look after you."

As they moved swiftly out of Nairobi towards Athi River, Claire marvelled how she had been taken on face value, just because she was a European. She thought, '*she must make more of an effort to learn more Swahili.*' Jim was really quite fluent, because he lived at the coast. Upcountry Africans, particularly Kikuyus, were often rather insulted if you spoke to them in Swahili, as it rather indicated that you did not think they had been to school and therefore were not educated. She thought that Tanzania had been more sensible by making Swahili the '*Lingua Franca*'. Kenya had made English its main language.

She asked Daniel where his home was. He said he came from Kwale. Claire remembered Jim saying how there was a small Game Park, south of Mombasa, in Kwale District which he wanted to take her to. She remembered him teasing her and saying she would not see any lions mating, so she might find it a bit dull. She remembered, with a blush, how she had pushed him on to the bed in his bedroom, kissed him hard and said.

"We don't need any lions, mount me from behind. I want to feel you inside me now, now, now." She was rather worried. Was she a nymphomaniac? Why did she want him so much?

However, she just quietly answered Daniel and said she did know of Kwale, she had blood tested some goats there. Also, she wanted to go to a Game Park there.

"That is Shimba Hills," replied Daniel. "It is very beautiful. There are two large types of antelope there. In English, they are called Roan and Sable. In Swahili they are called '*Korongo*' and '*Palahala*' or '*Mbarapi*'. They are quite rare in Kenya but I understand they are much more common in Southern Africa.

Claire said to Daniel, "I suppose, as you come from the coast, you speak '*safi Swahili*' (Grammatical Swahili). Will you teach me some, on the way down to Mombasa?" Daniel said he would be delighted. The journey flew by and they were soon at Hunters Lodge, having travelled 100 miles. The tarmac ended there but, after their stop, they were soon off on the '*Murram*' road. Claire continued with her Swahili lesson, as she ate a large '*samosa*'. Daniel said he hoped they could get all the way before it got dark but at least, if they could get to Mackinnon Road in the daylight that would be good, as the tarmac started again there. They were now going through Tsavo

Game Park. Claire learnt lots of Swahili words for animals and birds. They saw Elephant, *'Ndovu'*, Giraffe, *'Twiga'* ,Impala, *'Swara Pala'*, Warthog, *'Ngiri'*, Ostrich, *'Mbuni '*, Secretary Bird, *'Karani tamba'*. Claire hoped she would remember them, to impress Jim. She asked Daniel why he called Elephant, *'Ndovu'*, but she had heard them called *'Tembo'*. Daniel was not sure but he thought *'Ndovu'* was correct and that *'Tembo'* was half an English word.

The time and distance marched on. Although Claire was worried about Jim, she was really enjoying the trip. She felt like a young girl again, on her way to an adventure, a messy girl at that. She knew she was covered with dust. To keep cool, they had had the front vents of the dash board open so every time they came up behind a lorry, dust poured in. The dust had stuck to her everywhere, particularly where she had broken into a sweat. They had stopped at a garage at Voi to get more fuel. Claire had gone for a pee and found her white knickers absolutely orange with the dust. Back in the Landrover she went quiet. What if Jim did not have Malaria and only was hung over. What if he had some friends coming around for a drink and supper? She would blunder in looking a real sight. Then she thought how kind he was and that he would always make her welcome. She could always have shower and wear one of his shirts and a *'kikoi'*. She knew everything was much more relaxed at the coast. She loved that. She really was not happy with all the formal dinners and posh occasions in Nairobi. She remembered the wonderful nights on safari, when she could cuddle up with Jim and they could watch the camp fire die and the moon come up. She came out of her reverie, when they went over a bump and the noise of the tires was different. They had reached Mackinnon Road.

"That's good," said Daniel, "it is only just past 6 'o'clock. It will be dark as we come into Mombasa, but only just. I am sure *'Memsahib'* Grace would want to see you but I expect you would rather go where you are staying. I can easily pick you up in the morning, to take you out to the farm to see her. I think the Bwana will want to off load all the stores tonight."

Claire said, "Daniel it would be great if you could drop me off on the island. My friend lives next door to the Katherine Bibby Hospital."

"Do you mean the house next door to the PC's house?"

353

"Yes," said Claire.

"I know," said Daniel, "Dr Scott's house. I have often been there to pick up *'dawa ya ngombie'* (Medicine for the cattle). He is a very nice *'Bwana'* and a very good *'daktari ya ngombie'* (Veterinary Surgeon). He often comes to the farm." Claire thought to herself, *'how lovely it was that everyone liked Jim.'* She was now longing to get there. Very soon they were coming down the causeway.

There were no lights on, when they drove up the short drive up to Jim's house. Lucy ran out barking but stopped as soon as Claire, who had got out, spoke to her. Katana came out and said how pleased he was to see Claire. He was so worried about Dr Scott. He wished Dr Scott had sent for the doctor. Claire said he was not to worry, she would nurse him and send for a doctor if necessary. Claire shook Daniel by the hand and thanked him so much for being so kind to her. She hoped he would get home safely and perhaps he could bring *'Memsahib'* Grace here sometime tomorrow morning. With a wave he was gone and Claire went into the house with Katana. She was very apprehensive but was determined not to show it. She enquired from Katana if Jim had eaten anything. Katana said he had had nothing for two days, only tea and water. She asked Katana if he would make some tea for Jim and for her, and climbed up the stairs to the slow thumping of the fans. There was only a bedside light on and Jim lay naked on his back on the bed. She put her hand to his forehead, it was burning. He moaned as she touched him. She tried to understand him but his voice was incoherent. He was absolutely bathed with sweat. The sheet under him was soaking. She tried to rouse him to drink.

"You must drink, my darling."

"Yes, yes must drink," replied Jim. It was obvious he did not recognize her. When Katana came up with the tea, she got him to help sit Jim up. With Katana's help, Claire managed to get quite a good quantity of water into Jim. There was a packet of *'Nivaquin'* beside the bed but only four tablets had been peeled out of the wrapping? Claire made Jim take another four immediately. She then asked Katana to bring a bowl of water with some ice in it, together with some towels. It was only when she was slurping a cup of tea herself that she realised, here she was with a naked man, in front of his servant. The two of them had been so discrete in the past. She bathed Jim down with the wet, ice cold towels. He certainly felt a bit cooler. With Katana's help she moved the other bed in the room up close to Jim's bed. It was made up with clean sheets. Then they both managed to roll Jim onto the clean bed. Without being told, Katana pulled off the wet sheet and went to get a clean one. Claire managed to get the top sheet from under Jim and draped it over him. He still had not recognized her.

Katana came up and said he had prepared some food for her. She went down with him. It seemed very strange eating all alone in Jim's dining room. Actually, she was starving and ate all the cold ham, tomatoes and baked potato. *'How had Katana managed it?'* He even produced an apple pie and custard, which Claire ate with relish. When she looked carefully at Katana, who actually was quite an old man, she realised how tired he looked. He had obviously nursed Jim for the last 48 hours on his own. Claire said, she felt, that he should go and rest now and she would look after Jim and she would see him in the morning. She heard him downstairs and she knew he was clearing up the supper things. Then she heard him come up the stairs again. He gave her a small bell. He said Dr Scott had never used it but, if the *'Memsahib'* needed him in the night, she had only to ring and he would come. Claire could have hugged him. It meant so much to her that she was not alone. Jim seemed a little quieter so she had a good shower. She felt clean but knew she wasn't, as the towels were orange with the dust. She put on one of Jim's shirts.

Three more times in the night, Claire had to cool Jim down with ice cold towels. She got him to keep drinking water and twice she managed to get him to drink some fruit juice. He was delirious most of the time and got quite violent, when she made him have four more *'Nivaquin'* tablets. He spat the second two out. Claire was at her wits end. She rang the little bell. Immediately, she heard Katana on the stairs. He firmly held Jim, getting him to sit up in the bed and Claire managed to get two tablets into him and almost a pint of water. Katana helped her move him into the other bed which had new clean sheets. She thanked him and urged him to go back to sleep. He shuffled off with the sodden sheets and she only realised later, that he had taken her dust covered dress and even her filthy knickers. She felt so ashamed.

Claire was exhausted. She sat in the chair next to the bed. She must have dosed off, as she awoke hearing Jim croaking her name. With tears of joy in her eyes, she whispered to him,

"I'm here, my darling." He croaked again,

"I knew you would come. I feel so cold." Then his teeth started to chatter violently. With a rush of maternal emotion she took off his shirt and got into the sweaty bed. She lay on her back and cuddled him to her. His head fell on to her breasts. After a few minutes, he fell into a deep sleep. Then so did Claire.

That was how Grace found them, at eight 'o'clock in the morning. Grace lightly touched Claire's arm. Claire was instantly awake. There was a look of horror in her eyes but she did not say anything. She carefully slipped out of Jim's embrace and off the bed. She put on Jim's shirt and followed Grace out of the door. She shut the door behind her and felt totally vulnerable and ashamed. To her surprise, Grace put her arm around her and hugged her.

"Well done, my dear. I image his teeth started chattering. You are very brave to get in a sweaty, wet bed and cuddle him. Now you must have a cup of tea and some breakfast. We can then get the doctor up to examine him. These doctors are funny, in that they are quite happy to see a sick woman, but a well woman with no clothes on seems to frighten them. Katana has told me how marvellous a nurse you are. I will introduce you, to Dr Macbrian, as my niece. He is slightly deaf and a myopic old chap, but he is a good doctor and has seen a vast number of cases of malaria. He will be able to advise us whether this is a cerebral case." Claire had tears in her eyes, when she thanked Grace for being so understanding. Claire wrapped a 'kikoi' around her waist and did up the buttons of Jim's shirt.

Katana beckoned Claire into the dining room, as Grace brought Dr Macbrian up the stairs. When Katana was certain Claire had everything she needed for breakfast, he took a tray with tea, fruit juice and bread and honey upstairs. As it was, Claire did not have to meet the doctor as Grace brought him down the stairs. She offered him breakfast or a cup of coffee but he said this was his first call, and he had a busy surgery waiting for him, so he would not stop. Grace came and sat with Claire. "Good news, the doctor said that the malaria was serious, as it was Jim's first time. However he was sure it was not cerebral. He has injected Jim with 'chloroquin' (An injectable anti-malarial drug) and left some '*Quinine*' (The first natural drug), as he says there are some nasty strains of malaria now, which may be slightly resistant to '*Nivaquin*'. The '*Quinine*' will make Jim a little dizzy and he will hear roaring noises in his ears, but the doctor says the fever has broken and he will be fully recovered in two weeks. However, he stressed that Jim will be very weak and should not be allowed to get tired. Sadly, this type of malaria will reoccur, from time to time, for about ten years, but each attack will get less severe. What I suggest is, we get Jim up in a few minutes and then you both come out with Daniel and me to the farm. We have a separate '*rondavel*' with its own bathroom. You will both be able to rest and recover there. I will stay out on the farm, as I am meant to be ill. You can put a call through to Sir Richard to say all is well, but you should stay and nurse me for a few more days. Daniel is keen to give you some more Swahili lessons. I will have to make sure Guy does not tire Jim out, with too much farming talk. You will both need lots of rest and maybe a little fun." Grace said this with a chuckle and Claire blushed scarlet. Grace hugged Claire and said, "I was not always an old woman, you know."

Claire managed to dress Jim in an old track suit, while he was still lying in bed. Then, supporting most of his weight, she got him down stairs and into Grace's car. She grabbed some '*kikois*' and some of his clothes. Katana was a kikuyu and rarely smiled but he did manage one when Claire asked him always to call her Claire. He was a little shocked, when she hugged him to say goodbye. Claire hoped he would get some rest, as he looked exhausted.

Jim looked brighter, in the fresh air and sunshine. Claire thought she must look dreadful. Grace chatted away as they drove to the farm. When they arrived, Grace said they both should go to bed immediately. She would send Jonathan, the kitchen '*toto*' (child), down to the '*rondavel*' with water and fruit juice. Jim could not walk, un-aided, the 20 feet from the car to the *rondavel*' but he managed with Claire's help. He just flopped on to the bed and let Claire pull off his track suit and cover him with a sheet. She kissed him on his dry lips and whispered,

"I thought you were going to die in the night." Jim gave a small smile and said,

"So did I until I saw you by my bed."

Once Jonathan had brought the juice and water, Claire helped Jim with some of each and some quinine. Then Jim lay back and instantly slept. Claire was pleased that it was a relaxed normal sleep. He did not thrash about, or mumble like he had done in the night.

Claire loved the look of the 'rondavel'. She soon made it their home. There was one big bed and a little dressing table. She was appalled by her reflection in the mirror. She immediately went into the bath room and was delighted to see there was a large bath. She turned on the taps and ran herself a hot bath. She washed her hair three times, before she was satisfied it was free of dust. She used a big loofah to make sure all the dust-ingrained sweat was off her. She let out all the dirty water, cleaned the bath, and then refilled and had another soak. Then she dried herself, wrapped her hair in a towel and got under the sheet next to Jim. He did not stir. With a smile, she reached over and felt his now very small penis. She thought, I wonder how long it will be before just the touch of my hand will make it swell. I hope not too long. She rolled on to her side and was also soon asleep. They did not wake until darkness.

In the meantime life went on as normal. Guy came in for his lunch and was hungry for news, as well as food. Grace made him ring the High Commission and speak to Sir Richard. The call took nearly an hour to come through. Grace had given him careful instructions. He told Sir Richard that Claire was resting now, having been up most of the night. He said what a marvellous nurse she was. He did not actually lie, as he did not say who she had been nursing. Sir Richard, who actually had been nursed by Claire when he had a very bad vomiting and diarrhea bug, said he knew how good she was. He said all was well at the High Commission. His secretary had cancelled all her appointments for the next ten days and so he was happy for her to stay as long as Grace needed her.

Gerard relayed this message to Grace, who laughed and said, she knew Claire would be delighted. Both Guy and Grace were also delighted, but for different reasons. Guy was delighted with the thought of having such a lovely young girl about the place and Grace because, as she was meant to be ill, she could not possibly go to the boring social things like coffee mornings that she normally had to go to!

Jim made a rapid improvement. He was still very weak and the effort of just getting out of bed to go to the lavatory, made him puff and pant but he never became delirious, although he slept for most of the time. Claire spent time just reading a book by his side and making him drink, whenever he woke. She knew he was getting better, as when she was helping him to sit up to drink and his head was on her breast, he said,

"It is lovely to feel your tits. The feel of them is better than any medicine." Claire laughed and said,

"I remember you looking down my cleavage when we first met and saying they weren't big enough."

"Bloody rubbish," replied Jim. "You took advantage of my embarrassment and twisted what I said, to tease me."

"You were so shy," answered Claire. "It was so easy to tease you." She put her hand on his brow.

"You are much cooler now, shall I come to bed? But remember, you must not do ANYTHING to over tire yourself! "

"Yes nurse," replied Jim. Claire could see how weak he was and that he really meant it. She remembered how, actually, she had been shy when they first got together and was embarrassed being naked in front of him. Now she just took off her clothes brazenly in front of him, walked into the bathroom without shutting the door, had a wee, wiped her bottom, washed her hands and brought toothpaste on his brush for Jim to brush his teeth. When she had brushed her teeth with the same brush, she blew out the candles and got in beside him.

"Do we need the mosquito net?"

"I don't think so," replied Jim. "Being up just a thousand feet, seems to cut down the mosquitoes. It is so much cooler without a net." Claire actually had goose bumps and cuddled up to him, under the single sheet. They were soon asleep.

It was only after ten days when Claire, who knew she ought to return to Nairobi, dared to get Jim aroused. They had started going up to the main house and eating with Grace and Gerard. Jim looked very much better but still found even a twenty yard walk exhausting. They got back to the 'rondavel' after an early supper and Jim sat down on the bed, where previously he had flopped onto it, so Claire had to help him to undress. As he was sitting Claire knelt in front of him and undid his shirt and then his shorts. Jim lent forward and lightly kissed the top of her head. Claire looked up into his eyes and saw, not only love, but desire. She mischievously, slowly, undid the buttons of her shirt so he could see her lacy bra. She looked down and saw his penis swelling.

"I have been looking forward to this moment for several days, but I did not dare try to stimulate you, as I was sure it would worry you if you did not get an erection."

"You are a kind, lovely girl. I love you so much." They made love very slowly, after they had taken their clothes off. It was so different from normally when they had not made love for a long time, when they were almost in a frenzy. Claire lay on her back and Jim lay facing her, on his side, with his hard penis on her tummy. He slowly rubbed her with his hand until she whispered,

"Please rub me harder. Yes that is it." Claire was squeezing her nipples. Then she gave a gentle sigh and said,

"Feel inside me. I am so ready for you now." As Jim inserted two fingers into her vagina she started to thrust upwards. Then he pushed his fingers vigorously and rhythmically into her. She moaned.

"I want you inside me." As he rolled on top of her she came and her hands held hard on to his bottom, as he ejaculated and then collapsed on top of her panting. Claire was distraught.

"My darling, I am so sorry, I could not stop myself. Are you OK?"

"I am fine. That was blissful." Claire did not mind that he was almost instantly asleep. She cradled him in her arms and slept with him.

It was with heavy hearts that Jim and Claire left the Middleton's, when Andrea drove them back to Jim's house. Katana and Lucy were delighted to see them but, after a cup of tea, Jim drove Claire to the airport. They could not kiss goodbye but just held hands conspiratorially in the vehicle.

"Please take care, my love, and go straight home and have a good long sleep before you go to work tomorrow."

"Thank you for nursing me back to life. I love you."

Claire got out and walked to the terminal. She turned and gave a small wave before disappearing inside. Jim did as he had been instructed and had a long sleep when he got home.

Chapter 28

Hijack

Tuesday 17th November 1967

Claire was really down in the dumps. It seemed ages since she had seen Jim. She was sure he was back to his normal self. She listened to him on the radio, just to hear his voice, but that was not like chatting on a telephone. Making a call to Mombasa was an absolute nightmare, as it meant going to a telephone box and waiting for about half an hour for a call and the risk of one of her friends seeing her was very real. She wrote passionate letters to Jim, at the Veterinary Office as Jim said that was quite safe if she made up a bogus name, on the outside, as the sender. Claire had organized a private PO Box for Jim to write to her and she also had a second private PO Box for Jim to send his reports to Colin Shaw, her alias. She loved getting letters from Jim as, not only were they passionate but he also had a wealth of funny anecdotes which made her laugh. She was not laughing this morning. Christopher Martin-Jenkins had come in, while she and Sir Richard were having morning coffee, to announce, rather smugly, that Sir Richard had been summoned back to London. Claire's hopes rose, thinking she was going to be left to her devices, but Richard had immediately told Christopher to book two first class tickets to London, as he said Claire would enjoy a shopping trip to London. Claire could hardly refuse.

She was now writing a letter to Jim, telling him the bad news. She said she might be desperate to contact him, so she might try to telephone from a friend's house in the UK, but it would be risky. She ended by saying she ached for him and that he must please take care, as he was so special to her. She knew it would have little effect. He was always taking risks either on the rugby field, flying, deep sea diving or treating dangerous animals. Only a few days ago, he had to dart a buffalo for the Game Department and Claire knew they were one of the slyest of the so called 'Big Five'. Luckily, Claire thought, *'Jim had only routine reports to send in to her as her alias, Colin Shaw, and there were no risky trips pending. She just loathed the thought of being 7000 miles away from him.*

Initially, Sir Richard thought Claire was suffering from lack of sleep from the overnight flight. He had slept really well, as first class was quite luxurious, but he assumed she had not. They had a suit at the Savoy. Richard wondered if the memories of the first night of their honeymoon had made her depressed. He always was grateful to her for staying with him. He wondered if she had had an affair, but there had been no gossip which he had heard. He was very busy at meetings and Claire did do some shopping and met up with some of her old girl friends, so he just let time go by. They had been in the UK for a week, and had another ten days before their return when the shit hit the fan.

A BOAC VC10 had been flying from Heathrow to Nairobi. It had stopped in Benghazi, in Libya, to refuel. Four passengers had got on in Benghazi at 2.00 am. At 4.00 am, when most of the passengers were sleeping, they had hijacked the aircraft. Real information was sketchy but they were said to have automatic weapons and had placed explosives in the toilet behind the cockpit. The plane had landed on schedule at Nairobi Embakasi but they had not allowed any passengers off. They were demanding gold, American dollars and a helicopter to take them to an unknown destination.

Sir Richard and Claire were having breakfast in their suite when they received the news, by telephone, from the Foreign Office (FO). Sir Richard hardly said anything to Claire but rushed down to get a taxi to the FO, saying he would be in touch later but they would very likely have to fly back that night. Claire had had a clandestine meeting with John David, earlier in the week. As soon as Richard had left, Claire rapidly packed both their bags and got a taxi to Regents Park. She told reception to tell any callers for her that she had gone to the Zoo. She went to the bench, where she had met John David before. Sure enough he soon joined her.

"Thank you for coming Claire. I knew you would come here and the fewer people that know about this meeting the better. The firm thinks it is not a coincidence that Sir Richard is out of the country, but we have no firm evidence. The High Commission is in total disarray. The Kenyans have refused our offer of SAS assistance, on the grounds that they feel any violence will wreck the tourist trade. Martin-Jenkins has left to go to the airport to negotiate. He is as wet as a wet week in Wigan and the firm does not trust him on any level but, of course, he is the most senior FO person in the country, until Richard gets back tomorrow morning. The FO will only send Richard on a scheduled flight, as they say anything else will raise tensions. It would appear that the Kenyans want to accept the hijacker's demands. The British policy has always been the opposite, but the lines of responsibility are blurred. If the plane had returned to Heathrow, things would have been straight forward. The firm wants you to return with Richard and then take charge, when you have a secure telephone line in the High Commission. I know this is a big responsibility, but we would not be giving it to you if we did not think you were up to the task.

On that flight will be four SAS officers, two men and two women, disguised as tourists. They are there for Sir Richard's protection but will come under your direct control when he is safely in the High Commission.

We are also sending in an all male SAS team, disguised as a Rugby team from RAF Cyprus. They will travel in a Hercules on a 'training flight' and land at Entebbe in Uganda. They will come with all their equipment, including Landrovers. They will come into Kenya overland, on the foot hills of Mount Elgon, without the knowledge of the Kenyan authorities. They will contact you, at the High Commission, by radio. I will give you all the details. Any questions so far?"

Claire looked grave and replied, "There is really a 24 hour vacuum. Who is in charge until I am back? Couldn't I travel in a jet fighter to Eastleigh? The FO will only be worried about Richard's arrival not mine.

John David, replied, "You are right, the boss was not happy with the delay and so he has tasked one of your operatives in the country, to use any means to stop the hijackers getting away." Claire had a horrible sinking feeling when she asked,

"Who?" John David was not prepared for her reaction, when he replied,

"Animal Boy, I thought it was just up his street, after his extraction of Somali One." The colour drained from Claire's face and she groaned.

"Why? Have you a problem with his choice," said John David, "the boss has already instructed him." Claire, trying to compose herself, said,

"I know my operatives and I don't like them sent to their likely deaths. Animal Boy will take too big a risk, an older, less impetuous man would be more likely to get out with his life."

"And not get the job done," countered John David. "I am sorry Claire, it is a done deal."

"Fuck you both. The least you could have done, would have been to consult me first. I was in bloody London, for Christ's sake. I demand you get me back on station as quickly as possible."

"I admire you Claire but I don't like being threatened by my juniors. However, in everyone's interest, we will forget that outburst. Let's get on with the job."

John David was good to his word. Claire was helicoptered to a secret RAF base in North London. Kitted out as an observer and flown in a RAF jet, to Nairobi via RAF Cyprus. However, although she got to the High Commission by 8.00 pm, she was too late to influence events. The Kenya Government's negotiator had agreed to the hijackers demands. A Kenya Air Force helicopter had been ordered to Embakasi. Christopher-Martin Jenkins was already at the Airport with the gold and dollars. The hijackers had demanded that he stand alone, in the flood lights, with the ransom and they would check it for authenticity. The Kenya Government was keen for the incident to end peacefully, as quickly as possible. The hijackers were worried they were being double-crossed. They had several of the hostage passengers tied up, lying face down on the tarmac. They were very aware of a likely strike by Paramilitary forces. Negotiations were protracted. It ended with Christopher Martin-Jenkins being used as a hostage, together with the helicopter pilot, who, with the money and gold, together with Christopher Martin-Jenkins and the four hijackers took off at first light.

Claire, at the High Commission, was in despair. She had had a nightmare journey with obviously, no sleep. She had no way of contacting Jim. She had no idea what he was planning. Richard, and

364

the covert SAS team, were in the air not due to land until 7.30 am. The other assault team had landed at Entebbe. They were now journeying by road into Kenya. She just could not do anything constructive. Equally, she could not sit and do nothing. She went to her room and tuned the LWR to the veterinary frequency and prayed that Jim would broadcast.

Jim had not been idyll. Obviously, he knew Claire was in the UK. As soon as he received his instructions, in the morning he drove to Mombasa Airport and hired the Tripacer. He told the Veterinary Office he had had word from LMD that there was FMD at Bodhei Holding Ground and he was going to check personally. He loaded the plane up with as much fuel as he dared. He took enough food for three days with two, four gallon plastic jerry-cans of water. He took his rucksack, which could take one of these jerry-cans, his shot gun and some ammunition. He filed a flight plan to Bodhei and took off.

The flight was uneventful and, although the airstrip was rough, Jim had no problems landing. On the way up, Jim had been listening not only to the local Kenyan radio, 'Voice of Kenya', but also the BBC World Service. He therefore knew that the hijacked aircraft was still on the ground in Nairobi and negotiations were in progress. He also heard the hijackers had demanded cash, gold and a helicopter to fly them to an unknown destination. He knew that helicopters did not have a long range and he guessed that the hijackers would not be concerned about any return journey. He therefore reckoned that they would be aiming to land approximately one hundred miles north of Bodhei. Unlike Jim, with his fixed wing airplane, in the helicopter they could land on any of the open areas in the bush. He thought they would be unlikely to land on the main road from Galole to Kolbio but somewhere near so they could use bush tracks to disappear into Somalia, without being caught by either the Kenyan or the Somali army. Jim's orders were specific. He had to use all possible means to prevent the hijackers escaping. His London control had intimated, that the Kenyan authorities would do a deal to let the hijackers go, if there was no loss of life on the VC10 but the British Government did not want to be seen to be dealing with hijackers, or there would be more attempts. Jim guessed that the British Government would have SAS teams on their way but, at that moment in time, he was on his own. If he had miscalculated and the hijackers were aiming for

365

Ethiopia or the Southern Sudan, there was little he could do. He had to just hope his hunch was right.

With this premise in mind, he took off and started patrolling, on grid lines across the area, as if he were counting game animals or cattle as he had done several times before. He was looking for a group of at least two Landrover type vehicles. He thought they would be parked under trees, so he had to be fairly low to see them. He flew for three hours, until the light was failing, before returning to Bodhei. He was lonely when he landed, so he thought he would risk lighting a small fire. If a Somali or Orma tribesman found him, it might be scary but he might get some information of any vehicle movements. The holding ground was actually in Coast Province and was not normally a target for 'shifta'. He slept under the wing of the plane, with his loaded shot gun beside him. He actually slept well for at least eight hours, before he woke an hour before dawn. He ate his standard 'safari' breakfast of banana, cornflakes and UHT milk. He did not relight the fire. He had parked the plane ready for immediate take off and had filled up with most of the fuel so, after doing his preflight checks, he just sat in the cockpit with the door open waiting for the dawn and listening. He heard nothing. It was hardly light when he took off and continued patrolling. He listened to the BBC. He heard that the hijack was over and the hijackers had escaped. It was now solely up to him. Jim transmitted on the veterinary frequency to substantiate his story about FMD. He confirmed that he could not find any cattle at Bodhei and therefore the FMD story was just an idyll rumour. Suleiman, the LO Lamu, came on and asked if Jim could come to Lamu. He had several problems which he hoped Jim could help him with. The reception was poor, but Jim said he might get a chance to fly in. Suleiman said he would send 'Upindi', the larger veterinary boat, to wait at the jetty on Manda Island where the Lamu airstrip was located.

Jim had been airborne for an hour when he got lucky. Two vehicles, going fast with a trail of dust, were going down a track which Jim could see was heading for the Galole/ Kolbio Road. He doubted that they would see him as they were travelling, but he climbed quickly to make it harder for anyone in the vehicles to see him. The Tripacer was so slow that Jim had no problems following them. Near to the road, they stopped near a dried up water pan. Jim flew two miles back towards Somalia and circled in large wide circles. Should he wait and hopefully see the helicopter. They would then certainly see him. No, he decided to land on a straight piece of the track, about four miles from the Landrovers, out of hearing and hope he didn't damage the aircraft. Jim came in with full flap, at little over 50 miles per hour, and landed with hardly a scratch from the low bush beside the road. He was glad of his slow speed, as he had to brake hard as there was a sharp bend in the track, round some much taller bush. He cut the engine and got out. Quickly he ran round the bend towards the Landrovers. It was an ideal ambush spot. The airplane would not be visible until the first driver had turned the bend. Jim took his kit, food and water out of the plane and hid it behind a tree, some 50 yards away. He spread the remaining petrol around the plane in the sand. Breaking open a dozen cartridges, he laid a fuse to the side of the road where he could hide in the bush. He waited. He was not sure if he heard the helicopter but then all was silent.

The wait was agonizing. Had he done the correct thing? At worst he could turn the plane around and take off the other way. When he was airborne he could then locate the vehicles again and maybe the helicopter but how would he then stop them, except by flying the Tripacer straight into the leading Landrover and killing himself? Not a pleasant thought. He thought of Claire, worrying in England. He had not even said goodbye to her.

Then he heard the faint noise of a vehicle. He had two lighters ready in case one didn't light. Suddenly, the vehicle noise got louder. He lit the fuse. The fire raced across the sand. The two Landrovers were coming fast on a sand track, which the drivers knew well. They knew it was clear, as they had already driven down it that morning. The leading Landrover came around the corner. The driver tried to stop but skidded on the sand straight into the Tripacer. The noise of the crash was immediately replaced by the 'boom' of the petrol igniting. The second driver had no chance and skidded into the first Landrover and the blazing inferno. There was a second 'boom', as it too exploded. The thick bush protected Jim, but he was still stunned by the blast. The bush then started burning. He had to run back, almost to his kit, to get out of the heat. He stood, horrified to watch what he had done. He was sure there could have been no survivors.

As the heat became less intense he approached the burnt out shells of the two Landrovers and the Tripacer. The front Landrover contained two Africans and a European in the cab, and the body was full of metal crates. The second Landrover contained three Africans in the cab, and a fourth sitting with more crates in the back. There was nothing Jim could do, so he did not wait for the fire to cool. He obliterated all his tracks and set off in the bush towards the proper road, keeping parallel to the track, so that he did not get lost. He carried his kit, his food and the full water can on his back, in the rucksack. He carried the shot gun in one hand and a quarter full water can in his other hand. It was a heavy load and Jim soon got extremely hot but he knew he was going to need all the water, as he had a long way to go either to Bodhei or to Galole. In less than an hour, he came to the helicopter. The Kenyan pilot was dead having been shot in the head. Jim left the scene, having been careful to remove any trace of his presence. He continued to walk off the track so there were no, easily seen, foot prints. However, it was not long before he arrived at the Kolbio/Galole Road. He turned right to Galole. He expected army vehicles to arrive at anytime, as the fire must have been visible from a considerable distance. Of course, from the ground, the fire might have been thought to have been in Somalia. With the present tension, Kenyan army vehicles would keep well clear of the border areas. He had only been walking on the road for a little over a mile, before he came across a track to his right, heading back to Somalia and a track to his left, heading to Ijara. Although Jim would have been delighted to be picked up by a vehicle, he was reluctant to get involved. His story was going to be that he had had an engine failure in the Tripacer and had to land on the track. He had then walked towards the coast, where he knew he could get help. He would say he had seen the fire from a distance, but did not know its origin and that he had not seen the helicopter and the murdered pilot. He set off for a long hot walk. He drank plenty of water, as that would lighten his load. He ate little as he was too hot to feel hungry. He knew from his map, that he had 40 miles to walk to Ijara. He was not 100% sure, but he thought the Kenyan Army Camp was still there.

Claire's prayers were answered, when she heard Jim reporting about FMD. She hugged herself with joy. He was alive. She was still worried that he would get in a fight with the hijackers, but he had a plane. She hoped he would leave the helicopter well alone. She guessed that his report was total bullshit and was just a cover for his trip. She also heard his conversation with Suleiman. She knew Jim loved Lamu. In fact, he had promised to take her there. So, she hoped that he would fail to find the helicopter and make for Lamu. She decided, after she had reported to London and spoken to Richard, she would pick up the four person SAS crew and make for Lamu.

It was obvious that John David was not happy with the release of the hijackers but he could not blame Claire for that. At least he felt the Firm was doing something, when she told him 'Animal Boy' was patrolling the area in a light airplane. The High Commission was calm. Andrea had been dispatched to Embakasi to pick up Sir Richard. Claire knew it would not last. She knew Richard would be furious with the turn of events, and furious with Christopher Martin-Jenkins for getting involved. Claire was uncertain of his reaction, to finding out that she was a local spy master. Would he be angry that she had deceived him, or would he be proud of her for doing something for her country, rather than just attend coffee mornings and get a tan by the swimming pool? Anyhow, she would soon find out. Claire packed a small bag, ready for her trip to Lamu. She rang up an Air Charter firm and booked a Cherokee Six, to take five people from Wilson to Manda, near Lamu. She got the staff to order her a large taxi for a local journey in the Nairobi area.

Richard arrived at the High Commission. He went straight to his office, waving away Eli who offered him coffee. Claire followed him in and shut the door. He sat behind his desk. Rather than be treated as a junior secretary, Claire sat down in an armchair with her arms in her lap and said nothing. Richard looked at her and suddenly smiled. "I know I am a non-starter in the bedroom but you must admit, I cannot be faulted on my choice of a wife. Not only are you very elegant and attractive, you run this High Commission like a ship's wardroom and you are also the best intelligence officer in Africa. Please bring me up to date with the current crisis." Claire was dumbstruck, but immediately gathered her thoughts and brought Richard up to speed with everything which had happened since he left London. She said, she thought Christopher Martin-Jenkins was a traitor and was now likely to be on his way with the hijackers, together with the bullion and money to Somalia. She had only one operative who could actually do anything and he was totally on his own. She said she was trying to remedy that situation. She said it was not appropriate to divulge any facts to him, as High Commissioner. However, she could tell him that she was proceeding to the area, with help from a small SAS team now in Nairobi, in the guise of tourists. She could also tell him that a very much larger, better equipped, team was on its way from a neighbouring country to the West. She said that she had briefed her controller in London. She said that it was not her place to advise him but that she thought it would be in the interest of Her Majesty's Government, if he could delay any involvement by the Kenyan authorities until she and her teams had assessed the situation on the ground. She would report direct, if she could, to her controller in London who would brief the FO, who would then brief him. If she could not contact London, she would contact him and try to convey information in an oblique manner.

Sir Richard got up from his chair and walked round his desk. He lifted her hands from her lap and looked into her eyes.

"Thank you, Spy Master, for that report. I will implement your advice immediately. Your status here will not be mentioned again. However, as my wife, please take care of yourself. I am beginning to think you are more important to me than my career. I wish you God's speed." Claire was lost for words. She mumbled,

"I will get going. Good Luck. I will send Eli in with your coffee." She went into the hall and spoke to Eli. He surprised her by saying,

"Of course I will take the coffee, 'Memsahib', and organise the commission until you return. Please do not forget that you and Dr Jim are very highly thought of by my clan. You both have many friends in the area, who are happy to help you both. 'Bahati muzuri'." Claire walked down the steps in the bright sunshine, to the waiting taxi, reflecting that her servants probably knew more about the situation than London, her or her husband.

Claire had not rung ahead, but she had no trouble finding the two SAS couples sitting chatting by the swimming pool. She introduced herself and said that, as they had had the courage to continue their holiday in spite of the problems at the airport, the High Commission, as a PR exercise, was going to take them on an airborne safari to a dream island and she was going to be their guide. They all got to

370

their feet and shook hands. The older man who was, Claire guessed, in his early thirties, introduced the other, slightly younger couple as Gordon and Frankie Nelson. He said he was Neil Townsend and his wife was Catherine. Gordon said they were all good friends and thought the troubles at the airport were likely to be hyped up by the Media. They would be delighted to go on an airborne *'safari'*. They were just discussing, over a coffee, what they were going to do with their holiday. Neil summoned a waiter and asked for another coffee, for Claire. Claire told them all that they would be going in a light airplane to Lamu and, if they were happy, she had kept her taxi in the hotel forecourt and they could leave immediately. She said, sadly, that there was not much room for luggage so, if they could just take 10 kg each, she would ask the taxi to take the rest of the luggage back to the High Commission for safe storage. The girls left to go upstairs, to rearrange their packing. Gordon said he would check out and then help the girls with the luggage. Neil said he would finish his coffee with Claire and hear more about the safari.

It was obvious to Claire that Neil was the boss. She took an instant liking to all of them. She thought it was such a shame that she was so worried about Jim, that she could not relax in their company. They all had a job to do so, she had better man up and get on with it. She told Neil that they would fly to Lamu but would be dropped off at the airstrip on Manda. They would then take a boat across to Lamu Island. Jim had romanticised about Lamu, so she knew quite a lot about its geography. She said the four of them would stay at the best hotel on the island, 'Peponi', which was on the Northern tip. She would stay in the very old fashioned hotel in Lamu town, called Petley's Inn. She said a friend would contact her there. Neil was no fool and he immediately realised that it was an agent who would be meeting her. He had been warned, in the UK, that the High Commissioner's wife was involved. He had not thought that she would be so young and attractive, or that she would actually be operating with them. He could tell, by their body language that the rest of the team liked her. They all had imagined she would be a stuck-up, matronly character.

They all chatted like tourists on the way to Wilson, with Claire pointing out some of the sights. The girls were all dressed in various T shirts and shorts, as were the men. Claire was relieved to see they

371

were all wearing sensible, light-weight, walking boots. She guessed that they were not long back from some assignment in a hot country as they were all tanned. They certainly fitted their cover. The pilot of the Cherokee Six, recognised Claire from the High Commission. She remembered his name, Billy, as Jim had described him as a bit of an old Billy goat who, in Jim's words, would raddle anything. Claire smiled inwardly as Billy was well past his prime, with a beer gut and, unless he had a very long penis, would have a job to reach! Billy obviously liked the look of the two girls but, one look at their tough 'husbands', made him behave himself.

There was actually quite a large amount of room in the Cherokee six as, in reality, it could take seven i.e. six passengers and the pilot. Gordon and Frankie sat in the rear seats with the luggage behind them. Claire sat with Catherine in the middle, with the seventh seat folded away and Neil, who mentioned that he was an amateur pilot sat, in the right hand seat next to Billy the pilot. They were soon airborne and heading east, directly to Manda. Neil chatted to Billy about the country and the terrain. Claire realised how clever he was. He sounded like he was just an interested tourist but Claire knew he was getting as much information out of Billy that he could, without actually grilling him. Claire chatted to the other three. She told them what she had told Neil, while they were packing. She longed to know if either of them were an item. Either way, they were good actors. They asked casual questions about the guide they were going to meet in Lamu. Claire could be quite truthful about Jim. All the while, she was just praying he was safe. After an hour or so, Neil persuaded Billy to tune in to 'Voice of Kenya' and then on to the BBC World service. There was very little new news, just that the Kenya government were vigorously tracking down the hijackers but that ALL the hostages on the plane were safe and were either at their hotels or had been met by friends etc. Claire was pretty certain that Richard was putting immense pressure on the Kenya Government, with full backing from London, to allow unspecified British personal to take over. After all, he would argue it was British funds which had been stolen and a British national, in fact his number two, who was still a hostage. Billy actually confirmed that there did not seem to be any air traffic in the area. It was only when they were fifty miles out from Lamu that Billy pointed out the fire, near to the Somali border.

Claire was instantly alert. She leant forward and asked Billy if he could raise the Tripacer 5YAJH on the radio. Naturally there was no reply. Her heart sank. Neil picked up on the vibes, although Billy was oblivious. He suggested they flew over the area, keeping well away from the border. Claire was distraught when it was obvious that there was a burnt out, crashed plane and two Landrovers. Neil also spotted the helicopter. As they continued on to Manda, Billy wanted to radio in the position of the crash and the helicopter but Claire, who was having great difficulty in not breaking down, persuaded him that her husband, the British High Commissioner, should be the first to know. Luckily, Billy was obviously in awe of Sir Richard. He promised not to mention anything on his way home, but to make a full report when he got to Wilson. At Manda, they unloaded their luggage. Billy went off for a pee. Neil said nothing but just squeezed Claire's arm. The others said nothing. Billy returned and said goodbye to them all. Claire said they might well charter him for the return journey in a few days, but they would contact him through the hotel. Claire and Neil set off down the path to the jetty. The others hung back slightly to give them space. With rigid control, Claire told Neil that it was likely to be Jim, a vet who they were planning to meet, who was involved in the crash. She said he had been ordered to stop the hijackers by any means. Her anger stopped her from breaking down.

Claire put on a brave face when she met the veterinary department boatmen. It helped that they held Jim in high regard. It was only a short boat journey to the Government jetty for Lamu town. There Claire got off, saying she would go to the veterinary office and report to the High Commission and book in to Petley's Inn. She would then walk along to their hotel before dark. She asked Neil quietly to report to London and try to find the whereabouts of the Uganda team. The boat took the SAS team on to the Peponi Hotel.

Darky, the proprietor of Petley's, gave Claire a warm welcome. He obviously knew Jim well and said she could have Jim's usual room. Claire left her bag and went the very short walk to the veterinary office. Joseph the clerk greeted her warmly. He too obviously liked Jim. He said there was a twenty minute delay for calls to Nairobi but he would place one immediately. He told Claire that Mr. Suleiman had been worried by Jim's radio message and so he had gone himself to Bodhei, with timber to repair the crush. Joseph said he would send the boat, as soon as it was back to Mkowe, to the jetty on the mainland to pick up Mr. Suleiman. The call came through and Claire was immediately transferred, on his order, to Sir Richard. She explained what she had seen. Sir Richard did not guess how upset she was, but said it sounded as if the hijackers had been stopped and so her man had done well. He said he would report to London. He wished her good luck and rang off. That was too much for Claire and she thanked Joseph and went out into the street, in floods of tears. The next thing she knew, was a very large strong hand gripping her shoulder. It was Leonard Baloala, asking her if he could be of any help. She could not stop herself. She clutched and sobbed into his very clean white shirt.

Leonard, who was destined to climb very high in the Kenyan administration, was no fool. He immediately realised that Claire was in real distress. He had heard, from the game scouts, how this iron girl had stood her ground and held the torch high when the hippo charged. This was no wilting violet. This girl needed his help and she was going to get it. He made out, from her sobs, that there was a light airplane crash near Ijara on the Somali border and Jim, a Kenya civil servant and his friend was involved. He knew very well there was a relationship between Claire and Jim, although they had hidden it very well. He also gathered that Claire was responsible for some 'tourists'.

He immediately sent the DC Lamu's boat to Peponi to pick up the 'tourists' and bring them straight to Mkowe. He came back with Claire into the veterinary office and asked if Joseph would allow the Veterinary boat to take him and Lady Rochester to Mkowe. The boat could then wait there for Mr. Suleiman. Joseph had no problems with that. He said he would also have the small veterinary boat on hand as well at Mkowe, if further water transport was required.

The reason Leonard was in Lamu was that he had been meeting with Stanley Kimani, the DC Lamu. They were friends and neighboring DCs. He sent word with Abdul, the veterinary office messenger, to Stanley to say he would be going home via the northern part of his district to visit the sight of a possible incident and, that he would report back to Stanley when he reached Galole.

They then set off to Mkowe. Claire was now fully back in control of herself and explained the bogus reason for the High Commission helping these 'tourists'. Leonard guessed otherwise but said nothing. He could see the DC's boat bringing them along behind. The DC's boat was faster and they arrived almost together. There was quite a gathering at Mkowe Jetty. Claire was nearly knocked into the water by Dubi as she stepped ashore. He had come in Leonard's Landrover and was delighted to see Claire who he held in very high respect. He wrapped his thin arms around her. Neil and the rest of the SAS team, were very perplexed. Claire hugged Dubi and then made some of the introductions. She had never met Mr. Suleiman so she let Leonard carry on with the further introductions. This included a tall, grey-haired, thin African called Kassim, who had been taking in all the talk concerning the airplane. Kassim gripped both of Claire's hands very firmly and leant towards her and said very quietly, *"Bwana Jim hodari mno hapana kofa* (Dr Jim is a very brave man, he will not die). *"* Claire did not really totally understand but did realise that this old man must worship Jim and, somehow, knew that Jim was special to Claire. If she had not broken down when she saw Leonard, Claire would have been a wreck, with the greetings she had received from Dubi and Kassim, but she had dug deep into her ingrained spirit and she took strength from their presence. It was only later, on the journey in the Landrover, that she remembered Eli's words at the High Commission.

Leonard organised the *'safari'*. His driver, Claire and Leonard were in the front of his Landrover. The SAS team was in the back with Dubi. Suleiman with Kassim drove the Veterinary Department Landrover behind. Suleiman said that there was no need for Leonard to stop at Bodhei as there was no one there, but they had seen that Jim had spent the night there. Suleiman said he would stop at Burgoni, the much larger holding ground, to alert the staff there and to pick up extra stores, as there would be no help on the road or in the area in general. He said he would soon catch them up. He also said that The Kenyan Army had left their camp at Ijara, two months ago. Suleiman said that they should be prepared, as the road deteriorated markedly after Bodhei. The LMD had paid for the road to be graded up to Bodhei but from then on, nothing had been done since his last *'safari'* there, soon after the rains. Suleiman and

Kassim talked about that '*safari*'. They had met Jim many times since then. They knew how resourceful he was. They thought it was very unlikely he had been killed in the crash, but these hijackers were bad men and they might have caused Jim's death.

The fifty mile journey was a grueling experience for everyone, particularly the 'tourists' who, although well trained for desert combat, were not used to Kenyan roads. Catherine and Frankie were not used to being enclosed in the back of a Landrover. Although the very back was open, this was hardly a blessing as it funnelled in the dust. Dubi seemed oblivious to this discomfort. Although Jim always spoke to Dubi in Swahili, his English was quite good. He gave the SAS team a large amount of information. Frankie had been born in India and remembered the conditions of her childhood, especially the heat and the dust. Catherine had only been in the Middle East and the Western Desert, and was affected by the remoteness of the road. The lack of people, with Bodhei being deserted, affected them both. They were glad they had Neil and Gordon. They both guessed that Jim meant a lot to Claire. They both felt sorry for her. They admired her bravery. Dubi had told them about the hippo. The whole team realised Jim must be a pretty tough cookie. They also realised that he must be a born leader, as all the Kenyans seemed to look up to him. They hoped and prayed, for Claire's sake, that he had not been killed. They were brought out of their thoughts when the Landover violently swerved and then swerved from side to side, as it slowed down. They had had a blow out in the outside back tyre. Everyone clambered out. Claire thanked the driver for driving so well and preventing them from rolling over. The driver, whose name was Kofi, beamed with her praise and immediately got out the jack and wheel-brace from under his seat. He gave the wheel-brace to Dubi, who jumped back into the back of the vehicle and started undoing the wheel nuts holding in the spare tyre. Gordon was already lying on his stomach, pushing the jack so that it rested under the axle onto the firm middle track of the road. Leonard thought, '*these are not our normal tourists.*' Catherine was in the back of the Landrover helping Dubi with the heavy spare tyre. She handed the wheel-brace to Neil, so he could loosen the nuts on the punctured tyre, before they started jacking up the vehicle. Claire was offering around cokes, which she had bought in the '*duka*' at Mkowe and which were still coolish, but covered in dust. As soon as Dubi and Catherine were out of the back, with the spare tyre, Kofi started turning the long handle of the jack with Gordon keeping it in place, until the weight of the vehicle held it firmly.

Neil was just tightening up the nuts of the new tyre, when they heard the noise of the Veterinary Landrover. Suleiman and Kassim accepted cokes from Claire. Suleiman announced that he had brought two more extra spare tyres and all the kit and hot patches for repairing further punctures. They set off again, in convoy.

It was dusk when they reached Ijara. The duka, which as far as Claire could see only sold cokes, was still open. Neil bought everyone, including Dubi a coke. Dubi was particularly pleased, as normally he would have been considered a '*toto*' and would not have been included. The Somali '*duka*' owner had no news. Leonard questioned him very carefully about the directions from Ijara to other villages. The main road to Bura, the village across the Tana River from Galole, Leonard's home, was obvious. Apparently there was a track heading South, past the site of the old army camp, back towards the Tana River not far from Garsen. The track, which Leonard was interested in, ran north out of the village towards the Bura/Kolbio road. Leonard knew, from the map, that it was approximately sixty miles long. The '*duka*' owner said that no vehicle had been along it since the Kenyan Army had left. He said that the army had swept it for mines and found none. He did not think there was any likelihood of '*shifta*' planting any, as there were no vehicles passing along it. Leonard was a leader but he also listened to others. He particularly listened to Suleiman's advice. He got Neil to say, on the map, where the crash was likely to have occurred and what he had seen from the plane. Leonard decided they would take the track going northwards, even with the light fading. If they hit the Galole/Kolbio road, without finding the helicopter or the crash, they would have to think again. Everyone was happy with this initial plan.

They set off, with the '*duka*' owner's young son running ahead to show them the correct track out of the village. Dubi ran with him. As soon as Dubi was happy they were on the correct track, the Somali boy left them and ran back to the village. The light was fast fading but Dubi ran on, as he was worried that the small track would not be visible to Kofi. However, Kofi flashed his lights and shouted that he

377

could see the track and therefore Dubi should get back into the Land rover.

As they set off again, Claire lightly touched Leonard's arm and whispered in his ear. "Thank you for being so kind to me and taking all these risks. I am so grateful that you let us carry on tonight." He chuckled and said, so Kofi could hear,

"I have to look after my winning darts team, even if poor Kofi gets turned out of his bed to drive us home." Claire could see Kofi's smile, in the light from the dash board.

There were obviously some seriously big thorns on the track as they had two more punctures but, with everyone's help each time, they soon got going. The second time, Kassim did not help but indicated to Claire that she should walk with him, forward down the track. Neil and the SAS team were apprehensive but did not follow, as everyone else seemed relaxed. After they had gone at least a quarter of a mile Kassim stopped, sniffed and cocked his ear to listen. However, neither of them smelt or heard anything. Kassim said something in Swahili to Leonard on their return. When they were moving again, Leonard translated for Claire. Kassim had said that now he was getting old, young girls had better hearing than him. When he was young he could hear a lion cough two miles away.

Chapter 29

Jim is found

Thursday 16th November 1967

Jim was now exhausted. He still had some food and, actually, at least half the plastic can of water, which was heavy on his back, but he was bone weary. He still did not regret coming on this desolate, narrow track as he knew, deep down, he had the energy to make it to Ijara. Although the road to Galole was much bigger he doubted any help would come that way. He was certain help would come from the Burgoni holding ground. He stopped for a ten minute water stop. He admitted to himself that these were getting more frequent, even though the sun had set now and the air was slowly cooling down. Then he heard the distant noise of an engine. He stood and listened with more concentration. The noise was definitely coming towards him. He had a dilemma, should he hide? No, definitely not. If the vehicle went past him he knew he would never attract their attention from behind. The sound was coming from Ijara. Why should they be enemies? He shouldered his rucksack and kept walking. If he had to run, he needed to take his water with him.

Claire was dozing when Kofi shouted, *"Bwana* Jim *uku kule* (Dr Jim is not far ahead)."* Claire's eyes sprang open and there he was in the headlights. As the vehicle stopped Leonard nimbly got out, letting Claire get out from the middle seat. She was not fast enough. Dubi raced ahead shouting, *"Bwana* Jim. *Habari gnarni. Wewe hapana kufa* (Dr Jim, what is your news, you have not died)."* Dubi wrapped his arms round Jim's waist. Claire had time to collect herself but she knew there was love in Jim's eyes for her. She reached up to kiss him on the cheek. He whispered in her ear, "Animal Boy reporting." Then he kissed her on her lips as her mouth opened with astonishment. They all clustered around him. Leonard, Kofi, Suleiman and Kassim pumped his hand. Kassim was laughing with Jim asking, in Swahili, if he had been looking for cattle or mines. Claire could not share their private joke but, to Neil's amazement, she flung her arms around the old man and said,

"You old bugger you said he would survive." Kassim reached up and stroked her blond hair. Claire then introduced Neil, Gordon, Frankie and Catherine as special tourists. Jim instantly recognized them as British backup. He could really relax now. However, before he spoke he remembered the protocol. He was a Kenya Government Veterinary Officer and Leonard was the DC.

"Sir, I know we are just outside your District but can I make my report to you?" Leonard put him at his ease.

"Of course Jim, please carry on. We are all friends here and we were worried about you." Jim told them what they would find 35 miles away. He apologised to Leonard for disturbing the crime scene but he said he had no equipment to bury the pilot, so he had left him in the helicopter so he would not be eaten by predators. He said, as he was looking for suspect cattle infected with FMD, his Tripacer had suffered an engine failure. He had managed to crash land. He had got his kit and water out of the plane and was just sitting under a tree, when two Landrovers had come racing down the small track at great speed. There had been a multiple collision and both vehicles and the plane had caught fire and exploded. Jim said he was not sure whether they had died from the collision or the fire, but all seven occupants were dead. He had set off walking and that's how he found the helicopter. He had walked on, hoping to get to Burgoni for help. Suleiman chipped in and said the men at Burgoni were always helpful. Would everyone like some food? He even had some cold Cokes hidden at the bottom of the '*Jablo Box*'.

After Jim's tale, the mood was sombre but they were all hungry, so they relaxed and ate leaning against the front Landrover. Claire managed to stand next to Jim. Her hand stroked his thigh when she thought no one could see. After they had eaten, Leonard said he was sorry to cause them trouble, but he had a duty to investigate the two scenes and he felt they should all stick together, as they were in such a remote area.

They all climbed wearily back into the Landrovers. Jim knew Leonard would offer to let him sit next to Claire but, before it was awkward, Jim said he would ride with Suleiman, so they could discuss cattle problems and make good use of the time. Jim suggested they went first, as Jim knew the way to the helicopter. After they had gone several miles, they reached the Galole/Kolbio Road. Then they soon came to the left hand turning and on to the helicopter. It was as Jim had described and Leonard only took a few minutes to look around. They then set off again. The Landrover multiple crash site soon arrived in the headlight beams. Kofi parked next to Suleiman and they both left their lights on. Leonard looked at the bodies and said, although they were charred, he thought one of the three in the front Landrover was a European. He said he thought the boxes would hold all the money and the gold. He said they should be loaded into his Landrover and the Veterinary Landrover. The crashed vehicles had cooled down but it was still a horrendous task. He said they would leave the bodies in the burnt out vehicles, as the crime scene for the Kenyan Police. As it was in Garissa District, he would contact the Garissa DC, to set things in motion, first thing in the morning.

The journey back was a nightmare. With all the boxes, the seating was very cramped. It was a miracle they all got in. They did not stop at Ijara, which was totally dark. They all felt safer when they crossed the border into Lamu District. They had one more puncture but, thanks to Suleiman, they had enough spares so they did not have to actually repair a puncture with a hot-patch in the dark. Things were slightly better when they dropped off all the tyres at Burgoni Holding Ground. When they arrived at Mkowe, the two Veterinary boats and the DCs launch were still there. The faithful boatmen were still on duty. They transferred all the boxes onto the three boats. Kassim lived at Mkowe. He said Dubi could stay with his family, so they said their goodbyes on the jetty. There was no electricity on Lamu Island, except the DC's generator and the generator at Peponi Hotel on the Northern end of the Island. The water front was lit by hurricane lamps provided by the County Council. The only vehicle on the island was the DC's Short Wheel Based (SWB) Landrover. As they were unloading the boxes, Leonard went to the DC's House. Stanley, the DC, soon arrived and said there were no inmates in the jail, which was the Old Portuguese fort. They could use his Landrover to move the boxes to the fort, which was nearby. There were already two 'askaris' on guard but he would double that. The doors of the jail were seriously thick. Everyone felt that they would be safe. Leonard went home with Stanley. They said they would all meet at the DC's office in the morning. Neil and Gordon had obviously been talking together. They elected to stay at Petley's Inn. It was obvious to Jim and Claire that they were going to keep an eye on the crates, just in case. Suleiman said he would go with them to the Inn, which was just nearby. He asked the long suffering boatmen to take Frankie, Catherine, Claire and Jim down to Peponi. The other two boats were moored up.

If they had all not been so tired, the boat journey would have been idyllic. There was no light pollution. The stars were bright and the moon shone. They chatted like real tourists and Jim joked with the boatmen in Swahili. Apparently, they had been employed just as subordinate staff, like garden boys, but Jim had managed to get them re-employed as boatmen and paid a much higher rate, like drivers. For obvious reasons, Jim was a bit of a star. There is no jetty at Peponi. Normally, smart tourists walk down a very precarious plank off the boats onto the sand, without getting their feet wet. That was not for Jim and the girls, who jumped off the boat, up to their waists, into the surf and waded ashore holding, their few belongings above their heads. They shouted, *"kwa heri'* (Goodbye)" to the laughing boatmen, and walked up to the hotel. Suddenly, the hotel was lit up as the generator fired into life. A tall dark figure wearing a fez walked down to meet them. Claire did a double take. How had Eli got here? The figure laughed at her surprise and said.

"Welcome to Peponi. I am Elisha, Eli's brother. I hope you will be comfortable here."

Jim said, "These are friends from England. How is your family in Wajir?"

"They are all well *Bwana* Jim. I am sure my father would send his *salaams,* he thinks the camel is in-calf. I have kept some soup hot and we have bread, butter and cheese. Of course we have a large selection of fruit. Why not sit and have some food and a beer on the patio. Don't worry about your wet clothes, the chairs are wood and the cushions easily washed. Where are the other two '*Bwanas*'? We have four double rooms and no other quests."

"They have stayed at Petley's. They wanted to see the only upstairs long-drop in the world," replied Jim.

"It won't be quite as good without your illumination," laughed Elisha.

Of course, while they drank their beers, Jim had to tell the girls how he had dropped his torch down the long-drop, when he was having a crap in the middle of the night and it had landed, light up, in the muck at the bottom of the long-drop. Apparently, it had shone for the next twelve hours and had been viewed by most of the populous. Although it was a wonderful view over the shore and the sea, they did not spend long on their supper. Jim and Claire got up and walked to the edge of the patio and gazed at the ocean. Frankie and Catherine saw they were holding hands. They thanked Elisha for the supper and said they were good friends, so they would share a room. They said they thought Jim and Claire were also friends and would share. Elisha said that there was hot water and he would leave the generator going for another half an hour, so they could wash. He said there were candles and matches in the rooms. He asked if they would like tea in the morning. They all said they would.

They went to their rooms, each of which had its own verandah at the front, and a bathroom at the back. As Frankie climbed into her bed, she said to Catherine,

"This bloody beats anything Hereford has to offer." They were both instantly asleep, as not only had they had one hell of a day but they had spent the previous night on the VC10.

Jim had the first shower. He was truly filthy. He was washing his hair for the third time, when he realised Claire was standing naked, just gazing at him. She came into his arms and sobbed quietly.

"I thought you were dead, it was the most horrible day in my life." Jim said nothing but slowly shampooed her hair. He repeated the procedure three times. He kissed her on the forehead and started to wash her body. Claire lifted her arms above her head and opened her legs. Taking the soap, she looked into his eyes and washed his body. Then the lights went out. They both laughed and were initially quite blind. The water continued to run down their bodies. Their eyes slowly adjusted. Claire said,

"Bugger it, we are going to have filthy towels and sheets but I can't worry about it. I can't worry what Frankie and Catherine think, or what Elisha thinks. You are alive and I love you."

"Claire, if I have thought about you once today, I have thought about you a thousand times. I love you with all my heart. Let's try and dry ourselves in the dark and crawl into one of those small beds and cuddle until dawn." That's what they did and were rapidly asleep. However it was long before dawn when Jim woke, to feel Claire rolling him on to his back. She whispered, as she moved on top of him and straddled him with her legs wide apart,

"I woke to feel that rock hard cock of yours up my back. I felt, what a waste, I want him inside me. I am wet enough so he will slip inside and then we can go to sleep again." Claire kissed Jim's neck as she felt him enter her. Normally, there was no way that they could sleep like that but they were both so tired that they fell asleep again. They awoke to hear Elisha calling,

"*'Hodi. Chai tiara'* (Can I come in tea is ready)?" Jim answered, "*Asanti sana Elisha watcha uku* (Thank you very much Elisha. Can you leave it there)?" Jim was still inside Claire. Very quietly, she bent her legs and sat up on top of him. Then she moved her pelvis quietly forward and back all the time rubbing herself above her vulva. Jim grasped her bottom to help her. She could see, by the look on his face, that he was about to ejaculate. Somehow that stimulated her, and she felt her vagina and abdominal muscles tense. She leant forward and kissed him, as he thrust hard upwards. They kept kissing as their breathing came back to normal. Claire moved her body up Jim's body and she felt his semen pouring out of her, on to his tummy. She whispered,

"Lie still and I will get a flannel to clean you up. I love you." Soon they were clean and wrapped in *'kikois'*. Claire's, around her body and Jim's around his waist. They were sitting drinking tea when Frankie and Catherine came onto their veranda.

"Those wraps are both pretty and useful. Can you get them in Kenya?" asked Frankie.

"Yes, all over, but the best selection is on the coast," replied Claire.

"I am sure they are available in Lamu town," said Jim. "We will take you into the market." Elisha had come onto the verandah with a breakfast tray.

"There is no need to go into the hot town. I will ask two ladies to bring a selection here for you, so you can look at them at your leisure. They will compete against each other, so you will get a good price, provided you remember to haggle. '*Memsahib*', I have taken the liberty of booking a call to the High Commission. Eli is on the other end. He is enquiring if he should he call Sir Richard? "

"Yes of course, thank you, Elisha. I had totally forgotten. I will come with you." Poor Claire thought Jim. They had not really discussed anything. He had not told her exactly what had happened. However thank goodness Elisha had rung. It was better to get it over with. Claire was also worried. She should have rung last night but, she was so pleased that Jim was alive that logical thought had escaped her.

Claire stood next to Elisha as he asked Eli, his brother, to transfer the call to Sir Richard, as Lady Rochester would like to speak directly to him. There was a click and Sir Richard asked, as if they were having coffee in the drawing room.

"How are you my dear? Have you made any progress? I hope the lack of interference has been helpful? There is nothing much in the papers, except a possible sighting of a plane crash in Garissa District. This was made by the pilot who flew you up to Lamu. Eli did ascertain that you and the tourists arrived safely." Like Richard, Claire was well aware that half of Lamu and anyone in Nairobi were listening in on the conversation.

"The tourists are fine. We have retrieved the British packages. The sad thing is that the Kenyan helicopter pilot was murdered by the hijackers. CMJ was killed in the road crash, which involved two Landrovers and a light aircraft, which was parked having made an emergency landing on the track after engine failure. The pilot had left his aircraft and was walking for help, when we picked him up. The British packages are safe here with me. Any British help to remove them would be useful. They require two Long Wheel Base Landrovers (LWBs)."

"Well done, My Dear that is excellent. If you don't mind looking after the tourists and the packages in the meantime, I will arrange their collection. I look forward to your return."

Once again, Claire was surprised by her husband. She supposed she would have left him long ago, if he had not been kind and extremely intelligent and perceptive. She turned to find Elisha. She realised like Eli, he was also was very well informed and perceptive.

"That was very thoughtful of you to make that call Elisha. I am very grateful." With a totally blank expression, Elisha replied

"Not at all '*Memsahib*'. I knew you were tired and had other things on your mind. I expect you would like a cooked breakfast."

"As always, you are right Elisha! Yes I was preoccupied and I would like a big breakfast. Also, like your brother Eli, you have earned the right to laugh at me on special occasions." Elisha's face cracked into a smile as he replied,

"I hope there are many special occasions. However, there will be no smiles if I forget to send Pawpaws and special Lamu Mangos home with you, for Sir Richard's breakfast. Eli is my elder brother and his orders are to be obeyed." Claire was pretty certain he winked at her but, of course, that might have been a grain of sand in his eye.

Claire returned to the veranda, where Jim and the girls were tucking into breakfast. Jim said, "Elisha is keeping your breakfast hot."

"I am sure he will bring it soon," said Claire, "I am bloody starving."

Frankie said. "Before I met you, Claire, I thought you would be a stuck up bitch. I am so sorry, I was so wrong, you are so normal and so special in some ways."

Claire laughed as she replied, "Well, that is better than Jim who said he expected me to have buck teeth and a massive bosom. Then, he looked down the front of my dress and said my tits were too small!" Jim went bright red. "I am glad you don't try and deny it," went on Claire, "You went just as red then, if I remember correctly."

Both Catherine and Frankie were laughing now. Catherine, with a smirk said,

"You had better check us out Jim, before we buy '*kikois*'. Have we got time for a swim Claire?"

"Of course you have all the time in the world. Jim and I will walk along to the town and relieve Neil and Gordon, and send them back for a swim. I have no idea when, but I think some more tourists will be arriving from Uganda. Then you will all have a long '*safari*', with the boxes from the jail. Hopefully, you will see plenty of game. I think there had been too much happening in the area, for you to see anything yesterday."

Jim chipped in, "Sadly, you don't see much in the area we were in. Could you come out for a longer holiday soon? Claire could meet you in Nairobi and then you would see masses, coming down through Tsavo to stay with me." Claire stood up and ruffled Jim's hair.

"That's unlike you, Jim, to invite two girls to stay without checking their tits for size." They all laughed. Jim said. "Come on, Lady Rochester, you had better get some clothes on before we go into town. They may not be very strict but they are Moslems.

Suleiman had anticipated their needs and, as they were dressing, Jim heard the chug of 'Upindi', the Big Veterinary Boat, drawing round the headland. He shouted to Claire to only wear bikini bottoms and a shirt, but to carry her *'kikoi'* and shoes. She playful punched him as she joined him on the veranda, saying,

"I thought it was girls who changed their minds. First you want me to be dressed respectfully, now you want me in a skimpy bikini bottom." With that she jumped on his back and said,

"You can carry me to the boat." Catherine, Frankie and the boatmen laughed as Jim got his shorts wet, carrying Claire through the waves.

Leonard, Stanley, Neil and Gordon were on the jetty talking, as they arrived. They all greeted each other before Stanley took the lead. "Leonard needs to return to his base in Galole, and so my boat will take him to Mkowe now. We all agree that the boxes will be safest in Lamu Fort, in the short term." Claire agreed, and said she thought the High Commission was making arrangements for their collection but, as yet, she did not know when. She thanked Stanley for his help. She suggested that Neil and Gordon went to the hotel in 'Upindi' and relaxed as special tourists, as they must be tired. Leonard and Stanley smiled, but they obviously knew differently. She said that she would use the Veterinary Office phone and Jim also said he needed to phone, as he had missed his normal radio call this morning.

Jim and Claire walked with Leonard to the DC's boat. Claire said, "We owe you a very big thank you, Leonard."

"Think no more of it," replied Lenard. "Just make sure you are not too long before you come and see me again." Claire hugged him and Jim shook him firmly by the hand. They waved to him as the launch moved off. Claire shouted,

"Give Dubi a hug from me." Leonard shouted back.

"Have no fear, I will look after him."

There were lots of people who wanted to see Jim, at the Veterinary Office. Claire sat in the relatively cool interior of Suleiman's office, for a phone call to the High Commission. She watched Jim through the open door. It was all she could do, to stop herself running out and hugging him. Eventually, the call came through. It was Cynthia, who obviously felt she was very grand acting for Sir Richard. She said he was in a meeting. He had left word that the transport for the packages would arrive at Mkowe tomorrow, around 10.00 am. Would Claire arrange boat transport to pick up six more special tourists? They would come over to the island and help bring the packages to the mainland. Then, all the special tourists would leave. In case of delay, Cynthia said that she had been instructed to book a charter flight on the day after tomorrow, to bring Claire back to Nairobi Wilson via Mombasa. She hoped all would go well. Then she rang off.

Everything stopped at noon on Lamu, for a two hour lunch break. Rather than use 'Upindi', Jim and Claire said they would walk along the shore. Suleiman said he thought they were mad, in the heat, but wished them well. He said he would have both boats ready in the morning, waiting at Mkowe.

Jim and Claire walked along the water front and then onto the sand. When they were some distance away, they reached for each other's hand. Claire asked, "When did you realise I was Colin Shaw your control?"

Jim replied, "I had an idea, that first night at the High Commission, you seemed to know too much about me. I thought, if my control was a man, he would have made his presence obvious to me right away. Your official instructions, after we had met, always contained phases like, 'take care'. A man would never say that. So I love you, Claire or Colin, or whoever you are." She squeezed his hand harder.

"What actually happened to the Tripacer?" Claire asked. Jim told her. Claire laughed, "I knew you would take risks, as soon as John David said in London, he had instructed you over my head. I was so worried, upset and angry, that I said to him 'fuck you'. It is a miracle that he didn't give me the sack. He didn't and, in fact, managed to get me out here by fighter jet, so that I could take charge. Richard now knows that I am the High Commission 'Spy Master' but we will never mention it, as he has to take a 'holier than thou' stance. I am sure he does not know you and I are lovers, but Eli at the High Commission does know and, of course his brother Elisha. The 'tourists' have all guessed, together with Leonard of course. However, my love, they all hold you in very high regard and, somehow, they seem to like me, so I think it will remain under wraps. That Kassim is a wise old buzzard, he knew we were lovers. He would give his life for you." Jim mumbled, "I would for him."

"I think he knows that all right. Now let's forget about the recent past and have a fun afternoon on the beach with our tourists. Both of the girls have great tits, so you will be happy!"

"I only have eyes for you."

Claire punched him playfully. "You bloody liar, Jim Scott."

It did turn out to be a fun afternoon but not quite as Jim had expected. They borrowed a beach volley ball set and walked east along the deserted beach. They set it up between two trees and were having a great game, boys versus girls. Claire and Jim now knew that, in fact, they were not couples. They played their parts well and were obviously good friends. They were probably better friends after their experiences. The game was soon interrupted by the shouts of a little Arab boy, running down the beach from the hotel shouting, "*Bwana*' Jim, come quickly, the donkey has fallen down the well." Grabbing their shirts and '*kikois*' the six of them ran with the little boy, called Abraham, off the beach into the interior of the island. It was a hot, strenuous run. They were all fit but they were all sweating well, by the time they reached Abraham's home. He was unaffected, and looked as if he had just had a quiet walk on the beach.

The donkey was indeed in the well. No one knew how it had happened, but his back end and chest were in the well. His head and fore-legs were sticking out. He did not seem in pain and, in fact, looked rather comical. Abraham's mother and sisters were standing round looking anxious. Their heads were covered but they were not wearing veils. Jim thought they would not be concerned by the presence of three men or by the girls, who were fairly well covered

389

by T shirts and '*kikois*'. There was no solid structure above the well. Obviously, they drew water by just throwing down a bucket on a rope. Jim asked if he could borrow the rope. He asked Abraham to see if he could get some more. Abraham and his sisters spoke quite good English but Jim used Swahili to talk to Abraham's mother. Jim asked her if she had any old cloths which they could wrap around the rope as padding. Jim described his plan to the others. They would prepare a giant tripod over the well, with some wooden beams which were beside the house, obviously intended for a future enlargement. Then they would place a padded, wrapped, double rope under the donkey's backside. Then they would be able to pull vertically. Jim realised that, just pulling on the donkey's head and front legs would help, but would not be sufficient and might hurt the animal.

The donkey was amazing as it just sat there, while they constructed a tripod above it, and managed to get the padded rope under its bottom. With all the noise, many neighbours had arrived, to see what all the fuss was about. Jim managed to get all the help organized, so there was the right number of people on each rope. The majority of the helpers were women and older children. On Jim's command, they all started to pull - particularly the 'tourists'. It was not only the 'tourists' who dispensed with the '*kikois*' to cover themselves, but the villagers lent into the task and head cover was forgotten. Jim had put on the donkey's head collar and, now that its chest was out of the well, he started to pull horizontally. Suddenly, the donkey became free. Jim gave a large pull on the head collar, slipped back on the sand and the donkey fell on top of him. Claire was aghast and ran forward to him. Jim shouted,

"I am fine but please be careful of its legs. I will just wriggle out from under it." The donkey, mercifully, just lay still, getting its breath back, as Claire, with Neil's help, pulled Jim free. No one was hurt and the donkey, as if it understood the problem, lay still until all the ropes were clear. It then got onto its front legs and kicked up with its hind legs and stood up. The villagers gave a cheer. The donkey was a little wobbly but it was soon eating the cut grass it was being offered by the children.

Abraham's mother led Jim, as team leader, into her house. He was given a cup of sweet African tea, which actually was very welcome. The circus was over. The villagers drifted away and the six '*wazungu*' said their goodbyes, to much gratitude from Abraham' mother. Abraham led them along a track, which was the quickest way to 'Peponi Hotel'. He said he would bring the volley ball stuff to the hotel.

At the hotel there was a discussion about the sleeping arrangements. Catherine and Frankie insisted it was their turn to stay at Petley's. However, Neil thought that word about the gold might now have got around, and so he suggested all four of the 'tourists' stayed in Lamu town. Jim offered to come as well but Neil said there was absolutely no need. After some tea and fruit, the four 'tourists' walked into Lamu along the sand, leaving Jim and Claire alone. There was little point in them sleeping in separate rooms as they had shared the previous night so, after an early, supper they were soon in bed. There did not seem to be any mosquitoes, so they did not bother with nets but let the sea breeze cool them. Their love making was gentle but no less thrilling. They made the most of the night together, before their planned separation on the following day. Just before they went to sleep, when Jim had his head laid on Claire's breast, she said,

"This reminds me of when you had malaria. I suddenly felt all maternal. I am sorry, I must be over tired." She started to cry. "I was so worried you were going to die." Jim gently kissed her wet cheeks. He stoked her hair until he felt her drop off to sleep.

Chapter 30

Skinny dipping

Friday 22nd December 1967

Jim and Claire had not been able to meet since the hijacking. They were both desperate to see each other but it was difficult, as Claire was rather in the spot light. They knew that they would be apart at Christmas. Then Jim's parents were coming out to see him, which would certainly restrict their movements. Claire could not face separation for any longer and so, on an excuse of coming down to see Grace Middleton, she got a commercial flight down to Mombasa. She got a taxi from the airport to Jim's house and arrived before he got home from work. She was a bag of nerves in the taxi. *'What if he had friends coming for supper? Even worse, what if another girl was coming on a date?'* Claire was so relieved, when Katana told her Jim was due home for supper on his own. Claire had learnt a lot more *'Swahili'*, so she got quite a bit of news from Katana, who was normally very taciturn but obviously warmed to Claire's pleasure at seeing him again. They had a close bond after Jim's malarial attack. Katana said Jim might be home at 4.30 pm but more likely would go and have a water-ski, but he would certainly return before dark.

Claire sat having a cup of tea, on the upstairs verandah. She still had butterflies. *'What if he met a girl at the water ski club and brought her home? Why should she expect him to be on his own?'* She heard the Landrover and totally lost he nerve. She hid in his bedroom. Then she heard voices and a rush of footsteps on the stairs. She was in his arms and all her fears were gone.

They had a quiet meal at Jim's house, on the upstairs veranda, and were drinking cups of coffee, when Claire said,

"Let's go for a walk on the beach in the moon light." Jim's dog, Lucy, was asleep in the Landrover so they took her with them. They went over the Nyali Bridge up onto the North Coast. Jim knew a track down to the beach.

They parked the Landrover among some coconut palms, facing the silver expanse of the beach. The surf of the ocean could be seen breaking out on the reef, which fluoresced in the moonlight. They left Lucy to guard the Landrover and walked, bare foot, and hand in hand, down to the water's edge. They kissed passionately, with their feet in the surf. Claire lifted Jim's shirt over his head and buried her face in his chest kissing him all the time. Jim, in turn, lifted Claire's dress over her head and turned his attention to kissing the tops of her breasts, before reaching behind her to unclip her bra. Claire arched her breasts towards him, to be kissed. She moaned softly and then hopped up, with her arms around his neck, and her legs around his waist. Jim walked up the beach and let her down on the dry sand. She kissed him again as she undid his shorts. Then, Claire stepped out of her pants before hopping up on him again. Her legs held him like a vice around his waist and she hugged his neck with her arms. Jim's hands held her bottom and moved her up and down. Removing one hand from behind his neck, Claire felt under her thigh for his penis and carefully pushed inside her. Jim thrust gently and felt is penis going deeper and deeper. Claire whispered into his ear. "I feel so ready and wide open for you but you can't hold me up for long. Come, my love, come." It was all too much for Jim and he had an orgasm with one more thrust. His knees started knocking but somehow he managed to keep holding Claire's bottom, as she kept kissing him. At last he felt his shrivelled penis fall out of her. With a sigh, Claire let her legs fall from his waist and drop to the ground. Claire said "That was marvellous. I don't know how you have the strength?"

Jim said "Let's go skinny dipping?" They left their clothes in a small pile, ten yards above the high water mark and walked, hand in hand, down to the water. Claire's white breasts seem to glow in the moonlight. Jim and Claire kept stopping to kiss. Soon they were up to their knees in the water, which was surprisingly cold. "Cuddle me tightly," said Claire. "I have got goose bumps." Jim held her gently, rubbing his hands up and down her back, as they kissed.

"Come on, I feel braver now," said Claire as she broke away from him and ran splashing into the water. She dived into the water and

Jim got a glimpse of a little white bottom in the moonlight. He ran after her and dived. The water felt wonderful against his body. It was great having no clothes on. Jim swam out deeper. He jerked with alarm, as he felt something grasp his penis and testicles. As he spluttered he could hear Claire's giggling.

"A little fish nearly bit off your 'willy', but it let go to try and find a bigger mouthful." Claire laughed. Jim grabbed her.

"I have found bigger mouthfuls," said Jim squeezing her bottom. Jim still had his feet on the sand as Claire clung to him, not only with her arms around his neck, but also her legs around his waist. Once again Claire reached down below Jim's thigh to grab his penis. She whispered into Jim's ear,

"Poor little willy, that fish or the cold water has given him a real fright. Let's get out. He will be all salty and I want to give him a suck and say I am sorry for frightening him."

"I won't quarrel with that," said Jim. He carried her out of the water and laid her down on the wet sand. He knelt with his knees either side of her shoulders. She reached up with her mouth and started to suck his penis. She drew away and giggled.

"It is a bit like sucking a hard boiled, salted, quail's egg." She then sucked some more. He started to groan. Claire said.

"Jim, please come for me, in my mouth, I want to taste you." She kept sucking and then Jim ejaculated. He flopped forward on to his outstretched hands and then rolled off her. She slid up him and started to kiss him again. Jim could taste salt and his own semen. He was surprised it was not that unpleasant. He asked, "Have you ever done that before?"

Claire said. "No, but I might like to do it again, you sexy animal."

They walked back into the water, to wash off all the sand. "I think the tide has gone out while we were having fun. I wonder where our clothes are?" said Jim. "I remember they were in a line directly in front of the Landrover. I can't see them anywhere."

"Neither can I." said Claire.

"Don't worry, I will walk up and let Lucy out of the Landrover. She will find them quick enough." However Lucy could not find them. She kept coming back to a spot directly in line with the Landrover. There were plenty of foot marks but no clothes.

"Well, I'm buggered." said Jim. "Someone has stolen them."
Claire hugged him.

"It is rather spooky," said Claire. "To think someone was watching us."

"I imagine they picked them up and scarpered pretty quickly. Thank goodness I left the keys and my wallet in the Landrover. Did you have any money on you?"

"Occasionally I put a twenty shilling note in my knickers, for emergencies," said Claire. "But I didn't tonight."

"I must remember that," said Jim. "When I am strapped for cash I will put my hand in your knickers."

Claire kissed him and whispered, "You are welcome anytime, but now we had better get home before anyone catches us, stark naked, wearing satisfied smiles."

All they had in the Landrover was some tools, veterinary gear and Lucy's old very smelly blanket. Claire was not impressed.

"Put the blanket in the passenger foot-well and lie down with your head in my lap. If we have to stop and someone is going to look in, you will have to grab the blanket and cover yourself," said Jim.

"Oh no, you sex maniac don't, even ask. I am not giving you a blow job covered in that filthy blanket," said Claire.

"I will just sit up and look the person in the eye and say I got a little hot! Bloody hell, I will have a job living that down at the Muthaiga Club."

As it was, although they passed several cars going home, none of them could have a good look into the Landrover. Jim parked, as near to the door of the house as possible, and then they both slipped inside. They had a good shower. Claire walked into the bedroom. Jim shaved his face, in the mirror above the basin, before joining her.

"Now Romeo, look what I have just tripped over?" It was the length of rope Jim had meant to take, a month ago to the 'Chini Club' to help Claire get into the water.

"It is payback time for covering me in a filthy dog blanket, compared to silk wrap, which I am used to" said Claire with a wicked grin.

"On your back on the bed, you rogue". Jim could hardly resist an order like that from a beautiful naked girl. Claire was instantly on top of Jim, straddling him, and tied his left wrist pretty tight to the bed

395

post. He could feel her pubic hair tickling his tummy. He tried to reach up and kiss her breast.

"Oh, no you don't. You wait until you have your orders". His right wrist was quickly tied to the other bed post. Claire was left with a very long loop of rope. She leant forward to push it all over the top of the bedstead. Jim brought up his knees and tried to push his now erect penis into her. Quick as a flash, she grabbed his balls really quite hard.

"Do as you are told, slave, lie still!" She was quickly under the bed bringing the rope under the foot end of the bed and tied his left leg to the corner post. Jim just giggled as she tied his right leg to the other corner. He was now helpless. His penis was back erect again, having suffered no ill effects from his balls being squeezed.

"You just lie there while I get myself a cold drink from downstairs. That was hot work," said Claire, as she disappeared out of the door. She was soon back in the bedroom with a pint glass of water and ice.

"Now, let's see if that little chap wants a suck?" She then straddled Jim again, but this time with her pretty erotic bottom towards him. He craned his neck up to lick her.

"Not yet, you eager beaver licker, there will be plenty of time for that soon," said Claire as she straightened her knees slightly, to move out of his reach. She reached round behind her to the bedside table.

"Just need a little drink before I get sucking," said Claire. So she was going to suck me off what bliss, thought Jim.

"Wow, bloody hell" Claire had sucked some ice and then had immediately sucked his penis into her freezing cold mouth.

"Oh dear, he has gone all small. I don't think he will be much good, so you will have to use your tongue." Claire turned right round and brought her thighs up beside Jim's ears. He could smell her sex. God he wanted her, even if his penis had had a nasty shock. He did what he was told and licked, as Claire rocked forward holding on to the bed head.

"You are bloody good at that, my darling. Sorry I am such a tease, but you are so innocent in some ways but I love you for all that". She reached behind her and gently squeezed his penis, which was waking up fast. He licked her tiny, sensitive clitoris. He kissed her thighs. He brought up his smooth chin and rubbed her with some pressure. She was breathing hard now and getting really excited. He pushed his tongue as far, and as hard as he could into her. She pushed back towards him. They pushed in and out in rhythm. Jim felt the muscles in her thighs push hard against the sides of his face. He pushed one last time and she collapsed on top of him gasping, "Yes, yes, yes". Her smell excited him. She slid down him so she could kiss him. Her taste seemed to inflame them both, as they kissed passionately. As she had slid down Jim, she had pushed his erect penis up between her legs. She was so wide open, that he only had to push up with his pelvis and he entered her. She kissed him madly and ground her pelvis into him. He could not stop himself from thrusting up into her. She moved her mouth from his and said,

"Push harder. That is wonderful you feel so deep inside me." Jim gave a gasp and convulsed with ecstasy. They were both sobbing, as she totally collapsed on top of him. It was bliss for them. It took several minutes for their breathing to come back to normal and Jim felt his penis shrivel and slip out of her. Claire whispered in his ear,

"I love you so much. You may not have the biggest prick in the world and you come so very quickly, but I know you will be back for more in no time. In fact, I think I can feel him already". She slithered down the bed and kissed his penis and then started to suck it. It was quite remarkable. It started to swell again. Claire stopped sucking and sat up.

"Well, my darling, you are still my slave you know."

"You have got the most marvellous tits. Can I suck them?"

"Flattery will get you everywhere," said Claire as she bend forward so that her breasts were near his mouth. The tips of her nipples were hard, as he kissed and then sucked them gently.

"You are teasing me. Suck harder." Jim continued to suck very gently.

"So slave, you are being very disobedient. I will have to tease you in return." Claire sat up and then twisted around, so she was facing the foot of the bed. She then moved down with her legs outside of his legs so she was just above his now erect penis. Her hands grasped the rail at the foot of the bed. She then lowered her bottom slowly so he could just see and feel his penis entering her. She stopped and raised her bottom up, so the tip of his penis was not touching her. Jim strained upwards but she just kept out of reach. Then she just touched his penis again allowing it to enter but, before he could enjoy the sensation she raised her bottom up. Claire had Jim at her mercy. She just kept stimulating him but never letting him thrust home. Jim was breathing hard and getting, not only very excited, but very frustrated.

"Is it nice being teased?" Claire mocked him. He was so stimulated that he begged, "Please let me enter you".

"That's what I wanted to hear. Of course you can, my darling, I am going to give you the ride of your life." With that she lowered herself again and this time let her whole weight rest on him. Jim gasped

"I have never felt so deep inside you. I am in ecstasy". She slowly and rhythmically moved her bottom up and down and also forward and backwards. She was leaning forward, so there was pressure from the bottom of his penis on her clitoris. Claire moved faster, so she was panting. He could see her beautiful bottom undulating. He tried to stop ejaculating but suddenly he felt her muscles tightening and he could not hold out any longer. His spasms seemed to rock them both. Somehow, Claire managed to untie him and they cuddled together, until their breathing subsided. In seconds they were asleep.

They woke together, with the sun streaming in the windows. Claire kissed him and whispered,

"That was the most marvellous night! We must go skinny dipping again if it leads to that!"

It was Saturday morning. Jim did not need to go into the Veterinary Office, as he had organized a flying trip to see some cattle, owned by villagers on the Tanzanian border, which were reported to be dying. After he had visited them he was going to fly Claire back to Nairobi.

They both were a little sad, as Claire was leaving the coast again and going back up country but they were determined to enjoy the little time together. Much to Katana's amusement, Claire hugged him as she said goodbye. They left Lucy with him and went in Jim's Landrover up to Mombasa Airport. Jim had managed to hire a Cherokee 180, so they covered the ground much quicker than in the old Tripacer. As soon as they were clear of the airport, they set a course slightly north of east. They could see the hill called Kasigau, which rose up five thousand feet above the dry hot plain. Jim encouraged Claire to fly and got her to aim for Kasigau. He loved watching her concentrating on keeping on course and keeping the plane level. He stroked her thigh. Claire did not look at him but said,

"Mmm, that's nice. You will have to stop as I just can't concentrate."

They flew within a hundred feet of Kasigau and kept on the same heading. The ground was bare below them. They were too high to see any plains game and there did not seem to be any elephants. They came abreast of Taita Hills and then Jim could see Lake Jipe, on their left. Claire said, "You take control, I am knackered with all the concentration. You hardly have to concentrate. I will have to fly more and then I will get better."

Soon they saw the wide '*murram*' road heading for Taveta and the Tanzanian border. Then they saw the railway and immediately the Taveta airstrip. They lost some height and joined the circuit downwind. Although Jim called on the radio, there was no other traffic. They landed into the wind, which was blowing at ten knots from the east. As planned the LO Taita, Louis Mbeya, was at the strip to greet them. Jim introduced Claire and took his small sample and post mortem bag with him, out of the plane. It was hot but not as hot or humid as Mombasa. Louis took them on a small dirt road northwards, which ran parallel to the Tanzanian border. They came to the village of Chala and then followed the Lumi River up to a cattle dip and cattle pens, where they met the villagers who had lost some cattle in the last few days. There were two sick animals for Jim to see. Both of them had high temperatures and swollen lymph glands. Jim was certain that they had ECF but he took samples, just to make sure. He gave these to Louis and asked him to check them back at the Wundanyi Veterinary Office. Sadly, he told the villagers that there was no treatment. He suggested, as the disease was not contagious to man, they killed the animals to eat them. Jim thought, '*at least they won't suffer any more and the villagers will get something out of the disaster.*' Jim took a sample of the dip, which he asked Louis to send off to Kabete. He also suggested that they empty and clean out the dip. Then he suggested that they refill it with dip at the correct strength. He told them all that the deaths would continue for up to three weeks but after that they would then stop. It was a sad scenario but also so very common, in areas where there was the 'Brown Ear Tick', which spread the disease of ECF.

At the village of Chala, they stopped to buy some cold cokes. Louis was reluctant to leave them but Jim said they were going to go exploring on foot, and that Louis must go and enjoy his weekend. Louis had to return to Wundanyi by road, which would take him at least an hour and a half. After they had said goodbye, Claire and Jim set off to walk up the extinct volcano, near the village. There was a good track but it was a steep, hard climb. Jim had brought plenty of water which they kept drinking, although the water was warm. They did not see anyone, so they both soon unbuttoned their shirts. Claire took off her bra. They kissed but it was too hot to cuddle. At last they made it to the crater's edge. It was a spectacular view. The crater walls were a bright green with actively growing bush and, in the middle, was a blue lake. The path went down into the bush. It was still a good track and they followed it eagerly downwards. Very soon they were at the lake's edge. They could now see why there was a track, as there was a small wooden hut which contained a pump. There was a pipe running directly up to the craters edge. Obviously, this was Chala's water supply.

"I feel bit guilty," said Jim. "This is the water supply but I think we can have a swim if we get away from this pump. There is a massive dilution factor so I don't think we will really pollute the water." They clambered round the lake shore, which was clear of bush but was very rocky with lava boulders. After they had come about two hundred yards, they came to a big boulder of larva jutting out into the lake. Behind it, they could not be seen from the place where the pump was. The bush hid them from the crater's edge.

"We must not swim too far out or we will be visible from the top," said Jim.

"That's fine," said Claire. "I will stay near the edge and skinny dip, like last night. It will be so cool and refreshing."

It was heavenly. They crept out of the water to a spot, where they were sure they could not be seen. Jim sat on his rucksack and Claire sat astride his legs, facing him.

"Your tan marks are so sexy." They kissed and Claire pushed her pubis hard up against his erect penis. Jim started fondling and kissing her breasts.

400

"I can just feel the underside of your penis against my clitoris," whispered Claire into Jim's ear. "Can I move like this? It feels so good. It is just in the right spot."

"Just knowing it is good for you, makes it lovely for me."

Jim sat still and continued to suck her breasts as Claire moved just a couple of inches up and down. After a couple of minutes of panting, Claire sighed and flopped against him.

"Did you come?" asked Jim.

"Oh yes," replied Claire. "I feel all lovely and weak. I think the exertion of the climb has taken all my strength."

After ten minutes Jim started to get cramp in his legs. Claire was still, weak as a kitten but, with his help, managed to stand up. He carried her carefully into the cool water. Eventually they came out and got dressed. Then, hand in hand, they clambered round the shore until they arrived back to the pump. Claire leant against Jim.

"My love, I don't know how I am going to manage to get up to the top?"

Jim gave her a good draught of water from his rucksack, which was now pretty light.

"You put this rucksack on and put your arms around my neck and I will give you a piggy back."

"You can't my darling."

"Rubbish, you are as light as a feather. Give a little jump."

Jim held her thighs, and with her arms around his neck started upwards. Claire was indeed not very heavy but Jim only managed to get half way up, before he had to stop for a rest. Claire leant against him and then said, "I feel stronger now. I can walk. We will go up the rest of the way hand in hand. I love you so much, Jim. You will have a heart attack and that would destroy me."

They made it to the top and both felt better when then walked down to Chala. The cold cokes were like nectar. They sat outside the 'duka' and had a second one. Then, in answer to their prayer, they saw a bus coming down the road from the north. It was packed with people but they managed to clamber aboard. The pack of people kept them upright. They were asked where they had been. When they said they had been into the crater, their fellow passengers said that they were absolutely mad. The bus was going to Taveta Township but it stopped, for them to get out, at the airstrip. Claire sat on the ground under the wing, while Jim checked the aircraft. Then, she climbed in after him. Claire kept the door open, to let the air from the prop rush in, as they taxied to the end of the strip. She shut it as Jim turned. They were soon airborne and the temperature dropped. Claire was soon asleep. Jim flew over the foot hills of Mount Kilimanjaro. He did not wake her but the view of the summit was spectacular. Claire slept all the way to Wilson Airport. She only woke, when Jim parked up at the aero club and cut the engine.

"How do you feel, my darling?"

"I feel like that lioness in Nairobi Game Park. Totally shagged out but very satisfied. You must be exhausted. You know, I have got to be on parade at the High Commission. I feel so bad leaving you. Please don't do anymore flying today. It would be dark anyway, before you got half way to Mombasa."

"Don't worry, I will be fine. I will get a room here at the aero club, after I have taken you to the Residence. I just feel so sorry for you, having to make polite conversation, when all you want to do is go to bed."

"I will be fine in a taxi on my own. There is no need for you to come. In fact, it would be safer. We don't want to be seen together."

They said their sad farewells and Claire left for the Residency. Jim was tired but he also thought he was hungry, so he had a big mug of tea and a fry up after he had showered at the aero club. Jim was sure there was no chance of Claire joining him later tonight, as she had done after the Muthaiga Ball. He was certain she was just too tired.

He was wrong. It was not long after midnight, when he felt a soft sexy body getting into the small single bed in his room.

"My darling, how did you manage it?"

"It was only a 'drinks do' and so Richard and I had a late supper. When it was all quiet I crept out. I have brought my running gear so it will look like I have been for a run, tomorrow morning. I could not bear to say goodbye, after being such a wet rag after our adventure. You even had to carry me. I was so ashamed."

"You must not think badly of yourself. Think what I was like when I had malaria."

402

They were both tired but they soon excited each other and they quietly made love, so as not to wake any of the other pilots staying at the aero club.

Jim awoke first and gently reached his hand between Claire's thighs.

Claire rolled on to her back and murmured into his ear.

"How I miss that hand, when we are apart! I sometimes rub myself, but it is never anything like you doing it for me. I am beginning to get wet already. I want you inside me." Jim must have been more worn out from the previous day's climb in the heat, than he realised. They moved together rhythmically but he did not ejaculate quickly, so that they eventually climaxed together. He was still lying on top of her as Claire whispered into his ear,

"I know what I am going to do, when we are going to make love next time. I am going to make you climb up a mountain, with me on your back, until you can't carry me any further. Only then will I let you inside me. That was wonderful." She wrapped her legs round him.

"I can still feel you inside me. I can imagine all those sperm swimming like hell to reach my egg. It is lucky I am on the pill. Otherwise, I am sure I would get pregnant now. I feel so satisfied and relaxed." Jim kept kissing her neck and they both dosed off to sleep. They woke again soon and Claire crept out to the shower, without anyone seeing her. When she got back, Jim was up.

"Don't get dressed just for a minute. Let me look at your beautiful naked body, like I did the first time in Nairobi Game Park. What a wonderful picture to take home, in my mind, back to Mombasa." Claire kissed him tenderly.

"You lovely boy, thank you! I hope you always enjoy my body."

They crept out together and walked holding hands down the Langata Road until they found a taxi.

The period over Christmas and New Year was a routine drudge for Claire. She had to host the High Commission Christmas party and attend all manner of other functions. She longed to spend time with Jim but knew any contact was impossible. She knew he would be working and be on duty but she also knew he would be out to parties at the Sailing Club, the Water Ski Club and the Sports Club. In her heart, she knew Jim was totally in love with her but she knew, as a young man, surrounded by girls wearing very little in the sun drenched holiday resort, that there was temptation around every corner. What most annoyed her was that she was jealous, but knew she had absolutely no right to be possessive. She day-dreamed of being Jim's wife, having children together, and living in the UK in an idyllic rural setting. In reality, she knew it was just a pipe-dream and that she would never leave Richard. Equally, she guessed that Jim would find another girl, settle down and have a normal relationship ending in a white wedding. Claire was pragmatic. She was going to make the most of the exciting present. She was rushed off her feet, running the High Commission and her agents in the field. She did not have the time to be love-struck and moon around, like so many expatriate wives.

On the morning of the 7th January she was particularly depressed. She had to fly down with Richard to Dar es Salaam, to a weekend get together of High Commissioners and their wives from neighbouring states. She would be away, when Jim would be up in Nairobi meeting his parents who were flying in, on the morning of the 8th. They could have met at the hotel near to the Residence that night, if she didn't have to attend this bloody gathering. She did her best not to be grumpy with Richard, who was only doing his job.

They arrived at The Kilimanjaro Hotel, in Dar es Salaam, in the late morning. There was an official get together before lunch. In the late afternoon the men were going to play golf and the ladies were meant to going shopping. Claire managed to avoid this and spent some time at the pool. So it was, that she was the only one of the party at the hotel, when a call came through from London. Hastily wrapping herself in a 'kikoi' she ran to reception and took the call in a booth. The message was unambiguous. Intelligence sources suggested there was going to be a long-haul flight hijack, that night. All High Commissioners were ordered to return to their stations.

Such a crisis was Claire's forte. She was not only a superb organiser, but also she could think on her feet. She made an instant decision. She went straight to the airport, while the hotel staff got all the men back from the golf course and straight into a coach and on to the airport. She arranged evening flights for them all back, to their respective countries. She left the wives in Dar es Salaam, to return either the following day, or later if it was not dangerous for them to do so. Claire was well aware that at least one airport would be in chaos. Of course it might actually be Dar es Salaam, so the wives were much safer where they were. The wives could also bring the luggage home and, perhaps more importantly, any sensitive papers which husbands might have in brief cases.

It was only when Claire was boarding the plane with Richard that she was aware she was travelling in a bikini, '*kikoi*' and flip-flops. The Tanzania High Commission had been asked to retrieve their luggage, and return it to Nairobi after the crisis was over. They were rapidly boarded, as they only had Claire's handbag. She handed Richard a new Wilbur Smith novel.

"Darling you are amazing and extremely thoughtful." It was his only comment before burying his nose in the novel.

Claire's mind, having been totally focused, was now in a whirl. '*Would Jim be at the normal hotel? Would she get a chance to be with him? Would his parents be involved in the hijack? How could she prevent him being involved and taking some dangerous risk?*'

Once back at the Residence it was all go for Claire. Richard was based in his office, fielding all the important communications. Claire, still in her bikini and '*kikoi*', was flying round making arrangements. London confirmed that Nairobi was likely to be the flash point. Two SAS teams were on their way by air, which required clearance to arrive at Eastleigh, the Kenyan Military Airbase. A large group, were on their way from the British Army Training Team based at Isiolo and were going to camp on a ranch, between the International Airport and The Athi River. Eli stopped her and gave her a very welcome cup of tea. He whispered,

"I took the liberty of sending two of my younger brothers, who are staying with me, to Dr Scott's Hotel. One has returned with this note. He, of course, is available to return with a note, if required." He handed Claire a note, in an envelope, addressed in Jim's distinctive hand. Claire tore it open.

I will camp out at Embakasi and meet my folks at 7.05 am. I love you with all my heart.

Claire brushed a tear from her eye and looked up at Eli. "Thank you Eli that was most kind. I will write a quick note and I would be very grateful if it could be delivered." She squeezed his hand.

"Certainly '*Memsahib*'." Claire tucked the note into her bikini top, where it gave her a warm feeling. Her return note was terse.

I love you too much for words. Don't take any unnecessary risks.

The High Commission was at high alert all through the night. Andrea drove Claire to Embakasi, to arrive at first light, after she had done her best to smarten herself up. There, she found Jim in the arrivals hall, sitting outside the book shop. Either side of him were Eli's two brothers. He was helping them to read. She so longed to take him into her arms but instead, she sat down beside them, ignoring the dirty floor and telling them not to get up. The airport was as normal. Obviously the police had not been put on alert. Then, to Jim's amazement, there were his parents being ushered through like royalty by BOAC ground staff. Jim grabbed Claire and, followed by the two Somali lads, ran to meet his parents. He hugged his mother and shook his father by the hand. He immediately introduced Claire. "Mum, Dad. I would like you to meet Claire who is a pal of mine. However did you get off the plane first? I know you weren't in first class."

Jim's mother did not answer the question, but immediately concentrated on Claire. She kissed Claire on the cheek and whispered,

"I was worried Jim would not let us meet. You are the angel that nursed him, when he had malaria. I am so grateful."

Claire replied in a soft voice,

"Equally, I did not think he would let us meet. Fate has helped us as I am here officially." Jim's mother's eye brows went up. "How come? Are you something to do with BOAC? There were some high jinks on our flight, which Roy sorted out. That is why we were allowed off first."

Claire said, "Let's get out of the airport before the pressmen arrive?" She led Jim's mother out, holding her arm. "The men folk will sort out the luggage." Once they were outside and walking to the car park, they could talk freely.

Claire said. "I am the wife of the High Commissioner and so we have all been worried about flights, coming into Nairobi this morning. I am here to report back to my husband. Jim and I are close friends and, naturally, I was particularly concerned for you and, to be honest, I was even more concerned that Jim might do something foolhardy, if you were in danger."

"Claire dear, I understand perfectly. Thank you for being so honest. You have no need to say more. I can read between the lines. It is certainly ironic that the villains were on our flight. When they tried to take over the flight, waving guns about, Roy knocked out one with a bottle of duty free and two of the replacement air crew sorted out the other. I am afraid it is like father, like son. I hope you realise what you have let yourself into."

"I think I do. Do you mind if I call you Lydia?"

"I would be sad if you didn't. We are only here for two weeks. I do hope you will be able to spend some time with us? I feel close to you already."

"For a start, let's persuade Jim to let you stay in Nairobi tonight, to recover from your ordeal. I would love to come and have dinner with you."

"Definitely. Here come the men folk. Those two young lads obviously think the world of you and Jim."

"Their elder brother is our butler, at the High Commission. Jim spends time with their family up in Northern Kenya." Turning to Jim, Claire said. "Can your Mum and Dad stay tonight at the Norfolk? I do think they need a little rest before that long drive down to Mombasa."

Jim replied, "That's a great idea. Is that OK with you, Dad?"

"That's fine with me. I hope this young lady will come and have supper?"

Claire kissed him on the cheek. "You are the hero of the day. I will forgive you forgetting my name. I suggest you get going, before the pressmen grab you for a story. I will get Andrea to take me and these young men back to the High Commission and I will see you tonight."

On the way back Claire thought, *'what lovely people, I can at least dream that one day they will be my in-laws.* She had no time to day dream when she got back as there was chaos still at the High Commission. She reported to Richard, who was very relieved at the outcome. He made no objections to Claire going out to supper. With a conspiratorial wink he said,

"If you get caught out, you can turn it into good PR."

By lunchtime, everything was back to normal. Claire thanked Eli for his help. Eli laughed and said his brothers thought Doctor Scott's father must certainly be a '*Bwana Mkubwa in Ulaya* (A very important person in England).'

Claire managed to get four hours' sleep in the afternoon. She was delighted to get a note from Jim, saying he would pick her up. She was going to wear a very demure dress but thought, '*bugger it.*' She wore a very short skirt instead, knowing that Jim would love it. They behaved very properly when he picked her up, but his hand was on her thigh as soon as she was in the Landrover. She felt nervous but then was completely relaxed, when Roy Scott wrapped his arms around her, and said he would never forget a girl's name that had such wonderful legs. Lydia was obviously pleased to see her. Lydia insisted Roy ordered Champagne. Jim and Claire tried to dissuade him but to no avail, saying it would cost an arm and a leg but they lost the argument. It was a lovely meal. Lydia made Claire promise she would meet them for a night in Mombasa and also for a night in the Masai Mara. Jim took her home really quite early, as none of them had slept more than a few hours, including their rests in the afternoon. Claire was elated, being able just to walk into the High Commission, without having to go furtively around to the side door, dodging the '*askari*'. She had a nightcap with Richard, before they went to bed.

It was a tiring journey for Jim's parents, down to Mombasa, although they were delighted with all the game they saw on the way. Jim's mother was not impressed by the lack of furnishings in his house, on her arrival. She said nothing. She was pleased to meet Katana, who hastily made a light supper for them, soon after their arrival. Both his parents were delighted with the view from the house and all the wonderful fruit for breakfast. Jim had arranged for Chaiko to pick him up for work, so that he could leave his Landrover for his Dad to use.

He arrived home to a very different house. The main changes were to the beds, which had new bedclothes. Apparently, new curtains had been ordered and would be up by the following evening. When Jim suggested it was not necessary, his mother retorted that she and Roy did not mind roughing it but surely Jim could not entertain Claire in such bachelor-like conditions. Jim then cheered up, as he realised that only two bedrooms had been upgraded. Obviously, his mother had realised that he and Claire slept together and she had no objections. He marvelled at her perception.

Chapter 31

An almost normal family

Monday 15th January 1968

Jim had a busy day at work, so Roy and Lydia were at the airport to meet Claire off the early afternoon flight, from Nairobi. Claire was really touched that they gave her such a warm welcome. Roy drove the Landrover and Claire sat in the middle seat. She was wearing a linen dress with quite a short skirt. Claire could not resist teasing Roy, by saying she hoped he was not going to put her knee into third gear like Jim often did. "Certainly not," said Lydia. "I will keep these men under strict control. It is a very pretty dress, my dear, I imagine it is lovely and cool being linen."

Lydia was really pleased when Claire hugged Katana. Obviously the old man thought the world of Claire, as well as of Jim. Katana showed all the changes in the house to Claire, as he carried her bag up to Jim's bedroom. Claire was doubly delighted, as she realised that not only were the improvements for her, but that she was expected to sleep with Jim.

They had tea on the veranda. Claire thanked Lydia for making the house so welcoming. She said now she would be able to come out of the bathroom in her pyjamas without turning the bedroom light off and thereby risking being seen by half of Mombasa. Claire laughed with Katana as he brought in the tea. There were two types of cake. She told Lydia she never got cake normally.

"That is my fault," said Lydia. "When Jim was a little boy and he had done something naughty, he was not allowed cake at tea. Instead of sulking, Jim had just eaten a large amount of bread and butter." Claire laughed.

"I don't even get bread and butter!"

"You poor girl. What is Jim thinking about? You have a beautiful figure. I will certainly stop him starving you."

"You have no need to worry, Lydia. Katana looks after me."

"I am glad to hear that. I hope you will enjoy the steaks Roy bought us all for supper. However, let's tuck into the cake."

They went on talking so no-one heard Jim arrive.

"Wow Mum, cake for tea. Hope you had a good flight Claire?" Claire jumped up and hugged him. "I have been admiring all the changes. I am glad nothing fundamental has changed. You still smell of cows!" They all laughed. Jim said. "After tea I will have a swim, off the end of the garden, and then a good shower. I will let you check me out before supper."

"Can I come for a swim, even if I don't smell of cows? Do you mind if I have wet hair? You may have noticed, the establishment does not run to a hair drier, Lydia." said Claire, laughing.

"Of course not, my dear. Rest assured we will rectify that deficiency tomorrow."

After Jim had finished his cake, he turned to Claire and said, "I do hope you can stay for two nights, as I had to visit Grace and Gerald this morning and they have asked us all to supper tomorrow night."

Claire replied. "That will be great." She then told Lydia and Roy about meeting Grace on the train, having had too many '*waragis and tonics*' and getting caught in her racy pyjamas. Jim was amazed that, not only had she dared to tell the story, but also that his mother found it funny. He was delighted, because it showed him that his parents had totally accepted Claire.

His parents came down with them to the bottom of the garden, when Jim and Claire went for their swim. His mother was very complimentary about Claire's new one-piece swimming costume. Jim could see Claire was pleased. His mother also said she was glad Jim was looking after Claire properly, as he had brought down her neoprene diving gloves, so she would not hurt herself climbing up the coral wall. In fact she did not really need them as, when she came to get out, Jim's Dad gave her his hands and just lifted her out as if she was a child.

"You are as light as a feather."

Without thinking Claire hugged him.

"Oh my goodness, I am sorry, you are soaking." Roy replied,

"I would have even enjoyed a wet hug like that in a wind-frost."

They all had showers before their pre-dinner drinks. Lydia asked Jim if he had any '*waragi*', as she would like to try some. Jim found a bottle and Katana brought, not only cold tonic, but also ice and pieces of lemon. Roy poured the drinks saying,

"I will give you a good measure of '*waragi*', Claire. Hopefully I will see the racy pyjamas." Claire laughed and stuck out her tongue at him.

They all enjoyed the meal. Claire was delighted when, as they were saying goodnight, Jim asked her if she would like to come to treat some cows with him in the morning.

"What about your Dad? Surely you would like to go Roy?"

Roy said. "Don't worry I have been with Jim for several outings. You, I am sure, don't get much time together." Claire kissed Roy impulsively.

He laughed and said, "I am glad I have not had another soaking!"

When Jim and Claire were cuddled up together, she whispered to him.

"Your parents are really lovely. I am going to adopt your mother. I wish I could remember my mother." Jim felt her tears on his bare chest. He did not say anything but gently stroked her hair. They kissed gently and went to sleep, cuddled up like two spoons.

They were up early to drive to the cattle, so they did not wake Jim's parents. They both came back for lunch, smelling of cows. In fact, Claire had cow shit on her shirt.

Lydia called from the veranda.

"That's marvelous, you can have a shower and try out the new hair drier!"

After lunch, Jim had to go to the Veterinary Office to do some paper work, so Roy drove Lydia and Claire to Nyali Beach Hotel. They had coffee, sitting around the pool, before going for a walk on the beach. Claire and Lydia seemed to have so much in common they never stopped talking. Claire told Lydia how she had never know her mother, as she died when she was born, so she was going to adopt her. Lydia was delighted. When they got home Katana came out to meet them. He had a message from Jim. Claire was so glad she had learnt more Swahili or translation would have been very difficult. It appeared that one of Gerald's cows was in difficulty, having a calf. Jim had got Chaiko to give him a lift to the farm but would Claire,

411

Lydia and Roy come as soon as they could. Claire explained that Grace and Gerald were very relaxed and so it did not matter what they wore. So, saying goodbye to Katana, they left immediately.

Grace greeted them when they arrived and told them the news. The calf was too big to be born naturally and so Jim was going to do a caesarean section. She asked Roy if he would take a churn of hot water down to the cow shed. Claire said she would go to show him the way. Lydia stayed with Grace at the house. They were soon laughing together, drinking tea.

It was all go at the cowshed. The cow was trying to kick Jim, as he was injecting the local anaesthetic. Roy immediately grabbed her tail and held it straight up like a flag. Gerald was holding her nose. Claire started to help Jim by filling syringes with local anaesthetic.

"Thanks Dad. If you can hang on, that would be great, as I don't want to sedate her as that will weaken the calf, which is weak anyway. I should never have had a go at pulling him. He is much too big."

Claire was too worried about Jim being kicked, to notice she was standing in her best flip-flops in liquid shit. She did manage a '*Jambo*' to Chaiko and Gerald's headman. At last, Jim was on the final syringe of local. He asked Claire to draw up a dose of penicillin. She was so glad she knew which bottle it was, as she remembered the operation on Judas.

Jim already had his shirt off. He asked Claire to wash the cow's left flank where he had injected the local. "Be careful. I don't think she will kick, as Dad has got her tail up." While she was doing that, Jim scrubbed up and instructed Chaiko to start opening up the sterile kit. Luckily, Chaiko had done it before. When Claire had finished, Jim asked her to scrub up. She whispered. "Can I keep my shirt on? I feel shy."

"Of course you can but you will get plastered I'm afraid."

Jim started making his incision. To take Claire's mind off the small artery, which was pumping blood over their faces, he told her how there was much more room to make the incision on a cow compared to Eli's father's camel. Soon Jim had the calf out and Gerald was supervising its resuscitation. Jim got Claire to hold the uterus, so he could start stitching. "I am sorry it will be hard work as the uterus is contracting. Will you be OK?"

"I will do my best."

As he was stitching, Jim asked his father. "Do you remember Dawn Doubleday, Dad?"

"I do indeed. I saw her, with her father at the Fat Stock Show before Christmas. I forgot. She has started at Cambridge Vet School. She sent her love and, I remember now, a very strange message. She said she hoped you kept your mouth clean, before you kissed any girls." Claire was all ears as Jim had never mentioned a 'Dawn'. Jim laughed and, while he was stitching the abdominal muscles, with Claire keeping the tension on the catgut, he told them the story of him spitting on his handkerchief to clean the meconium off her face.

"Poor girl, she must have been frightened to death," said Claire.

"I don't think so," replied Jim. He then told them the story of her turning to an awkward farmer and saying, "A strong woman is much better than a weak man."

"Good for her," said Claire with feeling. Claire was even more pleased when Jim told how, when they were saying goodbye before she went back to school, he thought when she asked him for a handkerchief, she was going to cry, but that she wiped his mouth before allowing him to kiss her.

"She certainly sounds quite a girl."

Roy added, "I think she must be. Not many girls get into Veterinary College. She has done well getting to Cambridge. I know her father hopes, eventually, she will take over his farming enterprise."

Jim said, "Cambridge turned me down. I was lucky to get to Bristol."

Gerald said, "Well I am bloody glad you went somewhere, as the calf looks really good now. He is holding his head up."

Eventually, the operation was finished. Chaiko could go home to the Veterinary Office. Gerald, Claire, Roy and Jim made their way back to the house, leaving a happy headman with the cow and calf.

When they were getting out of the vehicles, when no one else could over hear, Jim whispered to Claire,

"I hope you are going to wash those tits before I kiss them?" Claire looked down and laughed. Her shirt had the wet look and the blood had soaked through onto her bra. "I look as if I have done a murder. I borrowed Grace's shirts, when you were recovering from malaria. I am sure she will lend me one again."

Grace took charge. Pointing at Jim and Claire she said,

"You know your way, off you go to the '*rondavel*' and have a good bath. I will send Jonathon down with clothes and a couple of G & Ts. You can be really decadent and drink them in the bath. Gerald, you take Roy off to the spare room and show him the shower, and lend him some of your clothes. When Lydia and I have finished preparing supper, we will have a drink on the veranda."

Jim and Claire went, hand in hand, to the '*rondavel*'.

Claire said, "It feels like home. I was so worried about you, when you had malaria. We will just stay in the bathroom and then we won't mess up the bedroom." As she bent over the bath he put his hand up her skirt. She turned and kissed him. "No hankie pankie, Jonathon will be here in a minute but, if you are really good, I will let you wash my tits before you kiss them. In fact, I am going to get in the bath. You can meet Jonathon. You can be a ladies maid and undress me." She held up her arms. Jim was just pulling down her knickers when he heard,

"*Hodi.*" at the door.

"*Asanti* Jonathon, *mimi na kuja.* (I will come)"

Jim brought the clothes and the drinks through to the bathroom. "Here you are, my lady."

"Thank you, Jeeves. Can you put my drink on the table and then wash my hair!"

"It will be a pleasure, my lady," answered Jim with a smile. They had a lovely bath and a little bit of hankie pankie.

Supper was a riot. The men kept teasing Claire, as it was obvious that she did not have a bra on. Jim had a constant smile on his face, as he was the only one who knew she did not have any knickers on either. They were all a bit pickled, so Roy asked Jim to drive home, as he knew the road. Gerald helped Claire into the back of the Landrover. She teased him. "You are a real gentleman, or are you trying to look down my shirt?"

"Would I? You must all come again. Have a safe drive home."

When Claire and Jim had eventually got into bed, she whispered. "Have you got Brewer's droop? I feel a bit frisky but we must be quiet." Jim did not reply, but started kissing her neck very gently. He

414

was lying behind her. "Mm, that's nice." Jim brought a hand around her and gently pinched one nipple. Very slowly he brought her to an orgasm after, he had brought his hand up to her mouth so she could not cry out.

"That was lovely," whispered Claire, when her breathing came back to normal.

"You feel rock hard now. You are so lovely." She rolled and started sucking him. In a couple of minutes Jim sighed as he came into her mouth. She wriggled up the bed and gave him a really erotic kiss. They were soon asleep.

Breakfast was fairly leisurely. Jim soon had to go but, as his parents were taking Claire to catch an 11.00 am plane, there was no rush. They planned their trip to the Mara. The plan was for Jim to fly his parents up to Nairobi, with all their luggage, in a Cherokee Arrow. Although they had quite heavy luggage they would be OK, as there were only three of them and they would be taking off at sea level. They would leave the majority of their luggage at the aero club at Wilson. Claire would meet them and then the four of them would fly the 170 miles down to Keekorok Lodge, in the Mara, for three nights. Claire knew she was taking a bit of a risk, as local Kenyan friends might stay at the Lodge but she thought Jim's parents would make everything look OK, at least on the surface. If the worst came to the worst, Jim could pretend to be sleeping on the floor of his parent's room. Claire knew his parents would not let her down.

They got to the airport in plenty of time for Claire's flight, so they had a coffee in the terminal. Lydia asked Claire what clothes they would need for Keekorock. Claire said they obviously would need safari stuff, as they would be going on some game runs. They would need swimming costumes, as there was a pool. Claire thought they should have some good clothes, as she thought it was quite smart in the evenings. She told Lydia that she need not worry too much about the weight of luggage as her things were very light and Jim, she knew, would be unlikely to worry about being smart.

"We will see about that," said Lydia. "Roy and I will try and smarten him up. It will be nice for you, my dear, not to rough it all the time. I think you are marvellous going with him, out in the wilds."

So it was that Jim flew up to Wilson, with a new pair of smart trousers and two new shirts. Claire had rung the control tower so she was at Wilson to meet them, as she knew their ETA. She introduced Andrea, the High Commission driver to them and said there was a slight change of plan, as she had booked their last night in Nairobi at the Norfolk hotel. She said that Andrea would take their luggage for storage at the Norfolk, rather than leave it at the aero club. They set off in high spirits. Claire insisted Roy sat in the front, so she could sit in the back and chat to Lydia. The flight was a little over an hour, as the Cherokee Arrow had a retractable under-cart and was really quite speedy. They bussed, the lodge so a Landrover came out to the air-strip to pick them up.

"This is the way to travel," said Roy. "That Landrover journey down to the coast was interesting, but jolly tiring."

Once they had checked in, Jim and Claire opted for a swim. Roy and Lydia sat by the pool and they all had tea. There seemed to be very few other guests. The waiter said they were quiet and the few other tourists had gone out on an evening game run. Claire was very relieved, as there was no-one there she knew. She had quickly looked down the guest list, in the hotel register.

When they went back to change for dinner, Jim said,

"I have a small surprise for you." He had brought the new hair drier. Claire was delighted. He suddenly was sad when he remembered Fiona, in his hotel room in Edinburgh. He wondered how she was. Claire realised something was wrong. She said nothing but put her arms around him and gave him a hug.

"I think you were remembering another girl. Was it Dawn?"

"No, it was a girl called Fiona. I met her in Scotland, when I was doing my tropical medicine course. I bought her a hair drier, as we used to go running together and she liked to wash her hair afterwards."

"Maybe you were not quite as innocent as I thought," said Claire. "I thought you were a virgin in Nairobi Game Park. Were you?"

"Well, yes and no," replied Jim

"I hope you did not leave the poor girl pregnant?"

"No, we were very careful."

Claire laughed and said, "You weren't very careful in the Game Park."

"No, that was really bad of me and you were so incredibly sexy and desirable. I still dream of your lovely brown thighs and the moment I realised you did not have any knickers on."

"You should not feel bad. I really wanted you. What's so lovely, is that I still really want you now. I can feel that you want me too." Without another word they made love, slowly and gently, and with a lot of satisfaction.

Dinner was quite smart and Claire was really pleased that her hair was dry. Lydia was very complimentary. They were not late to bed as they had booked a game drive in the morning. They were up at dawn, having been woken with a cup of tea. They set off, with a driver and a ranger, as soon as they were ready. Breakfast was scheduled for later. They drove out on the road past the airstrip. Jim relaxed when he saw the arrow was safe, and still tied down how he had left it. In the half light, there seemed to be game animals everywhere. Jim and Claire were particularly pleased for Jim's parents, as everything was new to them. Jim was very impressed that Claire knew all the Swahili names and chatted to the driver and ranger in Swahili. The ranger had obviously done his home work, as they soon found a pride of lions. It consisted of two females and their cubs. There were no males. Claire squeezed Jim's hand. Then they were really lucky. The sharp eyed ranger saw a leopard in a tree, with a dead baboon. It was magic for them all, as none of them had seen a leopard in the wild before. When it started getting really hot they stopped, under a big spreading acacia tree, and had a lively camp breakfast. There was hot tea in a thermos, loads of fruit and cold milk, also in a thermos, so they could have real milk, rather than UHT milk with their cereals. Jim noticed there was cold butter in a wide necked thermos.

"Look Claire that is a good idea. We should do that. It would not last for a long safari but it would be good for a short one. I have seen some camp toasters which go on an open fire. Toast and butter with honey would be great."

Claire turned to the ranger and asked,

"*Iko nyuki hapa* (Are there bees here)?"

"*Idiyo Memsahib. Lakini nyuki hapa kali sana.* (Yes Mistress, but the bees are very aggressive here)" Claire translated for Jim's parents. Jim teased her, saying her Swahili was as good as coastal

Swahili and that perhaps she should go around bare chested like a Giriama. She put out her tongue and said she had never really forgiven him for saying her breasts weren't big enough. Lydia was cross.

"What a dreadful thing to say, Jim." Claire laughed and told Lydia the story of when they had first met, at the High Commission, and that actually Jim had said she was beautiful, but he had expected an old matron with buck teeth and an enormous bosom. Lydia was mollified. They actually saw a lot of game on the way back to the lodge but they were hot, when they arrived, and they all had a swim in the wonderfully cool pool.

The next two days and nights flew by. They all had a wonderful time. They even saw a cheetah and masses of elephant and buffalo. The only disappointment was, they did not see a rhino. At the final breakfast, Jim said, "As you haven't seen a rhino, you will have to come back for another trip."

They made good time on the flight back to Wilson. Jim did not stop long after lunch, as Claire and Lydia were both worried he would go to sleep on the flight back to Mombasa. He kissed his Mum and Claire. He shook hands with his Dad and, sadly, walked across to the plane. They watched him do his preflight checks and then he waved both his arms got, into the plane, and he was off. Claire took his parents back into the aero club, while they waited for a taxi.

"Well, I have got one more treat for you tomorrow afternoon, as your plane does not go until 9.00 pm. Would you like to go horse racing?"

"I would love that," said Roy.

Lydia said. "That is really kind of you, Claire. Roy loves racing but I will give it a miss. I will do the packing. I am sure the hotel will let us use the room until the evening, if we pay extra."

The three of them went back to the Norfolk Hotel. Claire made sure they were checked in OK and then promised to meet them for an early lunch the next day.

Roy had the time of his life at Nairobi Race Course, escorting a very glamorous young lady. Claire could never have come with Jim, as questions would have been asked, but entertaining Roy, was well covered by her remit as Lady Rochester. Claire really enjoyed herself and often held Roy's arm. When they picked a winner and she jumped up and down, she thought how like Jim, Roy was. He turned to her and said,

"When you do that you make my glasses mist up."

"You old rogue," she replied and kissed him on the cheek.

When they got back to the Norfolk, Lydia was delighted to see them. She hugged Claire.

"That is from Jim. He rang half an hour ago, to wish us a safe journey and he said to give you a big hug from him." Lydia did not miss the tears in Claire's eyes, although she tried to hide them.

"We have had a wonderful afternoon. Roy has come back with some winnings."

Claire insisted on staying for an early supper and taking them to the airport. Andrea drove them, so Lydia was not worried about Claire going back in a taxi on her own. After Claire had left, Lydia turned to Roy. "What a sweet girl. I think we have certainly gained a daughter."

"Sadly, I think there will be difficulties ahead," replied Roy. "We will just have to give them all our support. You always say Lydia, children are only lent. I just hope we don't lose that one."

Chapter 32

A trip to Marsabit

Saturday 10th February 1968

Organising his leave, to coincide with when Claire could get away, had been difficult for Jim. However, after the hijack Sir Richard had been very relaxed, and providing Claire was discrete, he did not hold up any objections. Claire's cover was that she was going to stay on a ranch, with friends, in Laikipia district for ten days. She said that she was going to be picked up at Wilson airport early on Saturday morning. She was seriously excited and got an embassy car to take her at 5.00 am. She knew Jim was going to drive up, after work on Friday, and would camp, as he had done before, behind the aero club. They could then get out of Nairobi before dawn, hopefully without anyone seeing them. Claire thanked the embassy driver and said she would be fine and pretended to walk into the aero club, as if she was going to be picked up, to go by plane at first light. As soon as the driver had gone, she went around the club building and there was Jim's Landrover. Lucy was inside, guarding it but no Jim. So, having been licked to death by Lucy, she got into the middle seat and hid in the dark. In five minutes, Jim came out to the vehicle swung open the door saying to Lucy, it's only me, and got in. He nearly jumped out of his skin when he felt her hand on his thigh and then she was kissing him passionately.

As they broke apart Jim said,

"Christ, it is good to see you. We had better be going as I would like us to be well out of town before dawn. Please sit in the middle seat and cuddle up to me."

"I certainly will," replied Claire. "Have you heard from your parents? I was really touched by Lydia's letter to me. She said some sweet things about me and even you."

"Thank you for being so kind to them. They had a great trime. Dad loved his trip to the races."

They made good time out of town, through Thika and on northwards. They did not go into Nyeri but bi-passed it and carried on to Isiolo through Nanuyki. They filled up every jerry can they had with petrol at Isiolo. They also had five 4-gallon plastic cans, which were already full of water. With the extra two spare wheels, the Landrover was seriously overloaded.

They had a cold coke each at the garage, went through the police barrier with a cheery wave to the *'askari'*, and they were off into the NFD. In 35 miles, they came to the bridge over the Ewaso Ng'iro, at Archers post. Samburu Game Park lay to their left but, 15 miles ahead of them, the massive 6000ft lump of rock called Lolokwe, reared up out of the hot, flat country. They were in totally new territory for both of them. Even Lucy seemed excited. Jim knew they had to find a small, left-hand turn off before Lolokwe, as they did not plan to go directly to Marsabit but across west to Lake Rudolf and then back to Marsabit, before coming back home down the bigger road from Ethiopia.

Claire saw the turn first, which actually was quite clear, although there was no sign post. It was a narrow, sandy track through the sparse bush. There were some very squat acacia trees but the whole area was virtually a desert. Soon another peak arose from the plain, on the right, even higher than Lolokwe. This was Warges. At its foot was the very small village of Wamba, which was a couple of miles off the road. They did not stop, but continued with the Mathews range on their right. Jim hoped to make a wide sand lugga, called Seiyia, to camp for the night. It might or might not have water in it. The light was failing fast and they very nearly drove into the lugga. It was wide, maybe 200 yards. Jim took the precaution of walking across, before they drove through. The river bed was now dry but the sand was firm. There were some larger trees on the far side which would make a good camping spot, so they decided to risk a crossing.

Back in the Landrover, Jim gave Claire's thigh a gentle squeeze before pushing the red gear stick forward, putting the Landrover into low range four wheel drive. They were soon flying across the lugga and up the other side. They drove about half a mile up the bank of the lugga away from the road, before stopping to camp. It was blissful to stop, turn off the ignition and listen to Africa. It was still very warm but, now the sun was down, they hoped they would cool down. Although it would have been easy to actually camp in the lugga, they kept to the high ground. If there was rain in the Mathews Mountains there would be a flash flood in their camp site. Jim had also heard that there were sand flies, which got through mosquito nets and lived in sand luggas, in the west of the NFD.

While Claire lit a fire and got the old tin bucket near it, to make them some hot water, Jim got their bed ready on top of the Landrover. He did not bother with the tent, as it was so warm and rain, down on the plain, was extremely unlikely. He managed to string a mosquito net up from a bough of a tree, so that they could just sleep on the big mattress under the net. They had pillows and sleeping bags if they needed them. Jim fixed up the shower and said to Claire, in a very formal way,

"Will you join me in the shower? I promise I won't let you stand there, like I did once before?"

"Too right, you won't." Claire ran at him, wrapped her arms around his neck and hoisted her legs around his waist.

"Now, I have got you," she kissed him.

"Have we any cold beers?"

"So, it is just cupboard love. You don't really want me. You just want a cold beer! Luckily, I have just four. I did not bring anymore, as we have no way of keeping them cold. Come on, let's have them. You get the pewter tankards out and I will find two beers in the cool box." So they sat, side by side, on camp stools looking into the fire drinking the moderately cold beer.

"Look, the stars are coming out. This is so lovely, Jim. Thank you for taking me. I can't believe it, a whole week on our own. No High Commission, no British Government, no Kenya Government, just us. I am a very lucky girl. Can I get you the second beer?"

"That would be lovely. Then come and sit in my lap. I know I am sweaty, dusty and smelly, but I want a hug."

"You will get more than a hug after we have had our shower. I think because it is so hot I have lost my appetite. Shall we just have a bowl of cereal, UHT milk and a banana?"

"Yes, that will do me well." Claire brought him his second beer. She put hers on the table and found the bowls for supper.

"I don't know why we are wearing clothes. It is pitch dark and I don't think there is a human being for thirty miles." With that, she took off her shirt and undid her bikini top. Off came her shorts and knickers. All Claire had on were her gym-shoes. She took a swig of her beer and started getting the supper ready in the bowls. Jim took a big draught of his beer, got up and took off his shirt and shorts. As normal, he was not wearing pants. He kept on his safari-boots as there were plenty of thorns about on the ground. Watching her naked gave him an erection. Claire brought his bowl over. She bobbed down and kissed the tip of his penis.

"I am glad he appreciates my body. He is a bit salty and very dusty!" She had another swig of her beer, brought her bowl over and sat down next to him, as if it was the most natural thing in the world.

After they had washed up supper, they had an enjoyable shower together and clambered up onto the mattress on the roof-rack.

"Come on, how long does a naked girl have to wait to get ravished?"

Jim was still trying to fix the mosquito net. Claire sat up and sucked his penis.

"Still salty but not so dusty," Claire declared. Jim finished and pushed Claire onto her back and buried his face in her bush. Soon she was gasping and thrusting up with her pelvis. Claire wrapped her legs together, around his chest. Jim had difficulty in breathing, so he slithered up her body. Claire helped him to enter her and then gave some more thrusts. Jim groaned and ejaculated. He kissed her neck gently.

"That was marvellous," said Claire. "I can still feel him hard inside me. I won't mind if you go to sleep. In fact, I will probably just stay awake, as he wilts and slides out of me and then I will be asleep as well." The night was that hot that they slept cuddled together, without any covering except the mosquito net.

They awoke as the sun started to come up in the East, giving the earth a golden glow for a brief minute. Claire stretched out and said,

"I had a weird dream. I dreamt I was on a bed with a man. He would rather play with a mosquito net than ravish me."

"That is odd," said Jim, "I dreamt I was on a bed with a sexy girl, who was so keen for my body, she did not mind being bitten to blazes by mosquitoes."

Claire rolled on top of him and sat on his tummy with her knees against his body. "Well, this rather boring girl is going to ask this man to sort out his bloody mosquito net, while she gets down and has a pee. Then she wants to sit on top of him, rub her fanny up and down his prick, until he begs her to let him enter her." With that, she wriggled out from under the net and clambered down the ladder. She realised, she had gone to sleep with her shoes on. She let Lucy out of the Landrover, who came with her. She just got out of the camp and squatted down for a pee. As she came back into the camp, Jim gave her a mug of water, which she gulped down. She climbed up the ladder, as Jim drank some water and then went and had a pee. He gave Lucy a bowl of water. Claire was on her knees, when he came up the ladder. "Come on slow coach, get on your back I want to ride you like a trotting pony."

So they were fairly late setting off towards Lake Rudolf. Jim reckoned they had fifty miles to go, on this small road, before they joined a bigger road coming north from Maralal. They drove with the Karisia Hills on their left, which separated them from Maralal. The road obviously was hardly ever used and so it was quite a smooth sand track, with sparse grass growing in the middle. They actually made good time. Jim had taken the windows off the Landrover, which let in a good breeze. He could not think why he had not done that yesterday. Claire had just put on her bikini, just in case they met another vehicle. They met no one. Sadly, when they met the bigger road it was not in good condition. Obviously, the odd truck had used it after some rain. It was bone dry now but had lots of ruts, so Jim had to go slowly. Throughout the journey they chatted away, mostly about the look of the country and what game they might see, if they were lucky. They arrived at a tiny village that Jim found out was called Baragoi from an old man standing on the road side. It was meant to have an airstrip but this was very badly over-grown with bush and Jim thought it would be seriously dangerous to use, except in a dire emergency. When Jim asked the old man the state of the road, he replied one needed good shoes. It was not long before Jim and Claire realised what he meant. After they had climbed up to a pass in the Ndoto Mountains, the road turned into larva steps. Even going really slowly the Landrover juddered constantly. Jim turned to Claire and remarked,

"This road makes your tits vibrate. They look very sexy."

"I am glad you like them, but it is very uncomfortable. I am going to put on my proper bra." Claire got on to her knees and rummaged in her bag. Jim could not resist stroking the inside of her thigh.

"Normally, that would be lovely darling, but I think you need both hands on the wheel," said Claire, as the Landrover gave an extra big lurch. Jim enjoyed the bikini to bra change but was sad, as Claire put her shirt on. She said it would look idiotic, wearing a dust covered white bra on its own. As a concession, she had most of the buttons of her shirt undone.

The larva road continued past the tiny village of South Horr. Initially, it climbed and then started descending between the rocky peaks of the Nyiru on the left and smaller range on the right, called Ol Doinyo Mara. They were both getting really weary, when Claire spotted Lake Rudolf.

"Hurrah," she cried out, "I can see the sea. It certainly is well named, The Jade Sea. Let's keep going and we can have a break on the shore. Can we have a swim?" Jim was hesitant and replied,

"I think we jolly well deserve a swim. There are masses of crocodiles, some of which are really big but apparently, there are so many big Nile Perch that they don't need to eat anything else. Please be careful, My Darling, I would never forgive myself if anything happened to you."

"I would be devastated, if a Tiger Fish bit this little chap," said Claire, as she calmly rubbed Jim's crotch.

The rubbish road was forgotten, as they could see the vast lake before them together with large South Island, which had a peak nearly 2500 feet high. Once they were through the Kibrot pass, the road became even worse as it descended.

"Thank goodness we are not coming back this way," said Jim. "This would be a bastard to climb." As soon as the road started to run parallel, about fifty yards from the shore line, Jim stopped the Landrover. They had not seen another vehicle all morning, so Jim just left the vehicle in the middle of the road as there was no possibility of pulling off up the verge, as it was at least a two foot step of hard larva. They both walked carefully towards the lake. Even Lucy went slowly, as the Larva was so sharp and treacherous.

425

"I think there are black larval dust beaches but I don't think we have found one," said Jim.

"We will have to keep our shoes on," replied Claire.

"Also, you must be careful with the water in your eyes, as it is pretty salty. We must not let Lucy drink too much." A little will not hurt her, as the local tribes; the El Molo and the Turkana drink it.

"All the same, I am looking forward to my swim," said Claire. "At least we won't lose our clothes, like we did last time we went skinny dipping."

The water was by no means cool but it was certainly refreshing. They all enjoyed themselves swimming. Jim helped both Claire and Lucy to get out of the water. It was not easy, as the side was steep and the larva was sharp and hot. They walked back, naked, to the Landrover. They were dry within seconds and their skin had a soapy feel, but at least then it was no longer dusty. They got dressed again as they knew there was the site of an old hunter's camp not far away, on the shore. Whether there was anyone there they did not know. It took another three quarters of an hour to reach the camp, which was deserted. It was fairly derelict but there was no litter. "Let's camp here?" said Claire. "I know it is only 3.00 pm but we are both tired and we can have another swim at dusk, and again in the morning. Tomorrow, we will have the hot dry desert. If I remember right, you told me it was 200 miles to Marsabit. I will be so sad to leave the lake."

So they made an early camp. They found an old wooden table and chairs, plus a Bar-B-Q. Jim had brought some charcoal. They grilled some frankfurter sausages out of a tin. They made baked potatoes, in tin foil, and had a tin of tomatoes. It seemed like a feast. Even better, they found a crude water system which must have collected rain water in a big tank. After their second swim, they washed themselves and Lucy in this water. They washed their hair. They felt really clean, for the first time for two days. Claire was amazed that her long hair was dry so quickly, in the hot dry air. A slight wind had got up, so they felt very refreshed. Claire laughed and said,

"Give me a cuddle Jim. Look I have got goose bumps."

The view was beautiful as the sun sank over the lake. When they looked to the East they could see mount Kulal, which was nearly 7000ft.

426

"One day, we must make a safari there," said Jim.

Although there were some beds in the lodges of the camp, they were frightened to risk the bed bugs, so they slept on their mattress on the top of the Landrover. Jim managed to rig up the mosquito net with two poles. He did not think they would actually need it, as there did not seem to be any mosquitoes but he wondered if they might come at dawn, if the wind dropped. They were soon in bed, not really to sleep, although they were tired from the heat, but too lazy to make love. They did actually cuddle up in each other's arms to sleep, as the breeze kept them cool. They did not stay cool for long in the morning, when the sun came up and the wind dropped. Still naked, they had their normal safari breakfast of UHT milk, cornflakes and tea. They filled all the water cans with the rain water, as they knew the desert was coming. They had one final wash in the rain water. Apart from her shoes, Claire only had on her bikini bottoms.

"Hopefully, I won't need a bra. The road has not been so juddery since we have been down by the lake. My breasts have really taken a tan now. It is lovely not to have strap marks. Are you going to surprise me, by taking me to a ball on Mount Marsabit?"

"No," replied Jim, "but we will have a smouchy dance in the Chalbi Desert. I don't remember packing that lovely gown with the slit up one side."

"I will think of something," said Claire, "I still remember you touching me up. I can't believe how naughty you were. I can't wait to feel your leg between mine in a smouchy dance. Roll on the Chalbi Desert." They set off along the side of the lake, due North, with El Molo bay on their left. After about half an hour, they could smell a reek of rotting fish.

Jim said. "That must be the El Molo encampment. Shall we give it a miss? I gather they are not really fond of strangers."

"I totally agree. The place must really stink when you get near. I will have to put some clothes on and we will get sweaty. At least there is a little breeze, when we are moving."

"I don't think you need worry about clothes, they are totally naked but we will keep going."

They kept going northwards, climbing away slightly from the lakeside. The road became slightly better as there was no larva. It had hardly been maintained and they guessed that it was only used by intrepid travellers. They had discussed the trip and knew they were taking a big risk going with only one vehicle. Sadly, they had no choice if they wanted to be discreet. They both felt it would be such a waste of their precious holiday and time together, if they had to sleep apart and pretend they were just pals, if they were in a big group. They did feel very nervous, as the country was so remote and they had not seen any sign of another vehicle. They kept going and when they were getting really worried, they found a small track off to their right, which they knew led off to the small Turkana village on the Lakeside, called Allia Bay. Claire was all attentive now as they knew, from the map, that there should be a second turn off to Allia Bay. Sure enough, they found it in eight miles. In a further eight miles Claire saw a dried up water hole, which they guessed, was Gusi. Now, it was really important that they found a small road off to their right, to the Chalbi Desert. They could carry on and go to North Horr Police Post but Jim would rather avoid this, as he was concerned that they might be stopped as a single vehicle. They were going slowly now, even though the road was quite smooth. They were looking for a small track to the right, which should be only three miles from Gusi. Jim saw it first, as it was on his side. They speeded up, as they had about ten miles to go, before they should look out for the right hand turning that they needed to take. They agreed that if they did not see it in twelve miles they would turn around and back track as, in about fifteen miles, they would arrive at North Horr. They came over a small ridge and Claire saw North Horr in the distance, at the same time as Jim saw the right hand track. Luckily, there was some bush and they thought it was extremely unlikely that they had been seen. This small track ran for eight miles to a T junction at a water hole, called Woroma. This was also dry. The T junction was obvious, as it was a bigger road. However, it was still only single track. The left turn went back to North Horr and the right went on to Marsabit, through the Chalbi Desert. They were about one hundred miles from Marsabit Mountain.

Jim turned to Claire, and asked. "Do you want to stop for a lunch break or shall we press on and camp in the middle of the desert. I know you need time to make this ball gown for our dance?"

"Let's keep going. Now we are in the desert this road looks great. It is like a sandy beach." The going was indeed marvellous and they were making a steady forty miles an hour. Lucy was enjoying it as she had the airflow coming in the left-hand window. Jim had the same through the right-hand window. Jim felt Claire move next to him. She was taking off her bikini bottoms.

"I'm bloody hot. In fact, I feel really wanton," said Claire as she spread her legs wide apart and put her feet on the windscreen to make maximum use of the airflow.

After over an hour, when Jim was thinking that they could draw a little way off the road, disaster struck. At forty miles an hour they topped a small rise and dipped down the other side into a vast sea of tracks, in a very wide lugga. The Landrover slowed markedly and started to groan. Jim reached quickly between Claire's legs and pushed down the yellow knob to put them in four-wheel drive. They still kept going but they were losing speed quickly. Still between Claire's legs, Jim rammed the red knob backwards to put them into low range, which was also four-wheel drive but, after another thirty yards, they ground to a halt and Jim felt the wheels digging themselves into the soft sand. They were stuck, good and proper.

"I'm sorry, I have got us stuck," said Jim.

"It's not your fault, darling. You did your best. I knew we were in trouble as soon as you put your hand between my legs, but could not spare the time to stroke my thigh!"

They got out of the Landrover. It was mid afternoon and it was still very hot. They were pointing south so there was a tiny slither of shade on the left hand-side of the vehicle. Lucy immediately lay down in the tiny bit of shade. Claire was totally naked, except for her shoes. She put her arms around Jim. She kissed him on his dry lips and said,

"My guess is, the dance will have to wait until tomorrow? What is the plan? I could take some water and walk back to North Horr with Lucy, while you guard the Landrover?" Jim hugged her.

"No, we will all stick together. It is normally best to stay with the vehicle. We have plenty of water, but in this heat we could not carry much, so I think we would be risking dying of thirst. I have got two sand ladders on the roof. I know they will only get us a few yards but, I think if we totally lighten the vehicle we might be able to keep going. Also I reckon we are just over half way across the lugga, so we will carry the stuff to that ridge on the far side. I have got a winch

429

but there is absolutely nothing to anchor it to. I have read that you can anchor it to the spare wheel, if you bury it, but let's try the ladders first."

The carrying began. Jim started with the jerry cans, one on each side. Claire tried but they were just too heavy for her, so she brought anything else, table, chairs, tent, etc. It was very hot, hard work. They had to trudge through about four hundred yards of soft sand. Jim insisted that they always had a mug of water every journey, so that they did not get dehydrated. They gave Lucy a bowl of water. She came with them on the first two trips but, when she realised what was happening, she just lay in the shade. Slowly the sun started to go down and the pile of stuff on the far ridge got bigger. They took everything, including the spare tyres, the tools and the passenger seats. The only thing they left was one spare tyre to put the high-lift jack on and the two sand ladders. It was totally dark, and well after 8 pm, before they had finished. They had not needed torches, as they could just follow their tracks and see the vague outline of the dump on the far ridge.

"My darling, we are both totally knackered. I suggest we have a little food, brew some tea and then get some sleep. I think we ought to sleep near the kit, although I am, sadly, one hundred percent certain than no one will come along. I am sorry but I don't think we should waste any water washing. We will both stink like an El Molo but what the hell," said Jim. "I think the thought of your naked body, is the only thing that has kept me going for the last half hour."

Claire said nothing but hugged him. She realised that he had taken his shorts off, when the sun had gone down. She reached down to his tiny penis and said,

"Poor little 'willy'. I will make him big and strong again, when we get to Marsabit."

After they had had their meager supper and two mugs of tea, Jim asked,

"Have you had a wee since we got stuck?"

"No," replied Claire.

"I think we both ought both to drink another two mugs of water each," said Jim. "I am so worried we will get dehydrated and then not think clearly. Then we might get in a real muddle."

"You are right," replied Claire. "Let us make it four mugs. Normally I would not want a stomach full of water before bed because we would be making love but, I am sorry my darling, I just don't feel like making love."

"Even dreaming of you, there is no way I will have an erection. However there is a little breeze building up, so we may need to cuddle up before the night is over." Claire was pleased as, after about an hour she got up for a wee. Jim croaked,

"I will come with you." The moon was up, so they could see each other in the moonlight. They lay down again, naked. Claire said, "I have cooled down so can you cuddle my back?" She was relieved, as she felt his penis hardening as they fell asleep.

In the morning, the Landrover looked very small and forlorn as they trudged out to it, after having just a drink of water each. Jim had put on his shorts, as he was worried his white bottom would get burnt. Claire was still naked. Jim thought to himself, '*she is so lovely I must not be dehydrated, I feel like ravishing her right now.*' Somehow Claire knew his thoughts.

"I want you, my darling, but let's get to Marsabit and really have fun. It is so lovely for me that, whatever we are doing, you want me. Some of my girlfriends have to get into all manner of sexy clothing to excite their husbands. I love it that I only have to touch your thigh and you get an erection." She turned and kissed him.

They jacked up the front of the Landrover with the high-lift jack, in the middle of the strong bumper, and slid the sand ladders under the front wheels. Although Claire did not want to, Jim made her drive. He said she was lighter and he could push better. She got into the driving seat and started the engine. Jim helped her get the Landrover into first gear and reached across her naked thighs to check the red knob was in four-wheel drive low range. He stroked her thigh. Claire said.

"I hoped you would do that." Jim said good luck.

"If you get going just keep going don't wait for me. I will get behind the Landrover. When I am ready to push I will shout go"

The first four times they only managed about four yards each time but then Claire must have got the reves just right, as she shot forward. Jim fell flat on his face in the sand but Claire did not look back, she kept in the same gear and the same reves and eventually made it up the slope on to hard sand and over the ridge. She turned the engine off and raced back to him. Laughing, "We did it, we did it!"

Jim dropped the sand ladders he had under each arm and hugged her.

"They will want you in the East African Safari. They call Jogindar Singh, the flying Sikh. I wonder what they will call you if you drive wearing no clothes? What about Lady Godiva Rochester? "

Claire said, "You keep carrying the sand-ladders I will run and get the jack." Jim reached the Landrover and dropped the ladders and then threw them one at a time on to the roof rack. He turned to see poor Claire really struggling with the heavy jack. He ran to her and said,

"My poor darling, you will hurt yourself?"

"Rubbish," said Claire. "You can get the tyre, then we have got the lot."

They brewed up some tea and started packing the Landrover again. After Jim had put the mattress on the top, Claire disappeared behind the Landrover and put on a T shirt. She poured water down the front and came round to find Jim.

"Will I do? Come on this girl wants to be ravished on the top of the Landrover." Before Jim could grab her she was going up the ladder. The sight of her bottom had Jim out of his shorts and up after her. She was lying on her back with her legs wide apart smiling at him. As Jim knelt down, she guided his head to her bush. He kissed and sucked her until she pulled his hair to bring him on top of her. Then she guided him into her. Jim must have been tired and weak because normally, if he had not made love for some time, he would come in a few thrusts as soon as he felt her round him. However, this morning, he did not ejaculate but came out of her and knelt and then drew her bottom on to him. Then he started to thrust again as Claire rubbed her clitoris.

"Wait, my proud lion," said Claire. "Take me from behind like our first time." She rolled onto her tummy and, with her face on the mattress, pushed her bottom up and back to him. Jim guided himself into her and then, holding her waist thrust vigorously again. They were both panting when Jim came and collapsed on top of her. Eventually Claire said,

"That was bloody good, we must get stuck more often."

They set off across the desert and, once again the going was really good. Jim made certain to slow down whenever they came to a ridge. He would not have minded a repeat of the love making but he certainly did not want to be carrying all their stuff again. Claire was wearing only her T shirt, which she had wet again.

"This is a great way of cooling off. Is there a way we could cool the beer down like this? Could we have a couple of bottles, wrapped in a towel, in that canvas bucket?" They stopped and prepared their cooling device. Jim secured it to the Landrover. He turned around and there was Claire, quite brazenly, wiping between her legs with a wet flannel.

"Is that to bring you on bull?" laughed Jim. Claire looked up and slowly licked her lips lasciviously.

"That's a good idea but actually it is to wash off your sticky sperm. Look how it has run out of me, down my legs and got covered in dust. Any more comments and I will make you lick if off." Claire gave him a big kiss.

"It is pretty boring but I will have to put my bikini on as, look, there is Marsabit Mountain on the horizon." Sure enough, there was a big green haze on the horizon to the south.

Chapter 33

Marsabit Mountain

Tuesday 13th February 1968

It was a beautiful drive. The road through the desert was good and all the luggas were flowing in their direction off the mountain, so they did not have to cross any. All the while they climbed gently towards what looked like an enormous green hill but, in reality, was over 5000ft. The air not only became cooler, but moist. Claire remarked,

"I feel like Merry and Pippin coming into Fanghorn Forest in 'Lord of the Rings'."

"Don't worry," said Jim. "I think your feet are just dirty. I don't think you are getting hairy feet like a hobbit!" They were nearing the top of the road on the Mountain when they met the much bigger road coming in on their left, from Ethiopia. The airstrip was ahead of them.

"It is a difficult place to land," said Jim, "as it is often covered in cloud. There is a much lower strip on the south side, where you can wait for the cloud to clear."

They stopped in the town, to fill up with petrol and water. While Jim was sorting that all out, Claire and Lucy went shopping. Claire was excited when she came back. She had managed to buy two steaks, which they could Bar-B-Q and some fresh tomatoes. She had also bought some cold beers.

"I felt the beers in our experimental cooler and they are not too bad, considering how hot they were when we put them in. I thought, if we started with cold ones, we perhaps could keep them cold."

"Let's hope we can. I feel like a party tonight. Here is a cold coke for now, which I bought when I paid for the petrol." Claire poured some water in a bowl for Lucy, before gulping down the coke. She said,

"That would make a good photo for 'Tatler'. Lady Rochester on safari, necking a coke from the bottle wearing a shirt open to the waist and her bikini bottoms, in the middle of town."

"Well, I love her like that. Bugger what London expects. It is interesting for our report that we have not found any sign of drilling up here in the North West." Soon they were making their way through the town. The population was fairly cosmopolitan, as this was the District HQ. There were civil servants from all over Kenya. There were some Arab and Asian traders. The majority of the population were the tall good-looking Boran. They were the same tribe as Leonard Baloala. After two enquires, they hoped they were on a track which would take them to a crater lake called, 'Lake Paradise'. It was only eight miles out of town, on the eastern side of the mountain, but the road was bad and it took them well over an hour to find it. Jim's plan was to camp in the edge of the forest, on the lip of the crater. They would try not to make too much noise and keep Lucy in the camp. Then, he hoped, they would see some game at dusk, as the animals came to drink.

When they found a good spot, Jim started unpacking the table and chairs. Claire found the two pewter tankards and poured two beers. "I reckon we bloody well deserve these," said Jim. "Come and sit on my knee."

"I hope the old chair will take us both," said Claire. "We will look a right pair of idiots, falling down into the lake." Claire sat across the chair with her back against one arm of the chair and her legs over the other. Her arm was round Jim's shoulder. Jim idly stroked her thighs with his free hand.

"This is the life. What I would like to see is, either a Bongo or a Greater Kudu come down to drink." They were not that lucky but they did see some Bushbuck, a family of Bush pigs and a pair of duiker. The duikers were very small and Jim thought they might be Blue Duiker. He had never seen them before. Initially they thought they were Dikdik but the light was quite good and they were both certain they were something different. They also saw some Waterbuck. Claire whispered.

"I think we ought to put the windows in the Landrover tonight, so that Lucy is safe. I bet there is a Leopard near here. I want you to cuddle me properly tonight in the tent, not just lie on your back and

435

snore. I know what you are like after a few beers. Would you like another one?"

It was getting really dark now as Claire sat down in his lap again and passed him a beer.

"These are still lovely and cold. They have been in the cool box," said Claire.

Jim said. "Can you take your bikini top off now that it is dark?" Claire did as she was asked, thinking Jim was going to kiss her breasts. Instead he said,

"Would it be nice having a cold bottle against your nipples?"

"Let's try, I will try not to giggle and frighten the game away. Wow, that feels odd. It is not as nice as you sucking them." Jim put down his beer and obliged her.

It was getting quite chilly when they lit the Bar-B-Q. While Jim cooked, Claire sorted out the tent on the roof. The fresh meat and tomatoes with some baked potatoes was really tasty. They had a third beer. Claire said.

"I feel a bit pissed, can we leave the washing up and use the water you have heated in the bucket, to wash ourselves and our hair?"

"Great idea," said Jim. In turn they knelt in the camp bath and washed each other. It was not very successful but they got the worst of the dust off. They put Lucy, with her blanket in the Landrover. Claire was now shivering so they clambered up the ladder, into the tent, and zipped up the ends. Luckily, there did not seem to be any mosquitoes. They soon warmed up, as Claire had managed to zip their two sleeping bags together but they were both tired and a little pissed, so they did not make love but just cuddled up together and were soon asleep.

They both awoke together, not long after midnight. The Landrover and their tent were being rocked gently. Jim whispered in Claire's ear.

"There is an elephant rubbing his arse against the Landrover. Lucy must be terrified."

"She is not the only one," whispered Claire. "Now I have woken up, I need a wee."

"Me too," replied Jim. Soon the rocking stopped and there was silence. They waited but could hear nothing. Jim un-zipped the tent-flap, very quietly. They both looked out but could see nothing.

"Move your bottom over the edge of the roof-rack," said Jim. "I will hold you." Claire managed to wee over the back of the Landrover. On his knees, Jim did the same. Carefully he zipped up the tent and they both snuggled back into the joint sleeping bag. Jim was cuddling Claire's back.

"I will never get to sleep with that hard 'willy' between my thighs. You must be quiet." Jim felt Claire helping him enter her. He could only just reach and he felt her push her bottom back. She started to rub herself. Jim moved very slowly in and out. Claire's fingers kept his penis in her. She whispered,

"I can't really feel you. Let me roll onto my tummy, with a pillow under it. That's better. In fact, that is really good. Can you keep going? That's marvellous." Jim could not speak as he was trying to stop ejaculating. To take his mind off her, he was imagining the elephant coming back. He could hear her stifled gasps. Then she wriggled her bottom and it was too much for him. He seemed to ejaculate forever, probably because he was still a bit pissed. Claire gave a deep sign and moved the pillow, so she could rest her head on it. She kissed him.

"Now I will sleep like a log, even if the elephant comes back. Sleep well, my darling. Your smell is better than any sleeping tablet." He kissed her neck and they both slept.

The elephant did not come back and they slept well past dawn. Jim woke to see a naked Claire bending over and unzipping the tent. He thought, '*that was a sight worth waking up to, better than a Bongo or a Greater Kudu,*' His reverie was soon shattered, by a shriek from Claire, and she came flying up the ladder into the tent.

"It was mortifying! I was squatting to have a pee and there were two '*Askaris*' standing watching me and grinning. Don't you laugh Jim Scott; a girl must have some modesty! Now, of course, neither of us have any clothes. Your turn to go and say '*Jambo*', dressed in a smile. I am sure they are not like the elephant, they are not going to go away."

Jim wiped the smile off his face and knelt to go out of the tent. He felt Claire's hand on his penis as she giggled,

"He looked a bit small so I thought I could make him look his best."

"You wait, Lady Rochester!" was all Jim said. He climbed down the ladder, reached for his shorts which were on the chair, put them on and turned to the two smiling *'Askaris'*. *"Jambo, habari, ndovu nakuja hapa usiku* (Hello, Rangers. How are you? An elephant came here in the night)*"*

"Ndio, habari bwana (Yes, How are you?)*"* They replied.

Jim invited the *'Askaris'* to have some tea and put the kettle onto the small gas stove. Then he found some clean shorts and shirt for Claire and handed them up to her, via a very discrete hand coming out of the tent. It transpired that these two *'Askaris'* were the night shift, guarding the world famous elephant called 'Ahmed'. He was also guarded by two old bull elephants, one of whom had rocked the Landrover last night. Claire came down the ladder from the tent and shook the *'Askaris'* by the hand and then made them all some tea. Jim asked the *'Askaris'* about the chances of seeing Greater Kudu and Bongo, here in Marsabit. The *'Askaris'* said, if they stayed here, they might well see Greater Kudu but, sadly, there was no chance of seeing Bongo. As far as they knew, there were no Bongo left on Marsabit Mountain. They said the only place they knew to see them was on Mount Kulal. After they all had finished their tea, the *'Askaris'* asked if Jim and Claire would like to see 'Ahmed', his tusks were said to weigh more than 100 lbs. each.

Obviously, Jim and Claire were overjoyed at the chance to see 'Ahmed' so, grabbing the camera and a water bottle, they set off following the two *'Askaris'*. They skirted Lake Paradise and set off into the forest. Soon they came across a whole heap of elephant dung, which was still steaming. The *'Askaris'* indicated, with a finger to their lips, that they should be quiet. They walked on and soon they could hear the elephants pulling boughs off some trees. They could also hear their tummies rumbling. They crept on and soon were staring at three enormous elephant's bottoms. One of the *'Askaris'* indicated that the one on the left was 'Ahmed'. The *'Askari'* crept forward. Jim felt he was being deafened by the noise from their tummies. The *'Askari'* took Jim's hand and reached up with it to 'Ahmed's' tail. Jim knew what he had to do. It was a sign of manhood if you could pull an elephant's tail hair and make it into a bracelet. No way was Claire going to miss out. Jim felt her right close to him. They both reached upwards and wound a piece of hair, which was a thick as a piece of raffia, around their fingers. With his other hand Jim indicated a count of three and they both pulled down hard. 'Ahmed' gave a loud grunt and took two steps forward. Then there was silence. Jim had his arms tight around Claire. He could feel her heart thumping in her chest. He could also feel his own heart.

Elephants have the unique ability, if they are disturbed, to stop their tummies rumbling. Presumably, this is so that they can use their very acute ears to good effect. Jim knew they were listening now and also using their trunks to smell. One of the elephant guards was not happy. Suddenly he trumpeted and the three elephants lumbered, away deeper into the forest. The '*Askaris*' both smiled and one made a rude gesture, that Jim and Claire should now copulate. Jim and Claire were very hot anyway and they both blushed crimson. The '*Askaris*' indicated that they would have to follow the elephants and that two more '*Askaris*' would come this way soon, to take over guard duty from them, so they could go and sleep. Jim and Claire thanked them and shook hands. The '*Askaris*' had melted into the forest within seconds. Jim and Claire went back the way they had come. They met the new '*Askaris*' just at the forest edge. Jim told them the direction of their friends and the elephants had gone.

Claire and Jim were soon at their camp. They each still clutched the elephant hairs. Claire reached up and kissed Jim.

"I want you. Come on." She was up the ladder, quickly followed by Jim. She had her shorts off in a second and pushed Jim onto his back. She was immediately on top of him, kissing his lips, while he was fumbling to take his shorts off. She found his now hard cock and pushed herself on to it. Then she rode him, as if she was winning the Derby. Soon they were both gasping and came together. Claire collapsed onto him. She laughed.

"Look, I still have the hair in my hand."

"Mine is in my shorts and scratching my leg," answered Jim and they both collapsed, giggling like little children.

When they had recovered their breath, Claire said, "I had better make myself decent, in case the '*Askaris*' come back. You are a naughty boy, you did not find me a bra or knickers."

Jim replied, "I don't think they will come back. I think they will be ready for some food. Anyway they told us to make love."

They had a hearty breakfast of corn beef hash and baked beans, washed down with lots of mugs of tea. They tidied up the camp. Jim set up two canvas bags, to cool some beers, while Claire, using a small nylon bracelet as a pattern, started to make the proper elephant hair bracelets for each of them. It was rather a domestic scene as Jim sat next to her, scanning through a book on the wild life in East Africa, to make sure he would know what a Greater Kudu would look like if he actually caught a glimpse of one.

They then took Lucy for a walk around the lake. They both felt a little sorry for her, as they had left her shut up in the Landrover when they went to find the elephants. Jim laughed when he told Claire he had taken his camera when they went with the '*Askaris*', but he had forgotten to take any pictures. He took several pictures of Claire after she had insisted on doing most of the buttons up on her shirt, as she still had not bothered to put a bra on. When they got back to camp they had a beer each, as they reckoned they were cool enough. Then, feeling sleepy, they clambered up in the tent, opened both ends so there was a little breeze and had a siesta. They were both tired as they had had a broken night, thanks to the elephant. It was not as if they were well rested as the safari, up to now, had been quite tough. They slept until six 'o'clock. They had left out one of the plastic jerry cans in the sun, so they had some warm water. They had a shower together. They knew they could be seen but doubted if any of the locals came near the forest. They would be frightened of the elephants. Jim set up a spot-light just in case some more game came down to drink. It was wonderful sitting watching the lake, as the night came down. They both had another beer. The temperature was just right, as the altitude took some of the heat away. After a light supper of cereals, bananas and UHT milk, they made a coffee and put some African Cream Liqueur into it. Because they were out on safari, and in the moonlight, it tasted like nectar. They thought, because they had slept during the day that they would not sleep but they were wrong, they both slept like logs. They languidly made love when they woke, just before dawn. They lay on their tummies on the mattress looking out over the lake. As it was quite chilly, they pulled the sleeping bags around them. It was rather eerie as there was a light mist over the lake. As it lifted they were in luck, as there was a solitary Greater Kudu male, with his long spiral horns, grazing by the lake. They were delighted. Without saying a word, they cuddled up together and slept until the sun was really up and had cleared the mist.

They had a leisurely breakfast and packed up the camp. Jim and Claire were slightly sad, as this had been a beautiful camp overlooking Lake Paradise. They were disappointed to leave. On the other hand Lucy was bouncing around. She had been a bit restricted. She also may have been frightened, because of the presence of leopards. They had not seen any evidence of their presence but they had certainly heard one. They had always been careful to shut Lucy in the Landrover with the windows on, at night. Now, Jim took the windows off as he knew they would be driving again in the hot country, once they had come down off Marsabit Mountain.

They set off at mid-morning, on the track leading South West through the forest. In about an hour they reached another crater lake, called Gof Bongole. They surprised a group of ten Waterbuck, which was drinking. On the way, they saw several Dikdik and a flock of Guinea Fowl. Jim hoped they would see some more, when they were out of the Game Park, and he could shoot one for supper. After a further hour they met the main road, leading south from Marsabit to Isiolo. This was in good condition and so they made good time, as they were losing altitude. It was getting hot. Jim had not bothered to put a shirt on but Claire had been slightly worried about the 'Askaris' coming back so she had put on a bra and a shirt. She delighted Jim by undoing the buttons of her shirt and taking her bra off. She teased him by saying he must keep his eyes on the road. Naturally, he disobeyed her. She had no worries about being semi-naked, as there was no traffic on the road. There was not even a barrier at the Game Park boundary. They were now going through the Kaisut Desert but on a proper road, so that Jim was not concerned that they would suddenly go into a sand lugga. In fact they did come to one, called the Milgis, but that had a concrete bottom.

They had put two coke bottles in the canvas bucket, wrapped in a wet towel, which Jim had tied to the wing-mirror on his side of the bonnet. Claire decided it was time for a coke but they would not stop, as they would get so hot. First, to Jim's delight, she took her shirt right off and half sprawled over him and managed to reach the canvas bag. Once she had got the cokes into the car, she flipped the first cap. Coke fizzed everywhere.

"So, Jim, I did not take my shirt off for you to get a glimpse of my tits. I took it off to stop it getting covered in coke."

"They are lovely tits," replied Jim. "I will remember, when you are all scrubbed up at the Muthaiga club, to say to you, as I hand you a coke, Claire, take all your kit off I don't want to get coke on your dress!"

"You are a naughty, over-sexed boy, but I love you. I still can't believe you putting your hand up my skirt and getting me all excited by the roulette table. In fact, can you slow down and rub me now?" She undid the button on her shorts and drew down the zip. Jim could feel her springy bush and her slightly swollen lips. Claire lent back her head and sighed.

"Christ that is good."

The next minute Jim nearly swerved off the road, as there was a big blast of a horn, from a safari type Landrover overtaking them. Jim had forgotten that, as he had slowed down, there were other road users who wanted to go at a decent speed. Poor Claire- her shirt was wide open and the passengers in the other vehicle had seen all. She had hardly done her shirt up, before a second safari type Landrover came by followed by a Bedford 4 X 4 lorry. It was a professional hunter, taking his clients back to Nanuyki and probably on to Nairobi.

Jim could see that Claire was annoyed. Her face, neck and what Jim could see of her chest, were crimson. Jim would have laughed but instead he looked at the road and said nothing. Then he felt her hand on his thigh.

"You have no need to look so crest fallen. I am certainly not blaming you. I invited you to put your hand down my shorts. In fact, I undid the button and the zip to help you. I am blaming myself for being such a nymphomaniac. I just enjoy sex. I love you. I enjoy feeling you touching me. I just should not be such a fool to do it in public. It was not really my fault, squatting down naked in front of those 'askaris', but having an orgasm at forty miles an hour on a dirt road, was totally barmy."

"I love you for it," said Jim simply. "If you had not taken me to Nairobi Game Park, you would have remained my unknown controller. However, I was totally bowled over by you at first sight, so I would have come after you whatever."

"Would you really? Would you have risked all, before you got to know me?" asked Claire.

"Certainly," replied Jim. "You are a remarkably beautiful girl. Add to that, your wicked sense of humour and fun, makes you irresistible to me."

"Well, that is a very sweet thing to say to a girl, who has just made a perfect dick of herself. Thank you. I do not feel so bad now. Now I am going to ask you something but you can say if you don't want to tell me."

"Try me," said Jim laughing.

"You obviously had not had a lot of sexual experience before Nairobi Game Park. In fact, I think you told me so. I certainly have told you that I have only had one fling, with my father's groom. Somehow, now we both are, I would have said, very experienced. With your limited experience, am I a nymphomaniac?" She squeezed his thigh as she asked.

"You don't have to answer."

"You definitely are not a nymphomaniac," replied Jim.

"I trust you Jim, and I think you answered that honestly and, obviously, it was the answer I wanted. However, I think for you to be quite so certain, there must have been a girl in your past who was a little like me. Did she want sex all the time?"

Jim laughed. "Yes there was. I did love her very much. We were both very young and the time was wrong for both of us. It nearly broke my heart leaving her. I hope I did not break her heart."

"I hope you didn't hurt her too much. Do you still contact her?" replied Claire.

"No, we agreed not to write, as we both thought it was better that way. She was a very brave girl."

Claire lent forward and kissed Jim's neck.

"Thank you for being so kind to me. I love you." Then with an impish grin, Claire said, "As soon as we stop this hot, noisy, old Landrover and we are somewhere private, will you put your hand down my shorts?" Jim said nothing - just slowed the Landrover, drove off the road and headed for some thick bush about 100 yards away.

"You darling," said Claire and started taking her shorts off. They made love up against the Landrover, behind the bushes. Lucy lay down in the shade. Claire could see a mountain about five miles behind Jim. She told Jim, as he was doing up his shorts.

"I think that is called Losai and, knowing my luck," said Claire, "those hunters are up there looking at us with a telescope!"

"They should be so lucky," said Jim. "I think that means we are not far from our destination, which is the sand lugga near to the airstrip at Laisamis. We must not camp near to the lugga, as apparently the sand flies are really bad at night but, if we can camp a quarter of a mile away, we can have some good sand-grouse shooting in the morning."

They got going again. Jim had been right. The airstrip was on their right. They found some big trees to camp under. It was pretty hot but the cokes had kept cool and were very refreshing. Claire laughed and said there was no way she was going to open her shirt, so that she did not get coke on it. For the rest of the day she was going to be very well behaved. She would only have a shower after dark. Jim reckoned that was a little boring, but he would wait for the dark. He went off to collect some dry wood to make a fire. They were well out of any game park and Jim fancied a big blaze. Claire would look lovely, having a shower in the firelight.

Claire was busy setting the camp up. Something made her uneasy. She was sure she was being watched. She said to herself, not to be such an idiot just because she had been caught out earlier in the day. Then she looked up and screamed. There was a leopard up a tree about ten yards away. She took two strides and jumped head first into the Landrover onto Lucy. Jim came running to see the leopard running away into the bush.

He shouted. "Claire, are you OK?"

She shouted, "Look out, there is a leopard." As Jim came up to the Landrover, he could see that Claire was safe.

"You are safe now, my darling, I saw the leopard run off. Come on let me give you a hug." He could see Claire was very pale. She must have been really frightened. Slowly, she got out of the Landrover and came into his arms. He stroked her hair. Jim could feel her relax in his arms. Claire said, "What really scared me is that he must have been watching me, or even us, for some time. It was like a voyeur."

To cheer her up Jim said. "Well, at least you had your kit on and you won't be meeting him in the Muthaiga Club."

Claire smiled and relaxed more, so that she laid her head on his shoulder and placed one of his hands on her breast. They stayed like that for a couple of minutes. It was mid afternoon and very hot. There was no wind and no sound. Claire revelled in their closeness. She kissed him on the mouth.

"Well, this won't get the camp set," she said. "Let's have a really big fire tonight?"

"Great minds think alike. I thought the same, as I was collecting the wood. I was looking forward to our shower in the fire light. I think this is a hot place but there may be a breeze at dusk to bring you up in goose bumps." He kissed her and then they went back to their chores. Jim was careful not to go too far away, gathering wood. He was lucky as there was plenty around. They soon had a good fire going. They heated their big metal water bucket and also a kettle, so they could have a cup of tea. With the heat and all the excitement, they had forgotten they had not had any lunch, so they had their usual of UHT milk, cereal and banana. As they were sitting sipping their tea, Jim was assessing where they could hang the shower to be nice and near to the fire, but not too near so they would get burnt.

"Penny for your thoughts," said Claire.

"I was just thinking where we could put the shower, so that I could see as much of you as possible in the firelight, without burning you. The fire will keep the leopard away, so I will have you to myself. We will still have to shut Lucy in the Landrover when we go to bed, as the fire will die down and the leopard may come back. I think, if we want a wee in the night, we should do it over the back of the Landrover like we did when the elephants were about."

They read their books for a time and then they took Lucy for a walk. Jim took his shot gun in case they saw supper. They were in luck and saw a pair of Yellow-necked francolin. Jim managed to shoot one. They were delighted as, of all the game birds in the NFD, they are the tastiest.

They had an excellent supper having cooked the francolin, wrapped in tin foil, on the fire. It was now dark so Claire said they could have a shower together, as surely no one would be spying on them now. As Jim was shampooing Claire's hair in the shower, he said. "I have a proposal for you."

"As you have a bloody great erection, let me guess . . . it is I bend over and you roger me from behind."

"That is an excellent proposal but actually, it was about the night after next, which is our last night of our holiday. When we reach Nairobi we will be pretty dirty. We could check into a hotel and get cleaned up and then have one more night together, before I drive back to Mombasa. I know we said we were going to camp behind the aero-club. I know there are showers there but you might get seen and we can't go out and have a nice meal."

Claire turned to face him, now he had rinsed her hair and the water had run out of the shower.

"It is a great proposal but the sad thing is it would be much too risky to stay at the Norfolk or the New Stanley as we would be bound to run into someone we knew from up country."

"I agree but I was not thinking of those hotels but, say we checked into the Panafric? I know it is not the best in town but, on the whole, only air crew or tourists stay there. You would never see an upcountry farmer dead, in there."

"That's a great proposal. Let's do it. I am sure they will have a room. If they don't, we can always do plan B and camp at the aero-club."

"That's agreed then. Now let's do your proposal. Bend over."

"You cheeky monkey, I was guessing that's what you had in mind it was NOT my proposal. However, if you will brush the knots out of my hair, I will sit on your lap if the chair will bear us."

Brushing the knots out was good fun. When the task was completed to Claire's satisfaction, she announced that she wanted to let her hair dry, so she wanted to have her back to the fire. Jim put some more wood on the blaze and Claire sat in his lap, with her legs over the arms of the camp chair. Somehow, as she was wiggling and getting comfy, Jim entered her. They started to kiss and Claire rubbed herself and rocked her bottom. It was not long before she shuddered and let her head fall forward on to his shoulder.

"That was magic, my darling. Can I stay like this and feel you shrink and all your semen run out of me but, of course, some energetic sperm will be swimming up through my cervix to meet an egg. I am sad really, that I have to be on the pill. I would love to have a little Jim, to suck on my breasts." Jim lent forward and kissed them.

"I must say, it is rather nice when a big Jim does that."

After a peaceful night they got up just as the sun was climbing above the Rusarus plateau. They walked down to Laisamis Lugga. Jim took his gun and Lucy bounced about with excitement. As if at the flick of switch, the sand-grouse started to fly in to get a minuscule amount of water. These species came in the morning; other species came in the evening. It was great shooting. Jim managed two 'left and rights' but he stopped after he had shot eight in total. He did not want to kill any, just for killings sake. He just needed breakfast.

When they got back to the camp, they took off the breasts and fried them in a frying pan. With a baked potato, cooked in tin foil in the fire, they were delicious. They packed up camp and set off in good spirits, even though Jim reckoned they had about 200 miles to go. He hoped he would be able to find the track through, a private farm, up into the Mount Kenya forest. They had been going for about two hours, when they could see the northern face of Lolokwe, where they had turned off to head west. It seemed a life time ago. Jim squeezed Claire's hand as it rested on his thigh. To lighten his mood, Claire said,

"It is going to be very cold up Mount Kenya, you will have to hold me very close tonight." Jim squeezed her hand again.

They stopped in Isiolo for a coke each but did not bother to fill up with fuel, as Jim wanted to empty the jerry cans. After the barrier, they had the long climb up to Timau. The 'murram' was good, as it seemed to have been recently graded. Jim remembered the track was just before the tarmac, at Timau. Needless to say, they over shot it and had to do a U turn and then look for a track on the right. The cloud was down on the mountain. It looked very forbidding. They both hoped they could set up camp before any rain came. They reached the clearing in the forest, where Jim had been before, after a long hard climb. The Landrover, which was tuned for the coast, took singular exception to the altitude. Strictly speaking, they were in the national park but there was no gate on this little used track. They had actually three hours left of daylight but it did not feel like that, because of the gloom. Claire sorted out the tent on the roof rack and Jim brewed some tea on the stove, to keep them warm. Claire even put on a pair of jeans. Jim made a small fire in a circle of stones where there had been a fire before. Although the wood was damp on the outside it was actually old, fallen wood so it burned well, once the fire got going. Jim heated the bucket with the water but there was no way they were going to have a shower. Jim bravely stripped to the waist to wash his top half. Claire remarked,

"Bugger that, you can put up with my smelly body!"

They had their old favourite of corn-beef hash and beans, washed down with relatively cold beers. They ended the meal with a hot mug of coffee laced, with a large slug of brandy. They washed up together. Claire said.

"I am embarrassed to ask you but do you mind coming with me? I need the loo and after that leopard, this place seems rather frightening."

"Certainly, I will come with you. We will take Lucy as she has not really had any exercise since breakfast." They did not go far into the forest. Jim made Claire smile, as he dug a small hole for her with the 'panga'. Claire had no sooner dropped her jeans and was going to squat, when there was a noise in the bush behind her. She shot up. "Don't worry," whispered Jim, "it sounded loud but I think it was quite a small creature."

"That was close," said Claire, "I nearly pooed my pants. I love safari with you. You are so relaxed I would feel so embarrassed with anyone else." When she had finished Jim covered in the hole. He turned to find she had taken her pants and jeans off. He raised his eyebrows.

"I am going to have a bottom wash when we get back to the hot water in the camp." She led him back to the clearing with her white bottom acting like a light, guiding him home. While she was washing, Jim brewed another mug of coffee and laced it as before. Claire sipped it and sighed.

"I feel quite tipsy, I am sure we will sleep well tonight."

They shut Lucy in the Landrover. Claire had not bothered to put her pants or jeans back on, after her wash. As she started up the ladder, she felt Jim's had on her bottom.

"I hoped you would do that. That's why I said I was tipsy. Come on, I want to kiss that clean upper body of yours. There is no way I am going near your bottom half." However, Claire did allow Jim to take his shorts off when he got into the sleeping bag. It was jolly cold, so Jim did not take Claire up on her offer to kiss his upper body. They both snuggled down in the two sleeping bags, zipped together, with their shirts and sweaters on but naked from the waist downwards. Actually they slept very well cuddled up together in the warm sleeping bag but in the cold tent.

They were rewarded for their efforts in the morning, as Mount Kenya came out of the cloud in all its glory. They had a cereal breakfast, watching the Mountain cloud over. Then they packed up, made sure the fire was totally out, and headed back down the track to civilization. There was tarmac all the way to Nairobi. They made good time and clocked into the Panafric in the middle of the afternoon. While Claire took Lucy for a walk, Jim packed everything off the roof rack, into the Landrover. He did this mainly for the journey down to Mombasa, but also he thought he had better, in case there were any light fingered gentlemen about. Lucy could only guard the inside of the Landrover not what was on the roof rack.

They only took their clothes bag up to the room. There were a few aircrews by the pool but otherwise the hotel was deserted. In some circumstances, a swim would have been nice after the hot drive, but they thought it was pretty antisocial in their filthy state and after, they had two baths to try and get themselves really clean, they snuggled up in bed. They slept for a couple of hours. When they awoke they were both hungry, so they got presentable and decided that they could risk going down to the restaurant. Sadly, the place was well lit. It was not somewhere to take your beloved for a romantic candle-lit dinner. The food was good and they both got stuck into, first some 'talapia' fish cakes and then large rump steaks, washed down with G&Ts followed by a bottle of red wine. They did not notice four men looking at them from a nearby table. They had some ice cream followed by coffee. The men finished their meal and got up to go to the bar. As they went past their table, one of the men said,

"I think I recognise you. Weren't you driving down from Marsabit, three days ago? I hardly saw your face but you have got great tits. Claire blushed to the roots of her hair. She did manage a repost of,

"I am glad you like them. My boyfriend does as well!" The men went on, laughing loudly.

"Well, of all the bad luck," said Jim, as they walked out to give Lucy a final walk.

"Well, it could have been a lot worse," said Claire. "They could have been local residents. My guess is, they are up-market tourists on a photographic safari. Thank the Lord, they did not have their cameras ready. Richard is very understanding but he would not tolerate a picture of me topless, with your hand down my knickers."

They had a great night, bouncing about in a proper bed. They were in no rush in the morning. Jim went down to let Lucy out. He ordered breakfast to be brought to their room. He made sure he warned Claire what was happening, so that she was not wandering about in the nude. They were both really sad as they finished their breakfast. Claire outlined a plan for Easter, when Jim was up sailing. She suggested he booked into the Oxford Hotel, near to the High Commissioner's Residence, where he had stayed after the second Tana River trip. The rooms each had French windows, looking out on to a small swimming pool. All Jim had to do, was to hang up one of his shirts, outside the curtains, and she would know which his room was. She suggested his blue-stripped T shirt, which was very distinctive. Claire laughed and said it would be just their luck if a pole-fisher stole the shirt (this was a practice, where the thief had a pole with a hook on it, which he would poke through the bars of the windows and steal any clothes he could reach) and then she would not know which room he was in. Their holiday was over and they knew it would seem like an age until they could meet up again. Jim put the breakfast trays outside the door, with the do not disturb sign. Claire was getting dressed. She laughed and said,

"Come on, let's make love one more time. You take my underwear off. I know you like doing that. They only just managed to vacate the room by noon, as was required. They gave Lucy another walk. Then Jim drove sadly out to Wilson airport. The plan was for Jim to drive off to Mombasa and Claire to ring for an embassy car, as if she had been dropped off by a light aircraft.

Claire said, "Do you mind taking the real dirty bits of my washing? The staff will think it really odd, with my clothes that filthy. Particularly, any of your finger marks on my knickers." Jim knew that she was trying to cheer them both up and he loved her for it. "Of course I can. I will keep them and bring them up when I next can get up here, which will be at Easter." Jim then laughed.

"I would love to see the rugby lads' faces if I put them with my kit. They will think I have become a cross dresser. I think some of the chaps, and all of the girls, wonder why I haven't got a girl friend. They will put two and two together and make five." They stopped, up a side road near to the airport, to have one last kiss. Claire was crying openly but said she would be OK long before the embassy car arrived. She told Jim that he must be really careful not to go to sleep, on the long hot drive. He tried to lighten the mood by saying that if he felt sad, he would bury his face in her knickers. Claire tried to smile and said.

"I wish I could bury my face in your crutch." Then she got out and Jim got the Landrover moving, waving frantically out of the window and watching her waving back in his wing mirror.

Chapter 34

Sailing match

Thursday 11th April 1968

Jim was picked to sail for Mombasa against Naivasha, in the yearly match over Easter. This year the Mombasa team was away. The previous year he had sailed very well with Claire, in a Hornet in a local, club match, and beaten the 505s so he had been picked as Naivasha had two Hornets. However, Jim had not been able to get away the previous year for the away Naivasha match, because of the Rinderpest outbreak.

Jim managed to get off in good time on the Thursday before Easter, as he arranged to have a meeting up in the Taita hills. As soon as the meeting was over, he set off to Naivasha. He managed to meet up with the rest of the Mombasa team at Mitito Andei, for lunch. It was a boisterous lunch as all the team was pleased to be having an Easter Break. However they were not looking forward to the long, hot afternoon drive. They still had over 200 miles to go and had to negotiate Nairobi traffic. Jim had told the rest of the team that he was staying with a pal in Nairobi. In reality, he had checked into the small hotel near to the High Commissioner's residence, which he and Claire had agreed to, when they last saw each other. He had remembered to pack his blue and white stripped T shirt. The rest of the team was all booked in to stay at the Lake Naivasha Hotel.

He arrived at the Oxford Hotel before dark and checked in. The hotel had a small pool. Jim's room had some French windows which opened on to a veranda, in front of the pool, which was surrounded by a beautiful garden. He had a quick shower to wash off the dust off and then had a good swim, which was lovely after the long drive. He had an early supper and went to his room. He hung up the T shirt as agreed but he thought it was unlikely that Claire would come tonight, as although she knew he planned to stay on the Thursday night she would imagine that he would have arrived very late. He went to bed and was soon fast asleep.

There was no official function at the Residence on Thursday night, so Claire went to bed early. She told the cook that she would go for a run before breakfast. She planned to go out, when everyone was asleep, in her track-suit and see if the blue striped T shirt was hanging out of any of the windows. If it was not, she would come back and then go for an early morning run. She went to her room and changed into her track-suit. She soon heard Richard go to his room and so she decided to risk it, and crept out on to the landing. There was nearly a disaster. Eli and another of the servants, were still clearing up the coffee things. She froze on the top landing. Luckily neither of them looked up. With her heart pounding in her chest, she crept down the stairs and let herself out of the back door. She easily dodged the patrolling 'askari' and jogged out of the Residence. Twice on the road she had to quickly dive into the bushes, as a vehicle went past. Although it would be unlikely it would be anyone who knew her, to any driver it would be really odd to see a European woman running alone, along a road at night.

She soon reached the hotel. Once again, she had to evade the 'askari' to get around the back of the hotel. There was an outside light on by the pool and there was Jim's T shirt. No one had stolen it. She quietly opened the French door, having grabbed the T shirt, went into the room. As she closed the door, she could hear Jim breathing. He often lay on his back and snored when he had been drinking. There was no snoring tonight. She suddenly felt very naughty and wanted to play a trick on him. She took off her clothes and went round to the side of the bed he was facing, lying on his side. Then, very carefully, she burrowed under the sheet and blankets about, where she thought his groin would be. Being under the sheets, it was completely dark. She did not want to touch him with her hands, as she was sure she would wake him. She was like a mole, as she pushed forward with her face. His smell excited her. She was just too far down his body, as her nose touched the tip of his penis. She tilted her head, managed to reach it and licked it. This had the desired effect. She felt him become erect, just by the feeling of her tongue. She opened her lips and very carefully took him into her mouth. As she was under the covers she did not hear him grown. Then he thrust his penis forward and ejaculated into her mouth. He then immediately rolled on to his back, kicking off the covers. Claire had tasted him before but was amazed at how it excited her. She wanted him passionately and pushed herself on top of him. He woke, but was confused and thought he was dreaming. She held his wrists, was kissing him and rubbing herself against him.

"Darling, it's me." Jim was totally awake.

"Christopher Columbus you gave me a shock. I think I had a wet dream."

"You did, into my mouth. Please rub me I am so excited. I want to come now, now, now." She brazenly rolled on to her back with her legs wide open. Soon she was gasping. "Please don't stop. Yes, that's it, yes, oh yes."

Then Jim was on top of her. He had become erect again. She guided him into her. He was thrusting hard and she was thrusting towards him. He grabbed her bottom with both hands. He kept thrusting. Claire had an orgasm and then another, before he eventually ejaculated. He kept kissing her neck and squeezing her bottom. Normally, Claire would feel him shrink but he kept hard inside her. Claire held him tightly with both her legs and arms. She revelled in a wonderful warm feeling, deep inside her. Eventually she gasped. "That was bloody magic."

"It felt like bloody magic to me, as well. You are a very naughty girl. I just could not believe what was happening."

They cuddled together and slept until dawn. They had a shower together, without making any noise.

"I hope we didn't wake up any of the people in the next door rooms," whispered Claire.

"I don't think there are any. This is a pretty quiet hotel, except for seductive young ladies arriving at all hours!" replied Jim.

"Sadly, I will be much later tonight as there is a 'do' on at the Residence. At least I know which room to come to, so you won't need to risk getting your shirt stolen."

"Think, if you had got the wrong room last night?" Jim sniggered. "You are a very naughty and very sexy girl. I can't wait until tonight."

Claire got quickly into her track-suit. She had to just hope no one knew she was not staying at the hotel and saw her running across the garden. She was in luck. No one thought it was odd when she ran into the Residence. They just thought she had been running and they had not seen her leave.

As soon as Claire had left, Jim had to get going. He ate a hearty breakfast, in double-quick time, and drove down to Lake Naivasha. He turned off left, before Naivasha town on the lake road. He was going to be late. He was cross with himself for taking so long over breakfast. He had decided he would not stop at the Lake Naivasha Hotel, as he was sure the rest of the team would have left. He was wrong. Just as he passed the entrance, a car swung out behind him. In it, were the four girl members of the team. They hooted and flashed their lights. Jim relaxed, at least he was not last. He knew the four girls quite well but had never taken any of them out. There were two sisters, in their very early twenties, who lived in Mombasa with their parents. The eldest, Carolyn, had taken a shine for Jim but, although he liked her, he just did not find her in the least bit attractive. The younger, Peggy was quite pretty but definitely did not like Jim, probably because her sister was always throwing herself at him. The other two, Lizzie and Geraldine, worked in Mombasa and shared a small house in Nyali.

They all arrived at the Naivasha Sailing Club, on Crescent Island, at the same time. There was a hive of activity. The Mombasa sailing captain was not pleased that they were late for the briefing. Seeing the light wind, he had made his crew and captains allocation. He had already drawn lots, with the Naivasha captain, for the boats. Each team would have four 505s and one Hornet. The captain, and his petit wife, would have the lead 505. Then three other men would take the other 505s with a girl crew. Jim would take the Hornet with Geraldine. There was some grumbling, as Carolyn wanted to be with Jim. When she was told it was already decided, she said very bitchily.

"You always need a really heavy crew in a Hornet." Jim could see Geraldine was furious but he didn't say anything. Jim knew this was a team event. All he had to do was to beat the opposing Hornet, the fact that, in the light wind they would be left miles behind by the 505s was irrelevant. He turned to a red faced Geraldine and whispered,

455

"Don't worry about her. I am up here to have a fun Easter. Let's go and get changed and then we will be ready. We will have a laugh together, I'm sure." Geraldine squeezed his arm.

"I wish I was not so fat. I am always trying to diet but nothing seems to work."

"Don't worry, I will enjoy helping you do up your life-jacket. It is not very sexy helping a skinny girl. Make sure I don't put my hand down the front of your bikini by mistake!"

"You are a naughty boy. After Carolyn's remark I was going to wear my one-piece but, bugger it, I will wear a bikini to give you a good view!"

There was certainly a lot to see down the front of Geraldine's life-jacket but that did not stop Jim concentrating on the sailing. Jim and Geraldine did not hang about and they got their hornet into the water quickly. While all the other crews were getting ready, Jim took the Hornet round the tip of Crescent Island and got Geraldine practicing going about. She had never sailed in a Hornet before, but she soon got the hang of the sliding seat. She really threw it across the boat. She was not nearly as quick as Claire, in getting out on to the end of the seat but, because she was much heavier, she had just as much effect. Then when she did move her formidable backside on to the end of the seat, she made a big difference. In the light wind, Jim did not need so much weight to keep the boat upright, so he moved his weight inboard. In that way, he realised he would be able to trim the craft to perfection. Jim heard the five minute gun, so he quickly came back round the point of the island and moved up towards the start. He pointed the other Hornet out to Geraldine.

"That is the boat we have got to aim to beat. Don't worry about the 505s they will go much faster than us, in this light breeze. All we have to do is beat that one boat."

"OK Jim, you are the skipper. I think I am going to enjoy sailing with you. You are so relaxed. You don't shout at your crew."

"I know, if I do shout at you, then you will never bend towards me, so I can get a good view."

The one minute gun went off. They were quite a long way from the start line, running with the wind. Geraldine was in her correct position looking forward. She quickly swung round to face him and bend forward.

456

"Hope you enjoyed the vista. That was to wish us luck!"

She swung round into her correct position. She smiled as she could hear Jim chuckling. She knew she had lost them a couple of yards but she was pleased that Jim did not seem to mind. She thought, '*Up yours, Carolyn! You might have a bloody marvellous figure but I have got a happy skipper.*'

Geraldine really enjoyed the race. Jim gave her clear instructions and never moaned if she was slow with the seat. He even had time to tell her some funny stories about his work. She forgot all about the other Hornet they were trying to beat. She just concentrated on the seat and the jib. In fact, her sailing was ideal for Jim as she might not be quick but she was entirely predictable. It allowed him to trim the boat and get as much speed out of her as he could.

On the first two circuits, Jim carefully followed the other Hornet, as he knew the skipper was a local and would be likely to follow the best line. They both totally disregarded the 505s, which had finished the race when they were only half way round the third and final circuit. Jim had noticed, on the first two circuits, that the wind was stronger further away from the shore so he took a line which would take them further out for the final run, with the wind for home. As soon as they rounded the buoy Jim got Geraldine to back the jib and move her weight backwards, so that she was sitting on the gunwale in front of the cock-pit. This brought the bow up slightly so they just managed to come up on the plane. They soon overhauled the other Hornet, so that they beat them by at least two boat lengths. As they passed the finishing line Jim said.

"Well done, Geraldine, you are a star. We beat them. The Sailing Captain will be pleased with us."

"But we were miles behind all the rest of the boats and we were second to last," replied Geraldine despondently.

"Don't worry," countered Jim. "All we had to do was beat that one boat. Trust me."

"I hope you are right. I bet that bitch Carolyn will have some snide comment to make."

Having shaken hands with the Naivasha team, sailing the other Hornet, they walked up to the club house, where most of the sailors were gathered around the score board. Indeed, they had come in second to last and had got almost the lowest number of points. Carolyn made a point of saying to Geraldine,

"Well done, at least you didn't come last." Geraldine went a bit red but just ignored her.

The Mombasa sailing captain came up to them and, smiling, said,

"Well done, you two. You beat your opposite number and got us some points. As we had already finished, I was watching you with my binoculars. It was clever of you, Geraldine, to move back into the cockpit with Jim so that you could overtake them on the run in. However did you think of that?"

With a totally straight face Geraldine replied, "Oh, I only did that to reward Jim for not shouting at me during the race, with a view down my cleavage."

The sailing captain laughed and said, "Lucky Jim."

Geraldine had the pleasure of seeing Carolyn's face, which would have soured fresh cream.

The afternoon went really well for Geraldine and Jim, as the wind got up. They not only beat the other Hornet but, because of the handicap, they beat three of the 505s, including Carolyn's boat. Geraldine was ecstatic.

"As soon as we get somewhere private, I feel I should reward you by taking my bikini top of!"

Jim laughed, "That would be a reward. Tomorrow I will try to win out-right, to earn a full frontal!"

"Now, that would be very greedy and very naughty."

Jim could tell that, given a few drinks that might be on the cards. However fate had something else in store for Jim. All the Mombasa team, except Jim, went back to the Lake Naivasha Hotel when the racing finished, so that they could shower or bath in their rooms. Jim, like many of the Naivasha team had a shower at the sailing club. The Naivasha team was a friendly lot. Jim particularly liked a family of three girls, whose father was called Fred. They often seemed to be laughing together.

Jim knew there was no chance of Claire being free until very late, so he drove the short distance to the Lake Naivasha Hotel to socialise with the rest of the team. When he arrived, before supper, the party was in full swing. Jim did not want anything alcoholic to drink as he thought he might go to sleep, driving back the fifty miles to his hotel in Nairobi. He sat down and chatted to the team captain, who seemed to want to distance himself slightly from the raucous behaviour. Jim did not see what happened but, apparently, Geraldine who had done some martial arts, had challenged one of the men that, if he ran at her, she could use his momentum to toss him over her shoulder. Unfortunately, she had slipped and the man, who was quite heavy, had landed on top of her. Not only that, but Geraldine had landed on to the leg of a fallen bar-stool. She had winded herself and then had fainted. Lizzie had got four of the men to carry Geraldine to the room which she and Geraldine were sharing. None of the team had any medical training, so Jim was sent for.

There was a general hubbub in the room when he arrived. He politely suggested to everyone, except Lizzie, that they should go back to the bar and continue with the party. He came over to Geraldine, who had recovered consciousness and was lying on her bed. She looked ashen. He felt her pulse which was a bit rapid but steady.

"You know I am only a vet, but would you like me to examine you and try to work out how you have hurt yourself?"

"Yes please, Jim, the drink went to my head and I started showing off. The next thing I remember is waking up in here."

Jim had a good look at her pupils, which were normal and then he felt the back of her head. There were no lumps and she said that it did not feel sore.

"What really hurts is my chest."

"Are you really sure you want me to go any further? I could easily get a doctor. There must be one in Naivasha."

"I feel less faint now. Let's not bother a doctor, it is a Public Holiday."

"OK, but I think I am going to hurt you. Lizzie will help me and I will try to be gentle. Can you put your arms above your head?"

"Yes, that hurts a bit but it is not unbearable."

"Now, Lizzie and I will pull your sweater over your head, I think it will hurt like whoop."

Geraldine gasped but did not cry out.

"Well done," said Jim. "You are a very brave girl. You have got a massive bruise on your chest. Can you take her bra off, Lizzie? Luckily it undoes at the front, so it should not hurt."

Geraldine managed a weak smile. "Lizzie, I suggested to Jim that I might take my bikini top off, as we had done so well this afternoon but I had not thought it would be like this."

Jim gently lifted Geraldine's large left breast.

"Does that hurt?" Jim asked.

"No, not at all," was her reply.

He felt under her breast and she winced.

"I don't think you have hurt your breast but I do think you have broken a rib. That is going to be very painful for four to six weeks. Now, as you know, I am staying in Nairobi so I am happy to run you into Nairobi Hospital for an X-ray to confirm my diagnosis."

"Will they do anything that you can't do?"

"Not really. I can easily strap it up for you. You just must not laugh. Sneezing will be agony."

"So make sure you don't tickle me."

"I will slip out to my car and get some sticky bandages. Hopefully, I won't have to speak and explain to anyone."

True to his word, Jim was soon back.

"Are they horse bandages?" enquired Geraldine.

"Yes, but you won't start neighing, as that would hurt. Now, I want you to sit up. Lizzie and I will help you."

When she was sitting up Jim said.

"Now Lizzie, I want you to cup her breasts and hold them up, while I bandage around her chest."

Geraldine was obviously feeling better, as she said with a grin, "I have a better idea. You cup my breasts and Lizzie will put on the bandage."

They strapped Geraldine up and did up her bra. Then they found one of her shirts, as that would be easier to put on than a sweater. She was quite happy to stand up.

"I suggest you take a couple of Aspirin now and then two more when you go to bed. I would stay off the grog tonight but you will be fine to have a drink tomorrow.

Geraldine lent forward and kissed Jim on the lips.

"Thank you doctor, you have been very kind and gentle. Let's go and have some supper?" In fact Geraldine managed very well. Jim could see she was in quite a bit of pain. Jim was button-holed by the Mombasa captain.

460

"I gather Geraldine won't be sailing for the rest of the weekend. I can give you a male crew but a girl would be better. I suppose there is no chance you could persuade that beautiful girl, who crewed for you a year ago, to crew for you. It would be legal, as I remember that I proposed her for membership of the club."

"I am going back to Nairobi tonight. I will see what I can do but it is rather short notice. Let us hope I can contact her and she says yes."

Jim sat next to Geraldine at dinner. He felt sorry for her because now she was stuck up in Naivasha and could not sail. However, the rains had yet to come and the sun would be shining in the morning. Watching the sailing, reading a book or having a quiet drink would not be all bad. After dinner, Jim said his goodbyes and set off for Nairobi. He got back to the hotel by 11.30 pm.

After a shower, he got into bed having left the French doors open. He was soon asleep, only to be woken by a lovely warm body cuddling up behind him. He rolled over and they kissed passionately, as if they had not seen each other for months. When they broke apart, Claire asked, "Have you been a good boy and not been tempted by any of these sailing girls in their bikinis?"

"Actually, I have been a very naughty boy. I masqueraded as a doctor and fondled a girl's breasts." Claire was on top of him in a second, pinning his arms above his head.

"These are the only breasts you are allowed," said Claire pushing them out towards his mouth. Jim did not try to move his hands but just reached up with his mouth and kissed them. Claire moved her body down his and felt his erection.

"You are a very naughty boy, but at least you haven't got 'Brewer's droop.'" She kissed him.

"You had better have a good explanation, or that little man stays on my tummy and I will tease him until you beg for mercy. Jim had that wonderful sensation, as he felt her bush rubbing on his shaft. Jim told her the whole story.

"That poor girl, she has to put up with you all day, trying to look down her front, then she breaks a rib and has to put up with you groping her while she is being bandaged up. Then, she has to put up with another woman coming and taking over as your crew. I bet I am right, you persuaded the Mombasa captain to let you get me to crew for you?"

461

"No, I promise, he suggested it." Jim knew she believed him and actually was pleased, as she reach behind her bottom and put him inside her.

"Actually, I could come with you tomorrow but I am afraid we would have to get back as I have got to be hostess at another function at the Residence. Could I persuade you to come?" She tantalizingly moved up so his penis was only just in her.

"Only if you don't wear any knickers under, what I am sure will be, a very seductive dress?"

"That condition gets you a little further in." She lowered her bottom slightly. "If you want to come in all the way you will have to promise there will be hundreds of 'Lee ho's."

"It's a deal," murmured Jim as he cupped one breast and rubbed her clitoris.

"It's more than a deal. That is bloody lovely. Just don't stop. Please don't stop," begged Claire

Luckily, Jim must have been tired, as he did not ejaculate immediately but kept thrusting and rubbing until Claire collapsed on top of him and then he let himself go. Claire nuzzled his neck. It was still dark went they awoke and made love again. They had a lovely ten minute cuddle before Claire had to get into her running things and creep out. She told Jim she would meet him on the road, after they had both had breakfast.

"Remember, plenty of Lee ho's." Then she was gone.

They had a great drive down over the escarpment, looking down at the Rift Valley stretching away into the distance. Jim put his arm around Claire and hugged her to him.

"We are so lucky to be in the vastness of Africa."

"I am so lucky to have a strong man's arm around me, to protect me. Now, I want you to be really nice to Geraldine. I won't be at all jealous. We have both got to be on our best behaviour as we are on parade all day."

Jim told her about Carolyn.

"I will keep my eye out for her. So Carolyn has the hots for you, does she? Poor Geraldine, she will feel really down today. Did she get a Lee ho?"

Jim laughed. "I save those only for you."

462

"I expect that is a fib, but I would not have you any different. Mind you, I will murder you in the bedroom tonight if I catch you!"

She stroked his thigh and his penis popped out.

"Well he still fancies me," said Claire with a laugh.

They turned off onto the lake road.

"Back in your box, you little tinker," said Claire, as she tucked Jim's penis into his shorts. Luckily, he had calmed down by the time they reached the sailing club. The Mombasa captain made a big fuss of Claire. He must have noticed her wedding ring but he did not say anything. Luckily, no one else seemed to recognise her. Jim went straight over to Geraldine.

"How are you? I hope you are not too sore?"

"Well, it was my own silly fault. Thank you for being so kind last night." Claire came up and Jim introduced her.

Claire said, "I am sorry to be taking your place but I can't say I won't enjoy the sailing. However, Geraldine, I want you to take care of me. I gather Jim fancies himself as a doctor. I want you to make sure there is no inappropriate touching."

Lizzie came up and said. "Hello, I am Lizzie. I think I made a very good nurse. I will look after you. What is your name?"

"I am Claire. I am rather nervous as I have only been sailing with Jim once and that was over a year ago."

Geraldine piped up. "He is really kind and never gets cross. But you must watch him when he helps you into your life-jacket." Jim blushed.

"I think I will go and get a life-jacket now and get one of you to help me." Claire turned to Jim and said. "Then I will be ready for orders, captain." Jim went to take part in the boat draw. Lizzie whispered to Geraldine.

"She will keep him in order. She looks nice. At least you won't have Carolyn gloating all day. I saw her as I came in. She looks really miffed. Claire has a much better figure than her. Claire is so beautiful, she could be a model."

So the racing began. Jim and Claire were a great team together. There were lots of lee ho's, lots of giggling and laughter. Somehow, the hilarity seemed to make the boat go faster. In the stiff breeze, they not only beat the opposing Hornet but, because of the handicap system, they beat the 505s as well. The Mombasa captain was delighted. He was not the only one. Geraldine enjoyed the miserable look on Carolyn's face. At the buffet lunch in the sailing club Claire, with her normal poise, circulated and said all the right things to all the right people. Jim sat next to Geraldine and kindly got her food and drink, so she did not have to get up as she was obviously very sore. She never complained at the pain and managed to whisper to him that, if only they were alone, she would get him to adjust her bandage.

"Of course, I mean purely in your medical capacity!"

Claire came over and whispered to Geraldine, "I think I have pulled a muscle in my groin jumping over the seat. Do you think I should get Jim to examine it?"

Geraldine chuckled. "I think the wind must have changed when Carolyn was frowning earlier. She seems to have a permanent frown now." They both laughed conspiratorially.

In fact, the wind had not only changed but it had dropped to a mere whisper, so Jim and Claire were rubbish against the 505s in the afternoon. They only managed to beat the home team's Hornet by a couple of yards, thanks to Claire moving her weight backwards on to the rear gunwale. It was strange that she seemed to sit on Jim's hand! The Mombasa captain had good cause to ask Claire if she could come and be a crew the next day. Claire said she would be delighted. She was just sad that she could not be with them tonight but she had an engagement in Nairobi and so it was that Jim and Claire left very soon after the racing finished.

Once they were on the road going to Nairobi, Claire moved into the middle seat of the Landrover, so their thighs rubbed together.

"Do you think anyone guessed our relationship?" asked Jim.

"I don't think they did?" replied Claire.

"Obviously, the word will have got around that I am the High Commissioner's wife but, except for Geraldine and Lizzie they are all so 'up themselves' that I doubt if they would have considered well behaved, kind Jim Scott, who is obviously fond of Geraldine, would have the audacity to shag the wife of the High Commissioner! I think we have got time to call into your hotel, if we are really careful."

"Yes, I could do with a cup of tea," said Jim, stroking her thigh and grinning. Claire stroked his thigh and asked. "We might even have some cake?" They giggled like kids all the way back to Nairobi. Getting into the hotel was a doddle, as it was still only late afternoon on Easter Saturday and the majority of people were still out doing things. They made good use of the short length of time they had together, in the bedroom. As Claire was putting her clothes on, she said,

"I almost feel this is home." Jim kissed her on the neck.

"When you come tonight, could you bring your sailing gear then it would give us longer in bed. You must be in desperate need of sleep."

"That is a good idea but don't let's waste time sleeping! I have thought of the dress I am wearing tonight. I promise I won't wear knickers but it does not have a slit up the side, so you will have to take me on trust. However, much I might have enjoyed it, please do not repeat what you did at the Muthaiga Ball as it is just too risky." Claire kissed him on his lips.

"You will just have to wait to feel me. I must go. I can feel myself wanting you again."

With that, she left out of the French Windows and walked, very sedately, across the lawn, turned and waved and was lost from Jim's sight. She was a happy girl when she went in the side door of the Residence. She went to find Eli.

"I feel guilty, Eli, I have been sailing all day and have not helped you with any of the arrangements for this evening." Eli smiled at her. A thing he never did to Sir Richard.

"Everything is in order, Lady Rochester. There will be twenty three sitting down for dinner. I assume Dr Scott will be unaccompanied?" Claire lent forward so she could say in a lowered voice.

"You did not wink then, did you, Eli?"

"Yes, My Lady, I must have got a speck of dust in my eye. Please can you convey my family's *salaams'* to Doctor Scott?"

"Perhaps you could place him near to me at the table and then I will definitely remember."

"Certainly I will, my Lady. You must get him to tell you and the other guests about his trip to Mandera last year. When he sat down for supper with my parents, he said it was like sitting down for supper at his home in *'ulaya'*. That was a very memorable evening

465

for my Mother. My parents have eight children already but I am sure my Mother would like to adopt him into the family. She is always asking my Father for news of his exploits."

"I will certainly ask about his trip. I had better go and change, or I will be in trouble. Thank you for all your help, Eli."

As she went upstairs Claire thought, '*I knew Eli guessed our relationship but I bet he also knows I am his control.*'

Claire quickly showered and dressed in only a figure hugging, low cut black dress, without any underwear. She knew Jim would love it. She thought. '*I wonder what Eli would tell his mother.*' She went down and waited for the first guests to arrive. These functions were very much part of their routine. She knew Sir Richard did not enjoy them, anymore than she did, but they both accepted them as part of the job. There was no doubt, that the Residence and the High Commission were happier places, since Christopher Martin-Jenkins' demise. Sir Richard's timing was immaculate. He was almost at the bottom of the stairs, as Eli showed the Japanese Ambassador and his wife in through the door. They had all met several times before. Claire liked them and was fascinated by Yakki's petit figure. She wondered if Jim would find her attractive. She was certainly very different from Geraldine. Claire asked Yakki what she had done today.

"I have been painting," she replied.

"Could I come over, one morning to see your work?"

"I would love to show you my work."

Claire said impulsively, "Could I come on Tuesday?"

Yakki leant forward and delicately touched her arm.

"May I call you Claire? Please call me Yakki. I would love you to come to my house. Could you come for lunch?"

"That would be great, Yakki. That will be something for me to look forward to, after the holiday. I have been rather energetic, sailing on Lake Naivasha today."

"I used to sail when I was a school girl, with my father."

"Why don't you come tomorrow? There is a regatta and races but I am sure I can get you a sail?"

Yakki turned to ask her husband but he was busy talking to the Commander of the Kenyan Navy.

"I will say, yes please, unless my husband says no." Yakki replied, with a conspiratorial smile.

Claire thought, '*I wonder what Jim will say. It will certainly help with the wagging tongues.*'

Lots of guests started to arrive and Claire was busy greeting them all. Jim was not the last and made her laugh, by saying,

"As your captain today, I hope I am allowed a kiss?" He promptly kissed her on the lips. Claire was slightly taken aback, but managed to say,

"Of course you are and, as we won one race, I will give you another one." She playfully pushed Jim on into the Residence. She looked round to see Yakki looking at her,

On the way into dinner Yakki quietly said to her.

"Please don't ask me sailing. You must really value your time with him?"

Claire whispered, "Oh dear, Yakki, was it that obvious?"

"No Claire, it was only obvious to me as I am, as you say in English, 'in the same boat.'

"You must come tomorrow, Yakki, and we will have a long chat. Tonight we will be well behaved wives."

"Of course we will be, Claire."

Eli had been good to his word and Claire was sat opposite Jim at dinner. As usual she was a little monkey. She kicked off her shoes and put her foot up and caressed his groin. By chance, Yakki was sitting next to Jim, and her husband, who was a lot older than her was opposite, next to Claire. Claire had introduced them to Jim, but had not had a chance to mention anything about the sailing. She got Jim talking about his veterinary work and, as Eli had suggested about the very long and arduous trip to Mandera. Even the elderly Japanese Ambassador laughed, at the Landrover arriving through the wall of the office. Both Claire and Jim drank little, as they were well aware there were many eyes around them. The Japanese Ambassador drank heavily. He said little and became rather morose. Yakki drank little and tried to make conversation.

The conversation shifted quite naturally onto the day's events about Jim and Claire sailing at Naivasha, after the talk about moving the Hippo on the Tana River, to avoiding Hippos while sailing.

467

Claire thought it was a good opportunity to ask Yakki for the following day.

"Why don't you both come and watch the sailing tomorrow? The number of spectacular birds on the lake is worth a visit, apart from the sailing." The ambassador replied,

"I used to sail in my youth, when I was in the Navy but sailing brings back unhappy memories, of drifting in the Pacific Ocean in a lifeboat, having been torpedoed in the war. You may go, Yakki."

Claire then remembered that he had been an Admiral, before he became an Ambassador. There was a noticeable silence. Claire was so grateful to Jim, who said, "That must have been a dreadful ordeal Ambassador. It must have been almost as bad as, when I was a school boy having to learn the names of all the forty nine biggest islands of Japan!" Unlike the others, the Ambassador did not laugh. Jim could feel Claire's toes rigid with apprehension.

"Do you remember them now?" enquired the Ambassador. "Or only that the British helped the Americans to build the atomic bomb?"

Jim did not rise to the jibe but laughed and said, "Oh I remember them alright. I would have been beaten otherwise. One day, I hope to visit Japan."

Claire's foot squirmed in his groin. Jim started to chant the names of the islands. Soon the Ambassador started to smile. Jim felt a delicate hand on his thigh and a sexy foot in his groin. He prayed that the hand would not touch the foot. He kept chanting, until he had remembered the forty-ninth island. To the amazement of the whole table, the Ambassador clapped his hands loudly and declared,

"Young man, I will be very pleased to be your host, when you come to Japan."

Yakki smiled and added, "It was lucky you did not forget the last island. My husband and I were born on that island. I like it because it is very beautiful, with lots of flowers and blossoming trees. My husband likes it because it has a very strong naval tradition. His father and grandfather were both Admirals, as were both my father and grandfather. The Ambassador smiled like the 'cat that got the cream'.

The rest of the meal went by without incident. It was very drawn out, with cheese then a dessert. There were chocolate truffles with the coffee. Jim longed to have Claire by herself and, at last, the guests started to leave. Jim was one of the first. He said his goodbyes and gave Claire a demure peck on the cheek, as everyone was watching. He shook Sir Richard's hand and left to get in his Landrover. Obviously, he did not need a vehicle and could easily have walked, but he did not want to publicise that he was staying in a hotel so near to the Residence.

When the guests had gone, Claire went into the kitchen to thank the staff for doing so well. As she came out, she met Richard and they both went up the stairs together.

"Young Scott did bloody well with the Japanese Ambassador. It was kind of you to ask his wife sailing. There was no way you could have anticipated such a reaction. Jim certainly saved the evening. Can you thank him for me when you see him tomorrow? Sleep well, my dear."

"I hope you sleep well, Richard. I think these functions can be very stressful. In fact, they are bad enough to give us both nightmares."

Claire went into her room and closed the door. She was about to take her dress off, then she thought, '*I have left my sailing stuff with Jim, why don't I slip out now and just wrap myself in a black shawl?*' Claire therefore arrived, through the French windows, into his room much earlier that he had expected. He was naked as he came out of the bathroom.

"Wow, you gave me a real start," whispered Jim.

"In that gear, you look like that sexy Scottish widow selling pensions. You can have all my money anytime. Let me see you in that fabulous dress? Let me feel those sexy hips? Now, lean forward. You are truly stunning."

"Well, Richard thinks you are a star for pacifying the Japanese Ambassador. You are a bloody brain-box. Fancy you remembering all those Japanese Islands."

"It was bloody difficult to concentrate with a girl's foot in my groin and another girl's hand on my thigh. I was worried stiff the hand would touch the foot and then the fat would have been in the fire."

"You need not have worried. Yakki guessed, right away, that we were lovers. She also has a lover. We will ask her about him

469

tomorrow. It is good to see you like the dress," Claire pointed at his erection.

"Was it nice having Yakki's hand on your thigh?"

"I am sure it would have been, if I had not been so scared."

Jim came up close to her and held her tightly to him. He kissed her and nuzzled her neck.

"You are so bloody sexy, I want you right now." Before she could stop him, he had turned her around and had reached down to the floor and put his hand up under her skirt.

"As you promised, there are no boring knickers to hinder me." Claire was slightly moist and he slipped two fingers inside her. With his left hand around her slender waist, he rubbed her until she climaxed. He let her fall forward on the bed. He, very carefully, unzipped the back of her dress. Claire giggled and pushed herself up on her arms, so the dress fell away.

"I think I will employ you as my ladies maid. You unzipped my dress so gently. Let's get into bed before we get cold?"

They made love and fell asleep in each other's arms. Luckily, they woke in time for Jim to go and have some breakfast. He brought some bananas and a roll, back to the room for Claire. Claire had showered and so, took the food out to the Landrover and ate it on the way to the Japanese Ambassador's residence, which was only two miles away. Yakki was waiting at the gate, talking to the 'askari'. She quickly jumped into the Landrover, next to Claire, who had bagged the middle seat. She put her small duffle-bag in the back.

"Thank you both so much for taking me. I think, deep down, my husband wished he was coming. He is a silly old man to bring up the past. I am so sorry, Claire. His behaviour nearly ruined the party."

"You must not worry, Yakki. Just forget it and enjoy today. Do you get any chance to see your friend?"

"Sadly, very rarely. He is an airline pilot based in Japan. We were childhood sweet-hearts. He occasionally gets leave out here. We make the most of our time together." Yakki replied, with a giggle.

"Your English is amazing. How is that?"

"We had an English governess. I think my father was very shrewd. He saw how the world was changing." Yakki laughed again.

"What about your amazing Japanese, Jim?"

"It was your hand on my thigh that encouraged me," replied Jim. Claire chipped in.

"Are you trying to steal him from me?"

"Of course," replied Yakki with a little laugh. Then, in a serious voice, she added, "Japanese girls are very loyal to their friends. You are my friend, Claire. I promise I won't try to take him away." She leant over and touched Jim's thigh and added.

"It is fun to tease. I have not touched a hairy leg before."

"Jim is a very naughty boy. You must not encourage him." Claire said,

"I think, in fact, he is quite shy. Am I right Claire? "

"Yes, but if you give him an inch he will take a mile."

"We have a similar expression in Japanese."

Claire and Jim told Yakki about sailing. Then they came to the edge of the Rift Valley. Yakki thought it was beautiful. She said she must visit more of the country. When they reached the sailing club, the Mombasa team was in disarray. The Captain came up to them and said that Carolyn and one of the skippers had got very drunk last night and said that they could not race this morning.

"Maybe we can help," said Jim. "Yakki is a friend of ours and, I am sure she will crew."

"That is marvellous," replied the Captain. "Would you mind crewing for me, Claire? And could Yakki crew for you in the Hornet, Jim?"

"That will be fine," said Jim. When they were out of earshot, Claire said. "I think the dirty old goat has been dying to get me in his boat all weekend. There will be no lee ho's for me from him for that matter I am wearing a shirt and trousers."

"What is a lee ho?" asked Yakki. Claire whispered a reply in her ear.

"Jim, you would not dare to give a lee ho to an Ambassador's wife?" said Yakki, with a delightful smile on her face.

"Don't you trust him, Yakki? He is up to all manner of tricks. No girl is safe with Jim Scott." Claire squeezed his arm playfully.

Jim noted, with pleasure, that Yakki obviously was not at all worried. She wore a one piece costume, which showed off her petite figure to perfection. She giggled provocatively as she handed Jim her life jacket, asking him to help her to do it up. She said the smallest

471

ladies size would fall off her, so she thought a child's one would be better. She asked Jim about his T shirt. On the front it said, "These boots are made for walking." On the back it said, "Start walking boots." Jim told her that Claire had bought it for him. The lines were from a song by Nancy Sinatra, daughter of Frank Sinatra. Claire knew Jim liked the tune and also that he fancied Nancy Sinatra, so she had bought Jim the T shirt. Yakki laughed and said, in Japan a man would never let on to his lover that he fancied a singer, and certainly a woman would not buy a T shirt reminding a man of any other woman.

Once they got the boat into the water, Jim gave Yakki a hand to get into the boat. She slipped as she stepped onto the gunwale. Jim put out a hand for her to hold, to steady herself.

"Thank you Jim. I thought for one lovely minute I was going to get a lee ho."

"I think, Yakki, you are just as naughty as Claire. Come on, we must get sailing and practice. I will sail us around the corner of the island, so we are out of view."

"My English is a little rusty. Are we going round, the corner to practice lee ho's?"

"You, young lady, are a real tinker for an admiral's daughter. I hope you will be a good sailor, like an admiral's granddaughter." In fact, Yakki was a very good sailor. She picked up what she had to do very quickly. They were soon racing across the water in the strong wind. Jim wished Yakki was a little heavier but, to make up for her lack of weight, Yakki soon started to use her agility. Where taller crews would have sat on the end of the sliding seat, with their feet resting on the gunwales, Yakki crouched, like a monkey, on the far end of the seat giving more leverage. When Jim heard the five minute gun, he started to come around the headland to get near the start line. The Captain and Claire came near them, on a converging course. When Claire saw Yakki, squatting on the end of the sliding seat, she shouted,

"Look out Yakki, or he will dunk you in the lake. I should just enjoy the lee ho's." Yakki shouted back, "Make sure you win, so I have a good report for the admiral." As it was, the Captain and Claire did win. Jim and Yakki came third, which was good for a hornet." Lunch was good fun, as Geraldine and Lizzie were on good form. A very pale Carolyn did not appear until the afternoon, when they were back to their normal crews. Claire whispered to Jim that she thought the Captain had enjoyed enough excitement for one day and wanted to keep an unbeaten record for the trip. As the wind had really got strong, Jim took both Claire and Yakki with him. The extra weight worked wonderfully and they beat all the 505s. Yakki was really delighted and said she was sure the admiral would be delighted. They stayed for a celebratory drink and then headed back to Nairobi. They dropped Yakki off, with Claire promising to come to see her on Tuesday. Yakki turned to Claire and said,

"As he was such a good boy and there were no lee ho's, am I allowed to kiss him goodbye?"

"Of course you can. We will see if we can make a safari down to Mombasa to see him." When Jim dropped Claire off, she whispered, "Hopefully, I won't be too late but you go to bed and I will creep in beside you." So Jim had an early supper, after a shower and was fast asleep when Claire snuggled up in bed with him. He woke when she kissed the back of his neck. They gently made love and then both of them slept until dawn, when they made love again. They were both sad but were determined that they would get together again soon. Just as Claire went to leave, in her running gear, she realised that her evening dress was hanging up on the cupboard.

"I will keep it, to remind me of the sexiest girl in Nairobi. I will use it for an excuse to come up to Nairobi, to bring it back to you. Take care, my darling." They both had tears in their eyes, as Claire darted out of the French Windows and across the garden.

Claire went to have coffee with Yakki on the following Tuesday. Claire was very impressed with her beautiful Japanese painting. It was obvious that Yakki had a real talent.

Claire never spied on Yakki, as she was reluctant to use a friend in such away. The British Government did not really require clandestine knowledge, as it was blatantly obvious that Japanese cars and trucks were flooding the market in Kenya. Claire rarely saw the Ambassador. He was always very courteous when they did meet. Sir Richard could see no reason, why his wife should not be a friend of the wife of an old enemy. So it was, that the two girls became very close friends. In many ways, they had a lot in common.

Chapter 35

A night at the Castle

Friday 11th October 1968

The rugby season had finished and, with the pressures of work Jim was unable to get to Nairobi. The phones were unreliable between Nairobi and Mombasa and letters seem to take forever. Although Jim loved to receive letters from Claire and he enjoyed telling her all his experiences, love, at a distance, was very frustrating. He longed to see her again and hold her in his arms. At night he would lie awake, trying to think of ways so that they could meet. He would concoct coded messages, to send over his morning veterinary radio round up. He knew Claire listened in but could not reply.

He was up in Wajir. He only had a day's work left, blood testing cattle for CBPP before he could at least drive back to Mombasa and enjoy a little life in civilization, even if he could not see Claire. The blood testing was a non-event, as they had not found any CBPP in Somali cattle for years, but it was a chore which had to be done. The disease was common in the west of the NFD, on the other side of Lake Rudolf. It was also common in Masailand.

Jim got up at first light after young Michael, a trainee veterinary scout, had brought him a mug of tea. He got the blood testing team started. The day went well and they managed to get all the cattle through the crush, by 1.00pm. The team had still to test a large number of samples but, at least they did not have to get any more cattle through the crush. As each mob of 200 came through, each animal was numbered on its side, 1 to 200. Then, if there were any positives, the owner would be given a note to say he would be paid, at a later date, at a predetermined rate. The animal would be slaughtered. The meat was then given to the staff, herders etc. The disease was not infectious to man. Jim would do a post mortem. He would then take samples to confirm the diagnosis.

They had done over eight thousand cattle and had not had any positives. Jim packed up his Landrover. He had already filled up with petrol and water. He chatted with Wenceslas Matua, the LO in charge of the BTT, while the team were finishing off doing the remaining blood tests. Wenceslas said they would stay the night here, in Wajir, as they needed to pack the mobile laboratory up carefully, to avoid any breakages of equipment. They would then move off slowly and head for Nairobi. Jim, on his own in the Landrover, could go much quicker. They all had to go through Mado Gashi but there, Jim had to turn left and head for Garissa to cross the Tana River Bridge.

He would soon turn left and head for Garsen before turning due south for Mombasa. Jim decided he would leave as soon as the last animal was tested to be clear, so he could at least get some of the long journey done before nightfall.

They were all done at 1.45pm, so saying goodbye to Wenceslas, all his staff, the local Wajir staff and particularly Eli's family, Jim set off to see how far he could get. He had five hours of daylight. He was delighted that he managed nearly two hundred miles. He reckoned he was only thirty miles short of Garissa. He knew, if he reached Garissa in the dark, he would get into trouble with the police. He saw some lights off to the left. He thought he ought to investigate. He might turn up something that would interest Claire and London. He turned off the road and travelled over three miles into the bush. It was still just light and he came across vehicle tracks. He followed them and they led him to the lights. He reckoned he was within five miles of the Tana River. This was no seismic survey camp. This was a proper drilling camp. Jim was sure this was not known about, by London. There was a line of parked vehicles, so Jim drew up beside them. There was a line of tents on the other side, making a sort of square. He got out of the Landrover, leaving Lucy inside. He did not see or hear his attacker. The next thing he remembered, was bouncing around in the middle seat of the Landrover flanked by two men. Whether he hit his head again or not, he was not sure but he woke with a stinking head ache, slumped over the steering wheel, with water pouring through the vehicle. The window frames were still out as he had not put them back from the journey. It seemed very dark. There was no Lucy. Then he really woke up. He was in a river and the Landrover was sinking and the water level was rising quickly. He got out in the wide space above the door and had to swim a few strokes before he felt the sandy bottom. Then, he stumbled over sand, rocks and tree roots to get to the bank. As soon as he was out of the water, he sat on a big rock to take stock. He felt a big, egg sized swelling on the back of his head. He had obviously been hit with a brick or a rock. He did not feel woozy, so he did not think he had been drugged. Suddenly, he was being licked on his face. It was Lucy.

Jim started to think clearly.

He realised he must be on the bank of the Tana River. He guessed his attackers hoped he would drown and it would look like an accident. His first job, now that he knew Lucy was safe and well, was to rescue his gear and the Landrover. It was difficult in the dark, but he knew he had a good tow-rope wrapped around the front bumper. If he could get that off the front of the vehicle and attach it to the tow-hitch on the back, then he could use it to anchor the Landrover, so it did not sink further into the river. He set to work. The water was quite cold which, in fact, helped to wake him up. Getting the long tow rope off was not that difficult but it was hard work, dragging it the forty feet up to the biggest tree on the bank. He secured it and then could relax a little, as he now knew the Landrover would not totally disappear.

The next task was to unload his gear. He remembered how long it had taken him and Claire to carry it all across the lugga, in the desert. At least now it was relatively cool and he only had fifteen yards to move it. However the journey was partly in waist deep water. He started with the lighter, soft stuff like the bedding and mattress. This was on the roof rack and was not even wet. Most of the other stuff in the Landrover was soaked but, slowly, he got it out and made a camp up on the bank of the river. He was getting exhausted so, as he thought it was likely that his assailants had long since left, he could risk making a fire.

There was plenty of dry wood and twigs. The petrol lighter worked fine and so he soon had a fire going. The water cans were sealed and so he had plenty of clean water. He made himself a large mug of sugary tea. He now had the task of attaching the hand winch to the back tow-hitch on the back of the Landrover and low down on a big tree on the bank. It was not, fun fumbling in the dark in the cold water. Eventually, he managed to secure the winch. The hand winch could lift two tons vertically, so he hoped it would pull the Landrover backwards out of the river. Pushing the handle was very hard work. He had to keep stopping to rest but, slowly, the Landrover got nearer to the bank. Dawn began to break when he was totally exhausted. He had only about six feet left to go but he just did not have the strength. He could now see how lucky he had been. A big rock had stopped the Landrover's slow progress into the river. He spread out some of the wet gear to dry, as the sun came up. He knew it was dangerous if his attackers returned but he just could not make an effort to do anymore, so he lay on the mattress and slept. He hoped Lucy would bark, if danger threatened.

He slept for just over two hours. He still had a headache when he woke up but he did feel stronger. He got back on the winch. The river must have moved some sand but it did seem easier. Soon, he had the back wheels on the bank. Ten more movements of the handle, brought the bonnet clear of the water. He then had another rest and made more tea and ate a tin of baked beans. Ten more movements and, he guessed, the radiator fan was clear of the water. He opened the bonnet and could see everything was wet but at least the distributor; the coil and the fan were no longer under water. It was worthwhile now drying them. Obviously, Jim had to dry the inside of the distributor. While he was doing that, the river must have washed more sand away, so it was relatively easy for Jim to do more work with the winch.

He then got into the Landrover with Lucy, so there was no danger of running over her, and tried to start the engine. After three times the engine fired and then it started running smoothly, he engaged low range and reverse. The tyres gripped and he managed to move the vehicle back two feet. He put on the handbrake and got out, so that he could tighten the winch. Now the back wheels were nearly out of the water. He had not much strength left but he managed to get the winch to pull the Landrover another six inches up the bank. He got back into the vehicle and tried to reverse again. This time he was successful and the Landrover came right out of the water, up to the tree. Once again, he engaged the handbrake and, this time, took off the winch. Then he had the difficult job of turning the Landrover so that he could back it up the bank, avoiding the tree. He took several goes at the procedure, as he did not want to go back into the river and get stuck. When at last he last managed it, he moved the Landrover near to his baggage dump. He had another brew of tea and a sit down. He had to think what he was going to do now. The easy option was to return to Mombasa and report the incident, via Claire, to London.

Jim was very angry, as his attackers had definitely tried to kill him. It was the lucky position of the rock and his hard head, which had saved him. Somehow, he was even more annoyed that Lucy could have died out here. Certainly, she had water to drink but she soon would have been taken by a leopard, as he was certain she would just have waited by the river. The fact that she had found him so quickly, meant that the camp he had found must be quite near.

Jim made up his mind. He was definitely going to find out who had made that camp. He packed up all his stuff and loaded up the Landrover. The inside smelt really revolting but he would have to put up with that. Then, the dam thing would not start. Jim had to re-dry the distributor before it fired into life. He followed his tracks. He soon found the place where a second vehicle had turned around. Eventually he came to the main road. He had no way of knowing whether to turn left or right. He studied the edge of the road very carefully. It certainly looked as if, when his Landrover had turned off the road, it had been travelling in a northerly direction. He decided to go south. He still had a headache, so he revised his plan. If he came to the turnoff he had taken into the bush the previous night, he would do some investigating but, if he came to the other main road without finding it, he would drive on to Mombasa.

He was lucky. He had been travelling fairly slowly and after only five miles, he found the tyre marks off the road. He did not want confrontation, only information, so he drove past the place for about four hundred yards and then turned off, in a similar direction, so that, if he drove into the bush he would be running parallel to their tracks. He drove about twenty yards and then stopped. He returned on foot and obliterated his tracks. Returning to the Landrover, he drove for another sixty yards or so, to a group of acacia trees which were not only thick, but also higher than their neighbours. He parked as near to them as he could get, to give Lucy some shade. He made sure she had a good supply of water in a big bowl, and also that she could not get out of the vehicle and follow him. He then took his compass; his binoculars; his bush hat; a large bottle of water; his smaller water bottle and his *'panga'* and set off on a heading parallel to the road. He made a blaze on every tree, as he passed it, so he could find his way back. He soon found the much frequented track, which he had followed the previous evening. He did not walk on the track but stayed in the bush, to its right, and continued towards the camp. Eventually, he heard activity before he actually saw anything. He stealthily approached, until he could see the drilling rig above the acacia trees. From then on, he moved very carefully and the noise from the camp got louder. He could see the line of vehicles. He then moved back into the bush for few yards and headed in a direction so he could get round the camp, on to the other side, where he had seen the tents on the previous night. When he thought he had gone far enough he once more turned in the direction of the camp. Soon he saw one of the tents through the bush. With great care, he approached the back of the tent. He could hear voices coming from the other side of the tent. He crept right up to the canvas and stood absolutely still. He expected to hear Italian being spoken but it was not a language he knew. He had done Latin and ancient Greek 'O' levels at school. It certainly was a Latin type language but definitely not French, Spanish or Italian. He was sure it was not Greek. He knew Hungarian was a Slavic language and totally different. His best guess was that it was Romanian.

He felt rather cowardly, but he crept away. He had made sure he had not been dreaming the night before and that he had not just driven into the Tana River. He was careful to stay well out of sight, until he was well away from the camp. He followed his original path back to the Landrover. He was glad to see Lucy safe and sound. He made his way back onto the Mado Gashi road. He turned right and, in twenty miles, came to the T junction where, if he turned left he would be going towards Somalia and, if he turned right he had eight miles to travel before he reached Garissa. There was actually another road which went straight on which followed the north eastern side of the Tana River.

Jim, with some relief, turned right to Garissa. It was just after four in the afternoon. He had no problem at the police barrier. He filled up with fuel in Garissa and had a coke at the garage *'duka'*. He casually asked if there were any *'Wazungu'* camped up near to the Tana River to the North. The Somali, filling up the Landrover, said he thought there were some *'Wazungu'* but they never came into Garissa. Jim did not waste any further time but took the Nairobi road out of Garissa. Ten miles out of town he turned left, to take the Galole/Garsen road. He was pretty knackered but he somehow managed to drive the fifty miles to Galole. He knew his friend Leonard would let him stay in his rest house.

Leonard was not at home, as he was attending a Provincial Meeting in Mombasa, but his staff were delighted to see Jim. Jim was too tired to sort out the Landrover so he just left the windows open and hoped the smell would go. He was soon in bed and asleep. He felt so much better in the morning and set off early to drive back to Mombasa. There was quite a wait at the Kilifi Ferry, so he wrote a rapid report to Claire and posted it on his way through Mombasa. There was still some day light when he reached his house so, with Katana's help, he got everything out of the Landrover to dry. He had to oil up the tools so they did not rust. Jim was actually quite relieved, as nothing was missing, and he thought the soft stuff i.e. the tent, mattress, etc would just smell for a little while, but would actually be fine.

Next morning at the Veterinary Office, was somewhat of a letdown, as he had not been missed. No one had expected him back on the previous day!

He made his report for the PVO, through Silas, and then started to go through his mail. He was over the moon. There was a letter from Claire.

Darling Jim,

I know this is at the last minute, and will be a massively long drive for you, but we could have two nights together this weekend. Could you get to 'The Izaak Walton Inn' in Embu on Friday night? If you park five hundred yards up the road, I will come and meet you at midnight. I am so excited. It has been so long since we have been together. I will listen out on the veterinary frequency.

All my love. I can't wait. Claire

Jim also could not wait to reply but he had to, as the veterinary radio time was in the early morning. It was easy for him to concoct a coded affirmative the following morning. He also managed to arrange a veterinary job, at MacKinnon Road, early on Friday morning. If he could get that done by mid-morning, he could skive off and he was already fifty miles up the road to Nairobi. From Nairobi, he would then have a further ninety miles to drive to Embu. He decided not to camp, as it would be cold and wet, on Mount Kenya. He had heard that you could rent an old forester's house called the 'Castle Station', which was near to Embu.

He got to the cattle at Mackinnon Road at day break. He managed to blood test the two hundred, in record time, and so was on his way to Nairobi by 10.00am. The two hundred and fifty miles took him five hours. So it was 3.00pm when he had filled up with petrol and was on the road to Thika. The road to Thika was good tarmac, so he covered the twenty five miles in less than half an hour. Luckily, the rain held off but it still took Jim well over an hour to get to the Forestry Department office on Mount Kenya, on the road up to the 'Castle'. Jim paid for the accommodation for two nights. The forester was very apologetic but said the man who normally looked after people at the 'Castle' was on leave. Jim was delighted, as it meant he and Claire could have the place to themselves. The road up to the castle was very rough but not too bad as it was dry. Jim had over an hour of daylight to get some preparations done. He lit the outside fire to heat the water. He also lit the fire inside and brought in a good supply of wood. He brought in the bedding and prepared the double bed in one of the rooms upstairs. He had brought clean stuff, as his normal safari bedding still smelt from the Tana River. There was no electricity, so Jim brought in lamps and torches. He made some supper, on a portable gas stove, and brought in his food supplies. He read a book, in a chair, in the lamp light. He did not want to go to sleep. He filled a hot water bottle and put it in the bed, before he left to go to Embu.

Jim left the Landrover five hundred yards up the road from the hotel, so that when he restarted it he would not alert anyone. He left Lucy on guard and walked down to the big tree just outside the gates. He knew Claire would have to pass him, if she walked up to the Landrover at their arranged meeting place. It was quite chilly, so he wrapped his anorak around him and sat on a log, under the tree in the dark. He was early, as it was twenty minutes before midnight. It had been a long day and, although he was excited about seeing Claire, he dosed off to sleep.

The next thing he knew, was a hand over his mouth and a soft voice in his ear.

"I am not sure who is snoring louder, you or the '*askari*'?" Claire removed her hand. "My poor darling, you must be tired out after such a long drive"

Jim whispered, "I am fully awake now. It is so lovely to see you again. It has seemed ages. Let me hold you for a second and then we will go." They embraced. She kissed his neck and Jim kissed the top of her head. They walked, in the pitched dark, up to the Landrover. Jim opened the driver's door, so Claire could climb into the middle seat. He fondled her bottom.

"I hoped you would do that. I do so love it, particularly when I have only got my bikini bottoms on. I put jeans on, as you said it was going to be cold." Claire threw her small rucksack into the back of the Landrover.

"Yes, it is going to be bloody cold tonight. I have joined two sleeping bags together and brought several blankets, so we will be fine. It is just the time between getting naked and getting into bed, which will be freezing."

"Who said I was going to get naked. I have brought very thick pyjamas! If you are a very good boy I might let you hug me," said Claire with a laugh.

They set off. Initially the '*murram*' road was good but, as they climbed, it got worse and it started to rain heavily. Jim had to keep his wits about him to keep the Landrover on the road. After a really bad skid, when they reached a flat bit, he stopped.

"It is no good, we will have to put on the chains. If we slide off the road it will be a real pain and we will have to sleep in the vehicle. I did not think to pack the tent and bedding which was stupid of me."

"Don't worry, I will help you with the chains but I have never seen them used before, so you will have to tell me what to do."

"That would be great. I have left the engine going and the lights on. If you move into the driver's seat, when I have the chains in position I will get you to drive forward about two feet, onto the chains, then I will quickly do them up." Jim got out of the cab and got the hessian sack, containing the chains, out of the back. He got each chain out of the sack and laid it on the ground in front of each of the four wheels. Then he asked Claire to move the vehicle forward, so that the wheels were in the middle of the chains. Then he asked her to stop and put the handbrake on. He started to do the chains up. The clip on the inside of the wheel was always difficult. Jim was getting covered in mud and was struggling, in the dark beside the vehicle. Claire got out and helped him, by holding the torch and one end of the chain, so he could clip it up. Claire also got covered in mud but the job was eventually done. They both were wet, as well as muddy, when they got into the Landrover. Jim felt Claire shiver and turned up the heater to full blast. As they had been standing still with the engine running, it gave out a lovely blast of hot air. They set off again. They ground along through the mud in four wheel drive. The chains allowed Jim to keep the Landrover on the crest of the road. There was little danger of slipping off the camber. At last they reached the 'Castle' and drew up by the veranda, in front of the front door. It was still raining so they both, together with Lucy, bolted onto the veranda. Jim lent into the back of the Landrover and grabbed Claire's rucksack and a torch. There were still some hot embers in the fire, so Jim put on some dry wood which soon blazed merrily. He handed Claire his hipflask.

"Have a slug of cherry brandy? It will warm you up."

"Oh thanks. This is a bit like coming into the chalet after skiing."

"Now, let me tell you our problem. I have made our bed up in one of the two rooms upstairs. There is no fire up there, so it is freezing. The bathroom and loo are down stairs, in that room there." Jim pointed to a door.

"The water should still be hot, as I had a really good fire going earlier under the forty four gallon tank outside. I suggest, as we both are so filthy we have a hot bath, dry ourselves in front of the fire, and bolt upstairs before we freeze to death."

"When do I get a chance to show you my new, racy, very revealing nightie?" asked Claire with a beguiling look. "I was only joking about the thick pyjamas."

"I don't want to miss that. How about down here, in front of the fire, but please be careful as I don't want you to burn yourself?"

So Claire, with one torch, went into the bathroom to run the bath and Jim went outside, with another torch, to give Lucy a quick run. It was still raining, so Lucy soon did a wee and jumped into the front of the Landrover. Jim came back into the house and, without knocking, came straight into the bathroom. Claire was naked, sitting on the loo having a wee. She looked up and Jim bent down and kissed her.

"You are so lovely, Jim. You make a girl feel wanted even when she is peeing."

She got off the loo and bent over the bath to test the temperature of the water. Jim took off his sodden, dirty clothes.

"I will get in first and then you can sit in my lap." Claire did not do that but, instead, got in facing him with her knees between his legs. She brought the torch.

"I want to make sure you wash your face. How you managed to get such a muddy face, I can't understand?" She reached for a flannel, in the bath holding the torch in her other hand. Before she could stop him, Jim buried his face in her breasts.

"You rat. I know why you did that, so you have to wash my tits."

"Too right," said Jim with a grin. Water went everywhere, as they fought for the flannel. Jim won. He washed each breast very carefully and then insisted he washed between her legs. He did not rinse the flannel but washed his face.

"That was nice. I got a lovely smell of you."

"Jim Scott, you are totally weird but, when you do things like that, you make me feel sexy so I guess I am weird as well. We must be made for each other."

Soon they got out of the bath. Claire went to the fire to dry herself. Jim quickly washed their muddy clothes and brought them through, to dry them on the furniture in front of the fire. Claire put her arms around him.

"I do love you so much. I cannot imagine any other man washing the clothes. You have even washed my knickers." She kissed him, pushing his lips open with her tongue, and then lickling his tongue with hers.

"Come on, I want to see this nightie." Claire bent down to hunt through her bag. It was too much for Jim. He pulled her bottom to him and tried to put his penis into her. Claire dropped the torch and the rucksack, opened her legs and put her palms on the ground to support her. Then she pushed her bottom back to him. With a sigh, he entered her. Then, to her surprise, he did not thrust but gently rubbed her clitoris. Claire loved the feeling of him hard inside her and the gentle stimulation of his hand. She whispered,

"Yes, just there. That is so lovely." Soon Jim thought he could feel her muscles around his penis and he started to thrust against her. He came with a moan.

"My darling, I'm so sorry, I just could not wait." Claire straightened up and he dropped out of her. She turned and hugged him.

"I love you, you impatient old bugger. Come on upstairs. I have not had an orgasm and I bloody well want one. My sexy nightie can wait until the morning. I know what you are like, if you have not had me for some time you are liable to just rip it off me anyway." She grabbed the torch and ran up the stairs naked, with Jim close behind her.

She hesitated at the top of the stairs.

"Left hand door," called Jim. Jim had been right, it was freezing up there. Claire flashed the torch on the bed and saw the blankets and pillows. She was into the joined sleeping bags like a shot.

"Come on, you lovely man. Thank you so much for my hot water bottle. It is still warm." Jim jumped in behind her. Claire was cuddling the hot water bottle to her tummy. Jim cuddled her back.

They soon warmed up and Claire kicked the hot water bottle to their feet and then lay on top of Jim.

"Now, I want you to hold on this time and wait for me?" She guided Jim inside her. They kissed and Jim started to thrust upwards.

"Slowly," whispered Claire. "In fact, let me rub him with my lips." She raised her bottom and pulled Jim's erect penis out of her and let it fall on his tummy. She then slowly rubbed her clitoris on the back of his penis by rocking her pelvis. Slowly she became more excited. So did Jim. He gripped her bottom, holding her tight against him.

"My darling, that feels so good I am going to come again," gasped Jim. Claire stopped rocking.

"Please, oh, please wait," pleaded Claire. She reached down and gripped the base of his penis really hard with one hand and with her other hand rubbed her clitoris. She buried her face in his neck. Jim felt her hot breath. She began to gasp and then pushed his penis back inside her. She started rocking and panting. Jim tried to hold back but, suddenly, he could not wait anymore and he thrust hard into her. Claire moaned. "Yes, yes, yes." She flopped on top of him.

They both were soon asleep and did not stir until a clear dawn broke over the mountain.

Jim got out of the sleeping bag very carefully, so as not to wake Claire. She stirred but did not wake. Downstairs, he put more wood on the fire which slowly crackled into life. He put on a shirt and a sweater, which made him smile as they hung down longer than some of the mini-skirts which he had seen in Nairobi. He went outside and let Lucy out of the Landrover. He had a pee in the garden and walked around to the back of the house. The fire, under the hot water, had gone out. Luckily, there was a small wood store, with kindling and wood chips, as well as dry wood. With a little care, he lit the fire. He saw Lucy was happy wandering around in the rough garden and so he stayed by the fire and got it going really properly. The clear dawn did not last for long and very soon, cloud covered the two peaks of Mount Kenya. He went back inside, having put Lucy back in her beloved Landrover. He would let her into the house later but, he thought if she came in now, she would wake Claire. He stoked up the fire inside and boiled a kettle. He did not hear the bare feet, as Claire crept up behind him. He jumped when she put her arms around his waist, under his shirt. Her hands were cold on his chest. Even her lips were cold on his neck.

"Thank you for making up the fire. This place is bloody freezing. I am so glad we made it here last night as we would have been frozen in the Landrover." She hugged his back, as he poured out the hot water into the camp teapot.

"I hope you weren't cold in the night?"

"No, I had a lovely hot man to cuddle. What do you think of the skimpy nightie? One should wear racy, lacy knickers but I thought you would prefer me without."

Jim turned to look at her. "Wow that is really sexy. I can not only see your nipples but also your bush."

Claire looked down at his now erect penis.

"The nightie certainly had the desired effect. Let me have a wee. You take the tea upstairs and we will have it in bed. I need warming up." Jim poured out two cups and carried them carefully upstairs. He was getting into the sleeping bags when Claire came rushing up and jumped on to the bed and wriggled in beside him.

"Can you open your legs?" As soon as he did she put her freezing feet between his legs. Jim groaned.

"Those feet are seriously cold. They have cooled down my ardour from that lovely nightie. Why don't you put your feet and knees under my shirt? I still have my sweater on. It must be warm there. I should have put more boiling water in the hot water bottle. That is cold now. Somehow, Claire managed to get her feet up beside Jim's body and warm them. Jim had a lovely view down the front of her nightie. Claire could feel his penis tickling her bottom. She laughed.

"Even with my cold feet, what woke him up again?"

"I can tell you," said Jim. "It is the lovely sight I have, down the front of your new nightie."

"I will never understand you, Jim. You see me naked all the time and yet, one peep down my cleavage, gets you all aroused. They were lying, side by side, facing each other. Claire had her legs flexed, with one under him. She kissed him and pressed her body towards him.

"Is he long enough to reach me?"

"I think so, but we won't be able to move much."

Claire reached down and guided him. She kissed him again and pushed as hard as she could towards him. He was quite well inside her now. Claire giggled.

"I think this is very good training for you. You cannot thrust as you would like to, or you will come out of me and you don't want that to happen. You have to just stay put. It is a nice feeling for me. I can feel you getting bigger. Do you want to roll on your back and then I can ride you? Yes, that is seriously good." Claire went to take her nightie off.

"Don't take it off or I will lose my good view."

"I thought you might want to suck my tits," replied Claire.

"That would be good." Claire took her nightie off after all. Jim sucked gently on each nipple, in turn. Claire said.

"That is lovely. Will you suck my pussy?" This took quite a bit of manoeuvering but soon Jim could look up and see Claire, who was now on her back, with a glazed ecstatic look on her face. He kept sucking and brought his right hand up. He pushed two fingers into her, now well lubricated, vagina. He brought his other hand up to feel her tummy. Jim loved the feel of her tummy muscles contracting, as she got near to having an orgasm. She came and Jim realised how hot he was, as he still had his shirt and sweater on. He took them off and they lay again side by side. She cuddled into his arms.

"That was so lovely, we must not stay apart from each other for so long. God that was good."

"How did you manage to get two nights with me," asked Jim. "What are you doing up at Embu?" Claire explained, how Richard had been asked up to go duck shooting on the Mwere Rice Scheme. Wives had been invited for the Friday night dinner at the Hotel. The other three girls had said they would get bored in Embu and so had elected to go to have a beauty treatment at The Outspan Hotel at Nyeri, which had a spa. They would be in the taxi at this moment. Claire had said she would probably go with them but at the last moment had lied and said she would go back to Nairobi. Now she was up here and nobody knew or cared.

"This is so good. We have a whole day and another night together. In fact there is no rush tomorrow morning. Now, you must tell me what happened up at Garissa. I was worried when I read your brief report. I was worried about your head." Claire stroked the back of his head.

"You still have a bit of a lump. In fact, you might get delayed concussion, so I am afraid you must not have any more sex this weekend." Claire ordered. Jim murmured, "Perhaps you are right." He moved his hands up to her waist and started to tickle her under her arms. She could not stop herself giggling and laughing.

"Stop, oh Jim, stop."

"Only if you say that more sex would be good for my head."

"No way Jim, no more sex." He started tickling her again.

"OK. Stop, please stop, we will have more sex."

Jim stopped tickling her and said, "Before we do anything, I must go down and make the fire up downstairs and also the fire outside, heating the water. You stay here in the warm."

"No, I will come with you and we can take Lucy for a walk." Claire replied.

"OK, but just stay put while I bring your bag up and give you some clothes. You can put them on in bed."

"Don't worry. These will be nice and warm," said Claire, as she put on Jim's shirt and sweater.

"So, I have to go down stark naked?" moaned Jim.

"As a reward you can kiss my naked pussy, by the fire downstairs," said Claire, as she raced down. Jim ran down behind her and grabbed clothes out of his bag. Claire was bending down, putting wood on the fire. Jim grabbed her and started kissing her. He lifted her so she was kneeling in an armchair. She bent forward over the back of the chair and relaxed with his kisses. In three or four minutes, she sighed with the pleasure of an orgasm. They then both put on more clothes and went outside. Claire went to Lucy, while Jim made up the outside fire. Although it was cloudy it was not quite as cold as they thought it would be. They had a brisk walk into the forest. They let Lucy run ahead, so they did not actually see any game, but heard plenty of rustles in the bushes. They walked back a bit slower, with their arms around each other.

Claire made some scrambled eggs when they got back, while Jim toasted some bread in front of the fire. After they had eaten, Jim made up the fire while Claire cleared up and made a cup of tea. With a mischievous grin on her face, Claire said. "Let's take our tea back to bed. We will let Lucy lie by the fire."

Once back, naked, in the bed. Claire said,

"These two sleeping bags stink of sex but somehow that excites me. However, you must tell me about your attack. So, cuddling her back and fondling her breasts gently, Jim told her what had happened. Claire listened without comment but Jim felt her tense, when he told her about the knock on the head and the near drowning in the Landrover.

"I contacted London as soon as I got your first report. Their first instruction was very specific and I fully endorse it. No further contact must be made with that camp without specific instructions from them, in London." Claire turned to face Jim and kissed him long and hard. She broke off.

"I really mean that Jim. London thinks they are a rogue Romanian group, who has bribed someone in the Kenyan Government. London is fairly certain that they won't find any oil and therefore they are not a problem. London is happy just to wait and just monitor the site, from the air. Now, you sex maniac I want you to do two things. First, to promise me you will go nowhere near that camp and secondly make love to me." She immediately rolled on top of him and pinned his wrists above his head. Looking straight into his eyes she said,

"Promise me."

"I promise," replied Jim. They kissed again and languidly made love.

The day and night seemed to just fly by. The rain stopped and they had a long walk in the afternoon. They had a good supper, washed down with a nice bottle of red wine and they were soon in bed. Once there, they started making plans for a '*safari*' together, at the start of Jim's home leave, which was due in two months. Claire thought she could get away for ten days, if she planned it carefully.

On Sunday morning, they had a leisurely breakfast before packing up. It was raining yet again, which dampened not only the kit, but also their mood. Jim had a difficult drive getting them down the wet, greasy road off the mountain. They said little on the journey and, as they got near to Nairobi, Jim realised Claire was crying. They were just near Thika and Jim easily found a place to drive off the road, near the fields of pineapples. He put his arm around Claire. He asked, "What's the matter, my darling?"

"I know I am being a premenstrual old bag. I so worry about you. You just don't seem to see danger. If you see it, you just take it in your stride."

"You mustn't worry. What's brought this on?"

"I suppose I am tired and sad that I won't be seeing you for so long. You just drove down that horrendous road without a care in the world. Hug me. I will pull myself together in a minute."

"I have an idea. If I fly up a week on Saturday and book into the Panafric Hotel. Could you join me for the night?"

Claire smiled and tears were still running down her face.

"I am such a bloody fool. I will then worry about you flying."

"Oh, no you won't, you will remember joining the mile high club. I will be fine."

They agreed to meet and both their spirits lifted. Claire tidied herself up as they drove the last few miles into Nairobi. She got out of the Landrover about a quarter of a mile from the High Commission residence and came around to Jim's door. She gave him a big kiss and said.

"I will see you at the Panafric Hotel. I am going to shag you to death and, if I hear you have given some young girl a lift to Nairobi, I will kill you." Before Jim could reply she was running down the road waving.

Chapter 36

Meru Game Park

Friday 13th December 1968

When Jim and Claire had met for the night at the 'Panafric Hotel', in the middle of October, they had started to plan a ten day trip in Meru Game Park. Jim had been there once before, when he had only been in the country a few months, before he had met Claire. At that time, a friend of Jim's had been in charge of the Game Park. He had managed to import seven White Rhino (Thick Lipped Rhinoceroses). Two of these had been mature females. The Warden had wanted to know if they were incalf. They were relatively tame and so he built a stockade, with a suitable race and crush. All Jim had to do was examine the rhinoceroses *per rectum*. All had gone well and Jim had felt a calf inside the first rhino when suddenly, something startled the rhino. It had clamped down its anal ring and Jim had not been able to get his arm out. Jim thought he was going to spend the rest of his life with a rhino on his arm! Fortunately, by carefully pricking the anal ring of the rhino with a hypodermic needle, the rhino was encouraged to release Jim's arm.

On this same visit, Jim was privileged to have supper with George Adamson, the husband of Joy Adamson who wrote 'Born Free'. George lived in a camp, which was as if he was an animal in a zoo. He was in the cage and the lions lived free on the outside. Before supper, George took Jim for a walk outside the cage. They had not been walking long before a fully grown male lion, with only one eye, called 'Boy' came charging up to them both. As he did not know Jim, he decided to lick Jim's bare legs at the bottom of his shorts. Jim was sure each lick took off at least one layer of skin.

Having had such an interesting time in Meru Game Park before, Jim was keen to take Claire on a safari there. He was due to take his home leave on the 13th December 1968, having completed a two year tour of duty. Jim and Claire decided they would try to have a ten day safari together. Claire could get away OK, provided she was back at the High Commission on the 23rd December, for the time honored staff Christmas Eve party, the following day. Jim could fly out on an evening flight on the 23rd, arriving on Christmas Eve, and spend Christmas in the UK. Jim would store most of his stuff at Kabete, so it would be ready for his next posting. When they had finished their *'safari'*, he would leave the Landrover at Kabete and get a Government vehicle and driver to take him out to the airport. Claire's cover was that she would be staying with some upcountry, friends near Nanyuki. As she had done in the past, Claire would get a High Commission driver to drop her off at Wilson airport, as if she was being picked up by a light aircraft but, in reality, Jim would pick her up in his Landrover. As Lucy was not allowed in Meru Game Park, Jim arranged to leave her with his friend Ed, at Ol Kalou.

Everything went as planned and it was a very excited couple who set off on *'safari'*. Unfortunately they had not allowed for all the upcountry families who had decided to spend some time in Meru Game Park, before Christmas, as the school holidays had begun. All the campsites were full and the rangers were adamant that Jim and Claire could not camp, except at the recognised campsites. There was no way that they could risk being recognized, so they decided to head off on their own into the NFD.

They found a great place to camp in the Nyambeni Hills. The view of the NFD was spectacular, as they were well over five thousand feet. It was also quite cool so, although they made a small fire they were soon, in bed after their supper. They cuddled up naked together in the two joined sleeping bags. Jim lay on his back and Claire lay on top of him with her head on his chest. He gently stroked her hair.

"I have been longing to get away," said Claire. "With all that *'matata'* (trouble) at the game park, I thought we were never going to get on our own."

"What news is there from London, about that oil drilling camp near the Tana River?" asked Jim.

Claire replied, "To be honest with you, I am glad we are heading west. If we had tried to camp illegally in Meru Game Park, we actually would not have been that far away from it. I don't want you to be hit over the head." Jim continued to stroke her hair.

"I am glad you burst into tears, on the way back from the castle. If you hadn't, we would not have had a night at the 'Panafric Hotel' and would not be here together now," said Jim. Claire lifted her face to his and they kissed.

She said, "We are like an old married couple, worrying about each other." They kissed some more.

"London did not know anything about the oil drilling camp. However, there is a British Army Training Team based near Isiolo, so they have been tasked to get further information. Therefore, there is no need for us to worry about the problem anymore." They were both soon asleep.

It was a beautiful morning, so Jim and Claire were soon packed up and ready to go, after a quick breakfast. They came down from the Nyambeni Hills and met the road, which went from Isiolo to Kula Mawe. They turned left back to Isiolo. This brought them into the township, to the North of the Police barrier, so that they did not have to answer any awkward questions as to where they were going. Having filled up with fuel they headed north, towards Archer's Post, but soon took a left to pass to the South of The Buffalo Springs National Park. They headed for the ford across the Ewaso Ng'iro River, at Barsalinga. They hoped the river would be low enough for them to cross. They reached the ford at noon. The river was not that low, so they stopped and had some lunch while they decided what to do. They both were reluctant to go back, as they had sixty miles to travel back to the main Isiolo to Archer's Post road.

After lunch, Jim took off his clothes and, wearing his gym shoes, waded out into the river carrying a long pole, to test the depth of the river. It was about fifty yards across. Initially, the water was just above Jim's knees. The bottom was very rocky but the rocks were firm. Jim had to test a path the width of the Landrover, to make sure one wheel did not drop into a hole. Half way across, to Claire's horror, Jim dropped into a deep hole up to his chest. This hole was downstream from the direct crossing so Jim made a mental note to keep up stream. After this hole the bottom rapidly became shallower.

When he got back to the South side, even though he was wet Claire wrapped her arms around him.

493

"I thought you were going to drown. We can't possibly get across. We can easily go around."

"I think we can make it, provided I keep well up stream and aim for that big 'Fever Tree'. However, just in case I roll over in the river, can you wait on the bank here and direct operations?"

"No way, where you go, I go." Claire jumped into the Landrover. Her look brooked no argument. However, before they started to cross, Jim lifted up the bonnet and took off the fan belt. He did not want the fan to splash water onto the plugs and distributor. They started across the river in low range, which automatically meant that the Landrover was in four-wheel drive. Jim knew to keep the engine revs up, so that water did not block the exhaust. He aimed for the tree but he did get one wheel in a dip. Water came in the window over Claire but, because he was going fairly quickly, they lurched back and made the other bank. They both burst out laughing. They got out of the vehicle. Jim was still naked, so he did not really care about the water that had come over them. Claire started to strip off her clothes.

"James bloody Scott, the lengths you go to see me with no clothes on!" She wrapped her naked body around him.

Now that they had crossed the river, they really were in the wilds of the NFD so they both rode on naked, as if it was the most natural thing in the world. A few miles north of the crossing they came to a T junction. If they went right they would go to Wamba, where they had been on their previous safari to Marsabit. Instead they turned left, as Jim said he had a surprise for Claire, which required her to put her bikini on. In twenty miles they came to a turning off to their left. Jim stopped the Landrover and said. "It's time to get our swimming gear on." Mystified, Claire dutifully put on her bikini and Jim put on his swimming trunks. They took the turning. In half a mile they came to an old sign announcing 'Kirimun LMD holding ground'.

"Why do I need my bikini on, to visit a holding ground? Surely I should be properly clothed, so as not to upset the veterinary staff?"

"You will soon see," replied Jim. They soon arrived at the holding ground HQ. It was deserted. There was a row of junior staff houses and one senior staff house. The later faced south, overlooking a nearly dried out large dam, containing some very green scummy water.

"Oh no," said Claire. "I don't mind being half drowned by brown river water but there is no way I am swimming in there!"

Jim said nothing and just drove up to the house. There, in front of a long veranda, was an empty blue swimming pool. Claire was gob smacked.

"Well Jim, please explain the mystery."

"Kirimun used to be a well used holding ground, for bringing cattle out of the Maralal area. They were all held, vaccinated and blood tested here, before being sold to ranchers in Laikipia. Today, LMD bring out Somali cattle through the Isiolo holding grounds."

"That does not explain the unused swimming pool?" interjected Claire.

"The LO in charge of Kirimun, used money ear-marked to construct three cattle dips to make this swimming pool. He only got caught when a bright clerk, at the Ministry of Agriculture, queried the need for blue paint!"

"Well, I am really disappointed in you, Jim," said Claire, as she climbed down the steps into the empty pool. "You could at least have got it filled up for my arrival."

While Claire was not looking, Jim filled a canvas bucket up from a water-butt and poured it over her. Claire squeaked.

"You rat, that is bloody cold." She had difficulty getting out as the steps did not go down to the bottom of the pool. However, when she did manage she hugged him with her wet body. Jim loved it. It was a day for wet bodies.

The house was locked but they put up their table and chairs on the veranda. They cooked their supper on a gas stove and ate it, sitting on the veranda, admiring the view over Laikipia. Over supper Jim explained to Claire, as his controller, that the move to bring out Somali cattle was a political thing but he hoped that LMD would start bringing out Samburu cattle again, as there was serious overstocking. He said that they would need to build the cattle dips, as he knew this was a bad area for the 'Brown ear Tick', which spread East Coast Fever.

They slept on top of the Landrover and needed to cuddle up, as they were at about three thousand feet and it was distinctly chilly. In the morning they were, once again, up early. It seemed odd to be on 'safari' and yet to be eating at a table on a veranda. They soon packed up and were on their way. In twenty miles they came to a T junction, which was on the bigger road going north, from Thompson's Falls to Maralal. They stopped to let Claire put on a pair of jeans. Even Jim had a sweater on, as it was seriously cold and Maralal was shrouded in mist. They had intended to stop but it had begun to rain so they just filled up with fuel and carried on. As soon as they got passed Maralal, they started descending the Losiolo Escarpment and the weather brightened. It did not get really warm until they had traversed the Lopet Plateau and reached the right hand turn off, which they remembered from the previous '*safari*', from Wamba up to South Horr. They had to be vigilant after South Horr, as they were looking for a turn off to their right. Jim reckoned it was roughly twenty five miles from South Horr, before the road started to descend to Lake Rudolf. Claire, who was now in a bikini, said,

"I remember the dreadful descent to Lake Rudolf. I had to put on a sports bra as the Landrover juddered so much. I hope the way we are going is not so bad."

"I really don't know," replied Jim.

"As soon as we find the turn, we will stop for a break. I could do with a beer. They will still be nice and cold." The road started to get rough, when Jim gave a whoop.

"There is our road. It looks nice and sandy. Now, you can take your top off." They swung off the road and, after a couple of hundred yards, they stopped. There were no trees for miles, so there was no chance of any shade. They both got out and stretched their legs and then went to the back of the Landrover. Claire opened the door and was leaning in to open the cool box. Jim kissed the back of her neck and undid her bikini top. She turned and kissed him.

"You are a very naughty boy, but I love you for it. I think you want my body more than a cold beer. In fact you can have both and I won't even mind you being too quick as, in this sun, we will get burnt in no time." Jim threw down a rug on the sand and, as he was taking off his shorts, Claire pushed him back on to it. She was naked and straddled him, holding up a cold beer.

"Which do you want first?"

"The beer," said Jim grinning.

"No chance," replied Claire.

"I will be doing all the work." She tucked his cock inside her and slowly lowered her bottom, so he entered her. Then, while she wriggled her bottom forward and back, which she knew excited him, she put the cold beer to her lips and drank several swallows. Then she leant forward and carefully put the bottom of the beer in the soft sand. They both pushed rhythmically together. Claire managed two more swallows of beer before Jim groaned and ejaculated. Claire rolled off him on to her back but would not let him have any beer until he had satisfied her with his lips. Claire sighed. "I am seriously hot now." They both stood up and Jim washed them down with a wet flannel, while they finished the beer. They put the rug over the red hot seats of the Landrover.

They set off down the sandy track, which went beside a lugga. Jim knew they had about thirty miles to go, before they should find the Balesa Kulal Waterhole. They weren't worried about wearing clothes as they were very unlikely to see anyone, except a tribesman who would not be wearing any clothes either! The Balesa Kulal Waterhole was an interesting construction which had been dug out by the 'Rendile', who were the northern cousins of the Samburu, who in their turn, were the northern cousins of the Masai. It was much deeper than the Waterhole at Addi, but not as wide. There was no one working the Waterhole, presumably because the rains in the area had failed for some years and there was no grass, or any other vegetation, for animals to feed on in the area. Taking two canvas buckets and some rope, Jim and Claire climbed down into the Waterhole via a series of large wide steps, which still had rough wooden ladders joining each step. Each step, or ledge, was about ten foot below the one above. As they descended, the area of the waterhole got smaller. The sun was no longer directly overhead, so it became darker. They were both naked and had been very hot on the surface, but the air became cooler as they descended. At the very bottom, they were about eighty feet below the top. The sand was wet. Jim had not brought a spade but, when he dug a few inches with his hands, water appeared. It tasted sweet and not at all salty. They both dug out a shallow basin a little larger, in diameter than the canvas bucket. Then they could collapse the bucket into the hole and it rapidly filled up with water. It was beautifully cool as they poured it over themselves.

"What a mission, to get the water to the surface?" said Claire.

"It would have to be hauled up, level by level, eight times before it reached the surface," replied Jim. "A cow, in the heat at the surface, would drink at least twenty of these half buckets every day. No wonder the place is deserted."

They climbed back up to the surface. Claire went first and, on the way, they stopped and kissed. Claire could feel Jim's erection. Claire laughed.

"How can you get aroused just looking up between my bare legs? I could understand if I had sexy underwear on."

"Then I would be even more aroused," replied Jim.

"We had better get back to the top. We would look complete idiots if someone had stolen the Landrover, with no Lucy to guard it. We would not get very far with a canvas bucket half full of water! It would be a lot more serious than being naked on the beach at Mombasa, when we went skinny dipping."

There was no one at the top and, after the cool of the waterhole, the surface air felt like a furnace. They soon got the Landrover going, to create some breeze. Claire rode with her legs wide apart, with the air coming through the front air vents directly onto her.

"That is just about bearable but I am too hot to become aroused. Anyway I don't think you would be much good if I was aroused," said Claire. "Let's hope we can find a cooler place? Is that Mount Kulal up to our left?"

"I hope so," replied Jim.

"At the waterhole, I saw a track off to our right which, I think, would have taken us to Marsabit. Soon we should come to a T junction and, if we turn left, the track should take us along the foot of Mount Kulal. The top is actually nearly seven thousand feet but if we can get up, say five thousand feet it, will be much cooler. It may even be cold, like Marsabit." Sure enough, they came to the T junction. The track to the left started well and they made good time. They crossed one quite wide sand lugga, which Jim thought was probably the underground source to the Balesa Kulal waterhole. Luckily the sand was only dry on the top and moist underneath, so that the Landrover had no trouble grinding its way over.

"It would be lovely to get some aid money, to bore for water here," said Jim. "However, although the water would help the local people I doubt if there would be enough to irrigate and, unless there was rain, the cattle would starve."

"It is so sad," replied Claire. "I don't really think this whole area, in fact the whole of Africa just south of the Sahara, is really meant to have anyone living permanently in it." With that thought they drove on, in silence. The track was noticeably climbing now. Jim realised that they had been going in a westerly direction, towards Mount Kulal. Now they were slowly turning to the north.

"I think, if we continue to follow this track, we will eventually come out on the road we went on last time, which goes to North Horr. If you are game, I suggest we turn left off the road and see how far we can get up the mountain."

"I am certainly up for it," replied Claire.

"It would be so lovely to find a stream, running off the mountain, and to gain some altitude so it was cooler tonight." When Jim found a flat, sandy area off to the left they turned west, directly towards the Mountain. They stopped and built a small cairn, so they would recognise the spot if they came out on the road at a different place.

They would definitely have got lost if they had not had the mountain to aim at, as they initially had to keep weaving, to avoid rocks and holes. As they got higher, the bush got thicker, so they had to weave even more. On some occasions, Claire had to get out and run or walk ahead, to find the correct line. When she got back into the Landrover, Jim said,

"I think we ought to swop around as I am so busy, looking at your lovely body running in front of me, that I am not looking out for the pot holes!" Claire looked down at his groin.

"I am glad I still excite you." She gave his penis a little squeeze. "Down boy, you will get some action when we get up the mountain."

It was slow going, particularly as the vegetation increased. They took it in turns to walk and drive. Dusk was falling and so the temperature was dropping nicely, even although they had not climbed very far. Jim was walking, when he came to a nice flat sandy area and suggested to Claire that they stop.

"I know we haven't reached our objective but this looks an OK spot. Let's camp here and, in the morning, go for a walk and see if we can find an easier way up?"

In fact, it turned out to be an excellent camp site. There was a tree to pull the shower up on, although the rose was only four feet off the ground. So they sat together in the camp bath, under the shower and washed their hair.

"Well, I never thought, when I first met you at The British High Commission as the glamorous Lady Rochester that I would be sitting next to you naked in a canvas bath, probably two hundred miles from the nearest European, out in the bush." Jim pulled Claire to him.

"Well, I never thought I would be sitting naked next to a cheeky boy, who was late for the reception and could not even tie his bow tie. However, when I came close behind that cheeky boy to tie his tie, I knew I would not mind being naked with him."

"Is that honestly true? I thought it was only men who lust after girls at first sight? I certainly thought, Wow, this is the most beautiful girl I have ever seen. I remember I did not immediately even twig, that you were Lady Rochester."

The water was finished in the camp shower, so Claire stood up and, facing him, said, "Well, my darling, what I want you to do is to brush my wet hair, which will dry in no time in this heat and then to take me to our bed on top of the Landrover and make love to me, like a male lion." Jim did not reply, he just nestled his face into her groin.

In the morning, Jim got up first. He climbed down the ladder and got the stove out of the back of the Landrover and put on the kettle to make some tea. He saw a troop of baboons about forty yards away, looking at him. He was not concerned but he walked with the 'panga' in the opposite direction to go to the loo. When he got back he noticed Claire must have come down, as the stove was off and the two mugs were not on the table. He shouted up to her.

"Are you OK?"

"Yes, fine. Come up, I have just had a fright." Jim washed his hands and climbed up. Claire looked a little flushed.

"What happened?" enquired Jim.

"I got down and was squatting a few yards away, having a wee. I thought you were creeping up behind me. I finished, got up and turned round and, about ten feet behind me, was a big male Baboon. I swear he was about to masturbate. He was holding his penis in a very provocative manner. It gave me a hell of a fright. I eyeballed him and he ran off."

"You must be careful, my darling." admonished Jim. Claire gave him a cheeky smile. "I think he was better endowed than you." Jim did not hear the two plastic mugs falling off the top of the Landrover, as he grabbed her and started kissing her under her arms, which he knew was her second most ticklish spot. When he reached her most sensitive spot, she was mewing with pleasure. So they had a much later breakfast than normal. After breakfast, they made sure that everything was packed up so that the baboons, if they came back, could not steal anything. Then they set off with the *'panga';* the compass; the binoculars and water-bottles, walking to find the best way up the mountain. At the start it was quite cool but, as the sun came up, it got hotter and hotter. All the time, they were climbing and marking the trees with the *'panga'*. The trees got greener and taller, which encouraged them. They found an open glade area, with three tall trees, and sat down on a fallen log, having first checked it for ants.

"This is a good spot," said Jim.

"I was hoping for a stream but everywhere is still very dry," answered Claire.

"I suggest we turn back and go to the Landrover and bring it up here. Depending on how we feel, we will have some food and then, maybe, set off again," suggested Jim.

This they did and in fact, got the Landrover up to the glade much quicker than they thought they would. As the bush, although greener, was not so thick, they decided to go on slowly in the Landrover, to conserve their energy, as it was now noon and very hot. Now the trees were so tall that they could not see the summit of the mountain, but Jim used the compass to keep on a westerly course and, if there was a choice, always kept climbing. They made slow and steady progress and soon the sun started to dip down, to aid navigation. Although they kept drinking, they both got very weary and probably a little dehydrated. They said little. Jim suggested, "Let's go for another half an hour and, if we don't find a stream, we will stop at the next convenient looking campsite?"

They were lucky as in twenty minutes, they came to small stream. They both jumped out and bent down to the water and washed their faces. They were both naked, so soon they were splashing each other and laughing. They left the Landrover and followed the stream. They

501

only walked about three hundred yards and they found a rocky pool, large enough for both of them to get submerged in. The water was lovely and cool and refreshing. Hand in hand they walked back to the Landrover and drove it up to their pool. It was an ideal camping spot, with several large trees which would give them shade all through the day. Jim collected dry dead wood for the fire, while Claire set up the camp. She did not wait for Jim to light the fire, but made tea on the stove and called to him when it was ready. He wrapped his arms around her and they kissed.

"This is the most beautiful campsite. Let's make this our base and go walking from here?" suggested Claire.

"Yes, let's do that. We could have five nights here," replied Jim. "We will just have to have one night on the way home to Nairobi, as we could not do it in one day from here. There is a good spot we could stop at in the Mukogodo, where I have camped before. Then we will be in striking distance of Nairobi. Now, we have five days when we won't need to start the Landrover or bump over rough roads. We will even have cold beer. My next job is to put a whole crate in the stream. I am going to enjoy this lovely cup of tea first."

Jim sat down and Claire sat on his knee.

"What are we going to have for supper tonight? I wish I had brought my shotgun, then we could have Guinea fowl or yellow neck but I thought we would get into trouble, if they found us with a gun in Meru Game Park."

"Don't worry," said Claire. "We have got lots of different tins of stuff. We won't have to eat 'Bully Beef' every night. You make a good fire and I will concoct something. Can we have some hot water to wash in? That stream is wonderfully refreshing during the day but I think I will freeze to death in it, when the sun goes down."

Jim got a good fire going and heated up his big metal bucket, full of water. He rigged up the shower. Claire got the tent up on top of the Landrover. She thought they would be able, in the early morning, just to look out on the stream and see some game. Without Lucy, they were more likely to see some really shy animals. She knew Jim would love to see a Bongo. Kulal was one of the few places where you might see them in Kenya. Jim had told her that they were almost plentiful, in the remote areas of Southern Ethiopia.

502

After their shower they put on shirts and long trousers. The beer was great and washed down the baked potatoes and tuna. They rounded off the meal with steaming cups of black coffee laced with 'African Cream Liquor'. They were soon cuddled up in bed and asleep, in a fairly alcoholic haze. Claire woke in the middle of the night as she needed a wee. She tried not to wake Jim but failed. "I will come with you, darling. I need a wee as well." They stood naked with their arms around each other in the moonlight listening to the stream and the African sound of the night.

"Come on," said Claire. "Let's get back in bed. Have you still got brewers droop? It was awfully boring when we went to sleep, not having a hard 'willy' between my thighs." She giggled and scampered up the ladder into the tent. When she got into the sleeping bag, she pretended to want to go to sleep. She yawned, lay on her side away from him and casually pulled his upper arm over her to fondle her breast, as she often did when they went to sleep. Jim felt his erection mounting but Claire kept her thighs tightly together and moved her bottom occasionally, as if she was trying to get comfortable. Claire could not keep up the pretence for very long. She giggled.

"I thought you said there was a mission station on Kulal. I am going to lie on my back and dream of England. I probably won't notice what you are doing." She rolled on her back but Jim did not roll on top of her. He very gently stroked her tummy and then slowly worked his hand lower. He tantalizingly moved his fingers into her bush and gently tugged on the springy hair. Claire's breathing became a little deeper. Jim kissed one of her breasts and sucked very gently, while he started to gently rub her clitoris. He knew she really liked him to suck harder and to rub hard, but he still kept up only a very gentle movement. Claire growled in his ear. "Give me a bloody good shag, you bastard, I know you want to."

"I thought you were playing at being a missionary girl?"

"Bugger that," was the reply. Claire pulled him on top of her. Grabbed his penis, put it to the lips of her vulva and thrust upwards. In the next movement she wrapped her wide open legs round him, so that he was deep inside her. Claire came a few seconds before him. As they drifted off to sleep she murmured.

"I must tease you more often, my darling. That was beautifully satisfying."

Claire must have been more tired than she realized, as she did not wake up when Jim got up. It was fresh but not really cold, so Jim just put on a track suit top and his boots. He got the fire going and heated hot water for washing and made himself a cup of tea. He went collecting wood and made a large stack, so they could easily keep the fire going. He was hotter now, so he braved a slosh in the stream. He got totally under the water and was shivering when he got out, to find Claire standing naked by the fire. She turned and smiled at him. Looking down she said,

"Still got brewers droop I see. I think I was a bit pissed last night!"

"That was a real understatement. I have never known you so raunchy. You kept grabbing my penis and saying, come on shag me. You are bloody useless." Claire's eyes opened with horror.

"I am so sorry, I was so pissed." She hugged him. Then she realised he was teasing her.

"I remember now. I pretended to be frigid and you got me all worked up by being really gentle. You are a rat, James Scott. Anyway you have got the smallest 'willy' I have ever seen!" With that Jim picked her up and carried her over to the stream. "Please don't drop me in. It will be freezing."

"It is," replied Jim. "Have I still got a pathetic 'willy'?"

"No, you haven't. Please carry me back as I haven't any shoes on." She kissed his cheek and murmured. "It is a bit small unless I really work on it." With that Jim carried her back to the stream but had mercy on her and slowly sat down in the shallow water with her sitting in his lap. Claire held him tight round his neck and tried, in vain, to keep her bottom out of the water.

"I do love you but you must admit, it is rather pathetic. I can't even feel it." Jim lowered her further into the water.

"No, I was wrong, your 'willy' is enormous. I don't know how I can get it inside me." "Really," said Jim lowering her further.

"Yes, it is really quite large. It is almost as big as that baboon's I saw, two days ago." With that Jim dropped her in the water and stood up. Claire hardly touched the water but sprung up and wrapped her legs around his body and her arms around his neck. "Please don't drop me again. I will do anything you want."

"Can I wash you, with the water I have heated up by the fire?"

"Oh yes, please. I will be a contrite missionary girl." Then Claire whispered, "Until I am nice and clean and then I will be a tigress!"

They had an extremely lazy morning. Most of it was spent making love. Somehow they just could not get enough of each other's bodies. While Jim was getting more wood for the fire, Claire made a cold lunch. While she was looking for food in the Landrover she found a slim cane box, about the size of a brief case. She brought it to Jim. "What's this? It looks old and exciting."

"It certainly is old. It was handed down to me from my great, great Uncle Frank, who is the only vet in my family. He was a full Colonel in the Indian Army. I have had a difficult job living up to his memory."

"Surely you would not have wanted to be a Colonel in the army?"

Jim laughed. "Oh, I certainly would not. It was the manner of his dying that is important in the family history. He fell out of the back of a dog-cart, which is a small cart, pulled by a pony, with a door at the back so a dog can jump in. He hit his head and died. 'The Bombay Times' reported that he was inebriated at the time!"

"Well, with all those beers you drank last night, you might well have fallen off the top of the Landrover and lived up to his illustrious memory."

"Come and sit on my knee and I will show you what it is."

"You are amazing, Jim. I love you so much. You have been shagging me all morning and most of the night and you still want me to sit naked on your knee!"

However, Jim noticed, she did not refuse his request. He showed her the Back Gammon set. Claire had seen one but did not know how to play. It was decided Jim would teach her, after lunch. As they ate, Jim explained that it was a great gambling game because of the so-called doubling dice. At anytime during the game, one of the players could request that the stakes were doubled. The other player could accept the double or, if he was doing badly, he could refuse and forfeit his stake. If the double was accepted, then the original doubler could not double again, but his opponent could. Then, if he accepted, he could double yet again.

"What shall we use as stakes?" asked Claire innocently. "It would be very sexy to have to take articles of clothing off. I might lose my shoes!"

"I suppose we could keep a running tally. When one of us is ten down, that person has to do something nice for the other; like bringing them a cup of tea in bed."

"I hope I win," said Claire. "I will get you licking my clitoris all day."

"I think I will just throw the game," said Jim mischievously.

"Would you now," said Claire thoughtfully. "I did not realise you enjoyed it so much. Why do you enjoy it?"

"It is because I love feeling you getting aroused. I love looking up at you and seeing your breasts move up and down. I really love feeling your abdominal muscles contracting."

"You are a funny boy. I will never forget the first request you ever made of me, was to see me naked. I was really touched. Now, unless I am cold, I try to stay naked all the time for you or have on a low cut top, so you can look down at my tits. I just love it how you never seem to get bored with looking at me. Come on, show me how to play."

Claire was enchanted by the game. She played in a very daring manner, while Jim was much more conservative. She seemed to understand the odds instinctively. After two hours she was thirty up. "Come on," said Jim, "let's go for a walk and see if we can see any game. If I lose any more I am going to be your slave for the rest of the holiday. I will never forget when you tied me to my bed in Mombasa. You got me so aroused I thought I was going to burst."

"I do so love teasing you. Come on, we had better take the 'panga' to mark the trees and the compass, just in case we get lost. Don't let's bother with clothes."

"Fine," agreed Jim. "I have already hidden the key of the Landrover and put your handbag and my wallet in the car safe. Let's go?"

In the end, they decided not to head off into the bush marking the trees but instead to follow the stream up wards. It was hot work and, even though they had no clothes on, they were sweating. After about an hour, they came to a much deeper pool than the one at the campsite. "Are we brave enough to go in?" asked Claire.

"Let's hold hands and go in together. No looking now, when my crutch is in the water. You will say my 'willy' is too small!"

"Would I be so cruel?"

"That's why I am holding your hand. One peep out of you and I will pull you in."

Like real wimps they slowly got deeper. "OK both together. One, two, three down. Bloody hell that's cold," gasped Jim. They both managed to stay in. It was not deep enough to swim but they could move about and splash each other. It was certainly bigger than the pool at the campsite. They both started to speak together and then stopped.

"I know what you are going to say. Don't let's move. It would be a hell of a job getting up here, as the bush is much thicker," said Jim.

"The cold water has sharpened up your brain," replied Claire. "I agree one hundred percent. Now, let's get out and I want you to wrap me in your arms and warm me up. It can count as one of your forfeits."

"The best forfeit I can imagine," said Jim.

"Really," said Claire lasciviously. "I thought you had another idea which, as you lost so badly, would continue until I drifted off to sleep in ecstasy."

"I think I will lose some more and the forfeit can last all tomorrow as well?" Jim laughed, as he wrapped himself around her wet body. Sadly they did not see any game on the way home and, in fact, they were very dirty as the dust had stuck to their wet bodies, so they heated up the water and had a warm shower together. Claire washed her hair and Jim combed it out for her. Then, he said he had got a surprise for her. He had hidden a lemon and a bottle of gin in the Landrover, under the tool kit. He had also put two big bottles of tonic in the beer crate, in the river. The G & Ts were delicious. They had a lovely evening and went to bed early, with the excuse that they were going to get up early in the morning, to hope to see some game.

In reality, Jim did wake at dawn but they did not get up. They just quietly turned the sleeping bag around so they could lie on their tummies and look out at the stream. A bushbuck and a klipspringer came and drank from different parts of the stream. They left but Claire and Jim did not move or make a noise. They were rewarded by the arrival of three Grevy's Zebra mares and their foals. These are the only type of Zebra seen in the NFD. Elsewhere in the country the Zebra, which one normally sees, is Burchell's Zebra which is also called the Common Zebra. Grevy's Zebra have narrower black and white stripes. They are taller and have larger ears.

Where they were camping, was only a few hundred miles north of the equator, so the sun was soon up. The Zebra melted into the bush. Claire whispered into Jim's ear, "Any chance of you paying me my winnings?"

"Certainly, I will go and make you a cup of tea."

"That is not quite what I had in mind."

So breakfast was late that morning, but Jim and Claire consoled themselves that they were on holiday. Romantic days and nights went by. They did not see the elusive Bongo.

Chapter 37

Tragedy strikes

Monday 23rd December 1968

Then on the given morning they had to pack up. They both had heavy hearts. They were heading back to civilization. They had talked about their route home. They decided to go back the way they had come so there was no danger of them getting stuck in an impassable piece of road. However they had agreed when they got to Barsalinga they would not risk the crossing but carry on, north of the river, and go through Samburu Game Park. It was very tempting to stay in the lodge, which was a beautiful spot on the Ewaso Ng'iro River but, as it was so near Christmas, it was much too risky. They would be bound to meet someone they knew. However, they did see a nice lot of game as they came through the park. They met the main road at Archer's Post and turned right for Isiolo. Ten miles later they turned off right at the track Jim recognised, heading towards the LMD holding ground north of the Mukogodo Forest. It was only a few miles when Jim saw the tall trees marking where he had camped before. The bush was thick but Jim knew he had managed to crash his way through it before to reach the trees. It was very nearly dark. They were both very tired and dirty but a warm shower revived them, after they had eaten a light supper. They were soon cuddled up in bed. Jim was too tired to go to sleep immediately. He just lay back, thinking of what good fun they had had. Then it hit him. He started counting the days again. They had got them wrong. Today was the 23rd of December. Claire should have been back at the High Commission tonight. Tomorrow was Christmas Eve. Claire realised Jim was not asleep and said sleepily, "What's the matter, darling?"

"We are in trouble. We have made a mistake with the dates. Tomorrow is Christmas Eve. You will be late back for the Christmas Party."

"Oh, bloody hell. Well at least we are in bed pretty early. If we get up at 4.00 am, throw everything into the Landrover and drive like hell, we can get back to Nairobi. I can get to the High Commission and you can catch your flight. I know you are pretty good at waking up, Jim, but you had better set an alarm."

"Yes, I will do that. I am so sorry, I don't want to get you into trouble. It does not matter about my flight. I never told my family I would be home for Christmas. I thought I would just surprise them."

"You must not blame yourself. I am as much to blame as you. Richard will be cross but he will forgive me. I thought I was ready to sleep but I am awake now, so I think you had better pay me my winnings. Once you have done that I will lie back like the good missionary girl I am." She giggled. "You will have to get me really fired up. That 'willy' is so big, it won't get in."

"Have I ever told you what a naughty girl you are, but I love you with all my heart."

Jim woke ten minutes before the alarm and gently woke Claire. It was not cold as they were much lower, here in the Mukogodo. Claire packed up the tent and sleeping gear on the top of the Landrover. Luckily, there was a brilliant moon so, with their eyes well adjusted, they could see quite well.

Jim was packing the Landrover when Claire came down. She picked up the '*panga*' and loo roll and walked off into the bush.

Jim heard a terrible scream. Jim ran in the direction she had taken. A lion was on top of her. Jim grabbed the '*panga*', which she had dropped and rushed at the lion in fury. He jabbed it twice in its face aiming for its eyes. It sprang at him with its mouth open. Jim jabbed into its open mouth with all his strength. The lion crashed onto him tearing his legs and body with its claws. Jim fell and must have hit his head on a rock and lost consciousness. He came round briefly with the lion on top of him and then passed out from blood loss.

On the 23rd December, at the High Commission, Sir Richard was worried. He was sitting in his study, having a brandy with his coffee. He knew Claire was flying into Wilson. Had there been a crash? He knew the odd rancher might come in a bit late in the dark. He decided to ring East Air Centre. The Canadian Air Traffic Controller told him that there had been no incidents reported. He also said that there were no light aircraft flying into Wilson from anywhere. Sir Richard was a diplomat. He did not show his concern to the controller but just thanked him for his help. He rang the bell for Eli.

As soon as Eli arrived, he asked. "Is there any news of Lady Rochester? I am worried about her. She has never been late returning from a trip before." Eli agreed. He was also worried and had enough sense not to say anything except to say he would bring some more coffee. On his way to the kitchen, Eli lifted the internal telephone and spoke to the duty signals officer, and said it was just possible that Sir Richard would need a line to London, so it would be prudent to book one right away. If he did not need it then it could always be cancelled. After half an hour or so, Sir Richard decided that, in view of Claire's position, he should phone London. The duty signals officer was summoned. Sir Richard was slightly surprised that a line to London was already available, but he was too concerned about Claire to worry unduly. He curtly informed John David, in London that Claire was missing in the NFD, having been travelling to an unknown destination with agent 'Animal Boy'. He did not elaborate but just hung up.

At Stagg Place Sir Anthony Stratton, Head of MI6, was not pleased as John David made his report.

"However you try and dress it up, John, I can't think of a bigger cock up. The best placed controller we could possibly want in East Africa goes missing, on the night before Christmas Eve, miles from anywhere while on safari alone with an excellent agent who is also missing. The controller is the wife of the British High Commissioner. The agent not only knows Abdi Mohamed who, we hope, will be the next President of Somalia but he rescued him, showing great bravery. Abdi Mohamed owes him a debt of honour. I smell a serious scandal. I will have to brief the PM. You had bloody well better find them quickly. You can use any reasonable resources but be discrete. You will report progress to me daily. Now get on with it."

John David wished he had been a religious man. He would have prayed as he left the room. He was trying to locate a couple, lost in the wilds of Northern Kenya, who had driven off in a Landrover and no one had been briefed on where they were going. They were late on their expected date of return. When John David had first met Jim Scott, he had taken a liking to him but, he had also observed that

511

girls found him attractive. Had he eloped with the High Commissioner's wife? They could have been travelling for ten days. It was going to be a big search. How the hell was he going to do it discretely?

His first job would be to contact the army training team, on the ground at Isiolo. This was not a job for Special Forces, certainly not the Kenyan Army, but reliable British troops, which were already in the country. He had to get out to Kenya without attracting undue attention. The simplest way would be to take a commercial flight. He was too late to get a BA flight, that, evening from Heathrow. However, the RAF pulled all the stops and managed to get him to Rome. MI6 delayed the BA flight in Rome, with a make-believe mechanical problem, so he could board it there. He was the only occupant in first class. He arrived at Nairobi next morning, Christmas Eve, without incident. He picked up a Landrover, hired from Avis. He checked it over and noted they had included the extra spare wheel, as he had requested. He set off for Isiolo. It was a long, hot, dusty drive particularly as they were repairing the road north of Thika. He stopped at the Falls Hotel for a cool drink and bought some fruit and had some sandwiches prepared. He filled up with fuel in Nanuyki and carried on up to the village of Timau where the tarmac ended and the '*murram*' road started, taking him down 4000 feet into the hot country of the NFD. John David was a very lucky man. At the police barrier at the edge of Isiolo Township was a Game Department LWB Landrover coming in the opposite direction. The Game Department staff were talking to the police. John David was appalled by what he saw and heard. In the back, stretched out, was a dead European woman and man covered in dried congealed blood. He had found what he was looking for. The Game Department staff was transferring the bodies to Nanuyki Hospital as that was the nearest hospital used by Europeans. John got in the back to definitely identify the bodies. It was a gruesome task. The woman was definitely Claire Rochester. To his horror, almost under her, Jim Scott was still alive. He was barely breathing. He got Jim's head lifted slightly and trickled water into his parched lips. He cleaned the blood from his face. He sent two of the Game department staff to buy blankets, sheets and, if possible, a mattress in Isiolo. He lied to the Police, saying he was a senior official from the High Commission and he would take over the case. He had another stroke of luck as while he was talking to the police a British Army Landrover drew up at the Police barrier. Inside were a driver and a young lieutenant, called Charles Nichols. They were on their way to Nairobi to pick up a newly arrived Major, who was arriving the following morning. John noticed they had a short wave radio. He persuaded Charles to let him use the radio, to speak to his CO. Colonel Jock McCosh and John David had been at Harrow together. John needed several favours. It was difficult as there might well be eavesdroppers. So John explained to Jock that he had a confidential problem and that he was sending a Game Department Landrover to him, with a note explaining what he needed.

He wrote. *Jock I am sending you the body of Lady Rochester wife, of the High Commissioner can you get a post mortem done by your army doctor and then have a burial. This needs to done with as few people involved as possible. Then can you send a reliable man, with the Game Department staff, to the place where they found the bodies. Can you recover the vehicle and any personal effects? Can you also look for any evidence of foul play? It looks to me like a straight forward lion attack. Harrow seems a long time ago. I owe you one.*
'Salaams'. John David

Chapter 38

Recovery

Tuesday 24th December 1968

Jim was hardly alive when they arrived at Nanuyki Hospital. Dr Singh, the houseman, took one look at him and said that any further stress from travelling, would mean his death for certain. While Dr Singh and the only qualified nurse Judith Davis admitted him, cleaned him up and prepared a drip line, Mr Dick Anderson, the only surgeon in the town, was summoned. A wound on the back of his head was discovered so his head was shaved and it was cleaned. There was no evidence of a skull fracture but there was certainly some subdural haemorrhage. Once the drip line was in place, Jim was given massive doses of antibiotics and steroids intravenously as well as fluids to combat the dehydration. Remarkably, there were no actual bite wounds only multiple, very deep scratches to his chest, abdomen and upper thighs. Even his penis was cut. There was no question of stitching as all the wounds were badly infected. At no point did Jim regain consciousness. In fact, most of the time Judith could hardly see him breathing and his pulse was hard to find.

Dick went out to find John David.

"As I see it, there is no point in moving him to Nairobi, even with the flying doctor. There is nothing they can do which cannot be done here."

John asked. "Has he gained consciousness?"

"No," replied Dick

"Well, I will just see him before I go." John went in and shut the door. He leaned close to Jim and spoke. "Can you hear me?" John thought he could see Jim's eyelids move. John said very slowly.

"Do not say anything about the incident to anyone."

John came back out and said to Dick. "I need to go to the High Commission now but I will return in the morning. Please can you make

514

sure he does not have any visitors, until he is stronger and the situation is clarified?"

"Of course. We will look after him and not stress him any further." John left, to begin the long drive to Nairobi, before the nightmare meeting at the High Commissioner's Residence. He had met Sir Richard Rochester, but did not know him well. He had admired Claire. He could understand how Jim Scott had fallen for her. He also could understand that Sir Richard was considerably older than her and therefore she would be likely to have a wandering eye. He now regretted that he had not followed the correct protocol and checked in with the High Commission but Sir Anthony had been at pains to stress that discretion was important. It was nearly 10.00pm when he reached the High Commissioner's Residence. He had not telephoned ahead as there was a minimum delay of 30 minutes on long distance calls from Nanyuki to Nairobi.

He was greeted by Eli, when he rang the bell on the imposing front door. "Good evening Sir. How can I help?"

"My name is John David. I am a visiting civil servant from London. I would be grateful if I could see The High Commissioner, urgently, on a very important matter."

"I will inform The High Commissioner of your request, immediately. Please take a seat. " Eli turned and made his way to Sir Richard's study. He knew that Sir Richard was in a foul mood and had left the dining table. He knocked and heard an acknowledgement. He went in with some trepidation. Nothing had been right for the last two days as Lady Rochester had not arrived back as expected.

"What now, Eli?" barked Sir Richard. Eli explained that although it was late, he had opened the door, and a *'Bwana'* called John David had arrived, and said he had an urgent message for Sir Richard. Eli was told to bring him in and bring them some coffee and brandy.

Eli showed John David into the room and then went to get the coffee and brandy. Sir Richard was in no mood for pleasantries.

"Well, we have met before, but what brings you here at this late hour, unannounced?"

"I am afraid I have dreadful news for you. Your wife is dead, having been gored to death by a lion, somewhere in the NFD. I thought it was quicker and better to drive here than to telephone, as they are so unreliable. I am extremely sorry."

Somehow, in his grief, Sir Richard remembered his manners.

"Thank you for all your efforts. I do apologise for my rudeness. I just knew something dreadful had happened, as Claire has never ever been absent without leave before. I have sent for coffee and brandy. Do sit down. After your long drive can I get some food prepared? The kitchen, I am sure, can organise something in double quick time." John David replied, that coffee and brandy would be fine. At that moment Eli returned, so the two men sat in silence. When Eli had left, Sir Richard asked, "I informed London yesterday of my concern. You are here very rapidly with this dreadful news which, in my shocked state, I find hard to believe. I assume you were in the country already."

"No, Sir Richard, I was charged with being discrete by Sir Anthony. I flew in on a commercial flight from London, which arrived this morning."

"I see and, in blatant disregard for the regulations, you choose not to inform me of your arrival and have been roaming about the country ever since. Damn it all, Claire is my wife. How do you know she is dead? How do you know she was gored by a lion? It sounds a very tall story to me. I suggest you drink your coffee, take a sip of that brandy and tell me exactly what you know and how you came by this information. Sir Anthony may be senior to me in the service but I am the High Commissioner here and I was very fond of Claire. I am sure you have read her file and will think otherwise but, I can assure you, we were very close and did not let our private life interfere with our duty to our country."

"No one is implying otherwise. Claire was reckoned to be the best controller in Africa. She was found with Jim Scott who is dying of wounds in Nanuyki hospital. He was rated as one of the best operatives in the world. You are very well aware that he liberated Abdi Mohamed who, the British Government hope, will rise to very high office in Somaliland and he saved the Government from considerable embarrassment during the Hijack when your number two was shown to be a traitor. I am sure I do not need to remind you, that the British Government is walking on very thin ice in this country at the moment. We do not need a scandal."

"Right John, I repeat my request. What do you know and how can you verify it."

So John was forced to tell his story. Sir Richard did not interrupt and only broke down when John described them lying in the back of the Landrover. When Sir Richard got himself together he asked what had become of Claire's body. When he was told that John had given orders that she should be buried, by the army, in the NFD, Sir Richard really lost it. He screamed at John.

"Stay right where you are. If you move I will have my men arrest you." He swung open the door and roared,

"Eli, get Sparks to get me a secure line to London immediately. I don't care how late it is. Then get Captain Williams here, with two of his Royal Marines. The two men then stood glaring at each other. In no time, a very white faced young man opened the door and said,

"Your line is available, Sir Richard. Would you kindly follow me so I can issue you with the codes?"

Sir Richard went to follow him and remembered that Captain Williams had not arrived.

"How come you got the line so quickly, Sparks?"

"Eli ordered it some time ago, I imagine, on anticipation of your order."

Sir Richard bellowed, "Eli, since you seem to be in charge here you had better guard this Gentleman until Captain Williams arrived. How the devil did you know I would require a line to London?"

Eli stood straight backed and replied, "As soon I heard the tragedy of Lady Rochester's death, I knew you would require a line to speak to London."

"Were you listening at the Bloody door?"

"No Sir. My father rang with the news as I was preparing the coffee. Everyone in Wajir is devastated. Please carry on with the call. I will attend to Mr. David."

Totally bewildered by the turn of events, Sir Richard followed Sparks to the radio room.

Eli came into the room and closed the door. John said. "It appears that you are very well informed. How is that?"

"Lady Rochester was very highly regarded in the NFD, in her own right, because she was a very brave and kind lady. She was extremely highly regarded, as she was Dr Scott's woman. I understand Dr Scott is critically ill, in Nanyuki. My father has pledged ten camels. Eighteen other traders have matched that offer. The money is therefore available, should a journey be required to England but I understand, at the moment that would not be advisable.

John replied in a very tired voice. "You are correct." He thought, *'what a disaster, there is no way this can be hushed up. What the devil am I going to do?'*

As if reading his thoughts, Eli, who had reached this highly responsible post by showing considerable intelligence and total discretion, said, "Dr Scott has an excellent servant called Katana who is, at present on leave, at his home at Karatina. Katana, with the help of Lady Rochester nursed Dr Scott through a very bad attack of Malaria. He nearly died. I am sure Katana would immediately come to Dr Scott's aid. Might I suggest a safe house, in the cool on Mount Kenya near to Nanyuki is obtained so, as soon as he is fit enough, he could be moved there? If I can give the matter some thought I am sure I can find a *'Memsahib'* suitable to nurse him. I imagine *'Bwana'*, that your main problem is a scandal in the English press. The NFD is a very large place but the number of inhabitants is very few. If you give instructions to me, I will have the word put out that information is not leaked. I know, by the look on your face, that your Government would have preferred Dr Scott to have died, as well as Lady Rochester. That may well be what Doctor Scott now wishes. However, he is young and we think he has an important part to play in the future of the NFD."

John sighed. He knew he should have thought of all these problems and their solutions but he was so terribly tired and he knew he was not thinking rationally.

"Thank you Eli. I also think Dr Scott is a good man. I will bear what you say in mind." Eli replied, "You can always contact me here at the Commission. Can I get you another cup of coffee and a glass of water? I think that will help you, Sir?" John was very grateful. He knew he should try to take charge but, somehow, lethargy had overtaken him. He hoped more water and coffee would get him thinking in a clearer way.

Eli returned with the coffee and ushered in Captain Williams. Captain Williams was a short, stocky Welshman who had played tight-head prop for Cardiff, as a civilian and now played for the Army, when he was in the UK. He was a seriously tough thirty-year-old. No way did he require two marines to guard one man. He had ordered them to sit quietly in the hall. He would assess the situation and call them if they were required. However Captain Williams known to his friends as Dai and, behind his back, by his men as 'short arse', was a kind man and much respected. He took one look at John and saw he was all-in. He held out his hand to him and said, "I am David Williams. My friends call me Di."

John replied. "I am from London. My name is John David. Naturally, Sir Richard is very upset, as I have had to tell him about the tragic death of his wife. I don't think there is any need to arrest me."

"Good," said Dai. "I wonder, Eli, if you could bring me a cup of tea and a couple of cups for my chaps who, as you know, are outside. I am sure some biscuits would not come amiss." Eli still stood, straight backed. He could have been a marine, if he had been wearing a uniform.

"Certainly Sir, I think we may even be able to run to some cake." He turned on his heal and went out.

John had now collected his thoughts and filled Captain Williams in on the situation. Dai did not interrupt him, except to endorse the usefulness of the British Army training team in the NFD. He did show some surprise, when John carried on with his briefing in front of Eli. After Eli left, John explained how Eli was already aware of the problems and that, in his opinion he was a man who could be trusted even with him being a Somali. He said, Eli was a Kenyan first and a Somali second. John intimated that maybe Dai was Welsh but his main allegiance was to the UK Government. When Sir Richard returned, he was a different man. All the anger had drained out of him and the career diplomat had returned. London, obviously, had strongly urged his cooperation with John. He immediately apologised for his bad temper and also for bothering Captain Williams so late at night. Captain Williams said Sir Richard should not apologise to him, as his job stretched far beyond guarding the Commission. He suggested he send a driver and a reliable senior sergeant, trained as field paramedic to follow John, in the morning in a separate Landover and to send a young Second Lieutenant with John, to help in any way required. Captain Williams said security was not a concern. One word from him and his men would keep total silence. He left the two civilians alone. He went to go and get everything organised, with a view to leaving at 7.00 am on the following morning.

John explained Eli's plan to Sir Richard but intimating it was totally his plan. Sir Richard said he would announce his wife's death and plan a memorial service for approximately ten days time. Sir Richard suggested that John David stayed at the Residence. They both retired to what was going to be a short night.

Good news greeted John David and Lieutenant Gibson, on their arrival at Nanyuki Hospital after a two and a half hour drive. Lieutenant Trevor Gibson was a good driver and John was glad he had accepted his offer to drive as he was still tired from yesterday's experience. They were in a good car so they arrived twenty minutes ahead of the Marine Landrover, containing Sergeant Cook and Lance Corporal Smith. John walked into the hospital, leaving Trevor in the car park to wait for the others. He met Judith Davis, who seemed none the worse for her long night. She told him the good news, that Jim had recovered consciousness. She said he had drunk some water and some tea but had not said anything.

Sister Judith, was a relatively young Kenyan widow. She had come out during the Mau Mau, with her army husband. They had both loved the country and its people. Her husband had been killed in a car crash. Judith had stayed on with her young daughter, Kim, who now was eighteen. Kim was home, having just finished school for Christmas. She was due to go to the UK, to try to get into University soon. Kim's best friend was Susie Cameron, who was having a gap year. Susie Cameron was up staying with Kim. The two girls both had walked down to the hospital to see what had happened to Judith. Kim was used to her mother keeping erratic hours but she knew that normally her mother managed to return for breakfast, after a night shift, particularly as it was Boxing Day. Susie Cameron wanted to be a nurse. Judith was a role model to her. As they entered the hospital the two girls were pleased to see Judith, still looking immaculate in her sister's uniform. Susie felt a cold feeling in the pit of her stomach when she heard Judith talking about a patient called Jim. Judith saw the two girls and she waved them over. She asked John if he would like a cup of coffee. When he said he would love one and he thought the lieutenant, called Trevor, waiting in the car park would also like one, Judith asked the two girls if they would make coffee for; John, Trevor, herself and themselves. Judith then took John in to see Jim.

Chapter 39

Recognising Jim

Thursday 26th December 1968

The girls swiftly made the coffee. Kim who had cast an eye over the smart young English officer in the car park quickly volunteered to take him his coffee. Susie, with some trepidation, went into the room containing the patient called Jim. She just knew it was Jim Scott. As John and Judith were facing away from her, looking at the patient she quietly walked forward as if to put the coffee onto the bedside table. In reality, she wanted to look at the patient. Her worst fears materialised. She immediately recognised Jim and was appalled by his waxy looking appearance. She thought he was dead, until he moved his head slightly to acknowledge a question being asked him by John. She wanted to run away and hope it was all a horrible dream but she steeled herself to place the cup of coffee on the bedside table and ask if John would like any sugar. Before he could answer, Judith said.

"Thank you, Susie, but could you take it back to my office. Mr. David and I need to talk and it would be more private there."

Susie replied, "Of course." She glanced at Jim and was sure he recognised her, as he opened his eyes and tried to smile.

Susie took the one cup of coffee to the Duty sister's office and returned to the staff room to collect the second cup of coffee. She duly took that to the sister's office. Kim was still outside, chatting to Trevor. Susie busied herself making her own coffee and one for Kim. When she heard Judith Davis and John emerge from Jim's room she took the sugar bowl into the sister's office. She heard Judith say quite sharply,

"This is most irregular. I cannot see the reason for all this haste and secrecy. I think the patient's needs should come first and he should remain with us until he is stronger. He will require much more than a servant to look after him. I can imagine your army sergeant even if he is a paramedic, will not be allowed to stay with him for very long. However, I can tell by the determined look on your face that my advice is not going to count for much. I am sure Mr. Anderson will agree with me but, I suspect, you will even overrule him. At least, Mr. David let me find a suitable nurse." Susie left the sugar and quietly left the office. She had made her mind up. She was going to nurse Jim back to health however long it took.

Susie knew that she might get in trouble but she was determined to risk going back into Jim's room. She went into his room, to find a young African trainee nurse in the room. In her most adult authoritive voice she said, "Nurse, I think there is a lady in the women's ward who needs assistance. Could you go and help her?" Susie moved to Jim's bedside as the young nurse left the room. She stroked Jim's cheek.

"Poor you, I know you are too weak to talk but just to tell you, I am staying within walking distance of the hospital. I also think they are trying to move you too soon. Is that right?" Jim just managed to nod his head slightly.

"I think they will want someone to nurse and look after you. Would you like me to if I promise not to have too many G & Ts and get into bed with you?" Susie was sure Jim was trying to smile. He certainly nodded his head.

"I will do my best to arrange it and I will certainly keep coming to see you." Susie lent down and kissed Jim's lips. They were on fire.

"Keep fighting, I will be back soon." Susie slipped out of the room without anyone noticing. She went out into the car park to find Kim and Trevor. They had been joined by Dougie Cook and Fred Smith. Susie asked if anyone would like some coffee. Trevor said he was fine but Dougie and Fred both asked for a cup of tea with lots of sugar. Susie said she would make the tea and see if she could find some biscuits. Kim volunteered to help but Susie said she would be fine. When she came back into the hospital, John was just leaving Judith's office. He did not look a happy bunny. Susie went straight up to him with her most radiant smile.

"Your other men have arrived. I am just making them some tea. Would you like some more coffee? I was going to try to find some biscuits. I am training to be a nurse. You look awfully tired. Would you like to come and sit in the staff room, while I make tea? The armchairs are old but very comfy." Susie was so glad she had on some short-shorts, which showed off her long legs.

John replied, "That would be good. I had rather a short night. It would be great to get my feet up for a few minutes." Susie could feel his eyes on her legs, as she made the drinks. She purposely bent down in front of him, pretending to look for the biscuits. She thought, *'I hope Jim likes my legs as much as this dirty old man does?* She gave John his coffee and several biscuits and said, "You have a rest here. I will just take the tea and biscuits out to your men."

When she came back into the staff room, John said, "You are a very kind, helpful young lady. I am sure you will make an excellent nurse. What is your name? I am John David. I am out here, from London, to help a young man employed by the British Government."

"I am Susie Cameron. My Dad is the Chief Veterinary Research Officer. He works for the Kenyan Government through MOD."

"Well, I am very grateful for your help. Have you lived out here all your life?"

"Nearly all of it I was born in England but came out with my parents and brother, when I was a baby. I rather think of Kenya as my home."

John was now thinking on his feet and threw off his lethargy. "I imagine you speak Swahili. Have you a driving license?"

"Yes, on both counts. I am staying up here in Nanyuki with Mrs. Davis, as I am friendly with her daughter. I am going to find a job here, for some weeks before going to UK for my nursing training."

"Could I be very forward and ask you for your address and telephone. I might just have a job for you?"

Susie wanted to punch the air and shout 'YES' but instead, she very demurely said,

"I will find a pen and write it down for you. I will just pop out to reception."

John replied, "That would be most helpful. The job may be slightly sensitive and confidential, so could you keep my request just between the two of us?"

"Of course, I am used to keeping my mouth shut as Dad's job has many sensitive aspects."

Susie quickly found some paper at reception and wrote out her home telephone number and the number for her Dad's secretary, at the Vet Labs. She knew her name, Vet Labs PO Kabete, would find her. She returned to the staff room and said, "There it is. I will leave you now to have a little rest."

Susie went out to find Judith and also to see if she could find out what exactly was happening. She thought, '*Surely they won't move Jim immediately?*'

Judith was actually looking for Kim and Susie. She found them outside with the army chaps and beckoned the two of them over. "Let's go home for an early lunch? I have been in this hospital long enough. I won't stay at home long, as I am worried as these army chaps might move my patient, but I must have some free time. I know Dr Singh comes on duty soon. He won't be bullied by anyone."

"Auntie Judith, would you like me to stay with the patient? I can be quite fierce if I mean to be."

"That's really sweet of you Susie, but you need some lunch."

"I am fine, I will get as fat as a warthog if I eat any more. I have been eating biscuits all morning."

So, everything was going as Susie had planned. She went quietly into Jim's room and sat on his bed. He was asleep and seemed to be breathing too fast. Susie thought it was probably the fever. Judith had said that he had terrible, infected wounds on his body. He was lying flat, mainly to the opposite side from where she was sitting, so she very carefully moved so she could lean against the headrest. He did not stir. She risked carefully lifting up his hand and resting it on her bare thighs. It felt very hot. She smiled when she remembered the night in Watamu, when Jim was so frightened they would go to sleep together. She blushed when she remembered how they had been completely naked and Jim had stroked her hair and said she was lovely. Please don't die, Jim. I could not bear it.

Jim groaned and she thought he was going to wake up but he slept on, with his hand nestling between her legs. The next thing was, she could hear some quite loud talking outside the door. Susie shot off the bed. She must have gone to sleep. She had time to lift his hand and to pretend to be taking his pulse, when Dr Singh came in. "Ah, Miss Cameron, how is our patient?"

"He seems very hot, so he must still have a fever. I would have thought the antibiotics should be working by now?"

Jim did not stir, as Dr Singh explained how lion wounds always contained a mixture of bacteria, some of which were very likely to be resistant to antibiotics. He said that part of the problem was Jim had been left so long, out in the bush, before getting treatment. However, he added to her fears by saying she must not give up hope. Susie really realised then how critical a condition Jim was in. It made her more determined to nurse him with all her strength. So it was that Susie, to give Judith a rest, walked down to the hospital with Kim after supper, at about 10 pm, to stay with Jim until another staff nurse came on duty at 6.00am. Kim went home with Judith, who was dead-beat.

Jim felt cooler to Susie, which she thought must be a good sign. He was still on a drip, but Susie had been told to help him to drink some water, if he woke up. This he did, around midnight. He was groggy but Susie thought he knew it was her. With one arm around his neck, she held a teapot like cup to his lips. She reckoned he drank a teacupful. As he lay back, he reached out to her hand and squeezed it. Susie did not dare get onto the bed as she knew she would go to sleep, so she moved her chair as close to the bed as she could. She now had a pair of jeans on but somehow she wanted to feel his hand on her skin, so she laid his hand on her lower arm. She felt him stroke her twice and then he was still. His breathing was much less harsh. In fact she could barely hear it. She struggled to fight off sleep, but it was a losing battle and she drifted off to sleep. She managed to give him two more small drinks during the night. After he had the second, he obviously wanted something as he pulled her hand towards him under the covers. Although she was only half awake, Susie guessed he wanted a wee. She thought that must be a good sign. She had seen the bottle during the day, under a white cloth, on the bottom shelf of the bedside locker. She brought it up to the bed and pulled down the covers. She lifted his night shirt and, with a little help from Jim parting his legs she got the bottle between them. She remembered feeling his penis in Watamu when it was all erect but she had also seen her brother naked, so she knew it was normally small, soft and floppy. She was horrified to see Jim's penis as it had been torn by the lion. It obviously hurt him as he flinched as

525

she lifted it, as gently as she could, and put it into the bottle. As she withdrew her hand, she felt him relax and she saw urine slowly going into the bottle. His bladder must have been full, as the bottle was at least a third full when he stopped. She whispered. "Have you finished?" Jim gave her arm a very gentle squeeze. She guessed that meant yes so she very carefully removed the bottle and returned it to its place. She pulled down his night-shirt and drew up his covers. Impulsively she kissed him on the lips. She just felt him move his tongue, so she touched it with hers. His lips did not seem as hot as before. She settled back in her chair.

Susie was awake at dawn as Florence, the African staff nurse, came into the room. She shook Susie's hand and asked how Jim was. Susie told her that he had drunk, three times in all, and had passed quite a lot of urine. Florence whispered. "That is good. The 'simba' has damaged his penis but I think he can still make children. I heard he killed the lion with a 'panga' so he has become a man and can take a wife now." Susie realised that Florence must be a Masai as that tribe historically required the young 'Moran' to go out in a group and kill a lion with their spears before they were eligible to get married. Florence then thanked Susie for helping out and asked her if she would be OK going home on her own. Susie said she would be fine, as the dawn had come and it was not far.

Judith was up when Susie came in and so they had breakfast together. Kim was still asleep. After breakfast, Judith urged Susie to go to bed. Susie certainly did not need any persuading. She was soon asleep. The next thing she knew, was Kim shaking her and saying, "Wake up your Dad is on the phone and wants to talk to you urgently about something important." It was now noon but Susie was still pretty groggy and slightly bad tempered as her father gave her a ticking off for still being in bed. Susie retorted, "I have been up all night nursing a very sick man at the hospital, who is in a critical condition. Auntie Judith ordered me to go to bed!"

"I am sorry, darling, I did not realise. Well done, I am very proud of you. I thought I had to speak to you as I have had a very senior man from the Foreign Office (FO) on the phone asking if he could employ you for three months. He said he had met you at Nanyuki and had been very impressed by your behaviour and that you had given him my work number. He was rather cagey about what you had to do but he intimated that it would fit in well with your proposed nursing career. I told him I would have to discuss it with you and your mother. I said I would ring him back after lunch. Susie thought, *'John David has not wasted anytime. My legs must be better than I thought!'* "That is fine Dad. It is really a nursing job. It will suit me OK. Auntie Judith will look after me."

"Good, I will clear it with your Mum, but I doubt if she will have any objections. I am sorry I criticised you earlier. I thought you had been out partying."

"I wish," replied Susie with a laugh so that her Dad would know he was forgiven. Kim had made her a cup of tea when she walked into the kitchen.

"What was that all about?" Kim asked.

"Oh Dad was just checking up that I had not been out partying all night. Thanks for this tea."

Susie was well awake now, so she and Kim walked to Nanyuki Sports Club for a swim and some sunbathing. They were home when Judith got back, just after 5.00pm. Judith looked tired but Susie could not wait to find out how Jim was.

"He is certainly a bit better but I think I should go back later to be with him. He is still very, very weak but I am sure he will live."

"Thank goodness," said Susie, "but you must let me do the night shift, to let you have some rest, Auntie Judith. I had a good sleep this morning."

"That is so kind of you Susie. I am still worried about him. He does not seem to want to talk. I think there is a lot more wrong with him than the mauling by the lion. I don't know about that chap, John David. I am sure there is another agenda but I can't unravel it."

So it was that Susie and Kim walked down to the hospital at 10.00pm and then Judith drove Kim home, leaving Susie to look after Jim. Obviously there were other nurses looking after the other wards, but none of the patients were half as ill as Jim. Susie was delighted, as Jim was certainly better. He managed a tired smile when she came in. He nodded his head, when she asked him if he was feeling better. Susie fussed over his pillows and managed to get him to drink some water. He was still on a drip but his colour looked better. She noticed today's paper on the chair, which she picked up as she went to sit down.

"Shall I read you some of the paper?" Jim nodded again. As was normal with 'The Kenya Nation', the front page was all about what The President Jomo Kenyatta had done that day. Then Susie read a small paragraph on the second page, which was an announcement from The British High Commission. It read; *the tragic death is announced of Lady Rochester, wife of Sir Richard Rochester. She was tragically killed by a lion in the Northern Frontier District. She has been buried, at her request, in the remote area in the NFD where she died. She had always loved the area and she was much loved by the local people. A memorial service will be held in Nairobi Cathedral on Friday.* Susie looked up, as she sensed something was wrong with Jim. He had gone a deathly white and his eyes were wide. Susie realised immediately that Jim was somehow involved with Lady Rochester's death. She had the good sense to say nothing but continued to read bits out of the paper. After a few minutes she sensed that Jim had relaxed. She continued to read, until he dropped off to sleep.

Susie's mind was in turmoil. There was no way she was going to drop off to sleep, even in the dim light of the hospital room. She thought. *'It was too much of a coincidence that this important lady had been killed by a lion and Jim had almost been killed by a lion, at a similar time. If Jim had been a professional hunter it was easily possible that he had been taking Lady Rochester on a safari and they had been attacked by a lion. However, Jim was not a hunter but a vet. She did know he often worked in remote areas. She resolved to ring her father in the morning, to see if he knew anything to aid her in solving the riddle. She remembered the letters they had both written, after their meeting at Watamu. As she had said when they parted her letters were about girlie things but she wanted him to tell her about exciting trips in the NFD. He had told her about learning to fly. He described the hair-raising trip to Mandera, to discover the source of the Rinderpest outbreak. She had loved the story about the hippo, at Addi, and the sad story of the removal of Judas' eye. He had described, in detail, his work on the cattle ranches and his work with the LMD. She particularly liked the work on the stock routes and the use of the blow up boat on the Tana River. All of their letters had been humorous and interesting but, although they were affectionate, they were never love letters and, although they ended 'with love from', that was just as if they were brother and sister. As time went on they became more intermittent and, in fact Susie had not heard from Jim for over six months.*

Susie was certain the letters held a clue to this mystery and, as she sat beside Jim through the long lonely night she mulled over them. After about three hours, Jim woke and Susie gave him some water. He was certainly stronger, as he could hold the teapot type cup on his own. After he had finished, Susie asked if he needed a wee. He was obviously embarrassed but he nodded his head. Susie whispered that he should not be worried, as she wanted to be a nurse and would have to help many different men. Also she said she knew, from last night that the lion had damaged his 'willy' and she would be very gentle. He smiled and said nothing but just nodded his head. Susie had already helped him to half sit up so it was easy for her to put the bottle between his legs. Susie noticed that, unlike last night, no urine came. She immediately realised that he was too embarrassed to wee so she whispered,

"Shall I whistle?" Jim smiled and started to wee. Once Susie had sorted everything out, she got Jim lying down on his side and encouraged him to sleep. She kissed him on his cheek. He was soon sleeping peacefully and Susie continued her silent vigil.

She kept thinking about the letters until suddenly, she remembered a newspaper story of the wife of the High Commissioner helping to transport a hippo to safety in the Tana River. In fact, there had been a photo of her standing with the DC. That was the connection. Jim obviously knew Lady Rochester. Maybe they were good friends. Maybe they were more than that. All this secrecy was obviously to prevent a scandal. Susie still resolved to phone her Dad in the morning, as she was sure he would know why Jim had been on safari. Susie then slept, until she heard the hospital begin to wake up. Jim was still sleeping when she was relieved by Florence. As it was getting light, she walked to Judith's house. Judith's house girl was up and she made Susie a cup of tea. Susie had started on a pawpaw, with a squirt of lime, when Judith came down.

Judith was really grateful and said she had had a really good night's sleep and that she was now back to normal. Susie told her how she thought Jim was improving and that he had had a peaceful night's sleep. She said he had only woken once, for a drink of water and a wee. Judith exclaimed.

"Susie, you poor girl I forgot you were not a nurse. You must have been terrified. How did you get on? Were you both terribly embarrassed?"

Susie laughed. "Jim was. I had to whistle quietly before he could wee but I was not bothered. I am not sure how I would have got on with a lecherous old man. Obviously I was very gentle with his penis, as the lion has cut it."

Judith replied. "As a young nurse you have to be careful in these situations. You have to be very firm and show no affection or men will take advantage of you."

Susie answered, "Of course I will be." However she thought, '*I wonder what Auntie Judith would say if she knew I had held Jim's penis when it was hard as a stick and we had both been naked in bed. He had been so kind then and he could so easily have, in Judith's words taken, advantage of me. In fact, I would have encouraged him. I will just have to love him back to health.*'

Judith must have read at least some of her thoughts, as she said, "Susie, it is very important that you do not become fond of your patients."

Susie replied, "Of course Auntie Judith."

Judith responded. "You are a very sensible girl. I am sure you will make an excellent nurse. Today you must have a really long sleep. With a little luck, the surgeon will let us take out Jim's drip line so he won't need so much supervision."

Susie asked, "Can I ring home before I sleep, just to see how they are?"

"Of course you can. Do send them my love," answered Judith.

There was little delay for Susie's call to Kabete. In fact, she wondered if it was too quick and that her Dad would not be in his office. However, he answered cheerfully. Susie laughed and said she was glad he was not still in bed and that he and Mum had not been out partying all night, while she had been doing her night nursing work. Her dad thought this was very amusing as he had left Freda, Susie's Mum, asleep in bed. He said that they both thought the nursing job was an excellent idea, for three months, and that he had said so to the FO chap who would be contacting Susie directly. Susie was delighted. She was even more delighted as her Dad suggested doing it for three months and then they could have a few days at the coast, before she went to UK to start her proper training. This gave Susie an easy lead in to asking about Jim.

"Dad, do you remember that great guy, Jim, who was in the Veterinary Department, that we met at Watamu? I have lost his address. Do you know what has happened to him?"

"I do indeed," replied Colin Cameron. "I have followed his career, as I thought he showed initiative and promise. He has done really well. His contract has been renewed and, when he comes back from leave, it is pretty likely he will get promotion. He is away for several months, as extra leave is accrued for working in dangerous and unhealthy areas like the NFD. I will keep you posted on his return. I could find his UK address if you want to write to him? He may be still in UK when you go. He would be a good contact, as the UK may be a little lonely when you first start."

"Thanks, Dad," said Susie. "I had better go to bed now as I may be on night shift tonight."

"Don't work too hard. Have some fun with Kim," replied her Dad before he rang off.

'*So the Veterinary Department think he is on home leave but, in reality, he stayed here in Kenya on safari with the High Commissioner's wife*', thought Susie as she snuggled up in bed. She drifted off to sleep, feeling his hands on her thighs when he was teaching her to water-ski. It was a very nice feeling.

Susie was woken by Judith's house-girl, in the middle of the afternoon. Auntie Judith was at work and Kim had gone to meet friends at the club, for a swim. The young girl, who did not really speak English, said there was a man on the phone for her.

"Hello, Susie Cameron speaking. How can I help you?"

"It is John David here. I am sorry to rush you but that nursing job has come up urgently. I need you to nurse and look after a sick man who will be coming out of hospital later today. I have organised a house. Could you be ready in an hour? I will send Trevor round to pick you up."

"That will be fine. I will be packed and ready when he arrives," replied Susie.

'Wow,' thought Susie. *'Auntie Judith will not be pleased. I will have to write her a very careful note. She will be very cross with me, if she finds out.'*

It was easy for Susie to pack quickly, as she did not have much stuff. The house-girl made her a cup of tea and found some cake. The note was difficult to write.

Dear Auntie Judith,

I am sorry to leave so rapidly but an auxiliary nursing job has come up, which Mum and Dad would like me to take. Many thanks for a super time. I will write as soon as I find my feet. Also, thank you for all your advice.

Lots of love to you and Kim, Susie

Having said goodbye to the house-girl and given her a small tip to thank her for her extra work, Susie walked down the road, away from the house, with her rucksack on her back, so that the house girl would not see who had picked her up. She had walked about two hundred yards before she saw Trevor coming towards her. She waved him down and hopped into the passenger seat of the Landrover, throwing her kit in the back.

"Good to see you again. Sorry we had to rush you but John wanted the patient out of hospital as soon as possible. His drip was removed today and he should be picked up some time after 5.00 pm," said Trevor. "We have found a lovely house on a farm on a very large ranch, called Ol Pejeta which is to the west of here off the Thomson's Falls Road. It is fairly isolated but has fantastic views of Mount Kenya and the Aberdares. I hope you will like it. I have picked up the patient's cook and he is cleaning the place. It is furnished and is in good order. There is a *'kuni'* stove for cooking and heating the water, which comes from a stream. Sadly there is no electricity or telephone, but I am sure you are a tough Kenyan girl and will manage. You will have this vehicle, which belongs to the patient. It is in excellent condition and I got Lance Corporal Smith to check it over. He also filled up all the Jerry cans with petrol so you will have plenty. John David has checked up on the insurance and it is insured for anyone to drive. Have you driven a Landrover before?"

"Certainly," replied Susie. "I am a tough Kenyan girl, remember." Although Susie was extremely apprehensive, mainly because she was worried they were moving Jim too early and Auntie Judith would be furious, she enjoyed the drive with masses of game. There was a stock fence to keep cattle in, set about thirty yards back from the road. A herd of Eland crossed the road in front of them. They jumped the fence with ease. It was a wonderful sight. Trevor, obviously, had not been in the country very long so Susie told him all the names of the animals. He was a nice enough chap but Susie did not fancy him. She wondered if Kim did, but Susie hoped he would stay in Nairobi as it would not be a good idea for Trevor to meet Auntie Judith. They arrived at the house, after going through several cattle gates which Susie opened. She took very careful note of the route and the lay of the land they passed through. There was still two hours before night. The house was set on a small rocky hill with, as Trevor had said fantastic views. There was a small house at the back, for servant's quarters.

They went in the front door and were greeted by Katana who introduced himself in '*Swahili*'. Susie could see he had done a good job cleaning. There was a hall with two bedrooms, one with a double bed and another with two single beds. Each bedroom had a basin. Susie put her stuff in the room with the single beds, so Jim could have the double bed. There was a big bathroom with a lavatory. There was a separate small room containing a lavatory and a small basin. The dining room led into a big living room with an open fire. Off the living room was a veranda. The kitchen with a stove was at the back, it was reached by a covered walkway. Next to the kitchen, was the '*kuni*' stove to heat the water. Both stoves were alight. There was a massive pile of logs, under a lean-to on the side of the kitchen. There were hard furnishings in all the rooms. There were good thick curtains on all the windows, which had bars, which were a remnant from the '*Mau Mau*' emergency. The soft furnishings were obviously all new, as were all the other household equipment. There was a new paraffin Fridge and also a new water filter. Susie asked Katana if they worked. He said they did. Susie thanked him for his hard work. He seemed a kind old man and Susie thought he would be a great help. He asked if he could make them some tea. Susie said that would be marvellous. She said she would go to the loo and then quickly unpack. Susie translated for Trevor. He said he would love some tea. He also said that he was not sure when the patient would arrive. Susie could see a fire had been laid so she asked him if he would light it.

After tea, Susie had a look to see what food was available. She suggested to Katana that he opened some cans of soup and make a cottage pie. There was some cabbage and plenty of potatoes. They could have fruit for pudding. Susie said she thought there would be six for supper. She asked Katana if he too had food, and he said the *'Bwana'* had bought him all he needed. He said there were torches and several gas lights with spare cylinders. He showed Susie the fridge, which had beers, tonic, fruit juice and fresh milk. He showed her several pints of UHT milk, a bottle of gin and a bottle of brandy. Katana said he had all of Jim's safari kit so, he thought they would have everything they might need.

Trevor and Susie were sitting on the veranda when they heard the two vehicles approaching. Susie ran out on to the drive to greet them. Corporal Smith was driving the army Landrover. Sergeant Cook was sitting in the back with Jim who was laid out on a mattress. Susie saw Jim looked very pale but was wide awake. She put a finger to her lips to indicate that Jim should not say anything and hoped he would not show any sign of recognising her. John David followed them in a hire car. He immediately greeted Susie and tried to take charge. However, Susie was having none of that. She said the patient still looked very weak. She asked if they could move Jim, on a stretcher, into the house. Susie suggested he was put in the double bed. She asked if he needed the loo. Jim nodded his head. Susie asked if they had a urine bottle. Sergeant Cook produced one. She then shooed them out of the bedroom and told them to get themselves some drinks and that Katana would soon have supper ready for them, on the table at the end of the living room. She firmly shut the door and locked it. She made Jim who was still in his hospital night shirt, comfortable. She whispered that it would be best if he pretended not to recognise her, and then helped him have wee. She gave him some water and asked if he would like some soup and some bread. Jim nodded and then squeezed her hand. She kissed him on the cheek. As she left she said quite loudly so the others could hear, "Just lie still and I will bring you some food directly."

The others were sitting on the veranda having drinks. Susie immediately went into bossy mode.

"Katana will bring some supper soon. Can you bring me up to speed with the patient and what medication he is on?"

John replied, "He seems unable to speak, having been attacked in the NFD by a lion. He has been much traumatised. I would be very grateful if you could nurse him back to health. His name is James Scott, but I would like to keep that confidential. I have written down a telephone number and a contact at the High Commission. The contact's name is Eli and I think he is entirely trust-worthy. You should not speak to anyone else except for these gentlemen here. In case of a real emergency they can contact me in the UK. On no account should Jim be moved. I am afraid that I must insist that there are no visitors. The ranch manager has been told to stay away. I expect you saw how isolated you are. However, you can leave Katana with Jim when you need to go to get provisions. I would prefer if you go to Nyeri as you may be known in Nanyuki. Sergeant Cook, would you like to discuss the medical details?"

"The patient has no further need for intravenous fluids. He should continue with oral Oxytetracycline for a minimum of ten days. He can have aspirin as routine pain relief. I have prepared this kit, which contains some emergency drugs, e.g. sleeping tablets but only two per night and to be avoided if possible. There is some Senokot for constipation and some Kaolin et Morph for diarrhoea, If he has a fever he should have Chloroquine, as it is possible he might have malaria. I have included ready prepared syringes of morphine. You can inject one into a muscle if he is in very severe pain. You can give him a second injection in four hours. If there is no improvement, you can take him back to Nanyuki hospital." John chipped in. "That is only in dire emergency. Now, I would like you to sign this form, which is the Official Secrecy Act. I stress that you are not to divulge anything that has happened or does happen to Jim Scott, other than to myself. The others here have all signed."

Susie thought, '*Bloody hell, this is way beyond my experience but I am going to prove to Jim, and myself that I can do it.*' She replied, "That is fine. I totally understand. I will sign and stick to the Act. I would be grateful if, when you get to Nairobi you could ring my father and say. I am perfectly happy and have settled into the job well and I will be writing from time to time. Obviously, I won't mention anything I should not in the letters. Can you ring him on his home number tonight, however late, as he will be concerned? You will have to make up some story about my employment and why I had to leave so abruptly from Mrs. Judith Davis's house. I wrote her a very brief note, saying I had a nursing job but she may not be satisfied."

"Can't you make up a story in a letter now and I will post it?" answered John. Susie looked him straight in the eye and said, "No. I will not lie to my father or Aunt Judith. You are asking a lot of me and that is my request."

John was obviously not used to his authority being questioned. He replied, "You are a very forceful young lady."

Before he could say anymore Susie said, "I think that is why you recruited me?" She thought, *'Or was it my legs.'*

John sighed, "Very well. I will send you a letter saying what I have said. I have included, in my notes, a P.O. Box number for you to use in Nyeri. Here is the key. I will also expect a weekly report, by air-letter, to the address in my notes."

Susie added, "If Jim was due to go home on leave, I imagine his parents will be expecting him. I hope you have informed them."

John David replied, "Of course, I have it in hand. They will be told he is on another contract which started immediately. They will be told he is permanently working in a remote area so not to expect any mail from him in the short term. Can you get him to write when he gets stronger?"

Susie was relieved that, at that moment, Katana called them to the table for soup. Susie immediately took some into Jim and told them to carry on without her. Jim did not look quite so exhausted and he managed to drink his soup from a normal mug. Susie was just worried he would burn himself. He ate some bread, which she had buttered. However, then he slumped back and, when she asked him if he wanted to eat some cottage pie, he shook his head. She suggested he had a little sleep now and then a banana and coffee later, when she had got rid of everyone.

When she got back to the table, the atmosphere was less tense. Susie gulped down her soup and let Katana bring in the main course. She talked to him all the while in *'Swahili'*, mainly to reassert her authority over John and the soldiers. She briefed Katana that Jim was slightly better but did not want any cottage pie. She would give him a banana when the *'wageni'* (strangers) had gone. Katana smiled and said in *'Swahili'*, "The sooner the better." Susie laughed.

They all started to eat. "This is jolly good," said Trevor. "Can you thank Katana for us?"

John added, "He must have really worked hard. Can you pay him, at the same rate that Jim pays him? As Jim is on leave he will have paid Katana his leave pay, so this is really re-employment. I don't imagine you have looked but, in the bedroom Jim is in, there is a walk-in cupboard. In it is a gun safe. There are no guns in it, but I have put some cash in there, with a cash book. Here is the key, Susie. Can account for all you spend on food, wages, petrol etc? Can we leave your wages until the end of the three month contract? Obviously, you can take an advance if you want to buy personal items. Rest assured, you will be well remunerated as I realise this is a big responsibility for you. Confidentially, I understand that Jim will definitely have his contract renewed by the Kenyan Government. He will, hopefully, start work at the end of his leave. He will get promotion to a higher grade of Veterinary Officer. His posting is, as yet, undecided but it will be somewhere upcountry, in a healthy climate like this. I will tell him this before I leave."

Then, turning to the others he said, "Eat up lads, we should be going soon, as we have a long drive back to Nairobi. Actually, I will forgoe my fruit and have chat with Jim now."

"Can you take him this banana?" asked Susie.

"Certainly," said John. At that moment there was a loud shriek from outside. All the men jumped.

"Don't be alarmed," said Susie. "That was only a tree hyrax. They are small, furry, rabbit sized animals. I think they are related to elephants. They do sound rather alarming." Susie was actually delighted that all the men had jumped. It rather endorsed her command of the situation.

John only spent a few minutes with Jim. Then he shook hands with Susie and said, "I am sure you will do fine. I am sorry if I was a little sharp with you earlier." The others all wished her luck and soon they were off.

537

Chapter 40

A different type of nursing

Saturday 28th December 1968

Susie and Katana both breathed a sigh of relief as they cleared away the supper things. Susie went in to see Jim. He was now lying down and was not looking too good. Susie said,

"I think you need to sleep now, we will leave cleaning your wounds until tomorrow. Here are your antibiotics. I will help you with the water to wash them down." Jim tried to sit up but he suddenly seemed too weak. Susie helped him with her arm around his shoulders. He rested against her. She said,

"You are a poor old thing. Would you like a couple of aspirins?" Jim nodded his head. After he had swallowed them, Susie fluffed up his pillows and got him comfortable.

"I will just go and say goodnight to Katana and then I will come and sit with you."

When she came back, Jim was almost asleep. She sat in a chair, beside his bed, and held his hand. He squeezed her hand and, within seconds, he was fast asleep. Susie sat for maybe half an hour, listening to the African night before she turned off the gas light in the room. She left his door and the door to her own room open, so she would hear him if he was troubled. Having had a wee and cleaned her teeth, she put on her pyjamas and got into bed. She made sure her torch was handy and then laid down and also was soon asleep. She awoke to a low moaning noise. It was Jim having a nightmare. By the time she had got to his side, he was thrashing about. Susie thought he was going to hurt himself so she tried to hold him still. This seemed to make him more violent. She then shook him and commanded,

"Jim, Jim wake up. It's alright I am here. It's Susie." He kept fighting but then suddenly he stopped.

"Poor you, Jim, that was a terrible nightmare. It was only a dream, I am here." He then seemed to recognise her and totally relaxed. Susie asked,

"Would you like some water?" Jim nodded his head and she helped him to drink. It was really quite cold but there was sweat on his face. She then helped him have a wee. Susie was shivering now with the cold, so she settled him down and whispered, "Good night Jim. I hope you sleep well now but shout if you need me." Jim nodded and Susie knew he had understood. She went back to bed. Luckily, there was still some warmth in her bed so she soon warmed up. Susie did not immediately go back to sleep, as she lay worrying about Jim. Obviously, he had had a dreadful, traumatic experience with the lion. Thank God he was still alive. The poor High Commissioner's wife had not been so lucky. He had two more similar nightmares. The first one, Susie went to him immediately and woke him and then settled him down. The second one, she was really sleepy and left him for some minutes but he started shouting and so she got up and was waking him when Katana came in with another torch. Katana helped Susie get Jim comfortable. Jim was soon asleep. When they were back in the hall, Susie said to Katana,

"That is the third nightmare he has had. What should I do?"

He replied, "I think you are very fond of him, like I am. You are a women and the bed is large I would get in and hold him until you both are asleep. I don't think he will wake with you holding him."

Susie said, "I don't think it is proper for a nurse to sleep with her patient."

"True," replied Katana, "but this is not a hospital and you are training and you are doing what you think is best for the patient." He squeezed her arm.

"Good luck. I am there in my house you only need to shout loudly and I will come. There is nobody else for miles to worry about." Susie heard him shuffling out to his house as she quietly got into bed with Jim. She remembered Watamu. She remembered how sensible Jim had been then and how kind he had been to her as a young girl. She was just worried how violent he was in his nightmares. Susie was made of stern stuff. She cuddled his back taking care not to put her arms around him and hurt his scarred chest. It was rather a nice feeling and she was soon asleep. Katana had been right and Jim had

539

no more nightmares. The next thing Susie knew, was Katana's hand on her shoulder. Jim was still asleep as she slipped out of bed and went to her bedroom. Katana had made her a cup of tea. She quickly got dressed and drank some of it, before going to find Katana.

"Katana, I would like to thank you so much for your help. Jim did not have any more nightmares. Do you think I should wake him as it is almost 9 am?"

"No, I would let him sleep. He is still ill and very weak. Remember, he nearly died. You must keep strong so I will make you a good breakfast. You can then help Jim with his breakfast when he wakes." Katana was not surprised when Susie hugged him. She was not the first of Jim's 'memsahibs' to hug him.

Susie ate a big fry-up and felt much better. When Jim woke, she helped him with a cup of tea and a banana. He even managed two pieces of toast. She gave him his antibiotics. Then she asked him if he wanted a poo? He nodded his head. Susie said,

"The soldiers did leave a bed pan but would you like me to help you to the loo?" Jim nodded his head very vigorously. Jim was very weak but, with Susie's help, all doubled over like an old man, he managed to get to the lavatory.

Susie said "I will be next door, if you want me, so just shout or if you have finished. Don't try to walk on your own as I don't think you are quite strong enough yet, but I am sure you soon will be." Susie left him with the door slightly ajar. She straightened out his bed and covered the sheets with a towel. She was just coming through from the kitchen, with a bowl of hot water to wash him, when she heard a croak. He had finished. She helped him back to his bedroom and then asked,

"Can you bear to lie on your front then I can wash your back?" Jim nodded. Very carefully she helped him get down on the bed. She then undid the hospital gown and washed all his back, together with his legs and arms. Then she asked him to lie still while she got some more, clean, warm water. She knew he would be embarrassed but she made him roll onto his back and said,

"We must try and get these infected wounds to heal." Very gently Susie started to clean the dried blood and pus away. The wounds were really horrendous. She knew he was going to have dreadful scars. There was a tap at the open door.

"Do come in Katana. Poor Jim has some dreadful wounds but they will heal eventually." Katana had brought some clean sheets, a pair of scissors and a jar of honey. He said,

"When you have cleaned the wounds just let them dry in the air and then apply this honey to them, very carefully. Then, you can cut the sheets and lay them on the wounds. Then you can put on his pyjamas. You will be amazed how quickly the wounds will heal."

It was certainly a novel treatment but Susie did as Katana had directed. She smiled up at Jim when Katana had left and said, mischievously,

"If you are a very good boy and do all I tell you, I will lick it off when the wounds have healed." With that, she put a little honey on the wound on his penis. Although Jim was terribly embarrassed, he did manage a smile. In fact, the honey was very cooling to the wounds and did not sting unlike the cream they had used at the hospital.

Jim's main problem was that he was totally devastated by Claire's death. He blamed himself for not guarding her properly and, in fact, taking her into such a remote place. He blamed himself for not getting to her quicker when she screamed. Jim was also hung up on preserving her memory. He was so obsessed by John David's instruction, not to talk to anyone, that he could not talk at all. He was honest enough to know he was attracted by Susie. She had developed into a marvellous girl. He was very impressed with how capable she was. He had a problem with their relationship as the edges were blurred. She was his nurse and yet when she came to him in the night, she was only wearing pyjamas which left little to the imagination. She obviously was a naughty girl. Her behaviour at Watamu had taught him that. She was not upset by his body with all its scars. At the moment he was very weak but, he knew, he would get stronger. Would he be able to resist her then? Did he want to resist her? He was sad, confused and depressed.

In reality Susie, with her bubbling vitality, was just what Jim needed. It was an added bonus that she really fancied him but, she knew in her heart, that he was not the man for her at the present time. She wanted to make her way in the world. She wanted to go to the UK and get a qualification to be a nurse. She wanted to get up the nursing ladder. She had no intention in walking in a man's shadow.

However, she had thought Jim was 'drop dead gorgeous' at Watamu and now she felt very maternal. Whatever, she was going to help him in the next three months. He had been very kind to her.

When she had got Jim settled in bed and in his pyjamas, she asked him if he would like her to read to him. Jim nodded vigorously.

"I am afraid I do not have a paper. Shall I look through your things and see if I can find a book you might like?" The soldiers had put all of Jim's stuff, from the Landrover, in the 'walk in' cupboard in his room. Susie found some non-veterinary books and sang out their titles. Jim picked, with a nod of his head, 'Lord of The Rings'. Susie was a good, inventive reader. She managed to change her accent for the different characters.

Katana could see that Jim was enjoying it, when he brought in the mid-morning coffee. It was now a beautiful, sunny morning so Susie suggested she helped Jim walk to a chair, on the veranda. It was a bit of an effort but well worth it, to be in the fresh air. When Katana had taken away the coffee things, Susie asked Jim if he would like her to continue reading. He nodded his head. "As it is so sunny, I know it is not very nurse like, but do you mind if I put my bikini on so I can top up my tan?" Jim could not help himself from smiling and nodding.

They ate a light lunch and Susie lay on a towel in the sun and did some serious tanning. Jim had a sleep. Susie thought she was starting to get burnt, so she put on her running things. She told Katana she would only be thirty minutes and went off for a run. Initially, she ran on the main track; which led away from the house but she soon found a game trail off to her left. In this way, she managed to run right around the small hill on which the house sat. As it was still the heat of the day she did not see any game, only a 'Blind Snake' crossing the path. Jim was awake when she ran up the road to the house. Susie was delighted at his wide smile.

"Isn't this a beautiful spot? Are you OK? Is there anything I can get you? I feel guilty neglecting my nursing duties. Do you want a wee?" Jim nodded.

"Come on," said Susie. "I will help you off the veranda and you can wee on Africa." She helped him and stood supporting him, having a wee as if it were the most natural thing in the world. Katana saw them and thought, '*If anyone is going to make the Bwana better it is this memsahib. I don't think she is very old but she has got guts.*'

It was getting chilly so Susie helped Jim back inside. Katana had laid the fire, so Susie lit it. She then went for a shower. Jim idly imagined her naked body in the shower. He felt the stirrings of an erection. He thought, '*Christ I will have to be careful when she washes me. Then he thought, I don't think she will be alarmed. She wasn't in the least bothered in Watamu. She is now over two years older why should she be worried now.*' He sat back, closed his eyes, and remembered the morning on the beach when the surf brought him in quickly and he bumped into her legs. He was brought back from his reverie, by Susie's hands on his shoulders. She just had a towel wrapped round her. She was smiling at him.

"You had a naughty, cheeky grin on your face Jim Scott. I hope you were not dreaming about your nurse in the shower? That would be most improper." Jim went bright red. Susie laughed. "I think you are getting better. I am so pleased but I think, as your nurse, I will have to wear more clothes. What would Auntie Judith say?"

Katana brought them some tea and biscuits and then he listed the things he was getting short of. Susie said she would go shopping, in Nyeri, tomorrow. She said to Jim she thought there was a half decent supermarket but not much else that would interest her. She had a biro, which she used to write the list for shopping. She handed it, with the pad of paper, to Jim.

"Why don't you write down the type of books which you like? There may be a bookshop. I could see what is on offer."

Susie read to Jim until it was getting dark. She lit the lamps and then Katana brought in the soup for supper. He had added some alcohol to it and it was lovely. He had even made some croutons. Susie thanked him. Jim nodded his head and smiled. Then they had a rich beef curry with rice. The soldiers had provisioned them well as there was some sweet mango chutney. By the way Jim tucked into the curry, he was really hungry and obviously liked curry so Susie knew to get plenty of ingredients. She also liked curry having been brought up in East Africa. They were half way through the curry when Susie leapt up.

543

"Let's have a cold beer? I am sure half a 'Tusker' won't upset your antibiotics." Jim nodded and Susie brought a beer out of the fridge.

They were early to bed, even with the difficulties of Jim moving to the loo and into his bedroom. He was still in his pyjamas so there were no dressing problems. Susie settled him down and turned off the gas light. She wished him good night and kissed him on his forehead.

"Sleep well," she said, as she went to her room. She did not shut either door. She was not long in the bathroom and quickly got into her pyjamas. She made sure she had her torch before she turned out the gas light. It must have been well past midnight, as the moon was up, when Susie was woken by Jim's nightmare. She quickly woke him, without trying to stop him rolling about and punching with his fists. She had to dodge or he would have hit her. She gave him some water and helped him have a wee. She sat with him and soon he was asleep. She slipped into the warm bed. She had hardly got cold. She cuddled up, as close as she could get to his back, and went to sleep. She awoke and it was now darker with the moon having set. She had rolled onto her back and Jim had rolled over and was facing her. She was sure he was still asleep so she rolled on to her side and wriggled into his arms, bringing his arm over her waist, which was bare, as her top had ridden up and her bottoms were low on her hips. This triggered an unexpected reaction. She felt his hand move under her pyjama bottoms and gently rub her bush. It was a nice sensation, so she opened her legs and his hand moved lower. He was now rhythmically, firmly stroking her. No one had ever done that to her before. Susie really started to enjoy the sensation. She felt a warm glow. She had actually never masturbated. She bit her lip and sucked in her breath. It was lovely. She stroked her breasts and then she started to pant. After a few delightful minutes she was extremely hot and was gulping air and, with a deep sigh she climaxed. She reached down and brought his hand up to her lips to kiss it. She smelt herself. She had a job to stop herself from waking him and begging him to do it that again. After she had calmed down, she cuddled up close to him and went to sleep.

They both slept soundly. Susie woke to the bright dawn coming through the curtains. She slipped out of bed and went to her bedroom, via the bathroom. She was almost dressed when there was a discrete knock on the door. Katana came in with a cup of tea. They whispered together, that it was best that they left Jim to sleep but Katana said he would bring Susie's breakfast onto the veranda. Jim was still asleep when she had finished. Katana said he was entirely happy to look after Jim so Susie took her shopping list and some money, and set off for Nyeri. Trevor had drawn a map for her as there was a quicker way from the house, off the ranch and on to the Thompson's Falls Road, to Nyeri. John David had stressed that he did not want her going anywhere near Nanyuki. The road through the ranch was rough but it was a glorious drive. There was so much game to be seen. Susie made a mental note to tell Jim what species she had seen. There were both Tommies and Grant Gazelle. They were really quite tame, just skipping away from the Landrover. The Impala were even tamer, standing still but constantly flicking their ears. She saw Waterbuck, Zebra and Warthog and, in the distance a herd of Buffalo. Baboons were constantly crossing the road. Susie thought when Jim was stronger he would love coming out. Bugger John David, it would be fine if they stayed on the ranch. Once she got to the Thompson's Falls / Nyeri Road, she turned left. There was still game to be seen either side of the road. The road was good 'murram' with some corrugations. Susie knew, from her Dad, that there was a trick to driving on this type of surface in any vehicle. If you were a real mad-hat you went that fast, so that you floated over the corrugations. However, if you had to brake quickly, for a game animal, you could easily lose control and slide off the road, down the steep camber on the sides. If you went at a medium speed it was safer, but the vehicle juddered all the time with the corrugations. The sensible speed, according to her Dad, who was a very important person in her life, was to go slightly slower, taking your time and enjoying the drive. You then had a smooth, safe drive and usually arrived only a few minutes behind the mad-hats.

Whether they were mad-hats or unlucky but Susie rounded a bend to find a car in the nearside ditch with its upper wheels off the ground, still spinning. Dust still hung in the air. Susie drove past the car and then backed up, well to the side of the road so as not to obstruct anyone else coming round the bend. She jumped out, praying that no one had been hurt.

It was a very pale family newly out from the UK on holiday in a hire-car. They were very shaken up but not hurt. The parents were a similar age to the Camerons. They had three daughters, the oldest was probably older than Susie. As both vehicles were safe off the road there was not much danger of another vehicle running into them but Susie suggested they all get right off the road. She ran back and pulled three cut branches, off the side of the road, onto the carriageway to warn on-coming traffic. Susie introduced herself and reached into the Landrover for the basket containing a picnic which Katana had prepared. She gave the parents a cup of tea each and the girls some cold cokes from the cool box. As she was hunting in the back of the Landrover for the tow-rope, she heard one of the girls say,

"Dad, I am sure she is younger than Mel and she is out here all alone." Susie smiled to herself and thought. *'You don't know the half of it!'* She found the tow-rope and lay on the ground under the front of the car. She tied the tow-rope to the middle of the front axle with an easy-release knot and then attached it to the hitch on the back of the Landrover. The father said,

"I can see you have done that before. I am Geoff Thimbleby. This is my wife Jean and our three daughters, Mel, Emily and Tina." Before Susie could reply, Tina piped up,

"Oh, you have now got yourself terribly dirty." Susie looked down. She was indeed filthy.

"Don't worry, it will all come out in the wash! I am Susie Cameron. Now, what I suggest is that you get in the car, Geoff, and make sure it is out of gear and that the handbrake is off. If you ladies can stand well back and I will put the Landrover into low range and slowly drag the car back onto the road." Susie was delighted, as the plan worked perfectly. Geoff got out and was leaning under the front of the car. Susie said, "Don't worry Geoff I will undo the knot as I know how I tied it." She lay on the ground again and the tow-rope was soon free.

Jean said, "Susie, you have been so kind. If it hadn't been for you, we would have been stuck here for hours. We are going to the 'Outspan' Hotel in Nyeri for lunch. Would you like to join us?"

"I would love that," replied Susie. "I have got some shopping to do so I will do that first, while you are settling in, and join you. You go first now, as you will go quicker than the Landrover."

It was still a lovely drive. Now the morning cloud was lifting, Susie could see the Aberdares on her right and the shoulders of Mount Kenya on her left. She thought, *'How lucky she was to have some independence. She was very fond of her parents, they had both taught her so much but she was sure now was the time to break away. She wondered if she was confident because she was in her comfort zone. Kenya, and its wild places, was her home. Those three girls and, in fact, the whole family were slightly out of their depth. Would she be out of her depth when she went to London nursing, in three months' time? She had had her first orgasm last night. Maybe Melissa had rubbed herself when she was only fourteen. Lots of her school friends had talked big and claimed that they had had all manner of experiences with boys. Was she very naïve for her age? Other than her brother, Jim was the only boy she had seen naked. He had had a wonderful body at Watamu when he was straining backwards, water skiing. Now, it was all scarred but it did not turn her off. She made up her mind that soon, when he had recovered, she would encourage him to make love to her.* Her groin felt hot thinking about it.

She parked in the main street in Nyeri. She knew she looked a sight, with dust and stains all down the front of her shirt and jeans. She saw a cheap clothing shop and went in and bought a new denim shirt with pockets and a short denim skirt. It was pretty hot in the sun so she did not loiter window shopping but quickly found a book shop. She bought one historical novel, set in Roman times and one travel log of six young undergraduates, driving from London to Singapore. She hoped Jim would enjoy them. She had brought both a cool box and two cool bags so she took them into the supermarket and packed them, really carefully, with all her purchases. Then she drove to the Outspan and parked in the shade. There was an *'askari'* on duty so she spoke to him kindly and asked if he would *'chunga'* (guard) the Landrover for her. She left the windows of the Landrover open to try and keep it as cool as possible. She walked in to the hotel with her new clothes. The Thimblebys were sitting at a table on the veranda. Geoff jumped up and asked what she would like to drink.

Jean looked a little surprised when Susie said she would love a really cold Tusker. Susie noticed that although Geoff and Jean had G & Ts, the girls all had cokes. Geoff said, "Would you like me to take you to our room so you can have a wash and change? I see you have bought some new clothes. You must let me pay for them as, if it had not been for us, you would not have got dirty."

"No way," replied Susie. "I am always getting dirty, but thank you for offering. I would love a quick shower. We could go via reception. I am sure they will let me have a towel."

The old man at reception smiled at Susie when she said, *"Tabu kwa gari,* (I had trouble with my car) *iko kitamba* (is there a towel)?" He handed her two towels.

"Asanti sana Mzee (Thank you Old man {this is a term of respect}). *Mimi safisha indarni numba a bwana hapa* (I will wash in the room belonging to this man here)."

Geoff asked, "Are you fluent in Swahili?"

"More or less," replied Susie.

The room had an en suite bathroom, separated from the bedroom by a curtain. Susie thought Geoff would go and so left her new clothes on the bed and went into the bathroom. She had a very quick shower, without washing her hair. She put on her bra and pants and came out into the room.

"You are very trusting," said Geoff. Susie was too surprised to be cross.

She replied, "I am sure you are a real gentleman." She put on her new shirt and skirt.

"Will I do?" She enquired. Before he could reply she added,

"I will catch you up. I just need a wee." She went back in the bathroom and heard the door close. She was washing her hands when she saw four packets of contraceptive pills sticking out of Jean's wash bag. On impulse she took one packet and put it in her pocket. She had never ever stolen anything before. She tried to justify her action by thinking, *'He was a dirty old man hanging about while I showered. I hope poor Jean does not get pregnant. I am sure she can get some more in Nairobi.'*

Susie reached the table, just as Geoff was bringing the beer. Jean said, "You look very smart and that skirt shows off your figure really well. You were very quick in the shower."

Susie replied, "I feel so much cooler now. It was kind of Geoff to guard me, as there is no door to the bathroom."

Jean said, "I hope you stayed outside to give Susie some privacy." Before he could reply Susie said, with a dirty laugh,

"Don't worry, I would have soaked him if he had actually come in the shower." The girls giggled and Jean looked daggers at Geoff.

It was a good lunch. The food was excellent. Susie chatted to Jean and the girls about their safari and what they might see. Geoff was quiet, probably dreading being alone with Jean and getting a bollocking. Susie could not worry about it. She thought he had been truly out of order staying in the room. She offered to pay for her meal but Geoff would not hear of it. They all came to see her off. Jean hugged her and said she was a wonderful girl and, she was sure they would still be beside the road, if Susie had not helped them. Susie felt doubly bad for stealing pills but she could not undo it now.

She made good time getting home and was delighted to find Jim sitting on the veranda, reading 'Lord of the Rings'. Susie ran up the steps and lent down and hugged him.

"Are you feeling better and well rested?" Jim nodded vigorously.

"I have brought a paper and two books, I hope you like them." Jim smiled and nodded again.

"I must get the shopping in the fridge." She took in two bags and Katana came out and helped her with the rest. He seemed relieved to see her home, safe and sound.

Susie left Jim with the paper and went in to help Katana with the shopping. They chatted as they worked and Susie told Katana about some of her adventures. He was very pleased with all the food. Susie made a pot of tea and took it, on a tray with some cake, out onto the veranda. Jim had obviously scanned through the paper. He looked relieved. He had obviously been worried that there might have been something about Lady Rochester. Jim could now totally feed himself. Susie chatted on about all the happenings of the day. She told him everything except stealing the contraceptive pills.

They had a great supper, which Katana had cooked with all the fresh ingredients. They washed it down with two Tuskers. Susie told Jim about all the game and how they could have fun when he was better, without leaving the ranch. Once again, they were early to bed. Not having electricity, encouraged them to go to bed early and to get up early if they did not have broken nights with Jim's nightmares. Before she settled Jim for the night, she remembered to do the accounts and write her report for John David. She had not sent anything so far, which was remiss, but she would send off something next time she went to Nyeri.

For the next week or so, the nights were totally predictable. Jim would have a nightmare. Some were more violent than others. Susie would get him off to sleep and then cuddle up beside him. She wished she could start the night with him so that they would not have a broken night's sleep. However, she did not dare suggest it. To her disappointment, there was no repeat of him fondling her.

Then one night he had a really violent nightmare. He was really aggressive. He ripped her pyjama top and hit her in the mouth so her lip swelled up and there was blood everywhere. Susie knew he was totally unaware of what he done but she was pissed off as it bloody well hurt. However, she still managed to calm him down and get him off to sleep. She still cuddled up beside him, which seemed to relax him. She resolved to tell him, in the morning what had been happening and suggest that they slept properly together. Although she was wide awake she did not brood on the problem and she was soon fast asleep, so much so, that she was still asleep when Katana woke her. She got out of bed carefully and put a shirt on, over her top, to make herself decent and went through to the kitchen to have a cup of tea with Katana. When he saw her face he was concerned but she explained that Jim did not know what he had done. She said she would take her tea back to Jim's room and stay in bed with him until he woke. Then, she would have a chat with him and suggest she slept with him all the time. Katana squeezed her shoulder and said he thought it was a good plan. Katana did let on that, when Jim had malaria very badly, he, Katana, had been at his wits end and Jim had been saved by a *'memsahib'* sleeping with him.

As Susie lay beside him she thought about Lady Rochester. *She must have really loved Jim. She must have taken a considerable risk to go to him when he was ill. Having an affair was one thing but nursing a sick man was another.*

With all the problems in the night, Susie was sleepy and so she was actually asleep when Jim awoke. He was very surprised to find her beside him. Susie woke and rolled onto her shoulder.

"How are you feeling, Jim? You had a rotten night. You had a really bad nightmare and you hit me by mistake."

Jim said, "You poor girl, I am so sorry." They both looked at each other flabbergasted. He had spoken to her. Susie burst out laughing from relief. Her torn pajama top fell down exposing her left breast.

In between giggles, Susie said, "I suppose you are going to tell me, ripping my top was a mistake."

Jim blushed and said, "I really am so sorry. Will you forgive me?"

"Of course I will, you old goose!"

With that she totally trashed her top and said. "Have a good look. I am quite proud of them. Now I must get up and wash my face and make myself presentable. What would Auntie Judith think of me, exposing myself to a patient?" With that, she was out of bed and heading for the bathroom and nearly bumped into Katana, bringing in the tea. He said,

"Mimi hapana jua wewe a Giriama, Memsahib? (I did not know, Madam you were a Giriama?)" Susie replied. *"Tittie ake hapana kubwa tutosha* (No, my breasts are not big enough)." {The ladies of the Giriama tribe are renowned for exposing their large breasts}. She heard Jim laughing behind her and she knew, somehow, everything was going to be all right.

In fact, Susie's lip healed very quickly. A new pyjama top was put top of the shopping list. When both Jim and Susie had finished breakfast, Susie said it was time Jim had another bed bath and then she was going to see how the scars were getting on with their honey dressing. Jim said he dreaded bed baths.

"Why, for goodness sake?" said Susie. "Surely they don't hurt?"

"It is just so embarrassing," said Jim.

"Oh, don't be such a baby. I have seen it all before. Anyway, how about you ripping my top and exposing my tits, so Katana says I am a Giriama."

"That's different," said Jim. "Your tits are beautiful and you are proud of them."

"Well, your willy is very different and distinctive. It may be more stimulating to girls when you make love?" retorted Susie. "Come on, lie down and let's have a look at you."

551

Susie was amazed how well the scars had healed. She bathed them, very gently, and then she suggested he just lay there and let the air dry them. She said she would cover him if it got cold. She said she only had a shirt on and she was not cold. Susie read more of 'Lord of the Rings' to him, as a treat. They both had a really happy day. Katana was also happy and made them a special supper of Spaghetti Bolognese. They both had two tuskers but they were still slightly embarrassed when they went to bed. Susie helped Jim and got him settled. Then, to make him feel better after she had been to the bathroom, with the gas light still lit, she stripped off naked in front of him and only put on her pyjama bottoms.

"I have got another pair of pyjamas but they are much thicker and I will get too hot wearing those." She got in bed beside him and cuddled up. Jim remembered her beautiful body naked in the moon light. He felt his erection. He prayed he would not roll over and frighten her. He also prayed that he would not have a nightmare.

He didn't have a nightmare but he did roll over and Susie woke in the night to feel his hard erection against her thighs. She opened them slightly to let his penis come between them. *'Time to start taking Jean's pills,'* she thought, with a smile.

In a few days, Susie made another *'safari'* into Nyeri. They had started going on short walks together, from the house so Jim said he would ride with her for three miles and then walk back to the house, to get some exercise. Susie popped into the kitchen to warn Katana what was happening. She was worried that Jim might not be strong enough. In fact he managed the walk easily and when he got back he started unpacking his things. He particularly wanted his binoculars and his bird book. He was tearful when he came across his camp shower, and remembered the happy times he and Claire had had together. However, he got a grip on himself and knew he must move on. He would never forget her but she was dead and nothing would bring her back. He thought, *'how lucky he was to have Susie and Katana to look after him. Susie was amazing, she seemed to enjoy cuddling up to his scarred body. He could not imagine any girl wanting to do that.'*

He was happily sitting on the veranda, identifying birds, when he heard his Landrover. He walked down the steps and was several yards down the drive when she drove in. She jumped out and hugged him.

"Are you OK," she asked anxiously.

"I am fine, I just came to greet you," answered Jim. Susie kissed him properly on the lips. He helped her in with the shopping. She had got him a paper and two new books. She had bought a whole crate of *'Tusker'* as it was so much easier to sort out the empties which had to be returned. She had bought some tonic water. She knew the soldiers had brought some gin. She thought some G & Ts would be good. She had bought some limes not only to go in the G & Ts but also to go with the pawpaw she had found. She remembered Jim saying how he had it for breakfast, most days at the coast. She had also gone to the Chemist. It had been really easy to buy the same pills that she had stolen from Jean. She had bought enough for two more months. She did not feel half so guilty now as she knew Jean could easily get some more.

That evening, Jim said he was sure his scars had healed enough to have a proper bath. Susie said OK but to be careful not to have the water too hot. He shouted to her, when he was out, "Shall I run one for you as there seems to be plenty of hot water?"

Susie replied, "That would be great, I will wash my hair."

For the first time, there were two really clean people having supper. Susie had bought two steaks. Katana cooked them carefully, so they were rare. Jim complimented him. Katana said how pleased he was to see Jim getting better. They had several G & Ts. Susie reminded Jim about her escapade at Watamu.

"Now, I don't need the excuse of being pissed, to get into bed with you. I have to cuddle up to you to make sure you get better. I think it is nursing, in a broad sense but I don't think I will tell Auntie Judith!"

That night, as they were going to bed, Susie said. "Don't you feel hot in those pyjamas?"

Jim was a little embarrassed and said, "I feel guilty, as I am so much better, I get an erection and I don't want to frighten you." Susie faced him, "You won't worry me. Several nights now, you have rolled over and I have felt your 'willy' against my thighs. I have just opened them a little as I like feeling him there." She started taking off his pyjama jacket.

"One night, when you were still asleep, you reached your hand down my pyjama bottoms and rubbed me so beautifully, I had my first orgasm. Will you do it for me tonight?" Jim stammered as she locked eyes with him and slowly removed, first her shirt and then her bra. Still looking at him she undid her jeans and pushed them down, together with her knickers. Then she took his hand and took it to her groin. She whispered, "I am little bit wet already." She put one of her hands by her vulva and then put her fingers in his mouth. Jim could taste her. He felt his penis rock hard.

"Come on, let's get into bed. I want you to make me have an orgasm. I can't wait." Susie turned out the gas light and got in quickly bedside him. Jim remembered the night at Watamu when he had so wanted to excite her. He had managed to stop himself then because he was worried she was too young. He could not stop himself now. He soon had her on her back panting and moaning softly. When she had really climaxed, she whispered,

"Can you come inside me? I want to feel you. I know it will hurt." Jim very slowly came down on her. Her legs were wide open and she guided him gently into her. She gave a little gasp and then thrust quite firmly up towards him. Jim said,

"We must stop. You will get pregnant."

"Don't worry, I am on the pill. It is a wonderful feeling." She kissed him passionately and then whispered.

"No other 'willy' has been inside me, for me to compare, but I am sure yours is special." Soon Jim climaxed. He thought he was never going to stop ejaculating. He collapsed on top of her. She hugged him with her arms and her legs. Jim had no nightmare that night.

Jim's total recovery was rapid from then on. The walks got longer and soon they were running together. Susie was a good housekeeper and Katana was an excellent cook and therefore they ate lots of healthy food. John David had left a considerable amount of cash, expecting Susie to buy expensive European type food but she bought locally grown Kenyan produce. They had beers and G & T's some nights but often they just drank water. They were no longer shy. Most of the time, in the bedroom, Susie was not a '*Giriama*' with her chest bare, but totally naked. Often, if she knew Katana was busy elsewhere, she would sunbathe naked to get an all over tan. They mainly got up with the dawn but often made love early in the morning, and cuddled until it got light.

Chapter 41

A strange request

Monday 27th January 1969

Jim surprised Susie one morning by saying. "Can we break the rules?"

"Do you want to tie me up, beat me and then make love to me hanging from the ceiling?" replied Susie.

"No, you silly, it's about my dog," said Jim.

"Now I understand, you want to mount me from behind. That's not breaking the rules. I love it like that."

"Will you be serious for once," said Jim and started to tickle her until she was begging him, first to stop and then to make love. When they eventually collapsed into each other's arms, Jim said.

"It is about my real dog, Lucy. She is with a friend at Ol Kalou. Could we go and pick her up?"

Susie replied thoughtfully, "I don't think we can, but I am sure I can. No one knows me at Ol Kalou."

"I would be worried about you going so far on your own."

"What rubbish it is not that far and if I set off early I would probably be home in time for lunch. I won't go to Nyeri tomorrow for the shopping, I will do it in Thompson's Falls. I will post John David's report in T Falls. I doubt if he will notice the post-mark. If he does, I will say I was worried that I was going too regularly to Nyeri. That will shut him up. It is odd, there has been no feed-back in the P.O. Box in Nyeri. I have checked it every time I have been. My guess is, 'out of sight out of mind'. Have you seen any crisis in the paper, which would concern the FO?"

"No, there has been nothing remarkable."

So, during the day, Jim made sure everything was 100% in his Landrover. He made sure there were two spare tyres and there was a jerry can of water plus a spare can of petrol. He knew there was a petrol station at T Falls. It was just a precaution, in case the petrol station was out of petrol, for some reason. Katana prepared a picnic breakfast, as well as some lunch, just in case Susie was delayed. The plan was that they would leave before dawn. Jim would ride with Susie for approximately ten miles when they would nearly be off the ranch. They would stop for a very quick small breakfast. Susie would then go on and Jim would run back home.

They were woken by Katana, with two cups of tea and were soon off. Susie drove very carefully, as there seemed to be game everywhere. They very nearly ploughed into a herd of Giraffe and then narrowly missed a Dikdik. Jim knew Susie would have been mortified if she had hit it. They stopped for breakfast. Then Jim said,

"I am worried about you. Ed, my friend, does not have a telephone but there is one at the Veterinary Office, if you have problems."

Susie replied, "You be careful on your run there may be buffalo or even elephant about this early."

They kissed. Susie said,

"Remember you are very, very, special to me. I won't say I love you because that implies a life time commitment but you were my first and you are a bloody good lover. I will never ever forget you. TAKE CARE."

She jumped into the Landrover and was off. They hoped, if the journey went well, Susie would reach Ed's home before he left for work. The fall back scheme if he had left, was for Susie to go to the Veterinary Office and try and find him there, or on his rounds. Jim had given her, carefully prepared, hand written maps.

Susie had been to T Falls before, when she was a child. She remembered walking down to the bottom of the waterfall. As a child it had seemed very impressive. She had also been to a fresh water lake near Ol Kalou, called Ol Bolossat, when she was a teenager. Her Dad had gone duck shooting there with two colleagues from Kabete. She remembered really enjoying it, as the other two men had made a big fuss of her and she had always enjoyed going on 'safari' with her Dad.

When she reached the edge of the ranch she turned right, rather than left which would have taken her to Nyeri. She could just make out the Aberdares, in the gloom ahead of her, as she turned. Initially, the road was not too bad but it deteriorated. She was glad when she eventually joined the road coming in from Nanuyki which was much better and took her into T Falls. It was now light but there were few people or vehicles about. She turned left at the cross roads in the centre of town. The right would have taken her to the spectacular ranching country, around Rumuruti. The left, which ran beside the railway ran due south to Gilgil or, if one forked right, to Nakuru. Susie had friends who had been at school at Gilgil.

This was real Kikuyu country. All the farms, which had been owned by Europeans, were now owned by African cooperatives. It was mainly a dairy area, with African small holdings having two or three cows. It was Ed's job to do the Veterinary work for these cows. The road was intertwined with the railway so Susie had to slow down at the rail crossings or the Landrover would have bucked like a horse. There were no railway crossing gates but Susie knew that trains were rare, maybe one a day at the most. Now it was properly light, she could see Ol Bolossat shimmering on her left. Ed's house was an old, colonial farm house just south of Ol Kalou, off to her right. Jim had not been certain but he thought there was a big white sign saying Ol Kalou Co-op on the road side.

Jim had been right there was the sign, and the house was a hundred yards up on the left. Jim said he thought Ed had a white Peugeot 204. It was parked outside the house. Susie drove in and parked beside it. She was greeted by a friendly Black Labrador who gave one rather feeble bark and then licked her hand. She went down to stroke her and said, "Hello Lucy, you are a lovely friendly dog." Lucy put her head in Susie's lap. Susie looked up and, standing in front of her, was a big strong looking chap about Jim's age. He had close cropped hair, and a smile, on a weather-beaten face. This was obviously Ed.

"Lucy seems to know you. I am Ed Fisher. How can I help you?"

"I am Susie Cameron, a friend of Jim Scott. I was with Jim up to two hours ago. I expect Lucy can smell him on me."

"Oh," replied Ed. "I thought he was on home leave. Come in, I am just about to have breakfast. I am sure Patrick can find enough for you. I was just cleaning my boots, on the step, when you drove up. I have been here for nearly a year and Jim has been my only European visitor. I go down to Nakuru when I want company. I am afraid the house is pretty rough and ready. It is not really fit for entertaining young ladies. I am surprised that you are all alone."

"I am sure your house will be fine. I am not really much of a young lady but really a Kenyan cow-girl. The house where Jim and I are staying, does not even have electricity. I would love some breakfast. Could I have a wee and wash my hands?"

"Of course, how remiss of me, Jim usually has a pee in the garden."

Susie laughed. "Is the loo that bad? I can easily squat in the garden. There does not seem to be anyone about."

It was Ed's turn to laugh. "The loo is OK and, at the moment, I even have running water but often I don't. Jim usually smells terribly when he arrives here and I encourage him to get straight in the shower, if I have any water. If I don't, we have a beer outside."

The loo had a door and was separate from the shower and basin. The shower had no curtain or door and was open to the passage. When Susie came into the dining room she said,

"I am glad you did not force me to have a shower. I may be a Kenyan cow-girl but I don't usually take all my kit off in a bachelor's hall way."

Ed chuckled.

"I will earn a large amount of kudos at the rugby club on Saturday when I tell them that a pretty girl arrived for breakfast and insisted on stripping off for a shower in the hall!"

Susie touched Ed's arm and said, "I think I had better tell you what has happened, as it is rather vital that no word of this visit gets out."

"I see," said Ed. "I know when to keep my mouth shut. Sit down and have some breakfast and tell me what has happened. I have a box load of mail for Jim, as he gave my address as his contact in Kenya while he was on leave. Can you take it to him?"

"Of course," replied Susie. "Can I take Lucy? I think Jim is missing her. He won't go back to UK now for any leave but will stay here and then go straight to his new posting."

"Lucy must go back to him. She is a lovely dog but the two of them are inseparable," replied Ed.

While Susie was eating the hearty breakfast that Patrick had managed to rustle up, at a moment's notice, or perhaps Ed would normally have had the whole lot, she gave an edited account of what had happened. She said that Jim had been very badly gored by a lion, when he was on safari in a sensitive area in Northern Kenya, where he should not have been. The British Government was rather embarrassed. Also, the Kenya Government did not want lion attacks to be reported as they were worried about the tourist industry. Initially, he had been found by the Game Department but the British Army Training Team had taken over and got him to Nanuyki Hospital. He had nearly died and now he was recuperating in a house, on a Ranch in the Nanuyki area. To keep it out of the press, he was housebound.

"Where do you fit in?" asked Ed.

"Well, I want to be a nurse and I go back to UK in about six weeks to train to be a nurse. I have been nursing him for some weeks, with the help of Jim's cook, Katana; my Dad thought it would be good experience for me. Jim is doing really well now. He was very badly wounded and traumatized mentally, initially."

Ed raised an eyebrow, "Are you only his nurse?

Susie blushed. "Well no, I am a little bit more than that."

"Jim is a very lucky lad. You have done very well. I can't think of any girl of your age who could cope in such a situation. I won't say a word to anyone except, can I tell my girl friend Liz? She is very close to Jim although I hope not as close as you!"

Susie laughed and replied, "If he is that close to Liz I will probably kill him! If you both can just keep quiet, until Jim officially comes back from leave. The fuss will have died down by then."

Ed walked out with Susie to the Landrover, carrying Jim's post. Lucy had jumped through the window and now was sitting in the passenger seat. Ed said, "There is a dog who knows what she wants."

Susie said. "Many thanks for my breakfast. If I am ever in Ol Kalou, I will drop in for a shower."

Ed replied. "I would like that a lot. How about tomorrow? On second thoughts, Liz would NOT be pleased. Have a safe drive and wish Jim well from me."

Susie drove off back to T Falls. She thought, *'What a nice guy. I am sure I can trust him. I am glad Jim has got great friends like Ed. I am going to feel wretched when I leave him. However, it will be easier for me as I have a whole new, exciting life to go to but Jim*

559

will just come back to work. Obviously Ed knew nothing about Lady Rochester. Jim must have been very discrete.

Lucy must have realised something, as she started licking Susie's hand. Susie said, "You will look after him, won't you Lucy." Lucy thumped the Landrover seat with her tail. As T Falls was so small, the shopping was really quick. Susie filled up with fuel and headed for home. She did not stop to eat Katana's picnic. Jim was standing on the veranda, as she drove up. He rushed down to hug her. Lucy went absolutely mad and rushed around them, jumping in the air with excitement. Then she rushed inside to find Katana. Susie had both her arms around Jim's neck and they kissed passionately. As they broke apart she laughed. "Ed is a great guy. I am driving over tomorrow to have another shower at his house." Jim grabbed her to him and squeezed her buttocks. "You are a naughty little girl. I know there is no door. You had better not let Liz hear you suggest that."

"That is exactly what Ed said," replied Susie.

"Are you hungry?" asked Jim.

"Yes, but I don't want food," laughed Susie.

They both ran down the road away from the house, behind an enormous Baobab tree. Susie stepped out of her knickers and stuffed them into Jim's pocket as he undid his zip. She lifted her skirt, wrapped her arms round his neck and her legs round his waist. Jim lifted her bottom and pushed her against the tree. It was only when they were spent, did they look down and see Lucy looking up at them with a puzzled expression. Susie laughed and said,

"We must not confuse Lucy. If she is looking, we must do it doggy style." They walked back to the house for their lunch.

After lunch, while Susie lay in the sun, Jim went through his post. It was all pretty boring stuff but he did let out a whoop when he read an official letter from Kabete. Susie snatched up her bikini top, which she had undone, and came up the steps of the veranda to read the letter.

"I have been promoted and my next posting is on the Kinangop. I will be Ed's next door neighbor. Susie did not bother to put on her bikini top but hugged him.

"I am so pleased for you. That is great news. However, I am sure Ed would prefer me to come to his house for a shower rather than you. Do you think my Dad would sanction the promotion if he knew you had just rogered his only daughter, against a Baobab tree, in broad day light?"

"I think there were mitigating circumstances. The daughter in question, had elegantly stepped out of her knickers and had put them in my pocket." Jim brought out the pink knickers with a flourish.

"I don't think that is much of a defence. I will say that, before I knew what was happening, you had pulled them down. Now what I would like to do is, to very demurely, put on my bikini top and to sit on your knee. I would like you to put my knickers back in your pocket and then put your hand down the front on my bikini bottoms and let me have an orgasm. You were so bloody quick behind the tree, that I did not get a chance to get really excited."

Jim looked crestfallen. "I am so sorry, I just got carried away. I think it was the casual and sexy way you took off you knickers that pushed me over the top."

"Don't be sorry. It is a lovely feeling for a girl to have that power over a man, so that he completely loses control. It is bloody lucky I am on the pill. I don't think you would have waited to put a condom on."

She nestled into his arms. They both decided it was a lovely way to spend an afternoon. From then on, the time went flying by. Susie continued to write her reports, keep the books and go shopping in Nyeri. On one trip, as Susie came out of the book shop, a very pretty Japanese girl came up to her and in excellent English asked,

"I am so sorry to stop you, but I could not help noticing your T shirt. I had a very dear friend who had a shirt just like that. I have lost contact with him. I just wondered where you had got the T shirt from."

Susie replied instantly without thinking.

"Oh, it belongs to a boy I know. It is really too big for me but being loose it is lovely and cool."

The Japanese girl looked directly at her and asked,

"His name is not Jim Scott, by any chance?" Susie was trapped. She had never been a good liar. She sucked in her breath and said, "Yes."

"Will you see him soon?"

"Yes," Susie answered in a very quiet voice. "Please don't tell anyone. I should never have said anything but I could not lie to you, as you said he was a very dear friend."

"I promise I won't say a word to anyone. I can assure you Japanese girls, know how to keep their mouths tight shut. However, can you give him this? I was going to give it to him for Christmas." The Japanese girl reached into her handbag and brought out a small Christmas parcel. Susie said.

"I will give Jim the parcel but please do not say anything to anyone, or I will get into a lot of trouble."

"Thank you. You are kind." Susie noticed the girl was crying as she turned and walked away.

Susie thought, '*I wonder who she is. Is she an old girl friend? Could Jim have been running two girls at the same time? I am a fool because I never looked to see if she was wearing a wedding ring. I hope to God she does not tell anyone. If it gets back to John David, I really will be in trouble with The Official Secrets Act. Why ever didn't I say I bought it in a market?*'

When she got back from Nyeri Susie was even more apprehensive about her meeting with the Japanese girl. Jim came down the steps to greet her and help her in with her purchases. She immediately told him she had been stopped by a Japanese girl, and been given this parcel after she had recognised Jim's T shirt. Jim went very pale.

"I am so sorry Jim, I wish I had lied and said I had bought it in a second hand shop. By being such a fool, I may have got us in trouble with John David and the Official Secrets Act."

"It is not your fault. My past is bound to catch up with me. You have saved my life by saving my mind. I just will have to man up. When I first regained consciousness, I just wanted to die. Now I want to live but I am still aching deep down inside. I will just take Lucy for a little walk." He walked away slowly, almost like an old man. Susie was appalled. She thought. '*This may have ruined his recovery. I have been such a fool.*'

Jim did not walk far before he stopped and opened the parcel. Inside was a very small frame containing a beautiful painting of a young woman. There was no mistaking who it was. It was an excellent likeness of Claire. He sobbed. He felt like hanging himself and ending it all. He turned and there was the baobab tree to which he had pinned Susie and made such urgent love that he had disregarded her sexual needs. He was forgetting about Susie. She would be heartbroken if he committed suicide. How could he consider such a selfish act? What about Yakki what would she feel like, if she heard he had killed himself when he received her present which she had sent in good faith. He remembered how fond Yakki had been of Claire. Yakki would have been devastated when she heard of her death.

Jim still had tears in his eyes as he walked back to the house but there was determination in his step. Susie ran to meet him. She hugged him. Without a word Jim showed her the picture.

Susie said, "I know how much you loved her. I also know people say that love fades. That maybe true but I am certain, physical things are not easily forgotten. I can still feel the touch of your hands on my thighs when you helped me to water ski. I can still feel your thigh between my thighs as I rubbed myself on you, in bed at Watamu. I don't think we are destined to be together 'til death us do part' but you will always own a part of me and I certainly will never forget you."

Jim said nothing but just took her hand and they both walked back to the house. They were both very subdued as they ate supper and went to bed. Susie wondered if they would make love. They went through their normal night time regime but once they were in bed it was different. Jim's hands moved slowly over her body, feeling her and fondling her. Susie became very aroused. He lay on his back and rolled her on to him, so his thigh was between hers. He held her bottom and helped her to rub her bush against his thigh. Susie was worried he might not be able to get an erection. Then she felt him hard against her. She could not wait then but straddled him and rocked until she came. She felt him give a deep sigh and knew he had ejaculated. They lay together and then she felt his semen running out of her.

"Thank you, Jim. That was wonderful."

"It was wonderful for me. Thank you, Susie. You will make a wonderful nurse."

They were soon asleep.

From then on, Jim got very much stronger. They ran further and faster. In fact, often Susie could not keep up so, to get more exercise Jim gave her a piggy back. They went for lovely long walks with Lucy and of course they often made love. When Susie got letters from home she replied, saying she really loved nursing and that she was definitely sure she had picked the right career. It was agreed that she would come home a week before she was due to leave, to get everything ready. That would fit in very well, as Jim could leave her at Kabete on his way to the Kinangop. Susie received a nice letter from Judith saying she had heard she was doing some private nursing. She wished Susie the very best of luck in the UK. Susie was very relieved that Judith had not asked her to visit as Susie was pretty sure Judith would guess she and Jim were lovers.

John David wrote and said he had opened a bank account in London which he thought she would need. He had deposited an extremely generous salary. He said she could keep any of the money which was left, after completion of the assignment. Susie paid Katana his normal wages and gave him a large 'buckshish'.

John David said they should leave the house, on the morning of the agreed day before 10.00 am leaving the keys on the table, on the veranda. He would arrange for the ranch owner to come at 10.30 am so they would not meet.

Jim and Susie had a very sad discussion and they agreed that it was best if Jim dropped her off, at the gates to Kabete. John David did not want her parents to meet Jim. Also, Susie said if they went to her home she would be bound to break down and her parents would guess Jim was the patient and however hard they tried her parents would know that they were lovers. They still had a week to go, so they enjoyed themselves to the full. They did not have to eat up all the food and drink as, Jim could take it to his new house on the Kinangop. Obviously, Katana and Lucy would be coming with him.

A day before they were due to leave, they both went into Nyeri. Jim actually did not need to report to his new boss, who was the PVO for Central Province, until the following day but they both thought it was better to show keenness and Jim said he was likely to be tearful on the morrow. Susie went to do a little shopping and Jim went into the Provincial Veterinary Office. He was met by the PVO's secretary who was a smiling, mature Kenyan lady. She confirmed that Jim was expected the following day but she said she was sure Mr. Turner, the PVO, would be happy to see Jim now. She knocked on the door of the inner office and put her head round the door. Then Jim heard a very jovial voice saying,

"Of course, send him in. I am happy to see him." Jim thought. *'This is certainly a better start than Mombasa.'* Mr. Turner was a big man, at least 6ft 2 inches. He came around the table with an out-stretched hand.

"Welcome to Central Province. I am Matt Turner. Kabete think very highly of you, young man. I have a big job for you and I am sure you are up to it. The Kinangop has had very little veterinary input. I am sure you can change that, but also I want you to really get AI going and to get every bovine animal dipped once a week in, up to strength, acaricide. I want you to be an example to the rest of the province. Ed has done well at Ol Kalou but he has many bigger farms, run as co-operatives. You have just small farmers, who are much harder to organise although they do have a co-operative milk collection system.

Jim said. "I will give it my best shot."

"Good, I have got you a good house. It is very isolated but I understand, you have worked a lot in the NFD so the Kinangop will seem suburban. You are a day early. That is keen. I will make sure they are ready for you at the Veterinary Office tomorrow afternoon. Good luck."

Jim realised that was the end of the meeting and so said, "Thank you, Sir."

Jim thanked the secretary and asked her name. "I am Mrs. Kiboi. Do call me with any administrative problems."

Jim found Susie back at the Landrover so they did not hang about but headed back to the ranch. They set about packing up all Jim's stuff, into the Landrover. It was not difficult, as there was a big roof-rack. It was just going to be a squash in the front seat, as Lucy would insist on looking out the front window. Jim suggested that Susie wore trousers but she said she would wear a skirt and risk getting scratched, as she wanted to rub her bare leg against his one last time. Then she burst into tears. Jim hugged her and did not know what to say.

Then she turned to him and said. "I am going to be seriously brave from now on. I will not cry again. I want you to love me all night. I will leave you at Kabete, walk away with my rucksack and wave and then set about making my way in the world. I will write, telling you how I am getting on but they won't be drippy love letters. You are a super letter writer, so I will rely on you to keep me amused. I want you to tell me if you find anyone else. I will do the same. I am sure we will meet again. However, we have the Official Secrets Act to consider so, sadly, we will not be able to reminisce. These months did not exist. Katana, Ed and Liz are the only people in the know, other than the army boys and John David. They will keep their mouths shut." Then her face lit up, with a mischievous grin. "When we meet, I will allow you to whisper in my ear, do you remember when I fucked you against a Baobab tree for all of Africa to see! Let's do it again?"

They did. Jim was more controlled this time but it was just as much fun. Lucy still looked confused.

Yakki was distraught when she read about Claire's death, in the Daily Nation. She knew all about their planned safari to the NFD before Jim went to the UK for his leave. She understood why there was very little information as obviously Sir Richard did not want a scandal. She went with her husband to the memorial service. She was surprised that Jim was not there but assumed he had gone to the UK. She knew he would be a wreck as, she was sure he would have been present at Claire's death. She did not write to his Mombasa address as she knew he would not be there. She was so very sad and longed to find him. She knew she would grieve, more because she did not know what had really happened.

She and her husband took a group of four Japanese business men up to 'Treetops'. This involved a night at the 'Outspan Hotel' in Nyeri which is when she saw Susie. She then received Jim's letter.

My Dearest Yakki,

I wept when I received your present. It is so beautiful. I almost killed myself, as my grief overcame me. In some ways, your love stopped me as I could not conceive of hurting you with such a cowardly act. I am much stronger now. I would so love to see you but I know you have commitments.

You can see my new address. It is quite OK to write to the Veterinary Office. You can telephone but it is pretty difficult to get through. I have no telephone at my house. I attach a map of where I live. My house is lovely and would be ideal for your painting. It is, in fact, only twenty five miles from Naivasha.

With Love

From

Jim

Chapter 42

Changing the Kinangop

Tuesday 15th April 1969

Jim drove silently to South Kinangop, after he had waved goodbye to Susie at Kabete. Katana knew how sad he was and so, very wisely, was quiet. Even Lucy lay still, on the middle seat between them. Not only did Lucy feel the tension but she also loved Susie and was sorry to lose her.

The Veterinary Office was part of an old colonial farmhouse. It also housed the District Officer DO and the Agricultural Office. Jim left Katana with Lucy and the Landrover, and went into the Veterinary Office. He was met by a friendly young man, who introduced himself as Michael. He was the Veterinary Scout for the South Kinangop area. Michael said, "Welcome to the Kinangop, Dr Scott."

"I am pleased to be here, Michael. This will be very different from the Coast and NFD. I will be relying on your help and guidance. Please don't call me Dr Scott. Everyone calls me Jim."

Michael introduced the other three men in the office. There was Julius, the office clerk, Timothy the office messenger and Salim, a visiting AI man. Michael said the Livestock Officer had already left. Jim heard later that he had been a heavy drinker and had been disciplined for 'borrowing' money from the cash box. Michael gave Jim the only key to the cash box. He asked Jim to open it, to check that the amount inside was correct as the amount registered in the cash book. Jim was very relieved that it tallied up correctly. Michael also gave Jim the keys to his house. He then drew a small map, to guide Jim. The house, he said was quite isolated and difficult to find. Jim thanked Michael for his help and said he would go to his new home as soon as he had made a courtesy call to the DO. This was easy, as his office was only two doors away. The DO was a very relaxed Kenyan, from the Coast Province. He had heard of Jim's exploits on the Kenyan Coast and gave Jim a warm welcome. He said he was delighted to see Jim, as the veterinary cover up to now had been far from what was required. He said if Jim needed any help, he had only to come to him and he would do what he could.

So Jim and Katana set off for their new home. It was a ten mile drive along a dirt road. The road had enormous ruts, which had obviously been made by the milk lorry. The road was dry so Jim could easily straddle the ruts but Jim knew, in the wet, it would be a nightmare even for a Landrover, as the smaller vehicle would slip off the raised track and into the ruts. They were so deep that, even with the big tyres Jim had on the Landrover, he knew that the two differentials would bottom on the road and then he would be well and truly stuck. He was pleased he had some wheel chains. He suddenly felt sad, as he remembered the time he and Claire had used them up Mount Kenya, on the way to the Castle.

The house was ideal for Jim. He was not worried about the isolation. He was pleased to be near the forest. There would be plenty of wood for the stove and for heating the hot water. There was a house out the back for Katana. They unpacked the Landrover. The house had hard furnishings, rugs on wooden floors and curtains at the windows. They had most of what they needed. Katana lit the stove and made a fire under the 44 gallon drum, which acted as a hot water storage tank. Michael had supplied Jim with government diesel, to run the big diesel engine which drove the water pump and the generator. They would only start the engine when it was getting dark. They were just getting straight, and Katana was thinking about supper, when a car drove up.

It was Ed. Lucy gave him a tremendous greeting. Ed came in. "I thought I would come and welcome you to the Kinangop. Can I stay the night? My house is forty five miles away."

"Of course you can. I am so pleased to see you. I am not normally lonely but I will miss Susie like whoop," replied Jim.

"She seemed a lovely girl and extremely capable."

"Yes, she was. In many ways, she saved my life. I was nearly dying and she sat with me, in Nanuyki hospital. Then she nursed me back to health. I was terribly depressed but she slowly made me realise I still had a life to lead. However, because she is so capable,

568

she wants to make her own way in the world. I always remember my mother saying, 'children are only lent.' No way is Susie a child but I feel I had to let her go."

"I can see your problem," replied Ed. "What is there for her, stuck out here all day, with you at work? She would have to get a job in Nairobi. I can't see her wanting to live with her parents. I am lucky Liz has got a good job in Nakuru which is not that far from me. You have both done the right thing but it is going to be hard for you. You will have to throw yourself into the job and sport. You will have to hope you find another young lady. I won't let Liz try and match-make, as that never works."

They had a pleasant supper before turning in early to bed. Ed would have to be up early, to get back to Ol Kalou. He had made a farm to the East of his patch his first call, which would help. Jim was very grateful to Ed as this first night, without Susie in bed beside him, would have been hell alone. As it was, Ed woke him once in the night as he had a nightmare but, luckily, only the single one. They talked about it over breakfast. Ed advised Jim to be very careful with alcohol and that he should not drink alone. Going to bed in a drunken stupor to stop the nightmares would be very tempting, but it would be disastrous.

After Ed had left, Jim got his Landrover already for work. He and Lucy set off, on the ten miles to the Veterinary Office. They were very early which was lucky, as there was a Veterinary Scout by the roadside who waved him down. The Scout introduced himself as Kenneth Kamau. He was the Scout in charge of this area. He had heard that Jim had arrived and moved into a house in South Kinangop and would be likely to travel along this road, to reach the office at North Kinangop. Apparently, there was a cow having problems having its calf in a plot only a hundred yards from the road. Jim was glad he had got his Landrover organised. He got out the equipment he was likely to need and, leaving Lucy to guard the Landrover, set off with the Scout to the cow. The calf was in a posterior presentation with its hind legs flexed. In human medicine this is called a breech presentation. Jim could only feel the hocks of the calf and its tail. Luckily this was a fresh calving unlike so many parturitions in Africa which had normally been left for days rather than a maximum of four to six hours, which was the time to examine a cow if it has not passed a calf. Smaller animals e.g. sheep and goats would be seen sooner.

Jim gave the cow an injection of penicillin, which would help prevent any infection, and then managed, with some considerable effort, to push the calf further back into the cow. He then was able to extend the back legs, one at a time. He put one calving rope on each leg and, using a bowline knot, attached each rope to a small pole about a foot long. Then they had to really work hard as it was vital, with the calf coming backwards that, once traction had started, the calf was quickly delivered. Jim was strong and so was Kenneth. They quickly pulled out a nice live calf. The farmer was delighted. Jim hoped that such a good start to his arrival on the Kinangop would be a good omen for the future of veterinary services in the area.

As they had started out so early even with this visit, they were still on time at the office. Obviously no one expected him to be on time but Michael, Julius and Timothy were present. Jim immediately got Michael to show him where all the different areas were and the names of the Veterinary Scouts for each area. Apparently, nearly all the road-side crushes needed radical repair. Michael was tasked to arrange a '*barazza*' at each crush, so that Jim could address the farmers and explain how he was going to arrange routine visits to each crush.

Jim also had a discussion with Michael, about the supply of veterinary medicines to the Veterinary Scouts for resale to the farmers. Jim said that, if he worked out a careful pricing system, the Veterinary Scouts could make a profit and so could he. Jim knew that the idea, for small veterinary practices to be run by the Kenyan Government, was not likely to happen in the near future.

They had nearly finished this discussion when Salim arrived, having completed half of his AI round. He could only cover a small area as his only mode of transport was a bicycle. He said that, on average, he did less than two inseminations a day. Salim's home was on Lamu Island so he knew of Jim. In fact, he had told them all in the Kinangop office about Jim's exploits. Apparently Kassim, the Head Veterinary Scout in the Lamu Office, told anyone who would listen how Jim was totally fearless and had virtually rid the area of '*shifta*' single-handedly. Jim instantly realised that Salim was more than just

570

an inseminator, so he sat him down and they had a long discussion, on motorising the AI service on the Kinangop as it was in other areas. Salim told Jim that there was an AI office in Naivasha and that there was an AI driving instructor there. Therefore, if Jim could persuade the Swedish Aid to provide a car then they could train up some drivers. Then, with a driver and inseminator, they could do the whole of the Kinangop in one motorised round, using the road-side crushes which needed to be repaired anyway.

Ticks were a problem because, not only they sucked blood and weakened the cows, but also because they spread disease. Jim knew that he would have to get more dips built. He knew there was a Danish Aid Group which specialised in building dips. If the local groups could raise half the funds, the Danes would construct the dip by providing the other half of the money from their aid budget.

All these ideas were an exciting new challenge for Jim and totally different from his work at the coast or in the NFD. Obviously his work and the area were of no interest to London, but Jim was glad to have nothing to do with them. It would be too painful to have a new controller. No one would be able to replace Claire, in his eyes. Jim threw himself into the work. His efforts were appreciated by the farmers. He was soon really respected, by the sixty two veterinary scouts and AI men. He made sure they all got proper leave and time off. He carried a reasonable stock of veterinary medicines, so they were all well supplied. In fact, this was a very good legal money earner, for both Jim and the veterinary scouts. He worked well with the DO and the officials of the cooperatives. Road side crushes were soon repaired and many new ones were constructed. The local groups collected sufficient amounts of money for the Danish Dip-building teams to stay permanently in his area. With Salim's help, he got the motorised AI rounds up and running. Jim got enough AI men taught to drive, so that leave and sick leave were catered for. He was glad he had opted for the, two men in a car option because he heard horrendous stories of accidents on the BSA Bushman Motorbikes used in other areas. The motorbikes were very difficult to control in muddy conditions but their worst problem was that as they had a two-stroke engine, oil went into the petrol. The oil lubricated the engine only when the revs were high enough. If, coming down a hill the driver free-wheeled then no oil got to the engine and it was liable to seize. This could be prevented by the driver revving the engine regularly. They often forgot and ended up flying over the handle-bars.

All Jim's efforts were noted, to his credit, at Kabete not only by the Director of Veterinary Services but also by The Head of the AI Service. Colin Cameron followed Jim's progress with interest. He told Freda, who then included bits of information in her letters to Susie. Obviously Jim and Freda were unaware of Jim's relationship with Susie.

Susie and Jim kept up correspondence. They both missed each other but, for both of them, time and distance dulled their feelings. Susie had a lot happening in her life, which was all new and exciting. It was inevitable that she would find someone else. When she did, she was honest with Jim and told him in a letter. Initially Jim was really quite upset. He was lonely. The work was going well. He was really very fit, as he was training at such a high altitude. His house was at 8500 feet but, somehow, his rugby was not up to standard. He could get into the Nakuru team OK but he was never picked for the Kenyan team or for an upcountry team, to play against an English club side on tour. He had lots of laughs playing mixed hockey particularly with Liz and Ed. He was not a good enough hockey player to get in the Nakuru Athletic Club (NAC) men's team. He was not much of a cricketer but he did play occasionally.

Jim's main problem was, he still had nightmares. He did not sleep well and so he seemed constantly tired. He remembered how he had slept so well, with Susie cuddled up beside him. Somehow, her finding someone else depressed him. He kept remembering the good times with Claire and then he would become all melancholy, knowing that she was dead.

One afternoon when his work had gone well, he was finished early and so he did not return to the office but came home. Lucy bounded in to greet Katana, who came on to the veranda and said, "A lady was here asking for you. That is her bag on the chair. She did not speak very good Swahili. She has gone off in to the woods. I hope she won't get lost?"

Jim guessed immediately that it was Yakki. Katana would have been confused as to what to call a Japanese lady. He would not call her a 'memsahib'.

"Which way did she go Katana? Lucy and I will follow and we will soon find her."

Sure enough, Lucy soon was barking at a stranger in the woods. Jim quickly called Lucy to heal and called,

"Yakki, where are you? It's Jim." Yakki ran down a path in the woods and ran into Jim's arms.

"I have found you at last. It was difficult for me to get away on my own. I did not write in reply to your letter. I was so sad and so confused, I did not know what to write."

"Yakki, my dear girl, it is so lovely to see you. I often thought of you when I was recovering from my wounds but I was told I must not contact anyone and then you sent the painting when you saw Susie wearing my T shirt. So I wrote the letter and here you are. Tell me your news."

"Jim, I miss Claire so much. As you know, we used to spend a lot of time together. You, like me, must be devastated."

"I was a complete wreck, physically and mentally. Now, thanks to Susie's nursing, I am physically fine but mentally I still get very depressed and get dreadful nightmares. Having said that, I do hope you can stay."

"I would love to stay. In fact, can I stay for two nights as I said to my husband, I wanted to be on my own and paint some different animals and scenes? He knows I have found life hard without Claire. Although he is much older than me he is very fond of me and wants me to be happy. He is away at a meeting in Kampala so he is happy I am away as well." Jim looked worried.

"Don't worry, I did not say anything about you. I just said I would stay near Naivasha, where I had so much fun sailing."

"Sorry, Yakki. I don't know why I am so sensitive. I must try to live a normal life. I don't want you to get into trouble. May I ask how your friend, the pilot, is?"

"He is fine and, in fact, he managed to get over three months ago for a weekend. It was so short and we had to be so careful but we had fun together. I know I should be happy but loosing Claire, as a friend, has made me so very sad."

They walked together, in companionable silence back to the house. Jim translated for Yakki, so she could communicate to Katana. Then he showed her his spare room. He explained about the

573

lack of electricity. Yakki teased him and said how primitive it all was but that would still not stop her coming to see him, if she could organise it. After they had supper, they sat together by the fire and Yakki asked, very hesitantly how Claire died. She said how little was in the paper and how she therefore did not really understand what had happened. Jim did not really know why he was so reticent but, somehow although he liked Yakki and knew she was a good friend he could not unburden himself to her. He told Yakki how they had a great '*safari*' and that Claire had been killed by the lion while she was in the bush going to the loo. He told her how guilty he felt that he had not protected her. He said he had been hurt and nearly died but, even to his own ears, the account sounded very vague. Yakki just leant over, held his hand and said, "Poor Jim."

Then she changed the subject and talked about what she could paint in the area, next day. Yakki was woken by Jim's nightmare but just lay awake and eventually the house became quiet and she slept. It was a beautiful day and they ate breakfast on the veranda. Jim knew that he had obviously woken her with his nightmare as his bedclothes were in a state but neither of them mentioned it. He took her down to Lake Naivasha before work and they arranged to meet at the 'Lake Naivasha Hotel' at 4.00 pm.

Jim felt guilty that she had come all the way to see him but that he was not looking after her. Yakki did not seem to mind and Jim could tell how her painting was so important to her. She was smiling when he returned, soon after 4.00 pm. They did not stop at the hotel for a cup of tea but headed back to Jim's home and had tea and cake there. Yakki showed him her paintings. They were exquisite.

"May I have that one of the Hippo coming out of the water? It will remind me of you." Yakki came into his arms and kissed him. "You old rogue. So I remind you of a hippopotamus, do I? I will show you. No more cake for me." It was just as if the sun had come out on a rainy day. Happiness seemed to return into their lives. Laughing together, with Lucy running at their sides, they went for a walk in the forest. Jim took Yakki to a small stream, with a pool of dark water which only just had the sun on one side because of the surrounding trees. He knelt down to look, to see if there were any trout visible. He lent out over the water. Before he could stop himself a little, but strong hand pushed his bottom. "Lee ho." He fell into the freezing cold water. Yakki was laughing. "Who reminds me of a hippopotamus? I don't need a painting to remember you!"

Jim's teeth were chattering when he got out.

"Come on, lets run home and I will warm up." Yakki could not stop herself from giggling. Luckily there was plenty of hot water when they got home, for Jim to have a shower and, when he came out, Yakki did the same. They had a fun supper with a lot of laughter. After supper, when the generator had gone out and Katana had left. Jim was surprised when Yakki came and sat on his knee, by the fire. She started to cry.

"Don't cry, Yakki. What has made you so sad?"

"I suddenly remembered, a year ago, when I put my hand on your thigh and I promised Claire that I would try not to steel you from her although she guessed that I found you very attractive. Now she is gone, and I think she wants me not only to tease you to make you happy but also to comfort you. Normally I don't find European men attractive but, from the moment I met you, and you were so forgiving to my rude husband, I have liked you. For Claire's memory, may I give myself to you to try to help you with your nightmares? I hated just leaving you last night, moaning and crying out. My instinct was to come to you but I was worried you would be cross. Now, I somehow know that you will not be angry."

"Of course I won't be angry. I find great big Japanese girls, who look like hippos, very attractive!" Tears were rolling down Yakki's cheeks. They were now tears of laughter.

"Because you are so naughty Jim, I will tease you by behaving like a proper Japanese girl and not letting you do any naughty Lee ho's." With that she sprang up and raced into the spare room. She came back, having changed amazingly quickly into a silk kimono. She knelt at Jim's feet and gazed into his eyes. Then she turned her head to the side and lifted one arm so that Jim got a little view up, under her arm, to her breast. Then she turned the other way, letting the silk slide over her small petite body. She then looked at Jim's groin and saw his erection. She slid a tiny hand up the leg of his shorts and delicately fondled his penis. Her eyes flew open. Jim laughed.

"Don't worry, Yakki. European men are not different. It is the damage the lion did to me."

"You poor boy, it must have hurt so much. Does it hurt now?"

"No, it does not hurt. It is lovely to feel your delicate little hand. Would a Japanese man be allowed to put his hand up the slit in the side of your kimono and give you a Lee ho?"

"No, a Japanese man would not think to give a girl pleasure. It is for the girl to give him pleasure. Would you like to give me pleasure?"

"Nothing would give me more joy than to give you pleasure, Yakki. I would love to feel you becoming really excited and then to have an orgasm."

"Even though I love my boy friend, I have never had an orgasm with him. Jim, will you give me a real Lee ho and I will be like a European girl."

Yakki got off her knees and undid her kimono and let it fall to the ground. She stood demurely in front of Jim and unpinned her hair. It was Jim's turn to be wide-eyed. When she let her hair fall and brought it down over her shoulders, it completely concealed her breasts and even her bush. Jim stood up. The fire had died down. He let Yakki take off his shirt and shorts. She very gently traced his scars and dropped to her knees to look at his penis. She softly held the flap of skin which fell down over the end like a turkey's snood. She kissed it and licked it so gently, it felt like the touch of a feather to Jim. He lifted her up and then, as she put her arms around his neck, he lifted her off the ground. She was as light as a young girl. He carried her into his bedroom and laid her, on her back, gently on the bed. He came to the foot of the bed and crawled up between her legs and, placing his hands under her little buttocks, lifted her to his lips. Yakki gasped and then relaxed as she felt his probing tongue. Initially he licked softly and then slowly licked harder. He rolled his tongue and entered her and drew her pubis hard against him. Yakki started to rhythmically thrust up into his face. She started to really push hard and then Jim felt her tighten the muscles in her buttocks and she relaxed, with a sigh. Her hands were in his hair and she drew him up her body, letting her knees fall apart to accommodate him. Her delicate hands reached for him and Jim thrust into her and ejaculated into her. Her legs came up behind him and held him deep inside her, as Jim lifted his body up onto his hands, so as not to crush her small body.

"I know I am like a big hippo but you are a big gorilla, but you are very gentle. I love your hairy arms and legs touching me. Sleep now and have no nightmares tonight. In the morning, when Jim awoke, she was gone but her exciting smell lingered on. He heard her showering, as he came and walked out on to the veranda, where Katana was setting breakfast. No mention was made of their love making but Yakki giggled, as she tucked into a big fried breakfast. "One day I will be as fat as a hippo."

After breakfast Jim drove her down to the Bell Hotel, in Naivasha, so that she could get a bus to Nairobi. Yakki asked him if he could come to Nairobi sometime. Jim said that he would enjoy that. So they made a date for him to come and have dinner, at the Japanese Embassy in three weeks time. Yakki's visit had really lifted Jim's spirits and he had no more nightmares.

He was very cheerful when he parked the Landrover at the Japanese Embassy. The Ambassador came out to greet him and shook him warmly by the hand. Yakki came up beside him and Jim was at a loss as to how to greet her. He formally gave a slight bow, raised her hand to his lips and kissed it.

"I think, Jim, you are a very correct Japanese man. I am glad you treat my young wife so well, even if she does remind you of a hippopotamus." The ambassador had a twinkle in his eye.

"Welcome to our home."

There were several other nationalities around the dining room table. Many, Jim recognised from functions at the British High Commission. He was relieved that Sir Richard was not there. He enjoyed the evening but was careful not to drink too much as he knew he was in for a tricky drive home, as it had been raining and the 'murram' roads would be very difficult. It was only when the guests started to leave that the Ambassador dropped his, for Jim, devastating news.

"I have not told my wife yet but I would like to thank you all, who have been our special friends here in Kenya, for being so kind to us. We are moving back to the east. I have been promoted and will be taking up the post of Japanese Ambassador in China. We will be very sorry to leave our good friends. Sadly, I do not think we will be as happy in China as we are here, but relations between Japan and

China may improve. It will be my task to try to achieve some dialogue."

There was a general hubbub of congratulations and commiseration. When it was Jim's turn to say farewell, he once again shook the Ambassador's hand and said,

"I wish you the very best of luck Sir. Whatever happens remember there is one Briton who may liken your wife to a Hippopotamus but he will always remember you both with affection."

"I think many of my countrymen would benefit from your humor, young man. I wish you good luck."

Yakki could not stop herself. She hugged him and said,

"Keep the painting and treasure the memories." Jim knew he would do just that, for both paintings. He only just managed to leave without breaking down. He had a horrendous drive home, through the mud. Lucy seemed to know things were worse than normal, as she lay in the middle seat with her head in his lap. Jim thought, *'Life is a bitch and then you die. Then he thought it was not fair to use the word bitch in a derogatory way. Lucy was such a marvellous companion.'* Lucy may have been a loyal friend but, that night, he had a very bad nightmare and they continued whether he was busy or slack at work. Exercise, mental stimulation or socialising did not seem to improve things.

Chapter 43

The twins

Saturday 14th June 1969

Jim played squash regularly at Naivasha Club, mainly in the league. There he met a farmer called Fred Day. Fred became a good friend. He was a widower, about the same age as Jim's father. He had three daughters but, sadly, Jim did not fancy any of them. None of them lived at home as they were either working in Nairobi or away in the UK at university. Julia was the youngest and made it very obvious that she fancied Jim. Jim had to be careful not to encourage her, when he had had several drinks. As he was lonely it would be all too easy to get into a relationship which he could not get out of, without hurting her. Jim spent quite a few evenings with Fred. They both valued each other's company. Fred played polo and so he persuaded Jim to be the 'vet on call' for their home matches. Jim liked some of the players but some of them were very wealthy and not really Jim's type. He enjoyed the polo work and it was a good source of income for him. In fact, with that work and the sale of veterinary medicines Jim was very well off. He spent very little on himself and ate inexpensive, local food so he saved money. He was paid a third of his salary in the UK, which he kept in the UK. He invested it in Government stock, which meant he did not pay tax on the interest as he was resident overseas. Jim had everything going for him but he was depressed and he could not drag himself out of his self pity.

It was a Saturday. Jim was driving down to Nakuru. He needed to do some shopping but there was nothing important. He would normally have been in a depressed mood but this morning, having received a very cheerful letter from Susie, he was almost suicidal. The rugby session had not started. He still trained really hard every night, as that seemed to be the only way he could sleep. He was still suffering from the same night-mare of the lion on top of him and he was struggling to get out from under it. Obviously, he did not know how long he struggled and yelled but, nowadays, he woke in a muck sweat with the bedclothes in a complete muddle. This morning he woke normally but did not feel refreshed, just empty and sad. He knew his self pity was overwhelming him. The work no longer stimulated him as he had everything that he wanted up and running. Even the accolades from Kabete did not lift him. Life was just a drudge. His only cosolation was that he had not taken to drink although he was very tempted most evenings now. Lucy was a great solace as she was always exuberant. Katana knew how low Jim was but, by nature, Katana was not a lively character. All the farmers and most of the veterinary staff were Kikuyu, and so rarely showed cheerful dispositions. Salim, who was a very cheerful man, had been promoted, on Jim's recommendation, and had been transferred to the AI centre at Kabete.

He was deep in thought, as he was just coming down the poor tarmac road into Gilgil when he saw two European girls, sitting on a rock at the side of the road. He was past them before he recognised them. It was the twins, Emma and Amy, from the coast. He immediately slammed on the brakes, sending Lucy falling into the foot well. Then he backed up. The twins were naturally apprehensive and had scrabbled up the bank at the side of the road. He ran calling.

"Emma, Amy it's me. Don't be afraid and run away." When they recognised him they almost flew down the bank and ran, one into each arm, as they had done when they were younger. Now they had grown, and were heavier, they knocked him over on the verge. They all landed in a heap laughing. Still on the ground the twins chorused,

"We have been warned to be careful of cars stopping. We never expected to see you. This is wonderful."

"How come you are out on the road?"

"We are at school here at Pembroke. It is an exeat for a long weekend. Everyone else has gone home with their parents. Dad is away hunting in Tanzania and poor Mum has been really ill with Denjie fever. She is still so ill that she is in bed. Mum is never ill and she is never in bed. We do hope she will get better soon. We are stuck here bored to tears. We just came out for a walk, to get out of the place."

"I have a great idea," said Jim. "I am free until Monday morning. Why don't I fly you down to see your Mum? Just seeing you will make her feel better. I have a farmer pal, who lives just two miles down the road. I saw him early in the week and he said I could hire his plane this weekend as he knew I was at a loose end as the rugby season has not started yet."

"That would be so cool," said Emma.

"We would have to get permission. That won't be easy," added Amy.

"Come on, both of you, hop into the Landrover and we will go and ask the Head Master. He is a friend of mine and we used to play rugby together. He can only say no. If he does, at least I am sure he will allow me to take you out locally. I live only forty minutes away. I was posted on to the Kinangop when I came back off long leave.

Jim went, in alone, to the Head Master. He knew it would be difficult for him to make such a decision as the girls were under his care. He heard Jim out and sat thinking. In the end he said.

"I am 'in loco parentis'. I know what both parents would say, both separately and together. Do it. So I am going to say take them but don't take any risks and I would be grateful if you could fly home tomorrow morning. Then by all means they can stay with you until they need to be back, with all the other pupils, at 6.00pm on Monday. I hope their Mother is soon better."

Jim said, "Thank you for your trust. I won't let you down."

The twins were delighted. Jim said,

"Do you need to pack anything? I image you have bikinis at the coast." They both smiled and whispered in his ears.

"We have to wear the tops now. We haven't forgotten you telling us to take our shirts off." Then shrieking with laughter they ran out to the Landrover. Jim could not be bothered to go back to the Kinangop, so they drove straight to the airstrip. Jim had already been checked out on his friend's airplane, so he called into the house, left a note and took the keys. It was full up with fuel and oil. He removed the pito-head cover and the chocks while the girls got in. He realised how grown up they were, as there was no argument as to who was going to sit in the front. Emma was going to on the way down and Amy on the way back. They took a delighted Lucy, who loved flying and always stayed on the back seat.

They were soon off. Jim decided to fly directly to the airstrip at Vipingo which was only about a mile and a half from the twin's home. He thought he would call in at Wilson on the way home, to fill up with fuel. The plane was a fast Cherokee Arrow with a retractable under cart, so it did not seem to take them that long. He let Emma fly on a heading, which she did with great concentration, with her tongue just out of her lips. He did not tease her as he knew how much she now wanted to be a young lady and cease to be a child.

He told them how he missed the coast but he was so pleased with how well work was going, on the Kinangop. Jim also told them how pleased he was that they were at school near him because he would love taking them out at weekends. They landed, without incident, at Vipingo. They found some big stones to go in front and behind the wheels as chocks. A Cherokee Arrow is a low wing aircraft and so Jim thought it would be safe, as there were no high winds forecast. The twins seemed to skip all the way to their home, with Lucy bounding beside them. Jim felt his spirits lift for the first time for months.

Jim warned the twins that they must expect Emily, their mother, to be very ill. He suggested that they should not make too much noise when they arrived, as it would be a big shock for their mother. Luckily, he thought, '*it was a good time to arrive as it was lunch time.*' The dogs barked when they arrived but they remembered Lucy and they soon settled down. The staff were all delighted to see the twins. Jim was pleased to see how grown up and sensible the twins were. Two years had made a big difference to their behaviour. The twins crept into their mother's room. She was awake and was overjoyed to see them. She insisted they bring Jim into her bedroom.

"Jim, you are a real angel to bring my girls down. You have no idea how much better I feel, just seeing them. I have been so worried about letting them down and that they would be all alone at Pembroke. As you know Denjie Fever, is not contagious but spread by mosquitoes so come and let me give you a kiss. Someone up there must be guiding me as I put on my best nightie this morning." Jim was slightly embarrassed. He had always found Emily very attractive. He was surprised when she kissed him on the lips. Emily held him near her and said.

"We should not have lost touch like we did when you went on leave. Now you must have lunch. Damn it, I am not going to lie in bed. I am going to get up."

With no more ado she pushed back the bedclothes and got to her feet. She had got to her feet too quickly and would have fallen, if Jim had not reached out quickly and held her. Jim thought, *'it is a long time since I have held a woman.'* Emily gasped and seeing how worried the twins looked, said,

"Thank you, Jim. I am a bit weaker than I thought. I got up too quickly."

After lunch Emily went back to bed, for a sleep, but she insisted they woke her for a cup of tea. "I don't want to waste any of the precious time while you are down here. I know you must leave tomorrow, by mid morning."

Jim and the twins took the dogs down to the beach. First they went for a long walk and then, when they got back to the beach opposite the house, they had a swim. The twins were not at all shy and just took their shirts off saying.

"Look at our smart bikinis." They did, indeed, look as pretty as pictures. Jim said he would keep his shirt on, as he was worried about the sun. Luckily his shorts could double up as swimming trunks. Many people with fair skin, went swimming in shirts and so this did not seem to be strange to the twins.

When they got back, the twins and Jim washed down in the outside fresh water shower. Lucy enjoyed being washed off. They were delighted to find Emily, in a pretty, dress having tea on the veranda. Jim said,

"You are looking good, Emily. How do you really feel?"

"Honestly, I feel so much better. It seems amazing that there is no treatment for the disease. At least with malaria, there is a treatment."

"I know I sound like an old granny but you must not do too much for a few days, while you get your strength back. Promise me you won't? The twins and I do not want to hear you have had a relapse."

"Mummy! You must take it easy," said the twins, in unison.

Emily said, "I will take it steady, I promise. Now, who would like a cup of tea and some cake? Jim, why don't you go into my bedroom and get one of Eric's shirts and a pair of his shorts? I noticed you all came down without any luggage. Lucy, at least, came down with her lead." They all laughed.

They had a happy, relaxed evening together. Jim was so pleased he had not only brought the twins down but that he had come back to the coast where he had had so many good times in the past. Jim could see Emily getting tired, so he suggested they all went to bed. The twins insisted on coming with him for a final walk on the beach, in the moonlight, with the dogs. Emily said goodnight to them all. She kissed them all and said how they had made her day. When Jim and the twins came back from their walk, the twins made Jim promise he would come for a swim, with them as soon as they woke up.

Jim still had a nightmare but it was not as bad as most nights. He thought he woke up quite quickly and so, he hoped he had not woken anyone else up. He knew his room was next to Emily's and he particularly did not want to disturb her. He woke not long after dawn. He had no pyjamas or kikoi, so he had slept naked. He got out of bed and stretched. At that moment Emma burst into the room, in her bikini, ready to go for a swim. She took one look at Jim's scarred chest and abdomen, and screamed. Amy came in right behind her and said,

"Oh Jim, what has happened to you?" They both burst into tears. Jim grabbed a towel and said to the twins,

"Come and sit on the bed and I will explain what happened." The 'askari' had heard the scream and came in with a spear. Jim said to him, *"Hapa taboo Ole Kipoi. Memsahibs hapana jua na simba na jiribu na kula meme"* (There is no trouble, Ole Kipoi. The ladies had not seen that a lion had tried to eat me).

"Bwana Jim wewe na chinja simba" (Mr. Jim did you kill the lion)?

"Ndio meme piga he kwa panga. He na kufa (Yes, I hit him with a panga and killed him)."

"Wewe na bwana wakubwa. Wewe kamata na bibi maramoja (You are a very important man. You must find a wife soon)." Ole Kipoi left with a smile on his face.

Jim put an arm around each twin's shoulder. Emma said,

"I am sorry I screamed, it is just that you are so badly scarred. The lion even got your willy."

"Oh that's alright," answered Jim. "I can still wee OK."

"But you need a 'willy' for more than having a wee," said Amy in alarm.

"Don't worry, it is OK for that too."

"Poor Jim, you must have been so sore. Did you really kill the lion with a '*panga*'?"

"Yes," answered Jim simply.

"As Ole Kipoi says, you can now choose a wife. Will you choose us?" chorused the girls.

"I will only choose you in my dreams. You two are so pretty, your bride price is more than a thousand cows each. You are way out of my price range. Come on, let's go for that swim?"

Jim put on his shorts but did not bother with a shirt and they all went for a swim. They came and had a fresh water shower together. Jim was so thankful that the twins did not seem worried now, about his scars. However, he dried and put on Eric's shirt and shorts. He put his shorts out to dry. The twins had gone down to the dairy to get fresh milk so, seeing Emily's door open and a tray with tea things on it on the table outside, he knocked quietly. Emily called,

"Come in. I hoped it was you, Jim. I am still in my nightie so shut the door for a second and come and sit on the bed. I want to talk." Jim brought her tea and sat down near to her, on the bed. He picked up her hand.

"How do you feel this morning? I am sorry about all the commotion."

"I am the one who should be sorry, Jim. It was very naughty of the twins to burst in on you like that. I heard it all. I thought you handled it very well. I did not know the twins were quite so well informed. Do you mind me asking? Is your penis really OK? Can you get an erection?"

"Yes, I can. It just has a flap of skin." Jim was awkward as he realised he still held her hand.

She drew him to her and said, "I have always fancied you Jim, from the first day I met you and you picked the twins up, so they would not get their feet cut on the broken glass. You paid no attention to your own danger. Equally, I think you fancied me. Am I right?"

"Yes," replied Jim. "I have always lusted after you."

585

"Wow," said Emily. "I will have to be careful." She reached inside his shirt. "A scarred chest would not worry me. However I trust you Jim with my body and, more importantly, I trust you with the twins. I think they will be very forward with you. I think you will be very tempted, but I know you will resist. I am feeling very much better. I think it is a good thing you are not staying for another night because I don't think I can trust myself. Off you go now for breakfast. I will get up and make myself attractive. I like the idea of you lusting after me."

Breakfast was full of laughter. They were all sad when they said goodbye. Emily said to the twins, very firmly,

"You may go and spent tonight at Jim's house, and go with him on his rounds in the morning, but you must behave yourselves. I know you will because you are so grown up now. I will come up, by car, to pick you up at the end of term. Take care."

Walking back to the plane, the twins were not sad for long, and they were soon running with Lucy through the sisal. Amy sat in the front and flew the plane up to Wilson, where they filled up with fuel. The plane owner, Julian Emery, was at home when they returned. He insisted they stopped and had coffee and home-made scones, which his wife Edith had just made. Jim paid him a cheque, for the hire of the plane. He said Jim was welcome anytime.

They went back to the school, to a very relieved Headmaster. He was quite agreeable for the twins to go home with Jim as their mother had given her permission, provided they were back by 6.00pm the next day when the exeat finished. He asked to Jim to a Bar-B-Q, at Gilgil club, as he knew lots of parents would be going after dropping their children off. The twins went into the school to get their pyjamas and some warm clothes for the evening.

That afternoon, as it was Sunday, Jim did not have any work to do. He took the twins up to Sasamua dam, to do some trout fishing. They both caught fish, which they cooked on an open fire in Jim's garden. They came in and the twins had a bath together and put on their pyjamas. They had had a long, tiring day and Jim could see they were 'all in'. He did not have to nag them. They willingly went to bed. By the time they were in bed the generator had gone off, so Jim brought them each in a torch. As he was kissing them goodnight, Emma said,

"Jim, I am so sorry I screamed when I saw your chest this morning. Will you forgive me?"

"Of course I will, you silly old goat. Now, both of you must pay attention: because of that lion, I often get nightmares and call out in the night. If you hear me, don't worry I will soon shut up."

"Do you have nightmares like us, Jim?" they asked. "We used to when we first went to Pembroke and they put us in separate dormitories but, as soon as they put us in beds next to each other, we stopped. You could easily bring your bed in with us." Jim chuckled when he remembered what Emily had said.

"Don't worry, I will be fine. Sleep well." Luckily he did not have a nightmare. Jim thought. '*If he had, the twins might well have got into bed with him, which certainly would not have been a good idea.* He reflected on what Emily had said. He certainly had been honest with her.

They had a good breakfast in the morning. The twins were really excited by the idea of going on Jim's rounds. Jim was worried it would be boring for them but they loved it. They insisted on being allowed to inject the cows. They were very strict and took it in turns. They were delighted to be allowed to do rectal examinations. Jim was amazed how quickly they picked up the technique. They could both feel ovaries and the uterine horns. They were delighted when they could actually feel a calf. Katana had packed them up a picnic, which they ate at the Veterinary Office, after they had really washed their hands. They chatted away to the staff either in English or Swahili. They stopped at the '*duka*' to buy cokes.

When they got back to school, before 6.00pm, they were quite happy to be back. They both insisted on hugging him and then kissing him on the lips as they had seen Emily do. He did not try to stop them, as he did not want to cause a fuss. He did notice Matron raise an eyebrow. As they walked in, Jim heard Matron say, "Emma and Amy, I don't think you should kiss a strange man on the lips."

"Don't be so silly, Matron," replied the twins. "He is not a strange man. He is Jim Scott and we have known him since we were little girls. He is terribly brave. He killed a lion with a '*panga*'. Mummy said we could trust him with our lives."

'*Well,*' thought Jim, '*It is sad that Mummy and I don't trust ourselves to be in the same house, alone together.*'

587

Jim went along to the Gilgil club. On the surface, it was a fun evening. There were lots of people there that he knew but, somehow, it made him depressed. Not long after he had finished the excellent food he was driving back with Lucy to his house. *'At least I have my job,'* he thought.

He soldiered on but spent less and less time socialising. Actually he was quite happy, in his own way, on his own. He did spent a lot of time reading. He bought lots of books in the second-hand book shop in Nakuru. *'He knew he was becoming an old bachelor but he was only 25. Somehow he had got to drag himself out of this low point in his life. Claire had faded but he still had the nightmares. Was it these which were depressing him? Was it the physical scars which embarrassed him? He certainly missed Susie. It was not just the sex, but the comfort of cuddling up with her at night. The nightmares had totally stopped then. The only other girls, who knew about his scars and the nightmares were Yakki, Emily and the twins. He knew they were forbidden territory. His thoughts often wandered back to Fi. He wondered how she was. He longed to write but he was sure they had done the sensible thing. A beautiful, loving girl like Fi would be engaged by now. Could easily be married and have a baby. No, he must just keep doing his job. Keep physically fit. Stay off the booze and wait and see what happens.*

Jim kept in touch with the twins. They were allowed out on Sundays and so they had an expedition and climbed Logonot, a large extinct volcano in the Rift Valley. They then had a high tea at the 'Bell Inn' in Naivasha. This cheered Jim up. He also enjoyed going over to see Ed and when Ed came over to see him. He still knew he was depressed. He had just loved Claire so much. Her death which he still blamed himself for, haunted him. He managed to keep off the drink but, when he had several broken nights caused by the reoccurring nightmares, it was very hard not to reach for the bottle. Christmas was on the horizon. It was a year since Claire's death. It was going to be doubly hard. He made himself train harder and tried to be optimistic. He was sure something would happen.

Sure enough, something did happen. A letter arrived at the office; it had taken over two weeks to reach him, as he did not have a private P.O.Box. A photograph fell out. It was a very sexy photo, of

Emily in a bikini. On the back she had written. *'Something for you to lust after on the cold Kinangop.'*

She wrote,

Dearest Jim,

I hope all is well with you. Thank you so much for taking the twins out on Sunday. They really enjoyed themselves. Going up Logonot sounded very energetic. When I next see them they will be bloaters, by the sound of the feast they had at the 'Bell Inn' at Naivasha. Can you come down for Christmas at the coast? I know the girls would love you to come. Eric will be home, so you will be able to talk 'safari' with him. I am now totally recovered and would really enjoy your company.

With Love

Emily

Jim was really torn. He had nothing really planned for Christmas except a possible rough safari, carrying his gear up into the Aberdares from his house. It would be great to go to the coast and have a family Christmas. Eric would be home and so there was no reason to worry and yet he did. He had never felt bad about his relationship with Claire as she, poor girl, did not have a normal marriage. On the other hand, Emily and Eric appeared to have a happy marriage. It was just that Eric was away for most of the time. Jim guessed that they were not that close, or Emily would have gone on *'safari'* with Eric now that the twins were away at school. So he took the letter home to think about it. He put the photo in a small frame on his bed-side table.

Then his plans changed. He received a phone call from the wife of a rancher who Jim had met at the polo club. She knew Jim was a bachelor and she had a favor to ask him. Her husband's birthday was on Christmas Day. He was going to be to be fifty. She wanted to take him away on a surprise fishing trip, to a very expensive fishing lodge at Shimoni which was sixty miles South of Mombasa. She knew her husband would not be happy leaving the ranch, with both of them away, unless there was someone really capable in charge. Would Jim fly down, at their expense, and look after the ranch. She knew he was very familiar with the area as he had made a stock route down to their ranch three years earlier. She said, obviously they would pay him. This was too good an opportunity to miss so Jim said he would be delighted. It also solved his dilemma with Emily.

He wrote to Emily, saying he was so sorry that he couldn't come for Christmas as he was looking after a ranch, north of the Sabaki but he did hope he would see her when she came to pick up the twins for the Christmas break. He did not think anything more about the holiday after he had made certain he could hire his friend's plane. That would fit in very well as he could fly direct from Gilgil to the ranch.

Ten days before Christmas, he came back tired from a long day at work which had started with a caesarean section on a cow at day break. He had not had time to catch his breath since. He immediately went for a run into the forest, which always relaxed him. He had not bothered to wash so he had blood and muck on his legs and face. He came back at top speed so he arrived home sweating and gasping for air. He went in to the house and took off all his clothes and then walked out on to the veranda. There was Emily, covered with mud. They looked at each other and burst out laughing. She ran up the three steps onto the veranda and was in his arms. They kissed. Jim carried her into the house, into his bedroom. Jim helped her pull off her clothes and they fell onto the bed. He kissed her lips then her neck and then moved down her body, until he was kissing and sucking her groin. She groaned in ecstasy and pulled him on top of her. She groaned again as he entered her. After he had climaxed, he tenderly kissed her neck and breasts.

"Oh Jim. That was better than I have ever imagined." She ruffled his filthy hair and, looking at his bedside table, said,

"I am glad you liked my photo. I got a tourist couple, who were walking on our beach, to take it. They thought I was most odd. I think the woman thought I was after her husband as I put on that lascivious grin. You must make sure you put it away if the twins come. In fact, you old rogue, I hope you don't let them into your bedroom. I have decided to take them to England after Christmas. They would have to finish at Pembroke in July, but I think they are being held back. They are much more mature than any of the other girls. I think they should move on to school in UK or they will never reach their potential."

"I agree with you," replied Jim. "They are amazingly grown up, for fifteen. You don't know but they can drive my Landrover really well. When we are vetting, they treat the farmers, my staff and me as equals, in a sensible mature way. I never have to show them how to do anything twice. I would love them to train to be vets but I think they have set their sights on becoming pilots."

"Oh Jim, I can't bear the thought of them joining the RAF."

"Don't worry, women are coming of age. I am sure there will be openings for them, as commercial pilots. I don't just mean bush pilots, here in Kenya, but long-haul big jet pilots. I will miss them as they have lightened my life up here, on the Kinangop. One thing I beg of you. Do let them stay together. They will be terribly unhappy if they are parted."

"How do you know that?" queried Emily

"They told me they had nightmares when they were put in separate dormitories at Pembroke, which stopped as soon as they had beds next to each other. They told me, when I told them they should not worry if they heard me having a nightmare. I was worried stiff they would come into my room and try to comfort me. I was so violent when I was first recovering that I hit the nurse and split her lip in a really bad nightmare."

"Poor girl, whatever did she do?"

Jim went very red and mumbled something that Emily couldn't hear. She held his shoulders and rolled him onto his back and kissed him.

"Somehow I think it is important. What did she do Jim?"

"She got into bed with me and cuddled me," replied a very embarrassed Jim.

"African girls are very understanding," said Emily.

"Oh it wasn't an African, it was a European girl."

Emily laughed. "There is no doubt about it. You are a real rogue, Jim Scott. I can't believe you seduced your nurse. You did seduce her didn't you? I can see from your face you did. All I can say is she was a very lucky girl if you could make her climax as beautifully as you made me come. In fact, I want you to do it again right now."

It was getting dark when they got into their dirty clothes and took Jim's Landrover down, to tow out Emily's car. In fact it was quite easy. Emily had jacked it up and put sticks under the back wheels but

591

she had no one to push her. The Landrover made the job a doddle. Katana greeted them, on their return, with a cup of tea. He said the water was very hot so they should be careful. He would have supper ready when they had finished their bath.

When they went into the bathroom Emily said, "How did he know we were going to have a bath together? I bet you bring lots of ladies up here and ravish them? And then bath with them?"

Emily now was naked and turned Jim to look her in the eye.

"I hope you have never bathed with the twins?"

Jim replied, "No, I haven't but I can tell you it has taken all my will power."

"I believe you. Now, you have an old bag nearly twice your age. I expect you to be really gentle with her."

"I will be gentle with you but it is rubbish about age. I happen to know how old you are, as you let slip that you were only seventeen when you had the twins, so you are only a year or two older than me and you have a figure of an eighteen year old. Look how perky your breasts are."

"Jim, you really know how to please a girl. Come on, let's get clean. I am starving hungry."

It did not matter to Emily that supper was only sausages. Supper tasted like nectar. Soon the generator died and they were sitting in candle light. Jim had lit the fire and it seemed quite natural for Emily to snuggle up, in his lap. They chatted about their lives and Jim opened up to her but he could not tell her about Claire. She told him about Eric and how they were going through a bad patch at the moment as she had found out that he had had an affair, with the wife of one of his clients. She said she had forgiven him and she would stick with him because of the twins. She said that it was not difficult, as they were still friends. It was just that she found making love to him was difficult. She said it was a bit like 'lying on her back and thinking of England', as Victorian wives were meant to do

Soon they went to bed. Emily teased him and asked if they needed to play nurses and patients for him to get an erection. He held her wrists with one hand and kissed and tickled her until she was begging for mercy. When she got her breath back she asked him, very seriously, if he would kiss her vulva and clitoris again because that was so marvellous. After she had come, he mounted her from behind and she cried out when she had another orgasm. They went to sleep, with Jim holding her body in his arms, his hands on her breasts and his erect penis between her legs. They awoke just before dawn. She turned round and kissed him. "I am bursting for a wee. I will go first. You keep the bed warm. You can go for a wee quickly when I come back. Then I want you inside me, one more time."

When they were both snuggled back in bed, Emily said.

"You must be a wonderful lover, Jim. You must get me totally wet and ready for you before you enter me because I am not in the least bit sore and you have been drilling me like a traction engine. Normally with Eric I am sore and I can't wait for him to go away again on '*safari*'." She took Jim's hand and placed it over her bush. It felt electric to Jim, as he softly entwined the hairs. "Mm, that's good," she murmured. "You are just teasing my clitoris. I want more of that. Oh yes, much more." She pushed up her pubis. Eventually she started playing the fool. She was on her back with her legs tightly around his waist rubbing against his tummy. He kept trying to push his erect penis into her but she would not let him. She could feel his frustration and she could feel him losing control. This suddenly made her extremely excited. She pushed herself on to him and undulated her bottom rhythmically. She climaxed and bit his neck. He thrust really hard and climaxed inside her and lay exhausted on top of her. She murmured,

"Jim, Jim that was wonderful."

After sometime they knew they had to get up. Jim just put on his shorts and shirt and went into the bathroom to brush his teeth. Emily cuddled his back and, shamelessly, took his brush and cleaned her teeth. Then, when he was washing his face with a warm flannel, he took it and washed between her legs. He did not rinse it but put it on to his face. He held it and said,

"I won't rinse it. I will enjoy your smell when I wash my face tonight. You know, I will always remember last night but we must pretend it never happened."

Emily replied, "You are right. The twins think the world of you. I am sure, when they are older, our antics will not worry them but, just now I think it would really upset them. Now I have got you and you can't wriggle away." She reached her arms around his back and, with

593

one hand, grasped his balls. "I want you to promise me you will fly down from the ranch for Christmas lunch."

"I submit," said Jim. "My neck is sore where you bit me, heavens knows what you might do to my balls!"

Emily released his balls and kissed his neck.

"I am not going to say I am sorry because it was totally your fault for getting me so excited. Bloody hell it was good." They had a leisurely breakfast. Emily thanked Katana as he had done all her washing, even her bra and pants which had somehow managed to get mud on them. She thrust really quite a large note into his pocket.

She told Jim that the twins would be going to the UK after Christmas. He said they were marvellous young ladies and he wished them the best of luck. Then Jim led her the easiest way back, so she could drive down to Pembroke School. They kissed on the side of the road. Emily held him close and said, "You are a great guy, Jim. Something is troubling you deep down and I don't think over sexed middle-aged women are what you need."

"Rubbish," replied Jim. "In my eyes, you are a lovely girl who gives her all to life. You have got two wonderful daughters. Rest assured I would give my life for all of you."

"You somehow say the most wonderful things, Jim. I will never forget you lusted after me or that you said I had got perky breasts like a young girl. I am looking forward to Christmas. I know we will have to behave but we can have fun as well. I certainly have got wonderful memories of the Kinangop."

She broke away from him and drove off down to Gilgil, waving out the window of her car. Jim went off to work. He had some routine fertility work and he had to make sure all the veterinary scouts had sufficient veterinary medicines, to last them over the Christmas holiday period. He had everything pretty well worked out and so he was sitting in the office doing paperwork. He thought he should be happy. He had just spent all night, loving a very pretty girl. Somehow he was more depressed than ever. It was not because she was older than him. In fact Emily, was not much older than Claire. What was the bloody matter with him? Being a vet, he tried to think of his signs and symptoms logically. He was not ill. He had a good appetite. He was physical very fit. He was not on any medication. At the coast he had constantly to take anti-malaria medicine but there was no need to take any up here on the Kinangop. He had not been drinking. In fact, he suddenly realised that Emily and he had been so wrapped up in having sex they had not even had a beer. What a bad host he was? He had wondered if he was just sad, because he was not having sex but now he had had enough sex to satisfy many guys for a month. In fact it had been really great sex. He had no feelings of guilt. He knew that if Emily turned up at his house tonight he would have a really great night. Certainly he was a little bit sad that he was not going to have the company of the twins next year, but that was no big deal. In fact, having two very attractive under-aged girls about, who had adored him, was quite a strain in itself.

Chapter 44

The Day Family

Saturday 20th December 1969

What Jim did not know was that he was probably suffering from Post Traumatic Stress Disorder. This is a condition which was only to be recognised thirty years later.

That day he went home promptly and went for a run with Lucy. Then, after a good bath he went down to the Christmas party at Naivasha club. There he met Fred Day and his three daughters. Fred seemed delighted to see him and bought him a beer. Amanda, the eldest daughter, was distinctly frosty. Julia who fancied Jim spoke quite sharply to her elder sister. "For goodness sake, Manda what is the matter with you? What has Jim done wrong, to give you a face which would curdle cream?"

"I saw him kiss two Pembroke school girls, on the lips, outside the school two weeks ago. I was truly shocked. They are only fifteen. I expect he will deny it but I saw it with my own eyes!" Jim roared with laughter. "Just to prove to you I like girls in pairs, how about this?" He kissed first, a rather taken aback, Annabel and then a very pleased Julia who squealed with delight.

"Well," said Fred. "I think I had better be the judge of this heinous crime before Jim totally corrupts my daughters. Where did the supposed crime take place, Amanda?"

"It occurred right in front of the school gates. He was delivering them back to school. Heavens knows what he had been doing with them?"

"Who were these girls?" asked Fred

"The Gurney twins," replied Amanda.

"Oh yes. I have seen them with the accused at Polo. Very pretty blonds, wearing very short shorts, I recalled," said Fred, who was warming to his task.

"What were they wearing on the occasion of the crime?"

"Their school uniforms but I am sure they had hitched their skirts up," claimed Amanda. Julia sniggered.

"So there was some provocation for the crime?" asked Fred. "Who did the kissing?"

"Well, I suppose, they did," said Amanda begrudgingly.

Fred then said very solemnly. "I think I am getting the picture of this character which is going to be a threat to my daughters. He has been kissed by two scantily clad school girls who were unchaperoned by the school gates."

"Oh no," says Amanda. "They were with matron." Both Annabel and Julia exploded with laughter.

"I think I must say, Amanda, the likelihood of a crime being committed is pretty thin. I therefore think Jim should, to show there is no favoritism, kiss Amanda immediately." Before the shocked Amanda could move, Jim planted a kiss on her cheek. There was further laughter from Annabel and Julia.

Jim said, "I am sorry Manda. I have known them, at the coast since they were little girls and they do spend a lot of time with me on the Kinangop. I am very fond of them. He was very tempted to add. *'Their mother was bouncing up and down on top of me this morning, as if she was posting a pony.'*

The evening was a great success. Jim had several dances with Annabel and Julia. He even had one with Amanda who, in a strange way seemed to have forgiven him. Jim wondered if his love/hate relationship was really because she rather fancied him but did not want to show it as she knew Julia was prettier and therefore might eventually reel him in. Jim thought. *'They are three nice girls but somehow I just don't find them sexually attractive. On the other hand, Emily and the twins were seriously gorgeous, but he must blot out all such thoughts.'*

When Jim drove home, he was certainly a happier man. He was looking forward to his flight down to the ranch, on the Sabaki, on the next day which was Wednesday the 24th December.

Jim arrived at the veterinary office, slightly early the following day. He had left Lucy with Katana. He had packed some clothes. He also had bought Christmas presents for the whole Gurney family in Nakuru having skived off work at lunchtime. He sorted out his veterinary gear. He knew the ranch would have medicines but he thought he might need instruments. The rancher was fairly knowledgeable but Jim thought it was unlikely he could do any surgery. He also took his shotgun in case there was a chance to shoot some birds. When he was happy everything was in order at the office he left and drove down to Gilgil. He quickly checked out the plane and took off in a south easterly direction. As he was all alone in the plane which had, not only a retractable under-carriage but also was very powerful, he climbed rapidly. He was glad he did not need to land at Wilson, in Nairobi as there was a large amount of air traffic.

He arrived at the Sabaki airstrip in less than two hours and taxied to the house. There was chaos and a massive family row in progress. A Turkana herdsman had been injured, on the previous night as a lion had broken into one of the '*bomas*' and killed a steer. The injured herdsman needed to be taken to Voi for treatment. The rancher had refused to leave as he said the lion was bound to return and kill again.

They did not even greet Jim, when he arrived. Jim just listened, in the background and formulated a plan in his own mind. He hated what he proposed but thought he was brave enough to do it. He spoke up. "I am here to take over running the ranch while you have a Christmas and big birthday break. You leave for the fishing trip. I will fly the injured man to Voi, in the Cherokee Arrow, which is very speedy. I will take two of his friends and the stretcher. They can take him to Voi hospital so I won't have to wait about. I will come back and do any cattle checking and then, towards dusk, I will sit up over the dead steer and shoot the lion if it returns. End of story. Now bugger off, you are only fifty once in your life." Peace returned to the house after they departed.

Jim went to see the injured herdsman. Jim immediately recognised the tall Turkana, standing patiently, on one leg, next to the man lying on the stretcher in the shade. It was the Headman he had met on his first day in Mombasa. It was a day he would never forget. "'*Jambo Loki, Habari?*'"

"'Mzuri Bwana Jim. Lakeni tabu mingi. Simba na kuja.' (There has been lots of trouble a lion has come)". Loki held out a very long arm. Jim grasped Loki's hand in both of his. They both smiled in recognition of mutual respect. Loki drew back the blanket covering the herdsman whose name was Luti. It appeared that he had run into a stake when he was chasing the lion. The stake had sliced into his scrotum. A testicle was hanging out. Jim did not dare give Luti a GA, so he bathed the testicle and surrounding area with warm salty water. He gave Luti two aspirins and a glass of water. He also gave him two Ampicillin capsules to swallow, to reduce infection. He squirted local anaesthetic onto the testicle and the cut edge of the scrotum. Luti did not move a muscle but it obviously stung badly as his colour became ashen. Very gently, Jim tried to replace the testicle into the scrotum. He failed as the scrotal wall was so swollen and had turned in on itself. Jim knew that the correct procedure was to remove the testicle, as Luti would be quite OK with only one. Jim did not dare, so he packed the now anaesthetised area with gauze soaked in saline. He then found a pair of his Y-fronts and put them on Luti to support the testicle. They carried Luti to the plane. Loki insisted on coming for the flight so Jim got all his equipment and luggage taken out. They took out the rear two seats and loaded Luti, and the two stretcher bearers, in the now large area in the back. Loki came with Jim in the front. Jim knew it was illegal to have five people in the plane which was only licensed for four, but he did not want Loki to lose face. The plane had plenty of power and the strip was of a reasonable length. They took off towards the Sabaki River. As soon as they were airborne Jim had the under-cart up and pushed the stick forward to build up speed. He did not try to turn until he had built up speed and gained a little height. He slowly turned to the right onto the correct heading for Voi. They saw masses of elephant as they flew low over Tsavo National Park. Jim pointed them out to Loki, who made a guttural grunt. The flight was not long and in fact because the plane was cool, Luti looked a lot stronger when they arrived and went to walk. Jim insisted that he stayed on the stretcher. Loki endorsed this and so there were no problems. Jim grasped Luti's hand and said, *"'Baharti mzuri.'*(Good luck)."* The stretcher bearers carried him off.

599

With no further conversation Jim got into the plane and Loki got in the right-hand seat. Take off was easy, as the plane was now much lighter. They made good time back to the ranch. There was still plenty of daylight time left so, after Jim had spoken to all the different headmen and had been assured that all the cattle were either well or had been treated, he sat down and had a meal of stew, potatoes and cabbage, washed down with tea. He was dreading the night to come. He got the equipment he would require: a camp chair with arms, thermos-flasks with strong sweet coffee, water bottles and sandwiches. He decided to take four strong torches and his own shot gun, together with the ranch shot gun. He took all the stuff out to the ranch Landrover. Jim was relieved to see Loki. He had faith in this mature man. They drove out to the '*boma*' and arrived before dusk. The steer had been killed in the '*boma*'. Jim asked Loki to move a small amount of the thorn barricade so that it was easy for the lion to get to the steer, which had only been killed but not eaten. Loki then ordered all his men to strengthen up the whole '*boma*' with cut thorn bush. In fact this need had been anticipated and, during the day large amounts of both cut thorn bush and fire wood had been collected. Loki placed his men and their fires carefully. Normally, most of the men would be sleeping in bivouac tents and there would only be the night guards like Luti, patrolling. Tonight Loki had all his men on duty. It seemed as if honour had to be restored by the death of the lion who had dared to kill an animal 'on their watch'. Loki explained very carefully, to all the men what was going to happen. He did not want any of them to be hurt by either the lion or by Jim's shots.

There was a baobab tree near to the edge of the opening in the '*boma*'. The carcass lay near it and was now blown and covered with flies. Jim positioned his chair, so that his back would be protected by the enormous tree. He got all his stuff around him. Luckily, the '*boma*' was several miles from the Sabaki River and so there were no mosquitoes. Jim had remembered to start taking anti-malarial tablets some days before. As dusk fell fast, the last of the cattle were brought into the '*boma*' and the fires were built up. Jim settled down to wait in the chair, with Loki sitting with two torches slightly to his right and two yards in front of him. Jim had the ranch shot gun, loaded with SSG shot, across his knee. He had his gun, also loaded, on the ground next to him. Both guns had their safety catches on. Jim was wearing an old settler's jacket with big pockets, so he had spare cartridges in them. He had a pee and then sat down and waited for the long vigil to start.

He was terrified. It was much worse than when he waited for the hippo, with Claire. He remembered how brave she had been allowing him to get a second dart into its nose. If she had run then and not held the torch, he would have died. Now she was dead. If only he had not let her go alone to have a crap. Their relationship had been so close, it would not have mattered if he had gone with her. She had done everything for him when he had been so sick with Malaria. There was no part of his body she had not known. In fact, there was no part of her body she had not enjoyed him touching. It was just Victorian nonsense that had made her go, on her own. If only he could have saved her. The darkness hid the tears trickling down his cheeks. Slowly he conquered his terror. He must man-up or the lion would kill Loki. Loki trusted him. Loki had his pride and his honour. Jim must have the same. He might have let Claire down. He was not going to let Loki down. He had his pride. He had his honour. Lions were killers, powerful and cunning but Jim was determined he was going to get this one. He even smiled to himself, as he remembered that he had not got permission from the PVO in Nyeri, to be absent from his station. If he got killed here, he would be disciplined! Who would actually care? Certainly Emily and the twins would weep for him. He knew they were very fond of him in different ways. Colin Cameron would be informed and so Susie would hear. Jim knew although she had someone else, she would be a little sad. They had had a great time together. They had been particularly close, as they were so isolated. Jim worried about Katana. He had made no proper provision for him. He must do that. Suddenly he felt tears coming again when he thought, *'Fi will not know I am dead. Don't be so fucking selfish. Why do you want her to know? You should be thinking about her happiness, not wanting her to grieve over you.'* Jim knew his parents would grieve but he had been away so long now that his memory must have dimmed.

It was time he stiffened his back. He must look fate and danger in the eye. He would not let his friend Loki down. The night crawled on. He drank numerous cups of coffee and ate all the sandwiches. He now was on water. Where was the dawn? Then he heard the lion. He

601

had not heard it come he just heard it snarl. Something deep in his over-active mind registered that snarl. What did the snarl mean? Everything happened very quickly. Loki turned on both torches. Jim stood up with the gun to his shoulder. The lion turned to him and opened its mouth to roar. Jim shot it dead with one shot through its mouth into its brain. He shot it again, for good measure, into its chest as it fell onto its side. Then his brain kicked in. The snarl. The lion had snarled not at him because it was unaware of his presence but at another lion. He dropped the gun, squatted and picked up his gun. The lioness charged. Loki covered it with his torch. Jim hit it on the bridge of its nose and then, with a second shot between its eyes. It died, in a massive ball at his feet within an arms length of Loki.

Jim snapped open the gun and reloaded. *"'Iko ingenyi?'"* (Is there another)

"'Hapana,'" (No) answered Loki. *"' Mbili tu tosha.'"* (Two is enough)

Honour had been satisfied. The killers were dead. There was no crowding round of herdsmen. They had been ordered to stay in their allotted places. There was no one going to get hurt, chasing in the darkness. There was no back slapping or congratulating, just a silence. Jim sat back in his chair. Loki, having turned off the torches picked up his spear and stood a silent sentinel, waiting for the dawn. Now it was just a non-event. All in a nights work, waiting time before the day job. Although when he was all hyped, Jim had loaded both shot guns he had put them on safety and returned them to their positions. He did not think other lions would come. He dosed and only woke again with a start when he dreamt the lion was coming for him again. Luckily, he was sitting up in a chair and not in a deep sleep so he did not have a nightmare. The dawn rose quickly. Loki gave instructions for the lions to be skinned while Jim unloaded the guns and packed the stuff into the Landrover. The fact that it was Christmas day was not relevant, out here in the bush. Life went on as normal. Loki said he would stay out with the cattle as normal and Jim drove back to the ranch headquarters.

On the road, Jim saw a 'Lesser Bustard' which is often called a black-bellied Flurrican. They are good eating and Jim was thinking of his evening meal, on his return from Christmas lunch with the Gurneys. He quietly opened the Landrover door, loaded his shotgun, rested it on door hinge, aimed and pulled the trigger. The bird dropped like a stone. That was not surprising as Jim had loaded with SSG by mistake. He found he had totally blown one side of the bird to smithereens! When he got back to the house, it really made the cook laugh. Jim had a hearty breakfast and left instructions for his supper. He had a shower. He put all his kit and veterinary stuff back in the plane as he never liked to be without it even though he knew he was only going to be away for lunch. There were no problems on the ranch so he thought it was fine for him to go for Christmas lunch. He had told the rancher and his wife that he had intended to go to the Gurneys, on the coast. Obviously they knew one another. They had said that would be fine. The journey, which by road would have taken ten hours, took less than thirty minutes by air.

When Jim had taxied up to a safe place, he chocked the wheels, locked up and put on the pito-head cover. As he had a pee, he suddenly felt he was being watched. He looked around but could not see anyone nor could he see a lion. He totally had lions on the brain. There were no lions at Vipingo. He set off to walk through the sisal. The next thing he knew, he had been tripped from behind. He rolled and the twins jumped on top of him. He struggled but let them win. "You little urchins. Happy Christmas."

"Santa Claus. Have you got any presents in that rucksack?"

"I have got a present for two young ladies but not for two hooligans who have terrified me. I suddenly thought someone was watching me when I was having a wee."

"We thought you had seen us, but we lay flat and still and your eyes went over the top of us."

"Now, I have become a young lady," said Emma getting up.

"Me too," said Amy. "Can we have our presents after all? Look, we are no longer urchins." It was true, it was only Jim who had got dirty in the dust, the twins had been on top of him. The twins had grown even taller and so they easily reached up to kiss him.

"Do our kisses help to convince you we are young ladies?"

"I think they do," replied Jim. "I got into trouble from Amanda Day, as she saw you kissing me at Pembroke."

"Silly old Manda, Young ladies are allowed to kiss men they love."

"I think it was because you kissed me on the lips. Perhaps you had better just give me a hug in future?"

"Like this," cried the twins and they buried themselves in his arms.

They walked, holding his hands, to the house. They chattered, on telling him all the news at the coast. Emily came rushing out shouting,

"Happy Christmas." She hugged him and, so no one could see, gave him a little squeeze in a very inappropriate place and whispered,

"You kept your promise. I must grab your balls more often to get what I want."

Then, stepping back, she looked at him and saw he was covered in dust. "What has happened to you, I expected you to arrive in your Christmas finery?"

"I fell over on the airstrip," said Jim with a straight face. The twins sniggered. Emily was not put off.

"Has it anything to do with you two?"

"It might have," replied the twins. "Jim has forgiven us now and says, as we are proper young ladies we can have the presents he has brought for us. Can we open them now?"

Jim gave the twins their presents. They were both carefully wrapped and labelled. They tore them open. "I have given you those colors because you had those colour shorts on when I first met you, years ago. I remember Amy saying,

To help you remember our names. Emma is wearing blue shorts and I am wearing green." The twins looked at him and both said in unison,

"You are the one person who has never made a mistake with our names. Even Mummy and Daddy used to make mistakes when we were smaller."

"It is probably because you were quite grown up when I first met you," answered Jim. The twins replied.

"We were discussing it two days ago. We think it is because you really know and love us, but in a different way to Mummy and Daddy. We think, maybe Ole Kipoi is right. As you have killed a lion with a '*panga*', like a Masai you should marry both of us."

Jim laughed. "I have been saving up but I am still far short of your bride price." Eric had come on to the veranda and said,

"The little horrors woke me up this morning. If you give me ten cows you can take the pair of them."

"Well, I don't know about cows Eric but here is a bottle of Port to wish you a Happy Christmas."

"Jim, you must share it with me. It looks a good bottle."

The twins were holding up their presents which were a pair of pyjamas each. They had cartoons on them and each had written on them, 'Boys are silly. Throw rocks at them!'

"They are cool, Jim. We will wear them tonight." They ran and hugged him. "Can we kiss you on the lips?"

Jim laughed and replied, "Yes, unless Manda is hiding on the veranda." The twins shrieked with laughter.

"What's all that about," asked Emily.

The twins replied in unison. "Silly old Amanda Day saw us kissing Jim goodbye at Pembroke. Matron did not mind but Manda gave Jim a hard time at Naivasha club."

Emily laughed. "She is a funny one I expect she has got the hots for Jim. I know Julia has."

"You had better watch out, Jim, Fred will want a lot of polo ponies for those three," said Eric.

"What are the hots? Mummy," asked Emma. Before Emily could reply, Amy piped up, "I think it is when you get a warm feeling in your knickers"

A rather embarrassed Emily said, "I think that is quite enough of that. I am really miffed. There is no present for me."

"Oh yes, there is," said Jim

Emily unwrapped a beautiful cream silk shirt. She glanced at the label and saw Jim had got just her size. "Well, thank you Jim, I am a really happy girl. I can put it on now. You girls will have to wait until bed time until you wear your presents." She went to her room thinking. '*He is a crafty one. He must have checked the size, from the clothes I left strewn about his room. He might have just judged my size, when he said I had got perky breasts like a young girl. It is quite see through. I don't think I dare wear it without a bra. I hope I get a chance to give him a private viewing. It is so sad he is here for such a short time.*'

Emily kept her white bra on and came out wearing the new shirt.

"Looks good," said Jim.

"Its fab Mum," said the twins. Emily kissed Jim on the lips and said,

"I will have to be really careful not to get anything down it at lunch. I won't have an alcoholic drink just in case. I will keep you company Jim, because you are flying again soon."

Lunch was a real success. The staff had been given the day off but Emily had prepared a large cold collation, which everyone enjoyed. After lunch, they had a sit down and played a game the twins had been given, called 'UNO', which was great fun. After that, they had a swim and a long walk on the beach. They had cups of tea and cake and then it was time for Jim to leave. They all walked to the airstrip to see him off. Emily managed to walk, near to Jim while the others were a little ahead. She whispered, "You look very tired. Is everything alright?"

Jim replied, "I had to sit up all night and kill two lions which had killed a steer the night before."

Emily's hand went to her mouth. "My God, you are brave. Oh Jim, I hope it won't make your nightmares worse?"

"Send me a picture of those perky breasts in the new shirt and I will have something much better to think about, than a couple of lions."

Then he started telling her about the lesser bustard and so she was laughing when they caught up the others. He had to tell it all again for Eric and the twins. He just said he picked up the wrong cartridges. He did not mention the lions.

At the plane, Eric shook his hand, Emily kissed him and the twins hugged and kissed him. He took off with a heavy heart. He knew Emily would be right, his nightmares would be worse.

All was well on the ranch. Jim cheered himself at supper, eating the smashed game bird, by recalling his first Christmas night in Kenya. That strip poker game seemed a life time ago. It was a life time ago, Claire's life. He then felt really miserable. He went for a walk by the river before he went to bed. The generator had been turned off and all mechanical noise was absent. The crickets and the frogs made a real racket. He thought he heard the sawing noise of a leopard. Even in his misery he knew the wilds of Africa were his home. He might be in for rough nights but at least he had faced the lions early this morning. He had not let Loki down. He wondered how poor young Luti was now. One stone lighter he guessed. He walked back to the house with its glorious view, in the daylight, across the Sabaki River.

Luckily the house was some distance from the other staff housing because when Jim woke in the morning, his bed was totally trashed. He felt exhausted, so he guessed he had a prolonged nightmare. Somehow he got through Boxing Day. Luckily there were no major problems. He went to bed soon after 8.00pm. He woke himself with a nightmare, soon after midnight and slept fitfully until dawn. He managed to get through the following day and also the following night. All was well on the ranch, when the owner and his wife arrived home. They were in high spirits. They had really enjoyed their break. The owner had caught a sail fish which weighed 78 pounds, so he was really pleased. Jim did not chat for long, as it was Sunday 28th December and he had to be back to work in the morning. He flew home to Gilgil via Wilson where he filled up with fuel.

On the drive up to Gilgil he nearly came off the road, as he must have dosed off for a second. He was highly relieved to get home. Lucy gave him a massive greeting. Katana seemed relieved that he was home safe and sound. Jim went for a long run with Lucy. He hoped the exercise would help him to sleep. He had a good supper and a deep hot bath. He went to bed thinking about Claire which he knew was bad but, in fact, he only had a mild nightmare that night. The following night was New Years Eve. Jim said he would meet Ed and Lizzie at the Nakuru Athletic Club (NAC), for the annual dance. It was not a dinner dance as such but there would be some food available and, of course, plenty of drink. Jim knew he had to be at work on the following day as it was not a public holiday but he was determined to have fun. He said to himself, that he must not keep thinking he was going to have a horrendous nightmare. He did a lot of dancing, particularly with Liz as Ed was happier propping up the bar. The Day's arrived and Julia made a 'B' line for Jim. She pulled him onto the floor. He teased her and said,

"Aren't you worried Manda will see me kissing you on the lips, at midnight?"

"Why wait until midnight?" She started to kiss him ardently. She was obviously a bit pissed. Jim suddenly had a desire to take her outside around the back of the club, rip her knickers off and take her up against a tree. His good sense prevailed and he managed to get away from her, by dancing with Annabel. Annabel was much quieter and calmed him down. After a couple of dances she said,

"I had better go and find Julia." They walked off the floor together, onto the long veranda overlooking the pitches. There was Julia, vomiting over the railings at the far end. They managed to get her to Jim's Landrover. Annabel said,

"I know I should not ask but do you mind taking us home? Manda will be furious if she finds out. I will just pop in and tell Dad. He and Manda can come home as planned after midnight. I will tell him Julia has a tummy bug. He will know exactly what has happened but he won't tell Manda."

So Jim took Annabel and Julia home. Julia sat in the middle seat and passed out lolling against Jim. Jim felt sorry for Annabel as Julia had wrecked her evening. He was so relieved that he had restrained himself. He could have got himself in a total muddle. Jim lifted Julia out of the Landrover. He noticed she had rather good legs, as her skirt was up around her waist. Annabel held all the doors open for him and he carried her all the way into her bedroom. Annabel said,

"Can you hold her up, while I take her dress off? She can sleep in her bra and knickers. I have a very good mind to tell her you ravished her, outside the club. She was certainly all over you. At one moment I thought that was going to happen. Were you tempted?"

"Actually, I must admit I was. She seems besotted with me. I don't really know what to do as I don't want to hurt her."

Annabel laughed. "We are like a Doctor and Nurse discussing an almost naked patient. I think Julia would be mortified if she knew. Come on, let's go in the kitchen and have a coffee or something stronger, if you like."

They covered Julia up. Annabel left the light on, in case Julia woke up. When their coffees were ready, they carried them into the sitting room. Jim had no great desire either to go back to the NAC or to go home. Annabel was obviously quite happy chatting away. They did not drink anything alcoholic but Annabel had a juice and Jim a cold coke. When the clock struck midnight Annabel, very deliberately got up, came and sat on Jim's knee, then turned and kissed him.

"You are a really good guy, Jim Scott. Somewhere, there is a very special girl for you. I see sadness in your eyes and I won't pry, but I think you have lost a girl you really loved. I can sympathise, as none of the family know but I had a boyfriend at University, in the UK, who had a motorbike accident and died." She quietly sobbed on his shoulder. Jim stroked her hair and said,

"Let's hope there is someone special out there for both of us." She sniffed and borrowed his handkerchief.

"Don't tell anyone, will you."

"Of course I won't. Thank you for trusting me."

Then they both shook off their melancholy moods and chatted about all manner of other things Jim managed to make her really laugh, by telling her about his Christmas supper. She stayed on his lap, with her head on his shoulder, and encouraged him to continue stroking his hair. They both heard Fred's car arrive. Annabel whispered to Jim,

"If it would not have hurt and embarrassed Daddy, I would love to have pretended to have gone to sleep with your hand up my skirt." She got up and walked towards the door. "Thank you for being such a good friend. I am sorry the Day family has wrecked your evening." She opened the front door and kissed Amanda as she came in.

"Happy New Year, Manda," She hugged Fred.

"Happy New Year, Daddy," She looked at her watch.

"Goodness, it is nearly half passed one. Jim and I must have been snogging since midnight! Oh don't look so appalled, Manda. I am only pulling your leg. Jim and I are good friends and have a lot in common. You must be going Jim, as you have to be at work in the morning." Jim gave Manda a peck on the cheek.

"Happy New Year Fred, I hope to see you all soon." Annabel gave him a proper kiss and he was off, back to the Kinangop.

As he drove home he reflected that 1969 had been a really bad year, following Claire's death in December 1968, perhaps 1970 would be better. The year was not yet two hours old and he had made a real friend. Because he was so tired, he did not wake or have a nightmare.

609

Faithful Katana woke him, with his normal cup of tea. Jim did not feel too bad. All went well at work on the Thursday and Friday. He got a phone call, from a very contrite Julia, on Friday afternoon.

"I am so sorry I made such an ass of myself on New Year's Eve. Can you come to supper with us tonight?"

"I would love to," replied Jim.

It was an interesting night. There was a polo pal of Fred's who Jim knew and liked. There was an old Kenyan farmer, who had sold his farm at Molo and now lived with a new wife on the shores of Lake Naivasha. There were two friends of Annabel's, who she worked with in Nairobi, and a new young girl teacher from Pembroke. Manda was as bossy as ever and Julia was very subdued. Annabel and her girlfriends seemed very interested in Jim's amusing veterinary stories. Jim should have driven home in a happy mood but, as soon as he was no longer 'on parade' and alone, he was even more depressed than usual. The night was horrible. At dawn, he woke to a totally trashed bed. His eyes felt as if he been in a sand storm. He had a luke-warm shower, as somehow it had not heated up enough the night before. Then he remembered that Katana had taken the weekend off, to go to see his family at Njoro. He should have remembered as he had taken him to the bus before, going to the Day's. Normally, if Katana was off, Jim took the lazy option and went away as well but, this weekend, he decided to stay totally on his own. If he wanted hot water he would have to keep the fire, under the 44 Gallon drum burning.

He took Lucy up for a walk in the forest. His spirits lifted when he surprised two elephants that crashed away. He thought, *'How lucky I am. Not many people can walk out of their back door and meet two elephants. I need a project. I will start studying elephant's teeth. I am sure their teeth must be related to their longevity? Maybe I am going about getting back on track in the wrong way? I should start using my brain more. I won't stop physical exercise but clearly it is not really lifting me out of my depression. General socialising does not seem to help. Chatting to Annabel had been therapeutic, as they both knew there would be no physical attraction between them. In some way, they were like an old couple who had been married for years and just enjoyed each other's company and did not want sex.*

He walked on through the forest, on a path he rarely used. Lucy walked along, close at heel. They met some Bush Pigs, who disappeared rapidly into the undergrowth. Lucy was too apprehensive to give chase and then, to his amazement, he came across a large, lonely giant forest hog. These animals are very rarely seen except at flood-lit salt licks, near treetop type lodges either in the Aberdares or on Mount Kenya. The hog obviously saw him and smelt both him and Lucy but made no move to run. It just tried to stare him out. Jim wondered if they were as intelligent as domestic pigs which are said to be more intelligent than dogs. Eventually, the old hog just turned and walked slowly away back into the forest.

At this point Jim realised he had walked a considerable distance and that he had not had any breakfast. He did not try and be clever but turned around and retraced his steps. Eventually, as he was nearing his home, he heard someone calling his name. It sounded like the twins but he could not really believe it. Lucy knew and raced away. Jim ran after her. Then he heard them shout,"It's Lucy! He must be here?" Then he opened his arms wide and they flung themselves at him.

"I thought you had gone to UK?"

"Would we have gone without saying goodbye? We don't go until tomorrow evening."

"Have you had any breakfast?"

"Of course, silly, it is almost lunchtime."

"Well, let's have lunch. I have had such a fantastic walk! I have seen elephant and giant forest hog."

"That's fantastic! We have only seen them at the 'Ark'."

"Where is Emily?"

"She is inside, I expect organising some lunch. We have been doing some last minute shopping in Nairobi but we brought some food, as we know what you are like. Cabbage, spuds and steak is your staple diet!"

Sure enough, Emily was inside and she came out onto the veranda and gave him a big hug and a kiss. She had been making lunch because it was all laid out on the table. She turned to the twins and said,

"Let's all have a glass of chilled white wine? Could you two bring in the wine and the beer, out of the cool box in the car? The twins scampered out. She turned to Jim.

"Has it been really bad? I looked into your bedroom and saw the state of your bed. I guessed last night was horrendous."

"Yes, for no good reason I had a very good night out, at quite a big dinner party at the Day's."

"Oh Jim, I wish I could sleep with you every night. I am sure the nightmares would stop."

"I am sure you are right but somehow, I have got to find my way through this. It was made worse by the lions at the ranch."

The twins came back in with the drinks. "Can we pour out a glass for you, Jim and I am sure we can for you, Mum?

"That's very polite and grown up of you. Will you join us?"

The twins were absolutely delighted but they continued the game. "I think we both would like that very much."

So they all sat down to a very good lunch. After lunch, the twins went outside and lit the fire to heat the hot water. Jim and Emily did the washing up. When Emily thought they were safe, she gave Jim a hug and said, "I feel really bad leaving you in your hour of need."

"Don't worry. You and I have had more fun in two nights than many couples have in a lifetime. I will never forget 'Miss Perky Tits'." He gave one breast a gentle squeeze and, luckily, turned back to the sink as the twins came in.

After lunch, Jim took them to a small waterfall in the forest. He had brought with him a four foot long harpoon which he had bought in Mombasa, together with an old scuba diving mask. In his pockets, he had stuffed four bin liners.

The waterfall fell into a crystal clear pool. Jim made them all cut holes in the bin liners for their arms and head. Then he showed them a secret way, through the rocks and foliage so that they could get right behind the waterfall. Obviously, they got wet but the bin liners kept off most of the spray. They could look through the falls to the sunlight. The twins were delighted with such a magical place. Then Jim got them lying on their tummies looking into the pool which formed behind the waterfall. They could see trout swimming there. When they put on the diving mask and put their faces in the water, they could see much clearer. When Jim took the mask he also took the barbed harpoon. He jabbed it in to the water and harpooned a trout. He hooked it out of the water. He estimated that it weighed over a pound. After a few missed jabs the twins, and Emily, had managed to harpoon one each. The twins were ecstatic.

They had a really good supper. Emily cooked the trout beautifully. They all helped, as there were three fires to keep stoked up. Then they all had baths and they sorted out the sleeping arrangements. The twins were going to sleep in the spare room, with the twin beds, where they normally slept when they stayed. Emily was going to sleep in Jim's bed. *'How Jim and Emily wished they could share it together but they both knew that was totally impossible.'* Jim was going to sleep in the living room, on the large camping mattress which was the same width as the Landrover. There was a lot of laughter before they went to bed as Jim turned off the generator when Emily and the girls were not expecting it. They all pretended to be terrified but, in fact, they found it hilarious. Jim found a bottle of Amarula, a cream liqueur made in Kenya. They all had a glass which pleased the twins. Jim made up the fire and they all went to bed.

Emily woke to hear a moaning sound from the next room. It was obviously Jim, starting to have a nightmare. She longed to go to him but she dreaded the twins finding them together. She knew she would not be able to stop herself from making love to Jim. They both would be mortified if the twins found them. The moaning stopped. Emily thought. *'Thank goodness, it does not seem to be a bad one.'* She drifted back to sleep. As dawn was just breaking she woke again. All was quiet but she needed a wee, so she crept out into the living room. She was initially horrified. Jim and the twins were lying on the mattress, mainly covered by a sleeping bag opened up like a duvet. They were lying on their sides like spoons. She breathed a silent sigh that they all had their pyjamas on. Jim had an arm over Emma and was cuddling her back and Amy, in her turn, was cuddling Jim's back. They were all fast asleep. As she was sitting on the loo she thought, *'As a mother, she should wake them and make a real fuss but then would that not be more harmful.'* She crept back to Jim's room, leaving the door slightly ajar. Surprisingly, she went back to sleep and woke to hear them talking. They were obviously all close together as the voices were quiet but, if she listened hard, she could hear the conversation. The thing which immediately struck her was that the twins were not talking together as a pair like they normally did but as individuals. Jim was saying very little in a very strained voice.

"Why is it so wrong, Jim for us to be cuddling up to you?" said Emma.

"You were obviously starting to have a nightmare and, as soon as we cuddled you, you stopped moaning and slept peacefully. I know I kissed the back of your neck but why is that so bad?" added Amy.

"It is just that you are grown up girls now and you should not be sleeping with men like me."

"You do talk a lot of rubbish, Jim. It is not like you are going to serve us, like the bull does to the cows at home?" said Emma.

"I don't want to frighten you Emma, but some men would," replied Jim.

Emma replied, "Well, you are not some men. I trust you. You would never hurt me or Amy."

'Oh well,' thought Emily. *'Perhaps it is for the best to have a kind teacher like Jim. All the same, I don't think this conversation should be happening with them all lying together in bed, even if they have their pyjamas on.'* She would not have been quite so relaxed if she had heard Emma and Amy talking, a little time later when they were alone taking Lucy for a walk.

"I think it is rather nice having a man cuddle you," said Emma.

"Oh yes," replied Amy. "I felt all tingly when I cuddled Jim's back. I enjoyed gently rubbing my breasts against him even with my pyjamas on."

"It was lovely feeling his hand actually holding my breast. I really had the hots then."

"I felt his 'willy' from behind and it was really hard. I think it would hurt a little if he pushed that inside me."

"I think you are right. I could feel it hard against my bottom. I wriggled and opened my legs a little. It was a lovely feeling with it against my pussy. I wish I had been naked."

"Too right! Oh well I am sure we will get another chance when we get home for the holidays. Poor Jim, he must be so sad and scarred to make him have such horrible nightmares."

Meanwhile, back at the house, Jim was lighting the wood stove. He had already put wood on the outside fire, which was still just alight. Emily was still in her nightie and came up behind him and hugged his back.

"I was very jealous of the twins being able to sleep with you, last night." Jim turned and kissed her.

"I'm sorry. I promise I did not know they were there until we woke up."

"I know you didn't. I heard you talking together. It was all very grown up. They are no longer children. I think it was you who told me that your Mother used to say, 'children are only lent.' I think that is so true. It is the same with me you know. I have lent you my body and that night was wonderful but it must not happen again. I do wish I could help you with these nightmares. Your subconscious must be very troubled."

"Emily, you are a lovely person and a beautiful girl. I will get over my problems. In fact things were getting so much better until those bloody lions on Christmas Eve. That brought everything back. That memory is very fresh but time is a great healer. We will keep in touch and I am sure I will still lust after you but I will totally leave you alone. I won't come rushing down to the coast. I still bloody well want you, you sexy kitten."

They had a long kiss and broke apart when they heard the twins returning. They all had a leisurely breakfast but it was soon time for them to leave as, although they did not have to check in until 6.30pm, for a night flight, they had to drop the car at a friend's house at Machakos and then get back to the airport. The twins gave Jim big hugs and Emily gave him a kiss. The twins promised to write from boarding school. Emily said she would keep in touch. Jim was devastated when they drove away. He went back into the house to clear up. He went into his bedroom and was putting his pyjamas under his pillow and found a photo. It was Emily, wearing her Christmas shirt without her bra. It certainly was very see through! On the back she had written, '*To my darling Jim this is a Polaroid picture, as I had not time to get any developed over the holiday period. It will fade. I truly hope your nightmares will also fade. Keep it by your bed as a talisman, to make them go away before the picture does. You have stolen a part of my heart. As the song goes*

"OH WHAT A NIGHT." In fact it was two lovely nights. From Miss Perky Tits.' The photo made him smile and lifted his spirits. He had plenty of jobs to do, so he was not that depressed when Katana returned. Jim welcomed him and asked him about his weekend. Apparently, all was well at his home. Jim told him about his visitors and said how he had missed him.

That night was one of the worst ever. Jim felt dead in the morning but he managed to eat a good breakfast and then got immersed in his work. It would be wrong to say Jim was constantly depressed but certainly he was not 'A Happy Bunny'. His relationship with Annabel did not really work out, as they had Manda and Julia never letting them be on their own, in the limited time, Annabel was home from Nairobi.

His work continued to go well and he really enjoyed learning about elephant's teeth. He kept fit and continued to train with Ed. The nightmares continued and so he was constantly tired. His determination kept him going. He was never actually suicidal but life was not good.

Chapter 45

Fiona

Sunday 4th December 1966

Fi was heart-broken when Jim left. It had been the most wonderful three weeks of her life. However Jim had been right, saying they should not write to each other. If she had been always looking for a letter she would have been a complete wreck. As it was she survived by just knuckling down to her job which, compared with many jobs, was quite interesting and she tried to enjoy life at home. Her brothers came to realise that now she was no longer a silly girl she had her uses. She was very gregarious and, therefore had lots of girl pals who she had been at school with and lived locally. Her brothers were growing up and looking for girlfriends although, in Fi's eyes, they still spent an idiotic amount of time watching football.

Fi still kept up her running. Her family did not like her running at night, on her own but Fi maintained that she was quite safe if she ran where there were street lights. She would run really quite long distances, dreaming of Jim. Gradually, she came to realise that actually running made her feel more lonely so, with a big effort she started playing hockey with Margaret and Jean who she had been at school with. Neither of them had boyfriends and so they decided to play mixed hockey, with the idea of meeting some boys. Because Fi was so outward going and actually very pretty, the boys always made a big fuss of her. Many of them were actually Jim's age and were quite mature but, somehow they never were quite interesting enough for Fi. She did go out on dates, but she was always careful how close she got to any of them. She found it really difficult as, if she did not let them kiss her they said she was frigid. Equally, although she found some of them quite attractive, she was always thinking of Jim and so somehow they were never that attractive.

Margaret and Jean were always waxing eloquently about their latest boyfriend. They pretended to have been intimate with some boy or other but Fi knew, by the way they talked that they were still virgins. There was no way she was going to let on how lovely it had been with Jim. Fi had trusted Jim not to let her get pregnant but she certainly did not trust these other boys.

Gran was marvellous. Somehow, she seemed to sense Fi's problem. She realised with all of them that Fi did not really find them attractive as she never brought them home. Gran just encouraged her to go out and have fun. She said it did not matter if she did not have a boyfriend she could still have a good time.

One Friday evening, two of her brothers were going out to the pub to meet their pals. Fi asked if she could come. They were hesitant, saying it was only the lads and anyway she would take too long to get ready. "Rubbish," said Gran, "go up and get ready quick sharp, Fi." Fi scampered up to her room. It was a warm July evening and so she put on a thin, tight black sweater and a really short black skirt that she had bought the previous Saturday afternoon. She knew she looked rather tarty but she thought, *'what the hell.'* In her haste she laddered her tights and found that she did not have another pair. Oh dear she would look even more like a tart now. As she had no time she hardly bothered with any make-up which, she thought, at least would soften her look a little. Actually she looked stunning. She had a good figure and great legs. The black emphasized her strawberry blond hair. The boys were waiting at the bottom of the stairs. They did not even bother to look at her but commented she had taken an age. Gran whispered, "Well done, that was quick! The other lads won't be able to keep their eyes off you."

Gran was right. Fi made a marvellous impression when she came into the pub and that's how she met Malcolm Bennet. Fi's brothers had been right, it was an all boys night out. There were six of them but, of course they weren't boys any longer. They were all over twenty and Fi reckoned some were nearer twenty five. *'Well,' she thought. 'I am eighteen and thanks to Jim, I am no longer virgin. I am up for a bloody good night out.'* She obviously had made a good impression as there was a rush to buy her and her brothers a drink. Fi would have loved a glass of wine but thought she would show them so she had a pint like her brothers. There was general chat about football. Malcolm sidled up to Fi. She did not remember him but he introduced himself and said he was friendly with her brothers. He looked a kind chap but was by no ways good looking. He was about five foot ten inches and looked fairly strong. Apparently, he was training to be an accountant. He lived in Edinburgh with his parents. Fi found him fairly easy to talk to but she also found him a little serious. He was not like Jim, who had made her laugh all the time. Fi made a mental note not to compare every man with Jim. She must move on. A rather greasy guy, called Dean, bought the next round of drinks. He made a point of buying Fi only a half as he made a thing about the fact that she had not drunk much of her pint. Fi just smiled and said that was fine. She was determined not to make a big deal about it. Actually, she did not want to drink a bellyful of beer. Dean obviously thought he was a lady's man and claimed that he had taken a girl out, during the week, who had worn an even shorter skirt than Fi's.

"Good for her," said Fi.

"Of course, she was up for it," said Dean.

"Oh really," replied Fi, "Up for what?" Dean went rather red and did not reply.

'Oh dear,' thought Fi, *'I am getting like my mother already.'* Then she smiled and said to Dean, "Sorry, I am a little defensive as I am the only girl in the group." Sadly that did not placate Dean. Fi thought, *'well, at least I tried.'* However, her retort had the desired effect and there were no more chauvinistic comments.

Otherwise it was a good evening. On the way home, Fi thanked her brothers for taking her. They both laughed and commented that her skirt would be mentioned for many a night and they were glad she had put Dean in his place. Fi thought no more about it but she was surprised when she got a phone call from Malcolm, asking her out to the pictures the next Friday. He was obviously pleased that not only did she say she would be delighted to come but that also, if it would help, she could meet him at the cinema. Malcolm was obviously shy and she realised that, as he knew her brothers, coming to the house would have been very stressful.

Fi laughed to herself as she was getting ready to go out and thinking about what she was going to wear. She never worried when she was with Jim. Jim had obviously found her very attractive and he said so all the time, in an open way not in a smarmy way like that chap Dean. Fi could not stop herself thinking back on how she had even gone to Jim's room, while he was asleep, and stripped off and got into bed with him totally naked. What can she have been thinking about? She had been so wanton. Fi was proud of her appearance as she walked to the cinema. Her skirt was not as short as the previous Friday night and, this time, she had some tights on. However her top was a bit low cut. I wonder what he will think.

There he was, waiting for her. She realised that he was extremely nervous as he could not really look at her and kept wringing his hands. *'He must be at least five years older than me, maybe even more. This is going to be hard work,'* thought Fi. However it was not as bad as Fi had imagined. It was a good film. Malcolm behaved impeccably. He did not even hold her hand, and although she offered, he paid for everything. They ate 'Fish and Chips' on the way home so there was not difficult silences, like there might have been in a restaurant.

So their relationship slowly developed. However hard she tried, Fi could not stop thinking about her relationship with Jim. On her second date with Malcolm she could not stop herself giggling when he asked if he could hold her hand. He was slightly put out and asked why she was laughing. Fi just could not stop giggling, as she was thinking that Jim had had his hand in her knickers when they had only known one another for two weeks. She did not know what to say, but mumbled that, perhaps asking her if he could hold her hand was slightly old fashioned. It took Malcolm over a month before he gave her a peck on the cheek. However he was kind and it did mean she got invited out. Her brothers got used to her coming out with them, as they thought of her as Malcolm's responsibility. Fi started inviting some of her old school friends. Initially her brothers moaned but, when she invited Jess, who had really big boobs and wore a low top, they were a bit more enthusiastic.

After a time Fi's Mum suggested she invited Malcolm for a family supper. Fi said she would certainly ask him but she thought he would be terrified. Gran overheard the conversation and said, "I will try to encourage him, dear."

Fi laughed saying, "That's what I am worried about, Gran. You will probably ask him if he has had his wicked way with me."

"Well, has he?" asked Gran.

Fi gave a lascivious grin and said, "I wish!"

"Fi, go and wash your mouth out with soap," said her outraged Mother.

"I was only joking Marjorie," said Gran, "I remember, when Malcolm was younger, he would not say boo to a goose."

So Malcolm came to a family supper. It was a disaster. He hardly opened his mouth. When one of Fi's brothers' teased him, saying he hoped Malcolm had honourable intentions towards Fi, Fi had put her hand on his thigh to encourage him. He jumped, as if he had a ferret up his trousers. Gran saw and knew exactly what Fi had done. When Malcolm had gone home and Gran, Marjorie and Fi were tidying up, Marjorie said what a nice boy Malcolm was. Gran said, "I am sure he is but he is a little serious for my taste."

Fi thought. *'Trust Gran to understand but maybe I can change him.'* That was a very foolish thought. Women often think men will change and they rarely do. Men often think women won't change but they often do.

Their relationship lasted several months. It did not really end but just fizzled out. When, eventually, Fi suggested to Malcolm that they stop going out, he seemed relieved. Fi thought she ought to have been sad but, in fact, she felt liberated and started to laugh again. She was always thankful that she was a cheerful person. In fact although sometimes her job as receptionist, at the School of Tropical Veterinary Medicine, was boring she could somehow always make the most of it.

Fi actually had quite a good singing voice, so she decided to learn to play the guitar. She had an evening class once a week and she used to hide away in one of the empty laboratories, during her lunch hour and practice. As she got more proficient she became more confident and did not mind if people listened to her singing and playing. It was during her lunch hour, when she was playing that she met her next boyfriend.

She was strumming and singing to herself one lunch hour when she suddenly realised that she was not alone. She stopped and swung around. There, behind her, was this 'drop-dead-gorgeous' guy.

"Please don't stop. I was enjoying it. You play and sing very well. Your haunting voice would sound wonderful out in the bush, in my home in Australia."

"Thank you. You are kind. Are you over in Scotland on holiday?"

"No, I am the houseman at the vet school. I am here to learn really but I do a little undergraduate teaching. Are you a student?"

"I wish," replied Fi. "I am only the receptionist at the School of Tropical Veterinary Medicine. I just come here and practice in my lunch hour."

"Well, I am pleased to meet you. I am Darren Joslin. I can tell, by your accent, that you are Scottish. Are you a local girl from Edinburgh? It is a beautiful city."

"Yes I live in Edinburgh with my family. You must not know many folk. Would you like to come and have supper on Sunday with my family? I think you would get on well with my three elder brothers."

"I would love to. I am a bit lonely really as the Professor of Surgery works me hard and has advised me not to fraternize with the students as that will make it difficult for me to teach them. I think it is a load of rubbish. Such segregation would never happen in Australia."

"I am afraid you will find such type of nonsense is common, in Scotland. I must get back to work as my lunch is over. Have you any paper? I will write down my address. My grandparents live with us, so we eat fairly early. Will 6 pm be OK?"

"I hope so. I have to give a contact phone number. Can you write that down? I hope I am not called out. It is not very likely."

Fi went back to work with a strange foreboding. *'He certainly was good looking and seemed a nice chap. She had certainly been very forward, asking home for a family supper. Perhaps she was worrying unnecessarily. She could not stop remembering when Malcolm came to her home.'*

When she got home that night, she told her Mum and Gran that she had asked this Australian back for Sunday supper as he seemed lonely and she felt sorry for him. Her Mum took it at face value and said he was very welcome and, perhaps, the boys could take him to the pub or to football. Gran was not so easily fooled and asked Fi, when they were alone, if he was good looking. Fi was honest and said he was very good looking.

"I am glad" said Gran and said no more.

On Sunday night Darren arrived at exactly 6 pm with a bunch of flowers for Fi's Mum, who was thrilled to bits. Darren seemed to fit in well with the men folk and they were soon happily talking about sport, not only football but rugby and cricket. Gran took an instant dislike to Darren but she kept her counsel and said very little. It was arranged that Darren would meet Fi's brothers down the pub, on the following Friday night. He said no special goodbye to Fi and just said cheers to everyone and left.

When Fi and Gran were alone, Fi asked Gran what she thought of Darren. Gran was just rather non-committal and said she was not sure but he seemed very interesting. Darren made no effort to see Fi during the week. She even wondered if he would be bothered to come out on Friday. On Friday night Fi put on a new, very short skirt and a tight black sweater. Her brothers teased her and said she must be out to impress the Australian. There were lots of folk they knew at the pub but there was no sign of Darren. Her brothers after they had had a few drinks, totally forgot about him but Fi didn't. After she had had a few drinks, she became rather irritated and so had more to drink than she would have had normally.

When the evening was well advanced and everyone was well away, Darren turned up. He said he had been held up at the Vet School but he was very smartly dressed in a casual way. He accepted a drink from one of Fi's brothers but said nothing to Fi or to say he was sorry that he was late. Fi was past being cross and thought he certainly looked sexy. Eventually, Darren came over to talk to her. He stood very close to her and stroked her thigh and said it was a pity the girls in Australia did not wear skirts as short as this. Fi knew she should stop him but she was pissed and she rather enjoyed the feel of his hand. She giggled as she remembered Malcolm. Darren took this as encouragement and moved his hand up higher. Fi pushed his hand away and said, "Not in the pub, Darren, someone might see." Fi was too pissed to realise what she had said. She had inferred that she was quite happy for him to put his hand up her skirt but not in the pub. Actually, she was not really happy. Things were getting out of control. It was closing time. Her brothers assumed she was with Darren and did not wait for her to come out of the loo. Darren said she had no need to worry, he would walk her home. The chill night air hit her and she felt very drunk. She grabbed his arm and they set of in the direction of home. Somehow they missed their way and Fi found herself with her back to a big tree, in the dark, in the 'Meadows'. Darren started to kiss her passionately but she kept moving her lips away and saying,

"No, Darren. I hardly know you." His hands seemed to be everywhere she pushed them off her breasts.

"No Darren. Please let me go. Let's go home." She was very pissed but not that pissed and started to fight him off. She tried to scratch his face.

"Oh no you don't, you little whore. You have been asking for it all night with that skirt." Darren was almost sober and he was very strong. He held both Fi's wrists in one hand above her head, against the tree and reached down up under her skirt and ripped her tights and knickers. Fi screamed but he immediately held a hand over her mouth. He was behind her and he pushed her forward onto her knees so she hit the top of her head hard against the tree. Fi was half stunned. He still had his hand over her mouth. She tried to struggle and turn but he pushed her head down with his head. Then he entered her. It hurt so much but Fi was powerless as he thrust a few times and then grunted with satisfaction. Fi just collapsed on the ground sobbing.

After a few minutes she sensed he had gone. She got to her feet. Her head felt sore from the tree. When she bent down to get out of her torn tights and knickers she was sick. She managed to get her shoes back on. She found her handbag and managed to get herself together. What should she do? She just could not face going to the police. She knew if she told her brothers that she had been raped, they would take the law into their own hands and then they would be in trouble. So she just walked home.

Luckily she managed to let herself in without making any noise. The house was quiet, so she crept to her room. Once she had shut the door she turned the light on. She had a basin in her room. She bathed her face and looked in the mirror. Although she looked a mess, there were actually no marks on her face. There was a lump, under her hair on the back of her head. Her knees and feet were muddy and she washed them. With warm water, she gently washed her sore swollen vulva. Then she got into bed and quietly cried herself to sleep.

She awoke early. She felt like death. She felt humiliated. She felt defiled. She struggled into her running gear and quietly went down the stairs and out of the house. She hoped the rhythm of her running would give her time to think. However she felt too sore and felt too rotten to run. She walked home after a hundred yards. Maybe she had been a bit stupid wearing such a short skirt and getting drunk but masses of girls did that on a Friday night and they weren't raped. However she decided she was not going to tell anyone but she would somehow warn the girl veterinary students to be careful. She actually did not know any of them well. There weren't many, as there were many more boys. Most of the girls were rather plain but Fi guessed they were rather clever.

Her Mum was in the kitchen when Fi came in. She just called, "Hi" and said she was going to have a bath after her run. She had a lovely long bath and washed her hair. She cried as she thought of, Jim as she dried it with the hair drier he had bought. Eventually she put some clothes and make up on and went down to breakfast. Dad had gone to work and had given Gran and Grandad a lift to the shops. The boys were still in bed. Mum gave her a cup of tea and a bowl of porridge. She asked if they had had a good night out. She said she thought they must have done as they all made a real racket when they came in. Fi did not let on that she had not come in with the boys and just said she was sorry.

"I am sure it wasn't you dear," said her mother.

"Those boys sound like a herd of elephants. Did Darren come?" Fi said he had been very late, as he was working.

Mum said, "Such a nice lad. I thought Australians were normally rather brash but he seemed very sensible." Fi just bit her lip and then continued with her porridge. Fi spent the rest of the day either lying on her bed, pretending to read, or watching TV. No one seemed to notice anything wrong. Gran thought she looked a bit pale but thought she probably had too much to drink.

On Sunday, Fi went for a walk on her own and climbed Arthur's seat. She thought it would make her feel better but it made her feel more miserable.

Fi dreaded going to work but she knew she must, for the sake of other girls. If she was not brave enough to go to the police she must do something. During her lunch hour she walked over to the Equine Unit of the Veterinary School. There, she was lucky. There was a group of ten students, two of which were girls, standing round a horse. There was no lecturer in sight so, with her heart in her mouth, Fi walked up to them and asked if Darren Joslin was around.

"No, thank God," said one of the girls, "he has taken his swag-bag and gone back to Australia."

"Good bloody riddance," said one of the boys.

"Oh," said Fi, "I thought he was here for a year?"

"He was meant to be but there were so many complaints, about his bullying of the nurses and the lab-staff, that he was given the sack. He packed his bags on Friday night and left. The final straw was he was caught trying to assault Jenny the radiography nurse in the dark room on Friday afternoon. Old Miss Steel, who teaches radiography, made such a fuss that the Prof sacked him on the spot."

"It sounds as if everyone is pleased. Thanks for your help."

Fi turned and left. Initially Fi was furious that no one had warned her. However, on reflection, she thought how could they? She did not mix with the students or the other staff at the Vet School. The School of Tropical Medicine was a totally different unit. Fi was still very angry but now mainly with herself. How could she have been such a fool? Just because he was good looking and she had been a bit lonely, strumming her guitar, she had been fooled. She wondered why she was such a poor judge of character. First Malcolm, who was so dull and then this bloody Darren who was a thorough, on-going bastard. Well, she thought at least she had been right about Jim, her first love. She was a bit of a wreck but she would have been totally destroyed if she had been a virgin. At least now Darren had gone, and she did not feel she had any responsibilities regarding warning any other poor unsuspecting female. She went back to work, her lunch break over. She would never forget what had happened but she would let it fade in her memory. Thank goodness she had her family and friends around her.

Poor Fiona, life had dealt her another cruel blow. Her period was late. She knew, after a couple of days, what the problem was. She was pregnant. She went to a chemist and bought a home pregnancy kit. It confirmed her worst fears. However there was no doubt in her mind. She was not going to have Darren's child. She did not delay and immediately booked in at an abortion clinic. They counselled her carefully but she did not let on she had been raped but just insisted on a termination as quickly as possible. She said her grandparents lived in her house and they were elderly and the shock would jeopardize their health. It was a private clinic, so there was no delay. Fi did cry, when she drew out the money she had been saving. She had not really admitted to herself but she had been saving up for a flight to go to see Jim. Fi was a very sensible girl. First things first, she would have to start saving again. What she did not realise was, how terrible she would feel after the termination. She thought that, as she did not need to stay a night in the clinic, she would be fine. She had taken a day off work. She was allowed out at 3 pm but did not want to go home. She felt too weak to walk anywhere so she just went to the library and sat, pretending to read a book until, it was near to the normal time she would get home.

When she got home, she had a cup of tea with her Mum and Gran and then said she had a diarrhoea bug. She went up to bed with a hot water bottle and said she could not face any supper. Luckily she had booked two days off work so she spent the following day in bed. She felt weak and weepy. Luckily her mother believed the story about the bug. Fi was not so sure about Gran but Gran never said anything and kept coming up for a chat and bringing cups of soup or tea. Fi was actually really pleased to chat, as it took her mind off the abortion. She felt guilty causing Gran to worry but consoled herself that, although she had been foolish, it was that bastard Darren who was really to blame.

Interestingly, Gran did ask if Fi had seen him after the Friday night. Fi could be honest and say she had not but she knew he had been given the sack, for assaulting a radiography nurse, and had gone back to Australia. Fi said it was good riddance as, although she had thought he was good looking, he obviously was a nasty piece of work. Gran said she had not said anything but she had found him too greasy by half. "Your mother might have liked the flowers but that was about all he was good for," Gran said, with feeling.

The next day Fi still felt rotten but went to work and actually doing something worthwhile, made her feel better. She knew she was feeling better as she played her guitar quietly in her room after supper. Fi slowly improved, but it was two weeks before she started running again. That Friday night she felt a bit more cheerful and went out to the pub, after supper with her brothers. When she went to the bar to help her brother with a round of drinks, she interrupted his conversation with the barmaid, called Jean. She was a nice jolly lass who everyone liked. She was saying how many hours they had to work as a rather drippy girl, called Rachael had given her notice in two weeks ago and they had not managed to replace her.

Fi asked, "Would they let me do the job?"

"I'm sure they would," replied Jean, "As soon as I get a moment I will tell Rodney, the manager that you are interested. I would love you to take the job."

Rodney was rather a tired, white faced forty year-old who looked as if he had never been out in the sun. Fi was glad she had a rather low top on, as her chest seemed to impress Rodney. She got the job, starting the next night. On their way home, her brothers decided they were proud of her but they thought the rest of the family would not be so happy. They were right. Mum and Dad were not pleased but Gran spoke out quite forcibly. She stressed that, as the pub was their local, everyone knew Fi and would be kind to her. Gran grabbed hold of Grandad's arm and said it was about time he took her out to the pub occasionally, so that they would sort out any man who was too familiar with Fi. Gran then turned to Fi's brothers and said, "It is a poor job, if you big strong lads can't look after your little sister." So it was agreed and Fi started bar work, as well as her job at The School of Tropical Medicine.

Fi really took to the bar job but she began to get very tired as the autumn days became shorter. Part of the problem was the bus journey out to Easter Bush. If she missed the 5 'o'clock one home, she hardly got anytime for her tea before she had to go to the pub. Gran came to the rescue. She persuaded Grandad to buy a car for all four of the grandchildren. Fi could have it to drive to and fro to work and the boys could share it in the evenings. It only took Fi two minutes to walk to the pub in the evenings so she did not need it. This arrangement worked very well. Fi even had enough energy to go running at the weekends. On a Saturday night she made extra money at the pub by playing her guitar and singing. Her whole family was very proud of her.

However Gran still worried about her. Gran knew Fi was very attractive to men. She had an excellent figure. Her face, framed with her strawberry blond hair, was very striking and yet she did not have a boyfriend. In fact, Gran realised that she did not seem to want one. She was quite happy, laughing and joking with men in the pub. She often flirted with them but she never encouraged anything further.

One breakfast when Gran and Fi were alone, Gran said,

"You must have saved up a bit of money now, as you have been working at the pub for over a year. Why don't you take a holiday in Africa and go and see Jim. Both of you were very sensible when he first went, but you are very much more mature now and I think you would find Africa fascinating. Think of all those wild animals." Fi admitted that she had been saving and, in her dreams, she had been thinking of seeing Jim again but she said,

"He is likely to have a steady girl-friend; he might even have a wife and children."

"He might," agreed Gran, "but somehow I don't think he has. Anyhow, if you wrote, he could always say no. I would like to know what has happened to him. I think something has gone wrong in his life. I remember him saying he got long leave after two or two and half years. That should have been due a few months ago. I am certain, if he was back in England, he would have contacted you." Fi started to cry silently. She gulped in air and said,

"Oh Gran, I also have been worrying. Many months ago I overheard John David talking to Jim Anderson, at work. I did not hear who they were talking about but John said, 'He is bloody lucky to still be alive'. Somehow I am sure they were talking about Jim."

"That settles it," said Gran, "You find his address tomorrow, at work, and you write to him. If you don't, I will." Fi hugged Gran,

"I do love you, Gran."

So it was that Fi found his address in Kenya, at The Veterinary Office, PO Kinangop and wrote a newsy letter. She ended by saying, she really hoped that Africa had worked out for him. She said Gran had urged her to go out to see what Africa was like, as there were so many good wildlife programs on TV. She said all the family sent their love, particularly her and Gran.

629

Gran told Fi that she must be prepared for disappointment and that she should now forget she had written and just continue as normal.

Both of them were amazed that there was a reply, in just over two weeks. It arrived on Saturday morning. Gran saw the airmail letter. She quietly took it up to Fi, who was still in her pyjamas, having had a lie in.

"I will just go and make you a cup of tea dear."

It was a full five minutes before Fi dared to open it. It was better than her wildest dreams. She had only written Dear Jim. He replied, *My Darling Fi. I was so delighted to get your letter. Do come out to Africa. It is a magical land. I had a real set back some months ago but have slowly got back to normal. It is the land which has kept me going. I used to live on the coast, with wonderful beaches which you would have loved. I now live upcountry at 8500 feet. It is quite cold at night. I live in a very primitive way with only electricity, for a couple of hours, in the evening. However, I know you are a tough Scot and won't mind roughing it. I can't wait to see your beautiful face and hear your soft Scottish voice. I know I have aged markedly in the last three years so I won't expect you to still fancy me but I know we will always be friends and will be able to share some laughs. I am not short of money, so I can easily pay your airfare. I have money in the UK. Let me know the cost of the fare and I will send you a cheque. My old cook, called Katana, a lovely old chap, knew something was up when I came home with your letter. He said I looked like an elephant that had found a field of maize. I have not stopped smiling since. So don't delay do come Love to all the family, particularly Gran and you. Jim.*

Gran came in with a cup of tea. Fi handed her the letter. Gran said,

"I can't read your letters."

"Of course you can. Without your encouragement, I would not have got it."

Mum came in to find Gran and Fi hugging each other with tears running down their faces. She said, "What's up with you two?"

Gran blurted out, "I am so happy for Fi but I am also sad as I know we are going to lose her. Grandad will have to use up some of his savings to take us all out to Africa to see her." Mum looked totally perplexed. Fi explained,

"I have decided to go out to see Jim, in Kenya. He has just asked me in this letter."

Mum replied, "Well I was only saying to your father, last night, that it was time you had a holiday. You work so hard with your two jobs."

So it was agreed, Fi was going to Africa. She thanked Jim for his really kind offer to buy the airline ticket but she said she would get it, as she had saved up. However, she stressed that she would expect champagne like their first night. Jim asked whether he should try and track down Archie Ledbetter to come as well. He also suggested that Fi get an open return ticket, as she might like to stay longer. This meant a lot to Fi, as it totally confirmed that he really wanted her to come out. Jim was useless when asked about clothes to bring. There was a discussion with Mum and Gran. Mum was appalled when Fi stated that, "the least she wore, the more Jim would like it!" As it was Mum totally disapproved of the miniscule bikini and the very brief shorts? Gran's only comment was,

"If you have got it, flaunt it." Fi thought a rucksack was a must, as she was sure there would be a lot of carrying to do. Certainly, some of her hair products were heavy. She definitely was going to take the hair drier Jim had bought. There must be some electricity!

She got a travel agent to book her ticket for the 4th April 1970, from Heathrow to Nairobi on BAOC with an open return. Mum, Dad, Gran and Grandad insisted on seeing her off, so it was decided they would make a trip of it and stay in London for two nights, leaving the three boys in charge of the house. It was quite a squeeze on the journey down, on the 3rd April, but they made it in fine spirits and had a good meal out in the evening. They did some shopping on the 4th April, as they did not need to be at Heathrow until 5.30pm. Fi and Gran were fairly relaxed, but the other three were as excited as children. Dad and Grandad particularly wanted to see the airplanes taking off and landing. Once they got to the airport Mum got quite apprehensive. Fi was glad she had not told her that Jim had a pilot's licence and would be flying her around. Mum would have had a fit. The big moment came when Fi checked in her heavy rucksack and then realised that, with her small travelling bag, she was about to leave them all. Mum burst into tears and Fi could see Dad was upset. She hugged them all and promised them she would write soon. She went through the barrier and turned to wave and somehow managed to back into a silver-haired man who was travelling on the same flight. Fi apologised profusely.

"Don't worry my dear, as I checked in directly after you we are probably seated next to each other." They compared landing cards and, sure enough, he was right.

"I know it is a little forward of me but can I buy you a drink, as I think you are travelling alone and I expect it is your first time to go to Africa?"

"I would love that," replied Fi. "I have saved up for this trip, by working as a barmaid in the evenings as well as doing a normal job, so it will be great to be on the customer side of the bar." They went through immigration together and were soon standing next to each other at the bar.

"I am going to have a Gin and Tonic. Would you like the same? It will stop you getting malaria," laughed the man. "Actually, that is an old wives tale. I gather malaria is really bad at the Coast. You must be careful if you go down there."

"I hope to, eventually but the friend I am going to meet lives upcountry so we will go there initially, as he has to work but he hopes to get some local leave soon. Yes, a Gin and Tonic would be lovely. My name is Fiona King but everyone calls me Fi." Fi held out her hand.

"My name is Fred Day. I will get some teasing from my three daughters, who are meeting me at Nairobi, as they always say I manage to sit next to a pretty girl on the flights when I have to come to UK on business. They are about your age. I am sure they would like to meet you. What is your friend's name?"

"Jim Scott," replied Fi. Fred laughed

"That explains everything. Jim lives only thirty miles away from us. He is not only our vet but he also is a good friend. I always wondered why he did not take out one of my daughters. Now I have met you, I know why. You are very pretty." Because of the gin, Fi blushed crimson.

"I am so sorry, I have embarrassed you. To make up for it can I buy you some supper? We won't get any food, on the plane, until well after ten." Fi had recovered her composure and replied that she would love some supper but it was not right that he should pay. Fred said.

"Rubbish, I insist." And so it was, that they had a most enjoyable meal. Fred was a mind of information and a great raconteur. Fi could understand how he could chat up the girls but he was a real gentleman so she had no worries. He was very complimentary about Jim. He said what a really good vet he was, not only with the animals on the farm but also with the polo ponies and the dogs. He also said what a kind man he was. He said his daughters went to watch Jim play rugby and they said he seemed to be absolutely fearless on the field but was a really polite young gentleman off the pitch.

"Well, it stands to reason he is brave. It is rumored that he killed a lion with a 'panga' in the NFD but he never talks about it."

"What!" said Fi aghast? "What is a 'panga'?"

"It's an African machete. It is about so long." Fred demonstrated a length of about thirty inches with his hands.

"My God," said Fi, "that explains something I heard at work. However could he kill a lion with little more than a long knife?"

"It's a mystery to me," said Fred, "he never talks about it. He obviously has not said anything to you. I am sure he will, when you are together."

It was a very enjoyable meal but the story about the lion really worried Fi and she could not get it out of her mind. She was glad she had met Fred, as they had to get off the plane when it stopped in Khartoum to refuel in the middle of the night and she would have been apprehensive if she had been on her own. As it was, she managed to buy Fred a cup of coffee and they shared a bar of chocolate. Fred had suggested it, because he said the Sudanese coffee was extremely bitter. He was dead right. After Khartoum, Fi was really tired and managed to get some sleep. In fact, she was still asleep when they turned the cabin lights on and brought breakfast. Fred did not wake her but made the stewardess leave her breakfast on Fred's fold-down table, so that she could have it when she woke. Fi was grateful, as she was hungry when she awoke and her mouth was dry so the orange juice was nectar. Fred warned her when they were getting towards Nairobi, as he said there was always a rush for the loo and it was as well to get in first. Once again Fred was right. She was doubly grateful, as she managed to smarten herself up. She wanted to look her best when she met Jim. She suspected Fred was being modest and a typical father and that his daughters would be pretty. Fred was certainly a good looking man.

The sun was well up and the air was warm, when they disembarked at Nairobi. It seemed to take forever to get through immigration, collect their bags and go through customs. Fi had real butterflies and she was glad she was with Fred. He tried to carry her bag but Fi insisted she would put it on her back. She wanted to look a real traveller. They came through the swing doors and there was Jim. Fi could not stop herself and she ran to him. He had his arms wide open and was laughing. "How can I hug you with that great pack on your back?" he reached up for her face and kissed her.

Fred's daughters were all hugging him. Fi noticed that there did not seem to be a Mrs. Day. Holding Fi's hand, Jim introduced Fi to Amanda, Annabel and Julia. Fi had been right they were pretty but she was sure Fred had been telling the truth and Jim was not involved with any of them. Surely he had not been celibate for three and a half years?

The Day's were all going to go into Nairobi first and leave for their home in Naivasha, which was fifty miles away after lunch. They invited Jim and Fi to join them but Jim declined their kind offer but said he had got to get back to work or he would be in trouble.

"What about poor Fi," cried Amanda, "She will be exhausted." Before Jim could say anything, Fi said, "I will be fine. Jim will look after me."

Amanda said, "He had better. I don't think he really looks after himself. Look at him." Fi thought '*Amanda was right. Jim had lost a lot of weight. Although he was tanned, his face had a gaunt look and his clothes were old and dusty. However I love him to bits and I will soon fatten him up*'.

"Don't be so unkind 'Manda', he is fine," said Julia. "Is there a game in Nakuru on Saturday?"

"No," replied Jim, "we are away in Kitali. It will be great to show Fi some of the country."

"Have a good time and make sure you win," chorused the girls as Jim, holding Fi's hand, led her away to his Landrover.

634

Chapter 46

Getting together again

Tuesday 5th May 1970

Fi thought as they walked to Jim's Landrover, '*Manda is right, Jim certainly does not look 100%. I hope the TLC I am going to give him will help.*' As if reading her mind, Jim said,

"I am sorry I look so rough but I am on the mend now. Just seeing you, has made all the difference. You look a million dollars. How did you manage that after such a long flight?"

"Having Fred Day with me was a big help, he is a lovely old man. Is there a Mrs. Day?"

"Sadly not she died in childbirth having their fourth child. Manda only just remembers her. My guess is she was a lovely lady, if the three daughters are anything to go by."

Fi squeezed Jim's hand.

"Were you not tempted by Julia, she obviously fancies you? Don't give me any bullshit about saving yourself for me. As far as you were concerned I could have been a married girl in Edinburgh, with children."

"Good old 'down-to-earth' Fi," said Jim, as he held the door open of the Landrover for her. His dog Lucy did not move from the middle seat of the vehicle but just wagged her tail vigorously. Jim said, as he got in,

"This is Lucy, my top guard dog, who loves everyone to death."

"Hello Lucy," said Fi, "You may not be a good guard dog but you certainly are very well behaved and very gentle." She stroked Lucy's ears.

"Well," said Jim laughing, "Have you left Mr. Right and two kids back in Edinburgh?" He pulled out of the car park and expected to hear Fi laugh but there was silence. He looked round and saw tears forming in her eyes. He went to pull off the road.

"Don't stop, Jim, please don't stop. I am just being stupid." Jim reached across Lucy and squeezed her hand.

"Down please, Lucy, I would like your new mistress to come and sit in the middle seat close to me."

"I am glad you haven't changed Jim," sniffed Fi, "You are even polite to your dog. Do I put my legs either side of the gear stick?"

"You will give me a lovely view if you do, in that short skirt," laughed Jim.

"Yes, you certainly haven't changed," said Fi smiling through her tears. Jim noticed however that she did not hesitate but put her right hand on his bare leg and lifted a long leg up and over the gear stick. She squeezed his thigh and said,

"Now you, Jim Scott, pay attention to the road and stop trying to see my knickers. They are black and match my suspender belt, if you are interested?"

"Ooh la la," said Jim. "That sounds really sexy."

"No, it is just sensible, as I thought tights would be hot on the plane," replied Fi. "Now these stockings are hot so, if you will kindly keep your eyes on the road, I will take them off." Jim did as he was told but somehow, feeling her moving next to him was even more erotic than looking. Then Fi really laughed.

"Look at Lucy, Jim. I think she is more embarrassed than I am." Sure enough Lucy was looking straight ahead with her nosed pressed against the windscreen.

"Now, can you put these in your pocket? And DO NOT get them out and blow your nose on them! It is the sort of damn fool thing you would do, in front of Manda, and she would think we had stopped for a quick romp on the road side."

"I promise I will behave," said Jim, "I am also sorry I upset you back there. I guess you were very fond of someone in Edinburgh. I won't pry. Don't say anything if you don't want to. I am afraid there is a skeleton in my cupboard which I am reluctant to talk about."

"I won't pry either, Jim," replied Fi, "but can I ask, were you in love with her?"

Jim answered, "Yes, I was absolutely devoted to her and I am sure she was devoted to me."

"Thank you, Jim, for being so honest." Fi sat looking like Lucy, straight ahead, at the colourfully dressed Africans on the sides of the road, as they made their way through Nairobi.

Fi broke the silence. "I would like to talk about why I cried. I have not talked about it to anyone at all, not even Gran. I trust you Jim. I always have and I know you will never tell anyone. I was raped." Jim's reaction was what Fi had hoped for but not what she expected. There was no anger in his voice, he just said,

"You poor, darling. You know I love you and you know I always will." He reached behind her with his left hand and drew her as close as he could to him. Tears were pouring from Fi's eyes but she made no effort to stop or to wipe them. In some way she knew they were cleansing her. She told him the whole story. When she finished, Jim just stroked her neck and said, "You did just the right thing not telling anyone but you must have felt so terribly alone".

"I did." said Fi, "but now I feel so much better, having told you."

"I am glad you did," said Jim. "Africa is here to heal you. Look to your left." Fi gasped. There was the Rift valley, in all its glory, stretching as far as the eye could see.

"That is one of my favourite views," said Jim. "Sadly I rarely stop, as you get set upon by hoards of Africans wanting to sell you those sheep skins. They are a nonsense, as they are not cured properly and soon start to rot and smell. However I have got several properly cured fleeces, so you will have warm feet when you get out of bed in the morning." They wound their way down the escarpment, on the wonderfully engineered road, to the bottom of the Rift valley past the little chapel built by the Italian prisoners of war, who built the road in the 1940's.

Fi was lost in the view and Jim was lost in his thoughts about what Fi had told him. When they reached the bottom, Jim broke the silence. "This road carries on all the way to Uganda; in fact we will be getting near to Uganda on Saturday, when we drive to Kitali to play rugby. We have to turn right here and climb up again to the Kinangop, which is a plateau above eight thousand feet, at the foot of the Aberdare Mountains which rise behind my house up to twelve thousand feet. I am afraid this is where civilisation ends, we are now on dirt roads. They are dreadful at the moment as the rainy season has just started."

637

They had not climbed very far, before Jim told Fi to look to her left. He said she should be able to see Lake Naivasha. He told her that's where the Day's had their farm.

"You still have not told me, why you have not made a play for the lovely Julia," asked Fi.

"I am not sure why exactly," replied Jim. "I like all the family and they have been very kind to me. I have had a very hard knock and have had a difficult job coping with it. I needed to be on my own somehow. I have not been a recluse but I have rather thrown myself into my work and the rugby. Sadly, although I am enjoying the work as always, I am not playing rugby well," said Jim ruefully.

"You certainly have lost some weight," said Fi thoughtfully, "Let's hope I can help to build you up." She sensed that Jim did not want to say anymore. She thought he would, when the time was right. What Fred Day had told her about the lion must have something to do with his reticence. She changed the subject.

"Now tell me about Katana, your cook, I hope he will like me. I hope he won't mind having a girl about the place."

"I am sure he will like you. I have noticed that he has been tidying up more than usual. He has put clean sheets on your bed, in the spare room. A veterinary pal called Ed often stays mid week. He lives 45 miles away but we often stay at each other's houses, to train together. You will meet him in Kitali. He is an excellent player."

'So Jim had not presumed he would sleep with me,' thought Fi, *'I think that is kind. I hope my story will not put him off.'*

"I hope I have not stopped Ed coming," said Fi.

"Don't worry, he will be staying down with his girlfriend, Liz, in Nakuru. Katana does not smile a lot but that is his nature. I am afraid he does not speak any English but he understands quite a bit. You will like him. Now, we have got a bit behind. I know Manda said I must look after you but, do you mind if we go straight to a road-side crush and see some cows. If I get working hard we will see all the cows, call in at the Veterinary Office and then we can go home. You will be exhausted."

"That is fine," replied Fi, "it is all so new and exciting, I don't feel tired at all. Will I be all right in these clothes?"

"You will be fine," answered Jim, "I bought a pair of wellies for you. I hope I remembered correctly. You are a size 6, aren't you?"

"Jim, you are impossible. I will look a right trollop in a short skirt and wellies!"

"No one will mind and I think you will look rather sexy."

'*I don't think I need worry I am sure Jim still wants me,*' thought Fi.

They arrived at the roadside. There were about thirty people milling about, both men and women, the latter were wearing brightly coloured dresses. They all greeted Jim. A tall, very black man, in a khaki uniform, stepped forward and shook Jim's hand. Jim introduced Fi in English. "This is my girlfriend Fiona King. Fi this is Heron, who is the local Veterinary Assistant for this area. He has organized all these cows to come for me to examine today. I come here every two weeks. Heron bowed slightly and shook Fi's hand. "Welcome Miss King," said Heron gravely.

"Do call me Fi, Heron, you will have to help me, as I am new to all this."

"Let's get into our wellies Fi and we can get started?" said Jim.

Fi thought '*there seem to be cows everywhere but they are really quite small, compared to cows at home. They also seem to be very tame,*' as a child dragged a reluctant animal up to the crush.

Each cow was brought to the crush and Jim, having soaped his arm in some water provided, proceeded to push first his hand and then his forearm into the cow's rectum. It did not seem to hurt the cow. Fi was, at first, horrified and then was fascinated. After each examination there was a chat between Jim, Heron and the owner. Sometimes, the cow would receive an injection. Once Fi had got the hang of what was going on, she came nearer to the crush. Some cows seemed to have a vulval discharge. The vulva was cleaned with the soap and water and Jim would carry out a vaginal examination. Usually, he would pass the tail to Heron to hold. When Heron was getting an injection ready for a cow, Jim said, "Fi could you just hold her '*mkia*'?"

What's her '*mkia*'?" asked Fi.

"Oh sorry, Fi, it is her tail. Do you want to feel inside a cow?"

"Yes, I will have a feel after you feel in the next one." '*What would Mum think of me now, wearing a short skirt and wellies and going to put my arm up a cow's arse?*'

Fi climbed over the crush, in front of Jim. She said quietly to Jim, "now half of Africa has seen my knickers."

"Lucky Africa," said Jim,

"Now, this cow has had a vulval discharge. Heron will clean her vulva and you slide your soaped hand into her vagina keeping your hand up on its roof, so that you don't hurt her urethral opening". Fi guessed, *'that was where she has a wee.'*

"Now push your hand in a little further and you will feel a hard thing with a hole in it. That is her cervix. Now come out and look at your hand to see what the discharge is like. Good, it is mainly clear with just the odd flake of pus in it."

Jim turned to Heron and said, "She does not need any treatment. It is best if she has one more heat and then she should have AI the next time."

"What is AI?" asked Fi.

"It stands for Artificial Insemination," replied Jim. "In this area there is a lot of breeding disease and so we prevent its spread, by not using any bulls."

"Now, you can put your hand in her rectum. If you feel the vagina, below your hand, you can work your way forward until you feel a hard lump, which is the cervix."

"She is pushing back towards me," said Fi with alarm.

"Don't worry, just let the poo come out around your arm? That's it. Now feel the cervix again. Now, in front of the cervix you can feel a sausage like thing. That is her uterus. Can you feel that?"

"Yes," said Fi who had completely forgotten her reservations.

"Now, a little bit further in you will feel a split? That is the uterus splitting into two horns." Fi nodded. She was frowning with concentration. Jim thought she looked enchanting.

"Now, this is the most difficult bit. Slide your hand along one of the horns and you may feel another hard lump, about the size of the top joint of my thumb." Fi nodded.

"That is an ovary. Well done, we will give her a rest now and I will tell you in the Landrover about what you will find on the ovary, so that you will know next time."

Fi was delighted with her lesson. It somehow made her feel closer to Jim.

They kept on working until they had examined all the cattle and the owners and helpers had moved away to their homes, or 'shambas', as Fi realised they were called. In fact Jim explained to her 'shamba' actually meant garden or smallholding. A home was a 'Nyumbani'.

Fi was surprised that she did not want a wee nor was she hungry. She imagined it was because she was hot. She was glad she had taken her stockings off. Her feet felt seriously strange, swimming in sweat in her wellies. They said goodbye to Heron and got back into the Landrover.

Fi sat in the middle seat and kicked off her wellies, as Jim opened the front air vents as they got going. Fi then put her feet up on the top of the dash board and said, "I don't care if the whole of Kenya can see my knickers. I have got to cool down. Sorry about my smelly feet. Actually, the air rushing up my skirt is rather nice." She turned to Jim and said,

"If you go any faster I think I will come 'on bull'. What would Gran say if she heard me say that?"

"I think she would roar with laughter." replied Jim, "But I think your Mum would pretend to be shocked.

They arrived at The Veterinary Office, which was, in fact, an old European Farmhouse and had been taken over, when the whole area had been bought from the settlers, by the British Government and then sold as small plots to the Kenyans who had worked on the big farms. Although the garden was rather wild, Fi was enchanted by the profusion of flowers, which not only were marvellous colours but also had a beautiful scent. Jim introduced her to all the staff. Timothy, the office boy, made them each a cup of African tea. Fi thought, 'this is a little different,' However she recognised the digestive biscuits which she was offered to dunk in the tea. Most of the conversation was in English but there was some 'Swahili'. Fi was determined to learn Swahili and also to learn about animals and veterinary work, not only because she thought Jim would like it but actually because she was fascinated. In fact this place was not dissimilar to Scotland. A little warmer perhaps but now, as the afternoon had worn on, there was a nip in the air. Lucy had stopped panting and was stretched out on the concrete. Fi obviously was tired, as she almost nodded off, but woke immediately when Jim said, "Manda will be cross with me, it is time I got you home. You must be worn out. It is exactly ten miles to my house. As we have not had any rain for a couple of days it will only take twenty minutes. If we have had a lot of rain it can take hours, but the Landrover has never let me down yet. I have always got home even if I have had to put on the wheel chains." He was pleased, as Fi always sat in the middle seat next to him. It was nice to feel her thigh. She never moved it away, even if he was sweaty.

Jim explained that there would be plenty of hot water as Katana kept a wood fire going under a 44 gallon oil drum, which heated the water up beautifully. He said Fi must be careful, as often the water was 'red hot'. He said he would start the generator as it was getting dark, so they could have some light for a couple of hours but he then had to turn it off, as the Government only paid for that much diesel. It was actually meant to pump his water up to a header tank and was not really for electricity. He said Katana cooked on a wood stove and the refrigerator worked on paraffin. Fi thought, *'am I on a different planet? Surely paraffin is used for heating not cooling down.'* Once again, Jim read her thoughts and explained how the paraffin burnt, under a little chimney at the back of the refrigerator and caused expansion of the gases which cooled the thing. However, he explained it was pretty 'hit and miss' but Katana was magic with it. It seemed the secret was for it to be on an absolutely flat floor.

Jim also explained that, as there was two and a half hours of day light left, he normally went for a run, but he totally understood if Fi just wanted to collapse.

"I would love a run. I have bought my running stuff."

"Wonderful," said Jim. "You must be really careful as we are seriously high up here, at 8500 feet above sea level. You must go steady and not over tax yourself until you have been here for three weeks and acclimatised." Fi laughed,

"You sound like Gran. I will be fine." Secretly she was delighted. *'He obviously wants me to stay.'*

Fi was delighted with Jim's house. It was small but newly built, in a pine forest surrounded by a little grass. There did not appear to be neighbours for miles. Perhaps he was lonely. Somehow Fi did not think Jim had a problem with that. Katana came out to greet her and shook her solemnly by the hand. Then, strangely he did not let go of her hand but led her by the hand into the house saying something to Jim in *Swahili'*. Jim translated, "Katana says he really welcomes you to this house. He says he hopes you will stay forever." Jim blushed and added, "He says, ever since I got your first letter I have been a different man and I have been getting my strength back." Fi burst into tears and stepped forward and hugged Katana. She looked at Jim and could see, for two pins, he would cry. Fi then said, "Come on old worry guts lets go for this run. I bet Lucy would like that."

"She will indeed," said Jim, "I will go and get your rucksack."

Katana went back to the kitchen and Fi had a look around. There was one big room which was a combined dining room and sitting room. There was a fire burning in a big fireplace. There were masses of book shelves, so it almost looked like a library. Fi thought, *'that's what he does in the evenings.'* Jim's bedroom was pretty Spartan but there was a large walk in wardrobe and just a double bed. The bathroom had a massive bath, a shower, a basin and a loo. Fi's room had two single beds and a dressing table. Only one bed was made up. Jim came in with her rucksack.

"You certainly travel light. I suppose girl's clothes don't weigh as much as boy's. I remember your running gear is delightfully skimpy."

Fi said, "I know it is a bit cooler than in the heat of the day but it still feels pretty hot, can I run in just a sports bra and no shirt, then my tummy will be cooler?"

"Yes, that will be fine. You could run naked here. We won't see anyone!" laughed Jim.

"You wish," answered Fi.

So they set off, with Fi setting the pace as she had done years ago in Edinburgh. Lucy showed her the way, as obviously this was the normal path into the trees. Jim followed behind admiring Fi's bottom in her shiny running shorts. He thought to himself, *'we are going a bit fast. I hope she will be alright but I don't want to be a worry-guts'.* The path started to climb up the hill. Lucy had gone ahead and had set up a Lesser Kudu, which came bounding back towards Fi. Fi suddenly saw it. She stopped dead, turned and gasped,

"Jim, what's that?" Then she fainted into his arms. Jim lifted her up and carried her to a nearby tree stump, which he sat on. He sat her on his knees and hugged her. He thought he should actually lay her down flat on the ground but, as he went to lift her up, her eye lids fluttered and she moaned. "Oh Jim, what happened?"

"Don't worry, you just fainted from lack of oxygen. How are you feeling now?"

Jim hugged her to him as he felt her strength returning to normal. Fi hugged him back.

"I'm sorry for being such numpty. That dark brown thing frightened me and then I felt myself going. You must have caught me as I have not scratched my knees like I usually do, when I trip when I am running."

Jim had his arm around Fi and his hand on her tummy which he was rubbing gently. Fi nestled her face into his neck and said, "That's nice. Don't stop." She wriggled her bottom in his lap and definitely felt his cock hardening. She wriggled some more and said,

"That's nice too. Can we stay like this for a couple of minutes, until my head clears?"

Jim replied, "We won't run anymore but just walk home as you still look as white as a sheet. By the way, that dark brown thing was a Lesser Kudu. They come out of the forest. You will see them grazing the grass around my house, at day break."

"Well, it scared the pants off me. Heavens knows what a Greater Kudu would have done?" said Fi.

Jim laughed and explained that she would have to go hundreds of miles north to find Greater Kudu on Marsabit Mountain. Fi was definitely sure Jim had an erection now. She kissed his neck.

"Come on, you still look pale so I will carry you home." He picked her up in his arms. "Don't be such an old goat. Put me down. I will be fine but it would be nice if you kept your arm around me for a few steps." So they made their way home, initially with Jim's arm around Fi, and then just holding hands.

When they got into the house Jim said, "You have the first bath. You had better not lock the door, in case you pass out again."

"Oh yea," smirked Fi, "I know that trick!" Then she laughed.

"I remember the first time I had a shower, in your room at Braid's hill hotel. I did not lock the door. I knew I could trust you but I just wanted to test you. Actually, secretly, I wanted you to come in. I was such a brazen little hussy." She reached up and kissed him on the lips.

"Actually, I still am." She walked into the bathroom and turned on the taps in the bath. Jim shouted after her. "Leave your water in. I will have a wallow after you."

"Will do", replied Fi. '*Well,*' thought Fi, '*I think I am getting the picture. He likes me, he wants me, he may even love me, he wants to look after me but I think he has a problem with me seeing his body. I am lucky if he had not made love to me before that bastard Darren, I might have had all manner of hang ups.*'

Fi felt so much better after her bath. She got out and, wrapping herself in a towel, walked through to her bedroom, calling,

"The bath is all yours. It is still pretty hot. I am like a lobster, but I feel so much better. Can I borrow another towel? I can then wrap my hair in it. Then, when you start the generator, I will risk the hair drier." Jim came into her room with another towel.

"Sorry, it is a bit threadbare." Fi walked up to him to take it. She grinned and said,

"I think you specialise in small towels, so I can't cover myself." Jim went bright red and spluttered, "I will jump in the bath."

When he eventually came into the living room, fully clothed but with shorts on, as in the day time. Fi was in her pyjamas kneeling in front of the fire drying her hair. Fi asked,

"Will it matter if I eat supper in my pyjamas?"

"Of course not," replied Jim.

"I will go and start the generator. Then you can have a go with the hair dryer. We will turn off most of the lights, then there should be enough power. Fi was delighted the dryer worked and so she had supper wearing one of Jim's sweaters and with dry gleaming clean hair. Katana had lit a candle on the table so that when the generator died and the pump had finished filling up the water tank, it was quite romantic. Fi reached for Jim's hand.

"I am sorry, I didn't take your advice to go slowly when we ran. I will be more careful in future."

"Don't worry about it; I was just rather worried about you, at the time. Now in the morning, at day break I planned to go and catch two trout for our breakfast. Fresh like that they are really delicious. You have a lie in but don't worry if I am not in the house when you wake. Katana will hear you get up and make you a cup of tea."

Fi realised she was still holding Jim's hand. She squeezed it and said,

"I know I fainted today but really I am not a wilting violet. Can I come fishing with you tomorrow? My brothers would never take me because they said it was a boy's thing and I would get bored."

Jim looked straight into her eyes and said, "I would love you to come. I will ask Katana to bring each of us a cup of tea in the morning. You can wear that sweater, as it will be quite chilly. There have been one or two mornings, where there has been a frost lately."

Jim carried away the rest of the dirty plates and Fi heard him talking to Katana in the kitchen. He came back in with two cups of coffee and set them on the small table near to the fire where there were two easy chairs.

"Let's drink them near to the fire?" Jim sat down. Fi thought, '*I do love him but something has really hurt him. I wish I knew what.*' She walked over to the fire as if to sit in the other chair and then sat on a sheepskin rug at his feet and lent back against his bare legs. She took off his sweater.

"Thanks for lending that to me. This fire is lovely and warm. Can I pass you your coffee?"

"Yes, thanks."

Fi got onto her knees, turned and gave Jim his coffee as well as a lovely view of her breasts. She went back to leaning on his legs and thought, '*I wonder if they still turn you on?*' Her unspoken question was answered, as he gently stroked her neck. They sat together like that for some time, in fact probably a long time, before Jim sighed and said,

"Come on, we must be away to our beds, you must be doggo?"

They both got up. Fi picked up Jim's sweater, turned and blew him a kiss and then went to bed.

Chapter 11

The fishing trip

Wednesday 6th May 1970

Fi slept like a log and only awoke when she heard Katana at her half open door saying softly,

"Hodi," Fi sat up as she said, "Oh my tea thank you so much Katana." He put it on the floor next to her bed, as there was no bedside table and left the room. Fi flopped back down and went back to sleep, only to awake again with horror to hear Katana and Jim speaking softly. She was out of bed in an instant and called out,

"Just coming." Fi took off her pyjama bottoms, could not find her shorts so just put on the skirt from yesterday. She could not find her knickers as there was only a little light from a hurricane lamp in the hall. She left on her pyjama top and quickly put on Jim's sweater. She grabbed her tea which was still quite warm. *'At least I can't have been asleep long,'* she thought. She remembered her running shoes and socks were in the hall. She scuttled into the bathroom for a wee and to clean her teeth. Then she put on her socks and was lacing up her shoes as Jim came through with a fishing rod.

"Cor, you were quick. Well done. I hope we catch some trout after all your efforts. *'Twendeni'.*"

Fi grabbed his arm. "I guess that means 'come along'. You are just like my father. Lead on." Jim had said they would go at day break but it was still dark. Somehow Jim could see in the dark or he knew the way so well that he led Fi off, without a torch. They followed a narrow track. They kept climbing. Fi kept up close behind him. In fact, so close that, when he stopped, she bumped into him. They both said sorry at the same time.

"How are you feeling? I don't want you to pass out again. I have come prepared. I have brought a stethoscope to listen to your heart."

"Jim Scott, you do talk a lot of rubbish." Then Fi saw that he was taking a stethoscope out of his pocket. In one movement she took off her pyjama top and his sweater. Jim looked up to see her bare chest.

Fi smirked, "Satisfied? I think, doctor, you should have a nurse present. I hope the end of that thing is not cold." Jim's bluff had been called. With a shaking hand he bought the head of the stethoscope just below her left breast.

"Well, what is my heart rate?" said Fi.

"Steady, at about 70. That is fine," said Jim.

"Right," said Fi, "Let me listen to yours." She felt up his chest from under his shirt. She thought '*My goodness that must be the scars from the lion. No wonder he does not want me to see.*' Fi made no comment except laughing and said, "Either you can't be very well acclimatised to altitude or you must really like my tits. Your heart rate is over a 100. Now, if you have seen enough, I will put my pyjama top back on as I am getting chilly."

Before Jim turned to lead on up the hill, he said, "I know why I love you. You are such good fun."

The African dawn was quickly coming up as after another quarter of an hour, they came out of the forest and crossed over 30 yards of grass to a six foot high, chain linked fence. '*How embarrassing, I haven't any knickers on and he will expect me to climb over that.*' Jim had not quite read her thoughts correctly. He knew nothing of the lack of knickers and so thought she was worried about the height.

"Don't worry, we don't have to climb it. I have found a small hole under it. The fence was put up to keep humans away from the water. This is Sasamua Dam and it is the water which supplies Nairobi. Some old settler brought trout out from the UK forty years ago. No one comes here now, except me so there are hundreds. Here is the hole. I will hold the bottom of the fence up for you."

Fi asked, "Should I go under on my tummy or on my back? It looks pretty tiny."

"I always go under on my tummy," answered Jim

"Hmm," said Fi. "I think my bottom is bigger than my tits so I will go under on my back. You had better hold that fence up."

She lay on her back, with her arms above her head, and started wriggling under the fence. She was doing very well until the waistband of her skirt snagged on the fence. The button pinged off. Fi laughed. "You are a lucky boy, Jim Scott. You only saw my naked top half in the semi-darkness. It is now light and I am going to give you a full frontal. I could not find my knickers this morning!" Fi wriggled her way through and stood up. Jim followed her but on his tummy. He got up onto his knees and looked up. She was standing right in front of him, smiling and lifting up his sweater.

"I wish I had a camera. The shocked look on your face was worth recording. Actually your sweater is quite long, so I am perfectly decent for fishing. My excuse for not wearing knickers, is that I thought I would be in the water. Can I swim?"

Jim replied, "My darling, I do not advise swimming as it is freezing cold. You have got beautiful legs."

"Thank you, kind Sir. Let us go and catch breakfast. I am getting hungry."

It was only another thirty yards of grass to the water's edge. Jim explained that the level was high, as the rains had been good so far. He explained that, as they were fishing for breakfast, they would cheat and use a thing called a spinner fly. This was a bright, shiny, spoon-like thing, which revolved as it went through the water. Behind it was a feather, 'or fly' which hid the three barbed hook.

"I will show you how to cast, if you stand in front of me."

"As always, I trust you Jim. If it was any other boy, I would be worried he was going to put his hand up under this sweater."

After two or three casts, Fi said, "What a pity, I seem to have got the hang of it. I was rather enjoying having your arms around me. Come on, take over and be really manly and hook a trout for us."

Sure enough, on his third cast, Jim felt a bite. He handed the rod to Fi.

"Go on, reel him in."

"Wow," said Fi, "He is quite strong. Won't the line break?"

"Sadly, I don't think he will break the line, he is not that big. However, look, he is definitely big enough for one breakfast." Fi pulled him out of the water and Jim took the hook out of his mouth.

"You keep casting and I will find a stone to put him out of his misery."

Even before Jim was back, Fi had hooked another one.

"That is fantastic," said Fi, "I can't wait to tell my brothers. They will never believe me."

"Hopefully, your Mum will not believe that you did not wear any knickers because you thought your pretty bush would attract the trout!"

"Don't you dare tell her, Jim, although you could tell Gran, on the quiet, she would certainly see the funny-side? I think I will tell them how well you are looking after me. How you insist on groping my tits, just to check that my heart is not racing. In fact, if it was warmer, I am sure your hand would make my heart race. Come on, we have got to get under that fence yet. I hope that will make your heart race.

When they got to the fence, Fi decided to go, like Jim, on her tummy. She did not ask for any help but she felt a gentle hand on her bottom, pushing her through. When they were both through and standing up, Fi said, "Thank you, your hand was most helpful." She kissed him on the lips, picked up her skirt and started walking back.

When they got back, Fi went straight to her room so that Katana would not see her naked legs but she guessed that he would not be bothered. Jim had told her he had two wives, seven children and two grandchildren.

The trout were absolutely delicious. Katana even put some almonds on them. Jim said he also liked them with horseradish, if he remembered to buy it in Nakuru.

That day, they had two separate road-side crushes to go and visit. Soon Fi was really in the swing of it and was injecting the cows, handing out the small antibiotic tubes to the farmers with cows with mastitis etc. She loved it and felt she was really part of the team. Katana had sent them off, with some sandwiches and a flask of tea for lunch. They had this on a patch of grass, under a tree near to the road, on their way to the second road-side crush. The noon-day sun made it really quite hot. Fi had brought a floppy sun-hat as she did not want to get burnt. It was great fun, Fi learnt so much about cows and about Kenya and its peoples. Jim never stopped teasing her and Fi did not miss an opportunity to flirt with him. They got to the Veterinary Office at 3.30 pm. The staff made a big fuss of Fi, who was immediately given a seat and a cup of tea. Lucy was given a bowl of water which she managed to slop everywhere.

A young clerk came through from the DO's office to say that Dr Jim was wanted on the telephone. When Jim came back he said it was Julia Day on the phone. She said there was a club night at Naivasha club, that night, and she had invited them to come. Fi laughed and said, "Manda must be worried you are not looking after me or the lovely Julia is still trying to get your attention." Jim scoffed but Fi noticed he went a little pink.

They went home promptly at 4.00 pm. They had another cup of tea and soon Fi was wallowing in a lovely deep bath. She was amazed at how dirty the water was. She let it out and started to run another for Jim. She shouted out to tell him. He came through to the bathroom to find Fi, naked, leaning over the bath saying,

"I am so sorry, I have used most of the hot water. It is only tepid." Jim spluttered and was about to back out when Fi turned and said, "Don't be an old goose. You have seen it all before. Don't deny you like what you see." She pointed to the large bulge in his shorts. She kissed him on his red face and walked past him to her room saying, "Do you mind if I take yet another towel to drape over my top in the Landrover, as I know there is no power yet and my hair will have to dry in the wind."

Jim opened and shut his mouth a couple of times and then managed to say,

"That is fine, I will get one."

So they set off on the forty minute drive to Naivasha, with the vents all open and Fi's beautiful hair blowing in the wind. She had a towel over her shoulders and a cardigan in her lap. She was sitting in the middle seat close, to Jim, who regretted that he had put on long trousers. Fi had a short skirt on, but no tights. He thought, *'it would have been great to have her bare thigh rubbing against mine.* Once again Fi somehow seemed to read his thoughts as she said, "I love sitting close to you. It suits Lucy as she likes the outside seat."

At Naivasha Club, the Day family were sitting at a table with their drinks, near to the door. They heard peals of laughter from Fi. Julia turned to Manda and said, "It sounds as if Jim is looking after Fi OK. I don't think you need worry."

They all greeted one another. Fi kissed all the girls. Fred asked, "What is the joke Fi, can you share it with us?"

"I suppose so but it is rather rude."

"Go on," they all said in unison.

"Well, Jim and I went fishing very early this morning. Katana woke me with a cup of tea but I immediately went back to sleep."

"You must be exhausted," said Manda, "I knew Jim would not be looking after you."

"She does not look too exhausted to me," said Julia, "Do be quiet Manda, we want hear this rude story."

Fi continued, "As you know, there is no electricity at Jim's house."

"What did I say," chipped in Manda, "Fi should be staying with us."

Julia stamped her foot. "Shut up Manda. Please go on Fi."

"Well I awoke the second time, to hear Jim talking quietly to Katana. I was in a panic as I thought Jim might go without me. I jumped out of bed, took off my pyjama bottoms but could not find any knickers so I grabbed a longish skirt and thought, Jim will never know. Off we go up to Sasamua Dam. Dawn had come by the time we reached the high fence, which surrounds the dam and keeps people away. I was in a panic as I thought there would be no way of getting over the fence without exposing myself. Jim somehow read my thoughts but obviously did not know what I was really worried about and said don't worry Fi we don't have to climb the fence, there is a hole under it. So, with Jim holding up the wire, I wriggled very demurely under it on my back. The waist band of the blasted skirt caught on the wire. The button came off and I was naked from the waist downwards."

Manda gasped and Annabel and Julia sniggered.

"As you can imagine Jim has been teasing me about it all day. As we came into the club, he tickled me in a very inappropriate place. His excuse was that, as I was so forgetful, he wanted to check I had not forgotten my knickers this evening."

They all roared with laughter except Manda who looked very shocked.

Fred Day said, "I don't blame you Jim, with a skirt that short, I imagine knickers are pretty vital."

"Father that is very rude" rebuked Manda.

However everyone else laughed.

The evening was a great success. Fi and Jim were giggling together as they drove home. Jim said, "I think Manda was totally shocked, by your story about the knickers. Everyone else thought it was hilarious, particularly Fred."

Casually he let his hand rest on her bare thigh. Purposely, Fi wriggled her bottom so her skirt rode up. Jim was driving so he did not see. Then she wriggled her bottom forwards so his hand moved up her thigh, but not as high as she wanted. Fi thought, '*to hell with it,*' as Jim did not take the hint. She placed her hand over his, lifted it up under her skirt and under the elastic of her knickers around her right leg. Jim got the hint at last and slowly massaged her pubis. She reached up and kissed his ear and whispered,

"I have been dreaming of your hand being where it is now, for the last three and half years."

Fi wanted Jim really badly when they reached his home. However, she still realised that there was something holding him back and so, to avoid rejection, she gave him a passionate kiss and said, "Can you wake me in the morning? I will need about half an hour to get myself together for the weekend, before we leave? Good night, my darling. Today has been wonderful." She went to her room and got into her pyjamas. When she thought Jim had finished in the bathroom, she slipped out, cleaned her teeth and had a wee before going to bed and having a good nights sleep.

Jim was dressed, when he brought her a cup of tea in the morning. Fi languidly stretched and asked if there was time for breakfast. Jim said there certainly was and Katana would have it ready in a few minutes. He was just making them some sandwiches and drink, for the journey. Fi felt good and quickly got dressed. She asked Jim if he had a small overnight bag she could borrow, as she did not want to take her big bag. Jim found one which he left on her bed while Fi was in the bathroom. Fi quickly threw stuff into it which she thought she would need and came in for breakfast. Katana had made a 'Full English'. Fi tried out her new Swahili,

'*Asanti sana*' (Thank you very much). Katana gave her one of his rare smiles. Jim teased her, as she was so hungry.

The journey up to Kitali was fascinating for Fi. Everything was new. She loved the Roschild Giraffe which they saw, as they turned off the Uganda Road to go to Kitali. Actually, what with the Landrover being a bit slow and Jim talking a lot and not driving very well, they cut it a bit fine for the game. Luckily, Jim saw Jean

653

Mackinnon and her two young sons. He introduced Fi to her and rushed into the club to change. Jean's husband was also called Jim and, like Jim Scott played for Nakuru.

Although Fi was the youngest in her family she was a natural with kids, particularly daring young boys. She soon had them climbing trees, which was much to Jean's relief, as the boys had been non-stop scraping in the car on the long drive up. Soon they were joined by seven or eight more kids of similar ages, who were Kitali kids. Fi really enjoyed getting them playing all manner of games. She did not even notice when the players came out on the pitch to warm up. Jim came out with his friend Ed. They jogged up and down the pitch together. Ed said,

"Wow, who is that stunning girl playing with all the kids?" Jim looked up and realised that he was talking about Fi.

"She is the girl I told you about, who I haven't seen for three and a half years. I did not know she was so good with kids."

Ed said. "Well, you have got a real beauty there. Come on, we better get ready and beat these buggers!"

It had been a great party after the game. Fi really enjoyed the robust rugby boys, who reminded her of her brothers. In fact she realised that, as an unknown girl she scared the pants off them. Fi could see what Jim meant about the paucity of single European girls.

In the last week, she had seen how well Jim got on with Africans and how well respected he was. Equally, she could see that it would be impossible for him to have an African girlfriend. Fi realised that, as far as the rugby crowd could see, Jim had not had a girlfriend for years. He had told her that he had had an affair which had ended eight months earlier at the time that he had been gored by a lion but they had kept it very secret. They certainly had, as none of the rugby crowd was aware of it. Fi could see that many of the girls were really fond of him, in a sisterly way. Fi was standing with one of them, called Liz, who seemed particularly close to Jim as did Liz's boy friend Ed. They were obviously an item. Ed and Liz did not live together but spent a lot of time socialising in Nakuru. Fi knew that Ed and Jim used to meet mid-week to train together. Jim and Ed had gone off now to get drinks. Liz turned to Fi and asked, "Have you known Jim long?" Fi answered truthfully that they had only known each other just over three years ago, for three weeks when Jim was on a course in Edinburgh. She was out to visit him and had only arrived four days ago "Oh," said Liz, "you certainly seem to have made a big difference to him. He is back to his old self, laughing and dancing. He played a really good game today much better than he has done all this season. He has never been right after being gored by that lion. It really seemed to get to him. Today he seems to have shaken that off."

Ed and Jim returned with the drinks. Ed asked,

"Who are you staying with tonight?"

"Mike, I think," replied Jim.

"I think he has gone," said Liz, "You will never find your way to his house in the dark, so you had better follow us and stay with Tommy." They stood chatting. It was obvious that the party was winding down the music had stopped and at least half the people had left, although there was still a hardcore of drinkers at the bar. Suddenly, a young 'kijana' (Teenaged boy) popped up and said, "Tommy sent me in to get you people. He is just leaving."

"Shit," said Ed, "we must go or we won't find our way either."

They gulped down their drinks. Jim said, "Help me Fi, I just can't drink any more or I will be sick." Fi knocked back the rest of Jim's beer and earned an admiring glance from Ed.

Ed said, "Come with us, Fi. Jim will get your bag." They all rushed out to the car park and bundled into Ed's car. They could just see tail lights of a car as it disappeared, a couple of hundred yards from the club gates.

Liz said, "If you want a bed for the night, you had better drive like a loony, Ed."

Ed set off at a cracking pace to try and catch Tommy.

"What about drink and drive?" whispered Fi to Jim in the back seat.

"No one really bothers about that, in Kenya." Fi clung to Jim as Ed raced round the corners and slid on the 'murram' roads. Ed managed to stick with Tommy, until Liz called out. "Turn left, that's his drive." Ed, very wisely, did not turn left but braked hard and then backed up. They turned up the drive and could see Tommy's dust in the lights. Tommy had already gone in as they got out of the car. There was one hurricane lamp lit on the verandah. They struggled out of the car, thanking their lucky stars that they were still alive. Fi realised her over-night bag had been left in Jim's Landrover. She only had her handbag. She didn't say anything as she did not want to make a fuss.

As they came in, Tommy was lighting some more lamps. He looked up and, when he saw Jim and Fi, said, "Oh dear I thought you were staying with Mike. You will never find your way back in the dark. Not to worry, I will show you what I have got." He led the way with two lamps. At the first room he said, "I only have two bedrooms, this is my room, and there is a spare bed in this room and a single bed in the small room, down the corridor past the kitchen."

"We will have the spare bed in your room Tommy. Will you two be OK in a single bed?" said Liz.

"Oh yes, fine," said Fi, "the nearer I am to this old codger the better then I can kick him when he snores." They all laughed. Jim was so grateful to Fi for not making a scene. Tommy said,

"You can find your way, if you take this lamp. There is a *'choo'* (lavatory) and basin in the room next door. The water is fine to drink." Jim and Fi found their room. It was tiny, other than the small bed there was just a little table. There was not even a chair. *'I think maybe it is lucky I haven't got a bag,'* thought Fi. *'I would have nowhere to put it.'*

"You keep the lamp, Fi and use the bathroom. I will go and have a pee in the garden." Fi replied, "Fine." As soon as he had gone she looked in his bag for some tooth paste and brush. She took the lamp into the *'choo'* and had a wee. She left the door open to help guide Jim back. She was cleaning her teeth when he returned. She handed him the brush and said,

"I hope you don't mind, I seem to have mislaid mine."

"Sorry, it is even more Spartan than my house and it is bloody cold."

Fi just hugged his back and whispered, "Not as cold as on Arthur's seat." She grabbed the light and said, "Race you into bed." Jim raced after her and rummaged in his bag for his *'kikoi'*.

"Beat you," sung out Fi. Jim turned to see her stark naked getting into bed.

"Hey, that's not fair, you haven't put on any pyjamas."

"No, because some numpty left my bag in the Landrover. Come on, I need warming up." Jim stripped off and jumped in beside her.

In the lamp light Fi could see the dreadful scars on his chest and upper thighs. She could see that the lion had also scarred his penis. She pulled the sheet and blankets over them and started to kiss the wounds on his chest.

"You poor boy, you must have been in agony. She kissed him lower down and felt that some of his pubic hair was missing and there was just scar tissue. She looked up and saw he was crying softly. She cradled his head in her breasts. He sobbed,

"If only I had been quicker I might have saved her." Fi was perplexed. She knew he had been gored by a lion and had nearly died but he had not said anyone else was involved. She just kept hugging him to her and stroking his hair. She did not say anything but thought, he will tell me if he wants to. She somehow knew he wanted to talk and that he had never spoken of it to anyone else. He moved his head up to her ear.

"Claire wanted a crap and took the '*panga*' and some loo-roll into the bush. I was packing up the camp. She screamed. I rushed into the bush to find this lion on top off her. I grabbed the '*panga*' which she had dropped, and hacked at his head. I must have really hurt him as he flew at me with his mouth open. I rammed the '*panga*' into his mouth as he knocked me over. I hit the back of my head on a rock and was out cold. I came round trapped under the lion. I was too weak to move him and passed out again. The next thing I knew I was in the back of a LWB Landrover with Claire beside me. I could tell she was dead. I was desolate. I have never been able to tell anyone else. I just pretended to have had a memory loss. I am sorry for breaking down. You kissing the scars, just pushed me over the top."

Fi said, "I am honoured that you have told me. You obviously loved her with all your heart." Fi started to cry, "I am so sorry for you." She did not know what to do or say. She did what seemed natural to her. She guided his mouth on to one of her nipples. He sucked hard. Fi had to move him on to the other nipple as it was so swollen it ached. She rolled onto her back and parted her legs. His damaged penis was only half erect. She had become moist with him sucking her nipples. She guided him into her. She wrapped her legs behind, over his lower back. He kissed her tenderly,

"Thank you Fi, I think it is you who is having your wicked way with me. It feels so good."

"My darling, it is good for me too." They both moved together as if they had been lovers for years. They fell asleep in each other's arms. The bed was so small, if Jim hadn't been lying on top of her, one of them would have fallen out. They awoke quite soon and both needed a wee. The lamp was still alight. They both had a long drink of water and got back into the warm bed. Jim fondled Fi as he kissed her. She gave him every encouragement, opening her legs wide and thrusting against his hand. Soon he was inside her and, to Fi's pleasure, kept thrusting. She kept pushing against him. Then he came but pulled himself out of her. "God, you will get pregnant."

"No, I won't you numpty I am on the pill. Put that 'willy' back inside me." It was way too late as there was semen all over the sheets.

In the morning, after a leisurely breakfast while the boys were clearing up the breakfast things, Fi brought their sheets through and said to Liz, "Where is the washing machine?"

Liz laughed and said, "Tommy has not got any power so there is no washing machine. Throw them into the bath and his cook will wash them on Monday. Were you OK in that tiny bed?" Fi replied. "We were a bit pissed but we were OK the first time, but missed the second time, hence the messy sheets!" Liz impulsively hugged Fi. "Kenya needs girls like you. Jim needs a girl like you." Fi smiled, "I think I need him and he needs me.

The End

Abbreviations

AHITI Animal Health International Training Institute
AI Artificial Insemination
BOAC British Overseas Airways Corporation
BTT Blood Testing Team
CBPP Contagious Bovine Pleural Pneumonia
CMJ Christopher Martin-Jenkins
DC District Commissioner
DO District Officer
DVO District Veterinary Officer
DVS Director of Veterinary Services
EATRO East African Trypanosomiasis Research Organisation
EAVRO East African Virus Research Organisation
ECF East Coast Fever
ETA Estimated Time of Arrival
FMD Foot and Mouth Disease
FO Foreign Office
G & T Gin and Tonic
GK Government of Kenya
GSU General Service Unit (Part of the Kenya Police Force)
HQ Head Quarters
KMC Kenya Meat Commission
LMD Livestock Marketing Division
LN Lymph Node
LO Livestock Officer
LPO Local Purchase Order
LWB Long Wheel Base usually a Landrover
LWR Long Wave Radio
MOD Ministry of Overseas Development
MOW Ministry of Works
NAC Nakuru Athletic Club
NFD Northern Frontier District
ODA Overseas Development Administration
OIE World Organisation for Animal Health
PA Personal Assistant
PC Provincial Commissioner

PD Pregnancy Diagnosis
PPL Private Pilots License
PR Public Relations
PVO Provincial Veterinary Officer
SWB Short Wheel Base usually a Landrover
TLC Tender Loving Care
UHT Ultra Heat Treated Milk
VIO Veterinary Investigation Officer
VO Veterinary Officer
VPL Visible Panty Line